"A UNIQUE HEART-POUNDER."
—The Hartford Courant

"Rewarding . . . Perry infuses his novel with everything he's got: some introspection, some magic, lots of action."
—*Newark Star-Ledger*

"Perry is creating a niche as enticing and solid as Dean Koontz or Tom Clancy with Indian guide Jane Whitefield. . . . Perry's strength as the third-person narrator is a knack for breakneck pacing, a wry unobtrusive wit that sets perfect hair-raising scenes, and inventive plotting with clever twists. He manages to build suspense, pull surprises, and keep his characters in such imminent danger that he seems ready to sacrifice a hero at any moment."
—*Memphis Commercial Appeal*

"Swift plotting. . . . The overall story is so good that the climax comes much too soon."
—*The Seattle Times*

"From the disappearance of Pete Hatcher during a Las Vegas magic show to the satisfying denouement, Perry's third Jane Whitefield thriller delivers in full: a well-paced and complex plot, intriguing characters (including a chillingly psychotic couple who make a living as killers), and enough suspense to keep the pages turning all day. . . . Perry leads his readers on a galvanizing chase along a twisting, thrilling course."
—*Publishers Weekly* (starred review)

Books published by The Ballantine Publishing Group
are available at quantity discounts on bulk purchases
for premium, educational, fund-raising, and special
sales use. For details, please call 1-800-733-3000.

SHADOW WOMAN

Thomas Perry

IVY BOOKS • NEW YORK

An Ivy Book
Published by The Ballantine Publishing Group
Copyright © 1997 by Thomas Perry

All rights reserved under International and Pan-American Copyright Conventions. Published in the United States by The Ballantine Publishing Group, a division of Random House, Inc., New York, and simultaneously in Canada by Random House of Canada Limited, Toronto.

http://www.randomhouse.com

Library of Congress Catalog Card Number: 97-97107

ISBN 0-8041-1539-7

This edition published by arrangement with Random House, Inc.

Manufactured in the United States of America

First Ballantine Books Edition: June 1998

10 9 8 7 6 5 4 3 2 1

For my mother
my sister
my wife
my daughters

Any person, whether old or young, male or female, might become possessed of an evil spirit, and be transformed into a witch. A person thus possessed could assume, at pleasure, the form of any animal, bird or reptile, and having executed his nefarious purpose, could resume his original form, or, if necessary to escape pursuit, could transmute himself into an inanimate object.

Lewis Henry Morgan, *League of the Iroquois,* 1851

Pete Hatcher pushed through the warm, dry night air that was trapped between the tall hotels and casinos, feeling the stored heat from the sun still rising from the concrete to his ankles. He had tightened his back muscles to keep his spine straight and his shoulders back, but it felt like a pose, so he tried to lose his self-consciousness and slouch a little. It was hard to do anything for so many days without ruminating on the way it must look, what they must think about it. He had tried to look formidable and alert, as though he would be hard to kill. The idea was worse than childish. It was the reaction of an animal trying to convince a predator that he wasn't weak enough to take down just yet.

The part of Las Vegas that he loved was the Strip, with the exaggerated shapes of its giant buildings lit up in candy colors that burned against the blue-black desert sky, but being downtown like this was different. The carnival neons and incandescents glared from all sides and bounced off asphalt and concrete, then washed across the faces of the people walking with him as a dead yellow-gray that cast deep shadows in their wrinkles and sunken eyes.

He followed a couple who seemed to sense it. Each eyed the other and the woman became uncomfortably aware that the ghastly light that had skinned the life from her beloved's cheek must have done the same to her own. She bravely forced a smile that only gave her face deeper hollows and the bared teeth of a skull. The pair reached the roofed-over mall, retreated to the nearest glass door, and escaped into the soft blue of a bar lit with the twinkle of tiny star-white bulbs. When they had taken a few steps into the cool, machine-made air, Pete saw them both give a little shrug-and-shudder to be sure none of the leftover street magic was clinging to them.

Hatcher followed them through the bar into the big casino, then skirted the margin of the gaming floor, ignoring the din of the bells on the slots and the rattle of coins in the collection pans that bounced off the walls above his head to excite the customers. He moved deeper, staying far from the blackjack tables and crap tables, where bright overhead lights shone on the green felt and turned the dealers' starched white shirts into semaphores. He stepped to the little window in the wall a few feet apart from the cashiers' cages.

He said to the middle-aged woman behind the glass, "There was supposed to be a ticket for the midnight show left for me."

"Your name, sir?" He had somehow assumed she would know his face, but her expression was only attentive.

"Pete Hatcher."

Hatcher took the ticket and read the seat number while he was still in the light, then handed it to the girl in the fishnet tights and frock coat at the door and let her lead him into the show. Hatcher never looked back to see whether the two men were still following. They were.

The round walls of the room were lined with big plush booths in three tiers, and the space in front of the stage crowded with rows of long, narrow tables arranged like the spokes of a wheel so nobody in the cheap stackable chairs along them could see better than anybody else.

The woman he had been told to call Jane was already seated in the dark booth when he got there. She was thin, with gleaming black hair braided behind her head, a long, graceful neck, and bare shoulders that showed no trace of a line in the tan and made him want to believe that she was in the habit of sunbathing naked. He felt an unexpected, tearing pain when he looked at her, so he glanced at the stage. This was what he was about to lose—not the money or the fancy office or the clean, hot desert air. It was the women, ones like her. They weren't ever from here, but this was where Pete had always found them. It was as though they were the winners of some quiet beauty contest, judged not by a bunch of potbellied Chamber of Commerce types but by the women themselves, before they were even women. They seemed to take one look in the mirror and know that the creature looking back at them didn't belong in Biloxi or Minneapolis.

The woman said, "Pete?"

"Yes?"

"Kiss me." He turned in surprise and she was offering him her cheek in that strange way the best of them did, so he could press his lips against that incredibly smooth place just in front of her ear and smell the fragrance of her hair. He lingered there for a moment to whisper, "I thought we were blending in. You mean beautiful is the worst you can do?"

She ignored the question, drew back to end the kiss, and said, "Good enough. Dates want you to kiss them; hookers don't. If the management thinks I'm in business, they'll have their own people watching me. Did you know you're not alone?"

"I haven't been alone in two weeks," he said. "My phones are bugged, my apartment, even my car. When I'm asleep they switch on a camera with an infrared lens that's above the smoke detector in my ceiling."

"That's a very good sign," said the woman. "If the bugs and cameras had disappeared, that would be a very bad sign. It would mean they expected that pretty soon the police would be taking a close look at everything you used to own."

"It's not the sort of sign that makes me want to rush out and buy next year's calendar."

"Don't worry about what didn't happen," said the woman. "Worry about what you have to make happen."

"What?"

"The instant that the box opens—"

"What box?"

"Just listen. When the box opens, you get out and walk—do not run—to the exit door that's facing you. Go outside, get into the black Ford that's parked in the reserved space at the end of the lot. Drive north on Route 15. It will take you to St. George, Utah. That's about all the time I can buy you. You'll still be an hour from Cedar City. Don't stop to pee or something, just keep driving. There's a small airport in Cedar City, and your ticket is reserved at the Southwest Airlines desk under the name David Keller. From now on, that's you. The papers I promised you are in the wallet under the seat of the car. There's a suitcase in the trunk. You'll just make your flight, and you'll be in Denver before daylight."

"What about the other stuff?"

"Everything you'll need at first is in the suitcase. The diplomas, honorable discharge, bank books, and so on are in your new apartment."

"And?"

"And what?"

"That gets me out, but what about you? They've seen you with me. They'll have nobody to take it out on but you."

Her eyes settled on him in puzzled curiosity, studied his face for a moment as though they had found something rare and unfamiliar there, then drifted toward the stage. "I'm good at this, and you couldn't help me anyway. Don't think about me. Think about what you have to do."

"Anything else you haven't told me?"

"Volumes," she said. "I like to spend more time with my runners before I set them free, but you don't have it to spare. All you really need to know is that if you never make a mistake you'll live forever. Right now, just concentrate on tonight. If you live through this, you'll catch on."

"What if they've got somebody waiting at the back door for me?"

She placed her long, thin fingers on his hand, and her voice went soft and low, like a mother talking to her child. "Then hit him fast, and hurt him as badly as you can. He won't have the stomach for a one-on-one fight for keeps. It takes much more courage to spend two weeks pretending you don't know you're in trouble than it does to join a pack stalking a lone man. I've been watching you, and I've been watching them. You can do this."

He sighed, but his lungs had taken in so little air it came out in a shallow puff. "I sure hope you're right. I assume you took your fee out of the money when you took it to Denver?"

She shook her head. "It doesn't work that way. A year from now, maybe two, you'll think about the way your life is. And you'll remember how you felt tonight. And then you'll send me a present."

He raised his eyebrows. "How do you know that?"

"I don't. But over the years I've gotten a lot of presents."

As the house lights dimmed, Pete raised his eyes to see where tonight's shadows were. He found them in the tier above, seated in a booth where they could catch a glimpse of him in profile whenever they wished. He leaned back, hiding his face from them, but the woman gently leaned on his back and pushed him forward as she whispered in his ear, "Let them see you. Keep your face where they can see it."

A small projectile spitting sparks like a comet streaked over their heads. It exploded at center stage in a loud bang and a billow of lighter-fluid flame six feet high, followed by a fog of dry-ice smoke that quickly spread from curtain to curtain and drifted over the footlights into the audience.

A bright spotlight beam appeared and frantically swept across the wall of smoke, trying to penetrate it and find some solid object. In a moment a few wisps seemed to congeal and resolve themselves into the shape of an old, bent, wizened woman in bulky rags, leaning on a cane. She hobbled forward out of the fog haltingly, then seemed to notice the audience for the first time. Pete looked at the people around him. They were hushed with surprise, as though they had forgotten that they had bought tickets and sat here sipping watered drinks waiting for this.

The old woman glared at them, then gave a low unearthly cackle and lifted the cane into the air. As it reached the height of her shoulder it shortened and narrowed, and as it went over her head it was clearly a wand.

She tapped herself on the top of the head and the rags instantly incinerated in a flash of sparks and smoke. The spotlight fought its way through the smoke and found in her place a young, shapely woman who stood erect and wore a sparkling gold spandex skin that seemed little brighter than her mane of honey-blond hair. The deep, resonant voice of the announcer shouted, "Ladies and gentlemen . . . Miranda!" and then was drowned in music and applause.

Pete leaned to the side and said, "She's got my attention. I hope she's got theirs."

The woman beside him watched his eyes. "If she doesn't yet, she will. She used to strip."

Miranda paced the empty, dim stage like a cat, doing the impossible for the willfully gullible, receptive crowd. First she reached into the air and began plucking things out of it: white doves that couldn't have been hidden in her brief costume and flew out over the audience, then returned to a perch at the back of the stage; a single rose that she tossed over her shoulder onto the floor; then, one after another, four rabbits. It was as though she were completing the compulsory round of a conjurers' competition, executing a sampling of the standard tricks.

Only slowly did it occur to the audience that something strange and unplanned was happening. The rose she had thrown behind her was changing. It grew longer and longer, then arched upward a little. Then it began to writhe and slither. Miranda produced a magician's top hat, put it on her head, then took it off and held it before her stomach. The rabbits, one by one, ran toward her, leapt into the hat, and disappeared inside it. She collapsed the hat and flicked it offstage like a Frisbee.

The audience was distracted. The rabbit trick was a bit out of the ordinary, but the audience was captured by that rose. It was now seven or eight feet long. The petals had fallen off, and now it arched its back, slowly raising its head behind Miranda, and spread its hood. It was a king cobra, its green-black skin looking oily in the lights. As she took her bow, it coiled to strike. Miranda seemed to sense something was bothering her audience. She frowned at them, then reached up into the dark air again, produced a pearl-handled revolver, pivoted gracefully, and shot the serpent through the eye. It jerked spasmodically, then fell. A wind passed across the stage, swirling the smoke in little eddies. The snake crumbled into dry flakes that blew away, leaving only a new, fresh rose in its place. Miranda squeezed the pistol in her hands until it became a ball the color of mercury, threw it into the air, and watched it explode.

While Miranda took another bow, Jane studied the audience, trying to detect anyone watching the two shadows for a signal. After a moment she was satisfied that they had come alone. A company like Pleasure, Inc., could afford as many as they wanted, but they wouldn't put more than two on Pete Hatcher. Pete wasn't crazy enough to attack even that many. She leaned close to him and whispered, "Your time is here. Take one last look at it, and then never come back. This part of your life is already over."

He turned to look at her face, but it was veiled in darkness again. The music grew loud and frantic, and the audience murmured and then drew in its breath as Miranda took a little run and jumped off the eight-foot stage onto the floor. She danced up the aisle, glanced at a man sitting at one of the tables, reached into his ear, and extracted a pair of satin and lace panties. The man grinned appreciatively, but the woman beside him looked, then bared her teeth in something that wasn't a smile. Her left hand moved furtively along her haunch.

The audience gasped its religious conviction that the hand was quicker than the eye, and as Miranda danced along the tables, their approval drowned out all but the beat of Miranda's music.

As she drew near Pete Hatcher, he turned his eyes away from her toward Jane. She said, "Good luck, Pete," and Miranda's surprisingly strong, sinuous fingers wrapped themselves around his forearm. Pete looked up into Miranda's face as he rose to his feet, but when she was this close he saw nothing soft or reassuring there. Her unnaturally perfect teeth were set in the performer's clench, so she could be nervous or winded without showing it, and between the black eyeliner and the blue-gold eyeshadow, the eyes themselves had that mad, manic stare that they all had, not seeing him at all because she was living in her mind a minute or two ahead of everyone else. Her mask of makeup was not the color of a human being, and it reflected light in tiny metallic sparkles that were not what mortals were made of.

Pete let her lead him by the hand down the aisle to the stage, and he let the polite applause that acknowledged he was a good sport carry him to the steps until it was overwhelmed by the audience's celebration that Miranda had returned to the stage. While the spotlight had followed Miranda to Pete's booth, unseen hands had been busy up here. There was a couch placed at center stage. Miranda led him like a woman leading her lover. She spoke to him only in a hard, professional tone as they went. "I'll walk you through this. For now, just lie there. Don't move, don't touch. Got it?"

"Yes," he said. He lay on the couch and discovered that it was hard, a board with a layer of cloth over it. The audience roared again, and he could tell it was because Miranda, facing away from them, had snaked a hand up behind her back and unsnapped the top of her outfit. Her hands went to the waist of her tights and made a first, tantalizing tug. She stepped closer to Hatcher, placed a knee on the couch, and everything happened at once. At the front of the stage there was a flash and a big puff of smoke. For a second Hatcher could see streams of smoke piped upward at the footlights, and then he saw nothing. He felt an abrupt jerk as the silky material under him separated, yanked toward both sides of the stage by unseen wires. He felt the dislocation of air as Miranda flailed around in the dark a few feet from him, but he saw nothing.

The light came on, and the first sight was Miranda, this time wearing a Victorian-looking black corset with garters and black stockings and holding a long silver stiletto. She said, "Mug for them," so he looked her over uneasily. When Miranda had timed the laugh, she stepped closer. "Good. Now stand up and look at the couch."

He got up and stared down at it. The couch was now an

ornate lacquer-and-silver box about four feet long. She opened the top and said, "Climb in. When it's closed, bring your knees up to your chest."

He wasn't surprised to see the box. Jane had mentioned the box. Pete took one look out at the audience. He could see Jane sitting alone in the booth, now illuminated by the bright houselights, and fifty feet behind her and to her right, the two shadows. One was the guy he had seen outside his window after dark on Tuesday. He had the melancholy, tired look of a cop who had been on his feet too much. The other was short, stocky, and bullnecked like an Irish middleweight, with a round, reddish squint-eyed face.

As he stepped into the box he gazed past them at the ridiculous baroque lounge, its oversized booths with scrollwork molded from sawdust and glue and painted purple, then fitted with cushions of foam rubber upholstered with shiny fabric. He loved all of it, being part of it. He loved to see the women looking at it: the ones from the Midwest who wore crisp pastel dresses you could never quite see through and took the long way out of Caesar's to look in the windows of the shops at yellow diamond necklaces and solid silver samovars and sable coats, not because they wanted them but because they were placed there to be seen, just like celebrities. He loved the dealers in their little pressed man-outfits and bow ties and shiny shoes, and the tall dancers in costumes that made them hard and gleaming like human jewels, and the women from the dry plains who tiptoed out to the pool with hotel towels wrapped around their hips because they were having second thoughts about their new bathing suits—maybe not even how much skin they showed, so much as what owning a suit like that might mean about them. Hatcher lay down in the box, let her slam the lid on him, and waited.

Jane watched Miranda work through her variation of the ancient conjurer's tricks. Miranda whirled the box around on its casters, watched the mechanical feet at the end of the box kick and wiggle while she sliced the box in half, then wiggle again when she separated the two boxes. Finally, she flung open the lids of the two boxes, and there was nobody inside at all. She closed the boxes, whirled them around a bit, then had two burly assistants in turbans lift one on top of the other. She opened the single door, and out stepped Pete Hatcher. He bowed, shyly received a kiss from Miranda, and walked toward the steps.

As he reached the floor of the lounge, the lights swept back to Miranda. She was climbing into the box herself. The two assistants turned the box around a few times, tapped it with Miranda's discarded wand, and a big flame shot upward. All the while, the silhouette of the good sport she had drafted from the audience could be seen making his way in the darkened room to Jane's booth.

He sat down and said in Miranda's voice, "He's on his way, Jane."

"Thanks, Miranda," said Jane. "It's a great show."

On stage, the two befuddled assistants opened the box. Out stepped a man who looked very much like Pete Hatcher. The spotlights quickly searched the room. When they found Pete Hatcher's booth, the figure of Pete Hatcher leapt to its feet, threw off the coat and wig, stepped out of the pants, and became Miranda. She milked the applause, curtsying and throwing kisses, then ran back to the stage. She tore a curtain from the back of the stage to reveal what looked like Pete Hatcher lying stiff and seemingly asleep, floating three feet off the ground. She covered him with the curtain, levitated him a few feet higher, where he would be out of her way, and went on with her act. Jane looked at her watch.

Miranda proceeded to keep the audience confused and agitated with her smoke and mirrors and costume changes. From time to time she would bring up other members of the audience to shill for her, and when they had done their parts, she would cover them with cloths and levitate them too, until after two hours there were six men and women floating above the stage. As Miranda was taking her final bow, she suddenly seemed to remember something. She turned, looked up at the six bodies floating in the air, and hurried toward them. She stepped to the first, snatched the cloth away, and revealed that there was nothing at all under it. She pointed to a table at her feet, and the woman who was supposed to be floating smiled at the audience and waved happily. One by one, Miranda snatched the cloths out of the air and revealed each of her volunteers, sitting in their seats watching the show. When she pointed at Jane's booth, the man sitting beside Jane gave a graceful little bow that ended in an outstretched arm lifted toward Miranda in a gesture that began in appreciation and ended in surprise.

The audience's eyes shot to the stage in time to see another flash and puff of smoke, and Miranda was gone. Only the pile of cloths lay where she had stood a moment before. The smoke grew in volume and thickness, and slowly, the pile of rags stirred and began to rise. The hydraulic platform under the stage pushed Miranda upward, and as she rose through the cloths, they hung from her like thick draped clothing. She was, once again, the old, bent crone who had begun the show. She limped to the edge of the stage where she had left her wand, tapped it once on her palm, and it grew into the walking stick. She winked slyly at the audience and slowly walked through the smoke and disappeared.

The doors opened at the rear of the lounge and the audience filed out with the lights still low, Miranda's eerie music still in their ears and wisps of theatrical smoke still in the air. Jane and her companion made their way toward the door with the others, deep in the gratified, chattering crowd. Before they stepped into the light of the casino, Jane said, "Thanks," and the man, one of Miranda's assistants, stepped to the side and was gone.

Jane walked purposefully across the casino alone, under the enormous crystal chandeliers, where she could be certain the two shadows would see her. She went into the lobby and stopped at the front desk to pick up her room key.

She made her way back across the casino and up into the bar that overlooked the long rows of green felt tables. She sat down at a table for two and waited. In the mirror above the bar she could see Pete's two shadows. The tall one was wandering around looking over the heads of the gamblers to see where Pete Hatcher could have gone. The second man was behind Jane and to her left, just at the perimeter of the bar, where he could slip away if he needed to.

She waited a few minutes for the barmaid to show up, then ordered a martini and a scotch and water, and watched the barmaid throw down two napkins, one in front of the empty chair, then head for the bar to get the drinks. The sight of two drinks on the tray coming back to the table seemed to make all the difference to Pete Hatcher's shadows. They were reassured, almost as though they were watching Pete. They might not know where Hatcher was right at this moment—the men's room, somewhere in the labyrinth of slot machines, where they had not looked for him—but they knew where he was going to be in a few minutes. The few minutes accumulated into a half hour, then forty-five minutes. The small shadow left to see if Pete Hatcher's car was still in the lot and came back to report to his friend that it was, but they weren't feeling confident anymore. Something was wrong, and they weren't yet sure what it was.

She glanced at her watch. Katie ... she corrected herself: Miranda ... had promised to transport Pete Hatcher out the stage door near the start of her act, so the show had given him a full two hours to make the Utah border. Jane's little pantomime of being stood up had bought him the third hour to get to Cedar City. His plane would be loading passengers just about now. It was time for Jane to start making herself disappear.

She left a twenty-dollar chip on the table and stepped out of the bar. The two men hesitated for a second, then followed. They had to give her plenty of room and try not to look interested. Jane walked toward the elevators, and she knew they had no choice but to follow. If they lost her, they had nothing. She took the elevator to the fifteenth floor, went into her room, kicked off her shoes, and called the garage. "This is Miss Seymour in Room 1592. I'd like my car right away, please." As she

listened to the parking attendant's answer she was already stepping out of her gown.

She heard the doorknob rattle a little. She looked at the door,
but it didn't budge. She could see the shadows of feet under the
door. Jane kicked the dress under the bed, slipped on her
slacks, pulled the sweater over her head, then heard a sudden
thud. She looked at the door. The double-edged blade of a knife
had pierced through the thin oak veneer of the hollow door
beside the lock. She froze. An unseen hand worked the blade
around a little and withdrew it. There was another dull thud,
and the blade punched through again.

She snatched her purse, quickly slipped out through the curtains to the balcony, and quietly slid the door shut. She had
misjudged them. They should not have been willing to take a
chance like this yet. Maybe she had been too eager to get Pete
out of sight and she had missed some sign, forgotten to ask
some question. There was no way to fix it now, no time to
think. She had to get out.

She had nothing with her. This was not the hotel where she
had been sleeping. It was just the room she had rented to disappear from. In a few seconds those two would have the door
open. She looked around her at the balconies of the other
rooms. They were narrow and far apart, and even if she somehow managed to reach one of them without falling, she would
only be in the next room. She leaned out as far as she could and
looked down. On the floor below her there was a balcony just
like hers, but it had to be twelve feet down.

Jane saw a thin wedge of light fan into her room as they
opened the door as far as the chain would allow. She unclasped
the leather strap of her purse, clasped it around the bottom of
the vertical railing support closest to the wall of the building,
tossed her purse to the balcony below, stepped over the railing,
and lowered herself into the empty air. She was trembling with
fear and awe at what she had done as she dangled there, six feet
above the railing of the fourteenth-floor balcony. She wanted to
drop but found her hands would not obey the command to

open. It looked as though she would fall, scrape the outside of the balcony, and plummet two hundred feet to the pavement.

She bent at the hip and began a gentle swing. The first sweep brought her out away from the balcony and tipped her down a little so she had to look directly through all that empty night air at the tiny figures on the lighted concrete below. After a sickening pause at the end of the arc, she began to swing forward. When she judged that the balcony was under her, she let go.

She dropped and hit the concrete balcony hard, slid a little, and bumped the railing so it gave a low vibrating sound like a tuning fork. She turned and saw that the sliding door into this room was closed. As she stood and reached for the handle, she knew that, whatever else happened, she was not going to put herself outside the railing again. She tugged on the door and it wouldn't budge. She lay on her back, covered her face with her purse, and kicked out at the glass with both feet.

The glass gave a loud crack, but it didn't break inward. She went to her knees, lifted a long jagged shard out, set it beside her, then used her purse to push a bigger one inward. She crawled inside, hurried across the empty room, burst out into the hallway, ran to the elevator, and punched the button. But as she glanced upward she saw that the number lit up was fifteen. The elevator was coming down from above.

She turned and ran for the sign that said EXIT, slipped inside the door to the stairwell, and waited. The bell rang, the elevator doors parted, and she saw that nobody was inside. She ran for the elevator and got past the doors just as the big man emerged from the stairwell and dashed toward her.

She rode the elevator down to the garage level. When the bell rang she took a step toward the opening doors, but then the space was filled with a blur of moving flesh and gray fabric as the shorter man with the pink swine face charged inside the elevator. He slapped the button and used his body to block the opening while the doors slid together again, trapping her inside with him.

Jane predicted his half-formed strategy, because the small space made it inevitable. He had enclosed her in a tiny compartment, so he would sweep her into a corner before she could do much flailing and use the strength of his upper body to keep her there and stifle the screams. She put up both hands in a weak defense, half cringing before the blow, half supplication that it wouldn't come. The man lunged toward her.

Jane's right hand jabbed out, more to stagger him than to do harm, but he was moving faster than she had expected. Her knuckles glanced off the bridge of his nose and into his left eye. His hands went up, too late, and Jane rocked back against the wall to deliver the kick to his knee that she had planned from the beginning. She felt the knee break; he dropped to the floor, gasping in pain.

She sidestepped past him and hit the OPEN DOOR button. As the doors slid open his hand shot out to grasp her ankle. His grip was so strong it hurt, tightening like the jaws of an animal as he pulled her toward him. She said quietly, "Think. If you drag me back in there alone with you and your broken leg, are things going to get better for you, or worse?"

She felt the hand slowly, reluctantly release its grip. The door closed, she stepped away, and hurried toward the valet loitering beside her rented car. She was already chattering. "It's here already? Gee, you guys are really fast. I'm sorry it took me so long. Thanks a lot."

She slipped a ten-dollar bill into the hand of the valet, threw her car into gear, and drove out along Bonanza Road and into the darkness to the west.

2

Jane drove out of the desert into Los Angeles while the morning traffic was still moving and the glaring sunlight was on the back of her car instead of in her eyes. The car was rented on a MasterCard that said she was Wendy Aguilar, so if someone in Las Vegas had seen the license number, then asking the right questions would lead the chasers to a fictitious woman who had disappeared in Los Angeles.

She never used her own name, never started off in the direction of her final destination, never missed a chance to mislead, but never bet her life on any plan she had made in advance. What had kept Jane alive during a dozen years as a guide was not mechanical precautions but unremitting watchfulness. She lived by scrutinizing the fluid events and configurations around her—momentary gatherings of people, minor financial transactions, crowded travel routes—for opportunities to deceive.

As she drove the rented car up Century Boulevard to return it to the agency, she spotted a convenient place to acquire a small extra measure of safety. She turned off the street beneath the tall white sign that towered above the car wash and stopped at the entrance to the tunnel lined with spraying nozzles and whirling brushes. She slipped out of the car and let the two men loitering nearby climb into the front and rear seats, steer it forward until the conveyor track caught the front wheel, then ride it through the tunnel to wipe the prints off every window and piece of chrome and vacuum the inner surfaces to pick up hairs and threads. Even if these men overlooked some trace of her and the clean-up crew at the rental lot missed it too, the process put two more people with their own clothes and hair and prints into the car. She used her ten minutes away from the car to stand in the shelter of the cashier's kiosk and watch the street to satisfy herself that no other car was idling nearby to wait for her.

When the men had finished, she pulled forward to the full-serve gas pump to have the tank filled, so any prints on the gas door or cap would belong to still another man. She drove the car around several blocks to dry it, crossed her own trail after a few minutes, and returned to the lot where she had rented it two weeks ago.

She took the shuttle van to the airport with six other people. It was always crowded in the morning at LAX because anybody who wanted to be on the East Coast by the end of the business day had to be in the air by eight. The shuttle van stopped at the loading zone, so she was only in the open for five quick steps, surrounded by men and women who were in as much of a hurry as she was. She had nothing but the canvas carry-on bag she had kept in her trunk.

Jane shopped for a flight on the television monitors on the wall as she walked. This time she decided that American Airlines Flight 653 to Chicago was the right one. From there she could go anywhere without much delay. Until a few years ago she would have paid cash for the ticket, because that gave her the option of making up a name. Now they checked identification on every flight. She rummaged in her purse and selected Terry Rosenberg's driver's license and credit card, because the name was common enough and wasn't definitely female. Years ago, when she had just begun as a guide and had seen these trips as a series of brief adventures rather than an accumulating succession of risks, she had sometimes made up names like those of heroines in romance novels. Dahlia Van Sturtevant had been one, as had Melinda-Gail La Doucette. Over the years she had slowly, painfully refined the whimsy out of her routines. A name like Terry Rosenberg might actually send a tracker off in the wrong direction: Destiny Vaucluse was a taunt.

She went through the metal detectors and walked to one of the more distant ladies' rooms because they were less heavily frequented than the ones near the entrances and because nobody she met after the security check was likely to be carrying anything that would make killing her a neat, quiet task.

Jane had no reason to believe that the men who had been watching Pete Hatcher in Las Vegas represented any danger to her. Even if they had seen her rental car and had the license number, it would take them a day or two to learn that she had returned it near the L.A. airport. They had seen the Miraculous Miranda make Hatcher disappear, but they had also seen her make him reappear, and they had followed him out of the show into the casino. If their employers were grounded firmly enough in reality to know that there was no such thing as a coincidence—that nobody vanished from the stage and the world the same night without planning—it would get them very little.

Miranda was a Las Vegas headliner because she was a spectacular performer. She was a headliner at Bogliarese's Inside Straight because Vincent Bogliarese Jr. waited for her in her elaborate dressing suite after each midnight show for a frolic while she was still in makeup, sweaty and excited from her triumph. There was a rumor that they were married, but Jane didn't know if it was true, and it didn't matter. As long as Vincent was nearby, Miranda was not a woman that anyone but an old friend could safely approach to ask even an easy question.

Jane washed off her makeup in front of the sink, dressed in a pair of blue jeans and a black silk blouse with a print of bright chrysanthemums, put on a pair of sneakers, threw her old clothes in the trash, and covered them with a newspaper she found on the counter. She let her long black hair hang loose and brushed it out, then put on fresh makeup and a pair of sunglasses. She inspected herself in the mirror, decided she looked as different from the woman who had been in Las Vegas as she needed to, and went out.

She bought breakfast and waited for her flight in the cafeteria, because fewer people could pass close by and look at her face here than in the waiting area. Every move Jane made while she was working was calculated to shift the odds a little more into her favor. Taking Pete Hatcher out of the world from a standing start had presented special problems and forced her to accept special risks.

Usually the ones she took out of trouble could be taken more quietly. A woman with bruises would show up at a shelter in the middle of a big city a thousand miles away and talk to a counselor. After an hour or two of listening to options and remedies that had already been tried and gotten her more bruises, she would tell the counselor that what she really wanted was magic—to simply have it all end and start again as somebody else. The counselor would pick up the telephone, and maybe the woman would notice that the counselor's other hand was busy erasing her name from the sign-in list.

The ones who were children usually arrived at Jane's door in the night, holding the hand of some adult who didn't think of herself as a hero, who maybe hadn't even run the inventory of statutory punishments for what she was doing but already knew that the punishment for doing nothing was worse.

The usual victims were the helpless, and they were almost invisible to begin with. The authorities who had not seen their agony were no better at noticing their absence. Their names were simply added to the enormous list of people all over the country who were missing, and after they had left Jane's hands those names were no longer theirs. The petty criminals—the adults who had burned up one life by an accretion of small mistakes and infractions—were almost as easy. They often came to her at a time when they, at least, believed they were in no immediate danger. That meant they had no friends, no plans, and no temptations to keep their minds off the emptiness they had created for themselves.

Pete Hatcher had been the other kind. He was already trapped, and she had to get him out while their eyes were on him. He had been a successful middle manager in a town where the locals were all in the same business and engaged in ferocious competition to dominate it. Once he had come under suspicion at Pleasure, Inc., there had been little that could happen to dispel it.

When he asked why he was being isolated and kept out of meetings, they decided he must have been waiting anxiously for signs that his disloyalty had been discovered. When he mentioned the possibility that it was time to find a new job, they thought he had been conspiring with a competitor who had already prepared a safe haven for him. When he offered to resign with no job in sight, they figured he must not need one—had probably found a way to skim casino proceeds or helped an accomplice fix a game. It was when he did nothing that their worst fears were aroused. They suspected he was staying in place because he had made a deal with some federal agency and had been bullied into collecting evidence for them. They had watched him for weeks, waiting to find out which it was so they could clean it up after they killed him.

Casinos were like a lot of businesses. A tenth of what went on was disguised by showmanship, and the rest was invisible. Part of what wasn't easy to see were their gigantic security departments. They had people to guard and transport the vast sums of cash that appeared each day, other people to watch the dealers, cashiers, and croupiers to be sure that the nimblest fingers in the world never palmed anything, others to investigate possible high rollers, still others to find them if they didn't pay. They had more to simply protect the casino itself—people who watched for undesirable visitors who had come to prey on the guests and quickly, quietly hustled them away before they disturbed the unreal tranquility of the gambling palace. It had always struck Jane as ironic that probably the safest place in the country for a woman traveling alone was inside any of the big Las Vegas hotels.

In a way, the security was what had saved Pete Hatcher. Without that enveloping but unobtrusive protection, a woman named Paula might not have felt comfortable enough to go there by herself, and certainly wouldn't have dared get friendly with a gambler like him. A year later, when he was in trouble and trying to think of places to stay that his bosses wouldn't know about, he had remembered Paula's number and she had remembered Jane's.

Jane heard her flight announced over the loudspeaker, picked up her canvas bag, and walked toward the gate. She held herself with her spine straight and looked directly ahead, never allowing her eyes to focus on those of the other travelers, never turning away to give them permission to study her. She walked quickly, joined the line after it had begun to move efficiently but was long enough to include a lot of other people who would be more interesting for a bored observer to stare at than she was, and disappeared into the loading tunnel.

As soon as the plane was in the air, Jane pushed her seat back as far as it would go and closed her eyes. She had been anxious for two nights, trying to work out a path for Pete Hatcher that wouldn't lead him in front of a gun muzzle, then spent the third running. She knew she could sleep only fitfully now, because she had not dreamed in four nights and her mind was holding a jumbled backlog of jarring impressions that would plague her sleep. But lying with her eyes closed prevented other passengers from trying to talk to her, and that was another of her precautions. The road home was where the worst of the traps were, because she had already given dangerous people a reason to want her. That was when they would be making their best attempts to track her or place friends of theirs in her path.

Jane got off the plane in Chicago and found another, under the name Tracy Morgan, that took her to Rochester, New York. In the airport store she bought a packet of pipe tobacco, then drove a few miles southeast of the airport to Mendon.

Jane parked her car along the road above the bend of Honeoye Creek and walked to the quiet little park at Mendon Ponds. She sat where she always sat when she came here, at a picnic table with a surface scarred with carved initials, took out her manicure kit, and trimmed and buffed her nails.

The two little lakes were glassy and greenish. The tall, thick trees along the bank away from the road grew out of the water from submerged roots and protected the ponds from the tiniest breeze. The only ripples came from long-legged water bugs that skittered across the surface now and then.

Three hundred feet away, up the grassy bank, a mother with very white legs and feet sat in the shade of a sunhat and big dark glasses, watching her two little golden-haired children digging with plastic shovels in the muck. If the mother wasn't careful, they might actually find something, Jane thought. The People had lived here once. That black mud made it easy to grow corn, beans, and squash with a digging stick, and the weeds came right up with a tug.

The village was called Dayodehokto, a phrase that meant "a bend in a creek," so the rows of longhouses had probably been close to the stream on the far side of the trees, but the cultivated fields had stretched for a couple of miles in all directions. A Dutchman who came through here in the 1670s counted 120 longhouses with twelve or thirteen fires in a line down the center of each one. On opposite sides of each fire were a pair of compartments, where two adult women slept with their husbands—when the men were home—and their children. After allowing for the usual exaggeration, Jane guessed the village would have contained nearly three thousand people on June 23, 1687, when this quiet little spot had its moment of importance in global politics.

For twenty years, Louis XIV, the Sun King, had been ordering successive governors of New France to exterminate the five Iroquois nations, but particularly the Senecas, who lived the farthest west and were most disruptive to the fur trade with the Indians of the western Great Lakes.

He had received no satisfaction in the past, but this time he had found himself a soldier. The Marquis de Denonville efficiently assembled the total military force of New France—probably a thousand soldiers, traders, and trappers. The Sun King sent him two thousand French regular troops, half the number he had requested, along with a regal apology about being strapped for cash. Denonville gathered six hundred allies from the Indians of the west—Miamis, Illinois, Potawatomis, Hurons, Ottawas. They all met at Fort Niagara, where the river emptied into Lake Ontario, traveled in four hundred boats and canoes to Irondequoit Bay, and marched south along the trail to this village.

The army was confident that the people they were attacking were almost all women and children. Seneca men were out in the forests for most of the year, hunting or raiding distant tribes. The Senecas had no reason to expect an attack, because they had been assured that Louis XIV and their ally the English king James II were friends at the moment.

On the first day, the French expedition made good progress down the trail toward this spot. They marched with half the Canadian woodsmen and Indians in front, then the French army, and then a rear guard of Indians and woodsmen. On the second day they reached the edge of the cornfields but found them strangely deserted. At this time of year, the Month of Strawberries, the corn was still unripe and needed constant tending. The fields should have been full of women, chattering as they weeded and turned the soil. The marquis conceded that his tactic of surprise had failed, but he was sure the mission might still succeed if his men were quick enough. The French force ran toward the village in their eagerness to cut down the fleeing women and children before they could vanish into the forest.

The front of the column passed within a few yards of something they were not expecting—a group of Seneca warriors lying on their bellies in the brush. The Senecas waited until the vanguard had moved on, then tore into the center of the column, where the French soldiers were, first firing their rifles and then falling on the soldiers with tomahawks and war clubs. The French fell into disorder, firing at trees, bushes, or their Indian allies and then scattering along the trail in both directions. The Senecas killed over a hundred and then disappeared into the forest again.

It took the marquis the rest of the day to rally and reassemble his men, then force them to set up a secure camp for the night. In the morning he cautiously advanced into the village of Dayodehokto and discovered that the ambush had been a delaying tactic. The longhouses were already in ashes. The only living things left were two old men who had stayed to exercise the privilege of dying while defying their enemies. They were obligingly cut into pieces and boiled to make soup for the French allies.

It took Denonville's army six days to burn all of the corn-fields here and the fifty thousand bushels of dried corn that had been stored. When that had been accomplished, the marquis, less optimistic now, marched on to two more deserted villages, then returned to Montreal to contemplate what a lot of trouble he had gone to just to cook up two old men.

The Senecas and the rest of the five Iroquois nations retali-ated by making New France from Mackinac to Quebec a very dangerous place for a couple of years. They attacked Frontenac and Montreal, killing hundreds and carrying off hundreds more. French traders traveling in the far north disappeared. It would be a hundred years before the villages in Seneca country would be raided again. The next time it would be the Americans, and again the women would lead their children into the forest in time to escape the scheduled extermination, leaving the enemy to be satisfied with burning cornfields.

Jane gathered her nail clippings, smiled and nodded at the woman and her children, and walked along the perimeter of the pond into the trees until she came to Honeoye Creek. The area around the pond was a favorite picnic spot for people from Rochester, and not one in a thousand knew anyone had ever lived here. It had become one of the secret places.

Jane took out the package of tobacco she had bought in the airport. "Jo-Ge-Oh, it's me," she whispered. "Jane Whitefield." She sprinkled a pile of brown shreds on the flat bank where the Little People would be sure to find it. "Thanks for the break in Las Vegas. Pete Hatcher is gone now." There was no such thing as a prayer of supplication in the old religion, only ways of giving thanks.

She scattered the crescent fingernail clippings along the muddy bank. "This ought to keep the possums and raccoons away while you light up." The Little People had a terrible tobacco addiction, and they prized human fingernails because the scent kept away the animals that were bothersome to anyone that short.

Since she was a child, Jane had particularly admired the Jo-Ge-Oh, because they took the hunted, the wounded, and the defeated and hid them from their enemies. Time was different for the Jo-Ge-Oh, so the person they helped would simply vanish and then emerge from the forest thinking he had been with them for a day, but find it was now many years later, after all his enemies were dead and buried.

Jane liked to visit the Little People in places where Senecas had once needed to fade into the forest. The three hundred years that had passed on Honeoye Creek might not make much difference to the Little People. It might be a few days to them. And here was a Seneca woman, not changed much from the last one they'd seen on this spot, coming to bring them the customary present, as women like her had been doing for thousands of years.

3

The bus labored up Delaware Avenue out of Buffalo, building its momentum slowly after each stop, then coasting to the next one, until Jane saw her corner. She stood up, and the driver pulled over to let her out under a streetlamp. She walked along the uneven sidewalks across the south end of Deganawida in the dark, her canvas bag over her shoulder, her feet feeling without effort the places where the concrete slabs were pushed up by the big old trees, as Jane had learned to do when she was little.

She walked along Erie Street, unconsciously noting what was going on behind the lighted panes of glass without staring at them. She probably knew the occupants of every third house in the little city. Her parents had known more of them, and her grandparents still more, because they could have told her who was related to whom for generations back.

Jane felt so good about having these sidewalks under her feet, so glad to breathe the air in a place that made sense to her, that she allowed herself to think about what it would be like never to leave again. For the first time in two weeks, when her mind was drawn to Carey McKinnon she did not goad it away from him. He was going to ask her again if she would marry him. That would be in six months, and that was not much time to get ready. It occurred to her that if she had been someone else, getting ready would probably have meant worrying about trivia: dresses and china patterns. But what Jane Whitefield was going to have to worry about was how to make the bride invisible.

Jane let her eyes settle on her house as soon as she had turned onto her block. There were no lights, no curtains that had been moved since she had left, no cars parked on the block that she had not seen before. The reading lamp near the corner window in Jake Reinert's house next door was on, and she took a couple of steps along the sidewalk in front of his house until she could see a slice of light under the blind of the porch window. She saw the book on his lap and his thick, pink, callused right hand tilting it up a little as he read, to keep the lower segment of his bifocals on it.

He and her father had been raised side by side in these two old houses on this quiet street, and by now he seemed to be able to sense subtle changes in the atmosphere—a footfall on the porch next door would bring him to the window. She had even seen him stop what he was doing to stare if he heard the engine of a car going by that he didn't recognize. She had her house wired with a very good burglar alarm, but she had met people who made a living fooling better ones than that. She went to her car in the garage and took her house key out of the lining of the rear seat, then walked back to her front door, unlocked it, and slipped inside quickly to punch her alarm code into the glowing keypad before it could go off.

She stood in the doorway and studied the signs. The air in the house was stale, so no window had been broken. Before she had left the house she had vacuumed the carpet, leaving a pattern and the pile pushed upward. The carpet had no indentations from heavy feet. She walked to the table beside the couch and lifted the telephone off the cradle. The dial tone was clear and distinct, so nobody had disconnected the phone line to isolate the alarm system. She was home.

She set the telephone back on its cradle as the bell rang, vibrating her fingertips. "Hello," she said into it.

"Hi, it's me." His voice had a smile in it, as though his throat were tight. "Welcome home."

"Hi, Carey," she said. She blocked the little laugh of pleasure that almost escaped. Then she wondered why she had to and remembered that she didn't have to anymore. She was home, and this was Carey. "How did you arrange this?"

"I don't know what you're talking about."

"You're so full of—"

"Wait," said Carey. "I'm getting a psychic image. Take about five minutes to unpack that black bag you've got over your shoulder, take a shower—and I wouldn't mention anything so indelicate if I weren't a board-certified physician—but I sense you have to pee. Then the archetypal little black dress. And matching underwear: you might get into an accident, and the gang in the emergency room is very critical. Nothing too flashy, but not the jeans-and-sneakers ensemble you've got on now."

"Jake saw me come home and called you."

"Old people are so prompt. I guess it's because their dance cards aren't quite as full as they once were. You didn't eat dinner on the plane, did you?"

"I wasn't on a plane."

"The broomstick, then. Whatever."

"I haven't eaten. But what brings on this sudden manic outpouring? Did a rich hypochondriac move into town while I was gone?"

"No," said Carey. "But I'm hungry, and I keep seeing these 'Lost Dog' posters near the hospital cafeteria."

"Suspicion is a sign of a devious mind," she said. "I mean a big sign, not like all the other signs."

"I knew I could develop a quality that would appeal to you. So get ready. I'm on my way."

"I'll be listening for the sirens."

She dressed in a few minutes and left her front door open while she walked up on Jake's porch and rang the bell.

He opened it and smiled at her. "Hello, Janie. I'll bet you came for your mail." He stepped backward to let her in and pointed to the pile of mail in the shoebox on the coffee table.

She lifted the shoebox, shook it beside her ear, and listened. "Six bills." She shook it again. "Only three checks, all small." She frowned. "And my subscription is about to run out."

His sharp old blue eyes focused on her. "You're dressed like a girl for once," he said. "To what do we owe this honor?"

"You called him, so don't pretend you didn't. And it'll be on your conscience if I'm sweet-talked into doing anything."

"None too soon, either," said Jake. "If you're going to have anything to live down, you'd better get started on it."

She looked at him slyly. "Tell me something. When did he ask you to call him?"

"Some time ago. And I won't apologize. Judging from that get-up, the attention isn't unwelcome."

"How long ago?"

"I guess it was the day after you left. He came over here with that look they get when they're telling you that whatever they're going to do to you might be a little uncomfortable. I was sorely relieved when I found out it was something that was none of my business, so I jumped at it with enthusiasm."

"I thought you weren't going to apologize."

"I'm explaining." They both heard Carey's car pull up in front of her house.

"I accept your explanation." She turned toward the open door. "But don't let it clear your conscience, because you didn't apologize."

He sat down in his chair and picked up his book. "Tell him he owes me a favor. I know you won't admit *you* do. And close that door. There's a draft on my hind legs."

Carey was standing beside the passenger door when Jane stepped out onto the porch. She held up her hand, hurried to her own door, tossed the mail on the couch, set the alarm, and locked the door, all the time thinking about the first glimpse of him. He was wearing a dark gray suit that must be new, and it was one she might have picked for him. His long legs and arms seemed comfortable in it, somehow, and the fabric along the lapels looked so soft and smooth her fingertips wanted to touch it. The color made the thin sandy hair that never seemed to stay where he thought he was supposed to put it look almost golden under the streetlamp.

As she came down the steps she gave him a little smile. "You're not trying to impress me, are you?"

"Not me." He opened the door for her. "The only reason I'm bringing you along is I'm trying to make the car look good. I'm trying to sell it, and I notice they always use young women in the commercials."

"No flies on you," she said. "You're what Jake calls a 'go-ahead young man.' "

He drove slowly and carefully up the street. She liked that. It was something that only people who had been raised in places like Deganawida seemed to have the sensitivity to do. If people had to look up from what they were doing to see if someone was running over the kids or grandma they didn't forget whose car it was, or who was in it. Whoever it was forfeited part of his claim to being solid and respectable. In Deganawida that respectability meant that people would strain to put a benevolent interpretation on anything they saw, and a third party who asked prying questions would be enveloped in a fog of laudatory generalities that applied to everyone and no one.

As Carey drove along River Road to the south he said, "I missed you."

"I missed you too," said Jane. She looked out across the half mile of moving river at Grand Island. When she and Jake's girls were children there were still lots of places over there where they could walk across a swampy field and fight their way through impenetrable thickets to streams full of perch and sunfish. The lights of the Holiday Inn across the water were in the spot where there used to be pilings from the old ferryboat landing and a vast empty field of dry weeds like hay. Sometimes they would search the pebbly shore with sticks and find big, heavy pieces of rust-encrusted iron that did not suggest any known use but had probably come from old-time lumber boats.

Carey drove east out of Buffalo on Main Street into the open suburbs, until they came to a sprawling restaurant built around a coach stop from the early 1800s, along the road that was laid over the Seneca trail. There were big stone fireplaces where resin-soaked pine logs flared and crackled, fed a steady stream of fresh oxygen by the air-conditioning. The walls were lined with buggy whips and harnesses and Currier & Ives prints, and when the food came, the roast beef was served with Yorkshire pudding.

They sat at a table beside the front window. Jane smiled as she surveyed the dining room. "I forgot this place existed."

"Me too," he said. "I picked it because it's a good place to talk."

"You picked it because it reminds you of your house." Jane had seen an old Holland Land Company map that Ellicott, the company agent, had used for the sale of Seneca land in 1801. Clearly marked in its place was "McKinnon house." "What do you want to talk about—horses?"

Carey was quiet and serious. "Last time, you told me about your trip. Are you going to tell me this time?"

"I think I did what I wanted to do." Her eyes scanned the empty tables around her to be sure none of the waiters had drifted too near. "But it wasn't smooth."

"You mean somebody's looking for you?"

"Maybe, but not hard, and not for long. It had nothing to do with me." She scanned the restaurant again, and when her eyes returned to him, she smiled. "Sounds brave, doesn't it?"

"I'm awed, as usual," he said.

"Don't be. Twenty-four hours ago I was as scared as anybody alive. I could almost taste the strawberries."

He cocked his head. "What strawberries?"

She looked down and shook her head. "It's just an old expression." She paused. "Really old. It means you came so close that you could already taste the wild strawberries that grow by the path to the other world."

He looked down too, and then up again to fix his eyes on hers. "Want to tell me what brought that on?"

"I made a mistake—took a chance to buy some extra time for my rabbit. I ended up in a high place, looking down, the way you do in a bad dream." She patted his hand. "Since I didn't fall, I guess you could say nothing actually happened. What did you do while I was gone?"

"Surgery every morning at seven except Friday. Office visits from one to five. Hospital rounds five to seven."

"And then?"

"I thought about how to talk to you. You're not that easy. You have a long history of standing up and walking around whenever anybody says anything, so I decided to take you to a restaurant."

"Big talk, huh? Serious stuff?"

"Yes. You told me what happened on your trip in December. You said that I should think about what I'd heard. If I asked you again after I'd thought about it, you would say yes."

Jane said, "No, I told you I loved you. I told you that if you asked me again after one year, I would say yes. And if you do, I will."

Carey's long, strong fingers moved up his forehead and pushed back the shock of hair that had begun to creep down. "I'm a very quick thinker. I've been thinking about it for six months. No. Let me start again," he said. "You and I have known each other for almost fourteen years. We were sophomores that night at Uris Library when Sally introduced us."

"Right," she said. "You were doing sickening drawings of invertebrates. Compound eyes and mandibles."

"So whatever fundamental judgments we needed to make about each other have been made. That was what this was about, wasn't it? You told me something that I hadn't known about you. You wanted to be sure I didn't assume I could ignore it and then start mulling it over after it was too late."

"That's part of it," she said. "We have to be friends, because we are. We don't have to get married. That brings on a whole new set of rules and agreements that are very rigid and binding, and nobody should do it who has any doubts."

"Are we still talking about the same thing?"

"I'm not talking about one thing," she said. "I'm talking about everything at once, because that's what marriage is. You take all of the complexity of your life—Who is this person? Do

I approve? Where do I want to live? Who are my relatives? What time do I get up? What do I wear? What work do I do?—and compress all of it into just one question: Do I get married or not? That was why I picked a year."

"You made your decision in a day."

"I'm very introspective, and I spend a lot of time alone."

He shook his head and chuckled sadly. "I want it on the record that I haven't seen any other women since we talked about this."

"Come on, Carey," she said. "You're so dour and business-like. It's not like you. This is about being alive and happy. We're old buddies. We know way too much about each other to start making speeches. I'm glad to hear you're not molesting the nurses . . . anymore. But that's just my possessiveness. I'm not checking compliance with an agreement."

"You started it. In December."

"I had no choice," she said. "That was disclosure."

"It seems to be what's standing in the way now."

She sighed. "You are a person who spends his life taking patients who are probably going to die and fixing them up. It's an obsession. It's what you have instead of a religion. I told you because not telling you would have made everything else a lie. I had just come home from a trip where I had killed some people. I am, technically and legally, a murderer. That's not a small thing. It puts you in danger too—again, technically and legally. But also philosophically. Emotionally. I did something that is against everything you believe and everything you know."

"How do you feel about it now?" He lowered his voice. "Are you sorry? Afraid? Proud?"

Her eyes turned on him in a glare, then turned away again. "It's something to be avoided."

"Do better than that."

"It was the most horrible experience of my life. If the same circumstances came up tomorrow—no, right now, tonight—I know I would do it again. It would be much harder because I would know what it was going to look like. It also taught me some other things I had avoided knowing."

"Like what?"

"All these years I was telling myself that what I was doing was unambiguous. I was taking people who were in the worst kind of trouble and making them disappear. That made sense. Whoever was in danger of dying didn't, so nobody did. But I should have admitted to myself that one day I wasn't going to run fast enough, or I would take a wrong turn. Until it happened I didn't realize that what I was doing wasn't just saving people. I was choosing a side. There aren't any good guys in a fight to the death. So now I know, and you know."

"Yes," said Carey. "I know. I've thought about it every day for six months. My reaction is another surprise. I find it doesn't matter to me. It's another life, another time—like a war. What does matter is this: Is it over? Do you plan to stop making people disappear?"

"Done," said Jane.

"What?"

"I mean, Okay. I'll stop doing what I've been doing."

"It's that easy?"

"Answering quickly doesn't mean it's easy. It just means I didn't wait until now to decide. When I said I would marry you, that was part of the bargain." Jane shrugged. "I was a guide because it was the right thing for me to do in that time and place. If you're waiting for me to apologize for it, you'll wait forever. It's just not something you do if you're somebody's wife."

The waiter brought the check on its little silver tray and Carey set a credit card on top of it, then went through the ceremony of adding the tip and signing it. The waiters and busboys were all very solicitous and friendly, because Carey and Jane were the only patrons who had not left, and they meant to sweep away all obstacles to their swift departure so the shift would end.

The car was waiting at the door. As soon as they were inside and the car was in motion, Carey said, "I love you. I've done all the thinking I need to do. I want you to marry me now, not six months from now." He stopped at the edge of the highway and looked at her, but there was no answer.

"Drive for a while," she said. He turned left and went east, out into the country. She sat in silence and looked out the window at the dark landscape. There were woods now, and farmhouses.

"Are you thinking about it?" he asked.

"I'm thinking," she said. "I'm thinking about how to tell you everything that's in my mind." She drew in a breath and seemed to try to begin, then let the breath out. "There!" she said. "Pull over up there by that orchard."

"Where?"

"Beside the fence."

The car slowed, and then the tires ground on gravel, and the car stopped. "Oh, even better," she said. "Pull into that drive up there."

"What are we doing?"

"Just do it." She cajoled, "I want to show you something. I promise you'll like it."

He slowly drove the car through the opening in the fence and up a dirt road into the orchard. The road was pink with blooms that had spilled from the apple trees on both sides. He bumped along deeper into the orchard as Jane stared eagerly out the windshield. "Okay, stop," she said, opened the door, and stepped out.

She walked to the far edge of the orchard and sidestepped a few paces down a little slope, then stopped. She slipped off her shoes and walked down the hill a short distance, paused at the edge of a thick patch of ankle-high wild plants with round, serrated leaves that covered the lower slope, then turned and looked up at Carey McKinnon. "Come down," she said. "I knew I could find some."

He cautiously stepped toward her, looking down to be sure of his footing. When he looked up she was bent over, fiddling with something under the hem of her skirt. Then she pulled off her stockings and handed them to him. "Put these in your pocket for me, will you?" She walked barefoot among the thick, soft plants, then bent over and ran her hands into them, touching here and there in the dark.

Carey stepped closer and she held out her hand. In the palm were a dozen little round shapes no bigger than a half inch across. "What's that?"

"Dessert," she said. "Wild strawberries."

She popped one onto her tongue and squeezed it against the roof of her mouth, then chewed it. "They're perfect." She held out her hand again and poured the little strawberries into Carey's palm.

He tasted one and smiled. "They're good. Soft, sweet." But she was already bent over, running her hands quickly among the fuzzy leaves of the little plants.

Carey knelt on the weeds with her and picked strawberries until they had a double handful. Carey gave them to her and then spread his new coat in the weeds and they sat on it, feeling the warm June air and the intense darkness of the new moon and eating strawberries.

They turned to each other and kissed, then slowly and gradually the kisses grew longer and deeper and they leaned back to lie on the coat, the tall weeds now sheltering them on both sides like a nest. Carey's hand began to move along her body—breast, waist, hip—and the clothes Jane had chosen didn't need to be tugged up and pulled down tonight. In the darkness they seemed to melt away, and she hoped, knew he had asked her to wear them with this moment in mind. Or maybe his asking and her compliance and this moment were part of the same event, one long act of asking and complying, her wanting him to ask, even turn his eyes in some direction so she could offer before he even formed the desire. The kisses were long and hungry now, and the hands—the long, gentle fingers and the wide, smooth palms moving everywhere, touching and outlining her shape in the darkness, the skin feeling itself traced and caressed so she could see herself with her eyes closed, the smaller, graceful shape and the curves she had somehow forgotten were her until now, when he saw them, touched them, pulled her against him. The embrace defined them both, his body all tense, hard muscles, the skin tickly with hair, but the boundary between them gone.

There was only the smell of the strawberries and the taste of them on her tongue, the warm, dark motionless air that might never change at all, and this heartbeat and this indrawn breath. But there was time because the feelings were growing, moving down to her belly and thighs, too many breaths until it grew into a longing, an ache, and he knew it. Then she was relieved, so much better, happy, actually happy, out of time now entirely, because if this feeling went on forever it would not be enough, but it went on, and she heard her own breaths coming quicker, and her voice coming out with them, and it was going to go on until she was obliterated, burned up like a moth flying into a blast furnace. And in this moment of wanting and having, that seemed just fine to her . . . better, best. And then time came back because this could not go on, was about to pass, not gasping for breath, but filled with it, and then so light and cool, shivering almost and the word *delicious* coming into her mind and passing away again because contentment was too lazy and pleased to hold on to it.

They lay naked on the hillside in the little space of flattened weeds, smelling the strawberries again. She opened her eyes to extend the depth of her gaze far up into the night sky.

For the first time in ages, she heard his voice. "Were the strawberries what you wanted to show me?"

"Sort of," she laughed. "It's kind of a multidimensional experience. In the old days, they used to court in strawberry patches."

"I'll bet it wasn't quite the same."

"I'll bet it was," she said. "See, they would slip out of their longhouses at night and meet in a place like this."

"I mean they didn't make love."

"Of course they did." She laughed. "That was what they were doing out here in the middle of the night. Maybe right here."

"I can see why strawberries grow on the way to heaven." He

ran his hand along her hip, smoothing it gently. "Ripe and sweet and perfect and rare."

She sat up and looked at him with a tiny hint of a wish. "Just the opposite. The reason they were so precious was that they weren't rare at all. They grew from one end of Iroquois country to the other. No matter what, they came up every May and ripened every June. They were easy—always there, always as many as you wanted, and always just as good as the first one you ever put on your tongue."

He sat up and looked at her closely, his eyes blue-gray and shining. "That was what you wanted me to know."

"You're getting better," she said. "You have a shot at 'Most Improved Naked Man.' "

"I'd like to think I was already smart enough to appreciate you, and never let myself forget how special you are, even after a few years of getting our strawberries in supermarkets like other people." His hand moved gently from her shoulder down her side to her hip, thigh, knee, shin, foot. "But I'm glad you took me on the field trip."

"Me too."

He said quietly, "It's not like you to waste all this wisdom on the first naked man you meet in a strawberry patch. To make it worthwhile, you'd almost have to marry me."

"Yes," she said. "I will."

4

The boardroom for Pleasure, Inc., overlooked the Polynesian water slide. Somebody had once joked that the architect's plans had been folded and the contractor hadn't noticed. It sounded true because mistakes in Las Vegas were not little slip-ups that made a few chips fall between the floorboards. They were hideous, gargantuan blunders, like building a billion-dollar casino on ground that was a foot lower than the adjacent square mile of parking lots, so the whole place got inundated with water in a flash flood every five years. But the location of the Pleasure Island boardroom had been no mistake; it had been a suggestion from Calvin Seaver, vice president for security.

Seaver stepped from the elevator and stared out through the double layer of one-way glass at the beautiful waterfall and the rocks and the lush tropical plants and flowers. He saw a pair of boys—he guessed eight and ten years old from the memory of his own boys—and then the father, a guy in his late thirties with a little baby fat around his middle and a U.S.N. anchor tattoo that showed he wasn't troubled with neck pains from holding up his brain. They stood on the platform ten feet from Seaver, waiting for something. He guessed it was Mom. And there she was. Not bad. A trace of cellulite in the haunches and sag in the tits, but nothing for her to worry about. She plunked down at the top of the slide with them, and all four went slipping down, around, under the waterfall, and out of sight. Good for them.

Seaver was trained to feel a presumptive hostility, watching the guests for some sign that they were going to cause a need for his services, but the reason he was the best was that he could tell the sheep from the goats. These were sheep. They wouldn't know how to cause trouble, because it wasn't in their nature. During their stay they would never know that he was watching over them, protecting them while they played and while they slept, making sure that nothing disturbed the artificial tranquility around them.

Those four were evidence that things were going beautifully. They would stay maybe five days. Mom and Dad would get a taste of canned glamour and carefully controlled risk. The boys would spend some time in the virtual-reality arcades, getting the feel of paying money to get excitement, and ensure Pleasure, Inc., of repeat business for the next fifty years. The family would pay Pleasure, Inc., more than they spent on this year's taxes to their home state, and then they'd be gone.

The goats were different—card counters and con men and shortchange artists and call girls and pickpockets—always trying to fade in among the sheep, but restless. He knew half of them by sight, but he didn't need to. He could detect it in their eyes the first time he saw them. They were hungry. He had sensed something too eager in Pete Hatcher's eyes early on, but he had misinterpreted it. His mistake was in accepting the bosses' assurances that all Hatcher was after was pussy.

He glanced at his watch and moved on down the hallway. Seaver was probably the only one who could see this part of the complex clearly when he looked at it. The elevators and the long, narrow hallway gave his people plenty of time and means to isolate anyone who had some business that wasn't on the board's agenda. The double panes of one-way glass kept anyone from amplifying the vibrations to pick up a conversation or using any sort of photography. Being next to the water slide ensured that nobody who wasn't wearing a bathing suit could get close, and anybody scanning with a directional microphone from a distance would pick up the waterfall and eighty customers talking about nothing.

It wasn't the sort of security that an underground room would have, but it had worked well enough so far. What he was worried about these days was some kind of futuristic emergency—some loser driving a car bomb through the front entrance, or some Japanese cult releasing nerve gas in the climate-control system. He had consultants working on countermeasures, but so far nothing they had brought him was good enough to bring to the big guys. All the plans involved lots of rebuilding to make space for some strategy they could not guarantee would work.

The big guys were never reluctant to spend money on remodeling. What they hated was having to shut anything down while they did it. But Seaver believed in outside consultants, and he was confident that they would solve these problems, one by one. Security was a matter of batting down specific threats. Nothing worked all of the time for all purposes.

He opened the door to the boardroom, stepped inside onto the thick carpet, and quietly took a seat at the enormous rosewood table. The door closed silently behind him. The automatic closer had been Seaver's idea too. The time when people were going in and out was a gaping breach in the room's integrity. Anyone who managed to defeat the other obstacles could learn a lot by picking up a few seconds here and there and studying what he had heard.

This time there was no meeting of the Management Team. The only ones in the room were the big guys themselves, Bobby Salateri, Max Foley, and Peter Buckley. They met this way more often than people would think, to talk without the twenty upper-level functionaries who ran housekeeping or finance or public relations or security.

Peter Buckley first deigned to notice Seaver. "Morning, Cal."

"Peter," said Seaver. Then he added, "Bobby, Max," as the others saw him. Then he waited. They took their time, and it was a compliment to him.

"Having water misters all over the place is okay this year. It's okay next year," said Salateri. "How does it look ten years from now? I mean politically?"

"It's not exactly all over the place," said Foley. "It's just on the golf courses. The sun shelters are already plumbed. It's just a matter of installing these little fixtures around the roof. That's thirty-six misters. They'll make the players feel cool and comfortable."

"Yeah, I know," said Salateri. "It's nothing, really. But every single time some TV station does a report on wasting water I see footage of misters over some hot dog stand."

"The estimate says the trees around the shelters will catch some of the water and the shade will keep the mist from evaporating as fast. If there's ever rationing, it's just that much more water grandfathered in."

"That's a point I hadn't thought of," said Salateri. "I can buy it on that basis. How about you, Peter?"

"Sure," said Buckley. "If things really get stupid, we've got something we can give away: Pleasure Island shuts down misters to save water."

"I'll have them go ahead," said Foley. He turned to Seaver. "Little problem last night, huh, Cal?"

"Yes," said Seaver. "I wish I had some excuse. I don't."

"So where does that leave us now?" asked Buckley.

"Hatcher wasn't on any flight leaving McCarran, or a train. A bus is too haphazard for him. He undoubtedly drove out. If he had the sense to keep driving, he could be in Chicago by now." He reached into his breast pocket. "My resignation is ready, if you want it."

"Stick it in your ear," said Salateri. "This isn't the fucking army, where you get to resign your commission and hand in your sword and go write your memoirs. We've got a parasite that could eat us alive. We need you more than we did yesterday."

"Thank you," said Seaver. It was the only thing Salateri had ever said to him that could have been a compliment.

"How did he lose your people?" asked Foley. "Maybe that's the place to start."

"He met a woman at the Inside Straight for the midnight lounge show. The Miraculous Miranda picked him out of the audience, made him disappear a couple of times, and brought him back. The last time, she didn't. He probably slipped out the stage door. My men got suckered. They followed the woman and a decoy out of the show, then lost the decoy too. The woman was a pro. She got them to watch her for an hour, then split them up and cornered one of them in the elevator. She left him with a broken leg, a broken nose, and some damage to his eye."

"A professional what?" asked Salateri. "Boxer?"

"I don't know what term she uses on her business cards," said Seaver. "But I don't think Hatcher could have set this up for himself. I don't know what part in this Miranda played— maybe just picking him out of the crowd was enough, and magicians will sometimes do that as a favor if you send a waiter backstage and ask. Maybe—"

"It doesn't matter," interrupted Buckley. "I'm not about to start grilling Miranda, and I hope you're not."

"Only if you asked me to," said Seaver. "If she knows anything, there's no reason for her to tell me, and no way I can make her. If the woman is a pro, then Miranda probably doesn't know much."

Salateri shrugged and made a face of distaste. "I'll see if I can talk to Vincent." He sat quietly for a moment, then noticed the others staring at him. "Why not? You think if Vincent Bogliarese wanted to do us harm he'd do it this way—have his girlfriend sneak the guy off in a puff of smoke? Get real. He'd send eight hundred guys in shiny suits to pull our guts out and set fire to them." He added, to no one in particular, "I say that, of course, with the greatest respect, and in confidence. The man is a friend of mine. I'm not saying he'll find out anything for us, but it won't hurt to ask."

Max Foley looked at Seaver. "It looks to me as though we really have to handle this ourselves, Cal. This screw-up is yours, but the underlying problem isn't. It's ours, the three of us. We picked out Hatcher, we misjudged him, and we trusted him with a lot of things we shouldn't have."

"That's right," said Buckley.

Salateri nodded sadly. "He was smart, easy to be around, he

behaved like a man. Now we're in trouble, and we don't even know what kind."

"We can guess," said Foley. "No matter what he thinks he's going to do now, at some point he's going to end up in the hands of the F.B.I." He added, "Unless he doesn't."

Buckley leaned back in his big chair. "Do we have anybody on our payroll who can take care of this kind of problem?"

"No," said Seaver. "We've been very careful not to hire anyone like that full-time. They're not the sort of people you want to have around year in and year out. Other employees figure out what they're there for, and so on."

The three men sat in a row and looked at him. "You've been in the security business for a long time," said Foley.

"And a cop before that," added Salateri.

Foley continued. "Yes. You must know someone who would be able to do it. I mean a full-service specialist, who can find him and handle the rest."

"There's someone I can probably get," said Seaver. This was going to be the delicate part. He wasn't sure they knew what this involved. "I'll need a lot of cash. Maybe a hundred thousand to start, and more later."

"Cash?" said Buckley. "Well, hell, Cal. Cash is what we do. Go downstairs and give this to Eddie." He rapidly scribbled a note and handed it to Seaver, who glanced at it: "Give Seaver whatever he wants. P.B." Buckley folded his hands across his belly. "Who is this guy?"

"It's a Mickey-and-Minnie team. I'll talk to them today."

"Just don't bring them here," said Salateri. "I don't want to meet anybody like that."

"And if you're going to hire them, don't call them from here, either," said Foley. "A year from now I don't want some prosecutor going down the hotel phone bills and finding their number."

Seaver nodded. "Of course. I'll be flying to Los Angeles to talk to them in person. There are just a couple of things I should tell you. They'll give me a price, but expenses will be on top of that."

"This goes without saying," said Buckley. "What else?"

"Once they leave their house, it's done. I won't be able to call them off. They'll keep at it as long as it takes, and they won't check in with me or be any place I can reach them. If we find out tomorrow that Pete Hatcher was the most loyal employee the world has ever seen, it'll be too late. He'll already be dead."

"I guess this is the time to ask." Buckley looked at his two partners. "Are we all sure we aren't going to change our minds?"

"I'll chance it," said Foley.

They both looked at Salateri. He knitted his brows and held up both hands. "You know it would be too bad if we were just being paranoid. I mean, an innocent guy suddenly has his bosses decide he's the enemy, and then they get him tossed in a Dumpster somewhere. But he already knows we had him watched, and he knows we were considering getting rid of him. If he was our friend, he's not anymore. What good would he be to us now?"

Linda Thompson sat in her bedroom and rubbed the creamy mask onto the perfect white skin of her cheeks and forehead, staring into the lighted mirror. This one was blue, and it left three small round holes for her eyes and mouth. The white towel wrapped around her blond hair above her blue face made her look ghostly in the intense glow of the makeup light. She walked to the bed and lay down to wait. The blinds were closed, but the window behind them open, so they clacked back and forth in the dry, hot southern California breeze. She opened her robe and let the air blow across her naked body while it dried the facial mask. She had already covered herself with lotion, and the air made her skin tingle.

Linda was beautiful. She had never been anywhere since she was nine when somebody had not mentioned it, or looked at her in a way that made mentioning it seem like saying it twice. She knew it was the kind of beauty that was startling, because it seemed to take up space of its own. It was the initial premise of every transaction she had with other people. They didn't seem to understand that it wasn't a gift. It was a torment, because it was perfection, and maintaining perfection was a lot of work. Linda hated work.

It was only eleven in the morning and she had already done five point five miles on the stationary bike, worked for an hour on the exercise machines, and done a half hour in the pool. She knew she would have felt less bereft now if she could have had four fried eggs and a half pound of bacon, which was what Earl had eaten in front of her before he had gone out to work the dogs. Linda had not eaten since the cracker and asparagus last night, and Earl had thrown that nauseating mess into a pan in front of her and set off a racket of sizzling and popping and smelly grease. When she had said she didn't want any he had given that crooked smirk and eaten all of it himself. Wolfed it down, was the expression, and it was made for Earl.

He was tall and lean with big knuckles and a jaw that showed what he was: ten generations of white trash in assorted depressing hollows out of God's line of vision in the South, and probably the ten generations before that being the same thing in England, all twenty generations of them screwing with people only one or two branches over on the family tree, so they were all completely devoid of common consideration and never gained an ounce.

The air seemed to tear itself apart with a sound that wasn't quite a bark but a scream. She sprang from the bed amid low growls and the howl of the hound as it turned to defend itself. Linda didn't have the patience to run down the hallway to the living room, into the dining room, and out the door, so she raised the blinds, sat on the windowsill, swung her legs out, and jumped to the grass. She sprinted toward the kennel, muttering to herself, "He's absolutely retarded."

When she reached the high chain-link fence she could already see the bloodhound backed into the corner trying to keep the Rottweilers away from his hamstrings. His left ear had been chewed, and there was blood dripping from his muzzle.

Earl was standing in the corner of the pen, absently rubbing the bristle of his unshaven chin as he watched the big, heavy black dogs hurl themselves at the hound.

Linda spoke loudly enough for him to hear. "Call them off, Earl."

He turned slowly and looked at her, but she didn't wait. She barked, *"Halt! Aufhören mit!"* The two Rottweilers stopped and backed up until they were beside the fence.

"Oh, it's you," said Earl. "The face didn't ring a bell." She traced his line of vision and found herself looking down. She hastily closed the robe and tied it.

"What are you doing?" she asked wearily.

"Trying to see how two of them work when they've got something cornered."

"They bite the hell out of it until it bleeds to death. What more could you possibly find out?"

"I wasn't sure. That's why I did it. Now I know."

"And?"

"It might come in handy some time. I think I could beat two of them. Don't know anybody else who could."

"So what are you going to do with this thousand-dollar pure-bred bloodhound you brought home a week ago? You can't enter it in a show now that it's all chewed up. You can't even put it out to stud."

Earl glanced at the dog cowering in the corner of the exercise yard, not daring to move. He shrugged. "Science."

Linda walked into the house and opened the cupboard beside the sink. She pulled out the Heckler & Koch .45 A.C.P., pressed the button at the rear of the trigger guard to release the magazine, and checked it. She had to be sure Earl hadn't left it unloaded the last time he had pissed her off. No, there was a full load of ten Federal Hydra-Shok hollow-points. She slipped the big pistol inside her robe, clamped it there with her left arm, and stepped out the door.

When she reached the kennel, he had already let the bloodhound out of the pen into the run, and he was busily giving the Rottweilers chunks of red steak. She walked beside the fence of the long, narrow track to the spot where the bloodhound was lying on its belly trying to lick some of the gashes in its chest, but not really able to. She flicked off the safety, pushed the muzzle of the pistol through the links of the fence, aimed at the dog's round, bony cranium, and blew it apart.

The report of the big pistol brought Earl around the kennel into the exercise run. He looked at her blue face with the staring eyeholes, but he didn't speak.

She answered him anyway. "Any vet who got a look at him would have called the police."

He said, "You going to bury that?"

She had already started back across the lawn. Her blue mask had hardened, and now it burned against her skin as she whirled and snapped, "You know goddamned well I'm not."

Linda walked back into the kitchen, released the magazine, and left the pistol on the counter for Earl to clean. She knew if she cleaned it, he would clean it again. In her bathroom, she gently washed the mask off and patiently, thoroughly rubbed moisturizer from the tiny jar onto her face with her fingertips, staring into the mirror over the sink.

That was Earl. She had no doubt that he had figured out how to kill two Rottweilers attacking him at once. But the part that made him Earl Bliss was that if he hadn't been sure, then tomorrow or the next day she would, likely as not, find him out there in the pen with a Ka-Bar knife doing it. He was a severe annoyance between jobs. He could not rest.

She knew that this afternoon he would be out in the Angeles National Forest sighting in the new rifle for the fourth time. It was a British Arctic Warfare suppressed military sniper rifle with an olive-drab stainless-steel barrel and a Schmidt & Bender 50-millimeter scope. Everything about it was adjustable, from the pull and travel of the trigger to the recoil absorption of the butt plate, so Earl would spend days and days adjusting them. The plain A.W. military-issue model started at over three thousand dollars, but the suppressed model with the silencer was highly illegal and had probably set him back five times that, because he had never told her what the Mexican cop had asked for it. Earl always needed the latest and fanciest piece of equipment, and then he had to take it completely apart and put it back together to see exactly how it worked.

That combination of constant self-improvement and morbid curiosity was what she would have extracted as the most horrible part of Earl, but she could not even hold that thought firmly, because it was also the best part of him. And cutting things away from him wasn't possible. Earl had no surface, like other people: he was the same all the way through, like a chunk of steel. All you could do was move your head to look at the same qualities from different angles. That was how she had come to love and hate him at the same time.

He looked at everything the same—dismantling gadgets, testing the dogs to see how they worked, or her. Every time he heard or read or saw something that could be done to a woman's body, he would do it to her, watching with an expression between detached curiosity and, maybe she just hoped, fascination, to see how it affected her: to see how she worked. The result didn't seem to matter to him in any emotional way. It didn't matter if he had her panting like a bitch in heat, crawling to him and begging for more, or sent her whimpering into her room to lock the door for three days. He didn't take care to repeat the good things to make her happy, or avoid things that would remind her of something that had hurt her. He just wanted to see how she worked.

She had let him put her in a dark mood, and now she began to construct a fantasy about him. He would come in from burying the bloodhound. He would go to the sink in the kitchen to wash his hands. She would come in behind him while his hands were engaged and wet. She would put her left hand on his shoulder softly to show him she didn't give the dog issue undue importance, then use it to tousle his hair while she freed her right to reach into her robe.

But he was Earl, so it would take him a half second to realize from the feel of her fingers or the sound of her breathing that something was up. She knew she would not be able to say anything or he would hear the tension in her voice. She would use that half second to tighten her fingers on his hair, jerk his head back, and bring the fillet knife across his throat. She had been composing these little plays about him since she was in high school, when she first went to work filing and running errands at his detective agency, and as she had known it would, this one began to change.

He would sense her excitement instantly and give that little snort of a laugh as his right hand shot up like a striking snake to catch her left. The knife was still hidden under her robe, held there by the tie-belt on the outside, and she was afraid it would fall out, so she turned away and leaned her hip against the edge of the green marble surface of the island in the middle of the kitchen to keep it there.

The move gave him an idea, so he reached around her and pulled the belt of the robe so it opened, and put his big hand between her shoulder blades. He pushed her forward and she felt the shock of the cold, hard marble, first on her breasts, and then her belly, and the hard corner of the marble against her pelvis. She had no choice but to wriggle farther onto the marble to keep the fillet knife flat under her belly so it wouldn't slice her open or clatter to the floor, only that brought her buttocks up and parted her legs, and she had to hold herself absolutely rigid to keep from moving against the blade. And he—

The ring of the telephone beside her bed was like something breaking. She snatched the receiver off the hook and punched the button that was lit. She was too annoyed to see which number it was, so she said, "Linda Thompson."

"Hello, Linda." She recognized the voice, and her anger began to turn into hope. "Can you and Earl meet me someplace for lunch?"

A job, she thought. Thank God.

5

Linda sat beside Earl in the front seat and watched each shopper pull into the big parking lot, drive up and down a couple of aisles, coast between two diagonal slashes of white paint, then go through the ritual of checking the whole car: the mirrors to be sure the car's ass wasn't hanging out far enough to get clipped, the passenger seat to collect purses or glasses or hide a bag they bought in the last mall from the smash-and-grab crowd, then the lock buttons. The excruciating sameness of it was getting on her nerves. People were as predictable as gophers. You knew the next three things they were going to do before they did.

The car smelled like dogs, that nauseating dog-food smell they exuded from every pore. Earl had used the car instead of the truck again. She decided not to say anything, because it would spoil the next hour.

Earl was brilliant in his own way. Raising and training attack dogs was a great sideline for a detective agency that didn't do much business. In a city the size of Los Angeles you could pick up any breed you wanted from the pound for the price of the shots, which was up to sixty bucks now. Some of them had papers. You trained the dog to sit, heel, shit outdoors, and maul people, and you could sell it for fifteen thousand.

But Linda was ready to work now, and that was Earl's fault too. He had trained her practically from childhood to his rhythms. He was only really alive when he was hunting. Between times he only played at it and got more and more irritable.

Seaver was precisely on time, as she had known he would be. He was one of those guys who seemed to see himself as though he were still in the military. For the ones like him, that wasn't some kind of interruption in his existence but his initiation into manhood. She saw him pull the rental car between the diagonal lines, but he didn't behave like the others. He was out and walking as soon as the keys were out of the ignition. He still carried himself straight, only now there was a little gray at the sides of his short hair. The aviator sunglasses he used to wear had been replaced with plain black frames, but the gray summer suit with the bright white shirt still had that animal-in-clothes look because it was cut too snugly and the collar was too tight, the way the army had taught him to dress.

He got into the back seat and Earl drove off. "Hello, Cal," said Linda. "You're looking good."

"You too," said Seaver. She knew that he had thought of a compliment, but he had pressed his tongue against the back of his teeth because he had known better than to say it in front of Earl.

"Let's go to Ivy at the Shore," said Seaver. "We can talk business while we're on the freeway, and then eat in peace."

"When's your plane out?" asked Earl.

"Four o'clock," said Seaver. "If I'm back in my car by three, I'll make it. If not, I'll take another flight."

As Earl accelerated down the ramp onto the San Diego Freeway Seaver stared at the bottom of the first overpass. Some time soon it was going to be a bad idea to transact this kind of business on a freeway. Already the California Department of Transportation had tried placing cameras on the overpasses so when there was a traffic jam they could see what had caused it. And lately thieves had put machines on the bridges to capture cellular phone numbers and codes they could program into clones. He opened his coat, took out a thick manila envelope, and handed it over the seat to Linda. "In there is all the information I have about a target I want found and taken out."

Earl glanced at the unopened envelope. "What is all that?"

"Photographs, a surveillance videotape, two audiotapes—one on the phone, one live—his employment history. I thought I could save you some time."

Earl smiled. "He must be important."

Seaver felt a distaste for the tactics of bluff and barter. "The price is going to be three hundred thousand for him. We'll cover legitimate expenses."

"Hear that, Earl?" said Linda. "No illegitimate expenses this time."

"I mean," said Seaver, "that I'm not the client. I just picked you for the job. If it's too outrageous, the client is capable of getting rid of me and hiring somebody else to deal with you."

"I hear you," said Earl. "Why is this guy worth that much? Does he have something I have to bring back, or what?"

"No," said Seaver. "He's got information in his head. He can't hand it off or sell it, because nobody else can testify to what he saw. He'll have to be alive to do it."

Linda smiled at Seaver and he thought about what a strange creature she was. She had what used to be called cupid's bow lips, big, liquid green eyes. The smile would have been merely beautiful if it had been prompted by something else, but death seemed to excite her, and when her pulse went up the eyes got more green and there was a delicate flush in the pure white complexion. Her face was hypnotic, and the need to keep looking at it was like an itch. "Smell something, Earl? A Green Beret, right? No, I know. C.I.A. Forced retirement." She turned the eyes away, toward Earl, and the blond hair hid them like a curtain.

When she took the light of that face away from him, the frustration made Seaver involuntarily suck in a breath through his teeth. He quickly dispelled any hint that he had been thinking about anything but business by blowing the breath out through his lips in a contemptuous huff.

"The price is high because the client doesn't ever want to think about him again. I hire you, and you handle it. The end," said Seaver. "I don't think he'll put up any resistance. But I have no idea where he is. When he disappeared, he had professional help, so he's probably got reasonably good cover in place."

"How long ago?" asked Earl.

"Day before yesterday, about midnight, he drove out of Las Vegas. We don't know anything about the car."

"So the trail's cold. What about the professional help?"

"We don't have much on that, either. It was a woman, mid-twenties to thirty, tall, dark hair, probably brown eyes, but there are two versions. Very fit."

Linda laughed aloud, her voice somewhere between a taunt and a seduction. " 'Very fit.' " She imitated a man's voice the way a child would have: "Have I ever told you you're very fit? I want to look deep into your probably-brown eyes."

"She beat the shit out of one of my security men," said Seaver. "But even he said she was pretty. He didn't volunteer it, because it wasn't what he remembered most about her, but he didn't deny it."

"She sounds interesting," said Earl.

"Oh, now I'm getting jealous," said Linda. The lips came together like a kiss in a studied pout that Seaver knew should have been repellent but made him wish that Earl were dead. She brightened again. "Got her on tape, or any fingerprints? She might be the way to find him."

"Sorry."

"She would have been the one to leave the car for him," said Linda. Her voice was wheedling now. "She was there before he left Las Vegas, and she must have stayed somewhere."

"I know," said Seaver. "I've had my men watching surveillance tapes for twenty-four hours, and she hasn't turned up. The first time anybody saw her was the night she took off."

Earl Bliss swung onto the Santa Monica Freeway and watched his rearview mirror. Nobody in a car behind them seemed to change his mind and follow. The others said nothing while he pretended to be considering the offer. After a decent interval he said, "We'll get started on it after lunch."

* * *

It was after dark. Linda could hear him out in the kennel, giving the dogs their dinner. She had already heard him call Lenny on the phone and tell him they were leaving and to pack up and move in at seven in the morning. Linda walked through the house to make sure everything was as it should be. Windows had to be closed, valuables hidden away, checks written for the bills. She took the Heckler & Koch .45 out of the cabinet by the kitchen sink and the Para-Ordnance P-14s from the bedrooms, the den, and the garage and locked them in the gun cabinet behind her closet. Lenny would just stumble onto one of them and blow a hole in something. If he had some kind of trouble while they were gone, he would be more likely to survive it with the gun he always brought with him. Anyway, with a couple of the dogs running the perimeter he'd be safe enough. Nobody cared enough about Lenny to kill him.

Earl always left most of the packing to Linda, because she was the woman. She supposed that meant she was too fastidious to put dirty clothes in by mistake.

She heard his heavy feet on the walk outside, then heard them clomping into the hallway. She called, "You want to take these Colts, right?"

He came in and looked at the pistols she had taken out of the gun cabinet and set on her dresser. They were Colt Model 1911A1s, the most common handgun in the United States, and probably the world. Colt had made them since 1925, over a million of them during World War II alone, and other manufacturers at least that many. The government had kept issuing them for forty years after that, and every army and police force in the Western world had carried some copy with minor variations. The sheer age meant the cops had lost track of most of them long ago, and ballistics identification was a fantasy. Seven .45 rounds were plenty if you didn't plan to have anybody shooting back, and the bulk of the gun was only a problem on the way. You could drop it after it was fired.

Earl said, "These will do fine."

She could tell by the look on Earl's face that it was time for the ritual to begin, so she started. "I'm worried." She had to be the one who said the first words, because he liked it that way.

"There's a lot to worry about," he said. "This is a big job, and it won't be easy."

"I could tell as soon as Seaver started talking," she fretted. "He didn't want to look in my eyes. You spent the afternoon on the computer. Didn't you find anything?"

He pursed his lips and shook his head. "Seaver didn't miss much. No criminal record. No marriages, no out-of-town property. The only car he owned is the one that's still there. I found court records for probate when his old man died. He inherited a few bucks, and there were no other close relatives mentioned in the will."

Linda frowned. "Not much for us there. It will be hard."

"But this is one we've got to win," he said. "The money is good. If we do this one, it will get better on the next one."

"If we blow it, Seaver's bosses will send somebody to look for us." She knitted her brows. "He as good as said that, didn't he?"

"It's a Las Vegas hotel. It's got to be Mafia."

"Got to be," she agreed. "We do it right and we get lots of jobs and lots of money. We fail—don't find him, or try, and botch it—and they're not going to leave us alone."

"It's an important job. More important than anything we've ever done. Life or death."

It was working, and Linda could feel it. Already her breaths were quick and shallow, and her stomach had little quivers in it. The adrenaline was pumping into her veins. She could see Earl's eyes were beginning to get that narrow long-distance gaze. She searched for a way to turn up the pitch, and found it. "We're starting out dead, really. Because they already have us—know who we are, where we live. They'll kill us unless we get him."

That seemed to work for Earl. "He's got our life. We're dead until we get him. We have to find him to take it back."

Earl's anger transported Linda. Her energy was beginning to crackle out in little bolts of rage. "And who the hell is he to do that? He knew he was going to die—deserved to die—but he decided it wasn't going to be him. It was going to be somebody else."

"He knew what he was doing," said Earl. "He knew there would be somebody who had to come along and clean up the mess he left. Somebody like us would be put in his place, in a deep hole, and have to dig their way out of it." His throat was choked with anger.

"Oh, he's not worried about us," she muttered. "He's some-place laughing at us. Both of them are. That woman who got him out of Vegas. They think they're smarter than anybody who would need the money bad enough to come for them."

Earl stood up and began to pace. "Not just smarter. Better than us. Like even if we did luck onto him it wouldn't matter, because he'd beat us."

Linda's pulse was fast, hard, and strong now. She was trans-fixed with hatred and fear. Her jaw was clenched and her long fingernails were jabbing into the palms of her hands, leaving little red crescents. She could see the veins standing out in Earl's neck. He was moving again, too full of energy to keep still. He was picking things up and tossing them into his suit-case. He seemed to see what a mess he was making of it, so he went and gathered the two Colts from the dresser and headed for the door. He stopped in the doorway and said, "Just be sure you're ready by six."

Jane sat on the couch and stared around her at the baseboards in the living room. There were nicks that her father had patched with the best synthetic wood mixtures they had sold at the time, then painted over, but she knew where they were twenty years later. The one by the kitchen door was from the new refrigerator he had bought as a surprise for her mother, which was still on the other side of the door running right now. Jane remembered seeing the man pushing the two-wheel hand truck it was strapped to miscalculate and nick the doorway. The man who was supposed to be guiding him saw it, spit on his finger, and rubbed the spot, trying to believe it was just a dirt mark but feeling the groove.

The imperfections in the surfaces were events. Her great-grandfather had built most of the house himself, and her grandfather and father had painted and varnished it, and her grandmother and her mother had rubbed every square inch of it clean a thousand times, so if she put her hand here, or here, she was touching their hands.

She said aloud, "I got married yesterday," as a test, and it failed. The words didn't sound convincing, because they didn't have behind them the resonance of wonder. All of the people who would have come rushing in from the kitchen and the dining room, making noise and smiling—or maybe looking worried—were just memories now. Birth, marriage, death. That was all they put on tombstones, and that seemed to be about all anyone wanted to know unless you were pretty remarkable. Jane Whitefield had spent the past twelve years straining every nerve to keep from being remarkable, because attracting attention was dangerous. It seemed she had succeeded, and now she would have to succeed some more, because she had Carey.

Jane turned her attention to the pile of mail that Jake had left for her, setting the bills beside her and the advertisements on the floor for the wastebasket. She came to a stiff white envelope with no return address. Probably it was another wedding card. It would have the usual flowered bower with bells, and beneath it would be the archetypal stiff little people, one in white and the other in black. There was no way anybody could be expected to obtain one that was remotely evocative of a marriage between actual human beings. For some reason there was no market for such a thing. But this mail was old. It had come while she was in Las Vegas, and she had forgotten about it in the rush and excitement of getting married. This couldn't be a wedding card.

She tore it open and saw that it was a plain white folded sheet. Printed in ballpoint pen was "You told me I would be thinking of you just about now. So here's a present. Chris." Inside was a cashier's check with the purchaser listed as Christine McRea. The stub attached to it said "Repayment of Principal." Jane glanced at the machine printing on the check: one hundred thousand and 00/100 dollars.

Christine McRea had come a long way since the night when she had knocked on the door of this house. Her name had been Rebecca Solomon then, and she had made the mistake of assuming that when a judge said the names of people serving on a jury were confidential, that meant an enterprising reporter wouldn't be able to find hers and print it later. When Jane had met her, she had already used all the money she had saved on her secretary's salary just to get as far as Cleveland, and had hitched a ride the rest of the way with a pair of itinerant heavy-equipment operators who had begun to hint at things she could do to repay their kindness.

Jane tore up the note, slipped the check into the pile of bills, and got up off the couch, determined to accomplish something before Carey got here. She would need the address book in her office for the thank-you notes. A few of the people Carey had invited were reachable only through his secretary's computer, but almost everybody else was in her old book. She had known him for so long that their friends were nearly all shared. Most of Jane's relatives lived on the roads along Tonawanda Creek— Sandy Hill Road, Sky Road, a few on Judge Road. She could have sent all of those notes in care of the reservation, but the older ladies would not have approved. She set the floppy old leather book by the door and went upstairs.

She took a few favorite outfits and laid them carefully on the bed, then heard the front door open and close. "Carey?" she called. "I'm upstairs."

Jake's voice called, "Are you decent?"

Jane laughed. "No, Jake. But I'm married now, so I can be as indecent as I want."

"I mean am I invited up?"

"If you can make it up the stairs."

Jake came along the hallway toward her room. "It was a near thing, but I rested frequently and phoned my doctor for advice on the landing. Where is that quack, anyway?"

"He'll be here in a few minutes. He's helping me move a few things, so I thought we'd need both cars. Now that I look at it, I don't think we will."

"I wanted to tell you that I had a good time at the wedding."

"That's because your daughters came. Thanks for giving me away, though, Jake. There was never a man who looked as relieved to get rid of anybody as you did. Everybody make it to the airport on time?"

"Oh, yeah," said Jake. "The kids will make it to their final exams and the husbands will be at work Monday morning to keep my girls wearing the latest fashions and a bit too broad in the beam to fit them. The reception reminded me of when your parents got married. All the food and everything, a lot of the same faces, too, but of course we're all a bit the worse for wear."

Jane selected some of her shoes and set them in a cardboard

box. "Last night wasn't really a reception. It was another wedding. In the old days you just asked the two clan mothers if it was okay, and then everybody had a feast."

"I wish your parents could have seen it. God, I remember your mother in her white gown. She was probably the most beautiful woman I ever saw, close up. You're a pleasant-looking female citizen from a thousand yards out on a cloudy evening. But she could knock a rooster off a full henhouse with a veil over her face. She could have been an actress."

"She was an actress," said Jane. "She made herself up."

Jake was silent for a moment. Little Janie had gotten those arctic-blue eyes from her mother, but that penchant for saying the unexpected, like dumping a bushel of apples in your lap to show you what the bottom ones looked like, that came from Henry Whitefield without any dilution. He backed away from that part of it. "She was a wonderful woman."

He had never figured out how much Jane could have known about her mother's past. She had somehow found herself at the age of nineteen in New York City without visible means of support. No, that was exactly the wrong term. Spectacular, sure-fire means of support were still visible on her, well into her forties. Jake had never heard anything specific about how she had spent the years from one to nineteen, or even what part of the country she had started in. Maybe that was the deepest secret of all, and maybe his wife, Margaret, had heard all of that from her too, and found it too ordinary to repeat to her husband.

But she had spent the next few years downstate in the company of a succession of men who were accustomed to having their pictures taken twice—head-on and in profile. Maybe she had not made a choice. Women had a way of dancing with the man who asked, and a lot of the natural-selection business that determined who was first in line, or even who considered himself worthy, got settled among the men themselves.

Jane smiled. "She was a very smart woman. She had figured out that your life is pretty much what you decide it is. She picked the right person to be and spent the rest of her life being that person as hard as she could."

It was true. Whatever had happened to Jane's mother in the first years of her life, it had taught her something she never forgot. Whatever decisions she needed to make were all behind her before Jake had met her. Henry had a wife and Jane had a mother who could have come out of the television shows of the time—house neat and clean, something hot bubbling on the stove, and her looking fresh and crisp and reassuring.

Jake watched her daughter bustling around in the same house, and he unexpectedly had a vision of the future. It wasn't a vision he could take credit for. It was more like a prophecy that he had merely overheard. She was busy inventing Mrs. Carey McKinnon, the way her mother had invented Mrs. Henry Whitefield. He guessed the perfect wife wouldn't act the same these days as she had thirty years ago.

On that score alone, he expected that watching Jane over the next year or two would provide a supplement to his education. And Jane wasn't the same woman as her mother. Henry had made sure she got raised in the old Seneca way, where you didn't waste much breath telling kids what to do, so their self-reliance didn't get stifled. God knew the Whitefields had gotten a whopping return on that investment.

And Janie had a different order of determination entirely. She had consciously chosen to do something with the first part of her life that was more than heroic, because if you saved somebody's life once, that was bravery. When you did it a hundred times, that was pure stubbornness. If she had now chosen to be somebody else, the perfect wife, then letting your feet get in her path on her way to it would be a good way to lose a foot. This new person, this Jane McKinnon, was not going to be somebody you faced down eye-to-eye.

He heard the sound of Carey McKinnon's tread on the front porch and looked down at him through Jane's window. Henry would have been pleased. Jake could see Carey's head beginning to shine through the thin, sandy hair, so he was no kid anymore. Jake hoped he had enough sense by now to understand the nature of the gift he had been given, but he supposed he probably didn't. It often seemed to Jake that wisdom had settled on his own head like a wreath from heaven some time around age sixty, after it was too late to do him much good and was more of an irritation than a pleasure. He said, "Well, I've got to move on, or the damned dandelions will get a foothold on my lawn again and I'll spend the whole summer on my knees digging them out with a knife."

"Good. I thought you were just hanging around to get free medical advice."

"Not me. I want mine duly recorded in an office in front of witnesses so I can sue for malpractice. See you, Mrs. McKinnon."

"See you, Jake."

Jake met Carey carrying boxes up the stairs. "Take good care of her," said Jake. "I'll tell you why at your fiftieth anniversary, if you're not senile by then."

"Better write it down, Jake. Don Herbick keeps calling me from his mortuary to ask about your health. I say, 'Not yet, Don. But keep the motor tuned up.'"

"I suspected you probably worked closely with an undertaker, Dr. McKinnon. But I won't desert you now that you've got a wife to support."

"It's always good to have your unqualified endorsement, Jake. I could hardly ask for anybody more unqualified."

"It's a pleasure to serve." He walked out and closed the door.

Carey set the empty boxes on the floor and put his arm around Jane. "He's right about you. When I walked in, I could hardly believe it. You actually married me."

She smiled, craned her neck, and leaned back against his chest to give him a gentle kiss. "I'm glad to know that you're not here about a refund. But don't assume everything Jake has to say about me would make you happy. He's got no excuse left for illusions about women." She stepped away from him, picked up the dresses on hangers from the bed, and slipped the hooks over his hand. "To business. Take these down and hang them on the pole I've got across the back seat. Do not toss, crumple, or otherwise render them unsuitable for wear. Then report for further orders."

He walked off down the hall and clomped down the stairs. She looked around and began to pull things out of her dresser drawers and put them into boxes. Carey came back and stood in the doorway. "It just occurred to me," he said. "What are you going to do with this house? Sell it?"

She paused and looked at him. Why did she have to be the sort of person who already had calculated everything and made the decisions? "Come sit with me," she said.

They sat together on the bed. "This is one of the conversations we should have had before. I'm through being a guide. I will never take another fugitive and slip him to a new place with a new identity. But for a while, this house is going to be a problem. I can't place an ad in the paper announcing that I'm going out of business. It's more than a little likely that one or two people are going to arrive here in the next year or two expecting to find that kind of help. I know that ahead of time, and I'm prepared to accept the way I'll feel if I find out one of them tried on his own and didn't make it."

"How can you?"

"That's not going to be an issue between us. It's like what the insurance companies call a pre-existing condition. My problem."

"So you're going to keep it here, empty?"

"If we sell it, then maybe—no, probably—one night the new owners are going to be sitting downstairs watching television, and somebody is going to arrive and tell them things I don't want them to hear. Or even worse, one of the chasers will have followed him here. This isn't theoretical. It happened once."

"It's going to be a hard place to unload. I suppose you don't want the phone company reassigning your number either."

"I can afford to keep paying the bills. In a few years there will be fewer people who remember the address. The ones who do will know that it's not the solution to anybody's problem anymore. Then we'll cancel the phone, sell the house, and use the money for a trip around the world or something."

He laughed. "Don't be ridiculous. I'm not going to use up your money. We should have had that conversation before, too. I will support my wife. Keep whatever money you have safe, in case of an emergency."

"You're wrong," she said. "This is the emergency, tonight. Things are happening fast that will get set in cement, so we have to do all of them right. We take each other on, unconditionally. What I used to do has put you in jeopardy: not much jeopardy, but some enterprising F.B.I. agent could still stumble on somebody I helped, and you could wake up one morning to the smell of tear gas and the sight of men in bulletproof vests and baseball caps knocking down the door with a battering ram. There are also some very slimy people out there who still want to find some victim they didn't get to torment enough, and would be very happy to step over your body for the privilege of asking me questions." She paused to let the two unpleasant possibilities settle in his imagination. Then she smiled. "However. I did make a lot of money at it. You'd better share the rewards, because you've already taken on the risks."

He shrugged. "We can use it to buy a lot of life insurance."

She laughed and kissed him. "I'm serious. About once a month or so, you'll see a lot of mail from my two business managers. One is Stewart Hoffstedder. He's fictitious, basically just a mail drop in New York I use to pay bills for imaginary people, so you don't want to know about any of that. The other one is named Michael Mesnick, and he's real. He's a former I.R.S. agent. If you ever fall into the morass of my finances, call him or his assistant, Kim Henmi, and they'll straighten it out. Do not say anything about how ill-gotten my gains are. They think I'm a career consultant who spends too much money on travel and not enough on pensions."

He gave her a hug and stood up. "I'll try to remember." But she was still sitting on the bed. "That's it, right?"

She sat quietly for a moment. "Here is the rest of it. I don't think I want to have to say this twice, because it's a little . . . embarrassing. What I intend to do with the rest of my life is be your wife. I'm not reserving anything, holding anything back. This is the only life I expect to have, so I'm not willing to let it go wrong by little increments because I wasn't paying attention. I will always be available to you, at any hour of the day or night. If you want to talk, I'll talk. If you don't want to talk, that probably means you should try even harder to talk. I'll be listening."

Carey sat on the bed hard, as though his legs had given way. "The sweet old-fashioned girl? Jane Whitefield?"

"Jane McKinnon. Older than old-fashioned," she said. "Primal, actually." He hugged her again, but as he smiled at her, he saw she wasn't smiling. "The only thing I won't do for you is play dumb."

The supple, gentle touch of his arm around her seemed to stiffen, and after a second the arm dropped away. "I hope this is because you're getting everything out of the way at once—housecleaning day."

"It is."

"Then I guess I don't have any grounds to feel insulted. So I'll just say that I love you. I married you. If I had any reason to imagine I couldn't live up to the agreement, I would have to be insane. I don't expect to ever give you any reason to feel . . . insecure. Okay?"

She gave him a peck on the cheek. "Thanks. I'm sorry to bring that up again. Maybe we just know too much about each other. You're a very attractive man, Carey. And you're getting better instead of worse. You like women, and we all sense it, and so we all nuzzle up to you. And you're also a very successful doctor in a provincial town. Everybody likes to be around men like you. None of that is going to change just because you're married. What I'm saying isn't 'Watch your step because I'm onto you.' I'm saying, I know you like women a whole lot. And I like you a whole lot. You're used to variety and excitement and . . . whatever. I understand it. So here I am. I'm not everybody in the world, but I'm going to try to be everything to you. Just ask. No, you don't even have to ask, because I'm saying yes now, for all time."

"The strawberries," said Carey.

She threw her arms around his neck and squeezed him hard, rocking him back and forth. "I'm so glad. You don't know how relieved I am."

"About what?"

"You're nowhere near as dumb as you look. It's just the cheap haircut, after all."

7

Earl Bliss had once taken a locksmith course during the dead time while he was waiting for his next job to find him. Everybody in his graduating class had been a deep-bottom loser, with no serious hope of finding work fixing locks, but every one of them had learned to handle a pick and a tension wrench. Earl had gotten a great deal of use out of his set, and tonight he held them in his teeth until he and Linda reached the row of mailboxes in the lobby of Pete Hatcher's apartment building. He quickly slipped behind Linda while she watched the hallway, then set the tension wrench in the lock, pulled the pick out of his teeth, and opened the little door that said #6 HATCHER.

He handed the mail to Linda and walked on toward Hatcher's apartment door. Linda had always loved Las Vegas hotels, but the idea that the people who dealt cards and waited on her actually lived in Las Vegas had always depressed her. It reminded her of the summer when she was seven and her mother had gotten two days of work in a bikini movie. Linda had been allowed to believe that she was being permitted a rare glimpse at glamour. She knew now that her mother just had not had a place to leave her while school was out.

Linda had been dragged along and had watched a whole group of them waiting in line for a turn to climb into a dusty trailer on the hot, black road above the beach and wriggle into swimsuits handed out off a rack, all of them women like her mother—pretty, but at twenty-five already looking worn and a little bovine.

They were just supposed to play volleyball behind two men who got into a fistfight, but they knew even less about volleyball than the two men did about fighting, so as the sun rose higher and began to sear eyeballs and heat the sand enough to burn their feet, they got breathless and fell and bumped into one another, a couple of them crying. And then—she never was told how her mother had managed it—they had gone to live with Dwayne.

She recognized him as one of the men who had been up at the trailer that day. He was in charge of something or other—could it possibly have been lighting, on a beach? She remembered the long, dull, hot days of the summer living in that apartment on Winnetka Avenue, the doors of the apartments all open on the blindingly bright, lying promise of the empty pool, trying to catch a breeze that could never come because the building itself blocked it from entering the courtyard. Her mother had thrown Dwayne out in a rage one day and had to be reminded the apartment was in his name.

Linda followed Earl and watched him open the door lock with as little effort as he had needed with the mailbox. When she joined him he was already blocking off the bathroom window with towels and duct tape to keep the light from shining through it.

When Earl had finished, she closed the bathroom door, turned on the light, and took out the mail. They sat on the rim of the bathtub together and opened it. Before she even got to the bills, she could see they had something. It was a thick monthly bank statement with a stack of canceled checks inside. She curbed her eagerness and handed it to Earl, then opened the bills, one by one. There was the power bill, which was worth nothing. There was the phone bill, which was worth a lot because it would have the numbers he had called and the cities. There was a bill for rent on this apartment. When she saw the envelope with the Visa logo on it she felt hopeful, but then she saw it wasn't a bill at all but an offer for a new card. Earl stuffed the mail into Linda's purse and stood up.

They put on the latex medical gloves and began to search the apartment. She could tell that Hatcher had not been given much time to prepare before he left. There were objects here that were worth money and could have been sold or pawned—gold cufflinks and rings, even a good watch with a couple of small diamonds on the dial. But the same objects told her that somebody had given him a lesson or two about disappearing. Distinctive jewelry was as good as a scar or bright red hair. There were a couple of empty frames on the mantel, but not one photograph was left anywhere.

Earl came and shone his Maglite into the fireplace and carefully examined a pile of ashes. Whatever had been burned in there, it wasn't done for heat in Las Vegas in June. Linda could see that Earl wasn't going to be able to tell what it had been, so she left the room.

She found Hatcher's bedroom and systematically worked her way through it. From his pillow and the sheets under it, she gathered a dozen hairs and put them in a plastic bag. In the bathroom she made a list of all of the brand names she could find—toothpaste, shaving cream, razors, soap, shampoo, hairbrushes. She took the razors in case there was blood from a nick and gathered more hair from the brushes. They were more likely than the others to have been pulled out with the follicles. She searched hard for prescription bottles, so she could find the names of the doctors and pharmacies, but found none, so she moved to the kitchen.

She studied his eating habits. He didn't own anything even mildly interesting—a crêpe pan or a wok or a can of jalapeños or a jar of saffron. She dutifully noted the brand names in the cupboards and refrigerator, but they were all just the ones advertised on national television, and he had kept little food in the house. He probably had worked late at night and eaten in the hotel restaurants. She lingered at the refrigerator, opening bottles and unwrapping packages of food in the freezer because amateurs sometimes left valuables there, and he had left in a hurry.

Linda returned to the living room and found Earl busy unzipping each cushion from the couch to check inside the cover. The couch itself had been tipped over so Earl could look up among the springs. He had also tipped over the coffee table, chairs, and lamps. Earl heard her enter and said, "You get started on the bookcase."

Pete Hatcher had not been much of a reader. Linda wrote down the title, the author, and a description of each book, removed it from the shelf, looked behind it, held it up, and flipped through the pages with her thumb to see if anything fell out or had been taped inside, but found nothing.

At three in the morning Earl began to tip the furniture back onto the depressions in the rug where they had stood before, so Linda went from room to room making sure she had left no signs of her presence.

It was after five when they reached their motel. As soon as they were in the room Linda lay down on the bed and closed her eyes, but Earl was restless. After ten minutes, the sound of him shifting in the squeaky chair by the table and scribbling things on paper made her open her eyes. "Aren't you tired?"

"Nope," said Earl. "I'll sleep later."

"What are you doing?"

"I'm trying to get a picture of how to do this." He frowned and let his eyebrows bounce up once for emphasis. Linda hated that.

"How's it going?"

"According to Seaver, he had lots of friends. He was one of those guys who had everything. Everybody loved Pete Hatcher. Especially women." The contempt and envy in Earl's voice made Linda feel almost sorry for him. "He may have changed his name, but that isn't going to change. He's not the sort that's going to be lying low for long. He'll need company. He'll be out shaking hands and telling lies about himself." He looked at Linda and she seemed to remind him of something. "He'll be looking for women. According to Seaver, he's a regular old snatch-hound."

"That doesn't exactly limit his movements," said Linda. "Sex he can find anyplace. It would be better if there was one woman he couldn't live without. Her we could find."

"No sense thinking about what we don't have. What we do have has got to be enough to get us there." He consulted his notes. "He used a pro to get out of here. She had him drive out in a car instead of getting on a plane in Las Vegas. It wasn't a rented car, because then he'd turn it in wherever he ends up. So she bought it for him. If she's any good at all, she wouldn't let him stay in Nevada, right? It's too small."

"Right."

"So he's out of state, with the car. He's got to do something with it. If he sells it, keeps it, or abandons it, then it gets new plates and the old plates get returned to the Nevada D.M.V. There are only a million, two hundred thousand people in the whole state. How many cars? About half that many. How many of them are going to have their plates turned in this month?"

"I have no idea, do you?"

"No, but not many."

"What if it's in her name?"

"If it was, it won't be. He has to insure it in the new state, be able to get pulled over and ticketed without getting hauled in."

"He'll need a license to do any of that."

"If she didn't get him anything else, she got him a new license and birth certificate and Social Security card. Those I can't start with. But the new car registration I can probably get at the end of the month."

"Suppose he just drove it to an airport outside of Las Vegas? That's what I'd do."

"Yeah," said Earl. "We'll have to cover that possibility too. It's not going to be simple. This woman is a problem. She didn't let him make a lot of mistakes. There's nothing easy left: no personal letters, no pictures, not even any old credit card bills. Oh, that reminds me. Where's the bank statement we got? He just might have written a check to his new name."

"In my purse."

He snatched her purse off the doorknob where she had hung it, pulled out the statement, and opened it. He quickly shuffled through the checks, then sighed. "Jesus Christ," he muttered, then slapped the checks down on the table.

"What's wrong?"

"He had a balance of sixty-two thousand bucks. He wrote a check for sixty to 'Cash.' You want to know who took it and gave him the sixty in cash?"

"No bank I ever heard of would. . . . Oh, don't tell me."

"Yep. Pleasure Island Casino. The stupid bastards had him under surveillance, and they let him walk up to a cashier and write a check for his fuck-you money."

"That's got to be his idea," said Linda. "I'm sure he's seen them do it for gamblers. But he wrote it for less than his balance, so he doesn't have the bank and the police looking for him too. That's her."

Earl shrugged. "Her again. Yeah." He stared into space for a few seconds. Slowly, his jaw began to work, the knotted muscles grinding his teeth together. "Let's think about her. She sees, probably before he does, that his time is coming. They've watched him enough so if they were just going to fire him, he'd be gone already. She knows they're not going to take their eyes off him while he's alive unless she makes them. She tells him how to do a quick housecleaning. She gets him a car, and some papers. She arranges to meet him in the one place in Las Vegas where there aren't a million lights. She gets him out." Earl's face assumed a look of puzzlement. "But then she doesn't go too, she hangs in to buy him time."

Linda sighed. "This isn't getting me anywhere. So she bought him time."

Earl's irritated look froze her. "You're not thinking. You know any pros who are going to hang around to get in a fight in an elevator if the client's already driving out with a big head start?"

"No women, anyway."

"No men either. The pay doesn't go up any for bruises. She must have thought he needed the extra minutes, and that means he wasn't safe until a particular time."

"It can't be anything but an airport," said Linda. "He wasn't going to be invisible until the plane was in the air."

"How much time did she need to buy him?" Earl leafed

through the piles of tourist literature the maids had left on the coffee table. He found a number and dialed. "Yes. I'm interested in the midnight show, but I want to see another show, too. Is it one of those things where you have a bunch of warm-up acts? What time does the Miraculous Miranda actually get on stage?" He wrote something down. "Then when does the show end?" His pencil scribbled another note. "That's too bad. I may have to catch her act on another trip. Thanks." He hung up and studied his notes. "Okay. Miranda comes on right at twelve, first thing. She's on the stage for two hours."

"So what?"

Earl scowled. "So this woman figures Hatcher is going to have two hours to drive before the lights come on again and somebody sees he's not sitting next to her. He's driving to an airport, and she's planned on two hours. His plane has to leave pretty soon after he gets there, because she doesn't want him sitting in an airport when Seaver's people start looking for him. She wants him to arrive about the time the plane is boarding, so he can walk right in and disappear."

"Seaver said she bought him an hour after that."

"Right," said Earl. "She did it, but she couldn't know in advance that she could do it. How could this one woman think she could tie up those guys that long? No, she was counting on two hours, and whatever she got after that must have been insurance. Figure he drives sixty miles an hour, so there's no chance he'll lose twenty minutes getting a speeding ticket."

Linda stood up and pulled the map out of her suitcase. She measured 120 miles on a piece of dental floss, tied it to Earl's pencil, and ran it in a circle around Las Vegas. "Kingman, Arizona, on Route 93; Bullhead City, Arizona, on 95. Maybe Lake Havasu if he pushes it on Route 95 south. Baker, California, on 15 south. There's no airport for another hundred and twenty miles, so scratch 15 south. Nothing at all on 93 or 95 north, so scratch them. That leaves 93 or 95 south into Arizona or 15 north, into Utah. If it's 93, it's Kingman. If it's 95, it's Lake Havasu City. Both have airports."

"What about Utah?"

"No airport until Cedar City. About a hundred and eighty miles."

"Okay, scratch that too. We're down to two possibilities, then," said Earl. "He flew out of Kingman or Havasu City. Now what we've got to do is see what flights go out on a Tuesday night at those airports between two in the morning and, say, three. There can't be many."

"What if they go to Chicago and Dallas? Little airports usually just feed big ones."

"We'll just hope the other things we're doing give us a break, and tell us which one."

"What other things?"

He pawed through her purse and saw the apartment rental bill. "First thing is, put on some gloves and mail this in with some cash. I want to make sure his landlord doesn't evict him, in case we need to go back there."

"Okay. But where would he fly?"

"Put yourself in his place. This woman must have asked him what places he could go. He can't go to Atlantic City or Reno or some other place where they gamble. He's going to pick a place he knows a little about. A place he likes, right?"

"I would think so. The better he likes it, the longer he'll stay put, and the harder he'll be to find."

Earl clasped his hands behind his head and stared at the ceiling. "No close relatives, no permanent girlfriend, lots of friends, too many to narrow down . . ."

"Vacations?" asked Linda. "Business trips?"

"Maybe. If we can get a hotel charge on a credit report, we'll have a place to start."

Linda lay perfectly still. "I just thought of something. He knows he's in danger. He knows she got him out in the nick of time. He's never done this before, and he doesn't know if we're stuck in this motel or already staring at the back of his head, right?"

"That sounds right," said Earl. "But—"

"What's the first thing he's going to buy?"

"If he dumped his car at some airport, he'll buy another one."

"I'm not saying he won't do that," said Linda. "But what else do they always do? They buy a gun. If he flew out, he doesn't have one. If she set all this up in a couple of days, she probably wouldn't have time to get him one and leave it for him in the new town. Unless it's stolen, she'd still have the five-day waiting period."

Earl grinned and squeezed her so hard her neck hurt. "Whatever else he does, he'll do that. And that puts him on a list. It's a list we can get, because it's a public record. She'll probably tell him not to, but the minute he's on his own in a strange place, looking over his shoulder, he'll do it." He sat down and wrote more notes. "First, we've got to find out what airport he used, then what flight he took. Tomorrow I think we'll drive into Arizona and see if we can find a car with Nevada plates that got left in one of those two airports at two in the morning on Tuesday."

Linda Thompson pumped harder on the stationary bike, slowly adding speed, watching the digital readout on the little electronic podium in front of the handlebars. Thirty miles an hour, thirty-five, forty. She moved her legs faster, then pushed the thumb-lever forward to jump to a higher gear, and the speedometer told her she was going fifty. She gradually worked the gears back until the pedaling was almost effortless. She kept moving her legs for a long time to avoid getting knots in her muscles, but she had lost interest in the machine. Nobody went fifty on a bicycle. The scale was designed to give suckers a warm, cozy feeling.

She dismounted and looked out the glass wall of the exercise room. She was still alone. The gawkers were probably at their sales meetings. She went to the weight area, did a few more bench presses, a few more curls, then went to work on her latissimus dorsi, always using light weights and many repetitions to keep the muscles supple and avoid adding ugly body mass.

She had been eager to begin hunting, and it was frustrating

to be stalled for days right at the start. Hatcher might have been dumb enough to ditch the car at the Kingman airport or the Havasu airport, but the woman had not been dumb enough to let him. Earl wasn't saying it yet, but none of the flights out of either airport fit the schedule. The woman wouldn't set it up so that Hatcher had to drive out of Las Vegas at midnight and wait in an airport until seven for a flight. That was the kind of thing they did later, when she and Earl were getting close, and they were scared and desperate. At the beginning they still had a choice, and the first moves were smooth and efficient.

She walked into the tiny changing area and came out the other door in her swimsuit, cap, and goggles. She ran her toes along the surface of the water and verified that it was cold. It was a pretty good trick to have a cold swimming pool in a place where it was over a hundred degrees in the shade. She slipped in and endured the shock, then began to swim slowly up and down, warming her body and letting the long, slow strokes stretch the muscles and clear her lungs. It was already nearly eleven, so she decided she would do only a half mile and get out. Hotels started to get busy around noon, even in places like Havasu, Arizona. She resented having to do everything in the morning each day. Linda was a night person.

When she had finished her swim, she slipped back into the dressing room, and in a few minutes she was walking back up the hallway of the hotel. She opened the door and found Earl sitting at the table, tapping the keys of the laptop computer. Then she saw that the bags were packed.

"What is it?" she asked. "What are you looking at?"

"Airline schedules." Earl grinned that strange grin he had. At times like this his face seemed more animal than human. "I think I figured out why none of the flights he could have gotten out of Arizona fit."

"Why not?" She set down her gym bag and waited. She was relieved that he had not made her bring that up. But he must have found something else. He actually looked happy.

"Listen carefully," said Earl. "He takes the car from the parking lot in Las Vegas. It's about midnight. He drives two hours south toward Kingman or Havasu, Arizona. What time is it?"

Linda shrugged. "Two o'clock. Nothing takes off for four or five hours, and then it's just local stuff."

"Right. Suppose he doesn't drive to Arizona. Suppose he drives north about a hundred and eighty miles at sixty miles an hour. He's at Cedar City, Utah. What time is it?"

"Three o'clock."

"Nope. Four o'clock. He's crossed from the Pacific time zone into Mountain."

Linda sat on the bed. "But Utah is in the same time zone as Arizona."

"Yeah, but Arizona doesn't do daylight savings time. That's why we didn't have to set the clocks forward when we got here." He looked at her intently. "Okay. He's driven three hours to Cedar City. It's four o'clock. What time is it in Las Vegas?"

Linda lay back on the bed and stared at the ceiling. "Three o'clock. She's just finishing up with Seaver's men."

Earl nodded. "We ruled out Cedar City because it was too far to reach before Seaver's men started looking. I would have ruled out his flight, too, because it left so late. She couldn't have hoped to buy him enough time to make it, so why would she bother to buy him any time at all? But it wasn't late. It was just the amount of time she was buying for him. It's Flight 493 to Denver, at four eighteen A.M."

Earl looked at her expectantly, but she opened her suitcase, took out a comb, and walked to the mirror.

"Aren't you interested?"

"Interested?" asked Linda. "Oh, sure."

"Then why aren't you happy?"

She sat down on the bed facing away from him to comb her hair so he couldn't see her. "I was thinking about them. Hatcher and that woman. It's such a simple trick, and I'll bet when they thought of it they were laughing at us."

8

Jane heard a noise in the dark outside. She sat up and listened. The noise came again. She crept to the wall beside the bedroom window and leaned slowly to the side to bring one eye to the edge of the curtain to see. The wind was blowing from the east, making the long, leg-thick limb of the old maple tree behind the house bob its heavy foliage up and down. When it moved, there was a creak. There it was again, a rubbing sound that came once, then was quiet, a sound an intruder would make while he slipped into the house.

She stepped back from the window and watched the soft, hot wind blow the curtain inward so a little glow of moonlight showed her the room. Sprawled on the other side of the bed was Carey, his eyes closed and his jaw slack in an almost-snore, a long silence and then, after it seemed too late, a soft, gentle indrawing of breath. She admitted to herself that she would probably wake up this way for a few more months. She had slept—happily fallen asleep—beside a few men over the years, and Carey was one of them. But now she was sleeping in Carey's bed in the house where Carey had been a baby, which was now her house too. She had been in another life too long, a place where noises that might be intruders didn't always turn out to be made by the wind. She sat on the bed and spent a minute staring at him. She let herself adore the big foot sticking out from under the sheet, the long, hard muscles of the arm. She leaned over to stare at his eyelids. She could see his eyes moving in little nervous twitches underneath, and she knew he was dreaming.

She resisted the urge to touch him. She was his wife now, and that was different. She was supposed to take responsibility for the fact that he had to be at the hospital at six if he was going into surgery at seven, not wake him up and ask him what he was dreaming. She slowly lowered herself beside him, then lay on her back, closed her eyes, and listened to the wind fluttering the leaves of the maple outside the window until they made no sound.

After a time, she sensed from the way that the trees around her kept revising their shapes until she got them right that she was in a dream. It was night, and low, thin clouds made the moon a small ball with a rainbow ring around it. She didn't like the dream, but when she tried to fathom why that was, she found she had already known the answer before she had wondered. It was because the place where she was standing was familiar. She had not moved. She was still on the ground where Carey's house was going to be built some day.

She felt uneasy as she looked toward the street, because she saw only a narrow gap in the trees. There was no use trying to walk and find her way home, because if the path was there, the road was not yet on top of it, and the forest still stretched like this from the ocean to the Mississippi, and from the tundra to the Gulf of Mexico.

Jane tried to fight the growing sensation that she was being watched. She tried to force herself to be rational. This might be the Old Time, but that didn't mean there were such things as witches. There were no witches. If there ever had been, they had disappeared from the earth before Jane had been born. But her own memory told her she was lying.

She had been in the courtroom in Atlanta when the judge had looked past little Max Curtin, who sat behind the table that came up nearly to his chin, not seeing his pale face and thin bird-bones showing he hadn't just fallen down a lot but had not even been given enough to eat. The judge could see no grounds to take him away from his cousin. But the cousin had heard the words, and turned around quickly to gaze at Max Curtin's face, and the cousin's eyes had glowed, not only in triumph, but because he was drinking in the sight of the terror and despair that showed in the little boy's face. The Grandfathers would have taken one look at the cousin and known he was a witch.

She could feel the Workers of Evil were out there, feel them turning their attention to her. She had been thinking about them, and they had heard her thoughts, and now they were looking up, their faces vacant but alert. They were somewhere in the forest, and they began to turn and move toward her. She could feel the emptiness that was in them begin to fill up with excitement, anticipation. They were concentrating on her now, thinking about how happy she had been, and how easily that could be taken away from her. And they were coming.

Jane caught herself worrying about Carey sleeping unprotected in his bed, and she felt a jab of alarm. She had to force herself to hide him in the back of her mind, where they would not find him. She turned her attention to the witches. As long as she concentrated on them, they would see only their own reflection in her mind. There had seemed to be dozens of them when she first had thought of them, all pricking up their ears to search the air for her. But now she saw that they had winnowed themselves down to just two. Because they stood for all witches, they had to be a man and a woman.

There were footprints on the path, so sooner or later it had to lead to a place where people lived. Jane set off and followed it, then worked up to a run. It was hard for Jane to run on the trail at night, and she was ashamed of how clumsy she had become. She had been lazy for the past three months, and she began to get winded after only a hundred yards. Her foot hit the edge of the path, where it was higher, and she tripped. She gave a little gasp of surprise, and she knew it had reached the man and the woman and told them she had been flushed from hiding.

Although they were far behind her, only now reaching the clearing where she had started, she had no trouble seeing them. The man burst through the bushes, breaking branches and trampling the brush at his feet. He saw the path. He hunched over and stared down to read it for fresh tracks. He leaned forward on his knuckles, and his heels came up like those of a

runner at the starting blocks. He grinned with a horrible emo-
tion that looked like appetite, and his grin changed him. His
lips kept moving, curled upward, and his bared teeth seemed to
grow. His heavy jaw thickened, and he sprouted hair along his
back, and then his haunches and arms. His small, black eyes
lost none of their intensity as he started to move along the path
on four feet.

The woman was quiet. She seemed to materialize out of the
forest without moving a leaf, as though her feet didn't quite
touch the ground. She stood still for a few breaths, listening.
Jane didn't let herself think about what the woman was sensing
about that place, but it was why Jane was trying to draw her
away from there. The woman didn't hurry. She watched the
man lumbering away down the path, growing bigger and
heavier, his claws now long and black and the fur thick and
impenetrable. He was a wolf.

The woman smiled to herself and held her arms up, her long,
graceful fingers fanned out, made longer by her pointed nails.
She looked up at the moon glowing through the clouds, ringed
with the faint colors of the spectrum, and as she did, she
seemed to rise. Her fingers were impossibly long now, her neck
was elongated to look upward, and her face in the moonlight
was beautiful and ghostly. The bright, liquid eyes opened
wider.

Jane could see the fingers were the shafts of feathers, and
she watched the feathers spread along the woman's forearms
and then all the way to her shoulders. The woman's skin
glowed white and smooth and flawless, and she had a soft,
shapely grace that made Jane not want to turn her attention
away. The arms were definitely wings now. The woman's
white neck seemed to curve, stretching up toward the moon,
and Jane's heart beat faster—a swan! In the old stories, swans
were never evil. As soon as Jane allowed herself to feel hope,
it expanded in her chest and she almost cried with joy. The
female apparition wasn't a witch at all. She was probably some
powerful woman asleep somewhere, who was now entering
Jane's dream to help her. Jane had acquired an ally, a sister.

But the woman's face had not stopped changing. The eyes kept growing bigger and brighter, and now they seemed to ignite, to burn with a light from inside that looked like fire. Suddenly the woman ducked forward in some wrenching physical reflex like a retch. Her shoulders shrugged, her neck shortened, the flesh of her feet shriveled and left only curved talons. She was no longer human. She gave the great wings a flap, and she soared into the dark sky. She was an owl.

Jane was stung with shock, and in a few seconds the hurt threatened to soften and degenerate into heavy-footed despair. She strained to run harder, staring at the darkness ahead to discern the deeper black of the trail ahead of her feet, the empty air between the trees that could show her the way.

Jane could hear the wolf behind her and to her right, his body lean and hard but heavy, crashing through the underbrush. He knew the path because he was a human, and he was cutting across the curves. Jane stepped off the path and ran to the right, into the cover of the forest. She had to go more slowly now, slipping through thickets, sliding down inclines and then straining to scramble up the next rise, tiring herself just to get to level ground again. At the bottom of a steep, rocky hill she found the beginning of a stream. She turned with it and trotted for a few hundred paces, splashing along the stony creekbed until she came abreast of a rocky ledge and pulled herself up onto it just because it was difficult and the wolf would expect her to avoid it. Then she shifted her course toward the path, and in another mile she came out onto it again. She knew she had fooled the wolf. Her feet seemed light, running on the clear, even ground.

Then she felt rather than heard the sound above her, not so much a sound as a displacement of air behind her neck. She took two more steps and then whirled and swung hard at the same time so it would be her fist that arrived first instead of her face. Her knuckle felt the soft, downy brush of the breast feathers but swept past, hitting nothing solid at all.

The owl rose high into the air and a high-pitched screech came from its throat, then echoed from the rocky glen Jane had just left. The owl circled above her and called again. Jane could hear the sound of the wolf's claws scraping the stones as it came up out of the gully, then heavy paws thumping the leafy ground, and the grunting breaths growing louder.

Jane turned again and ran. There was no concealment now, because the owl flew low under the canopy of trees, its wings flapping only to make the curves, sometimes a few feet behind and sometimes so close that Jane turned to strike out at it, but always screaming with that almost-human voice to tell the wolf where she was.

Jane ran with a sob in her voice, feeling the futility of it. An owl could see better than she could, and easily avoided her blows, and a wolf could run all night if it could smell its prey. As soon as she had thought of smelling, she imagined she smelled something pungent in the air. Was it something she had invented because she wanted it so much, or was it really smoke? It must be smoke. All she had to do was follow the smoke to the village, a clearing somewhere ahead where people slept in their longhouses and tended their crops and made love and sang. All she had to do was reach a circle of light. She ran beside the path, weaving in and out of the big trees so the owl couldn't swoop in behind her neck with its talons.

The owl seemed to sense that it didn't have much time. Maybe it smelled the smoke too, and maybe it had known where the village was. It stopped screeching and swooped upward.

Jane stepped back onto the path and sprinted, lengthening her strides and holding her head high to open the airway, pumping her arms and knees. She smelled the smoke more strongly now, and she knew she was close. She would dash for the nearest longhouse, duck under the bearskin flap that covered the door, dive through the little anteroom where the corn and beans and squash were stored, and roll into the little circle of light thrown off by the first cooking fire.

She could see a sharp off-turning in the trail ahead, and she knew this must be the path that led up to the village. She cut across a patch of low three-leafed plants she thought were strawberries, but as her ankles slashed through, her skin began to burn. It was poison ivy, but she didn't care. She dashed up the path, climbing higher and higher. She reached the little plateau on top and stopped.

There, in the clearing, was a strange, horrible sight. The wolf had begun to change back into a man, and he squatted on human legs beside a pile of green brush that he had half-ignited with his human hands. It was smoking heavily but giving off no light at all. The man stood and turned his wolf snout toward her. She could see the sharp yellow teeth and the eyes that gleamed like pale gold-green beads. "Hello, Jane," he said. "Smell the smoke?"

Jane heard something behind her. The owl alit and began to change back into a woman. "You're ours now."

"No."

"We're going to make you into a skin woman. He'll flay the skin off you carefully, and I'll sew it back together, and we'll hang you from that tree limb over there. The soft breeze will fill you up a little and there will be a sound like a quiet song coming from your mouth. People passing by on the trail will look up this path and see you. Maybe they'll just want to pass the time, and maybe they'll be alone and running, looking for a place to rest and someone to help them. But they'll stop. They'll step off the trail and up this little path alone."

Jane threw herself on the woman, digging her fingers into the throat with her left hand and drawing back her right for the first punch. She could feel the witch changing shapes under her hand, first the scales of a snake and enough of the neck free so the head could curl around and sink its fangs into her forearm, then the scales turning into thick fur and the body widening into a lynx, the jaws now chewing to get free of the hand.

Jane swung hard and woke to the light streaming through the white curtains onto the polished hardwood floor of the bedroom. She held her eyes open in the glare, her breaths coming fast and shallow, afraid that if she closed her lids the dream would still be there. She spun her head and saw Carey, then slowly began to calm down. She was wet, covered with sweat so her nightgown clung to her. She sat up and waited for the dizzy feeling to pass, then eased her weight off the bed. She looked at the clock radio on the nightstand. It was almost six. She walked down the hall quickly, turned on the shower in the guest bathroom, pulled the nightgown off over her head, and threw it on the floor. In a few minutes she would be clean and clear-minded, and Carey could awaken to hear her making his breakfast downstairs.

As she stepped into the shower, she tried to get over the dream. Since she was a child she had heard people clicking their tongues and saying that dreams of the Old Time had begun to come back. The pessimists said it happened only to Senecas who had begun to forget who they were and what they were supposed to do. They were paying the price for repressing their true inclinations. There were others who said the dreams were returning because the supernaturals had stayed on the land with the Senecas all this time and finally gotten used to the way things were now, just as the Senecas had. They recognized that the people had not changed in any way that mattered, and so they had begun to touch them more often in sleep.

Jane felt the terror and claustrophobia of the dream beginning to wash away with the hot water and mental exercise. There wasn't much mystery about it. She had been holding down a quiet tension since the night when she had agreed to marry Carey. She had done the little she could do to make herself unobtrusive. She had taken a new name and moved into a house that no runner and no chaser could know about. She was living as quiet a life as a woman could. She had even been careful to leave untouched all of the things that pertained to Jane Whitefield: the old house looked occupied, the telephone was connected, the mail carrier still came every day.

She had told Carey that she had kept the house as it was because she couldn't think of a way to keep her old life from popping in to alarm the new tenants. It had not been exactly a lie, but it was part of the truth. What she had not mentioned was that anyone—victim or persecutor—who was able to satisfy himself that she had moved out of that house, and not merely gone on a trip, might keep looking and find this one. The old house kept them one extra step away from here—not much protection, just something that might buy her the time to see them before they saw her.

The dream had been her subconscious mind protesting, reminding her that the few small obstacles she had placed to hide her own trail were pitiful. No matter how fervently Mrs. Carey McKinnon wanted to ignore it, Jane Whitefield could not forget that the trail behind her was full of wolves.

9

Jane parked her car in the gravel driveway in front of the small frame house under the big hemlock tree. When she got out she stepped into a little cloud of dust that settled on her shoes. A dog in the back yard began to bark, then dashed toward her with menacing yaps. It was a little black mongrel with brown eyebrows, the kind that she had seen running around yapping on the Tonawanda reservation since she was a child, so she knew what it would do before it did. It ran up until it was five feet away, then straightened its forelegs, skidded to a stop on the grass, and began to hop up and down, wagging its tail.

"Maggie," came a deep voice from the porch. "Come." The little dog trotted happily around Jane once, then scampered up the steps onto the porch and ran through the open screen door to alert the others in the Peterson house. "Hi, Janie," said the man. He stood up from his rocking chair so Jane could see him over the railing. He was very tall and had the square-chested, long-legged look that she remembered noting in his father when she had come here with her own father for visits in the old days.

"Hi, Billy," she called. "Is this a good time?"

"There is no bad time," he said as he put a sprig that had fallen from the hemlock into his book to mark the page, set it on the stack on the wicker table beside him, then folded his reading glasses into his shirt pocket.

He met Jane on the walk and let her hug him, then leaned his head down and turned his cheek to catch her kiss. "Married life agrees with you, Janie."

He said it in Seneca, so Jane answered in Seneca. "The old man wanted to come too, but I made him go to work so I could keep being a grand lady who wanders around doing nothing."

As they stepped up onto the porch, he saw her notice his books, and reverted to English. "Just some reading for my undergraduate course in the fall. Basic abnormal psychology."

"What we used to call Nuts and Sluts."

"That's the one," he said. "The department makes me take a turn every third year."

The little dog pushed through the screen door again with its nose, and then a woman nearly as tall as Billy with hair like Jane's came out from behind it holding three glasses of lemonade on a tray. "Hi, Janie," she said. "I thought you might like a cold drink."

Jane took a glass. "Thanks, Vi," she said, and they exchanged pecks on the cheek while Billy took the tray to keep the other glasses level.

Violet Peterson sat on the porch swing with Jane and smiled. Jane looked around her. "Did you sell the kids?"

Violet said, "They're in school, believe it or not. Veronica's taking a computer class every morning, and Delbert's doing art." She glanced at her watch. "I pick them up in an hour."

"So serious," said Jane.

"It's great," said Violet. "If I don't make them do something in the summer they run around in the woods like—"

"Like we did," said Jane.

"Exactly," said Violet. "Kids are wonderful, but anybody who says they don't drive you nuts is in a state of denial." Her lips pursed and she said slyly, "You'll see."

Jane sipped the cold lemonade and listened. The red-winged blackbirds at the edge of the marshland a hundred yards away were calling to each other.

Billy said, "You have something on your mind?"

"You must be a psychology professor," said Jane. "It's kind of a delicate problem. Delicate politically."

"Politically?"

"I came to see my friends Billy and Violet, but before I go, I want to do some lobbying with Sadagoyase."

She could feel the weight of ages as he stared at her. Sadagoyase meant Level Heavens. It was the name that had been given to the member of the Snipe clan who held that sachemship in each generation since the first Sadagoyase, one of the forty-nine who had sat at Onondaga with Hiawatha and Deganawida to establish the Iroquois League. Each of them for a thousand years had probably sat in front of the doorway of his wife's house on a day like today, with the blackbirds calling in the hot sunshine, and listened to a woman like her who had come to talk politics.

"Is this about the gambling?" asked Violet.

"Yes, I'm afraid it is," said Jane. "I'll bet you're both sick of it."

"Not at all," said Sadagoyase. "It's good that you came, because I've been meaning to give you a call about it."

"Me?" asked Jane. "I thought I was being clever sneaking around to the sachem of another clan. Why would you call a Wolf?"

"You said it was delicate politically. It's been voted down four times, but it keeps coming back up. I need to know what key people think, the ones who are educated and can sway public opinion."

"I don't know," she said. "Everything I see about it tells me to leave it alone and let other people decide. I'm not here to offer advice about the general issue. I just wanted to make one little point and skulk away."

"But I'm asking your advice."

"I'm not the one to ask. Whitefields haven't lived on the reservation in three or four generations."

"Being a Seneca isn't a matter of residence."

"I had a mother who started out Irish. A colleen, as they say. It sounds like the name of a dog that's not quite a collie, doesn't it?"

"Cornplanter had a father named O'Bail. Mary Jemison was

a year out of Ireland when she was captured. She had thirty-nine grandchildren by Hiokatoo. You want to tell their great-great-grandchildren they're not Senecas? There's probably nobody within rifle shot of here who doesn't carry DNA from somebody who was adopted twenty generations back. It's a nonissue."

Jane sighed. "I would love it if the people could have a little dependable money coming in. There are already over a hundred Indian casinos all over the country, and I heard somebody refer to gambling as 'the return of the buffalo.' But I've got worries. If I say those worries out loud, people I love and respect are going to say things that hurt me."

"What will they say?"

"They'll remind me in that quiet, gentle way people around here have that I've never been poor. And I'll know that they could have said more."

"What could they say?"

"I'm one of them too. Maybe I would say it to myself. There I would be, this doctor's wife who lives in a house like a fortress in Amherst, driving Carey's BMW up to the dilapidated council building to tell them gambling money isn't good for the nation."

Sadagoyase raised his eyebrows. "Maybe living that life makes you objective. The traditionalists, the longhouse people, trust you because they know you're at least as conservative as they are. They're an important constituency."

"I'm an anomaly, and they know it," she said. "I'm a leftover Indian Rights radical from ten years ago. A lot of what I know comes from the Old People, but a lot doesn't. It comes from staring at old archives at Cornell and Rochester that were written by Europeans who studied us the way doctors study viruses. I'm not a radical now. I'm a spoiled rich woman who has a hobby."

"Good for you," said Sadagoyase. "I'm a professor teaching the theories of a dead man from Vienna. Now answer my question and I'll listen to whatever you came to tell me."

Jane shook her head and smiled sadly. "All right. Here goes.

I'm not a spiritual believer in the Gaiiwio of Handsome Lake. I don't believe there's anything left after we're dead, at least not in broad daylight like this. But whatever happened when Handsome Lake got drunk and passed out in 1799, he woke up with some sense. I think there wouldn't be any such thing as a Seneca now if he hadn't."

"You want to be more specific?"

"Don't sell any land. Accept as much education as you can get, but keep up the ancient cycle of celebrations. Drinking liquor might be fine for whites, but for us it's poison. Don't abuse your wife and kids the way whites do. And—here it comes—don't gamble."

She glanced at her old friend, but Sadagoyase was waiting in silence. She said, "He didn't mean don't play the peach-pit game or bet on snow-snake matches. He was a warrior, brought up in the Old Time. He got his scalping knife wet at Devil's Hole. He was saying, 'These are the temptations that the modern world is sending our way. Watch out.' I think he was right."

"What about now?" he asked. "Is he still right?"

She took a deep breath and let it out slowly. "For hundreds of years the Five Nations kept the peace, managed a unified foreign policy with fifty or sixty other nations, and played the Dutch, English, and French off against one another. Now on half the reservations there are competing governments and splinter groups, and Iroquois burning their own buildings and taking shots at each other. And every time one side looks like it's losing, they call for intervention by the New York State Police or Quebec or Ontario Provincials, or the Canadian or American federal governments. They've always gotten it, and they always will."

"Are you worried about hard feelings or loss of sovereignty?"

"I don't think those are two issues. They're the same. I'm not saying all of that would happen at Tonawanda. But it would be especially stupid if any of it happened here. Everybody around here knows that in 1838, when the state was kidnapping chiefs to force them to sign the land treaty, not one single chief from Tonawanda let himself be caught. I hope people remember that the reason for that was that the chiefs were willing to risk their lives to disappear, and the people were willing to risk theirs to hide them. That's not just why we're still here. It's who we are."

"So what you're afraid of is just that I'll get dehorned?"

"Not you, Billy—Sadagoyase. Once gambling comes in, you've got to think of what else happens. New York State will want a vested financial interest the way they did with the Oneidas, and they'll have to police the gambling and everything around it."

"That boat sailed in 1821," said Sadagoyase. *"The State of New York* versus *Tommy Jimmy."*

He needed only to allude to the case because it was one of the legal precedents that had established the boundaries of the modern Seneca world. A witch named Koquatau had murdered a man at Buffalo Creek, and Tommy Jimmy had been appointed by the council to act as her executioner. He had followed her into Canada and, as soon as he had her back on Seneca land, had cut her throat. He had been defended at his trial by Red Jacket, one of the greatest orators of his time, and acquitted on the grounds that he was following Seneca law. After that, the state had asserted its jurisdiction.

"Same principle, different consequences," said Jane. "There's a big difference between having the cops investigate a crime every ten years and having dozens of them move in with you to protect the financial interests of the legislature and its cronies."

"What cronies?"

"Building hotels and casinos can't be done without money from outside. That means some big corporation with investors and boards of directors is going to have more to say about what goes on here than we are. It may have occurred to you that Senecas haven't had a lot of luck trusting either the state of New York or corporations in the past. This state has a perfect record. It has never, even in the most minimal way, lived up to any agreement that it has ever made. It has never even felt itself constrained by federal laws."

Jane could feel that she had talked herself into an agitated heat. She paused, let the passion cool for a moment, and said, "I guess I'm working up to what I wanted to say. I read in the paper that there are already offers from gambling companies on the table. One of them is an outfit called Pleasure, Inc."

"That's right."

"If the decision is that we're not in the gambling business, forget I ever told you this. If there is gambling, make sure no agreement includes Pleasure, Inc."

"Why not?"

"I met a man who used to work for them. They're criminals in the usual ways: skimming money from the casino, feeding illegitimate cash into the games and redeeming the chips with checks and credits to launder it, investing secret profits in illegal enterprises. They're capable of killing people when it suits them."

"How in the world did you meet anybody who knew that?"

"It's just one of those crazy things that happens if you travel a lot. You meet people you wouldn't otherwise."

"You should have paid the airline for an upgrade," said Sadagoyase. "Why would he tell you and not the police?"

"He was afraid of them, and he wasn't afraid of me. I just have that kind of face."

"But—" he began.

"No more questions. I won't answer them, and that will spoil this beautiful day. Use the information as you think best. If you think it will help in council, you can use my name. I can't tell you his." Jane stood up to leave.

"What will you do if gambling comes in?"

Jane gave a little shrug. "I'll give myself an extra fifteen minutes to drive out here in the traffic, and another fifteen to find a place to park."

"All Senecas would be entitled to a share of the profits. Would you take it?"

She shook her head. "No. That I couldn't do."

He watched as she bent down to kiss Violet, her long straight black hair swinging to touch his wife's; she came to him and did the same. Then she turned and walked to her car. As she passed under the big hemlock and the sunlight fell in bright dapples on her head and shoulders, he felt himself losing perspective. He could not help feeling he had just received an official visit from his grandmother's grandmother.

10

It was nearly noon. The three men at the far end of the enormous conference table had begun to look bored. Calvin Seaver watched Stella Olson's eyes sweep down the page of her report to the summary. This was one of the reasons why Seaver was in awe of Stella. Some of the people in this room would have decided to hold the big guys' attention by tickling them with cheerful patter, or just droned on, insisting that if these three persisted in owning a casino, they would have to hear all about how it was run. Stella just said in her clipped, soothing voice, "Thirty-two hires, two terminations, eight on medical leave, four resignations, for a net gain of eighteen, which will cover all existing positions until the end of September." She sat down, closed her folder, and watched the three men attentively. Seaver saw Max Foley's eyes slip to one side, then the other, and come to some understanding with his partners. "Are the salary figures in the report?"

Seaver couldn't tell whether the three partners had decided to humiliate her because she had been the one to hire Pete Hatcher or to ask a polite question because Stella had earned the right to their attention, but he knew that probably Stella could tell which it was. She was a poker player, and she seemed to have a gift for reading faces. She came back at them without looking down at her papers.

"Salary and benefits on the eighteen new hires adds up to an additional \$52,500 a month. Lower starting salaries on the fourteen replacements offsets \$5,833 of it. So the extra cost is \$46,667 for this month only. On September first we lost eight regulars who went back to college for additional work, and eight shifted from full to part time. We have three scheduled retirements. We'll make up the $46,667 on October fourteenth."

Peter Buckley smiled. "That's marvelous work, Stella." Even Salateri seemed to make an exception to his habit of never praising and gave her a reluctant nod. Seaver decided they must have given Stella a slow one over the plate. That way when she walloped it out of the park, the others would see how it was done.

Max Foley looked around expectantly. "Anybody have anything to talk about that's more urgent than lunch?" The men and women around the table looked like statues. "No? Then you know where we are."

All of the twenty managers stood up and began to glance at watches, gather papers, and file out. A few of them chatted affably, but Seaver knew it was all harmless banter. He knew because he had periodically tape-recorded the whispers and murmurs, amplified them, and listened to them to be sure nobody said anything once the soundproof door opened that constituted a violation of security.

As Seaver stood to join the queue, Buckley caught his eye and lazily gestured at a chair near the end of the table. Seaver set his papers on the table and pretended to put them in order until the others had gone, then walked over and sat down.

This was one of the times when the three partners looked like one entity, some Hindu deity with six arms and three faces. They all turned to watch Seaver, but Salateri was the face who spoke. "Cal," he said. "We're wondering what stage we've reached on the Pete Hatcher thing."

It was Seaver's impulse to say, "It's taken care of," but he knew that was not what the triumvirate had held him apart to hear. He pursed his lips thoughtfully, then said, "I made the arrangement I mentioned. I gave them one hundred for expenses. We agreed on an eventual price of three hundred, plus any overhead they incur beyond the hundred."

"And?" prompted Buckley.

"They haven't asked for the rest yet."

Foley frowned. "What does that mean?"

Seaver said, "They haven't finished yet."

Salateri shook his head in disgust but said nothing. To Seaver's surprise, it was Buckley who pursued it. "Doesn't that make you . . . a little uncomfortable?"

Seaver resisted the glib, easy answer. "It's not as quick as I had hoped," he conceded. "But I'm not concerned. I picked these people because I was confident that they would be able to find him and take care of it quietly, without the sorts of problems these matters can sometimes cause." He held his palms up. "I still think so. The delay just means that the professional who helped Hatcher disappear also helped him stay hidden for a while."

Foley snorted. "I think it's time to ask a few specific questions. Just who are these people?"

"Their names are Earl Bliss and Linda Thompson. They have a detective agency in Los Angeles."

"Why did you pick them?"

"They've done a few things for me and for acquaintances of mine, and they've always delivered. The choice of specialists isn't very good. They're the best of a bad lot."

Foley's brows knitted. "A bad lot?"

"As a rule, paragons of mental health don't do wet jobs. Usually the people available for that kind of work have felony records. They look like they've spent a lot of time lifting weights in some exercise yard and have lots of memorable tattoos. They've all learned that you can get out of just about any sentence if you've got something juicy to tell the authorities about somebody else, and they're all certain to be in trouble again. So they can be a problem that doesn't go away."

"What's different about the ones you hired?" asked Foley. "Are they paragons of mental health?"

"I can only guess, and I would guess not. But they don't seem to have problems that get in the way. And these people fit the Pete Hatcher problem."

"How?"

"They've done a lot of skip-tracing and bail-jump cases, so

they're set up to find people quietly and without fuss. If they get noticed while they're looking, they can say they're on that kind of case, and show licenses to make it believable. There are two of them, and this kind of work is best done in pairs, which is why police officers work that way. If you have to, you can watch a building twenty-four hours a day, and it's very hard to slip behind someone who can look in two directions at once. And one of them is a woman. Two men together are probably a team of some kind, but two people of different sexes are just 'a couple.' "

Salateri seemed to be bursting, but he confined himself to a measured tone. "If they're so good, why is it taking them so long to find one guy? It's been almost four months."

Seaver sighed. "The Justice Department has seventy thousand people, and sometimes it takes them twenty years." He saw that this did not please the three men, and he regretted having let it slip out. "I don't mean to be flippant. But the problem isn't going out and finding the Pete Hatcher we knew. He has professional help. She's probably been doing everything for him. At some point he'll stop paying her, and he'll be on his own again. He'll float to the surface."

Max Foley blinked his eyes, took off his glasses, and set them on the table, then produced a white handkerchief and meticulously cleaned the tinted lenses. "How do I put this?" he asked himself. "The world is a complicated place, full of pieces that somehow fit together, and each one affects the others. Most people just don't know how."

Seaver could sense that what was coming was terribly important, and that he would need to catch every word and remember it. Then it seemed to him that they might be about to fire him. He waited anxiously.

Foley put on his glasses and his eyes widened to look at Seaver. "That's what we do—the three of us here. Together we know how the pieces fit. It can't be written down. It's too much for one person to keep in his head, so we each know one part completely, and some of the rest."

Buckley said, "We think we haven't explained our problem well enough to you."

Seaver began to wonder. There were worse things than being fired. Maybe he was about to hear a description of one of them. "Explained what—Pete Hatcher?"

Buckley nodded. His arm came up in one of his vague, limp gestures. "And so on."

Seaver could feel the danger. "All my life I've operated on orders," he said. "If I got the orders wrong, I apologize. Repeat them, and I'll do my best. But I don't need to know any more than I do."

"Who said you had a choice?" snapped Salateri.

Peter Buckley gave a deprecating smile and said, "You think we're going to tell you something that will make you a liability. That's perceptive, but I'm afraid there's nothing we could tell you that would make you more vulnerable than you already are." A moment went by. "Now you're thinking that we're going to tell you something intended to give you a better appreciation for the importance of Pete Hatcher: what we win if we win, what we lose if we lose. If that happened we wouldn't be sorry, but that's not why you're here. We're hoping that if we tell you more, you'll think of new ways to help us."

"I'll try," said Seaver.

"You know we gave Pete Hatcher quite an education," said Foley. "We started him in personnel with Stella. Then we had him work customer service on the hotel side for a while. First the tennis shop, then he was a starter at the golf course. Then we shifted him to the casino side. He worked the floor as a runner for the pit bosses." He turned to his partners. "Help me here."

"Finance," said Buckley. "First purchasing, then accounts. Then I think it was entertainment."

"Right," said Salateri. "Ticket sales, then booking." He glared at Seaver. "I think that was when we sent him to you."

Seaver nodded.

"Then we started promoting him. He seemed to have potential," said Buckley. "He was young, not a genius, but not stupid. He didn't care how hard he had to work, he seemed to get by just fine. He had one rare and special gift. That was the way he got along with people. Everybody liked Pete Hatcher: grandmas, little kids, people from foreign countries who might interpret some normal gesture as an insult."

Salateri looked as though he were sucking on something sour. "We gave him a taste of everything. We trusted him with little things, then tried bigger things. He never let us down."

Buckley sighed wistfully. "We began to rely on him. That was where we got into trouble. Las Vegas is a special place. There's never been anything like it in the world. When the country goes into a recession, we do better. People flock here in the summer, when you can burn your hand on the roof of a car. Sometimes it seems as though the laws of economics don't apply here. But they do."

"This is a business like any other," said Foley. "If this company is going to survive, it has to diversify, expand, form alliances. Staying put means dying. We've presented Pleasure Island as a family attraction. We may have done ourselves incalculable good for the future, but in the meantime, it has cut the number of dollars we take in per customer. Kids don't spend much. All they use is the beds and the food, which we practically give away to attract business."

"We've looked into other areas," said Buckley.

Foley said, "One we've been studying is off-site gambling. The attraction is obvious. At some point, the number of people who can fly here and bring serious money to the tables will reach a peak. Other companies have already figured out that they can start casinos near big population centers—first in New Jersey, then on riverboats in the Midwest, then Indian reservations. Each casino somewhere else clogs one healthy artery and turns the flow from there into a trickle. So we looked into growing some new arteries."

"You're thinking of building more casinos? When?"

Foley shrugged. "This has been in the works for several years. After some study, we decided that the most promising idea was Indian reservations. We put fifteen reservations under scrutiny, and came up with one we want."

"Where is it?"

"Upstate New York. Draw a triangle from Rochester to Buffalo to Niagara Falls, and it's in the middle. It's less than two hundred miles from Cleveland and Toronto, less than four hundred from New York and Philadelphia, less than five hundred from Baltimore, Detroit, Hartford, Indianapolis. It sits just off the New York State Thruway. If you go by car from one of those cities to the other, you may very well have to go past it."

Seaver looked at the three men, keeping his expression empty. He had no way of knowing whether it was a good idea or madness.

Buckley seemed to read his mind. "You're thinking that we're not exactly diversifying. But we are. Think of a full-service world-class resort. Casinos and hotels, of course. That's our strength. Only this time they would be exclusive, on land only we had access to. But best of all, we could offer things that nobody else can do, anywhere."

"You could?"

"An Indian reservation is a peculiar place, in the law. They can already sell tax-free gas and cigarettes. Why not foreign cars? High-ticket jewelry? Designer clothes? Appliances? Besides the tariffs, the sales tax in New York is eight and a half percent."

"Are you saying that's legal?"

"It hasn't been tried yet. We think we could use the precedent of those companies that sell tickets to police benefits. As long as they give a cent to the police, they can keep ninety-nine for overhead and profit. We give a cent to the Indians and they still make millions a year. This could all be in the open. But what would not be in the open is even more intriguing. Indians have exclusive hunting and fishing rights on their land, with no external regulation. We could have live hunts with game we release: bag a rhino in Upstate New York. We could build a private port a few miles north, on Lake Ontario, connect it to the resort by rail, and offer cruises: package tours for Mom and the kids. For Dad, maybe a members-only junket with high-stakes games and even some exotic companionship. We could rotate girls in and out maybe once a week. The port would also give us access to the St. Lawrence Seaway into the Atlantic. We could take anything out, bring anything in." He looked sad. "It was all intriguing. Very intriguing."

Seaver shook his head. "I never heard a word about any of this. I'm amazed."

The three smiled. "The world is a complicated place," said Foley. "No one head can carry all of the pieces."

"What about Hatcher's? Is this what he knew?"

Salateri muttered something to himself that could have been a curse. "Hatcher knew nothing about this, because none of it has happened yet."

"There have been delays," said Foley. "The Indians have to accept the idea, and we haven't really approached them yet, just left our card, you might say. First we needed to do feasibility studies, find out what wasn't possible, then make it possible. The big delay has to do with the Indian Gaming Act. The federal law says that gambling is okay under conditions established by the state where the reservation is. Before we go handing money to a bunch of Indians we needed to be sure that we could get the state legislature's approval. And we had to make friends in Albany and Washington."

"How do you do that?"

Buckley smiled. "We'll have to learn about the Indians—keep them in the dark while we study them. Politicians, on the other hand, are a tribe whose customs we know."

"Hatcher handled the payouts," Salateri blurted.

Seaver frowned. "I thought he didn't know anything."

Salateri scowled defensively. "It was all indirect. We didn't want to see a videotape with a time and date in the corner and a shot of Hatcher counting out hundred-dollar bills to some New York politician in a hotel room. We set up a fund."

"What kind of fund—cash?"

Buckley said, "It was a corporation that received some of its money in cash. We had a lot of land—here, in San Francisco, in Los Angeles—which we sold to the corporation for an imaginary sum before we brought Pete in. We converted various plots to parking lots—put asphalt over them. Pete was in charge of taking the money we said came in, and paying it to people we said were investors or creditors. He paid it to other corporations, middlemen, girlfriends, relatives, some to bank accounts in the Cayman Islands."

"And Hatcher didn't know what he was doing?"

"Never," said Foley.

Salateri said, "He might have suspected that the money that started the corporation came fresh from the casino tables. There were a couple of times when he told us the numbers on the official slips were lower than the count that night. Max told him that it was because we needed a lot of cash in the vault in case somebody hit the million-dollar jackpot on the big slot. That way we could take publicity pictures of the guy up to his ass in hundreds. The money only gets reported when it's taken out of play."

"He bought that?"

"Maybe for a while, maybe never. He stopped asking. The worst he would have thought was that we were still skimming cash and mixing it in with the take on the parking lots." Salateri shook his head. "Can you imagine that, after all we did for him? He turned his back on us because we were taking money out of our own casino—our own money! I still can't believe it."

Buckley shrugged. "We should make it clear that the corporation with the parking lots and so on wasn't the problem. There was nothing wrong with it but where the money came from, and there's no way he could have traced it. I think he resented the fact that he was the one who signed the slips with a short count on them." He gave a puzzled little smile. "You see, that was enough to cost him his virginity."

Seaver stared at the floor for a moment, then looked up at the row of three faces. "So the problem is that he can say he's pretty sure that at one time, money was being diverted from the

games and put into his own corporation. Then he paid it to a lot
of people he didn't know? I'd say let him."

"Let him?" Foley looked troubled.

Seaver said, "When I was a cop, we needed evidence of a
crime."

Peter Buckley looked at him kindly, sympathetically. "I'm
afraid you're missing the problem. Pete Hatcher doesn't know
anything. If he somehow strained his capacities and figured out
the names of the people in New York State who ultimately
received the money, he never heard of them. They're state leg-
islators and bureaucrats and party functionaries in a distant
place. People in their own state wouldn't know who they are.
But the F.B.I. would. And if they heard the little that Pete
Hatcher could be assumed to remember—say, four or five
names, dates, and amounts—they could trace the money backward to the accounts Hatcher controlled, and then forward to
find out where the rest went."

"But even if they did, the most they would be able to prove
was that Pete gave money to politicians. Maybe that it came
from here, but not who took it. If he signed for it, then he took
it. And half the equation is missing. You have no interests in
their state, and they aren't doing anything in return for the
money." When he saw that the three men were looking at him
without changing their expressions, he said, "You abandoned
the project, right?"

"No," said Max Foley. "Unfortunately, it isn't right."

"Why not?"

Salateri's impatience made him look as though he were
swelling up. "There are people in New York State who are
already in the gambling business. They are big, scary people.
In the twenties, if they didn't like you, they mixed a tub of
cement and put your feet in it. Now, if they want cement, they
make a phone call and five hundred cement trucks arrive, with
fifty government building inspectors to certify they did it
right."

"What have they got to do with this?"

Salateri's eyes narrowed. "You think we can go into their

front yard and set up a business they've been in for a hundred years and expect them not to notice? They needed to be consulted, mollified."

Seaver was beginning to sense the gravity of the partners' predicament. "Did Hatcher pay them too?"

"He doesn't know that either," said Foley. "The Justice Department would take about thirty seconds to figure it out. And what Hatcher paid them wasn't to buy them out. It was to buy them in. Without their help we wouldn't have known which politicians could be paid off, how to approach them, where to put the money."

Seaver frowned and considered. "I know I'm being slow, but let me be sure I understand where we are—"

"For Christ's sake!" Salateri shouted. "Hatcher doesn't know he knows anything! But if the F.B.I., the New York State Police, the Nevada Gaming Commission, or the fucking dog-catcher hear a word of it, they'll know everything!"

"It seems to me that if we could somehow separate the issues—"

Salateri was white with rage. "What did they teach you in the police academy—how to shake down doughnut shops? We have one deal that connects a Las Vegas casino, half the politicians in New York, and the Mafia. In one deal! That blows the politicians, who might have to go get a job. And that blows seven or eight fat old grandpas, who have to spend their last few years locked up with friends and relatives. But not us. We're not going to jail with them. They're not going to let us make it up the courthouse steps to hear the charges."

Buckley looked at Seaver with gentle regret. "It seems to us that we can't pull out of this and tell them we managed our business badly. We can't let them get an inkling that anything is wrong. We're staying alive one day at a time by convincing them that we move slowly, cautiously, prudently."

"This is something they respect," said Salateri. "For five generations they've been nibbling away at the world like termites, until now you can't pull a board off a toolshed without finding them behind it. The problem is, the longer we bullshit them, the harder they're going to take it."

Seaver squinted down at the carpet.

Peter Buckley said, "You're thinking we should tell them the truth and ask them to find Hatcher for us."

"Well," said Seaver, "I was considering it."

"Very alert of you," said Buckley. "They could certainly do it."

"Sure," said Salateri. "They have people in every city in the country. He couldn't run to Europe, because they had that sewn up before Great-Grandpa got on the boat to come here. In South America, Southeast Asia, North Africa they have drug suppliers with armies to protect the crop. I never heard of them having anybody at the South Pole, but I wouldn't rule it out. They'd find him. But he doesn't know much, and we know a lot. Who's the biggest threat? And they don't have to hunt around and find us to end it."

There was a moment of silence to give Seaver's mind a chance to catch up, to understand. "What would you like me to do?"

Foley said, "We're thinking of hiring a second team. Maybe a third. Pay all of them. Whoever succeeds gets a bonus. How does that strike you?"

"It makes me nervous," said Seaver. "Earl and Linda are good. Most likely, by now they know where he is, or at least what region. If they find him and there are other people nosing around, they'll notice them. They'll have to assume those people can only be bodyguards for Hatcher, or police of some kind. They'll kill them. Or try to."

"So what?" asked Foley.

"Then it's not a clean hit where an anonymous newcomer came quietly and went quietly and nobody notices. It's a fight between professionals with lots of gunfire and unburied bodies and blood."

"And?"

"And, as Bobby pointed out, no matter where this happens, it's in the middle of some Mafia family's territory. They're going to want to know who these shooters were, who they worked for, who they were after. It would be hard to imagine them not turning up Hatcher. If he's killed or wounded, he'll be identified. If he gets very lucky and escapes while our own shooters massacre each other, somebody will survive, and the local family will hear Hatcher's name."

Buckley stared at Seaver with interest. "Any ideas that would get around those problems?"

"Not offhand. I'll think about it."

"How about if we had somebody at least as good as Earl and Linda, somebody they know by sight, whose interest in Pete Hatcher won't require any explanation? Somebody they'll see as an ally?"

Seaver's collar tightened and he began to sweat. "I don't think they'd see it that way. I don't know where they are. There's no way to call them off, or warn them."

"But they wouldn't shoot you, would they? How could they expect to get paid the three hundred thousand if they killed their employer?"

"They couldn't, but—"

"Good," said Foley.

Seaver flailed hopelessly. "But what would happen here? Who would run security for the hotel? The casino?"

Salateri blew out a breath in a mirthless chuckle. "Your errand boy, Bennis, or somebody. Who cares? If you don't get Hatcher before he talks, we won't have a hotel and casino," he snapped. "There'll be a bunch of U.S. marshals in here running the place for the government, or a bunch of paisans running it for the ones we screwed in New York."

Buckley's voice became avuncular. "I think it's rightly your responsibility now, don't you?"

Seaver sat in the chair, helpless.

Foley scribbled on the pad at his elbow. "Give this to Eddie downstairs." He tore off the sheet and held it out.

Seaver glanced at the small note. "Give Seaver whatever he wants. M.F." Seaver stood up. He took a step, then paused and looked at the three men. He knew that there must be an answer, but he could not bring his mind to stop racing long enough to concentrate and find it.

"Good luck," said Buckley. His cheeks constricted to bring up the corners of his lips in a false smile, then went slack again.

"Don't let the door hit you on the ass on your way out," Salateri muttered.

11

Tonight was a sort of birthday, because David Keller was three months old. He had spent the time cautiously, patiently finding out who that was. He had spent the previous thirty-three years acquiring a working knowledge of Pete Hatcher, and now most of that work had been wasted. Any quality that David Keller shared with Pete Hatcher would probably get him killed. That was the most distinctive characteristic that David Keller had been able to establish about himself, and it determined all of the others. David Keller was a suspicious, fearful person. He lived in a two-bedroom apartment on the fourth floor of an old brick building in downtown Denver that had no elevator and overlooked a triangle of grass that wasn't big enough to be called a park. It looked like a spot where the surveyors had not been able to make three roads intersect and had to leave a scrap.

In the evening, when David Keller cooked his simple dinner and washed the dishes at the small, scratched porcelain sink, he could look out the window, across the tops of trees, and see the side of a topless bar with a turntable contraption over the door that had a female mannequin dressed in a sequined outfit revolving around and around like a mechanical dervish. The apartment was small and dark, built at a time when lumber must have been cheap, because everything was old, varnished wood—a built-in sideboard in the dining room and cabinets in the living room and, everywhere, ten-inch baseboards.

David Keller lived in his little apartment like a man holding his breath under water. In the two conversations that Pete

Hatcher had with Jane Whitefield he had memorized a few lessons that David Keller now followed mechanically. "Most people who don't make it get caught right away," she had said. "If you can put a break in the trail that lasts three months, they won't have much to work with, and there won't be as many people looking."

He had asked, "If I last for three months I'll be okay?" and she had shaken her head. "I'm just saying, if you're going to make a mistake, don't do it before then." Pete Hatcher had been the kind of person who had wanted to know all of the limits—where can I go and what can I do?—but David Keller was not.

David Keller carried the limits in his mind with a shuddering sense of awe that he should ever have considered going near them. It was lucky for him that he had somehow come to his senses before he had made some impulsive mistake.

Women had always taken up an enormous portion of Pete Hatcher's thoughts. He loved to look at them, to smell the scents that hung in the air close to their hair, to touch their smooth skin, to hear their soft, high voices. He savored the unconsciously graceful little movements they made with their hands. But Pete Hatcher had no philosophy. He had never set aside the time to sit by himself, wondering why things were the way they were. That never seemed to get anybody else anywhere, so how could he be so unrealistic as to think he, of all people, could figure it all out? He had simply known the obvious—that the standard, plain, no-frills human being was a man. There could be no purpose for women to be so radically different from men unless they were created to be enjoyed and cherished.

One afternoon nearly two months after David Keller had arrived in town he had gone to a supermarket on a Sunday afternoon. A pretty woman in her early thirties wearing a Denver Nuggets baseball cap with a long chestnut ponytail stuck out through the back walked past him, and their eyes met. A couple of times after that, when he went up an aisle, his eyes lingered on her again—on the black, skin-tight spandex bicycle shorts that the oversized sweatshirt didn't hang low enough to cover the way she pretended to think it did, because women bent at the waist to reach the lower shelves, instead of at the knees. Once, she had caught him appreciating her, and she gave a little smile of acknowledgment.

Suddenly, without warning, Pete Hatcher had struggled to come to life. The opening lines had begun to rise to his throat automatically: "Do you ride a bike?" he would say, just in case she didn't, and he had to talk about something else. "Riding in Denver traffic is taking your life in your hands. I guess I'm not as good as you are." She had been reading the label on a jar of wheat germ, so he could say, "I heard that stuff is good for you, but is there any way to get around the taste? What do you put it on?" There was nothing to saying the first words. It usually took him five or six syllables to see in the woman's eyes whether she was pleased that she had attracted him or startled that some creep had been drawn to her. He had never made a mistake after a whole sentence, because women were much more alert and aware of the people around them than men were. He knew that if he noticed a woman, she had noticed him first. She had already decided what she would do if he spoke.

He knew he had to push Pete Hatcher down, strangle him before he got David Keller into some kind of trouble. Then he met the woman again on the far aisle, which was lined with wine bottles. It was a bad place, because it was out of the way, almost private. He had to look at some labels and put a bottle in his cart to assert his right to be here.

But she came to him. She said happily, "I guess you don't like football either."

David Keller was startled. Football? Then he remembered. It was late summer, and preseason games must be on television already. He hadn't owned a television set in months, and what might be on it had slipped his mind. He smiled and shrugged. "I've been known to watch a game now and then, but it's such a beautiful day."

"Yeah, it's great, isn't it? I've been out riding my bike." Her voice was high and cute, and she moved in little explosions of excess energy that reminded him of the quick, abrupt dartings of a little bird. He was fascinated. He caught himself wanting to see her do things—any things, but he was already allowing his imagination to form preferences as to what they might be.

"Riding a bike?" he said. "Riding in the traffic around here is too much for me. I guess I'm not as good as you are. You're in better shape, too."

She gave him the hint of a smile. It said, "That already? Be patient." But her voice said, "It's not bad on Sundays. If you like off-road, you've got Bear Creek, Cherry Creek, Chatfield . . ." Her bright brown eyes narrowed. "You're new here, aren't you?"

He felt suddenly scared. "Yes."

"One more southern California refugee, right? Someplace hot and low altitude."

"Los Angeles." He lied with the best smile he could manage. She had instantly known he was a stranger and picked up the quarter of the country he had come from. What was wrong? What was he doing wrong?

She lifted her sweatshirt a few inches so she could reach the pen stuck in the waistband of the tight pants. The flash of white skin forced him to weather a flood of wishes. "Here," she said as she wrote something on her shopping list and tore it off. "If you need directions, just give me a call."

It was all right. She could hardly be less threatening. He took the paper. Above the phone number it said "Kathy." He smiled again and said, "Thanks, Kathy. I'm David . . . David Keller."

She raised an eyebrow. "You don't look like a David."

His heart stopped.

"Maybe a Mike . . . maybe a Jim."

He desperately reminded himself of all of the times when women had said things like this. She thought it was fun to nudge men off balance just a little. He smiled. "I'll give my mother a call and see what she can do."

"You might give it a try," she said. "I guess moms all want their babies to grow up to be Davids. Most of them grow up to be Buck or Ace or something." She was giving him a chance, buying him time to notice that he liked her and think of a way she could be with him that would preserve her self-respect.

It wasn't difficult for Pete Hatcher to think of an invitation. She would like to go pay for her groceries and meet him next door at the health-food place for one of those fruit drinks they made in blenders. She could even have been persuaded to meet him for another ride at one of those creek places she had mentioned and show him the bike route, if they went in different cars. Dinner would have made her feel at a disadvantage because it would mean she had picked up a man and made a date with him. But David Keller was not Pete Hatcher, could not afford to be.

"Well," he said, "I'd better get the rest of my stuff and get home. Thanks." He put the slip of paper in his pocket.

The disappointment hovered behind her bright smile, but she turned to look at the wine bottles on the shelf. "See you." She didn't push her cart away. Instead, she waited and let him move up the aisle away from her.

As he stood in the line at the check-out counter, he was filled with regret and sadness. But for the first time, that feeling was outweighed by something new. He was afraid of her. His disguise was transparent, his identity obviously false. He wanted to leave his shopping cart and slip out the door, hurry along the windowless side wall of the building, and disappear.

After that Sunday, David Keller always ate in his apartment, and when he needed supplies he walked to a small grocery store on Sixteenth Avenue after dark and paid cash for them, then carried the bag home in his left arm to keep the right one free to protect himself.

He had gone to a movie a mile away once, but he had been unable to get used to the sensation that people were looking at him. He knew, objectively, that they were. They might be wondering why a thirty-three-year-old man had nobody to go to the movies with, or they might only be looking at him because when the lights were still on in a theater there was nothing else to look at but a wall of white at the front of the room. But David Keller didn't want people looking at him, and he especially didn't want them wondering. When Pete Hatcher had walked into a room, people had lit up. He could still see them, hear their voices. "Hey, Pete. Have a seat." And he would see pleasure on their faces, and he would make a joke out of it. "What, you're so glad to see me, I owe you money, or something?" He had spent a good part of those thirty-three years learning about Pete Hatcher by seeing him through other people's eyes.

David Keller didn't exactly miss being Pete Hatcher. He had simply begun to realize that being Pete Hatcher had been easy. Being David Keller took a lot of thought, and there seemed to be no reward beyond waking up each morning and verifying that he was still alive. And because when he awoke he found himself still alone, he could regale himself with the strong likelihood that he would be alive to latch the windows and close the curtains that night.

He sat in his little dining room and stared past the gouged sideboard at the mirror above it. The glass had little black specks where the backing was showing through, but he could see himself well enough. He had gotten his hair cut short and lightened it, so he looked a little bit different from Pete Hatcher. The odd thing was that he didn't seem to look like anybody else, either. Some time in his childhood he had been given a game that consisted of a board with a pink oval and a collection of eyes, ears, noses, mouths, and hair. Usually, when he selected features, he could put them together and they would practically scream out what they were: a pirate, a Chinese mandarin, a cowboy. But once in a while, when he put the pieces together, nothing happened. It was simply an oval with two eyes, a nose, and a mouth. That was what he saw looking back at him in the mirror tonight: it was a face, but it didn't seem to belong to anybody.

He had lived for three months on a couple of conversations with a woman he didn't even know. "If you want to be invisible," she had said, "you have to do what other people do. Think average."

"What's average?"

"The average man your age makes about thirty-five thousand dollars a year." He had felt distress, wonder. Could that possibly be all? She had tried to mitigate it. "The good news is that he doesn't save any of it. But he's always doing something. Busy busy busy."

"Busy at what?"

"Watch people. Whenever they're out of their houses, they're engaged in some obvious activity. If you were a cop, you could stop every one of them and ask what they were doing, and they could all bore you silly with details. They're dropping clothes off at the cleaners, then stopping by the drugstore for dental floss, and then they're going to head home for dinner at the time when everybody else is too. An experienced cop wouldn't even have to ask them, because he can read it on them: the way they walk, the way their eyes are set. The people you have to worry about think like cops. Men between seventeen and seventy don't just hang out, sit on a park bench or something. If they're out in a park, they're jogging for their health or walking fast because they have someplace to go."

"Where do I live? What do I do?"

"You rent an apartment. It's in a large building, but not a building that's fancy enough so they do any checking before you move in. I've already found one and rented it for you. I used an identity that's old enough to stand up if it needs to. Nothing else is in your name. I'm your girlfriend. If anybody ever asks about me, we broke up and I moved out."

"What do I drive?"

"For now, nothing. I'll have to get you out quick, so I have no time to do it for you. Here's a short lesson. Leasing a car triggers an all-out credit search. Buying a new car on time does the same. But it's going to be tricky for you to write a check for the full price tomorrow or the next day, because it's what the people who have studied you think you'll do. So don't. What you want is to find a used car for sale by the owner: it's the only market where paying in cash is necessary, and it will keep you off a car company's customer list. Have a mechanic check it out. For most people that's just to see if it's any good. For you, it's also because he'll warn you if it's stolen. Register it and insure it under your new name. Car registrations are public records, and insurance companies sell lists of customers. There's no way to avoid that. Just don't do it right away."

"How long should I wait?"

"If you do it tomorrow, you'll be on a short list. The longer you wait, the longer the list."

"What else?"

"Don't do anything that brings you to the attention of the police, of course. If you see a fire or an accident or a politician, walk the other way. There could be news cameras. Don't vote, file any legal papers, serve on a jury, buy land, buy a gun, or get married, because those create public records."

He had heard the list, and none of those things had been anything he would have done anyway. At any rate, Pete Hatcher would not have done them. He looked at his face in the speckled mirror. The part of this that was beginning to weigh on him was that he had not had enough time to get used to the idea before he had done it. One day he had been Pete Hatcher, walking through the cavernous casino in his tailored summer-weight suit, and a few hours later he had been sitting here in this small, dark apartment in Denver.

She had asked him where he wanted to live, where he could live without being recognized. He had not been able to think of a place. She had rattled off a list of cities and when she had said Denver, he had said yes, just because it was a city where he had never lived, never been for more than an hour or two to change planes, and now even that was safe because it wasn't even the same airport. She had said Denver was okay, because it was only eight hundred miles from Las Vegas, and a person running for his life didn't usually stop that soon.

There were lots of things she had not told him, because there had been no time. She had not told him that David Keller would one day sit in this room and look at himself and find that he had not the slightest vision of a future—not just what to do, or what to expect, but what to want, who to be. And she had not told him that David Keller would be afraid.

It was late. Through the open kitchen window he could hear faint traces of the music from the bar floating up through the still, late-summer air, and cars hissing past it on Colfax. He closed the window and locked it, sat on the single bed in the small bedroom where he slept. He should have felt safe. She had chosen a fourth-floor apartment so he didn't need to worry about somebody climbing in the windows. It wasn't even in a male name, so it would be hard to trace him here. Pete Hatcher had left Las Vegas with over six hundred thousand dollars. He could live like this for ten or fifteen years without poking his head above the surface.

He took his shirt off and lay in the tiny, dark room, on the surface of the bed. He had found David Keller was not comfortable taking all his clothes off in a bed. There was something especially frightening about having them come for him while he was naked, so now he always kept his pants on and his shoes. He had forgotten something. He got up, walked into the kitchen, opened the drawer, and took out the butcher knife. He wrapped the blade in a dish towel and set it beside his left hand in the bed, so they wouldn't see it behind his thigh, and he wouldn't roll over on it. He rested his hand on the handle and lay back in the darkness, feeling the drops of sweat forming on his forehead in the airless room.

As he waited for sleep he thought of the woman in the supermarket. He wished, more fervently now than ever, that he could have responded to her differently when she had spoken. She had been in the market on a Sunday afternoon with nothing much to do, and she had liked him. She had not wanted to put him in danger. She had wanted somebody to play with—to ride bikes, like kids. He had thrown away her telephone number, but maybe he could still find her. He could buy a bicycle, go to one of the places she had mentioned, and just happen to meet her.

No, it was impossible. She would talk, and he would have to talk too—pay out to her an endless series of lies, like beads on a string. There was something too quick about her for that. She would remember what he said, see that bead sixty-seven wasn't the same as bead nineteen. Or she would tell people about him, even make him meet them, and then he would have two or three strings of lies going at once, then more. They would all get farther and farther out of control until he got himself tangled in lies. She would never be in this bed with him, lying with her soft chestnut hair on his chest. Not her, not anyone. The difference between being alive and being dead had all but vanished.

He awoke to the glare of the sun hitting the window above his head and throwing a square patch on the wall. He closed his eyes again and lay perfectly still. If they had come into the apartment while he was asleep, they would have gone straight to the bigger bedroom, and their muffled creaking and rustling would be what had awakened him. He listened for a long time, as he did every morning, at length satisfied himself that no sound had caused him to wake, and sat up. He sensed a change. The world was different this morning.

He went into the big bedroom, laid out some of his favorite clothes—the plain blue oxford shirt, the blue jeans between new and broken in—and stepped into the shower. This was the best part of the day. It always seemed to him that in the morning the universe was starting out clean and fresh. Anything could happen.

It wasn't until he was dressed and eating his breakfast under the open kitchen window that he recognized what was different. It was David Keller. He was through holding his breath.

He found the car after an hour of looking in the newspapers. He knew he couldn't buy something like a Mercedes. Even an Audi or a Saab was pushing his luck. It should be dull and American and cheap. The sliver of an ad said, "96 SL2, 4 door, air cond., automatic, PS. $12,000 OBO." He called the number and he could hear a baby crying in the background. The woman said, "You should probably come after dinner, when my husband is home. I can't answer any questions about it. I don't know a thing about cars."

He made his voice sound worried and disappointed. "Oh. That's too bad. I just got to town, so I've got nothing to drive, and I start work in a couple of days . . ." A little of Pete Hatcher seemed to come back to him. He could sense there was something bothering her. "Oh, I'm sorry. I'm being stupid. Your husband's not home so you don't want some stranger showing up. And of course, I don't want to buy a used car in the dark. So I guess I'm out of luck. . . . Hey, I have an idea. Is the car on the street?"

"No, but I could move it."

"Great. I'll just come by and take a look at it. If it's not what I want, I won't bother you."

"I guess that would be all right."

He took a cab to the house and stood beside the gray car for a time, peeked at the underside, cupped his hands to lean against the window to peer at the number on the odometer, wrote down the license number and serial number, examined the tires. He was running out of things to do when the door of the old duplex opened and a young woman came out on the porch carrying a one-year-old girl on her hip. She had a corkscrew strand of blond hair that kept coming down across her left eye. She had been watching him, as he had hoped, and decided he didn't look like a psychotic.

She said, "You the one who called about the car?"

"Yes," he said. "I'm sorry to come at such an inconvenient time." He smiled at the little girl. "Hi, cutie."

"That's okay," said the woman.

"Well, I'm interested." He looked back at the car. "Is there anything I need to know about the car? Any accidents?"

"No. My husband's dad bought it, drove it for a year, and died. He seemed to like it, and he took care of it. I'm not going to be working again for a while, so we'd just be paying insurance on it for nothing."

"I understand," said Keller.

"Would you like to drive it?"

Keller said apologetically, "If it's all right."

"I called my husband and he said it was okay." As she held out a set of keys, Keller sensed that she wasn't telling the truth.

He took the keys and said, "I'll be right back." Keller drove the car around the block and pulled up in front of the house. This wasn't exactly the way Jane had said to do it. It seemed better. The woman had seen him for a few minutes, could suspect him of nothing, and seemed too busy and housebound to talk to anybody about him. He got out of the car and walked to the porch, She came out and he held up the keys. "I'd like to buy it."

She brightened. "Well, wonderful." After a second she added, "My husband will be happy. It kind of reminds him of his dad."

"Do you know what time he'll be home? I'd like to get this done today." He showed her the envelope. "I brought the money."

"In cash?"

"I didn't want to have to wait for a check to clear. I'm not exactly an old customer of the local banks."

"We don't need to wait for him. Come on in."

Keller followed her into the house. She opened a drawer of the buffet, where she kept the dishes, and pulled out the pink slip. Keller handed her the envelope and watched her count the hundred-dollar bills. When she had finished, she leaned over the coffee table and signed the pink slip and handed it to him.

Keller glanced at the slip. It had been signed by Ronald Sedgely with the new owner as Maura Sedgely, and now she had signed it. The car was hers? There was no husband coming home tonight. Either Ronald Sedgely was her father, and she wasn't married, or she had gotten the car in a divorce from Ronald Sedgely. The discovery made him feel elated, filled with confidence.

He wasn't the only one. Everybody was lying. Everybody was hiding some vulnerability. Opening your face and telling people the truth about yourself wasn't normal. She was normal. She was a single mother trying to deal with a man who called on the telephone and might try to cheat her on a car deal, or might even be a maniac who would rape and kill her in front of her baby. Pretending there was some guy who had to approve the deal and knew all about cars, and just might pop in to protect her, that was the sensible thing to do. She was perfectly normal. He was normal.

Keller drove the car to the D.M.V. to register it, drove to an insurance office he had picked out in the telephone book to insure it, and found that neither was as difficult to do as he had feared. They wanted to know the answers to questions he had prepared for a month ago. Jane had assured him that his driver's license was genuine. It must have been true, because everybody's computer loved David Keller. He had no outstanding warrants, no problems of any kind, and not even any disturbing blank spaces. He had gotten a new license a year ago, after driving in New Jersey for twelve years.

As David Keller drove around town, he couldn't help feeling grateful that human beings were so simpleminded. All he had needed to do to break free of the depression that had been paralyzing him was to get out and drive around in a car on a summer day with his window rolled down. It was such a small improvement that it made him laugh.

It made him even happier when he looked at it in reverse. He had bought the right kind of car in the way Jane had said was the safest. He had bought it from the ideal seller, a woman who didn't even know his name. Maybe he had done it a little early for Jane's taste, but she had not known how invisible he had been for three months. He had made no mistakes at all. And the car made him feel safer.

He would park it somewhere away from his apartment. If they found the apartment, he could sneak down the fire escape, get in his car, and go. If they found the car, he would see them watching it before he went near it. He would hide some emergency supplies inside the car—money, maybe ten grand in a clever place. And what else would he need if they found him?

The clerk in the gun shop was a woman. She was short and gray-haired and probably had been pretty once, but her face looked as though she had spent some time squinting into the sun. When she walked around the counter and he saw that she was wearing a pistol in a holster on her hip, he thought at first that it was some kind of illusion. Then he noticed that everybody in the store was wearing one, even the stock boy with the broom.

She let him stare down through the glass case for a few minutes, then came up and stood beside him. "Anything I can show you?"

He shrugged. "I'm not sure. Yes, I guess so. I just don't know what."

She smiled like an aging dance-hall girl in a Western movie. "Let's narrow it down. You want to buy a handgun."

He smiled back at her. "That's right."

"Are you an old shooter?"

"No. I've never even fired one of these."

"What do you want it for? Target range or protection?"

"Protection. You know, burglars and so on."

She stared at him for a moment as though she were estimating his hat size. "Well, okay. You know, of course, that if somebody comes into your house, what he really doesn't want to see is one of these." She pointed to a short-barreled pump shotgun on the rack behind her.

"I suppose not," he said. "But I'd rather have something small."

She nodded. "And you've never fired a pistol. Are you mechanically inclined? Fix your own car?"

Keller shook his head. "Never."

She opened the case thoughtfully with a key on her belt, selected four pistols, and set them side by side. "There's this," she said. "It's a Beretta 92. A good, reliable nine-millimeter semi-automatic. A lot of police forces use it, and there's a similar model that the army uses. This is the kind of gun that you have to take apart to clean and oil, and put back together right. I don't recommend that for a novice."

"What do you recommend?"

She showed him a revolver with a short barrel. "This is a Ruger SP 101. It's a .38 Special and it's small and lightweight. It doesn't pop up and hit you in the face from the recoil when you fire it. It's easy to care for, and won't let you down." She leaned close to him and spoke from the side of her mouth. "It's the model we usually recommend for women who don't know anything about guns." She watched him for a reaction.

He smiled. "That sounds like just the thing. I'll take two."

"Really?"

"Is that a bad idea?"

"No," she said. "I'd be delighted to sell two." She pulled a set of forms from a tray behind the counter. "Fill these two out, and after the waiting period is up, you can come get your guns." She put away the row of pistols, then stopped, holding the one he had picked out. "As you know, it would be illegal for you to carry a concealed weapon. This is a model you have to be very careful with in that regard. It would be possible to put one of these in your coat pocket and go out without noticing it. Your friends wouldn't see the bulge. Of course, when you reached in and discovered your mistake, the compact size would be a great advantage because you could take it back home without embarrassment." She winked and locked the gun in the case.

12

Linda Thompson sat at the edge of her chair in the dark and watched the front door of Pete Hatcher's apartment building. She liked looking through the night-vision binoculars, liked the way everything showed up green and glowing. She even liked the fact that Earl had spent nearly nine hundred dollars on them. His aching need for the best toys and gadgets gave her a lever to keep him a little bit off balance. Any time he felt the urge to say something about what she spent, she had been able to point to a gizmo that cost twice as much. She was careful not to let Earl notice how much she liked looking through the binoculars. They made her feel as though she had the senses of some sleek, beautiful animal lying in wait in the jungle, its eyes bright and yellow, able to see its dim-sighted, clumsy, hoofed enemy stumbling through the underbrush toward her.

Tonight she could feel her heart beating in her chest, the blood carrying more oxygen to her fingers and toes than it had since they had arrived in Denver. The air was clear and thin here, and she had hated that until her body had adjusted to the altitude.

Linda was feeding on Pete Hatcher's fear and indecision. Five nights ago she had seen him walk down the street at about nine, and come back at nine thirty carrying a single big grocery bag back to his apartment. He had done the same thing three nights ago. Tonight, she knew he was thinking it was time to go get some more food. She was sure he wanted to get into his car and drive somewhere—to a giant supermarket in some other part of town, or to a good restaurant. He had not done it because he was afraid. He was afraid to go where there were bright lights and a lot of people, even though his craving for them was almost physical. Those moments in crowded public places must be precious to him because they felt like safety, but he seemed to know they were not good for him. People would see his face. His car represented the same kind of problem. He had probably bought it because it kept him from feeling helpless and trapped, but he sensed that he needed to keep away from it.

She saw him at the window of his apartment. He stood to the side in the darkened room and looked out, first at the little park, then up and down the street. She raised the magnification and studied his face. He was getting ready, and he was anxious. She saw him move away from the window. "I think he's coming down," she said.

She listened to Earl's voice behind her ear, but kept the binoculars trained on the front entrance of the apartment building. "Everything's ready," he said. "Don't worry." He was talking to her like one of his dogs, low and soft. She liked it. "Just keep him in sight. That's all you need to do."

She saw Hatcher stop inside the lighted entry and pretend to check his pants for his wallet and keys, just buying time while he studied the street outside for signs of danger. He would do one last thing, and she waited for it, holding her breath. He reached behind him and put his hand under his coat to tuck in his shirt. She had known he would tell her. He was carrying the gun, the cute Ruger SP 101 he had bought a week ago. He had bought it because he was afraid, and now that he had it, he was afraid of the gun. "He's got the gun in his belt in the small of his back, under his coat."

"Fine," said Earl.

"He's out. He's walking straight down the street toward the store."

"Time to go," said Earl.

Linda handed him the binoculars. While he was putting them in their case, he checked his watch. "It's nine twelve.

Give him until nine twenty-two to get there and get busy shopping. Be there at nine twenty-seven."

"Right," she said, and went out the door without letting herself look at his eyes. Let him wonder.

As she drove along the dark street, she teased herself gently. It would have been much easier to sit comfortably in the darkness of the hotel room and watch through the night-vision binoculars while Earl popped him with the fancy British sniper rifle through the window. The silencer on that thing would have made the whole episode sound like a bird bumped against the glass and broke its neck. But Earl could never feel satisfied unless he made Linda get a taste of it too.

Earl couldn't just crudely cut him down with a rifle. Linda had to fool him first, make him into an accessory to his own death. He wasn't going to be a leaking corpse lying on a kitchen floor. He was going to be one of those guys who walked off toward the grocery store and simply never came back. If the police got called in a week or two, they wouldn't know whether to look for a corpse or a rent jumper.

David Keller walked out of the small grocery store trying to evaluate the odds. If he continued to walk to Danny's to buy his food, he could just go on buying a little bit at a time and paying cash. If he went to a big supermarket and bought everything he would need for a couple of weeks, he would decrease the frequency of his trips. That would decrease his vulnerability. But he would have to take the car, and he would be seen by more people, and flash more cash, and that would increase his vulnerability.

He hurried to cross the little blacktop parking lot in front of the store where he was lit up by neon beer logos in the window and the yellow sodium light over the tall Danny's Market sign. He moved quickly onto the sidewalk, where he could stay out of the light. Jane had not had time to explain everything to him, but she had told him he would do well enough if he just maintained the right attitude. He reached behind him to feel whether the revolver was riding up under his coat.

As he touched the lump he felt a small twinge of anxiety.

She had implied that a gun was not a good idea. She had said, "You're out of Las Vegas, trying to live a new life in, say, Chicago. You see the same car outside your apartment for three nights in a row. On the fourth night, at midnight, you see the car pull up again. Two men get out. After a minute you hear a knock at your door. What do you do?"

"Do I have a gun?"

"Yes."

"I get it ready, hold it where they can't see it, and open the door to see who they are."

"Right hand or left?"

"Right."

"They're your new neighbors, young single guys who go out every night, a lot of fun. They noticed you watching them through the window, so they knew you were up and decided to ask you over for a drink. One of them holds out his right hand to shake. Or they're cops. The good guys. They're watching the neighborhood because somebody has been selling drugs. They came up to see who you are: maybe you're a witness, but maybe the reason they haven't caught the dealer is that there's a lookout, and it's you. At that hour they're going to ask if they can come in to talk to you. Or maybe you were right, and they're professional killers, come to get you. You have the gun in your right hand. You open the door with your left, so you're ready. They know who you are, but you don't know them. They won't hesitate. You will."

"What was the right answer?"

"What would you do if you didn't have a gun?"

He had shrugged. "I guess I'd figure out who they were without answering the door. You said it was after midnight."

"Good," she said. "Now you know the main thing about guns."

"I'm not sure I do."

"They make you act differently. And they're no good unless you're positive. You have to be so sure that you're willing to kill the two men at the door right away—not look closer, or ask them anything, just pull the trigger."

"If they come to my door, intending to kill me, shouldn't I do that?"

"That's up to you. What would you do after you killed them? There's been a lot of noise, and now there are two bodies bleeding in your doorway. Five quarts of blood each."

"Run, I suppose. Get away. I couldn't very well hang around to talk to the police."

"Good. What if you didn't kill them, just ran instead? Do you get anything from killing them first?"

"More time?"

"It's after midnight in an apartment building. You've fired at least two shots into a hallway. Your neighbors are up dialing 911. The response time on 'shots fired' calls in a big city averages around three minutes, and they usually redirect the helicopters at the same time."

He had said, "I give up. Forget the gun." Maybe he had known even as he said it that he had been lying. Now, while he walked down the dark, quiet street lined with big, dark houses that had been segmented into apartments, he felt a little better because of the gun.

He turned the corner and walked down the darker side street, carrying his grocery bag in his left arm. He saw the woman long before she saw him. She had the hood of her car open, and she was standing in front of it, leaning over and staring down into the engine with a little keychain flashlight.

Keller walked along the sidewalk until he was within twenty feet of the car. She reached out tentatively and touched something. It must have been hot, because she instantly drew back her hand, gave a little "Oooh!" and sucked her fingertips.

He could see her face in the dim glow of the little flashlight, and it looked so perfect that the air in front of him solidified and cut his speed by half. She had long, shiny blond hair that was pulled tight along the sides of her head and held back in an intricate braid, and skin that glowed. As she drew her fingers out of her mouth he saw long pointed nails that showed she had not spent much time staring into the engines of cars. She wore tight blue jeans and a jacket of some fabric that looked like canvas but couldn't have been, and the engine she was staring into belonged to a pearl-cream Lexus LS 400 that cost about sixty thousand dollars. She walked around to the trunk and opened it as Keller came abreast of the car. When the light came on and he could see her eyes welling with tears, he stopped.

Whatever anyone thought of women like her, none of them were in the business of ratting on fugitives. As it happened, David Keller liked women like her very much. He missed them. Instead of approaching and spooking her, he called to her from the sidewalk.

"I see you've got trouble. Can I call the auto club for you or something?"

She swung her head around, startled. She didn't seem to have remembered that she wasn't marooned alone on the surface of the moon. She studied him for a second, seemed to be noting that he had clean pants and a respectable sport coat on. But the fact that he was carrying a grocery bag seemed to make the difference. Jane had been on the money once again. If people could see that you were out on your own business, it was better than a pile of testimonials.

She smiled, and he could see the lush, ripe lips part to show perfect white teeth. She shrugged and held her shoulders in an embarrassed cringe. "My membership lapsed. I called them, and they ran me on the computer, and then I noticed my card was expired."

"I'm sorry," said Keller. He stepped a little closer to her car—not to her, but to the open hood. He would let her do the approaching. "I used to have one of these. They're usually pretty dependable . . ." The sentence died in his throat. He could not believe he had let that slip out. It wasn't like looking at a ten-year-old car and saying, "I used to have one." This one was new.

But he could see that the effect he had wanted to convey was the only one that she had caught. She was coming around the car to join him. She had snatched a clean red towel from the trunk, and she was wiping her hands with it. He said, "At this time of night, I'm afraid all the mechanics might be home teaching their sons to overcharge." He stared at the engine, pretending he knew what he was looking for. "How is it acting? Does it turn over?" He set his bag in front of the bumper.

She was right beside him now. He could smell the scent of her hair. Things must be going much better than he had imagined. She was much closer to him than was normal. They were almost touching. She leaned over the engine and pointed to a box bolted to the firewall that had colored wires plugged into it. "When I opened it, I could smell something burning over here."

He leaned in too, trying to see if the insulation on one of the wires was melted. He felt a light touch on the small of his back, and the hard, heavy weight of his pistol was gone.

Almost instantly, his head was pushed to the side. The pain was horrible, and it was coming from a heavy metal object pressed to his temple. He could feel the red cotton towel covering it, but he had no time to think.

She was speaking low, almost in a whisper. "Police officer. Come around to the back of the car." He hesitated, but she tugged his coat hard, and he tried to straighten so fast that he banged his head on the hood. When he reached the back he noticed that the light in the trunk had gone out.

"Get in," she ordered.

"Look," he said. "I can explain the gun. I was just trying to help you."

"You have the right to remain silent." She lifted the rag off her hand and he could see the gun now. It was big and square and ugly, with a muzzle that looked cavernous. "Get in the trunk, please. Anything you say can and will be used against you in a court of law."

Keller was dazed. His mouth was dry and he couldn't swallow. He was getting arrested by a Denver cop, a woman decoy. On an illegal weapons charge. They would find out who he was. There had to be a way out of this.

"You have a right to have an attorney present during questioning. If you cannot afford an attorney, the court will appoint one for you. Have you heard and understood these rights?" Her thumb with the beautifully polished, tapered nail came up and cocked the hammer.

David Keller climbed into the trunk. Why did she have to put him in the trunk? Didn't they have a second car with regular cops who hauled you away when they caught you? Of course. She wasn't a decoy at all. She was off duty. She had just seen the gun at his back, plucked it away, and stuck hers in his face. The trunk slammed down on him and the world went black.

Linda stood behind the trunk of the car, squeezed her eyes closed, and smiled, smelling the thin, delicious night air. She had found the mark, taken his gun away from him, and locked him up, all by herself.

Part of the pleasure of it was that she was not alone. She had done it from start to finish with Earl watching her. He had seen her pretending to burn herself and sucking her fingers and crying just a little bit, just enough to seem soft and feminine and vulnerable. And he had seen her stand on her tiptoes to bend over the engine in these tight jeans, just arching her back a tiny bit, enough to make the mark ashamed of himself for thinking that way, and enough to give Earl something to think about too. For Earl, part of the experience was that it made him want to hurt the guy, to break bones and teeth for Linda.

Linda didn't really think much about the mark once she had him. He was necessary, but he wasn't really a player in the event. She was just using him to act out for Earl's eyes how desirable she was. The mark was a mirror for both of them. He let Linda see how beautiful she was through his eyes, because she never could quite look at herself the way men did, and so watching them look was the only way. And Earl could look at the way she affected this mark, and it made Earl feel more that way about her—as though he were seeing her for the first time too, and because he was feeling desire, he knew exactly what the other man was feeling, and that made him wild. The night was filled with invisible sparks of energy shooting back and forth around her. It was magic.

This was the part of their lives that she craved. She loved it when they were out in the night hunting together, thinking hard together about the mark and his habits and what he would do, and deciding what they would do to bag him like this. And now the hunt was right at its climax, with Earl out there in the dark concentrating all of his attention on her. In a minute he would emerge from the shadows to obliterate the mark and reclaim her. They would drive him up into the mountains and bury the body before dawn. She felt as though somebody had taken one of those electric-shock machines they had in hospitals and pressed the paddles to her chest to jump-start her heart.

She saw Earl appear from the alley behind the little market, walking along briskly. He was primed. She stepped to the front of the car and slammed the hood. That let her see the police car.

Then it was pulling up beside the Lexus. The cop was young, and she could see his lips were straight across his face with no smile, but she knew it was waiting to come, because the eyebrows had that wanting-to-be-concerned look that cops sometimes got. He stopped the car, got out, and left the door open so he could hear his radio. He didn't do the things they did when they were suspicious—put their nightsticks in their belts, say something into the radio. She could hear the nasal voice of a female dispatcher squawking out meaningless words and numbers, but he didn't answer. Instead, he stepped closer to Linda and said, "Having car trouble?"

"No," said Linda. When she smiled she could feel that she had actually induced a blush. Her cheeks were hot. "I thought I heard something in the engine, but it was just my imagination. Everything is fine."

He glanced at the car, then back at Linda. "Why don't you start it up, and I'll listen?"

Linda sensed that it was a devious way of being sure the car wasn't stolen without coming out and asking for her license and registration. She was glad he was so young and handsome, because the sight of him right after Hatcher would be sending hot flashes of jealousy up Earl's spine mixed with the alarm and the wonder at how desirable the bait really was. She smiled as prettily as she could for both of them and said, "Well, if you wouldn't mind . . . ," then obediently opened the driver's door and sat behind the wheel.

The shot was so loud that her legs kicked out and pushed her back against the seat. Blood and brain from the cop had spattered the windshield. She scrambled out of the car as though it were on fire.

Earl's strong hand clamped her arm. She danced at the end of his arm, tugging to get moving, but he tightened his grip. "He's still alive, right?"

At first she thought he meant the cop. "How could—" she began, then remembered. Hatcher was still in the trunk. She held her panic in check as she hurried to the trunk, unlocked it, and lifted the lid three inches. She stuck her big Colt into the dark space, then pulled the trigger four times before Earl grabbed her and slammed the trunk.

In the sudden silence she could hear the sirens too. More police were coming. Earl dragged her toward the alley, his grip so tight that she could feel the blood beginning to collect below it, so her fingers throbbed. His voice was a raspy whisper. "Don't ever fire blind into the trunk of a car when your ass is that close to it again, you dumb bitch. The gas tank is right under it."

She had forgotten about the gas tank. Imagining the bright orange explosion she had flirted with gave her a giddy feeling of luck, but even better, she detected that the strain in Earl's voice was genuine concern. He had just dusted a cop to reclaim her, and he really didn't want to lose her. She let him pull her along the alley, then lead her up the dark space beside the market and over to the next street. In another minute and a half they were on the pedestrian mall along Sixteenth Street, far from the sirens and far from the cops cruising around looking for a getaway car.

When he saw her turn her head to look at the display window of a boutique, Earl gave a sullen nod and followed her inside. Linda bought a silk summer dress that made her feel light and pretty, a little bit like a butterfly.

Pete Hatcher was crouching on his knees, shaking. He could tell that he must have lost some of his sight and hearing. He had seen the trunk begin to open. He had just found the safety latch inside the lid by touch and gotten the courage to release it when he had heard the keys in the lock and seen the crack of light appear.

He had been terrified that the cops would see his hand near the lock, so he had reflexively recoiled, scuttled back into the corner of the trunk behind the loose spare tire and curled up. He had seen the pistol appear in the opening, but he had never expected the gun to go off. The blast, the flash, and the shower of sparks made him bring his knees to his chest, clap his hands over his ears, and close his eyes.

She had fired again and again at the spot where he had first lay down when she locked him in—first where his head had been, then his belly, then halfway back up, to his chest, then his head again.

He heard nothing now, but his ears were still ringing, so he wasn't sure that there were no sounds. The woman had every right to think he was dead, so now she would drive the car somewhere. He waited for the sound of the engine, but it didn't come. He tried to figure out what he should do, but first he had to know why she had shot at him. No, that was wrong. Somebody was going to open the trunk again soon, expecting him to be dead. When they discovered that he wasn't, they would certainly correct the oversight. He could die that way, or he could try to run.

He pulled the safety latch behind the lock and cautiously pushed the trunk open a crack. He heard the sound of a police radio, then saw the police car. He closed his eyes and felt sweet relief. She couldn't kill him if the other cops had already arrived. That was probably why she had done such a hasty job of it—to finish it before they got here. He popped the lid up, then swung his leg over the rear bumper, misjudged the height of the trunk, and toppled over onto the street. He began to sit up, then lay back down again and stared along the underside of the car.

He could see the body of a policeman lying on the street at the front, almost under the radiator. There was a big hole in his forehead as though the skull had been punched outward, and blood draining down over his left eye into a pool. Hatcher's brain tried to take all that it knew and make sense of it. Did she imagine Hatcher had killed the policeman earlier, and then think she was executing him for it? What was he thinking? It was impossible. She had killed the policeman. She was no cop.

His breathing stopped. He had no idea how long he had been hearing the sirens. He was alone with the body of a murdered policeman. He had just bought two guns, and this woman had probably used one of them on a policeman. It might be lying around here someplace, and if it wasn't, the police certainly had a way to know he had owned two and had only one left.

Hatcher stood and backed away from the car, his head swiveling around, first to see if the madwoman was still nearby waiting to fire, then to see if any of the people in the houses had come out, then just to see where he was going. He walked to the front of the car and picked up his grocery bag. He turned, and then his feet were pounding on the sidewalk, carrying him away, the momentum building and building, his mouth open in a grimace so the air hissed in and out through his clenched teeth.

His mind burned through the mass of impressions into a bare, heightened clarity as he ran. There was no moment of indecision, no wavering among choices, because he had no choices. He knew the police would come toward this spot from three directions at once, because there were only three ways for a car to come. They would flood each end of the block and come up the alley. He took the fourth way, entering the lobby of an apartment building that looked a lot like his own, walking through it, down the first-floor hallway and out the back door, then beside the next one and across the street, where he entered the lobby of the next one, so he emerged on his own street a block from his apartment.

He walked into his entryway and climbed the stairs for the last time. He knew that the madwoman almost certainly believed he was dead. Even if she had any doubts and knew where he lived, she would have had a difficult time getting here before he had. He opened the apartment door, slipped inside, and locked it behind him.

He had no difficulty working out the order of tasks. He made the telephone call first. She wasn't home, but he left a message. Then he collected the cash from its hiding places in the apartment, packed his clothes quickly, and wiped his fingerprints off all the surfaces he usually touched. He took all of the food jars and bottles out of the refrigerator, put them into the sink, and ran water over them until he was sure they carried no fingerprints, then put them all into a big plastic trash bag with his groceries.

He went out, locked the door, wiped the doorknob, walked quietly down the hall, and carried his suitcase and his trash down the back staircase. He put his trash in the Dumpster. Then he walked around the corner to where his car was parked, set his suitcase in the trunk, and began to drive.

Earl and Linda sat in a cowboy bar in Golden, a half hour into the mountains west of Denver, and watched the eleven o'clock news on the television set on the wall above them. The newswoman was reporting "the senseless, execution-style killing of a young police officer."

Earl knitted his eyebrows. "Now, that's typical, isn't it? They haven't found out why it happened, so they say it was senseless. They read the words on the prompter, but they don't seem to know what they're saying."

Linda could see the newswoman standing about twenty yards away from the Lexus, and behind her the police crew was dusting it for prints. The car trunk was open. "The police are urging anyone who has information about the incident to contact them. They have no solid leads as to why anyone would have shot the officer. One theory I've heard is that even though the new Lexus sedan had not yet been reported missing, the officer might have seen something suspicious and pulled it over."

Linda held her breath, waiting for Earl to notice what had not been said. Finally she knew that he already had. He swallowed the last of the beer in his glass, set it on the table, and said, "Well, we'd better go see if we can figure out where he's gotten to now."

"I'm sorry, Earl," she said. She wanted to waste some time in the bar, where there were people, before she blithely stepped into the dark with Earl. He was perfectly capable of hiding his anger until they were somewhere along a deserted road. "I'm really sorry. I don't know how I could have—"

"I did it," he said. "I stopped you before you could do him right." He added, "I keep thinking, 'So she might have put a round into the gas tank. If we'd been back a few yards it wouldn't have been so bad.'" He pulled her up by the arm. "Better than this, anyway. This is a joke."

When they reached the neighborhood where Hatcher had been living as David Keller, they drove past the place where he had parked the used Saturn that evening. For an instant Linda felt the thrill of surprise and anticipation: the space was not empty. But when Earl drove closer she could see that the car in the space was a Thunderbird.

Earl left their car a block from the rear of Hatcher's building and they climbed the back stairs. Earl opened the lock effortlessly and they stepped inside, put on their gloves, and began the search. As soon as Linda opened the refrigerator, she knew what the rest of the small apartment would be like.

After fifteen minutes, Earl sat down on the couch. "He's getting better at this."

"He doesn't have as much stuff to worry about," said Linda. "She made him travel light."

"Let's see," muttered Earl. "He's in the trunk of the car. You put four shots in there. You would think with four rounds rattling around in there and bouncing off things, one of them would have clipped him, wouldn't you?"

"Yes. I did. But it didn't happen. There's no blood anyplace."

"He knows he's a lucky man, but he's scared to death. He hears us leave, he pops out and runs like hell—probably through back yards, or the police would have picked him up. He's too stupid to do the wrong thing and run across town. He comes right back here. What does he do?"

"It looks like he spent some time cleaning up."

"Right. He couldn't have done that for us. We know who he is already. He must think the cops are going to come here looking for him. What else did he do?"

"He took his car."

"That's last. What's first?"

"He packed his stuff. Probably some money, the other gun he bought."

Earl nodded. "He did that. Put yourself in his mind. You're scared. You're so scared you just ran home as fast as you could. You clean up, throw everything in a suitcase. You're about to go out the door and drive until you run out of gas. Where are you going to go?"

Linda's eyes narrowed, and she bit her lower lip, then released it to reveal a little smile. She looked across Earl at the telephone on the table. "Does it have a redial button?"

Earl opened his briefcase and found the little microcassette recorder. "Testing," he said. "You'd better work." He clicked two buttons. "Testing. You'd better work," it said. Earl pressed two more buttons, then looked at Linda. He lifted the receiver, clamped the tape recorder to the earpiece with one hand, pressed the redial button with the other, and recorded the series of quick musical tones.

Linda counted the tones. "Eleven numbers. Long distance. An area code and a number."

Earl hung up before the phone on the other end could ring. Then he played back the recording of eleven tones and handed the recorder to Linda. "Get the numbers." He stood up, took a penlight, and began to shine it on the surfaces of the furniture.

Linda lifted the receiver and said into the recorder, "One," then pressed the one button and recorded the tone. She said, "Two," pressed the two button, and recorded the tone. When she reached six, she hung up to avoid completing a call, then got the last four numbers on tape.

It took Linda another ten minutes to decipher the recorded tones of the woman's telephone number. "I think I have it. Should I test it?"

Earl said, "Give it a try."

Linda said aloud, "One. Area code seven one six," then dialed the rest of it. After four rings she heard a woman's voice. "Leave a message when you hear a beep." Linda hung up. "It's the woman. She has her answering machine on."

Earl took his penlight and opened David Keller's telephone book. "Seven one six. . . . That's New York . . . Buffalo, New York." He closed the book and looked at Linda. "Maybe this time we got lucky, not him, and not her. She's got her answering machine on. He called her no more than an hour or two ago. Maybe it's on because she's already talked to him and gone off to meet him. But it just could be that he got her machine too, and left a message."

Linda looked at the phone as though she could see down the wire to the other end. "Most machines will play back a message if you're away. Ours will do it if you push a two-digit code. Some use codes with three or four, but it might be worth a try."

"There are only a hundred possible combinations. And we aren't paying the phone bill."

It was two o'clock when Linda heard a change. "Leave a message when—" and the recording stopped. There was a click, and she could hear the answering machine rewinding, then another click. Linda held Earl's tape recorder beside the earpiece of the telephone.

"Jane? Jane? It's me. I'm in trouble. Somehow they found me. A woman tried to kill me tonight. I've got to get out. I'm going to head north, to Cheyenne. No, too close. Billings. I'll try to make it to Billings, Montana. I'll call again when I get there."

She was laughing with delight when she played the recording for Earl, but he was staring at the wall, and he wasn't smiling.

When it ended, he sat in silence for a moment, then glanced at his watch. "We'd better get going. I've got to put you on a plane, and then head up north."

"Put me on a plane?"

He spoke so gently that she was afraid of him. "He saw your face, honey. Having you around isn't going to do me any good in Billings."

"You're sending me home?"

"Home?" His grin came like a sudden snarl. "No. You've got to go do something about her."

13

"Jane? Jane? It's me. I'm in trouble. Somehow they found me. A woman tried to kill me tonight. I've got to get out. I'm going to head north, to Cheyenne. No, too close. Billings. I'll try to make it to Billings, Montana. I'll call again when I get there."

The shock in his voice made Jane's scalp prickle, and a hot, sick sweat began to materialize on the back of her neck. The machine's inhuman voice said, "End of messages," and clicked off. She pressed the button again and heard Hatcher's voice. "Jane? Jane?" She listened to the rest of it, each word of it giving her bits of information that Pete Hatcher probably didn't know.

He had made a mistake, but even after he had seen the executioner, he had no idea what he had done wrong. He had stayed hidden for three months, so it had nothing to do with the escape route. He must have done something as David Keller that they had expected Pete Hatcher to do. He had gotten himself on some list.

"I'm going to head north, to Cheyenne. No, too close." She felt something clutching her stomach. He had been sitting in his apartment in Denver all this time, gotten up a hundred mornings and gone to bed a hundred evenings, and it had never occurred to him to plan the best way to get out if they found him. It sounded as though he were running his finger up a road map while he was talking, looking for a route that sounded safe to his panicked brain.

She had told him to prepare contingency plans. After some-

142

thing happened, he wouldn't be able to think clearly, he would forget details, leave things behind that he needed. But had she told him? She tried to remember their two conversations. She thought she had told him. She had tried to instill in him an attitude. Other people could make decisions at the last moment, but a fugitive could not. He had to know in advance the places where he was willing to show his face, what he was willing to do, what he was going to say when somebody asked him a question.

Jane slowly felt the suspicion harden into a certainty. She had not taught Pete Hatcher how to stay alive. The excuses began to flood her consciousness. Getting him out of Las Vegas had not been a question of redirecting a running man. It had been like staging a prison break. He had been watched, followed, suspected by people who seemed to have no other duties. She had needed to slip him out between the guards from a standing start, and then spend most of her energy delaying the pursuit. But repeating the circumstances to herself accomplished nothing. Words were enough to apologize for her haste, but not enough to absolve her if Pete Hatcher died.

Now he was on his way to Billings, Montana, a city with a population of no more than eighty thousand, where finding his car would probably be no harder than driving around for an afternoon and looking for it. She knew about the car from his telephone message too. If he had to decide in the middle of the night between stopping in Cheyenne and going on up Interstate 25, then he was driving a car he owned.

She looked around her at her bedroom. It occurred to her that she had taken very little out of here when she had gotten married. It was as though she had subconsciously tried to leave Jane Whitefield behind, where she could cause no trouble. There were most of her clothes, hanging in the closet with dry cleaners' bags over them, and there was her old dresser.

She walked along the hall and down the staircase, then through the kitchen to the basement steps. She turned on the light and looked around. The house had been built in the days when they used stones for basements, the beams under a house were just rough-planed tree trunks, and the floorboards were held to them with square-headed spikes. She walked to the old set of shelves her great-grandmother had used to store her preserves—sweet peeled peaches and pears in sugary water, stewed tomatoes, applesauce, corn soup, and strawberries, all in big mason jars with rubber gaskets and glass tops with a steel-clamp contraption that held them tight. The fall canning had lasted through her grandmother's time. Only the old jars had survived her mother's.

Jane went to the oil furnace, moved the stepladder beside it, then disconnected a section of one of the heating ducts. This was a round one that was left over from the days when the house had been heated by an old coal furnace. It wasn't connected to anything anymore, but it ran from the now-empty site of the coal bin, turned upward, and connected to the floor under the kitchen, where there had once been a wide brass grate. She looked inside, found the box, and set it on the top step.

She separated James Weiss's papers from the others—his birth certificate, New York driver's license, his credit cards, his Social Security card, his college diploma, the life insurance policy he had bought six years ago. James Weiss was one of the most credible identities she had ever assembled—certainly among the best of the adult males.

James Weiss had no pedigree, but his credentials had a long and complicated history. His birth certificate was genuine. Years ago, a man Jane knew had gotten a job in a county courthouse in Pennsylvania, where he had quietly added fifty birth records. Jane had bought twenty of them. She had liked the idea so much that she had allowed two women who worked in county clerks' offices in Ohio and Illinois to repeat it. The woman in Ohio had offered to do it because she had known a little girl for whom Ohio had turned into a dangerous place and knew that Jane had been the one to make her disappear. The woman in Illinois had made the new people and sent their birth certificates to Jane as a present on the anniversary of her own disappearance from a tight spot in California.

James Weiss had been one of the Illinois woman's creations.

Jane had gotten him a Social Security card and a driver's license by sending a young man who owed her a favor to apply for them. The college diploma was the product of another ruse she had invented at about the same time. She had searched alumni magazines until she found a James Weiss who had graduated from the University of California at Berkeley. She had run a credit check on him and gotten the information she needed to request a transcript and a duplicate of his diploma. Anyone who wished to could call and verify that they were genuine.

Jane had found an insurance company that did not require a physical exam for a life insurance policy under two hundred thousand dollars, so she had bought him one for a hundred thousand. She had kept building Weiss's identity in small ways over the years, just as she had a number of others.

For most of the people she had taken out of the world, Jane had bought false identities from professionals. But she had always been aware that professional forgers were not permanent fixtures on the landscape. Lewis Feng in Vancouver had been murdered. George Karanjian in New York had gotten too rich to take chances and retired.

Jane bought and used identities for herself by the dozen so she could travel unimpeded, then destroyed the ones that might have been compromised. But she also kept about fifteen that she had built on her own—some here at her house, some in safe-deposit boxes in banks in New York, Chicago, Los Angeles, and Toronto.

She selected six matched sets of papers for couples, added them to James Weiss, put the heating duct back together, and went upstairs to make her telephone calls. She called the airline first. The flight to Chicago would leave in two hours. Then she took a deep breath, let it out, and dialed her home number.

Carey answered. "Hello?"

"Hi, Carey," she said. "I want you to do something for me and not ask any questions until you get here."

"Get where?"

"Can you meet me at the house in Deganawida?"

He hesitated. "Well, sure. Do you want me to call somebody? Dress for dinner? Bring bail money?"

"Just come." She hung up. She wished she had laughed when he had mentioned bail money. It should have been funny. If she had been the wife she wanted to be, it would have been. She went downstairs to find the small brown suitcase she had left in the little office that had been her mother's sewing room. Then she checked the latches on the first-floor windows, changed the light bulbs of the two lamps that were on timers, and hurried upstairs.

She was packing the suitcase when Carey came into the bedroom. He looked at the suitcase, then looked at Jane. He said, "I hope you called because you needed me to help you carry a few things home."

Jane smiled a sad little smile. "There's something I want you to hear." She stepped to the answering machine, pressed the button, and watched Carey's face while Pete Hatcher's voice came on, scared, dazed, and breathless. "Jane? Jane?" When Carey had heard the message and there was the clatter of the telephone receiver being hurriedly set back in its cradle, she pressed the other button to erase the message, then stepped close to him. She touched his arm and it felt hard and stiff, but when she tugged it, he sat on the bed with her.

He said, "I can't believe this is happening."

She sighed and tried to find a way to begin. "I love you." That was the best way. "I love you. I don't want this to happen either."

"But you made a promise. You said it wouldn't. Not that you would be sorry if it did, but that you would do what was necessary so it didn't."

"This is something else."

"Jane," he said. "Everything is something else."

"Let me try to explain," she said quietly. "This is going to sound like some kind of legalistic excuse, but it isn't. I said that if somebody came to me and asked for this kind of help, I would tell them I wasn't able to do that anymore. I would have. This is a time when I need you to help me. I want to be honest and tell you everything, so you understand. You heard his voice. His name is . . . used to be Pete Hatcher. He worked for a big casino company in Las Vegas. They weren't honest. He learned too many details. He also made them suspicious. They were busy preparing to kill him when I took him out."

Carey shook his head. "What a shock—something so unprecedented. A gambling outfit that turns out to be dishonest. Boy, I'll bet Pete Hatcher was surprised. Who would have guessed?"

She looked at him apologetically. "That's part of being a guide. Some of the people I've taken out of their troubles weren't innocent, or weren't smart, or caused their own misery. Pete Hatcher is probably one of them. But he hasn't done anything that I consider a capital offense."

"You'd be amazed at how many people like that there are," said Carey. "Billions. Some of them haven't even committed a felony."

Inside, she winced, but she forced herself to say, "If Pete Hatcher came to me out of nowhere tonight, I would tell him no. But he happened before I made that promise. He could be about to die because I didn't do a good enough job. This isn't something I can ignore. It's as though you operated on somebody and left a sponge in his belly."

"It's not exactly an apt analogy," said Carey. "If I had been operating on a patient, I would have been doing it in the legitimate pursuit of my lawful profession, doing what I was educated, trained, and certified to do. I would perform surgery if it were the generally accepted way of correcting a serious and possibly life-threatening condition. I'm part of a system. I'm not just some guy who decided on his own that real doctors aren't doing enough surgery, or doing it well enough, so I try to do a few at home."

She hugged him. "You're right, Carey," she said.

"I am?"

She stood up and went to her closet. "Yep. When you're right, you're right."

"And?"

"And I was right to choose you. Not that there was any choice involved. We're not talking about some profession here, that I had to give up. It's just a trick I learned to do when I was too young and stupid to know any better."

"So you'll stay home—mail him another false ID and forget it?"

She looked at him in surprise. "Oh, I'm sorry, Carey. I didn't mean that." She went back to her packing.

"What did you mean?"

"I meant I'm much sorrier about this than you will ever know. You're my life now. When I get this over with, I'll spend the next few years trying to make it up to you—trying to give you back the confidence and peace of mind I just threw away, so you don't think that any time the phone rings I might go off to do something stupid. Because I won't. I just can't start being smart tonight. I can't pretend I didn't abandon a person out there where I know he'll be killed."

Carey went to her and rocked her gently in his arms. "Is there anything I haven't said that would talk you out of it?"

"No. You've done pretty well."

"You know how I feel about it, right? No point in going into all the stuff about how a man feels letting his beautiful young wife go off to some place where she might get killed."

"I know how you feel," she said. "I can't help this."

He brightened, then looked dispirited. "Threats don't work on you, do they?"

"Not very well," she said. "You could make me very, very sad without trying very hard."

"So whatever I do or say, all I can do is make a bad time worse for both of us." He stared at his feet. "Need a ride to the airport?"

She threw her arms around him and held him as tightly as she could, clutching him and letting the tears run down her cheeks. "Thank you, Carey," she said. She turned and went into the bathroom and closed the door.

Jane lifted the perfume bottle out of the medicine cabinet, opened it, and sniffed. It had a sweet, damp, earthy smell.

Periodically, for years, she had collected the roots of water hemlock, mashed them for their juice, then purified and concentrated it. This batch was fresh enough, and maybe stronger than the last. In the old days, when an Iroquois wanted to commit suicide, he would eat a hemlock root and die within two hours. The perfume worked much faster. She put the bottle into her purse and felt the tears coming again.

She rested her foot on the rim of the bathtub and began to run adhesive tape around her thigh. She wiped her eyes and carefully retrieved the boot knife she had hidden on the underside of the drawer of her vanity. It was thin and weightless and razor-edged, made of zircon-oxide ceramic instead of steel so it wouldn't set off metal detectors. She taped it to her thigh, then put her foot down and let her dress fall to cover it.

She walked into the bedroom and kissed her husband. "How do I look?"

14

The lights came up to reveal the Miraculous Miranda in a Victorian gown, standing behind tall glass windows in an octagonal set like a gazebo. The back wall of the little room was covered with library shelves. She stood on tiptoes to lift from a shelf a folio volume bound in worn leather, opened it, and turned the old parchment pages as she walked toward a small table. Finally she found a passage and read it with interest. She closed the book, set it on the floor, and snapped her fingers. A bottle of champagne appeared on the table. She snapped them again and a stemmed glass appeared beside it. She stared at the bottle with a scowl of concentration: nothing happened. She took a deep breath, stared harder, and the cork popped fifteen feet into the air. When it came down she caught it happily and held it while it turned into a little bird. She opened the window and let it fly away above the heads of the audience, then closed the window.

Miranda picked up the bottle and poured champagne into the glass, lifting the bottle higher so the stream of clear liquid caught in the spotlights appeared first green, then red, then blue, then the golden color of her hair. She sipped from the glass, then set it back on the small, graceful table, took a step away, and faced the audience to resume her act. But she changed her mind and returned to the table. She poured the liquid into the glass again. The bubbly liquid foamed to the rim, but she kept pouring. The foam frothed over the side of the glass and down the stem, off the table and onto the floor. She seemed to be intrigued by the way the foam kept bubbling and growing. Soon there was a sudsy puddle at her feet that threatened to cover the floor of the little pavilion.

Miranda seemed nonplussed. She righted the bottle and scrutinized the label with curiosity. But while she read it, she noticed that turning the bottle upright had not stopped the liquid from gushing out. It came faster and faster, first like a fountain, then like the eruption of a volcano. She set it on the table and backed uneasily away from it, toward the tall shelves of books.

The audience was enchanted, but Miranda seemed concerned about her long nineteenth-century dress. She held the skirts up with both hands as the sudsy champagne soaked her dancing pumps and rose to her ankles. She looked around toward the wings of the stage, but none of her helpers seemed to be able to see her around the walls of books at the sides of the set. She waved testily above the set at the lighting and music technicians in the glass booth behind the audience, but the fans who turned their heads to follow her gaze saw that the two men were shrugging and shaking their heads in dismay. The lighting man seemed to be the only one with any presence of mind, and he switched on a row of soft lights above Miranda so she could see what she was doing.

As the flood from the bottle rose higher, the audience could see that Miranda was on her own. She turned to the bookshelves, placed one foot on the lowest shelf, pushing the books back with her toe, and began to climb. On the sixth shelf, her foot caught on the hem of the dress and slipped. She lost her footing, dropped with a stomach-gripping jerk, grasped a shelf, and dangled there.

Miranda's toe found a purchase, and that freed one hand. She quickly undid the buttons on the front of the dress and let it fall to her ankles. She stepped out of it with one foot and looked over her shoulder in frustration. With her free hand she gave a hasty gesture, and conjured a wooden hanger floating in the air. She gave the dress a kick and it promptly flew through the air and hung itself on the hanger. She snapped her fingers and it vanished from sight.

Now that Miranda was dressed only in a corset, petticoat, and white stockings, her unnaturally strong and nimble acrobat's body seemed to scale the bookshelves effortlessly. She reached the top shelf at the rim of the structure as the foaming torrent sloshed behind the tall windows, turning the room into an aquarium.

Just as the audience seemed to make the analogy, the resemblance became inescapable. Brightly colored foot-long fish began to flit and glide out of the bookshelves, then swim down into the room to investigate the furniture. The mind struggled to go through the processes it had been trained to do: Are the fish alive, or mechanical, or holograms of live fish projected from offstage into the liquid? But the cogitation stumbled over itself and collapsed, because in Miranda's little pantomimes, guessing the method answered no question at all, and something else was always coming in to change the mixture.

Miranda was visibly fascinated by what she saw in the library below her. She seemed to forget the audience for a moment. She slipped off her stockings and put a toe in. She stood and paced along the top of the bookcase, looking into the pool, and as she did she loosed herself from the corset and stepped out of the petticoat to reveal a bright orange two-piece bathing suit. Then she ran back along the top of the bookcase, sprang into the air, executed a flip, and knifed into the water.

Through the row of tall windows the audience could see her swimming underwater with the bright blue and yellow fish. Suddenly, the unthinkable happened. There was a creaking, tearing sound, the walls collapsed outward, and the water poured onto the stage to be sucked away by invisible drains. Miranda was left lying on the carpet near the table. She stirred, then stood up suddenly, bowed, and blew kisses. Then she bowed very low. Her face assumed that strange, playful, mischievous look as she picked up something from the rubble on the floor and held it up.

It was a big painting from one of the collapsed walls. It was a painting of Lady Godiva riding on her white horse.

Miranda looked down at her bright orange bathing suit, then

at the audience. Now her smile was naughty. The audience roared, urging her to do whatever she was contemplating. She propped the painting against the table, picked up the old leather-bound book that still sat beside the bottle. She quickly leafed through the pages, found the right one and read it, and set the book down.

Miranda stepped back a few paces, gestured portentiously at the painting, and then, with a final mischievous glance at the audience, slowly raised her hand and pointed down at her own head.

There was a brilliant flash, a puff of smoke, and Miranda was gone. In her place stood a graceful white Arabian horse. Braided into its mane was a swatch of bright orange cloth that could have been the top of Miranda's bathing suit, and into its long tail, the second piece of orange cloth. The audience was laughing, shrieking, applauding its approval: if Miranda had been a horse, this was the horse she would be.

The horse walked to the table, nosed the old book thought-fully, as though it were Miranda trying to discover her mistake, then turned to face the audience, extended its foreleg, and low-ered its head in a final bow. There was another flash and puff of smoke, and when it cleared, the horse too was gone.

Seaver sat on the folding chair beside Miranda's technician and watched him engage the hydraulic lift, bringing the white horse the rest of the way down under the stage. The gleaming ten-inch cylinder shortened as the hole in the stage floor above snapped shut, the noise of it covered by the deafening music of Miranda's exit. As the black platform moved down to eye level, he saw Miranda was standing on it with the horse. She swung her leg up over the horse's back and mounted it, but she didn't sit up. Instead she clung to it, her hands caressing the horse's face, patting its neck while she spoke into its ear, crooning soft words into its dumb animal brain to keep it from remembering to panic.

When the hydraulic lift reached the level of the concrete floor she swung down from the horse, and now he could hear her words. "Great job, baby. Wonderful show. You made mama have a lot of fun."

A woman who had to be the horse's handler stepped forward with a halter in one hand and a few lumps of sugar in the other. Miranda took the sugar and watched the horse's big prehensile lips nibble them off her palm, then hugged the horse again.

Like a wild animal, Miranda seemed to smell the unfamiliar presence. Her eyes swept the dim concrete enclosure filled with machinery and electronic devices and found him unerringly. Her voice hardened. "Take the horse, Judy." She stepped to Seaver and stopped. The wardrobe mistress expertly slipped the black velvet robe up her arms and onto her shoulders, then receded. Miranda brought the belt around her and cinched it, hard.

She did not speak to him, but her sharp, angry eyes never left him as she called out to her staff, "Who is this?"

Seaver stood up and smiled. "Calvin Seaver. Vice president for security at Pleasure Island." He had known she would be difficult, so he already had in his hand his plastic-coated identification card, along with the backstage visitor's badge he had been issued at the Inside Straight. "Will King and I sometimes get together to check out each other's operations. Professional courtesy."

She studied the badges and looked back up at his face. "Sorry. You could have been a reporter or a trick thief. Real magicians don't do that to each other. Professional courtesy. If you saw anything you didn't know already, please keep it to yourself." She took a step away.

Miranda's stagehands and technicians all seemed to have been held frozen in a spell, not breathing. Now she released them. "Great show, everybody." They relaxed and began working again, moving around each other without pausing.

Miranda took a second step. "Your secrets are safe with me," said Seaver. "For the moment, anyway."

She turned on her heel and faced him. "What do you want?"

"Three minutes," he said. "Five at the most."

"Come on." She walked to the far end of the area below the

stage, around two more hydraulic lifts and a console that seemed to have been set up to control the explosive charges wired on stage. She stopped. "What's your pitch?"

"I'm looking for a woman."

"Smile more. They'll like you better."

"A particular woman. Dark hair, pretty, in very good physical condition. Three months ago she helped a gentleman named Pete Hatcher disappear. You might recall the evening, because you slipped him out the back door for her at the start of your midnight show."

Her left eyebrow arched. "Did I?"

"Yes. At first, I thought the dark-haired woman might be you. What you do on stage makes strolling out the door in a dark wig and getting two security men to look the wrong way seem like a small thing."

He reached into his coat pocket, snatched out an envelope, and handed it to her. "So I did a background investigation. All of your legal papers—licenses, birth records, Social Security— say your real name is supposed to be Katie Mullen. Even your union records and personnel file. You're from Ohio. But— funny thing—there's nothing on Katie Mullen that goes back more than eight years."

He watched her look at the credit report, then at the Social Security earnings report, then at the two lists of avenues checked, with "none" or "not found" beside them. She shrugged. "Not much happened to me before then." She folded the papers, tucked them in the envelope, and handed them back to him.

Seaver slipped them into the inner pocket of his coat. "No record of enrollment in a high school class in Ohio."

"You can't get that."

"I use a company that arranges class reunions. They feed all the names into their computer for mailing lists. They ran three years of them for me."

"I lie about my age."

"Your birth certificate says what you say. But I'll bet the paper the original is printed on isn't more than eight years old."

"I'm not the dark-haired woman."

"No, you're not. You're somebody she helped one time. There never was a Katie Mullen. She helped you disappear from someplace, so you helped her."

She leaned against the wall with her arms crossed over her chest. "So who did I used to be?"

He shrugged. "I don't care. All I want to know is who the dark-haired woman is."

"That's it?"

"That's it."

"Then good night." She pushed off the wall and took a step toward the corridor.

Seaver's hand closed on her forearm, and she looked down at it icily until Seaver began to wonder whether he had made a terrible mistake. He loosened his grip until it was too loose, and she snatched it away. "What now?"

"I want you to take one minute to think about what Vincent Bogliarese would feel if he knew what we were talking about."

She looked at Seaver with a sense of wonder. She had underestimated him. She turned to face him. Her impossibly golden hair had dried into a wild mane, the skin of her sculpted face was still covered with a makeup that had little metallic sparkles in it. She didn't look quite human. The big, unblinking blue eyes acquired the mischievous look they wore on stage.

"The back elevator over there goes up to my suite. By now, Vincent is up there waiting for me. Maybe he knows everything you know. Maybe he doesn't. Come with me." She took two steps toward the elevator, then stopped, turned, and looked back at him. Her face was a blank, like a portrait of a woman, but the eyes were burning him.

Seaver tried to decide. If he had been anything but positive, he would never have come here. She had once been in some kind of trouble. She had escaped because she'd had the help of a professional, who had given her false papers and set off whatever changes had transformed her into the Miraculous Miranda. She would not have slipped Pete Hatcher out for any other reason. Who would have the money to pay a performer like her to do anything? It must have been to return a favor, and a big one, at that. Now that he had met her, he was even more certain.

The incarnations he could trace were unbroken for about eight years: first Katie Mullen, the pretty assistant in the brief costume who opened trap doors and distracted the audience for a past-his-prime magician in worn tailcoat named Mister Zenobia; then Magical Miranda, playing kids' birthday parties in the daytime and, at night, doing gigs at supper clubs where part of the deal was waiting on tables. Then, three years ago, the Miraculous Miranda had materialized in Las Vegas.

But Seaver had miscalculated. The eight years should have made him at least suspect it. He had assumed that she had been running from some woman problem—maybe an arrest or two for soliciting, maybe a stint starring in pornographic movies.

Seaver studied her face, and was suddenly lost in amazement at her perfidy. She was trying to look as though she were bluffing, but she wasn't. She had already shown all her cards to Vincent. What she had been hiding was a whole lot worse than Seaver had imagined. She wasn't hiding some embarrassing period of her past from her boyfriend. That wasn't it at all.

She had told Vincent all about it, and that meant it wasn't that there were some videotapes of her going down on one of those pimply-faced druggies that were the foot soldiers of the porn trade. That would have driven a man like Vincent nuts. What she was hiding was a charge that wouldn't get stale after eight years—a class-one felony, like armed robbery or homicide. And of all the men in the world, Vincent Bogliarese would be the last one to write her off for homicide. His own father had a homicide conviction. Whatever Miranda had done in her early twenties, Vincent Senior had done more in his. For that matter, Seaver had always heard that these old families still expected a son to make his bones before he could be trusted with business matters, and Vincent Junior had been running the Inside Straight for at least ten years.

She was trying to get him to think she was bluffing, so he would go up there with her and get himself killed. There was no way in the world he was going to step into that elevator. He had never relished the idea, and now there was no reason to consider it. What he had come for was safe in his coat pocket. When he had handed her the papers, his purpose wasn't to show her he knew nothing. He had just wanted her to touch them. He would have to get one of his old buddies on the L.A.P.D. to run the fingerprints before he knew what it was he had. But he had something. Now it was his turn to let her think he had been bluffing.

"No," he said. "I don't think I'd like to speak with Mr. Bogliarese at this time. You go on without me."

Miranda's smile grew. She winked, spun around with a speed and grace that an ordinary woman would not have imitated, even if she could, because she had no excuse to be bigger than life. Miranda stepped into the elevator and let the doors close on her.

Seaver decided not to take the time to get upstairs and walk out the front door with the customers. Miranda wasn't predictable enough for that. Right now she might be giving her boyfriend some version of what had just happened. Seaver walked straight to the steel door at the back of the stage area and said to a stagehand, "Can you let me out?" There was a sign on it that said, EMERGENCY ONLY. ALARM WILL SOUND, but he knew they must have keys to it, because that was the way Pete Hatcher had slipped out. The stagehand opened it and let him out onto a long narrow asphalt strip beside the building where a few employees' cars were parked.

It took Seaver at least five minutes to walk all the way to the front of the building, then another ten to walk down the covered mall and out the other side to the lot where his car was parked. He patted the envelope in his coat pocket three times during the walk.

He got into his car and started the engine. He had already begun to back out when he realized that patting the envelope was not going to be enough. He stopped the car, pulled forward a little, and slipped it into neutral. He had watched Miranda touch the papers, so he knew exactly where her prints were, and he wouldn't make the mistake of smudging them. She had been hot and sweaty from the show, so the prints would be oily and clear. But thinking of Miranda's show during his walk had prompted a small twinge of uneasiness in him. This was a woman who was world famous for sleight of hand. Could he really be sure that what he had seen was her tucking the papers back into the envelope before she had handed it back to him? The same set of papers?

Seaver reached into the inner pocket of his coat and pulled out the envelope. He held it on his lap where no bystander could see it, placed only the nails of his thumbs in the slot and made sure that they touched only the envelope, then pushed the envelope's sides outward just enough.

There was a blinding flash of light, a sound like an indrawn breath, and a choking smell as though a whole box of matches were burning. A thin, jagged line of orange fire streaked from the bottom of the envelope up both sides until his thumbs held nothing, and a pile of black powder was settling onto his lap. He rolled to the side out of the car, slapping his pants furiously.

In a few seconds, he was sure his clothes had not ignited, and nothing had reached his skin. He stood beside the car for a moment and closed his eyes. He could still see a bright green patch floating behind his eyelids from the flash. He hated that woman. He knew exactly how she had done it. All of the big pyrotechnics in her act had been fired electronically by her technicians, but not the little ones. Somewhere in her costume she must have carried a supply of flash powder, so she could use it when she wanted it. Probably it was in pea-sized, airtight capsules. That way it would be safe and inert, until the mixture was exposed to oxygen and a tiny trace of white phosphorous ignited whatever else was in there. It had to be something like that, anyway, or it would have gone off before he opened the envelope.

He got into the car, opened all the windows, and drove out into the night. He was not going to stick a knife into the

15

Jane flew to Chicago as Karen Roth, then shopped for her next flight by walking along the concourse at O'Hare looking at the television monitors that listed scheduled departures. Hatcher had called her at around ten on Tuesday night, and she had not heard the message until seven the next evening, so he was already in Billings. She diverted her course to a pay telephone, called her answering machine, pressed 56, and listened. "Two messages," said the mechanical voice. The first was Hatcher's voice saying, "It's just me again." She clapped her hand over her free ear to block out the noise around her and waited, but there was a pause, then a click to signify that the call had ended. The second message was just the pause and then another click. Jane put the receiver back on the hook and went to buy her next ticket. Either Hatcher had not settled anywhere yet, or he had decided it was not safe to leave a number, or something had gone wrong with her machine to make it stop recording. Maybe it had failed to disconnect after the first call, and used up all the blank tape recording nothing. Maybe the clock battery had died, or the tape had tangled, or . . . she might as well stop kidding herself. Or when Pete Hatcher had made the first call, standing in a lighted phone booth at a rest stop on Route 25, he had hung up the phone, turned around, and had a .357 Magnum stuck in his face.

She flew to Missoula as Katherine Webster on a smaller plane and arrived at seven in the morning, then went shopping for a car as Wendy Wasserman. The car Wendy Wasserman selected was a two-year-old Nissan Maxima with low mileage and a finish that had been dulled by the first owner's failure to protect it from the winter weather. The owner had left on it a parking sticker that said UNIVERSITY OF MONTANA. Jane drove it to the campus and left it in a covered parking structure surrounded by busy dormitories, then walked northwest up Broadway until she found a car-rental agency.

She called her answering machine three times during the day, and each time the machine said, "Two messages." She drove the three hundred and forty miles eastward on Route 90 to Billings as the sun made its way toward the mountains behind her. The eastern side of the Rocky Mountains was high country and forested, but it was dry and hot, the very edge of the Great Plains. As she drove, the forests dwindled and were replaced by huge fields of wheat growing tall in the late summer sunset.

Jane arrived in Billings after dark. She drove the streets for two hours to get a sense of the city, then left her rented car in the parking lot at Deaconess Medical Center and began to walk. She bought a newspaper at a machine on a corner and studied it. There was no mention of a David Keller being found, no Pete Hatcher, and no John Does. If he wasn't alive, the police didn't know it yet.

She tried to imagine his steps. He would have come up on Route 25 until it merged with Route 90 and arrived in the middle of the night. He had probably checked into a hotel at noon. He would have been exhausted by then, and slept until dark. He would have gotten up, dressed, and then realized that he didn't have a good enough reason to go out there in the strange city at night. He would have eaten in the hotel, then returned to his room. He would know that the only place she could hope to find him was in a hotel, so he would stay there. If there was a problem with her answering machine, then he would send her a note in the mail. He would stay put and hope that she could get to him before anybody else did.

If she wanted to get to him and take him out without attracting attention, she would have to look as though she belonged here. Jane went to a shopping mall and studied the women around her. In the twelve years since she had begun doing this, fading in had gotten easier. She had read somewhere that between 1970 and 1990 a mall had opened somewhere in the country every seven hours. One of the changes this had brought was that women in one part of the country dressed pretty much the way they did in all of the others. Her clothes would do for a few days in Billings, but she could still make some purchases to improve her chances.

She found a store that sold T-shirts and bought one with UNIVERSITY OF MONTANA printed on it. She bought a pair of hiking boots like ones she saw on some other women.

She knew a little bit about what Pete Hatcher was going through. At times he would be sure that he had completely, miraculously lost his pursuers. But every time he heard a maid push her cleaning cart down the hotel hallway, he would feel all the muscles in his body go tense. He would try to reassure himself, then realize that he had no external way to tell whether he was perfectly safe or in imminent danger. So he would sit for hours looking out the window of his room for some piece of evidence that had not come from inside his own skull.

As she searched for the store where she would make her last purchases, she reconsidered what she knew about Pete Hatcher. The first time she had heard his name had been in a telephone call from Paula Dennis. Paula was an intensive-care nurse from Kentucky, and it wasn't until the call that Jane had learned she was also a gambler, and she needed help for a man she had met on a junket to Las Vegas. When Jane had asked her what she knew about the man's habits, she had said, "Pete Hatcher is a ladies' man."

To Jane that had sounded like trouble. Men who had that reputation left behind rivals and angry husbands and women who knew too much about them and were bitter enough to tell strangers. But Paula had said, "By that I mean he is a man who could have been invented by and for ladies. He is a perfect gentleman: attentive, thoughtful, kind, considerate at all times and in every situation. You could take him to visit your aged grandma in Charleston. He's also a very naughty fellow, if you know what I mean, but there are no hard feelings afterward. He's at his sweetest when he takes you to the airport. There are no lies, no chances to make false assumptions with Pete Hatcher. You can be sitting in a restaurant with him, and he will not pretend he's not looking at other women below the face. But the way he does it doesn't make you mad. It makes you squirm in your evening gown. One night I saw him doing it and told him so, and we had quite a conversation about a woman two tables over. He made me understand what he saw when he looked at a woman, and honey, it made me like myself better."

Jane had not been moved to enlist in Hatcher's cause just yet, but her curiosity had been piqued. "What, exactly, did he say?"

"He misses nothing—and I mean nothing—and he likes all of it. This is a woman on the downhill side of fifty. I'm thinking, 'A kind face. Nice clothes. Not impersonating a teenager, but not making up the seating list for her wake, either.' He starts telling me about the smile lines at the corners of her eyes, and the calm glow of the cornea that shows wisdom and receptiveness—which from Pete's side of the table seem to be the same thing—and the flecks and color variations. This is just eyes, remember. I'm leaving out the topographical features south of there, which he can talk about well into next week, if you're mature enough to stand it without hyperventilating and falling into a swoon. But he's never exactly wrong, because what he sees is verifiably there if you look for it. He sees what you wish they would all see. You're just this person getting by on whatever you have. You don't think about how you look most of the time. You think about what you're doing, and that's probably just as well, because it keeps us all out of trouble. Pete comes along and looks at you as though you were an object. No question about that, but the object is a flower or a bird or a tropical fish—something that has its own rules and purposes, its own course in life that doesn't have anything to do with his. If you want to come closer, that's okay with him. But if you don't, that's fine too, because he's just glad to be there and see the pretty colors. This is not a deep thinker. But if this is a man who deserves to die, I want the others all killed off first."

Remembering Paula's call made Jane irritable. It wasn't Paula's fault, and it wasn't even Pete Hatcher's. It was her own. She was already feeling a sick twinge in her stomach about Carey, and she was not yet prepared to set aside time to think clearly about it. She had no business leaving a husband of three months. She had no business breaking her promise, so something in some primitive lobe of her brain told her she was going to be punished. What Paula had said had nothing to do with Carey. It should not have made her feel this way.

When Jane had met Pete Hatcher she had understood what Paula had meant. He had been scared and psychologically worn, but while he was standing up politely to shake her hand, his eyes had taken the long route up to meet her eyes. What he was saying at the time was something good-natured and self-deprecating about needing her advice and help. It should have been incongruous and discomforting, but somehow it wasn't.

Carey would never do anything that simpleminded. He was much more . . . what? Highly evolved. Pete Hatcher appealed to women because he was guileless and optimistic. He made it clear that he was having a lot of fun, and that was a form of flattery. His expression said, "You delight me," and delight was contagious and reciprocal. It created a magnetic field around it stronger than gravity.

But women loved Carey because he knew all their secrets, including the ones that weren't any fun—wear and aging and imperfections and scars—and he was always on their side. It wasn't that they seemed glamorous for the moment, or something. His appeal was a quick and sensitive mind but, more than that, an air that conveyed a knowledge that didn't exclude things found in books but was full of things that he knew because of who he was.

Jane felt weak and foolish for letting Carey enter her mind now. She knew it was because she was about to do something that Carey would have had a right to object to. The bathing suit she chose was relatively modest. It was one piece, black, and not cut as high at the hips as the others in her size. She could have worn it at home without feeling uncomfortable. But she was buying it to wear for Pete Hatcher.

She had to be where the hunters weren't looking and Pete Hatcher was. They would be looking at lobbies and parking lots, and he would be looking at women. He would be hiding, he would be scared, but he had a lifelong addiction to studying every woman who passed in front of his eyes. He would look, because runners had a way of falling back into old comfortable habits to calm themselves. She bought a canvas purse and a wraparound skirt, a big pair of polarized sunglasses and a pair of slip-on rubber-soled shoes that she could run in if she needed to.

The next day she allotted two hours to each of the biggest hotels: the Rainbow, the Traveler's Rest, the Mountaineer. It was easy for a woman to get into the part of a hotel where Jane wanted to go. She entered at the end of a residential wing and walked down the corridor of rooms. She left it near the center of the building, before she reached the lobby, and stepped out into the courtyard. She knew that Pete Hatcher would not be in a ground-floor room, because he would not feel safe in a room where an intruder could walk up to the windows. If he had his choice he would be on an upper floor in a room facing the courtyard, so he could not be shot from the street.

At each hotel she walked to the swimming pool, found a big lounge chair, greased herself with sunblock, and lay back to feel the sun. At some point, Pete Hatcher would look out his window, and he would see her. A lot of people would notice that there was somebody out by the pool. Pete Hatcher would not leave it at that. He would stare at her hard, just because she was a woman between eighteen and fifty-five—and he would recognize her.

By noon she was glad that she had found some sunblock that was practically opaque. The sun came down clear and sharp at this altitude. She lay on her stomach at the Mountaineer and stared along the surface of the water in the pool, watching the sunlight break into spots on the surface and ricochet up against the concrete wall of the building.

She saw Pete Hatcher the second he stepped into the bar overlooking the pool. She stood up, put on her shoes, then wrapped the skirt around her and hooked her bag over her left arm while she watched him through the sunglasses. He was talking to a waiter. She walked quickly toward him.

She could see the waiter going to a cappuccino machine behind the bar that looked like the reassembled parts of a steam locomotive. Too late. The waiter was pouring a pitcher of milk into the boiler and flipping levers. She thought about what Paula had said. Pete Hatcher was standing there with a pulse rate that was probably nearing two hundred. He had just seen the arrival of what amounted to his last chance to blow out the candles on his next birthday, and his response was to order coffee for two. She stepped in the door. No, it was iced cappuccino for two, somehow even more absurd and courtly, because it was the right thing to order for a woman who had been lying in the sun.

He carried the glasses to the table, but Jane took his arm and moved him on to another that was out of sight of the door. The waiter was busying himself at the bar, so she leaned close and gave Hatcher a peck on the cheek before she sat down. "Very thoughtful," she said. In a whisper, she added, "Why didn't you call again?"

He looked pained. "I did. Your message ran, but then there was no beep to start the recorder. I said where I was, but I couldn't tell if it picked anything up. I guess it didn't." He leaned close and looked into her eyes, and she thought of Paula again. Those long eyelashes were part of it—he didn't seem to know they belonged to him. "I made a couple of mistakes in Denver," he confided. "I thought I was doing great, but I was absolutely clueless. That scared me. That's why I called in the first place. If you didn't get my messages, how did you find me?"

"Okay," said Jane. "It doesn't matter. You got through. Now, what have you got up in your room that you can't leave there?"

"One suitcase. The one you had me pack the last time. It's got my money in it."

"Give me the key," she said.

He handed her the key, and she looked at it before she slipped it into her purse. He said, "The number's not on it, but it's 605."

"Here's what we do," she said. "You sit here, sip your drink. If it takes too long, drink mine. Stay here with the waiter. If he leaves, don't go to the lobby or follow me to your room or something. If everything unexpectedly goes wrong, don't go to your car."

"How did you know I had a car?"

She smiled sadly. "If they haven't found you yet, all this is practice. If they have, what they've found is the car."

Jane stood up and walked across the deck outside, back into the corridor where she had entered. She followed it until she found a fire door that led up the stairs. At the sixth floor she stood for a moment with her ear to the door. She heard nothing, so she stepped out into the hallway, found 605, and opened it.

The suitcase was neatly stowed in the closet. She tipped it on its side and searched it. There was sixty thousand dollars in hundreds, fifteen little plastic folders full of traveler's checks, seven passbooks for savings accounts in Denver banks. She loaded the money, passbooks, and checks into her canvas bag and looked deeper.

When she found the box at the bottom she stopped. It was gold with a black stripe. It said, ".38 Special. 20 pistol cartridges." She felt almost relieved. He had gone out and bought himself a pistol and a car. There was nothing mysterious about the way they had found him. All they had done was watch lists that anybody could get, until one man's name had turned up on two or three lists. She put the box of cartridges into her bag with the money, then examined the suitcase for anything else Hatcher had neglected to mention.

She went into the bathroom, picked up his bag of toiletries, wiped the faucets and fixtures with a washcloth, then came out and wiped the desk, the television set, the table, the doorknobs.

Then she checked all the wastebaskets for receipts or papers that would hold a print. When she was satisfied, she closed the suitcase, put the sign that said MAID SERVICE on the doorknob, and slipped back into the stairwell.

She climbed to the top floor, then onto the roof of the building. She left the suitcase behind a big air-conditioning condenser and went back down the stairs. They would find it in a month or two and have no idea how it had gotten there.

Downstairs she found Pete Hatcher drinking his cold coffee and looking happy. "Time to go," she said.

"Just like that?"

"Just like that."

She led him the way she had come, down the long corridor and out the door at the end of the east wing to avoid the lobby and the front entrance. When they were in her rented car on the next street she started the engine and waited. "Tell me where your car is."

"It's parked down the street near another hotel," he said. "About three, four blocks down."

She was beginning to feel a little more confident. It wasn't a particularly cunning way to hide a car, but at least it showed he wasn't totally unconscious. He was thinking. She turned the corner and drove in the opposite direction. "I hope you're not too attached to it."

"No," he said. "Does that mean we're just leaving it?"

She sighed. "If things were different I think I would be tempted not to. I would find a very good spot so we could watch the car around the clock. Eventually, the people who want you might come along, and I could see who they were. I'm not that curious this time."

"I don't want to imply that I am, but why aren't you?"

"Several reasons. One is the way they found you."

"You know how they found me? Even I don't know."

"I'm not positive, but you did two things that I know of that a person does who's scared and running. You bought a gun and a car. That gave them two things to put together, two lists with the same name on them. So they might already be watching the car."

"How did you know about the gun?"

"Hardly anybody carries ammunition in his suitcase who doesn't have one," she said. "Tell me exactly what happened in Denver." She drove along the same street in the opposite direction and saw no other car turn to follow.

"There was a woman on the street when I was coming home from the grocery store. She looked like she had car trouble, and I walked over and took a look under the hood. She lifted the pistol out of my belt, stuck a big automatic in my face, and said she was a cop. She made me get in the trunk. A real cop came along right after that, and she killed him."

"How did you see that from the trunk?"

"I didn't, but when I got out, there he was."

"How did you get out of the trunk?"

"She opened it, fired four shots at me, and slammed it again. I'm lying there and after a minute, I realize I'm not dead. She actually missed. On most cars there's a latch inside the trunk. You pull it, and the trunk opens. I was alone except for the dead cop. I don't know anything else."

"That's about all we need to know," said Jane. "They managed to find you. I assume you walked to the same store by the same route regularly?"

He nodded.

"They knew that, and they knew you weren't the sort of man who could walk past a woman with car trouble. Not everybody would stop. They knew you were carrying a pistol, because otherwise she wouldn't have grabbed it before she showed you hers. The fact that she didn't pull the trigger means they must have been planning to drive you out of town where they could shoot you without having anybody hear and bury you without having anybody find you."

"Why do you keep saying 'they'?"

"Did this woman look as though she could carry your body by herself?"

"No."

"Then there was someone else who could. There's also the dead policeman. Denver has serious criminals, and a serious police department. Any cop who stops his car is going to be sure he's able to control whoever he sees. So probably he was shot by somebody he didn't see. Not for sure, but probably."

Pete Hatcher looked out the window and watched the display windows of businesses slipping past as the car moved west toward the interstate. "Then the one I didn't see could have shot me the way he shot the cop—while I was alone on the street. Why didn't he?"

"That's one of those bits of good news that's not quite as good if you take a second look at it," Jane said. "Your former friends from Pleasure, Inc., aren't hunting you themselves; they've hired professionals. The problems that raises should be getting obvious by now. Professionals know how to hunt. They know which ways to kill you are smart, and which ways are stupid. Taking you to a quiet, private place where nothing will be seen or heard is smart; blasting away in the middle of a city is not."

"But that's just what they did. They shot the policeman, and then—"

"They didn't plan to, and that's another side to it. When something unexpectedly goes wrong, professionals don't get emotional. Killing you is just a job, and anybody else who happens along is nothing but a little extra work. They know in advance that they might have to get rid of witnesses, so they're primed for it. They react quickly, and don't spend time asking themselves philosophical questions first."

She glanced at Pete Hatcher to see if he was listening. When she saw his face, her breath caught in her throat. His eyes were watering. Could he be crying? She pretended to pay attention to the road behind her for a few seconds. She glanced at him again. His big brown eyes were welling with tears. When he sensed that she was looking, he turned away and wiped his eyes on his sleeve. She waited.

"That policeman," he said. "He lost his life, and I got mine. It was a bad trade. You should have seen him. His head was half gone. I couldn't even tell what he looked like. The world lost him just to get a little more of me."

Jane blew out a breath slowly. "I don't think that's a train of thought you want to follow too far." She stared ahead at the entrance to the interstate, slipped her car into the center of the tight stream of traffic, and found herself silently talking to Paula. You didn't have a way to say it, did you? In all the talk about his pleasant disposition and nice manners you never told me why you called me.

In all her years of snatching rabbits out of the fangs of the wolves, she had almost never heard a rabbit so much as wonder out loud what had happened to the other rabbits. They weren't selfish. It always seemed to her to be physical, the body overpowering the mind to save itself. They never thought of looking back until they had run far enough. That was why a sensible nurse who had seen a lot of men would intercede for this one. The fact that he didn't have a fine and complicated intellect was about the same as saying he didn't have a twelve-cylinder Italian sportscar. He was a decent human being who was just trying to drive what he had.

When she looked at him again, she had an urge to give him something. "Okay," she said, "let's think practically. What do we do with what we know? You got a good look at the woman, right?"

"Right."

"And she got a good look at you. Wherever we go, keep looking for her in the distance. She won't be up close again, but she may be in a crowd, or in a window, or in a car that goes by. If you see her again, you go. No hesitation, no wondering if she saw you or not, no decisions. You go that minute. If you're in the middle of a date in a restaurant a year from now, you go to the men's room and never come back." She watched him to see if he understood, and he seemed to. "Only this time, you're going to know in advance where you're going and how to get there."

"Where are we going now?"

"First, we'll drop out of sight completely for a few days, to let the trail get cold. Then we'll start all over again, and do this right. I'll hide you somewhere, but I'll stick around this time until I'm sure we've lost them for good. I'll give you a few lessons I should have given you the first time. I'll help you get used to the next new name, new place, new life. Then I'll leave for good."

"You said the first thing is dropping out of sight. How do you do that?"

"The best way is to do nothing." She smiled. "Missoula looks like a good place to start doing it. We'll buy you a new suitcase, check into a motel, and see if you got lucky and lost them. In fact, that's the good part about what I was saying, and I almost forgot to tell you. They're pros, and from what I can tell, they're near the upper end of the scale of people who could be called that. That means we avoid them or we're dead: there isn't any mystery about the outcome. But the nice thing about pros is that they're in it for the money."

"So?"

"They get paid in two ways. One is that they get all of it when they've killed you. The other is that the client gives them some money up front for expenses, and the rest when they've got you. Either way, your best friend is time. They've just wasted three months for nothing, and spent a lot of money traveling. People like that could have made a lot in three months. Hardly anybody is very difficult to kill. If the client is paying for all this, then by now he's going to be wondering what he's getting for his money."

"I still don't get it. How does this help me?"

"If you wait long enough, pros go away."

"You're kidding."

"No, I'm not. They don't hate you. They're in a business. At the moment when they calculate that the job is a waste of effort, they quit. If they're getting paid for expenses, the time comes when the client makes the same calculation and stops paying."

"Then I'll be safe?"

She cocked her head and pursed her lips, then said reluctantly, "Not exactly. At least not yet."

"Why not?"

"The client in your case can afford to replace them. But the replacement would have to start all over again at Las Vegas. Pros aren't likely to turn over their information to competitors." She shrugged. "I'm not saying you're in the best position possible, but there are worse."

"What's worse than being chased by professional killers?"

She thought for a moment. "I guess the worst is if you've committed some really awful crime and people know it."

"What would you do for a person like that?"

"Nothing," she said.

16

Seaver drove along the desert highway, watching the long, empty gray road ahead wavering near the distant vanishing point as heat waves rose from the pavement. Now and then a dark reflective spot would appear on the road, the eyes would see it as water, but the brain would say "mirage," and it would diminish to nothing as he approached it. He drove quickly, feeling the slight lift of the car's springs as he reached the crest of each little rise, then feeling his body regain a few pounds more than its weight as the car came to the bottom and began the next climb.

Seaver was satisfied that he was going about this in the right way. The three partners had ultimately left the strategy up to him. Earl and Linda were probably getting close to payday by now, so whatever he did, he had to avoid getting in their way. He might have left a message on their answering machine, asking them to get in touch with him. But leaving a message like that on the answering machine of two professional killers required an absolute belief that they could not get caught, recognized, or traced on this job. The world didn't always work that way. Anybody who had worked in Las Vegas for ten years had seen the ball stop on the double zero a few times.

He had considered tracing their movements and trying to catch up with them. But Earl would not look upon his sudden, uninvited appearance as a favor. It was, in the way these people looked at things, a terrible insult and a violation of their agreement.

Seaver suddenly showing up would mean that there were

three people for bystanders to notice, instead of just two. And he would have traveled there by a separate route. That doubled the number of trails that later might be traced to Hatcher's body. He was not at all sure that he wanted to place himself in some distant city with those two at the precise moment when he convinced them that he was so unprofessional and unreliable as to be an actual danger to them.

No, what he was doing made more sense. Earl and Linda were looking for Hatcher. He was looking for the woman. After he found her would be the time to think about meeting them. Then he would have something to bring to the party.

He had assigned five men just to talk to people who were in the chase-and-find business—skip tracers, retrievers who worked for bail-bond outfits, freelance bounty hunters—to see if any of them had ever come across a woman like this. A few of them had heard vague stories, but none of them knew anything that could lead to an actual living woman. It was then that he had realized that he was going about solving the problem backward.

The people most likely to know about her would be the ones in the run-and-hide business. He had called an old friend from the police department who had quit at about the same time he had and had gone to work in the California prison system. Seaver had not described his problem but had described the sort of prisoner he wanted to talk to. He needed one who had been in lots of jails in different parts of the country and who had drawn a long sentence the last time out. But most important, it had to be one who had a history of trading information for favors.

Seaver saw the low, drab buildings, the fence, and the watchtowers undulating in the heat waves across a barren field far back from the highway. He turned up the long, narrow drive that led to the small parking lot outside the gate and glanced at his watch. The drive out here had taken longer than he had expected, but he supposed it wouldn't much matter. In order to miss this guy, Seaver would have to be about twenty years late.

As he turned off his car engine, he stopped to glance in the rearview mirror. Then he got out and put on his coat. He had chosen his clothes carefully. He wore a dark-gray summer-weight suit that cost more than his first new car. His white shirt was marine-pressed with the front and collar starched stiff, and the cuffs showed only a glimpse of his Rolex Oyster watch. A naive observer would have interpreted the bow tie as a whimsical touch, but Seaver didn't expect to meet any naive observers. He was going into a maximum-security prison, where it was well known that nobody with a functioning brain wore anything tied around his neck with a slip-knot.

He walked to the gate, handed his driver's license to the guard, watched him compare it to the list on his clipboard, then obeyed the invitation to step inside. He held up his arms and stood with his legs apart as the second guard ran a metal detector up and down his body, then ran a hand through several of his pockets. He submitted to the preliminaries patiently. Security was his business, and he knew that each stage of the process had two purposes. Scanning the human body for chunks of metal or contraband was the easy part. The hard part was studying the visitor to see if he had something hidden in his head. Each of these meaningless little steps was a test. A normal person would gradually get used to following the unfamiliar rules that applied in a place like this. The person hiding some rash and violent scheme would either feel his nerve draining out of him or get frustrated to the point of blind, undirected rage. Security was mainly a question of finding out whom you were letting breach your perimeter.

Seaver was directed into a small anteroom where he could be kept isolated until they were sure that he wasn't carrying anything that would make him a match for more than one man and that the identification he had given them was real. After ten minutes he was admitted to a room with a desk, where he could be observed while he signed in and had time to check off his compliance with each of the regulations listed on a form and acquaint the guards with the purpose of his visit on another form. It was only after his forms had been completed, read, and

determined to be satisfactory that the next door was opened
and his escort beckoned to him.

When he walked through the doorway, he noted with approval that there were two guards, the first to lead the way and
serve as turnkey and the second to follow a half step behind
and to his right, either to protect Seaver's weak side or take
advantage of it, as events dictated.

They took him on a long trek down hallways broken at inter-
vals by steel grates that had to be opened with a key and an
electronic code. They walked under surveillance cameras
recessed in wall niches that one prisoner standing on another's
shoulders could not reach and covered with plastic plates that
would probably stop a bullet. He admired the premeditation of
the system and felt a tiny twinge of envy at its blatancy. Here it
was an advantage to be obvious—to convince inmates that
escape was ludicrous, that movements inside the complex were
monitored, and that disturbances could be isolated instantly.
Seaver had to work under more difficult circumstances. The
few devices and precautions he could use legally had to be
subtle and decorative.

The two escorts led him into a windowless room with a bare
wooden table and two chairs. He sat down in the chair facing
the door and waited. He had sat for twenty minutes before the
two guards reappeared with Stillman, Ray Q. He was a little
above middle height, but he slouched the way violence-prone
convicts often did, the hips forward and the back hunched in a
question mark stance that invited an approaching stranger to
take the first swing.

When Stillman turned to hold his wrists out for the guards to
unlock his manacles, his back looked like the hood of a cobra,
spreading wide as it rose from the thin waist, and then rounding
inward at the top because of the slouch that kept the hands and
knees forward and the gut pulled back.

The guard wordlessly declined to unlock the manacles. He
simply glared at Stillman and left. Stillman's predatory eyes
focused on Seaver as he sat down, his thin lips coming up at the

corners a little to convey his interpretation of the demonstration: I'm too dangerous for you.

Seaver reached into his shirt pocket and produced a pack of cigarettes, pulled the strip to remove the cellophane, tore off the foil, and thumped the pack to raise a cigarette. He lit one with a match, then held it out. Stillman reached across the table with both hands, stuck it in the corner of his mouth, rested his hands in his lap, and waited.

Seaver looked at him for a few seconds, then said, "I'm Seaver. I can't get you out of here. I can't get you a new trial. If you ever get a parole hearing, I won't be there to tell them you cooperated in an investigation. I won't be there at all."

Stillman looked at him expectantly, and Seaver knew he had begun well. They were all experts in the ways that the system could be manipulated, and the ways that it couldn't. After about two convictions they also knew that false hope worked on them like poison, and they hated anyone who tried to force it on them. "Here's what I can do. Captain Michnik is an old friend of mine. If you have the answers to my questions, he will help you right now, starting today. You don't have to wait six months for an official letter that's never going to come."

"What kind of help are you offering?"

"A little slack. You'll get a better job, if what you want won't be so obvious it'll get you killed. If a guard is down on you, he'll be rotated to another block. If you've done anything recently that you need to skate on, he'll give you the benefit of the doubt."

"What does that cost me?"

"I heard something, and I want to know more about it."

"What did you hear?"

"I heard there's a woman who hides people."

Stillman blew out a quick puff of smoke. "A lot of women hide people."

Seaver slowly shook his head. "This one is a professional. If you're in trouble, you hire her to get you out of it. She comes and whisks you away—makes you disappear. I guess she must get you a new name and new papers, maybe a job."

"Which are you?"

"What?" snapped Seaver.

"You thinking of disappearing, or are you looking for somebody?" His head was cocked to the side, and his eyes squinted through the smoke.

Seaver gave a half smile and a snort. "Do I look like somebody who has that kind of problem?" He shot the cuffs of his immaculate white shirt so he could be sure Stillman saw his watch and the perfect fit of his tailored suit.

Stillman shrugged. "You look like somebody who might develop some problems if you got sent to a place like this—or even if somebody in here got out. If you know the captain, maybe you put some of them in."

"Could be," said Seaver.

Stillman nodded with amusement. "That's it, isn't it? Somebody you don't want to turn your back on dropped out of sight?"

"No," Seaver said. "I'm interested in this woman because she made somebody scarce that I want, but the last person he wants to see is me. I'd like to ask her about him."

Stillman shifted in his chair and lifted both hands to pluck the cigarette from his lips. He stepped on it with deliberation. When he raised his face again his blue eyes were opaque, but Seaver could tell he was taking the offer seriously.

"I don't know her." Stillman grinned and held up his chained wrists. "I bet you could have guessed that."

Seaver nodded. "But you've heard of her."

Stillman nodded too. "If you're in here long enough, you probably hear every way that words can be pulled together. I'd like to get a few favors. But there's another side to this. If you can get me goodies, you can also get my ass kicked or worse. What I know is just rumors: thirdhand stuff. I send you off, you're probably going to come back and tell the captain I shined you on. I don't know you, but I know him."

Seaver studied him. Something else was on his mind, and the only way to hear it was to get through the easy ones. "Okay, I've been warned. You tell me what you heard, and I won't

hold a grudge, as long as you don't add anything of your own."
Then he added, as a precaution, "Anyway, I know plenty about
her already, so I can figure out which parts you heard wrong."
He handed Stillman another cigarette and struck a match, then
held it out so Stillman could lean into it and puff until the tip
ignited.

Stillman leaned back and said, "Say there really is a woman
like this? There would be people in the joint who know about
her. Maybe they got helped by her once, then fucked up again
and couldn't get to her in time. Maybe they didn't get to her
even the first time, but they hope some day they'll make it." He
smiled and shook his head. "Even though a germ couldn't get
out of here, about one in five of these guys thinks he can."

Seaver's smile mirrored Stillman's. "A lot of sheets get tied
together, but you don't see many of them hanging outside the
walls of these places." He shrugged. "Anyway, this isn't that
kind of situation. I'm not interested in charging her with anything, or even putting her out of business. I want this guy, and
I'll pay her for him. She's nothing to me." He caught a hint of
skepticism in Stillman's stare, so he said quickly, "Of course, if
she draws down on me, I'll have to kill her. But even then,
nobody would know you told me about her."

Stillman put his tongue to his lips and spat out a flake of
loose tobacco. "Okay, then I know some things."

"Go on."

"It's probably none of it true. People talk about things like
that. There's a pair of Siamese twins in Vacaville they have
to let out every other week, because one of them didn't get
convicted. There's a four-fingered lawyer in San Diego who
knows one thing they forget to do in almost every trial, so
he can get anybody off who will send him a finger. One of the
contractors who built this place was getting kickbacks on the
materials, so just in case they caught him, he put a secret tunnel
under the infirmary. There's a woman who takes people out of
the world and gives them new lives."

"A little bit past her prime with blond hair, right?"

"Not in the version I heard. It was black. She had long black

hair, and she was nice looking. I don't vouch for that, because
in stories the girl is always that way. It wasn't like you said
before, either. I heard the way it works is, you have to come to
her. And you have to clean yourself before you do. If you want
to bring something you left behind—maybe what you stole,
maybe a girlfriend—she'll tell you you're not ready for her. If
what you want is another chance to kill the one who set you up,
she'll tell you to go do it and not come back. She's in the running business, not the fighting business. You don't just give up
your name, you have to give up everything you ever were, ever
saw or did. You're a new person, who doesn't know any of
that."

"I heard that," Seaver lied. It occurred to him that maybe
Hatcher wasn't planning to resurface after all—that maybe this
was all a waste of time. But it was way too late for that kind of
thinking. It just weakened him, distracted him. The partners
had made their decision, and they were waiting. "Where do
you go?"

"You mean where does she take you?"

Seaver spoke patiently, almost respectfully. "No. You're on
the run. You collect a pile of money for her fee. Where do you
take it?"

"I don't know."

"Who did you hear all this from?"

"I heard it a few times, and I can't sort out which part I heard
which time. The first one was seven or eight years ago, in
Alameda County Jail. It was an old guy, and he was telling a
kid. See, the kid was in for the first time. They had a running
tab on him. It started out as some kid thing—vandalism or
something. He tried to run: resisting arrest. He hot-wired a car
to get away: grand theft auto. He drove it fast until a police car
crashed into him to run him off the road, so it was attempted
vehicular manslaughter. He struggled, so it was assaulting a
police officer. On and on. He tried to hang himself, but the old
man cut him down with a shank he carried. He said to the kid,
'You got to get yourself in shape so the guards don't know
about this. On the day of your arraignment, you're going to get

out on bail for a month or so while they dream up more charges. That's your chance. But if they know you did this, they can keep you here and watch you.' He helped the kid get rid of the homemade rope and cover the welts, and then told him about the woman."

"In front of you?"

"No. The old guy never talked to me at all. He didn't like me from the minute he laid eyes on me. The kid came to me later and asked me if the old man was crazy—just jerking him around, or what."

"How did he tell the kid to get in touch with this woman?"

"That was one of the things that made me think it was bull-shit. He wouldn't tell the kid the address, because the kid was too green to make it that far. The kid had to wait until he was out and write her a letter, then let her say where to meet her."

"Do you remember where the letter was supposed to go?"

"A post office box in L.A. The next time I heard it, there was a house somewhere."

"Where?"

"I don't know."

"Who mentioned the house?"

"Some counterfeiter. Just what they do is so stupid that you can't believe what they say. They all get caught, then go out and do it again."

Seaver sighed and looked at Stillman. He had seen Still-man's record. The man had been in jails for twelve of his thirty-one years, and there was something he'd done before the adult record had begun that had put him in youth camp. If he ever got out again, he'd be a three-time loser before he even did anything.

Stillman went on. "He wouldn't tell me where the house was. He said the only reason he had the address was because his girlfriend gave it to him just before he got arrested. She didn't get arrested, though. She got away, and never got caught."

"Is that true?"

"I once saw a thing on TV where they said nobody ever saw a U.F.O. until somebody said he saw one in 1947. Once he said it, everybody and his brother started seeing them. Maybe that's the year when the U.F.O.'s got here. Maybe it's just that once somebody makes something up, then it's everybody's. It gets to be another way to seem important, to have something to tell, because nothing that's true about you is worth listening to. Bigfoot, the Loch Ness monster, God, all that."

"Do you think I could get to any of these guys—the old man, for instance?"

"The old man was here for a while, but he's been dead a couple of years. The counterfeiter, name is Bill Ortega, I heard he was in federal prison back east someplace. I don't know his girlfriend's name. If you've got a lot of connections in the correctional system, maybe you can track him down."

"What about the kid?" Seaver's hands moved unseen from his lap to grip the support under the table.

Stillman squinted up into the air and smiled. "Now, him I don't know about. I just don't know. For years I've been wondering. Once in a while, I ask around with the guys who have been in a lot of joints all over. His name was Phil O'Meara. Nobody's seen him, or seen his name on the count, or knows anybody who's met him." He smirked mysteriously. "Maybe he figured out to get the knot behind his ear and hung himself right."

Seaver's feet kicked out under the table and pushed Stillman's chair over backward onto the floor. Seaver sprang up, used one arm to vault over the table, and came down with his knee on Stillman's chest.

He spoke quietly, through clenched teeth. "You're one of them, aren't you? You think maybe, just maybe, they'll forget who you are one day and let you unload the grocery truck so you can strangle the driver. Let me tell you something. It isn't going to happen. And even if it did, and you got to her, she'd take one look at you and shut the door. You're an evolutionary dead end, a throwback. She can smell it on you as well as I can. She can't predict what you're going to do next, because even you can't. You're a bad risk. Don't hold out on me, because it's nothing you're ever going to use."

Stillman seemed to be immune to surprise. His face seemed to slacken, to go blank in the prisoner's stare. He looked past Seaver at the ceiling and said, "Two packs of cigarettes a week. A job in the library."

"Done."

"The box wasn't in Los Angeles, it was in New York City. It's Box 345, 7902 Elizabeth Street, in New York. There's some fake name attached to it—a man's name."

Hours later, Seaver sat staring out through the scratched plastic pane of the window at the baggage carts and fuel trucks slipping past him backward as his airplane was pushed away from the terminal by a tractor with a tow bar. He thought about Earl and Linda again. When he had hired them, he had known a lot about Hatcher, but nothing about the woman. It was just as well, because this way he didn't have to worry about bumping into them on this trip. With nothing to go on, they wouldn't have seen her as the way to find Hatcher.

Now he had a few bits of information, and soon he would have enough. He stared at his watch for a moment, then carefully pulled the stem and set it three hours ahead. When he got to New York, he would still have time for some sleep. The hotel reservation was guaranteed, so the room would be waiting for him. The overnight package from Nevada would probably be there when he awoke. He could assemble the pieces of the gun after breakfast.

17

The telephone directory said that the 996 exchange meant that the telephone answering machine was in Deganawida. The road atlas said that the population of Deganawida was only 22,000 souls.

Linda Thompson sat at the desk in the little suite she had rented on the south side of Buffalo, her face illuminated by the computer screen. When Earl had initiated her ten years ago, tracking a person still meant going to counters in below-ground floors of old county office buildings and turning the pages of bound books of records while some sour-faced old clerk watched her out of the corner of her eye. Then she would fill out some form with a ballpoint pen with a chain on it, pay a fee in some strange number like three dollars, or six, but never five, and wait weeks for the copy to come in the mail.

Now all she had to do was put herself into a screen-trance, tap in the secret numbers and symbols, and then conjure what she wanted out of the air. She watched the lighted screen as she put in the mixture of upper- and lowercase letters, periods, slashes, pound signs in their correct order. The screen exploded into life with the company's greeting, "Welcome to Probar Commercial Information Systems, Santa Ana, California." There was a graphic of the front of a building with a big closed door like the vault of a bank. "User number?" said the screen.

Linda typed in the Northridge Detectives account number, the door appeared to swing open, and the doorway expanded beyond the borders of the screen as though she were stepping inside. The door was replaced by the menu. It was longer than it had been a month ago. PCIS had been collecting for seven or eight years now, and it had thousands of public records databases. She scrolled down the list quickly.

She moved her cursor to select "Tax Assessor's Rolls." She selected New York State. She selected Erie County. She selected City of Deganawida. The menu disappeared and the screen said, "Access charge five dollars. Do you wish to proceed? (Y/N)."

Linda tapped Y. She was guessing that this Jane woman did not live in an apartment building. The business of making people disappear did not lend itself to renting. It was almost inevitable that from time to time a client might show up in person, and renters on the same floor would wonder about it. Any clandestine business was best conducted from a free-standing building without a landlord who might drop in, and the address had to remain the same.

This Jane had apparently operated in Las Vegas as though she were good at it, and the people who needed to disappear badly enough to hire help doing it probably didn't care what they paid. She could afford a house, especially in a backwater like Deganawida. Linda looked at the list that appeared on the screen. Now that she was in, she could manipulate the list. She asked it how many entries were on the list, and it said 5,864. Linda felt power begin to flow into her. The number was tiny. She ordered her computer to search for the word "Jane."

The computer found sixteen Janes, a Janeway, and fifty-two houses on a Jane Street. She made a copy of each of the Janes. She was feeling more and more excitement as she went along. She had been in western New York for only a day, and already she had the list down to sixteen.

Linda relinquished her hold on the tax assessor's rolls and returned to the main menu. She contemplated Jane. She was twenty-five to thirty-five years old, probably about thirty if Linda could trust Seaver's description. She was tall, thin, dark-haired. She operated a very strange little business from one of these sixteen free-standing buildings in Deganawida. Would she have the office disguised as some kind of business? Linda could not decide. Was Jane one of the seven married women, someone like Ronald and Jane Schwartzkopf, Tenants in Common? Or was she one of the nine sole owners listed—Jane Hanlon, Jane Whitefield, Jane Carmen Rossi? Most of the women listed alone were probably widows or divorcees. Some would be too old.

Jane the woman who made people disappear would have a driver's license. The driver's license carried date of birth, height, weight, hair and eye color. Linda selected the Department of Motor Vehicles records: "Access fee ten dollars. Do you wish to proceed? (Y/N)." She began with the first of the sixteen names and scanned the information that had been printed on the license: Jane Anne Hanlon, DOB 08-09-29. Jane Pildrasky was HT 5-02, WT 160, HAIR BLD, EYES BLU. Jane Rossi's license was RSTR: CORR LENS, DAYLIGHT ONLY. The Jane who had helped Pete Hatcher would never have picked a darkened room and a night escape if she could see only in bright light.

Before she relinquished the Department of Motor Vehicles records, Linda had eliminated all but four of the Janes who owned houses in Deganawida. All were HT 5-06 or better, HAIR BRN, DOB after 1960. She returned to the telephone directory and looked up the four names. She eliminated first Jane Sheridan and then Jane Whitefield because neither had the right telephone number. But then she discovered that none of the other Janes had it either. Of course. The Jane she wanted had to live a visible life in a small town. She would have a listed number in the book. It was the business phone that would be unlisted. Linda put Sheridan and Whitefield back in contention.

Linda stared at the main menu and let her reverie deepen. She picked up Jane and turned her around and around, looking at her closely, trying to feel her surfaces. Jane was a tall, lean, dark-haired, youngish woman who owned a house in Deganawida but was gone from it for periods of time. She probably operated much the way Linda and Earl did. She would get a telephone call, drop everything, and go to meet a client. Then she would come home and lie around for weeks, getting used to the time zone and letting her aches and pains go away. Linda felt herself coming closer and closer to Jane.

She selected the credit check: "Access fee, thirty-five dollars. Do you wish to proceed? (Y/N)." Y, of course. Now for the federal privacy law. "Please indicate your legitimate legal grounds for requesting the information. You are a Prospective: (a) Lender, (b) Employer, (c) Insurer, (d) Other. Please specify." Linda loved that part of it. They gave you a selection of lies to choose from. She chose insurer. Insurance companies could do virtually any kind of investigation they wanted on anybody, and they often hired detective agencies to help.

When the four credit reports came out of her printer, Linda studied them. Jane Sheridan was employed by the Deganawida School District. She was a teacher. She couldn't leave town every time the phone rang. Jane Finley was listed as a "homemaker," which was more promising, but her record was full of late payments, credit extended by appliance stores and car dealers, and interest paid to credit-card companies. It didn't make sense for the Jane that Linda was looking for to live that way. She didn't need to, and it made too many people interested in her. Jane Colossi was promising for thirty seconds. She was an attorney. She seemed to spend a lot of money, but the most recent big charges listed for each credit card were for the month of June in France and Italy, when the right Jane was in Las Vegas. Jane Whitefield was the last one in the alphabet. She worked as a "career consultant." She had the right kind of credit rating—excellent. Then Linda found it. Jane Whitefield had two telephone numbers. She probably didn't know the telephone company's computer had spit out the unlisted one when the credit bureau's computer had asked. She was Jane.

Linda looked down the list of debts. There was no mortgage on the house, and none listed as having been paid off. That interested her. Either Jane had paid cash, which would have raised eyebrows, or she had inherited the house.

Linda returned to Probar's menu and asked for probate court filings for the state of New York. She started the computer in

Santa Ana on its search for the name and waited. This would take some time.

Linda stared at the glowing screen while she thought about Jane. Linda was beginning to feel her now. She was—how had Seaver said it?—fit. That was it. She did exercises and pushed herself the way Linda did. It wasn't just because she wanted to get the attention that came when your abs were tight and your ass round and firm, but because she might have to run or fight. She had fought a man that night in Las Vegas, Seaver had said—not hit some old night watchman over the head when he wasn't looking, but faced off with a grown man who was trying to hurt her. That meant she was fast and dirty, because there was no other way it could happen. A man could be dumb as a buffalo and lead with his face, and there was still no way a woman, at most two-thirds his weight, could stand there and take turns throwing punches with him. She was probably a lot like Linda.

The computer screen flashed awake again with the probate documents Linda had requested. The former owner of the house was Alice Whitefield. Before that it had been Henry Whitefield and Alice Whitefield. Linda perused Alice Whitefield's bequest. She had died twelve years ago and left everything to her daughter Jane, age twenty-one. Everything had not been much—the house, contents valued at under thirty thousand; a ten-year-old Plymouth; a bank account with nine thousand in it.

Linda left the court files. There was one last piece of information that she needed to conjure tonight. She selected the records of the County Clerk of Erie County. Linda typed in Jane Whitefield's name and address, copied her date of birth from her driver's license. When the Probar computer found the document Linda was startled. She read it twice to make sure. Jane Whitefield had been married on June 21, to Carey Robert McKinnon, 5092 Dodge Road, Amherst, New York.

Linda felt a sense of fulfillment, of completeness. She was beginning to know Jane Whitefield now. Probably this Carey McKinnon had started her out when she was young, the way

Earl had started Linda. It had probably been about the time when her mother had died and she found herself alone with an old house and a cheap car and barely enough money for a good vacation. He had told her she was going to learn a lot and see a lot, and make a lot of money. And here she was, ten or twelve years later, out alone, risking her life to make people like Pete Hatcher vanish.

Linda went back to the menu and began to work magic on Carey McKinnon. It took her an hour to find out more about him than she knew about Jane. She glanced at her watch frequently now, because the time was almost certainly coming. She had given Lenny her telephone number as soon as she had moved in, so Earl would have it by now. The telephone rang at midnight.

"Hello, Linda."

"Hi," she said. She wanted to sound unperturbed and self-sufficient. "How's it going?"

"Not so hot," said Earl. "I found his car in Billings, between a couple of hotels. I plugged the gas line so it would turn over but not start, but he hasn't come back for it, and I haven't had any luck at the hotels. Where are you?"

"I'm in a little place south of Buffalo called the Meadow-green Suites. You get a kitchen and a refrigerator, but you don't have to make the bed."

"What have you got?"

"Her name is Jane Whitefield. She has a house in a little town north of Buffalo along the Niagara River called Deganawida. That's where the answering machine is."

"Is she home, or do I have to watch my back for her too?"

"I don't know yet. My guess is that she's already out there with him."

"When will you know?"

"Tomorrow morning. It's a little more complicated than I thought. She got married in June."

"Know anything about her husband?"

"What I know doesn't make too much sense to me yet. His name is Carey McKinnon, and he's a doctor."

There was a short pause while Earl ruminated. "It could be she dreamed that up as an identity for one of her favorite clients and then got him to marry her—you know, he says he's a doctor that's retired, and he doesn't have to explain why he's got a lot of money and plays golf all day."

"I thought of that," said Linda. "But his credit check says he's actually getting payments from a hospital, and from some surgical group. He's in the A.M.A. directory. They don't let you flash a fake ID and go operate on somebody."

"A double beard, then?" asked Earl. "Maybe he's queer and gets to hide it—nobody wants a surgeon who might have AIDS—and she gets to be that much harder to find. Does he have a separate house?"

"Yeah. But I don't know if one of them is empty. If they don't live together, she wouldn't be much of a beard in a town that size. I just got this stuff an hour ago, and I'm thirty miles from there, but I'll be out early to see if she's at his house or hers, or neither. You know, it occurred to me that he could be some kind of fanatic."

"What kind of fanatic?"

"We know she took Pete Hatcher out. We don't know why, or if he's typical, or one of a kind. There are these groups that take battered women and children out the same way, like the Underground Railroad. The first person to see somebody like that is a doctor. That kind of group might hire a pro like her to do the hard part, and that's how they met. Maybe Pete Hatcher was just the money for their honeymoon."

"Get on them," he said.

"What does it sound like I'm doing, Earl?"

"I mean really get on them," he said. "Hatcher has me out here in Billings, Montana, watching a parked car. I don't think he accomplished that alone. If she's home, I'd like to know it. If she's not, I'd at least like a picture of her so she can't walk up to me on the street and blow my head off. If her husband's gone, I'd like to know that I've got him to expect too, and what he looks like."

"I'll know if they're here in a few hours."

"If he specializes in plastic surgery and he could be busy making Pete Hatcher look like Miss Arkansas, I'd like to know that. I'm dead in the water out here. Whatever you can get me, whatever it takes to get it."

"Whatever?" She let her voice go soft and low. She savored the pause on his end of the line. There was the electrical charge, growing and growing, and the resistance was making the air hotter. There was nothing in the world like hunting, knowing that any click in the dark could be the slide of the pistol locking the first round into the chamber.

He was feeling it too. "I mean do whatever you have to, and then do some more. If you think they're going to pay us a couple hundred thousand and write it off after three months, you're dreaming. One of these days you're going to call home and it won't be Lenny that answers. It'll be Seaver."

"I know," she said. "I'll do my best, I promise."

"If she's there, kill her. I'll call tomorrow night." He hung up.

Linda put the telephone receiver on the hook, lay on the bed, and stared at the ceiling. She toyed with the fear, tested it for titillation. It made her heart beat fast, and a little electric shock clapped her back behind her lungs, then moved down the sides to her haunches like a shiver. Playing for death was better than anything.

But tonight there was something extra, something that made it better and more delicious. It was Jane. She was the attraction. There was an urge to take a risk to beat her. Linda was going to be the one who was smarter, faster, dirtier. She was going to be the one.

18

Jane left the rented car at the agency in Missoula and picked up the one she had parked on the university campus. Pete Hatcher watched everything she did and listened to her explanations, then nodded his head. He had stopped asking questions, and that set off a tiny alarm in the back of Jane's mind. It would not be out of the question for a man in his position to be contemplating suicide. It was also possible that he was only getting tired and passive. If that lasted long enough, it wasn't much different from suicide.

She drove him northeast on Route 200 away from Missoula, and stopped at a motel in a small town called Potomac. They sat in the car for a moment. She waited for him to ask a question. Finally, she pulled a small leather wallet out of her purse and handed it to him.

"What's this?" he asked.

"We need to sleep now. This is a motel. It isn't part of a national chain, so that makes its records a lot harder to get. If we do everything the way everybody else does, we're invisible. What everybody else does is that the man goes inside and registers. For the moment, we're going to travel as Mr. and Mrs. Michael Phelan of Los Angeles. I have identification that matches. Now go do it."

Too soon, he came out of the office and walked to the car. "They don't have any suites or anything like that," he said. "Should I rent two rooms?"

She closed her eyes and took a deep breath. He seemed to have lost his will to keep his mind working. "Pull yourself together and think. Mr. and Mrs. Phelan don't sleep in separate rooms. Get it over with."

He disappeared inside the office again and came out carrying a key. She watched him open the door, then started the car and pulled it into a parking space a distance from the room and went to join him inside. She surveyed the room. Her eyes rested on the king-size bed in the center of the floor. She forced them to move on. That was an extra problem with hiding a man. Dancing around in cramped quarters to keep the distances proper and the bodies covered became part of the job. She decided not to face that conversation yet. Anything she said now would not get a second bed in here, and would make him more passive and tentative.

She looked out the windows, checked the locks, examined the curtains, and continued her commentary. "When you check in, you take a mental picture of the world outside. The best way out of here is to the left, toward the car. I parked it in front of another door, away from the office. If somebody finds out we're here, he doesn't know which car is ours. If he finds the car, he doesn't know which room is ours. It's late now, so most of the other cars that will be in the lot are already here. Next time you look, what you'll be looking for is newcomers. You lock everything that will lock." She flipped the deadbolt and the safety latch. "If you do all the little things right, you'll sleep better."

She glanced at her watch. "I'm going out for a few minutes. When I come back I'll knock four times, like this." She rapped on the table.

"Where are you going?"

"To make a phone call from the booth at the gas station."

"There's a phone right here."

"There would be a record of the call."

She slipped out and walked toward the car in case the night clerk happened to be watching, then kept going past it and across the weedy margin of the property to the gas station, put a quarter into the telephone slot, and dialed zero, then the number of the house in Amherst. "I'd like to make a collect call. It's Jane."

She heard Carey pick up the telephone. "Operator." The word came out before he had even said hello. "Will you accept a collect call from Jane?"

"Sure," he said. The operator clicked off. "Jane?"

"Hi," she answered.

"You okay?"

"Yes. I found him, and I picked him up, and now I've got him hundreds of miles away. I think we're two hops ahead of them. Maybe only one hop, but it's a good one."

"Where are you?"

The question startled her. She had never talked to anybody at home while she was working—not really talked, because she had always lied. She felt a twinge almost like pain when she said, "I'm in a little town in the Wild West. At least I think I'm in town. There's not much here, so I can't be sure."

"A hotel or something?"

"Sure. It's not the Hilton, but I haven't seen any cockroaches either." She was saying words that were true, but she was lying. He wanted to know everything, and she was giving him breezy nonsense.

"You're staying with . . . him? That can't be safe."

The lie came easily, like breathing, really. "Well, no, not exactly. One of the tricks of the trade. He's in his motel room and I checked into another room across the parking lot. That way I can watch his door, and if anything suspicious happens, all I have to do is dial his room. He goes out the window on the side I can see is clear, and I pick him up on the highway."

She knew it sounded plausible. She had been lying for so long that it was almost a reflex. She had heard the trouble building in his voice, and she had flinched to evade it. She pushed the question and the answer into a corner of her mind and labeled the corner a special exception. She had been trying to save him some anxiety, and the anxiety would have been pointless, because he would have been worrying about a dangerous situation that she had no way to evade. Or maybe, in the back of his mind, he had been worried about . . . something else. That was something she simply was not going to do, so worrying about it would serve no purpose. She loved Carey McKinnon.

Carey was already talking. "I'm sorry," she said. "I missed that."

"I said, Do you know where you're going next, or when you'll be home?"

His kind, patient voice opened a wound in her, and she tried to make up for the small lie. "I'll tell you what I know at the moment," she said. "The attempt these people made was a little worse than I thought. He would be dead now if a cop hadn't happened along in time to take the bullet for him. So he's a mess—I mean psychologically. Guilty, scared, and, consequently, stupid. The hunters are a lot better at it than I had hoped, so I have to be cautious. At the moment the plan is to take him someplace where he'll be almost impossible to find, teach him everything he could possibly need to know, and split. That's what I should have done in the first place, but I couldn't."

Carey's voice was a monotone, as though there was hurt and anger that he was making an effort to keep out of it. "It's starting to sound like it will take a lot of time."

"It shouldn't," she said. Why was she talking to him as though there were lawyers present? "There is nothing in the whole world that I want more than to be with you. Right now. Tonight. But I think this could take a couple of weeks. I've got to be sure I've lost the hunters, and then get him settled. When that's done, I'll rush home and have a lot of fun being Mrs. McKinnon again. Forever. Maybe I'll lock you in the house for a month and see for myself if the bad reputation you have is justified. I'm pretty sure it is, but I'd like to double-check."

She heard him give a small, unvoiced chuckle. "I miss you," he said. She heard a sigh. "Well, I guess there's nothing much I can do except wait and hold you to your word. Do what you have to do, and get home."

She loved him. The lies were a pain in her chest. "I miss you so much I could cry." She wanted to tell him things. A big truck rushed past on the highway and a hot, dusty wind blew off the pavement into her face. "Stupid trucks," she said. "I'm going to try to jump around to a few of these little towns for a couple of days to see if anybody's looking for us, then leave some trails in the wrong direction. After that I'll put him in a place where he can stay for twenty years. But first, the little towns."

"Pick one, and I'll call you there tomorrow."

She felt a chill. "I can't do that," she said quickly. "I'll be using different names, and I don't know which one or where I'll be yet. If I did, I couldn't say it on the phone. I'll call you."

There was silence on the other end. Had he figured out that the name would be Mr. and Mrs. something?

"Carey?"

"Yeah?"

"I'll call you as soon as I can. I know this is hard. I love you." She had never known that "I love you" was what a person said when she had run out of words and couldn't say anything else. It was like reaching out a hand in desperation.

"I love you too. Just be careful, and come home in one piece."

"Don't worry. I've become a very cautious married lady." She took a deep breath. "That reminds me. I guess I ought to get going now."

"I could talk to you all night."

"When we're together," she said. "Then I'll talk until you want to smother me with a pillow. But I'd better go. Some people are born to disappear. This one takes a lot of hand-holding." She drew in her breath, leaned her forehead against the phone booth, and shut her eyes. It was the middle of the night. If Hatcher was waiting for her to come back, the story that they were in different rooms didn't make sense. She said quickly, "I love you," and hung up. She turned and walked to the motel feeling sad and empty.

Jane approached the motel by circling it to study the cars in the lot, the traffic patterns on the two roads that intersected beside it, and the businesses nearby. The town was tiny and clean and presented an unassuming business face. But she could not induce a feeling of safety here. It was not big enough to provide a crowd to hide in, and not remote enough to be hard to find. As soon as Pete seemed rested and presentable, she would get him back on the road.

She thought about her conversation with Carey as she walked. She had been vague and evasive, but she had heard herself say something that she now realized was accurate. She had almost no idea where the chasers were, or what they were thinking. It was possible that Pete, in his novice's panic and ignorance, had managed to leave them behind in Denver. They would certainly trace his car to Billings, but by the time they did, it would be in an impound lot and Pete could be anywhere.

Only if they were spectacularly good or phenomenally lucky—had an unseen person follow his car all the way to Billings—could they know he had gotten even that far. After that she had taken him out in a rented car, changed to still another car, and driven nearly eight hours. It was very unlikely that they could have followed without her seeing them.

If she kept Pete out of airports and big, well-lighted cities for a time, she would at least avoid squandering the lead she had on them. One way to do that was to keep him in suspended animation in the tiny resort towns up here, looking like one of the thousands of summer tourists.

She knew a little bit about the way the shooters must have found him the first time. They had looked at computerized public records and found out that the same man in Denver had registered a car and bought a gun at the same time. Probably they had run a credit check and found that he had also just arrived in town, and then they had flown in to take a look at him.

Now Jane would keep him from doing anything that got him on any lists for a time. Then she could control where and when he did anything else that created public records. She had already bought him a car under the name Wendy Wasserman. She would get him settled in his next apartment, find him a job, and help him fit in with the locals. He had already given in to the urge to buy a gun, and he still had it, so he probably wouldn't make that mistake again.

She allowed herself a small feeling of optimism. Eight hours was not a huge lead, but it was growing. When she knocked on the door of their motel room, she heard him go to the window, saw him move the curtain aside to look out, then heard him step to the door and open it.

She slipped inside, closed the door, and glanced at him. He was in a pair of blue boxer shorts, and he turned away and hastily slipped his pistol into a pile of clothing on a chair. She couldn't help being surprised by the sight of his body, but she fought to keep him from noticing. She had plucked the poor man away from Billings without his suitcase. She had not expected him to sleep fully dressed. She had not expected anything at all, and she reminded herself that she was going to have to anticipate his needs or she was going to wear them both out. She tried to formulate some words that would get them past this moment.

"It looks clear out there." The attempt disappointed her. After all, what he was wearing wasn't different from what men wore on the beach. She was a grown-up married woman. What difference did it make what he wore? Then it occurred to her that she was going to need to wear something to bed too. What she wore did seem to her to make a difference.

She pushed the thought aside and let the space fill itself with a trivial observation that had been prickling the back of her mind. "You did okay a minute ago, but all I've got to do right now is give you lessons, so here's another one. You heard the right knock, so you thought it was me. You looked around the curtain to see if I was alone. Good. But I heard you, and saw you, and that was not so good. If I had been the wrong person giving the right knock, you'd be dead."

"What was I supposed to do?"

"You were right to want to look before you opened the door. The very best time for them would be those few seconds while you and I were standing together with the door open. They could see us both in the light, and if they missed one of us the first time, they wouldn't need to break anything down to get the survivor. But you want to look without letting anybody know you're doing it. Do what the cops do on surveillance: don't move the curtain, just look over the top of the track it's on."

"You can't see anything but the wall," he said. "The track is above the glass."

She moved a chair to the far side of the window, and said, "Trust me."

Pete stepped on the chair and looked down over the top of the metal track. In the two-inch space he could clearly see the step in front of the door, the wall on either side of the door, and some of the sidewalk. "I can see more from here than I could when I opened the curtain."

"Right. It's a view that shows you the likely hiding places around the door. It's above them, which is good, because people seldom look up unless they know what they're looking for. They look to both sides, look behind, look down."

"I never noticed that. Why?"

"I don't know. Maybe it's just the way the skull is connected to the neck. Maybe it's some prehistoric instinct that serious trouble hardly ever comes at an animal our size from above the treetops. Notice anything else while you were up there?"

"It's an odd angle."

"Right. When you were at ground level peeking between the curtains, they could have seen you and shot you through the glass from the left, from the right, or from the parking lot. When you were beside the window and above it, the right side of the window and the parking lot were out. Anybody there couldn't see you. The only danger left was that the person at the door would look up and to his left, pull out a weapon before you saw him do it, and make a world-class shot that hit the thin slice of your body that wasn't protected behind the wall or the woodwork—all of that before you moved. Or, since you had a gun in your hand, before you opened fire on his completely exposed body."

"How did you learn all these tricks?"

Jane sat down on the bed and smiled sadly. "No matter how

much you learn, the people who chase fugitives are still better at it. You watch how they work, you pick up what you can, and you keep going."

"Why do you? What made you get into a line of work like this in the first place? Is the money that good?"

She shook her head and let out a little chuckle. "I did it once, I did it again. It never occurred to me to accept pay. Somebody pressed the point, and I said, 'So send me a present.' The jobs got more dangerous, and the presents got bigger."

"But why the first time?"

"Anybody who knows how to swim will jump in and pull out the one who's drowning. I knew how to swim."

"But—"

"Enough," she said. "Things were going to happen, and I made decisions about which ones I could live with, just as anybody does. The choices aren't always limitless. In case you haven't noticed, I was feeling sorry for myself tonight without this conversation."

"I'm sorry," he said. "If you want to be alone for a few hours, I could manage that much."

"Of course not," said Jane. "I didn't mean it that way." She felt ashamed. He was scared to death, and he was volunteering to go out and cower somewhere while she had a fit of the vapors or something. "You're a good guy, Pete. We're going to have to spend a lot of time together for a while. I'll let you know now that I enjoy your company, so you don't have to wonder or apologize for being here. We're going to pull you through this little bumpy stretch and get you started on a new life. Then I'll float off like the good fairy and go to work getting my own life straightened out. Okay?"

"Okay," said Pete. His smile was almost a laugh. He looked strong and comfortable. The muscles in his shoulders and legs elongated as he slouched in his chair. He had that unself-conscious, almost comical look that she had seen on fathers taking little children to the park. "I guess knowing how to shoot people doesn't do much for your social life."

She was surprised at her sudden need to keep him from

thinking she wasn't desirable. She drew in a breath to respond, then looked down at her watch. "It's late, and I'd like to get an early start tomorrow morning."

He looked at the bed. "I can sleep on the floor."

"Sorry, that's mine," she said. She took a pillow and the bedspread off the bed. "What I'm worried about is not you, by the way. Tonight I'm going to keep my eyes open for visitors." She busied herself with the bedspread while he got into the bed and turned off the lamp beside it. Then she went into the bathroom, brushed her teeth, and came back out. He was lying in the dim light with his eyes closed. She turned out the other light and lay on the folded quilt in the dark.

"Jane?"

"What?"

"Thanks again."

"Think nothing of it."

She lay in the darkness, staring up at the ceiling and testing the sensation of not being able to detect the difference between having her eyes open or closed. She closed them and thought about Carey. She knew that at this hour he was fast asleep in the big bed at home. She tried to reach out with her thought and place a blessing on him while he slept, but the mere knowledge that he was sleeping cut her off from him. He was dreaming, not thinking about her, like a receiver tuned to a different station. She opened her eyes again and she was back in the motel room in Montana.

As she lay there feeling the floor pressing harder on her spine, she contemplated the absurdity of pretending to stay alert for intruders so she could lie here on the floor when there was plenty of room on a perfectly good bed a few feet away. She knew that she would have the thought again and again, each time she awoke in the darkness waiting for the night to end. It was her penance for lying to Carey about the sleeping arrangements. She couldn't take back the lie, but she could suffer a little discomfort to make the lie almost true.

She dozed off for a few seconds and began to slip into a dream. The vague image of a man appeared and began to

19

Linda Thompson spent all of her time studying Dr. Carey McKinnon. He was attractive, with a lean body and gangling walk and big hands that made her wonder if he had made his way through college playing basketball. He always looked as though he was late, ducking out of the driver's seat of the BMW, unfolding those long legs, then taking two steps toward the hospital building before the door that he had flicked with his hand slammed shut. Then he would step along toward the entrance without looking to either side or slowing down as visitors did to be sure the automatic door would open in time, and then disappear inside.

When his shift ended, he would come out alone at the same speed, slip into the BMW, and drive off. She watched him travel the same route each time, back to his big old house in Amherst. After a few minutes she would see him moving around in the kitchen. Later there would be the glowing bluish light in a room on the upper floor from a television set. When it went off, he would sleep.

It took Linda two days to grow accustomed to his hours. He was at the hospital for surgery by seven and usually walked across the street to the medical building where he had his office at around one. Some time in the late afternoon he would walk back to the hospital and stalk the hallways, talking to patients in their rooms until at least seven, and sometimes nine.

After she became used to his movements and had adjusted her internal clock to his, she had long stretches of time when she could let him out of her sight. The mornings were good, because she knew that he wasn't going to leave in the middle of an operation. She spent some mornings with realtors. His neighborhood was wrong for her purposes. The houses were all big and expensive, sitting well back on vast lots. The nearest one that was for sale was two long blocks away, and the view of his house was obscured by a row of old maple trees along the sidewalk. The zoning apparently didn't permit apartment buildings, because there was not one on any of the surrounding streets.

She considered getting a job in the hospital, but only for a moment. Hospitals checked credentials to avoid lawsuits, and she could never create any that would get her a job that placed her in his path frequently enough. At best she would find herself emptying bedpans three floors away from him, with no excuse to leave and follow him.

Linda had an expert eye for bodies and could tell he was in reasonably good condition. He didn't jog or work out at home, so it was possible that he belonged to some local club. She looked up all of the ones in the telephone book, made some calls, and learned nothing.

His entry in the A.M.A. directory told her he had gone to Cornell and then to the University of Chicago Medical School. She opened an account at the bank listed on his credit report and shopped at the supermarkets closest to his house, but never saw him.

She visited the main library in downtown Buffalo and read old issues of the Cornell alumni magazine until she found the right obituary. A woman named Susan Preston had died six years ago in a plane crash. Susan Preston would have been five years younger than McKinnon, so they weren't in school together. She had been survived by various Prestons in San Francisco, so it was unlikely that McKinnon had known her family. Linda took the catalog off the shelf and studied the maps and photographs of the Cornell University campus, then memorized the names of professors and courses. If the university was going to be an entree to anything, she might need to be able to talk about it.

Linda called her house and reached Lenny. She told him to punch the name Susan Preston Haynes onto some blank credit cards, make her a California driver's license, and send them by overnight mail. It was a gamble to use a real name, but it would put her on the right lists, and adding a husband's surname gave her the option of being Haynes any time Preston seemed too risky.

After six days of stalking Carey McKinnon, Linda found an article in the *Buffalo News* about a benefit dinner to be held by the auxiliary of Buffalo Memorial Hospital. She called the number in the article and bought a ticket for a hundred dollars. Carey McKinnon seemed to do nothing but work and sleep, but maybe he would consider a benefit for the hospital a part of his work. She had just taken out the good dress she had brought from California in case she needed it in Las Vegas and begun her preparations when the telephone rang.

"Yes?" she said into it.

"It's me." Earl sounded angry.

"Hi," she said. "Have you got anything yet?"

"Zero," he said. "I've watched his goddamn car for a week. If he's in Billings at all anymore, he doesn't drive anywhere. He's also not visible in any hotel, motel, or park bench in the city. If you don't have anything for me soon, I think we might want to begin considering our alternatives."

"What alternatives?"

"Make some fake ID with Hatcher's picture on it that won't fool even a Montana cop, rent an apartment in that name. We salt the apartment with the ID and the mail we found in Las Vegas, and anything from the car that has Hatcher's prints on it."

"Then what?" She knew he wasn't serious. He was saying it because it sounded desperate and risky, and the thought that he was contemplating such a fraud would affect her.

"Pop some guy Hatcher's size and shape, put him in the car, and torch it. Once the police run the prints we leave in the apartment and identify the photograph on the fake ID, they won't have any reason to strain themselves with a lot of tests, and Seaver won't be able to. If anybody's real curious they might go to the Denver apartment the car's registered to and find more of Hatcher's prints there. We collect the rest of the money from Seaver. End of story."

"What happens if Pete Hatcher shows up later?" She sounded as worried as she would have been if she believed Earl would give up. Earl didn't need safety as much as he needed to win.

"Honey, if I can't find the bastard, you think anybody else is going to?"

"Of course not. Nobody's better than you, Earl. I'm just talking."

"If we wait too long, we might have to do it in reverse."

"What do you mean?" asked Linda.

"Cut and run before Seaver's bosses send somebody for us. Find a man and woman and make it look like this specialist Hatcher hired set a trap and killed us first."

"Please don't do anything yet, Earl," she said. "I won't disappoint you, I promise." Her own voice, sounding breathy and submissive, gave her an erotic shiver. She experimented with making her voice break, not quite a sob. "I've been trying really hard." The effect was good. "I'll have something for you in a few days."

"I sure hope so," he said. "I've got nothing. I've been running computer checks on the two names he used so far, her name, car rentals, everything. None of it leads anywhere in particular. So I'm beginning to think she picked him up and they were long gone before I got here."

"I know it's up to me," she said. "I won't forget it for a second."

Carey McKinnon stood in front of the mirror in the bedroom and studied the man who stared back at him. He had been aware long before tonight that he looked foolish in a tuxedo, but he had consoled himself by renting a tuxedo to look foolish in instead of owning one, and by picking out the plainest model that Benjy's Midnight Tux had to offer, with black cummerbund and white plastic studs and cuff links. Probably the last time this one had been out of Benjy's, it had been taken to a prom. The shoes were his, but only because Benjy's selection of shoes for big feet had the sturdy spit-shined look of military footwear.

With resignation, he brushed his hair into place one last time. The warring cowlicks would reassert themselves in the car. Then he turned off the light, walked downstairs, and stopped. He looked at the telephone before he opened the door. He had been looking at telephones all over the house for two hours, each time remembering that the way they looked had nothing to do with ringing.

It was two hours earlier in Montana, so it was still about five o'clock there. His mind warned him that thinking about time was the first step into treacherous territory. The second was to ask himself what she could possibly be doing that made a telephone call to her husband such a hard thing to accomplish at any hour of the day or night. That brought a hundred contradictory answers into his mind together, elbowing past one another to the front to be acknowledged.

He left the lamp by the door burning and hurried out to his car. As soon as he had started the engine, he noticed the fuel gauge again and cursed himself for forgetting. He hated to stop at the full-serve side of the gas station and wait by the pump helplessly until the attendant happened to glance out the window and notice him, then get so lonely and bored that helping a customer was all he could think of to do. But Carey was determined not to pump gas in a tuxedo. The unwritten laws of physics meant that the pump nozzle would backwash or the hose would leak.

He backed out of the long driveway quickly, drove up the street, and stopped at the light. He hoped the needle of the fuel gauge was still just working its way upward to its correct reading. The light changed, and he turned left to drive the familiar route back to the hospital.

When he reached his reserved parking space he found a big black Mercedes had been backed into it. He paused for a moment with his foot on the brake, then drove on into the visitors' parking lot, took a parking ticket, and found a space. As he walked toward the building, the argument the muscles of his mouth and tongue were rehearsing was that taking a surgeon's space in a hospital parking lot could cost the driver's child the five minutes that might have saved his life some time. He clamped the argument to the roof of his mouth with his tongue. He wasn't going to say it. He wasn't going inside to save anybody's life. He was going in there to kiss that Mercedes owner's rich ass with enthusiasm and sincerity, and hope it bought the hospital a new children's wing.

It was probably somebody he had met before. Around Buffalo, most big money was old money, handed down from the days of the Erie Canal, or at least the days of Civil War profiteering, enhanced by practices like buying up the tax liens on family farms in the surrounding countryside during the Depression and turning them into suburbs.

He walked into the foyer and glanced into the garden. He could see a few fat penguins and their bejeweled consorts loitering out there, flicking cigarette ashes into the shrubbery and sipping drinks where their cardiologists couldn't catch them at it.

He caught a glimpse of Lily Bortoni, the wife of his friend Leo, an orthopedic surgeon. She looked as serene and elegant as she always did at these affairs, every shining chestnut hair in place and with just enough makeup so her skin looked like the smooth surface of a sculpture. She was staring unperturbed through a cloud of cigar smoke at a potential donor as though he were saying something important, so Carey couldn't catch her eye.

As he walked on, a series of conflicting thoughts flashed through his mind. The sight of Lily made him miss Jane and feel annoyed with her at the same time. He felt sorry for himself for having to show up here alone, felt guilty that Leo's wife, Lily, had to work the crowd while Jane escaped it, dreaded having to explain ten times in the next hour why Jane wasn't here. Then he remembered that she could be running for her life right now. He forced the idea out of his mind: she was out finding a new address for some moron. It was unfair to Carey and inconvenient for her, but the danger was over. She was doing what she felt she had to do, and he would just have to cover for her until it was over.

He stepped into the cafeteria, and a hand patted his arm. He turned to look down at Marian Fleming. She had managed to confine herself in a beige evening gown with metallic filigree on the front that looked as though its purpose was to protect her from body blows. Her blond hair was sprayed and sculpted into a spun-sugar helmet, and her ice-blue eyes fixed him with a stare that told him he was not about to be offered any choices. "There's somebody you've got to meet," she said.

Carey understood the words "got to," so he waited.

"Where's Jane?" Her eyes flicked around behind him.

"She's out of town," he answered. "I'm on my own tonight."

He did not miss the tiny twitch above her eye as Marian's mind punched Jane's card. She was already pivoting to push him along toward someone, still talking. "Here's the doctor I told you about."

"You did?" asked Carey.

"Susan Haynes, this is Carey McKinnon. He went to Cornell too." She gave Carey a perfectly benign empty look. "So did his wife, but she's not with us tonight, so he'll have to do."

Carey looked at the woman and smiled. Her blond hair beside Marian's was the difference between polished gold and yellow paint. Her eyes were big, a bright green with flecks in them like malachite, and her lips were full, with a natural upturn at the corners. She gave a reserved smile, as though she were bestowing tiny portions of a powerful spice.

"Hello, Dr. McKinnon," said Linda.

"Pleased to meet you, Miss Haynes. I have a feeling you must have shown up in Ithaca after my time. I would have remembered."

She looked as though she was not surprised by anything men said to her, just mildly disappointed. "I was Sue Preston then."

"It doesn't help," he said. "I've been out about ten years, and you're only twenty . . ." He squinted at her. "Eight."

The big green eyes widened. "How did you know that?"

"I'm a specialist in looking at people as bundles of cells. Yours are twenty-eight."

She looked around her, but nobody was nearby bursting to explain it. "This is some kind of trick."

He shook his head. "Nope. You weigh one hundred and twenty-two pounds, right?"

"I don't know," she said. "I don't weigh myself every day." She lowered her head and conceded from behind her eyelashes, "That's close, though."

He leaned closer, and she turned her ear to listen. "Those guys at carnivals who guess your age and weight?"

"What about them?"

"They're all old doctors."

He could tell she was getting used to him now. She just smiled, showing perfect teeth and spilling a prodigal supply of the precious spice into the room, but it was all for him. "Now I know it's a joke."

"Some do it to save up for their malpractice insurance, some just hate golf. I think some of them do it just to get away from these." He showed her his beeper. "Ever have one of these?"

"I'm not the kind of person anybody needs urgently."

"Good. Don't ever start." He put his beeper away. "Well, I should introduce you to more people. Or you should introduce me. Just because I haven't met you at one of these things doesn't mean I know more people than you do."

"This is my first time," she said.

Marian Fleming drifted up with Harry Rotherberg. "There," she said. "I knew you two would have something to talk about. But I need to take Carey back for a minute. This is Dr. Rotherberg. He's the head of pediatrics, so he can answer any questions you have about the new wing."

Carey flashed a valedictory smile at the young woman and stepped away with Marian. "How am I doing?"

"You're my paladin," she said. "Right now I'm going to

jump you over a few pawns and get you to work this bunch over here."

"The captain of industry with the plaid cummerbund?"

"Yep. Know him?"

"I'm pretty sure I've seen his cummerbund at these things before, but his name doesn't leap to mind."

"He's Charlie Fraser. That's his tartan. He comes off as a dope, but he's not. He's given about a hundred thousand so far this year. Be nice to him."

"What a devious plan."

"Oh, and Carey?"

"What?"

"Since Jane isn't here, I've seated you with Susan Haynes. I'm counting on you to romance her a little for me."

"Why?"

"She doesn't know anybody," said Marian. "Harry's a great pediatrician, but ten minutes with him is an evening in Mister Rogers' neighborhood. She's got money and she wants to do good with it."

"I'll get it for you if I have to turn her upside down and shake her."

"I have no doubt. Your reputation precedes you." There was no trace of a smile as she expertly moved him into the space before Charlie Fraser. "Charlie, this is Dr. McKinnon," she said.

Carey shook Fraser's hand and smiled while Marian Fleming said, "And this is Honoria Fraser, his wife."

"I'm glad you could come," said Carey. "I had heard you had given us quite a bit of help in the past, and I wanted to thank you."

Fraser looked shocked. "Who are you, anyway? What do you do?"

"I'm a surgeon."

Fraser leaned over and kissed his wife on the cheek. She laughed, then put her fingers over her mouth as though it were a breach of decorum. Her husband said, "That's another one for you, Honey."

Carey said, "I don't understand."

"I made a bet with Honey two years ago. Every year I get a printed thank-you note with my name written on it so the I.R.S. will be satisfied. But to this day, no actual human being connected with the hospital ever walked straight up like a regular person and said thanks. I said nobody ever would, or if they did, it would be an administrator from fund-raising. You just won her the bet."

Carey looked worried. "Uh-oh."

"What's wrong?"

"If nobody ever did it before, maybe I wasn't supposed to. I guess this means you'll stop giving money now?"

"Do I look like an idiot?" asked Fraser. He looked down at his tuxedo. "Well, I suppose I do. But I'm not. I do lose most of my bets with Honey, but so would you."

Carey looked at Honoria Fraser and smiled. "I can believe it."

"Let me tell you something about fund-raising, since you seem to be sensible," said Fraser. "These dinner-dance things are a mistake. When I want to lure investors into my business, I take them to the plant. I let them meet the good people I've got working for me. They show them the machinery and computers and trucks. They let them see how we make our products, from the quality of the raw materials to the packing and shipping. They show people what Charlie Fraser's going to do with their money. Now, if I was an idiot"—he turned his head to survey the room—"I would put on something like this party."

"Charlie!" said Honoria sharply.

"The doc doesn't care," Fraser assured her. "He can tell I mean well." He turned to Carey. "There's nothing that makes a person who gives money cringe more than a fancy party. It costs money, and if he's reasonably intelligent he knows it's his money. He didn't give it so he could go to a party. He gave it so some poor kid gets his turn on a kidney machine. He'd like to see that. If it comes down to parties, he knows he could do a pretty good party himself for a few thousand, invite whomever he pleased, and serve better food."

Honoria said to Carey, "Charlie's quite the blowhard, isn't he?"

"Yes," Carey agreed. "You are, Charlie. But you're absolutely right. I can't talk Marian out of throwing these parties, but I can do the rest for you." He wrote a telephone number on his ticket and handed it to Fraser. "This is my office. Call any day, and I'll have somebody arrange a tour for you, and for anybody you want to bring. If you see where the money goes, and what it does for this city, I think you'll be proud."

"I am proud," said Charlie. "I'm just telling you how to get more." He glanced at the number on the ticket. "I will do this, you know."

"I expect you to," said Carey. "Bring some friends."

There was a chime, and people began to move beyond the screens dividing the cafeteria in half. "That's dinner," said Charlie. One of the waiters pushed the button to make the opening widen, and Carey could see white linen and gleaming silverware for the only time this year. "If you don't have anybody to sit with, you can come with us."

"Marian's got other plans for me," said Carey.

He drifted across the paths of a few familiar couples moving toward the tables and scanned for Susan Haynes. He found her standing with one arm across her chest and the other holding a glass of champagne, listening to Harry Rotherberg talking about the ultrasound machines the hospital was about to buy. Katie Rotherberg moved in ahead of Carey and separated them.

Carey said, "Dinner time. Don't worry if the meat tastes funny. You're already in the hospital."

" 'Please be seated and the maître d' will call you when your stomach pump is ready'?"

"I can see you've been to benefits before. Why this one?"

She shrugged. "I'm new in town, and I saw it in the paper. Hospitals tend to be everybody's charity. I thought it was a good opportunity to get a look at the local gentry and make it clear I'm one of the good guys."

He looked at her in mock suspicion. "You're some kind of businesswoman, aren't you?"

"Good grief, no." She giggled. "Nobody in my family has 'been' anything in ages. My father used to sit on boards of directors. That way he got mail and was allowed to own a briefcase. But he didn't actually know anything or do anything, or they wouldn't have wanted him around. His epitaph should have been 'He Voted Yes.' "

"Your mother?"

"She voted no. When I was about three. She turned up a few years ago, but we didn't have much to talk about. To complete the whole sordid family tree, I have an older brother. Come to think of it, he's something—a fisherman."

"A commercial fisherman?"

"No, silly. Trout. He spends his summers at his house in Jackson Hole and his winters in rehab places. They don't seem to have any therapeutic value, but it's a quiet place to tie flies, once his hands stop shaking."

"I'm sorry."

She touched his arm, and it felt as though it had been brushed by a bird's wing. "Don't sound so solemn. None of this just happened, you know. It's all old history."

As they reached the newly unscreened section of the cafeteria, Marian Fleming caught Carey's eye and nodded toward the front of the room near the head table. He gave his head a tiny shake, and she picked up two place cards from the front table, ushered Leo Bortoni and his wife from the back to Carey's place, and watched Carey take Susan Haynes's arm and walk her to the rear table. He could see that Lily Bortoni was delighted, having interpreted the move as a sign that her husband was appreciated. He liked them both, and he congratulated himself for having accidentally made them feel good. He pretended he had been looking past them for someone else, gave a little shrug, and continued toward the back of the room.

Carey and Susan Haynes sat at a table for four, but they were alone. He looked at her. "I guess this is where we're supposed to talk about Cornell."

"Do we have to?"

"Briefly. Uris Library."

"Cruel to put it at the top of a hill," she said. "Thought I'd die." One of the photographs in the alumni magazine had shown the view from the library, so its altitude was all she knew about it.

"Goldwin Smith Hall."

"Big, old, and cold." She said it with an air of profound boredom. She hoped that was the long, low one across the quadrangle with the statue in front, but whatever it was, the description seemed to satisfy him.

"Had enough?"

"More than enough." She leaned closer. "So what about your life story?" she asked.

"I was born in this hospital, and sort of never got out," he said. "My education was just a leave of absence. I'm a surgeon."

"Married?" He wasn't sure if she said it so quickly and adroitly because she didn't care, or because she did care.

"Just. Three months ago. She's out of town right now."

"Oh, yes. Marian said something about that. I forgot. What kind of surgeon are you—plastic surgery?"

"If you need anything cosmetic done, Buffalo isn't really the best place. There are hospitals in Los Angeles and Boston that do more of those in a week than we do in a year. What I do is mostly basic medicine. If you have no further use for your gall bladder or your appendix, I'm your man."

Her eyebrow raised in a perfect arch. "Do I look sick?"

"Hardly. But you could be a hypochondriac. The rich ones sometimes give money so they'll have a nice place to stay during their next anxiety attack. I promised Marian I'd explore every avenue."

"You're doing just great," she said. "I feel as though I'd been strip-searched. All my avenues have been thoroughly probed."

"Are you going to cough up the loot?"

She nodded. "Some. I told you before that if I'm going to live here, I have to establish myself up front as one of the good guys. That makes me eligible for unearned invitations and so on."

"What made you pick Buffalo?"

She turned the big green eyes on him and looked at him shrewdly. "I like it. Or maybe it's better to say that I don't dislike it, which is not true of certain other places. And real estate is cheap, so I can sell my house that's teetering on a precipice in San Francisco and buy something nicer here. As you may have guessed, my heart and Mr. Haynes's no longer beat as one. Before that, we spent some time being no longer a fun couple. I used to come through Buffalo when I was in college, and I decided it was the sort of place where I could be happy."

"Because it's not on the circuit you're used to."

"If you're tired of humanity, maybe it's time to meet new specimens. That's the theory, anyway." She brightened. "Did I pass my examination?"

"Sure," he said. "You're healthy as a young Hereford cow and as sane as Monsignor Schumacher." He glanced at the tables around him and nodded. "Evening, Monsignor." He turned back to her. "I think you'll like it here, at least for a time. It's smaller than you'd think, and people are clannish. But you're the sort of person who makes a good impression, and anybody who comes here voluntarily has passed the first test."

"And you've passed yours," she said. The caterers arrived and dealt out plates of food from a cart, leaning down to mutter into each person's ear, "Careful, the plate is very hot."

She tasted the salmon on her plate and said, "You can go unplug the equipment. It's very good."

"That's Marian's fault. She's always destroying cherished traditions. Usually after these things we used to spend half the night admitting people, giving upper GIs and so on. I have no idea what we'll do with ourselves."

She looked at him, her chin resting on her hands. "That brings me to something I'm a bit concerned about myself."

"Oh?" he said.

"Well, it's kind of embarrassing. I leased this big black Mercedes when I got to town, because I figured it would be good on snow and ice. But I'm not very good with it. I managed to steer it to the hospital okay, but about half an hour ago I went out to get my makeup bag from the front seat . . ."

Carey's lips slowly, involuntarily curved upward.

"This is nothing to smile about. I backed into an empty parking space and hurried to get inside, so I wouldn't be late and get stared at by a lot of people who knew each other. There's a color code and a sign, but I guess I didn't see it because I backed in. Anyway, I guess it was for some kind of emergency vehicle, and the police towed my car away. Why are you smiling?"

Carey's smile grew, and he began to chuckle.

"Are you some kind of sadist?"

"No," said Carey. "I'm very sorry. I saw your car when I got here, and I wondered whether I should say something. That's all."

"Then why on earth didn't you?" she asked. "I would have moved it in a second."

He looked down at his hands, then forced his eyes to meet her stare. "I didn't want to seem like a jerk. It was my parking space."

It took two breaths for her face to register confusion, then shock, then understanding. Her eyes sparkled, and her laugh was clear and musical. It seemed to linger on her lips. "You know where I can get a ride to the impound lot after this thing ends?"

"It's the least I can do."

20

Ultimately, it seemed to Seaver, all investigations came down to staring through a pane of glass at some doorway late at night. Sometimes it was sitting in a car that smelled like old cigarettes, and sometimes it was renting a rat's nest of an office like this one, barring the door, and trying to drink enough coffee out of styrofoam cups to stay awake until something happened.

This time the doorway was on a little storefront with a big sign that said OPEN TWENTY-FOUR HOURS, so the surveillance was worse than it had usually been in the old days. And Manhattan presented special problems. You couldn't sit on a street in a parked car for twelve hours without collecting a stack of tickets, and even if you did, there wasn't much chance you could use the car to follow anybody. Suspects in Manhattan scuttled underground to slip into subway trains, or stepped into yellow cabs that barely came to a complete stop before they were off again on a long street that looked like a river of identical yellow cabs, each of them blowing its horn and weaving erratically to keep going ten miles an hour faster than the speed limit. Or the suspect veered into a doorway a hundred feet away and vanished into a building that had fourteen elevators and sixty floors. Cars weren't much use. The quarry had to be stalked on foot and not taken down until he was indoors, away from the hundreds of faces that were always visible on the street.

Seaver had mailed a small package addressed to Valued Cardholder, Box 345, 7902 Elizabeth Street, New York, NY

10003. The outer wrapping was bright orange with iridescent yellow stripes on it, so he would have no trouble spotting it when the mail was picked up. He couldn't sit here waiting for the dark-haired woman to show up in the flesh. There was a better than even chance that the mail would be picked up by some intermediary, and Seaver would have to follow the package.

If the woman had been hiding fugitives for anything like the eight or nine years since Miranda's reincarnation, then the woman must have built some high walls between her and people like Stillman. She couldn't let people like him find her easily. She would know what Seaver had known—that even though some part of a career criminal's stunted brain believed that some day she might be his last chance of surviving, the reason he would need her at all had a lot to do with his inability to choose a future benefit over an extra pack of cigarettes right now.

Seaver was prepared for the intermediary. Inside the package was an expensive sports watch packed with a photocopy of a typed message explaining to Valued Cardholder that it was a reward from Visa for using a credit card. Inside the watch, and running off its battery, was a small radio transmitter with a range of a thousand yards.

If Seaver got lucky, the dark-haired woman might strap the watch to her wrist. Even if she didn't like it that much, she would at least see it was too good to throw away, so she would shove it into a drawer in her apartment. It didn't matter. As soon as she had it, he would have her. When he had her, he would have Hatcher.

Seaver reached over to the desk and pulled the plastic top off the next styrofoam cup of coffee. It was not much warmer than the air around it now, the white powdery substance that symbolized milk already beginning to coagulate in little gooey lumps that floated just under the oily surface. He covered it again and walked to the sink, ran the water until it was steaming hot, stopped the drain, filled the sink a few inches, held the cup in the water, and looked around for something heavy enough to keep the cup from floating up and tipping over.

He could find nothing in the little bathroom to hold it down, so he took the extra ammunition clip out of his pocket and carefully placed it on the lid. Since he had nothing else to do, he used the opportunity to urinate. That was another problem with doing surveillance at this stage of his career. He had not sat around like this drinking quarts of stale coffee in at least ten years, and his kidneys were treating it as a new and unpleasant experience.

He yawned, zipped up his pants, took his coffee cup out of the water, and set it on the edge of the sink while he washed his hands. When he carried the cup back to the window he could still see the bright orange package through the bronze and glass door of the woman's mailbox, so he sat down and took a sip.

He had a perfect view of the small shop from his office window. His elevation placed the rows of mailboxes in his field of vision, and he could see the surface of the counter and part of the workspace behind it where bored employees wrapped, weighed, and stacked packages, sorted letters, and sent faxes. The streetlamp in front of the shop threw a splash of light on the sidewalk outside the door.

He sipped the lukewarm coffee and watched. At this time of night, so few customers came in that his cop's brain wondered whether the purpose of keeping the shop open might be that other customers besides the dark-haired woman were doing something illegal: leave your money in some other mailbox on Tuesday, and come back on Wednesday and pick up your heroin from your own. But he had watched the boxes for a full cycle of shifts now, and he had detected no signs that he could interpret as commerce. Nobody who came in to open a mailbox seemed to take the time to look around him first for cops or thieves. Nobody seemed to bring anything in with him that ended up in one of the other mailboxes.

It was nearly midnight when he recognized the new clerk coming up out of the subway and walking toward the shop for the changing of the guard. The skinny kid with jeans and a black T-shirt came in the door, and the older man collected his belongings—a greenish brown sport coat that looked as though it had been picked up off a rag pile and a paperback book that he put in the side pocket so the coat hung down and made him look like the scarecrow he was.

But then he did something that made Seaver put his coffee cup on the desk and lean forward. He stepped behind the mailboxes. Seaver saw him reach into Box 345 and start sliding envelopes into a big padded mailer. Seaver watched as the orange and yellow package disappeared with the others.

Seaver snatched up his coat, stepped to the door, and ran for the stairwell. As he hurried down the steps, he switched on his receiver and watched the direction indicator for a base reading. He slipped it into his pocket, stepped out into the darkness at the side of the building, and walked slowly toward the street, his eyes on the lighted window of the little shop. He paused in the shadow until he saw the older man come out the door carrying the mailer under his arm.

Seaver followed the man along the dimly lighted street for three blocks, staying close to the buildings, sometimes keeping his silhouette obscured by the irregular outlines of pilasters and ornamental brickwork on the facades, sometimes pausing in the alcoves at store entrances to be invisible for a time.

The man turned left onto another street and Seaver broke into a run to shorten the man's lead. As he turned the corner, he saw he had misinterpreted the man's intentions. He wasn't on his way to meet the dark-haired woman and hand her the mail. He was walking in a diagonal course along the broad, empty sidewalk toward the curb, where there was a big blue U.S. Postal Service mailbox. When the man had taken the woman's mail with him, Seaver had been sure he wasn't sending it off again. But he was definitely heading for that mailbox. The woman must have given him orders not to leave any packages lying around the store with her forwarding address on them.

Seaver's mind was flooded with disappointment at the unwelcome news. There would be more airline trips, more nights sitting and watching doorways. No, it was worse than that. If that package went into the postal system before Seaver knew the address, he would have no idea whether it was going to an apartment a block away or to Ethiopia. He had to keep that man from reaching the mailbox.

Seaver called, "Excuse me."

The man glanced over his shoulder and straightened. He was surprised to see Seaver suddenly so close. He kept going, a little more quickly.

"Wait!" shouted Seaver. "Sir?"

The man went more quickly, his long legs taking steps that made him strain. Seaver had made a mistake by not letting the man get a clear look at him right away, on a lighted street. In the light, Seaver could easily have passed for a prosperous middle-aged executive coming home from a restaurant. But the man was acting as though he expected to be mugged. Instead of stopping, he went faster. He seemed to want to get rid of the package so he would have both hands free to defend himself. It didn't matter what he thought he was doing, or what Seaver had planned. The man was hurrying toward the mailbox.

Seaver walked faster, screwing the silencer onto the end of the barrel. "Sir?" he called. The man had obviously made his decision. Now he seemed to want to reach the big mailbox and use it as a shield.

Seaver stopped on the sidewalk with his feet apart, bent his knees slightly, extended both arms to steady his right hand, blew the air out of his lungs to keep the carbon dioxide from causing a tremor, and squeezed the trigger. The gun jumped upward and Seaver heard the spitting sound.

The man pitched forward. The mailer fell and slid a few feet, but the man had forgotten it. He was writhing on the sidewalk, bleeding.

As Seaver ran to finish him, he saw that a car had appeared near the far end of the block. He clamped the pistol under his left arm, knelt over the man, and said, "I tried to warn you. There was a guy in a car shooting. Lie still now."

The man seemed to barely hear him. He was squeezing his

eyes in an agonized squint and rolling his head from side to side on the pavement. Seaver glanced down at the blood on the shirt. It was bright crimson and bubbly, so the bullet must have passed through a lung.

Seaver saw the car pull up to the curb. It was a yellow cab. "Is he all right?" called the driver. Seaver could see only the dark shape of a torso and an oval head.

"He just tripped and fell," said Seaver. "He'll be okay in a minute." The wounded man struggled to reach out his arm toward the cab, and moaned.

"Does he need to go to the hospital?"

"No," said Seaver. "I'll take care of him." He returned his eyes to the wounded man, shifted his position slightly, and rested his right forearm on his knee. If Seaver heard the click of a car door latch, he would move the hand a few more inches and grasp the gun. He would use the time it took the driver to walk around the rear of the car into the open to pivot and fire.

The driver shook his head doubtfully, then stared anxiously ahead through his windshield for a moment. Just as Seaver acknowledged that he now had the task of killing this one too, the driver pushed a button to roll up the window and accelerated up the street.

Seaver felt an abrupt, wrenching tug, and realized that the wounded man was trying to pry the pistol out of his armpit. Seaver's right hand swatted the man's fingers away, and he straightened his legs so quickly that he nearly toppled backward. He pulled out the pistol, aimed downward, and shot the man through the chest. This time he judged that he had hit the heart. The man gave one spasmodic jerk and went limp. Seaver gave him a kick, but it prompted no reaction. Seaver decided there was no reason to keep wondering, so he fired one more round into the man's head, put the pistol into his inner coat pocket, picked up the padded mailer, stuck it into his belt at the small of his back, and covered it with his coat.

Seaver turned and looked around him. The little discreet sur-veillance had degenerated into a bloody disaster, a tangle of complications and obstacles and hazards. There was a narrow alley between two buildings to his right, but there was a high iron fence to block it. He could never lift a grown man's body above his head and push it over the fence. He thought he might be able to carry the body a short distance, but how could he do that without attracting attention? As he considered the problem, he saw another set of headlights come around the corner at the far end of the block and head toward him. He saw the lights jump upward as the car accelerated, but then they dipped and stayed low. The car was going to stop.

Seaver stared at it, and saw the color of the paint. It was yellow, and the little marquee on the roof was visible now. It was the same cab. Seaver waved his arm frantically, and the cab pulled to the curb. The driver stepped out, slammed the door, and looked at him over the roof.

"He's hurt worse than I thought," said Seaver. "We need to get him to a hospital after all."

The driver trotted around the rear of the car and opened the back-seat door. Seaver knelt and began to lift the torso of the body. "Give me a hand."

The driver squatted to lift the feet. He backed into the cab and set the legs on the back seat, but that gave him a look at the chest. "This guy's bleeding all over. He's been stabbed or something."

Seaver's hand was already in motion. The gun swung out, he fired into the driver's belly, then raised the barrel higher and fired into the driver's chest, then into his head.

Seaver returned the gun to his coat pocket and walked around the car to get into the driver's seat. He turned on the meter, then drove the cab to the rear of the building he had rented and parked it. He went up the stairs, through his little office, and into the bathroom. He washed his hands and face thoroughly, then examined his suit, shoes, and shirt for blood spatters. He saw none, but wiped his shoes with toilet paper anyway and flushed it down the toilet. He took a big wad of dampened toilet paper and wiped off the gun and wrapped it in toilet paper, then went about the little suite wiping off all of the surfaces he had ever touched. He collected all of his old coffee

cups and lids, boxes, and wrappers, and locked the door behind
him before he left. He dropped the trash in the Dumpster at the
rear of the building.

Seaver started the cab and drove at least twelve blocks south
before he found a dark alley between two stores that met a
second, longer alley, so he could turn and leave it beside a
loading dock. Then he walked a mile, stuffed the still-wrapped
gun into the fishy-smelling center of a trash bag inside a
garbage can, and replaced the lid. He walked another mile
before he came to a theater. People were streaming out onto the
street, walking toward parking lots and climbing into taxicabs.
He attached himself to the crowd, climbed into a cab, and had
it take him to an intersection not far from his hotel.

When he was inside his room, he pulled the mailer out of the
back of his belt. He opened it and poured the mail out on the
bed. The envelopes were all addressed to Stewart Hoffstedder,
C.P.A. That was something that gave him hope, at first, because Stillman had said something about a man's name. But
the mail was almost all bills, as though they were for a real
C.P.A. The bills were all for credit cards in different names—
female, male, even corporate names. Were they all for this
woman?

A horrible thought came to him. Stillman's brain was
probably not a perfectly developed organ to begin with. Since
the age of ten it had probably been shorted out by drugs and
jarred by blows. Maybe he had gotten the number wrong.
Maybe this was some real C.P.A., a business manager who
paid bills for a number of clients. The mail in the pouch
seemed to have nothing to do with the dark-haired woman. It
was possible that Seaver had scared Stillman so badly that he
had cooked up a box number on the spot.

Seaver laid all of the bills out on the bed in a row and
began to study them, looking desperately for similarities. On
August 8, Wendy Wasserman had rented a car in Missoula,
Montana. On August 10, Michael Phelan had rented a hotel
room in Potomac, Montana. Katherine Webster had paid for
lunch in Condon, Montana, the next morning. Seaver rocked

21

Carey drove up to the gate of the impound lot and parked. Susan stepped to the gate and rang the bell. Carey could hear the old-fashioned jangling noise a hundred feet away in the little shack in the center of the lot, and that meant trouble. There were no lights on in the windows. He stepped to the gate and stood beside her feeling useless.

Then he walked along the fence and around the corner. There was a small sign that said, LOT HOURS 6:00 A.M. TO 10:00 P.M. He walked back to Susan and frowned apologetically. "It's closed until six in the morning."

"No." She seemed to see herself from outside. She was standing in a dark, desolate part of the city in the middle of the night, wearing three-inch heels and a strapless evening gown. Slowly, the beautiful smile reappeared. She let her arms come out from her sides in a "look at me" gesture.

He said, "Come on. I'll take you home."

They got into his car and he backed out of the drive. "You can't really do that," she said. "It's all the way out in Orchard Park. If you could just drop me off at a hotel near here, you can go home and get some sleep."

"Why would you stay in a hotel?" asked Carey. "It's ridiculous." Why was it that people who didn't want to be any trouble always ended up being plenty?

"It's now after midnight. If you drive me all the way to my apartment, it'll be two before I'm asleep, and probably three before you are. So I'd get three hours' sleep, call a cab, and for eighty dollars or so, he'd drive me to the other end of the county to get my car. That's if I could even get a cab in Orchard Park at five in the morning. But if I stay here, I can be on the spot when the lot opens and drive myself home."

"Here's the problem with that. Look around you—factories, warehouses, and an impound lot. It isn't very scenic in the day-time, so there's a shortage of good hotels around here. By 'good' I don't mean famous, I mean safe."

"Oh," she said.

"On the other hand, I happen to have a perfectly good house about twenty minutes away, with six spare bedrooms, five bathrooms, and clean towels." He held his breath, hoping she would have a better idea.

"I hate to put you to that kind of trouble."

That meant "yes." He had no choice but to push the offer as graciously as he could manage at this hour, and make it sound easy. "I have to be at the hospital by seven, and I can take you to get your car on the way." He glanced at her. "I might even be able to scare up some clothes for you that won't look strange at dawn—like the bedraggled party-goer at the end of an Italian movie. Jane's about your size."

She looked at him with what seemed to be curiosity. "You would do that?"

"Sure." What choice did he have?

"Won't your—won't Jane feel . . . uncomfortable?"

"What for?" he said too quickly. He had been concentrating on his own discomfort, so he had not yet thought about what Jane would feel. He cautiously considered the subject. He had a sudden vision of Jane's eyes resting on Susan, taking an inventory—the long, golden hair, the little wisps on the nape of the long, delicate neck where they had escaped from the place where they had been tied, the impossibly smooth ivory skin—then focusing on Carey. But Jane's look would be completely unjustified.

What he was doing was a simple act of kindness—no, it was even more innocent: an obligatory refusal to be unkind. He imagined Jane hearing his thoughts, and the gaze turned ironic. No, he thought. That wasn't the way Jane would react at all—

unless she was just teasing him. He was being irrational and unfair to her. She would never give him that look just because the person he helped happened to be female.

Then he admitted to himself that his deepest motive for taking her home with him had been provided by the needle on his gas gauge. He hadn't insisted on driving her to her place, where she belonged, because he was afraid he wouldn't be able to find an open gas station at this hour on the long, unfamiliar drive to Orchard Park. He might run out of gas, and then they'd both be stranded.

He realized he was taking too much time inside his own head. "If she were here, she would be the one asking you to stay. She's always doing things like this." It sounded true to him, as far as it went. He couldn't quite get himself to feel certain that Jane would invite a woman who looked like Susan to stay in the house while she wasn't there.

She looked at him closely. "I'd feel a lot better about it if I heard her say it. I'd hate to get you in trouble."

He smiled and shook his head. "I'm not going to call her in the middle of the night to wake her up and ask her permission, no. But I'll mention it the next time I talk to her." He drove onto the boulevard and accelerated. "Of course, the first few times you meet her, you'll have to get used to my calling you 'Sister Mary Boniface.' "

She laughed the melodious, liquid laugh again. "Oh, well. I guess I'd rather just be your secret."

Carey was still contemplating those words as he pulled into his driveway. He idled near the front door, where he usually parked in the summer, then found himself touching the gas pedal again to let the car glide the rest of the way up the long driveway before he stopped again at the old carriage house, out of sight of the street. There was no sense piquing the neighbors' curiosity, he thought. The fact that what he was doing was innocent didn't make it a worse story.

He opened Susan's door, led the way to the back entry, unlocked the house, and let her enter first. He reached over her shoulder to flip the light switch just as she stopped to keep from stepping into a dark, unfamiliar room. It would have been much better if they had collided hard, but instead his body met hers softly. "Oops," he said. "Excuse me."

She half-turned to give him an utterly unreadable look, then stepped into the kitchen, looking around her. "Great kitchen," she said. "Do you entertain a lot?"

"No," he said. "At least I don't think we do. Jane might let me know I'm wrong at any time. It's big because that's the way they were in the old days. Everybody hung around the kitchen because it was warm."

She said, "Late eighteenth century?"

"The structure might be that old. Of course, it's been remodeled."

"When?"

"Beats me. If contractors worked the way they do now, they probably started in 1850 and finished in 1950."

He flipped a second light switch up as he went, but when he reached the doorway into the dining room, he paused to let her get a head start. She lingered.

He detected that she was looking toward the cabinets on the wall. He said, "Can I offer you a drink?"

She pretended to decide, then smiled. "Sure. It's a cinch I'm not driving."

"I don't have a lot here, so we'll have to rough it. Let's see. Malt scotch. McCallan. Terrific stuff. Makes you want to strap on your claymore and march against the Duke of Cumberland. Vodka. It's Stolichnaya, but I've run my Geiger counter over it to be sure it was made before the Chernobyl reactor went. Gin, of course. There's also some vermouth if you're good at making martinis. I've seen every James Bond movie, and mine still taste like poison. The usual mixers. Cognac. Wine and champagne in the refrigerator."

"Did you say champagne?"

"I think I did." He opened the refrigerator and found it. He set it on the counter and lingered over removing the foil and the wire. He would have to remember to buy another bottle. Jane would remember putting it in the refrigerator, and the missing champagne was not the best way to lead into telling her there had been a guest. He removed the cork, plucked two tulip glasses from the cupboard, and filled them.

The sound of the telephone was jarring. He snatched the receiver off the hook on the wall. "Hello?"

The operator said, "Will you accept a collect call from Jane?"

"Yes I will," he said.

"Hi, Doc." It was Jane.

"Hi. I was hoping you'd call." He looked at Susan as he said it, and she tactfully strolled off toward the dining room, then suddenly turned around and mouthed the word, "Bathroom?"

He pointed through the living room at the far hallway, and she walked in that direction. He felt relieved. "Where are you?"

Her voice was apologetic. "You know I can't say."

"That isn't what I wanted to know anyway," he said. "I should have said 'How.' How are you?"

"Tired of missing you. Tired of . . . all this."

"That's what I wanted to hear. When are you coming home?"

He heard her sigh. "I just don't know. I wish it were now. But I really don't want to have to do this again. And I really don't want to see this guy's picture in a newspaper."

"Or yours, either."

"You know why I'm doing this," she said. "Just put yourself in my place."

He craned his neck to look out the kitchen doorway and through the dining room. Susan wasn't visible. "Just put yourself in mine."

Her voice sounded worried, pleading almost. "Please, Carey. This is an aberration. It's the last time, a job that I thought was finished, and it wasn't. As soon as I've got him tucked away, I'm done. We'll start over again, from the beginning."

He was silent for a long time. "All right," he said. "One last fling."

"See?" she said. "I knew I could get around you if I batted my eyelashes loud enough."

He knew it had been meant to be funny, an ironic comment on men and women that they were both supposed to laugh at, but he snorted mirthlessly. He tried to think of words that would take his mind off the worry and the emptiness he felt. He stared at the kitchen floor. "Well, I'm exhausted," he said. "Tonight was the benefit for the children's wing."

She gasped, and he began to wish he had not mentioned it. "It was?" Then she said, "At least I missed that. What a relief." He knew he was supposed to laugh at that too, and he was sure he would have, if she were standing here in the kitchen, where he knew she was safe.

"Yep," he said. "You lucked out again."

"Did Marian Fleming ask about me?"

"Of course," he said. "So did a lot of other people. I told them you were in Morocco taking a belly-dancing course."

"Oh, no. I used that excuse last time. Now I'll have to do penance with committee work for the next thirty years."

"Maybe not," he said cheerfully. "But if you don't know how to belly dance, you're going to have to fake a hip injury."

Jane said, "I'll work on it." She said quietly, "I'd better go."

He said, "Do you have to?"

"I'm afraid so."

"Just let me know if you need anything." He knew he had said it that way out of self-pity. She had never needed anything from him, and he was positive that she would never have asked if she had.

"I love you," she said.

"Me too." He hung up the telephone and walked to the counter. He saw the champagne glass and it reminded him that he had a guest. He picked up the champagne and walked toward the living room, but she hadn't reappeared. He set the champagne bottle on the mantel and stared into the fireplace.

In the den off the bathroom, Linda heard the click and dialed the operator. "Can I have the time and charges on that call, please?"

The operator said, "Two minutes and seventeen seconds, billed at three minutes. That's four dollars and eighty-eight cents."

"For three minutes? That can't be right."

"There's a two ninety-five surcharge for an operator-assisted collect call, ma'am."

"Okay, but it wasn't international or something. What are the night rates from Billings?"

"That might be your mistake. The call wasn't from Billings."

"That might be your mistake. She thinks she's in Billings, and I'd bet on her. How could she be wrong about that?"

"It was Salmon Prairie, Montana. It's the same area code, but it's a different calling zone, and the pay phone is owned by another carrier."

"Oh, I see," said Linda. "My mistake after all. Thanks."

"You're welcome." The voice was imperturbable, but chilly.

Linda hung up and hurried down the hallway into the living room. She found Carey sitting on the couch looking at a magazine. He tossed it onto the coffee table. "Sorry. That was my wife."

"You didn't tell her, did you?"

"Tell her what?"

"About me. Sister Mary Boniface."

It caught him by surprise. "Oops. You're right. Forgot. Well, I'll have to tell her tomorrow." He had been wrenched from a sad contemplation of how close Jane had sounded, and how far away she was. Now he felt reluctant to let this stranger see that he was annoyed at himself for forgetting to tell Jane about her. He hated it when Jane called from a pay phone. It was impossible for a person to remember everything he had to say in a couple of minutes.

"You aren't going to tell her," said Susan. The smile was mysterious and amused now.

He was startled, and it irritated him. "Why do you say that?"

"Because this was the time to tell her, and now you won't be able to, because it will look as though you were hiding me."

The smile had a trace of sympathy now, the full lips pursed. Then there was mischief in the eyes. "If you try to tell her tomorrow, she'll think that you didn't tell her now because you were hoping to get lucky tonight."

"That's ridiculous," he said. "She's not that way at all."

"That's how women think," she said. "You shouldn't have decided to take one on full-time if you don't know how they work."

He suspected that she would have seemed bright and witty at about eight o'clock, but right now, he was not in the mood to be the butt of any more feminine teasing. "Well, I'd better show you where your room is. It's getting late."

She stood, but she took her glass with her and sipped from it as she headed for the stairs. "Just what I was thinking."

He led the way up the stairs and turned right to take her down the hallway. "This is the best of the guest rooms," he said. He flipped the light on and walked her into the room.

She sat on the bed, bounced a little, looked at the walls, the curtains over the big window. "It's very pretty."

He pointed to the door on the side wall. "Your bathroom is right there. Everything you need should be in the drawers—clean towels, shampoo, soap, even toothbrushes."

Susan glanced in that direction with little interest. She set her champagne glass on the nightstand, stood up, turned her back on him, and bent her neck forward. "Unzip me."

Carey stepped forward. He tried to lift her long hair out of the way without touching her neck, and carefully grasped the zipper without touching her back. He tugged the zipper down eight inches, to where he judged she could reach it, and stepped back. "There. If there's anything you can't find, I'll be in the room at the other end of the hall. Good night."

He began his retreat, but she said, "Not so fast." He stopped and turned. She was holding her hair up off her neck. "What do you think I am—a contortionist? I can't reach that."

"Sorry." He stepped forward, stopped three feet from her, reached out, and pulled the zipper down a few more inches. There was an instant—perhaps two seconds—when several things seemed to happen at once. She was still holding her hair up when she turned a little to say over her shoulder, "That's more like it." But her slight turn inside the dress seemed to spread the two unzipped sides of it apart. There was a tantalizing view of the white skin of the lower part of her back, where it softened and curved inward toward her hips. But worse, the front of the dress had nothing to hold it up. She quickly released her hair and hugged the dress to cover herself, but not before Carey had been presented with a glimpse of her left breast in profile.

"Good night," Carey muttered. As he backed quickly out the door and closed it, the last thing he saw was Susan Haynes facing him, holding the front of her dress up, her big green eyes looking into his with that knowing, amused stare. When he reached his own room at the end of the hall, he closed the door and leaned against it for a moment. The stare was still with him. "Taking her to a hotel wouldn't have been such a bad idea," he muttered. He locked his bedroom door, then undressed and got into bed. He lay in the dark with his eyes closed, but what he had seen came back to him again and again. "That," he thought, "is what the end of a marriage looks like."

At three o'clock, he awoke, lying on the bed on his back. He imagined for a moment that he could feel Jane's soft, silky hair on his arm. He turned to touch her, then remembered. He lay for a moment feeling sad and empty, and then he realized he could hear a voice. Someone was talking.

Carey sat up quickly and looked around him, but he saw nothing. He switched on the lamp beside the bed and squinted against the searing light to see the door. It was still closed, and the room was empty. It must have been a dream. As he reached for the lamp, he heard the voice again. It had to be Susan Haynes. It didn't seem possible that there could be somebody here with her. He got to his feet and walked into the hallway. As he reached the second-floor landing, he followed her voice and looked over the railing. She was facing away, sitting on the couch near the fireplace. The sight of her obliterated the lingering clouds of sleep. She appeared to be wearing only a bedsheet, her legs folded under her and her purse beside her. She turned to look up and the green eyes focused on him, and then she hung up the telephone.

She put a plastic card back into her purse, fastened the white sheet under her arm, and stood up. As he looked at her from a distance like this, the thought that overwhelmed all others was her perfection—the long shiny hair, the smooth, white shoulders and arms, the graceful veiled curve of hip and thigh. When she turned toward him, he saw she was aware that he had been staring at her intently. In order to look up at him she tossed her hair in a gesture that should not have been intriguing because it was self-conscious and calculated, but it was mesmerizing because she was posing for him, trying to look more beautiful. "I was just calling my machine in San Francisco. I didn't want to use the phone upstairs and wake you up. Hope you don't mind."

"Not at all," he said. "I just wondered—"

"Don't worry, though. I used a credit card, so it won't be printed on your phone bill."

He felt a sick chill. It had not occurred to him before that he had somehow become a man who was in the business of hiding evidence from his wife: first the champagne, and now the telephone bill.

Susan seemed to forget about him for a moment. She hitched her shoulder uncomfortably, then did a poor job of retucking the bedsheet she was using as a sarong. She frowned, unwrapped a little of it, and tried again. It was as though she had unaccountably forgotten she was not alone. But then she abruptly looked up into his eyes, pretended to follow his line of sight and be surprised to find her own eyes looking down at the translucent sheet that covered her body. As she tucked the sheet under her arm she looked up again with the knowing, amused expression.

"Something else on your mind?" The smile was still on her face as she moved up the stairs toward him. She walked so lightly that her feet seemed not to touch, as though she were floating.

He shook his head, as much to clear it as to communicate with her. "No," he said, already backing away. "No. I was afraid it was a burglar or something. But it was just you. See you in the morning." As he walked back to his room and closed his door, he wondered why it was that virtue had to be so clumsy and inept.

22

Earl sat up and looked out his hotel window at Pete Hatcher's car. He was through staring at its dusty finish, each day picking out new spots of birdshit on the windshield with his binoculars, never seeing a human being go near it. Now he needed to think ahead. He unfolded his road map and studied it, then picked up the telephone again and dialed.

He heard the sleep in Lenny's voice. "Yeah?"

"It's me," said Earl. "Listen. I want you to close the place up and get on a plane right away. Get a suite at the Rocky Mountain Lodge in Kalispell, Montana. Stay there until I call. It could be two weeks, or the phone could be ringing when you walk in the door."

Earl could hear rustling noises and groaning. Lenny must be sitting up in bed. Lenny coughed to clear his throat. "The place already is closed up. I went to bed an hour ago. What's up?"

"Did you understand what I said? This isn't a dream."

"Rocky Mountain Lodge in Kalispell, Montana. Wait there for you. Right." Earl could almost hear him thinking. "Hey— Rusty and T-Bone. What do I do with the dogs?"

"Bring them."

Earl hung up before Lenny could start protesting about the difficulty of flying dogs around. If people did it with fancy show dogs, then it certainly wouldn't harm two big, muscular beasts like the Rottweilers, and he didn't care what it did to Lenny.

He walked into the bathroom and turned the water on cold, then stepped under the icy stream. He gasped, then slowly let the water warm up. He was fully awake now, confident that he was thinking clearly. It would take ten minutes to dress, pack, and clean his prints off everything he had touched. It might take another ten minutes to check out and get on the road.

It had not escaped Earl that Linda had been talking in a whispery voice over the telephone at one in the morning. That was three A.M. in Buffalo. Linda would have called with Hatcher's location as soon as she could—the first minute when she could reach a telephone. If she was with this Carey McKinnon at three o'clock in the morning, worried that he would overhear her, then there wasn't much question what they were doing. She had been doing it with him for hours, letting him put it to her until he had used himself up and fallen asleep. This was not a simple flirtation where she got a fact out of him that he wouldn't remember saying and probably didn't even know was a secret. This was a full night of it, her hair probably wet with sweat and his sperm still dripping out of her, sticky and warm when she called to tell Earl.

He was enraged. He hated this man, and he felt a mixture of awe and disgust at Linda. She had said she would do anything to find Pete Hatcher. But what she had done was not brave or cunning. It was pathetic, requiring only a fawning sort of guile and a strong stomach. It was like biting the head off a chicken. She was soiled. Unclean. The only way he was ever going to feel right about this was to make it even. He was going to do the same to Jane Whitefield before he killed her. Then he was going to make Linda go back and watch him drop the hammer on Carey McKinnon. Maybe he would make her go back and do it herself.

He stepped out of the shower, quickly dried himself, and dressed, tossing pieces of clothing into his suitcase as he saw them. Then he remembered the way she had cut him off at the end of the call—quickly, abruptly. It was probably because McKinnon was awake again. He nearly reeled with the sudden realization that it was worse, more humiliating than he had thought. McKinnon was awake. She would have put down the telephone and needed to distract him. She was doing him again right now, this second, while Earl was two thousand miles away in a hotel room. He didn't dare close his eyes, because he knew that the sight of it was forming behind his eyelids.

He slammed his suitcase shut, stepped to the door, and hurried out of the room. He took long, purposeful steps down the hallway toward the check-out counter. He was in a perfect mood to kill somebody.

As Jane walked back to the hotel room along the road through Salmon Prairie, she considered whether she had succeeded in leaving the right kind of trail in the wrong direction. She had charged some plane tickets for flights out of Missoula and Helena to credit cards. The accounts were held by male identities that were unripe enough to attract the attention of a hunter who was using a computer network to search. She had made guaranteed reservations for hotels and rental cars in the destination cities so the charges would be recorded and would appear on credit reports.

Her temptation was to use ten identities to build twenty trails in twenty directions. There was no reason to save false faces for fugitives anymore. This was her last trip. But two identities were the right number. If the chasers picked out both of them, they would think that one was an innocent who was not running from anything but didn't have much of a history. But they couldn't pick out one and ignore the other, so they would split up. If she left twenty trails, they would sense that she had made them all and wait.

Everything about the way they had tracked and cornered Pete Hatcher looked like at least two people. A lone woman might play the broken-car game, pop him on the spot, and walk away, but she wouldn't put him in the trunk and expect to drive him away. There must have been at least one man waiting unseen to do the heavy lifting and solve problems. It wasn't easy to kill an armed cop when he was looking at you.

Jane was almost certain that she had made no mistakes since she had found Hatcher in Montana. They had been on the move for a month, traveling as husband and wife. They had spent a lot of time in the car each day, then used different names in each town where they stopped to check into a motel late in the afternoon. Pete was always visible to motel clerks and guests, but always imperfectly and from a distance. Jane would stand at the counter and sign a name, and Pete would be busy with his head under the lid of the trunk pulling out the suitcases, or under the hood checking the oil. Even if the searchers stopped at the same motels later and asked the right questions, the clerks would not have been able to give them a direction. Jane and Pete had gone slowly, taking detours like tourists who had all summer.

She knew that she was just thinking of reasons to turn Pete loose and go home. Carey had sounded as though her call had depressed him, and the knowledge stung her. When she tried to repeat the conversation now, everything that she had said sounded empty and foolish, and she could do nothing to change it.

Jane stared up the road at the hotel and gave herself a reprimand. The quickest way home was to concentrate on preparing Pete Hatcher for his new life. He had already gotten accustomed to using false names, and he had begun to develop a good sense of how to make himself invisible in public places. He had listened carefully while she had explained how the tricks were done and what to do when they didn't work.

Now she had to teach him something more subtle and difficult. The way he would defeat his enemies was to outlast them. While they were staring at computer screens or loitering late at night in airport baggage areas or sitting in cars outside hotels at check-out time studying each male who came out the door, he had to be somewhere living a normal, reasonably contented life. If he could do that for long enough, they would give up. Even the owners of a casino couldn't keep a team of assassins on the payroll forever to search for one man. And the longer he went without showing any intention of doing them harm, the more pointless the search would seem.

Jane had watched the changes in Pete for several days, and she was satisfied with his progress. When she had picked him up in Billings, his personality had already retreated into him like a turtle's head. Now he was slowly emerging, getting his sense of humor back, looking less like a person recovering from some illness. If she could get him to rebuild himself—not to return to the same old Pete Hatcher, but to see the man he now was as normal—then he had a chance. With a few cosmetic changes and a surrounding establishment—a job, a place to live, a car, a couple of promising friendships—he would be better off than the people who were hunting him.

The last danger that she would have to save him from was the biggest. She had to teach him not to throw away the advantages she had built for him, sink into a depression, and stop trying, or grow so paranoid that he jumped at every shadow and attracted attention. That had been her mistake in Denver. She had sent him off to isolation in a small, dark apartment and effectively severed all of his ties to other human beings. To a man like Pete, who seemed able to maintain a sense of himself only by watching the reflections in other people's eyes, the days of solitude had been like continuous, small doses of poison. She was going to have to keep being his buddy, build up his confidence, and make him strong again.

She reached the gift shop of the hotel and found it had closed hours ago. She continued to the room, gave her familiar knock, and used her eyes, her ears, and the soles of her feet to try to sense where he was at each moment. Finally he opened the door. "Very good," she said as she entered and locked the door. "I couldn't have done anything but fire blind through the door, and I would have missed."

Pete walked back to his chair and sat down. She could see he was watching something on the television that featured a lot of men flying upside down in fighter planes and shouting into radios. "Good," he said. "That's one for me."

"I just walked by the pool," said Jane. "There's nobody in it, and the lights are off."

"Then it's probably a septic tank."

"Nope. There's a diving board. I'm going for a swim. Want

to come?" She found the bathing suit she had worn in Missoula at the bottom of her suitcase. "We'll have to be quiet."

He glanced up from the television screen for a second, then shrugged. "Can't. No suit."

She reached into his suitcase, held up pairs of pants until she found a pair of jeans with a worn knee. "Are you saving these for the Levi Strauss museum?"

He seemed to consider. "I've heard I could get a good price for those in Tokyo. I don't know how to get there, though, so I guess that's out."

"Good thinking," she said. She put her foot on the bed and pulled her boot knife from her ankle, sliced the legs off the jeans, and tossed what was left in Pete's lap. "I'll change in the bathroom. Knock when you've got those on."

He knocked on the door sooner than she had expected. When she came out, she carried the two big towels from the rack by the tub, holding them in front of her casually to disguise the way the suit rode up at the hip. The suit seemed to her to be less modest than she had remembered it, but maybe it was just the unfamiliar feeling of wearing one at night; there was no sun to warm the places that weren't usually uncovered. She plucked the room key off the table. "Here. You have pockets."

He took the key and she approached him in a way that forced him to go out the door first and start across the lawn to the pool. She dropped the towels, then walked down the steps into the warm water at the shallow end of the pool. She ducked down and swam the length of the pool under water. The pool was so dark that when she reached the end, she nearly crashed into him. Her fingertips brushed flesh, and she came up to find his face a few inches from hers. "Sorry," she whispered, then sank, pushed off the wall and glided away again in the silent darkness of the water.

While her momentum was slowing, she felt a shiver of embarrassment. There was no reason for being so squeamish about touching his belly. She was the best friend he had right now, and she had not done it on purpose. She gave a kick and rose to the surface, looking around for him. He was invisible, under the glassy surface somewhere.

With a sudden start she felt his big arm hook around her waist and lift her in the water. She was held against his big body in a feeling that was at once smothering and too pleasantly familiar. She gave a little cry, and he spun her around to face him.

She could see the white teeth in his smile, and the whites of his eyes, much too close. She leaned away, but that brought her pelvis into contact with his, so she jerked back. The white teeth disappeared and she felt the brush of his shaven upper lip and the touch of the soft lips. "Time out," she said, too loudly. She put her hands on his chest, and she was aware of the hard, hairy torso as she pushed him away.

She could see the silhouette of his head and shoulders, but his face was in shadow. "I made a mistake," she said quietly. "I never told you I was married."

She could see him tilt to sink backward into the water like a man blown over by a sudden wind. He rose to the surface floating on his back, took a couple of shallow breaths, and bobbed to his feet again. "I'm the one who made a mistake," he said. "I apologize. Please, forget it ever happened. I didn't know, and . . . I guess that's just me. I meant no harm."

Jane found herself in a depth where her toes brushed the bottom, so she stood on them. "Look, don't overdo it," she said. "It's reassuring to an old bat like me. It's just that—well, you know—I'm taken."

She swam the rest of the way to the shallow end and sat on the bottom step with the water up to her neck. From here the light of a fixture on the wall of the hotel reflected on the surface and she could see him swimming. He was not very graceful, but he was strong, each armstroke pulling him a few feet. She knew he was trying to work out a way to face her after making a pass and being turned down flat. It occurred to her that it was probably a new experience for him.

Jane wished she had never thought of swimming at this hour. The night was unseasonably warm, and she had wanted to get him involved in something that was careless and fun. Now she was afraid he was going to withdraw again. But there was something worse going on, and it was something that she had not prepared herself to defeat. She had almost let it slip out while she was saying no, detected it crowding up behind the other words and put her face into the water to keep it from coming out. It was, "I'm not offended. I don't have anything against sex."

If she weren't married, if this had all happened years ago, she might very well have let Pete Hatcher's hand stay around her waist, might have stayed in the water and waited with great interest for it to move where it pleased. And even worse, if she had not considered the marriage vow unconditional and permanent, Pete was exactly the sort of man she might have chosen to disregard it with, and this was exactly the sort of time and place when it could have happened. The incredibly clear, warm night air with the strange brightness of the stars, the feeling of floating weightless in the dark water might have made it seem to be an exception.

Pete disappeared again and surfaced at her feet. He was smiling tentatively, the water gleaming on his smooth, hard shoulders. "I think we'd better clear the air," he said.

She nodded. "Good idea."

"I'll never put you in a position where you have to feel uncomfortable again."

"Thanks," she said. "I won't do that either. What you did wasn't exactly assault, you know. It was a question. The answer is no, that's all."

"You don't wear a ring, you never mentioned a husband. Maybe because we spent so much time alone, I've been holding you under a magnifying glass. I interpreted a lot of things wrong—movements, words, everything. I like you. You're not like anybody I've ever met, and—"

"Relax," said Jane. "I like you too. I've said that before, and maybe I shouldn't have, or I said it wrong. We'll still be just as close. Maybe closer, because of this. But I'm your sister, not . . . not anybody else. Have we said enough?"

"Hi." The quiet female voice came from the shadow beside the hotel doorway. Jane spun her head and saw the shape of a woman. Jane's muscles tensed, and she let herself slip lower into the water, but the balls of her feet found traction on the rough surface of the pool steps.

"Hi," said Pete. Jane's jaw tightened. If this was the woman who had tried to kill him in Denver, he had just helped her locate him in the dark water.

"Hello," said Jane. Maybe two voices would complicate her directional fix on Pete. She studied the silhouette as it took its first step toward her. The towel was wrapped around the waist like a skirt, but there could easily be a gun tucked in back. Then she saw a second silhouette step from the entrance, and for a half second she was sure. She took in a breath to prepare to move, but the two shapes stepped into the dim swatch of light from the lamp at the same time.

She could tell from their bodies that neither was a young girl—not seventeen or eighteen. The curve of hip and thigh and breast were too pronounced. She could see their faces now, and they were both mildly attractive, but to determine age she needed to see them in bright light, where the texture of the skin would show mileage. The thinner one with red hair stuck her toe in the water near Jane's face. "Oh, good. It's really warm," she said. She whisked the towel off and tossed it on the deck. Jane was satisfied that this one was not armed. The green two-piece bathing suit would not have hidden a razor blade.

The second one took off her towel and knelt to touch the water with her fingers. "You're right. It's perfect. Just like a bath." She was wearing a suit that Jane guessed had probably come from the same store, but on this one it looked even more obvious, almost indecent. She was shorter and blond, with big white breasts that seemed painfully confined by the top, and when she stood to dive in, Jane saw the lower part of the suit as a blue line bisecting a heart-shaped flash of white buttocks.

The blond one surfaced near Pete. "I hope you don't mind our coming in with you. We saw you from our room, and it just looked so good . . ."

"Not at all," said Pete. "We're glad to have you. This way we don't have to wonder if we're crazy, because you are too."

"I'm Pam," she said. Jane could hear something in the woman's voice. Then she decided it just sounded tense because she was treading water and in the effort her throat muscles had tightened. "And this is Carol."

Jane tried to analyze her unpleasant feeling. It was the way bodyguards must feel when their charges decided to go into a crowd. The bodyguard's adrenaline flowed, her muscles contracted for action, and then the threat turned into a mere distraction.

Pete said, "I'm Jim Holstra. This is . . . Mary. She's my sister." Jane's distracted thoughts suddenly crystalized. He was using her own words.

"Oh, really?" said Carol. She half-turned toward Jane and smiled faintly. "You two must get along pretty well, to travel together."

Jane had no direction of escape from this conversation. Was he doing what she thought he was doing? The distraction had blossomed into an annoyance. "Yes," she said.

Her mind was prickling with irritation. They were gently closing doors on her. She reminded herself that whoever they were, they weren't killers. They were making it obvious that they were intrigued by Pete. If anyone asked later if they'd seen him, they could hardly forget, but what could they say? She couldn't take them seriously as a threat to Pete's safety. She could not think of a reason why they seemed so threatening to her.

The one with the red hair glided out into the deep water and bent at the hips. Her bottom broke the surface and then her feet, and she disappeared in the direction of Pete and the blonde. Jane had to fight some inner resistance to bring the names back. The blonde was Pam; the redhead Carol. In a few seconds Carol emerged again, beside Pete. For a minute the three held on to the tile in the deep, shadowy end of the pool. She couldn't hear what they said. Then Pete floated out into the center.

Jane saw the copper head slip very close to the yellow head, cup a hand, and whisper something. The blonde gave a little squeal, and they started whispering again, then giggled like two unappealing children in a conspiracy. Then they began to swim slowly on either side of Pete. She stared at the two of them, and found herself thinking, Wait until he gets them under the light.

She was horrified at her thought. She was acting as though she were jealous. For the first time she was glad he had offered himself so she had gotten the opportunity to turn him down and acquit herself of that charge. Why was she suddenly feeling angry? The anger didn't seem entirely real. It occurred to her that it might be her mind's way of protecting her from something else, and she could even identify what that something was. It was regret at the loss of something that never could have been, something that would have been beautiful, but was now being transformed into something tawdry. Why did she call it tawdry?

She moved to the top of the steps and she realized that she had been unconsciously moving away, to escape the place where this was happening. She shivered when the air touched her skin. She stopped. If she left, went back to the room, these two almost certainly weren't going to try to kill Pete Hatcher. But if she weren't present to control the situation, they might ask him questions he was not prepared to answer, or even attract attention that would get him killed.

She felt the urge to hear what they were saying. She slipped back into the water and drifted toward them. Suddenly there was splashing. Pete was out of the pool walking toward the hotel room. He opened the door and disappeared. Jane looked after him in confusion.

The two women suddenly appeared on both sides of her, heading for the steps. "Your brother is really something." Pam laughed. Jane altered it: little turned-up nose, pink all over—Spam.

"Yes," said Jane. "He's a lot of fun." She loathed them.

"Aren't you coming?" asked the other one, turning to the side to wring out the long copper hair. She seemed hopeful.

"Coming where?"

"To our place, for a drink."

"Your place?" asked Jane. She let her feet touch and began to walk along between them.

"Yeah," said Spam. "We've got a little suite, and we've got supplies."

Jane's head began to ache, but she hid her distaste at the idea. It was after one in the morning. If these two got tipsy and festive, they could be loud enough to get Pete arrested. Then there would be fingerprints, public records for the killers to find. "Sure," said Jane. "We'll stop by for one drink."

She saw the look that passed between Carol and Pam. They were not pleased.

Jane was still twenty feet from the door of the hotel room when it opened and Pete stepped out wearing a dry pair of jeans and a T-shirt, carrying some glasses. He walked to a room two doors from theirs and waited while Carol unlocked it. She considered calling to him, but it would have to be loud if she wanted him to hear it. She tried to catch his eye, but he was looking down, as though he were staring at the lock.

The two women were busy pretending they didn't know he was looking at them, and they seemed to enjoy the task, giving little shimmy-shivers they could blame on the cold, then tiptoeing into the room ahead of him.

Jane stepped into her room. She stripped off the wet suit quickly in the bathroom and hung it in the shower. She glanced at her own naked body in the mirror and caught herself making the comparison that seemed inevitable at this strange instant in her life. It made her feel a little better: she was not the hag she was feeling like. She was pretty.

She stepped into a pair of jeans and pulled a sweatshirt over her head. At the door she stopped, stood absolutely still, and took a breath. Why am I doing this? Because if I sit in this room alone, I could wake up alone and wish I had kept him from getting himself killed.

She blew out the breath, closed the door behind her, and walked to the women's room. The light was on, so she was sure it was the right one. She knocked. The door opened a crack, and she pushed it cautiously to come inside. The connecting door to the next room was open, and a dim light was on in there too. Carol, the copper-haired one, emerged from the next room still in her bathing suit, set two glasses of brown liquor and bubbles on the table, and headed into the bathroom. She stopped in front of the mirror and began to blow-dry her hair with a loud dryer. She yelled over it, "Where are you two from?"

Jane picked up the drink that was closest to her and walked to the doorway of the bathroom. "More important, where are Jim and Pam now?"

Carol clicked off the dryer and began brushing her hair, an amused little smile on her face. "Didn't they come in there?" Then she stopped brushing. "Why, that little . . ."

Jane turned toward the open connecting door and Carol stepped to her side. "If you can't see them, do you really want to go next door looking for them?"

"Probably not." She took an experimental sip of her drink. It was warm and sweet, like bug repellent.

"Are you really his sister?"

"Sure."

"You don't look like him."

"Different fathers. Our mother was a magnet for bums." Jane wasn't sure why she had chosen to make up this kind of story, but it fit her mood. It occurred to her that Pete could easily be telling a different story. "Jimmy might not tell you that, because it's not nice. And I think men make up nice stories because they need a father they can admire. But we're all grown-up women here. Are you and Pam related?"

"Just friends," said Carol. She pulled down the top of her bathing suit and Jane looked away involuntarily to see if Pete was behind her seeing this. But the door to the next room was now closed. Carol slipped the tight suit down from her hips, and Jane looked at her objectively. She had been given to understand that men liked red hair, and hers was at least real.

Carol caught her eye and smiled. "We're on vacation together from the car agency." She cocked her head. "You wish we'd drop dead, don't you?"

"No," Jane lied. "Why would you think that?"

Carol found a small perfume bottle in the shoulder bag on the counter and dabbed a bit on her neck, then another on her belly, close to the patch of red hair. The little smile was conspiratorial. Jane's stomach felt hollow. Carol leaned close to the mirror and began to make up her eyes. "I don't know. That's what I was wondering."

"That's not the way I feel," said Jane. "But he's my little brother, and maybe I'm protective." She walked into the outer room and sat at the table.

In a few seconds Carol walked out to join her. Only then did she carelessly slip on a terrycloth robe and tie it. She sat on the bed and switched on the television with no sound. "I guess you should be protective," she said. "He's such a hunk. Of course, if you're his sister, he probably doesn't strike you that way."

"I can see," said Jane. She needed to add something malicious. "He seems to attract one after another."

It didn't seem to touch Carol. She shrugged. "Life is short. He might as well have some fun."

Slowly, against all of Jane's hopes, she began to hear faint noises coming from the next room. The walls were so thin that they muffled none of the sounds. There was a soft, female moan, and then the springs of the bed. She needed to talk. "You said you and Pam work together?"

Carol stared at the silent screen of the television set, but Jane could see she was listening to the sounds behind the door. "Uh-huh."

"And this is your vacation. Have you been up in the mountains?"

Carol looked at her, the blue eyes focused on something behind Jane's head. "A couple of hikes." The voice in the next room was up an octave now, and louder, sounding almost distressed. "Oh," it said. "Oh, oooh, yes. Please."

Jane considered that this was one possible way that hell could be. It was torment, and it was designed to make her know, and to feel, that she was bad and weak. She could do nothing but talk to this idiot on the bed, and talking to her was like looking in a mirror and seeing a grotesque parody of herself. Carol was lying there and the robe barely covered her anymore, but she didn't think to close it, and her face showed that she wasn't just hearing, she was listening, and wishing more fervently each second that it were she instead of her friend. "Are there any good hikes that we shouldn't miss?" asked Jane. "We've been sticking to the road a lot."

"No," said Carol absently. "I don't really think it's much fun." She turned to glance at Jane, then said to the television set, "You get hot, and sweaty, and out of breath." She lifted her glass to her lips, tasted it, and made a face.

"What's wrong?" asked Jane. Talk, damn you.

"These taste awful without ice. We need ice."

Jane almost sprang to her feet. "I'll get some," she said. "Do you know where the ice machine is?"

Carol shook her head. "I'll get it. It's around a couple of corners." She stood and walked to the door. Jane noticed that she put no shoes on her feet. She paused and studied the two room keys on the table, then seemed unable to remember which one fit this room and slipped both into the pocket of her robe.

For the first few seconds, Jane was relieved to be out of Carol's company. But as minutes passed, the sounds from the next room seemed to grow louder and more frequent. Jane tried not to hear them, then knew that there was no way not to hear them and let them induce clear, detailed visual images in the mind. She was ashamed, and she resented having to feel that way. Her mouth was dry and she detested the drink in her hand, and she needed to clear her throat, but if she did, then Pete and the blonde would hear her, and it would show them that it was impossible for her to be in this room without eavesdropping. She could not even deny to herself that she was listening now, feeling each minute that this was some low ebb in her life and that it was sinking lower, and she with it.

Then Jane heard a new sound. For a few seconds, she wondered why it had surprised her. It was the voice of Carol, coming to her through the connecting door like the other one. "Oh, Jim," it said. "Oh, Jim." Jane carried her drink to the bathroom sink and poured it out. Then she walked out of the room. When she reached her own room, she remembered that Pete still had the key in his pocket.

She was not going back. She picked a credit card out of her wallet without looking at it, curved it a little so it would fit between the door and the jamb to depress the plunger, then slipped inside and stood alone in the darkness.

She was amazed. She had left her husband and rushed all the way out here, maybe to walk in front of a gun muzzle, because that man had called for help. Then she had carefully piled up day after day of invisible, anonymous travel to let his trail get cold. Now he was busy burning up all of her efforts, making himself as memorable as any human being could be to two women who probably couldn't wait to meet the next strange man in the next hotel. She hated Pete Hatcher. He had done this to punish her for rejecting him—wanted to make her imagine, know what she had thrown away, and learn to want it. No, that was too simpleminded. It had been for both of them, to prove that he was still attractive, still manly, still Pete. He had done that better than she would ever let him know. The word *ever* struck her ear as accurate, so she said it aloud: "Ever."

23

She heard him before he put the key in the lock. She let him sneak in without acknowledging his presence, or the bright sunlight that shone in the door when he opened it. She had gone out twice during the night to walk the perimeter of the hotel grounds, studying the cars in the parking lot and the windows of rooms that were on the court, but had seen nothing that worried her, and then she had slept.

She waited until ten to get out of bed. While she was in the shower he got up too, and she found him packing his suitcase. "Good morning," she said, carefully modulating her voice to sound as cheerful and unconcerned as she could.

"Good morning," he answered. He stepped past her into the bathroom without meeting her eyes, and then she heard the shower for a long time.

She finished packing, latched her suitcase, and spent a few minutes selecting identities for the day. Today they would be Tony and Marie Spellagio, who had not yet made an appearance in Montana. She laid their credit cards and driver's licenses on the bed in a row, so that Pete could examine hers too.

Then she made her preliminary inspection of the grounds through the windows. It was another perfect late-summer day in the Rockies, with the sun glaring from what seemed to be just over their heads, and no sign that anyone was near enough to be watching.

Pete came out fully dressed and with hair wet from the shower, picked up his cards and both suitcases, and followed the usual routines. He set the suitcases down beside the car, dropped something so he could look beneath it, peered under the hood, and then loaded the trunk while Jane checked out. She came back and said, "You want to eat breakfast before we move on?"

"No," he said. "If you don't mind, I'd like to get down the road a bit before we stop."

Jane nodded and got into the passenger seat. She was not sure whether he was feeling queasy from the syrupy drinks or wanted to be gone before his little playmates woke up. As he drove off the lot onto the highway, he answered her question. "I don't want to run into Pam and Carol."

"Why not?" she asked.

"Because they want to travel with us for a few days. It came up last night. I can't think of a good way to refuse without hurting their feelings. Everything I tried last night had an answer. This way I'm a jerk, and that will burn off the attraction. Because I left them both, neither one will take it personally. In a day or two they won't mention me, even to each other."

Jane did not speak, because he was probably right. His famous understanding of women seemed to have come back to him. It shouldn't have been a surprise: he had given himself a giant dose of femininity in the past twelve hours. She studied her road map.

They stopped outside a big restaurant in Swan Lake. There was no evidence on the signs on nearby businesses that the name referred to anything but a lake that had once had swans in it. They walked inside and the head waitress noticed them. "Would you like to sit inside, or outside on the terrace?"

Pete glanced at Jane, who said, "Inside" and moved into the interior of the restaurant. "Is that booth over there taken?"

"No," said the waitress, "but I could seat you by the window if you like."

"No, thanks," said Jane.

When the woman had left the menus and returned to her post by the door, Pete said, "What's wrong? Are you hungover?"

Jane leaned forward, her forearms on the table, so she could talk quietly. "It's a beautiful spot, so most people want to sit where they can see it. This time you don't want what everybody else wants."

"I don't?"

"Sitting here is a precaution that costs you nothing, loses you nothing. It makes you invisible to anybody but the people to the side of this booth."

His eyes moved to the side. "There aren't any people to the side of this booth."

She smiled. "That's why I picked this one instead of another. Almost all precautions are simple and effortless. After a time you'll take them without thinking each one through. The important thing is that you look at each situation and modify it to make yourself comfortable. If there's a choice between a tiny bit of vulnerability and none at all, you pick none."

"I thought the best place to hide was in a crowd."

"It can be. If a crowd is immobile and on display, then it can't hide you. If what you want it for is to hold off shooters by surrounding yourself with witnesses, then twenty is better than a thousand, because they can't shoot even twenty, and all of them will see. So you don't stand in long lines to go to movies or plays or games. You do your waiting at home. When the movie has been out a month, you can walk right in."

"What if it's a game? You can't wait a month for that."

"Watch it on television. If it's so important to you that you still want to go, then it's important enough to pay for the safest seats in the stadium."

"Which are those?"

"Down near the field. The only ones who can see your face in a stadium are the ones below you. A hunter scanning for you would look up toward the seats in the back—not only because the back seats feel like a hiding place to an amateur, but because they're all the hunter can see. So you pick the front seats. Everything is a choice." She smiled. "You're getting a feel for this. All you have to do is keep trying it out in different situations until they're all automatic."

Another waitress arrived and took their orders, then bustled off to the kitchen window to clip it to a stainless-steel wheel for the cooks to read.

Pete stared at the table. " 'Different situations.' You're trying to be tactful about the mistakes I made last night, aren't you?"

Jane looked away for a moment, then back to him. "What was wrong last night? You tell me."

"We met two strangers. I let them get too close before I was sure they were okay."

"Go on."

"I went to their room. Somebody could have been waiting."

She waited, but that was all he was willing to say. "Or been called in by one of them while the other one . . . kept you busy. Prostitutes have been robbing clients for thousands of years, so the routines are pretty slick by now. You couldn't know all of them."

"For starters, they weren't prostitutes."

"I'm teaching you how to live by your wits, not by luck. Neither of us knew anything about them when they showed up. What about my mistakes?"

"Yours?"

"Sure. You can learn from those too."

He seemed shocked. After a moment, he said, "I guess you let them get too close."

"Good. I never saw them coming until they were by the corner of the building. I should have kept scanning the entrances to the courtyard while I was swimming."

"Like those Secret Service guys," he said sadly. "What a way to live."

"It would have been easier than that. All I had to do was keep my mind on the possibility, and looking would have been unavoidable. As it happened, it didn't matter. As soon as I saw them, I was certain they weren't dangerous."

"How?"

"They showed up in the skimpiest suits imaginable." She saw Pete wince, but she went on. "In certain situations that would be ominous. Maybe they had been sent to distract you, keep you from looking in another direction. But it also let us see that they couldn't be armed. And their presence wouldn't make it any easier for someone else to kill you: they might get hit in the dark, and they could hardly expect me to be stupefied by the sight of a girl in a bikini."

"Stupefied?"

"I'm sorry," said Jane. "Distracted."

"I'm the one who's sorry. Once again."

Jane's eyes flicked to his face and then around the dining room. He was miserable, and she wasn't being fair. "I guess we have to clear the air some more, don't we?"

Pete shrugged. His face was apologetic and appealing, like a little boy who wanted to be forgiven.

Jane took a deep breath and saw the waitress striding toward them on rubber soles, carrying a tray. Jane waited until the waitress had served them, said, "Enjoy your meal," and hurried away.

"Back to that air," she said. "I'm a guide. I lead people who are about to be killed to places where nobody wants to kill them. I give them pieces of paper that say they're somebody else. To the extent that I can, I train them to be the new person—how to look, act, think. If they're being actively hunted, I give them a few tricks that can fool hunters."

"And?"

"And then I turn them loose and go home." Jane stared into his eyes and watched him to see if he understood everything she was saying. There was light behind his eyes, but it seemed only to be the life force, the glow of the eyes of a big, healthy animal.

"What is he like?"

Jane stiffened. "That wasn't . . . I wasn't talking about him."

"No," he said. "You know everything about other people, but they're not supposed to know anything about you."

It wasn't a statement Jane could ignore. "It's true, and it's not an accident. It protects him, and it protects me, and it protects you. When I take on a person like you, we both have to be aware that some day I might very well be caught. Years from now I might be asked where you are and what name I gave you. There are things that could be done to make me want very much to tell. My promise to you is simply that I won't tell. If there's no other way, I'll commit suicide to avoid it."

"Really?"

"Really." She let the knowledge settle on him for a moment. He seemed unable to take the next step. "If I tell you about my family and friends, are you willing to do the same before you'll tell anyone?"

He thought about it for a long time. "I would want to. I don't think I could."

"And you don't have to, because you don't know about them. But I can't help knowing about you, so I'm stuck. I gave my word."

Pete nodded thoughtfully. "We're back to last night, aren't we?"

"If you want to be," she said.

"Why you said no."

She sighed. "Marriages are fragile. When you boil off all the nonsense, what they amount to is a promise."

She could tell he had no trouble understanding her. If she could break that promise to her own husband, then strangers like Pete Hatcher wouldn't stand a chance. "Okay. I won't grill you anymore."

"Keep asking questions. It's what we're doing together," said Jane. "I want you to learn everything you can. I want you to get as good at this as I am, because in one more day I'm going to take you somewhere, get you settled, and go home. You're my last trip."

He stared at her. "In a way, I'm glad," he said. "I'm a little scared. One more day isn't much time. But I'm glad for you. This is a crazy way to live."

"It took me a long time to reach that conclusion. I guess I had to find another way to live before I could admit it. But I'm taken care of. Let's get rid of what's still bothering you."

"I don't know," he said. "I seem to be having trouble imagining a future. That makes it hard to ask questions about it."

"I know some of it," Jane said. "You'll live in a place that's pleasant, but maybe has a few security features most people wouldn't pay extra for. This morning I was thinking that one of those small, gated developments might suit you. The identity I'm going to give you is terrific, so you could survive the checks they do on new residents. The rent-a-cops wouldn't present much of an obstacle to the people who are after you, but the entry gates make it difficult for them to drive through and browse. They're pros, so their main concern is getting out afterward."

"It sounds logical."

"We'll find you a job. You were a manager in Las Vegas, so we'll get you something at about the same level in the new town. It will have to be something where you have less contact with outsiders, so we'll pick a company that limits it, some-how—maybe one that sells equipment only to doctors, or physicists, or—"

"How?"

"How what?"

"How do I get a job at that level in a business I've never been in?"

She smiled. "That's something I'll help you with. I'm a rep-resentative from an executive head-hunting agency. I've got a promising prospect. I sell you to them. I've already checked all your references, et cetera, so the company doesn't have to."

"You can pull that off?"

"Sure. I do it by not cheating too much. Your résumé won't list your real college, but it will have equivalent courses from another one. Your references won't come from Pleasure, Inc., but they'll come from a company that has a similar corporate structure, and I won't lie about your place in the hierarchy. And I'll be very clear about my fee."

"You actually collect a fee?"

"Of course. It will be the same fee other companies like mine charge. Otherwise your employers would know I'm a fraud."

"So now I have a condo and a job. Good start."

"A condo in the center of the development, that can't be watched from outside the gate. A job you like and are qualified to do, that keeps you busy. All you have to do is keep from making mistakes."

"Mistakes—you mean the ball games and movies and all that."

"I said that I train you to be the new person, to the extent that I can. What I can't do is give you an identity that doesn't fit." She paused. "That's why I'm glad last night happened."

"You're working up to writing me off."

Jane smiled, but her brows knitted. "I thought we were past that game. You pretend to be shocked at your own behavior and deeply humiliated that I know about it. This forces me to choose between two roles—the scandalized schoolmistress who talks to you with pinch-faced distaste, or the conspiratorial madam who tells you it's cute. Either way, we evade the real issue."

"What is the real issue? My sex life?"

"Your life, period. Suppose I tell you that having sex with strangers is dangerous. Is that news? Does it change anything?"

He looked down, silent.

"How about that it's even more dangerous for you, because the people who are chasing you know that you do it?"

He watched her, but still said nothing.

"You could improve your chances a lot just by being slightly more selective. Women who go to church social groups are less likely to be decoys than ones who step out of dark doorways after midnight wearing two ounces of nylon. And church groups are notorious for being exactly what you need. Join a group for singles. Every woman there is looking for a man, and they outnumber the men two to one. Someone like you would be very welcome."

"Are you trying to help me, or get back at me for embarrassing you last night?"

"I'm being realistic. Even if I were trying to embarrass you, who cares? Will anything I think about your personal life matter when you're on your own? No, and it shouldn't."

"So where does that leave us?"

"When I sent you to Denver I hadn't had time to get to know you. I expected you to live like a monk. Maybe you did too. This time, let's get it right. Those security-minded condo places are that way because they're full of young, career-minded women. You'll find them hanging around the pools and the exercise rooms. Some of the owners' associations even have parties where the eligible women will push themselves in front of your nose. Take them. Enjoy yourself. But stick to your story. Never reveal anything that doesn't fit."

Hatcher looked at her sadly. "I thought you were just being the pinch-faced schoolmarm. It's way past that, isn't it? You sound like a scientist talking about rats."

She reached out and touched his hand, then regretted it and pulled back. "I'm sorry. I'm just being professional. If you're happy, you'll be able to stay in one quiet, safe place for a long time. If you're not, you'll take risks to get happy. So I need to make you happy for as long as I can."

"But you don't feel anything."

"I don't feel what you feel. You see any woman on the youngish side with round breasts and the right ratio of hips to waist, and you want her. I can know that, but knowing is all I can do. It's all any of us can do. And what you did last night wasn't shocking or particularly newsworthy. It was just something I needed to be reminded of."

"You're taking one incident and weaving it into a rope to tie around my neck."

"No," she said. "This is hard for me to talk about, so let me get it all out of the way. Last night I watched a young woman strip off a wet bathing suit to put on makeup at two A.M. so she could lure you away from her best friend. Ignoring the power, the need that makes people do that would be stupid. Will you personally take the chance of getting killed for sex? Sure. Scratch the topsoil anywhere on the planet and you'll find the bones of people who maybe didn't all know it, but who died over the instinct to mate. It's not an opinion, it's a fact. What I think about it, or feel about it, or what the implications are for romantic love or babies or families or anything else is irrelevant. All I can do is get out of the way. In this case it means putting you in the right location, so you'll survive."

"Why?"

"Why?" He had surprised her again.

"Yes. You don't think much of me today. When I ask you why you save people's lives, you say it's because you're a woman who saves people's lives. I want to know if you care about me. I know I have no right to ask you to care. I just want to know if you do."

Jane patted his hand and gave him a smile that was achingly false. "Of course I do. You're the best brother I ever had."

She turned her attention to the plate of food in front of her. He had been eating while she had been talking, and her scrambled eggs had turned cold and rubbery. She put some into her mouth. She could feel tears beginning to gather behind her eyes. Something was very wrong this morning, and she could not find a way to fix it. Maybe she had placed too much weight on her young, tender marriage. She had somehow gotten the impression that it was going to be a shield that protected her, kept her at a distance from certain kinds of hurt, certain ugly facts of other people's lives. If nothing else, it should have made her immune to feelings about men like Pete Hatcher.

Jane swallowed her eggs and turned her attention to the people filling up the dining room for lunch. There were the usual number of older people with gray hair, the women in shoes like nurses wore and the men in socks that matched their shirts, and lots of stuff in their pockets. There were two families with children who had sat in cars all morning and now fidgeted and thought of excuses to get up and wander in the dining room. She let herself wonder if some day she and Carey would be like this, threatening their kids in low voices to make them behave, or later, growing old together and wandering around like the couple in the next booth.

Then she saw two people who intrigued her. The woman was tall and thin with long black hair, dark almond eyes, and

high cheekbones. Around here the blood was probably Black-
foot or Kootenai or Flathead. The man was big, blond, and
broad-shouldered—not muscular, but fit in the way that tennis
players were.

The head waitress moved them from an inner table and
seated them at a table beside the window. They watched her set
their plates in front of them and talked quietly. Jane wished she
had not seen them. The woman looked a little like her, and so
she had wanted the man to resemble Carey. It was a childish
and primitive impulse to make the world bend into congruence
with what she wanted, to have the universe send her an omen
that everything was all right. She did not want to notice at first,
and then she did not want to acknowledge the truth. If the man
looked like anybody, it was Pete.

She looked away. But before her head had finished its turn,
she sensed that she had seen something strange. Her eyes shot
back to the couple, focused on the high hillside through the
window beside them. She gazed at it for several seconds, but
the sight did not come again. She had imagined a small, bright
flash of sun on metal. She stared down at her plate, not aware
that her brow was furrowed.

Pete noticed her expression and said, "What's—" just as
Jane had put the pieces together. She stood up quickly and took
a step toward the couple, and time ran out.

She saw the windowpane shatter and the man by the
window stop, his mouth open to receive the fork with a piece
of pancake on it. His head seemed to bob toward Jane, his ear
striking his shoulder, then bouncing back a little. Jane saw the
splatter of blood, bone, and dark tissue that had to be brain in
the air all mixed with glittering, sparkling fragments of glass.

The dark woman's eyes grew white-wide, her fingers curled
like claws, and she shrieked as the rest of the people in the
crowded dining room took in a single gasp and let it out in a
shuddering moan. People began to scramble. Chairs fell, plates
broke.

Jane dashed over the shards of glass, yanked the woman out
of her chair, and pushed her into the crowd that was backing

toward the doorway just as the second shot shattered another pane of the window. She turned to search for Pete and he bumped into her, then held her to keep her from falling. The details flooded her mind now: there had been no report of the weapon, so it must have a silencer; no crack of a bullet breaking the sound barrier, so the ammunition must be subsonic. It probably didn't have the velocity to pierce any walls. She said, "Hold on to me," and set off, with Pete's hands on her waist.

They threaded their way into the crowd cowering in the restaurant foyer. The cashier was shouting into the telephone and the dark woman was off to the right screaming while two elderly women held her. Jane's mind raced. If the shooter had finished firing and was already slipping away, then she should get Pete out of here before he discovered his mistake. But what if he wasn't running away? His rifle scope had enough magnification to let him put a bullet through the wrong man's temple from the mountainside. If he was using this time to creep down the mountain, then in a few minutes he would be close enough to see faces clearly.

Jane knew she had to do something that was not going to make her proud, and she had to do it now. She began to push toward the door and yelled, "I'm not going to stay here and get killed!"

The people who had been standing paralyzed, waiting for some voice to suggest a remedy for their terror, shifted in a single wave. The double door ahead of them opened, then began to wag back and forth as each person nudged it aside to get out.

Jane tugged Pete out in the middle of the throng. As she had expected, once they were out in the sunlight and fresh air, sanity seemed to descend upon the crowd. They saw how open and unprotected they were in the parking lot, so they began to spin like dancers, looking in every direction to see where the danger was coming from as they retreated toward the overhanging roof and brick wall of the restaurant.

Jane sprinted to the car and crouched until Pete had joined

her. As she had expected, her run—a definite, unhesitating move—seemed to some in the crowd to be shrewdly based on information they did not have. They ran to their cars, started them, and wheeled out of the lot to the highway.

"Drive," said Jane.

Pete ducked into the driver's seat and they joined the line of cars streaming out onto the road. Pete gripped the steering wheel hard, holding it steady with effort as though its natural inclination were to veer off into the woods. "I saw it," he said. "I couldn't think fast enough."

"Saw what?" said Jane.

"I was thinking they looked a little bit like us. Like you and me."

"Drive," said Jane. "Don't worry about the speed. Out here what they do when they want somebody is put up a roadblock. When they do, we'd better be on the other side of it."

24

Jane studied the road map while Pete drove. She traced the red and blue lines meandering through the mountains, searching for turnouts and alternative routes. It was the wrong part of the country to evade someone in a car. The Rocky Mountains didn't offer many vulnerabilities to road builders.

"Where do I go?" asked Pete.

"No choice but to keep going up 83 for a while," she said. "There's no place to switch until Bigfork."

"What then?"

"I'll tell you when I know. Right now, if you do that much, we're not dead. When there's a straight stretch, try to look behind you and make a list of all the cars you can see. Get to know them."

"How do I know if he's in one of them?"

"You don't. Most of them will drop out at Bigfork to look for a police station or a telephone. The one we need to worry about won't."

He drove for fifteen minutes, and Jane noticed no cars coming toward them in the left lane. Finally, three police cars flashed past, driving hard toward Swan Lake. She turned to look after them, then switched on the car radio. After some static and blurts of music she found, "The police have asked us to report that Route 83 is closed south at Bigfork and north at Salmon Prairie. It will remain closed until further notice." She switched it off and muttered, "Of course."

"What?" said Pete.

"I hadn't thought of that. They think they've got a sniper

back there still taking shots across a highway at a restaurant. They don't want to block the road out until they get people evacuated. What they're blocking is the way in, so nobody gets shot."

She went back to her road map. "All right. At Bigfork, turn right onto 35, to Creston, and keep heading north when it changes to 206."

She set the map aside and stared out the back window. Maybe the shooter had not made it to his car in time to follow. He had been up above on the hillside, at least three hundred yards away. As soon as she had thought of it, she knew she was being foolish. It wasn't likely that a pro would strand himself that far from his car and open fire. His car had been up there too, probably parked beside one of the firebreaks or timber roads cut into the forested hillside.

The reflection had not come from his equipment. All he had needed was a rifle and a scope, and the good ones were designed with that problem in mind. It was cars that were covered with chrome and mirrors. He was probably right behind them now, if not among the first few cars, then in the next pack.

"We have to talk," she said.

"You start."

"We have a problem here. I don't have any idea how they knew where we were."

"Obviously I don't either." He turned to her, eyes wide. "You don't suppose Pam and Carol—"

"No," she said. "If they had put two girls in your path to get you alone, that was when they would have killed you. And we left this morning before those two were up. They couldn't have told anybody where we were going, because they didn't know."

"Then what could we have done to tell that guy where we were?"

"Maybe they have some spectacular new way of instantly picking out charges on the credit cards we've been using. Maybe they somehow found out about this car the day I bought it, and hid a transmitter in it. Whatever they're using to trace us, it might as well be magic."

"You're making me more nervous than I am already, and I can hardly hold the wheel steady as it is."

They passed a sign that said BIGFORK 5. She said, "We have five miles to make a choice. What I'm saying is that they shouldn't be here. When I play this game, if my side wins a round, we get to play another round. If the other side wins one, the game is over."

"A nice, sporting way of saying I'm dead."

"We'll both be dead. I'm trying to tell you we haven't won any rounds. They had you in Denver, until the policeman got in the way. They had us twenty minutes ago, and that poor man took the bullet. They haven't got you, but they haven't exactly missed yet, either. It's important to remember that. In a few minutes we'll be in Bigfork. There are cops on the road there now, and more on the way. We could stop, tell them our story, and they would take over."

"You mean give myself up?"

"You haven't committed any crimes. They would protect you, beginning in four minutes. In a day or less, you could be a thousand miles away, telling the Justice Department what you know about Pleasure, Inc. They would keep you safe, at least until you testified in court."

"Yeah, but what then?"

Jane threw up her hands and let them rest on her lap. "I can't be sure. Probably they would do what I did: give you fake papers and a plane ticket. You'd be a protected witness. I'll be honest with you. They're very, very good at protecting you until you testify. After that you're a drain on the budget and not much use. At that point you come back to me and I'll try again."

"I can't go to the police," said Pete.

"You said that when I met you. Now is the time to be sure."

"There are three men who own Pleasure, Incorporated. I know enough about all of them to get the cops a warrant to investigate, and a few tips on specific places to look, and I'm done. I didn't see things happen. I put two and two together. I heard them tell Calvin Seaver, the security guy, someone was a problem, and then read an obituary. I saw a rough count of the day's take on a piece of paper, and then a lower number on the ledger in the computer. The paper's gone. I'm not an eye-witness, I'm a rumormonger."

Jane heard an edge in his voice. "You're not telling everything. You did something."

"The reason I was getting ready to leave was that I was expected to do things that could get me in trouble. I signed receipts when I knew the count was wrong. I deposited money that came in from side businesses I never saw, and sent it to investors without reporting it to the I.R.S. I never sat down and listed all the things like that, I just got out. I think the cops could find evidence against the owners, but I know they could find some against me. I'll let you out of the car in Bigfork, or anything you want, but I can't go to the police."

"The people you worked for think you can." Ahead, she could see the police cars parked at angles in the other lane.

"I've been over this in my mind a million times. They must think I saw more than I did, or took evidence with me, or God knows what. But I didn't. I won't end up in some protected place. I'll be in a Nevada State Prison, and they'll hire some lifer to kill me." He drove past the roadblock, and Jane felt a little twinge in her chest.

Jane watched him take the turn just before the buildings began to cluster at Bigfork. He swung onto the smaller road and accelerated. She said, "Creston is eight miles. Bear right again there." She turned around in her seat to stare out the back window. She saw a few cars go the other way, toward Kalispell and Whitefish, and wondered if that would have been the way to safety. The road always seemed to have forks in it, and all she could do was pick. Maybe what she was watching recede into the distance was her chance to ever go home again.

They were at the Creston intersection in ten minutes, then onto 206 and climbing again, higher into the gray mountains. At Columbia Heights they switched onto U.S. 2. The road curved around big stony outcroppings, always climbing. Ahead were towns too small to hide in—Hungry Horse, Martin City, Coram. Always Jane studied the map. The idea of moving around in these mountains, where there were places to stay and everyone was a tourist, had seemed to be a good one. But now the roads reminded her of the chutes in a stock pen. Each opening looked at first like a way out, but each was an irrevocable choice. The walls were too high to jump and the animal couldn't turn around. The animal had no way to go but forward, pushed by the ones behind it. Somewhere, waiting at the end of the chutes, was a man with a hammer.

The hunters could see what the map told Jane as well as she could. She could leave this road only by two routes—along the east side of Glacier National Park and then north on Chief Mountain Highway to the Canadian border, or north along the west side of the park by the Flathead River on 486.

She looked more closely at the map. Route 486 stopped at the Canadian border. There were no little flags there to indicate a point of entry, as there were on the Chief Mountain Highway. She couldn't risk choosing a road that might lead to a dead end with a fence across it. She turned the map over and studied the little detailed map of the area on the back.

The map showed Route 486 ending at the border. It showed the customs checkpoint on Chief Mountain Highway. But the checkpoint had a note under it in small black print. "Closed September 15–May 15." After September 15 there was only one way to Canada by car.

Jane looked at Pete, driving the car along the highway.

He seemed to feel her gaze. He turned. "What?"

"Take the entrance to Glacier National Park at West Glacier. If there's a store in any of the towns before then, stop there."

"Do you have it figured out?"

"I think I know a way out of this, if that's what you mean."

"Whatever it is, I like it better than your last idea about the cops."

"Wait and see."

* * *

By five in the morning, Linda had searched the house as thoroughly as she dared with Carey sleeping behind the closed door at the end of the upstairs hallway. There seemed to be nothing lying around downstairs that could tell her more than she already knew about where Jane was or what she was likely to try next. The pads by the phones had no useful jottings on them, and darkening the top sheet with a pencil revealed no impressions that Linda could read. There seemed to be no weapons hidden where she could find them, no papers that would give her the false names Jane and Hatcher were using. When she began to fear that Carey would wake up, she retreated into her guest room.

She told herself not to worry. She had not failed completely. She had given Earl the name of the town, and if Earl caught up with them at Salmon Prairie, it didn't matter what they had been calling themselves: they were going to be John and Jane Doe. But she had not come all this way and worked this hard to get into Jane's house only to have Jane's husband push her out again.

The thought made Linda's throat contract in an angry gulp. Somehow Carey had become the worst part of this job for Linda. The thought of him made her sick with humiliation and regret. She had used every opportunity to show him that she was available. Could he be so stupid that he had not understood? No, that was just a way of salvaging her pride. She had even given him an eyeful of what was being offered.

She looked in the mirror above the dresser. It was so unfair. That body was absolutely perfect. Her face was captivating. How could he go scuttling down the hall and lock himself in his room like that? Jane could not possibly be prettier than Linda was.

She walked to the telephone by the bed and forced herself to concentrate. First she looked in the telephone book and tried dialing a few numbers. She settled on one that belonged to a restaurant that sounded too fancy to serve breakfast. It rang twenty times before she hung up. She copied the number and began to dress.

At six thirty, Carey knocked quietly on the door. Linda stopped at the mirror, checked her hair and makeup, and then opened the door.

"Good morning," he said. "I hope I'm not bothering you."

She gave her best smile. "You're not. I don't sleep in an evening gown." She made her eyes twinkle. "As you know."

Carey glanced at his watch. "It's six thirty . . ."

Linda's brows knitted in apologetic distress. "I'm afraid I've got another problem, Carey."

"What's wrong?"

"I've been calling the impound lot since quarter to six, and they're not answering. Didn't the sign say they opened at six?"

"I'm pretty sure that's what it said." She could tell he was trying to look as though he were hiding his worry, but what he was hiding was irritation. "When did you call last?"

"A minute ago. I know you have to be at the hospital by seven . . ."

"Let's try it again. The only place for a phone is in that little building, and they could be out on the lot." He stepped into the guest room with her and picked up the telephone. "What's the number?"

She handed him the little pad from the telephone where she had written down the number, and he dialed. He let the phone ring longer than she had, and finally hung up. "It doesn't really mean they're not open. I'll drive you there, and if nobody's around, you can always get a cab at the hospital."

"Can I make another suggestion?"

"Sure."

"They're sure to be open by nine or so, right?"

"I would think so."

"Then it would make me happiest if you would just go to work. I'll call a cab to pick me up here at eight. If we're both wrong and the place is deserted, the cab can keep going and take me home. That way you don't leave some patient waiting on a gurney. Better still, I'm not left on the street in an evening gown in an unfamiliar city. And I'm not seen driving back to the hospital wearing last night's clothes with a married man whose wife is out of town."

She could see that the suggestion had the desired effect. It contained reasoning he could follow, and it also gently reminded him of what could have happened. He seemed flustered as he shrugged. "I'm sorry. Everything seems to have gotten complicated." He was fiddling with his keys. He handed her one of them. "Would you mind locking up when you go? You can just pop the key into the mail slot in the front door."

She took the key. "No problem." She touched his arm. "And I'm the one who's sorry. I didn't mean to be this much trouble."

"No trouble at all," he lied.

"I'm very grateful," she said. "More grateful than you know."

He backed away from her gratitude toward the stairs. "It's getting late."

"Oh, Carey?"

He stopped. "Yes?"

"I promise this is the last thing I ask. But do you think you could lend me something of Jane's—an old pair of jeans and a sweater or something? Just to get me home."

He seemed surprised, then reluctant, but as she had expected, he did not know how to refuse. "Of course," he said. "I offered last night and then forgot. I'm sorry. Her closet is in the master bedroom. Take what you need." He hurried down the stairs and out the front door.

At two thirty, Linda Thompson dialed the telephone and heard the machine in her suite come on. She pressed the two-digit code and listened while the machine rewound. She could tell there was something on the tape. There was a click, and Earl's voice came over the line.

"I picked them up at Salmon Prairie and followed them as far as Swan Lake. I drilled a man through a restaurant window from five hundred yards. Felt pretty good about it until I saw their car pull out of the lot with them in it. They took off to the north. They could be heading to Canada. Lenny's with me, and

we're going after them. When you find out where they are,
leave a message on the machine at home. As soon as I've heard
it, I'll erase it from here." There was a loud hang-up sound, and
then a beep. Linda put the receiver back on the cradle. Earl had
not said "If you find out." He had said "When."

Linda felt a shiver of fear that started in her shoulders, crept
down her spine, and shot back up again. She could tell from the
chill in his voice that he thought he had figured out exactly
what Linda had needed to do to find out about Salmon Prairie.

That made Linda feel afraid again. His voice had sounded
cold and detached on the answering machine, and that was
very bad. He was resenting her for it, and Earl's resentment
was always acted out.

She was in trouble. She had not done what he thought
she had done, but he was going to punish her for it. And here
he was, sending her back for more, knowing deep inside that he
was going to hate what she did this time even more than the
last, and he was saving it all up.

The telephone had not rung since Jane had called from
Salmon Prairie. Carey knew nothing more recent than that, so
no matter how devious Linda was about asking him where his
wife was now, he couldn't tell her. She would have to buy time.

The best way would be to stay very close to him—move in
with him, so she would hear the telephone ring and he would
tell her, not because she had asked but because he wanted to.
And the only reason he would want to tell her was to convince
her that his wife was still very far away, that she was not about
to burst in the door and find Linda with him. If Linda hoped
to accomplish that, then she would have to make Carey want
very much to keep her near him. Last night she had been
sure she had him. He had not been as adventurous as she had
anticipated, but there was no question he had been tempted.

Linda lay back on the bed and tried to coax from her imagination ways to make Carey interested in her. There was a special kind of titillation in the images she conjured, because even
as she planned, she could feel Earl thinking about her on the

bed with Carey and getting that strange combination of jealousy and arousal that was most exciting to her. Linda knew what her punishment was going to be, because she was going to submit herself for it.

She was going to make the big, wet tears come, and make her voice go small and helpless, and say, "Then he did this, and this, and this." And Earl, because he was Earl, would make her do again everything she described for him. She could already hear his voice, through clenched teeth, whispering, "Like this? Was it like this?" And she would be beside herself with excitement, because with Earl it wasn't like being with a man. It was like being possessed by a demon—part guilty, shameful sensation, but mostly fearing and sharing all of that power. A necessary part of her fantasy was that Earl would begin her punishment only after he had killed Carey. She liked to imagine that he would do it with a knife.

25

As the sign for Hungry Horse drifted past her window, Jane said, "Keep your eyes open for a sporting goods store. If we don't find what we need here, go on to Coram. If you see a military surplus store or one of those places for survival psychos, don't pass it by."

They both saw the store at the same time, and it seemed to be a little of each. The sign was big and crude, but the merchandise in the window included skis and toboggans. "Park off the street," she said. Pete found a space behind the building between two delivery trucks and they entered.

Jane picked out two of everything—compasses, canteens, sleeping bags, waterproof matches, flashlights. Pete hovered beside her to take the merchandise she selected, a worried look on his face. She whispered, "You wanted another option. Without this stuff we don't have one."

She carefully picked out their clothes: rainproof ponchos, olive-drab woolen pants with belted ankles, pullover sweaters, hiking boots, wool socks, long underwear, M-65 field jackets, gloves, and watch caps. Next she found a pair of ten-power binoculars, polarized sunglasses and Swiss Army knives for each of them, packets of dried food, a cook pot, and, finally, two backpacks to carry it all in.

Then Jane joined Pete at the counter, where he stood beside the pile of purchases he had built. As an afterthought, Jane picked up a small foam fire extinguisher, added it to the pile, and paid the clerk in cash.

When they had loaded all of the bags into the car, Jane began to sort out her purchases and pack the two backpacks while Pete drove. "There will be some kind of ranger station or visitor center at West Glacier. Stop there too, but put the car between two tour buses or behind a building or somewhere."

"Pretty authentic disguises," said Pete. Behind the thin sound of hope in his voice there was dread.

"I'm afraid they're not disguises," she said.

"They're not?"

She looked at him unapologetically. "Not exactly. It's something I stumbled on by looking at the map. We're brought up to see the world as a lot of roads. It's like a grid, with dots for the towns at the intersections and nothing between the roads at all. These people will keep chasing us if we stay on the lines. We have to stop now and then at one of those dots at the intersections, and they'll catch up. So we'll see the map differently for a couple of days."

"We're going camping? What does that get us?"

"I'm not sure yet, so I'm not making promises. I think they're using commercial computer databases to track us; the lists of people who buy handguns, cars, or rent hotel rooms. I've never used the same names or credit cards two days in a row, and that's always worked before. But it's not working now. I made some phone calls, but they were from pay phones. They don't transmit the numbers of pay phones for caller ID to pick up, so nobody can be intercepting the signal and finding us that way. Even if they managed to find out where I live and tapped my home phone, I never said where I was calling from. Our phone bill comes at the end of the month, so they're not reading it. I don't have any idea what these people are doing, or how. And that scares me."

"Isn't it possible that they just followed us?"

"Maybe. Maybe they out-thought me—figured what I would do, then drove along the right road and showed your picture to hotel desk clerks and waitresses. But it's not a great method if what you plan to do after you find the person is kill him. It's also possible that they're tracking this car electronically."

"How do we find out—search it?"

"Dump it."

"Where do we get another car out here?"

She gave her sad little smile again. "We don't. I'd love to get a new one and drive until the tread is off the tires. But we tried that, and a shooter turned up. I'd love to put on a blond wig and step onto an airplane to anywhere. But unless we know for sure how they're tracking us, we can't do anything that puts us in a predetermined airport at a prearranged time. The safest tactic I can think of is to do the opposite: go where there are no people to see us, no schedules, and no records for anybody to break into. It's not a great idea, but it's an idea. We've got to keep moving."

"Keep moving where?"

She sighed. "I think we have no choice but to dump everything we had when we walked into that restaurant this morning, and cross the border."

"Canada?"

"If they're using computer data files, it's possible crossing a national border will make it harder. A lot of businesses are national—not international. If their car gets searched at the border, there will be guns in it. There might be other advantages, but there are no disadvantages that I know of."

As the road wound up into the mountains, Pete seemed to be concentrating on his driving. "Shouldn't we leave this car someplace to mislead them?"

"I don't want to confuse them," she said. "I want them stuck."

"How do we manage that?"

"It's September thirteenth. In two days they'll close this road for the winter. If the chasers don't get this far by then, they'll have to go back. If, after that, they find out we left the car inside the park, they have the same choices we had: go on to the Chief Mountain Highway, drive to the border, and get stopped, because the customs station closes on the fifteenth too; go east to the next road that crosses at the Piegan-Conway crossing; or go all the way back along this road to Whitefish and drive up Route 93. Either way, we'll be in the space in-between, at least thirty miles from them with no road to get to us."

"And then?"

"And then we walk out of the woods in Canada and pay somebody to drive us far enough away to catch a bus. I'm not getting on any more planes until I know they haven't tapped the reservation system."

They drove into the park at West Glacier, bought a trail map at the ranger station, then joined the long single-file line of cars on Going-to-the-Sun Road. The progress was slow because the road was a Depression-era two-lane pavement with high, rocky cliffs on the right and Lake McDonald on the left. Drivers ahead of them pulled over whenever there was a turnout to take pictures and stare at the icy, glass-clear lake and the surrounding forests.

Pete said happily, "It looks as though we won't be needing that winter gear we bought. The weather's beautiful."

She turned in her seat to look at him. "I guess I should have asked you this before. Have you ever spent time in the woods?"

He pursed his lips. "Let's see. By woods you don't mean a bunch of trees next to the fairway, do you? I mean, this is a park, right?"

"I'm glad I didn't ask. Here it's seventy and sunny. The altitude is three thousand feet and it's three o'clock in the afternoon. In an hour or so, we'll be at seven thousand feet. The temperature drops about five degrees for each thousand feet. It could be fifty up there now. Sunset tonight is about six twenty. That's when it sinks majestically below the horizon if you're on the ocean, not if you have a mountain or two to the west of you to cast a shadow. It's also windy on mountains. So that fifty could already feel like thirty."

He frowned. "Thirty degrees? And you're sure today's the day the teddy bears have their picnic?"

She stared at him for a second, then laughed. "You've lost your mind."

"You know what?"

"What?"

"No matter what happens to me after this, it won't be anywhere near as interesting."

"I wouldn't give up yet."

"I know that sounds idiotic," he admitted. "I've been
thinking about it for a couple of days now, and I kept wondering if I'd bumped my head. Then I was thinking that if I told
you, I would just convince you that I was too stupid to be
scared. But I'm scared all the time, and it still feels true. If they
find me and kill me, it will just be a sharp pain, and then
nothing. If they don't, I'll try my best to live a quiet life. But
right now, every second is full of possibilities, full of things I
never thought about or looked at before. I've never wanted to
stay alive so much in my life."

Jane had not sensed that trouble was coming, and here it was
again. It was not that she would be tempted to have a fling with
Pete Hatcher. This was the fling, and she was having it. She felt
the same exhilaration he did. This time the hunters were the
best she had ever faced, and Pete Hatcher was her last client,
and after this great flaming burst of clarity she was either going
to die or let her life settle down to a steady unchanging glow
like a pilot light. From then on, when evil came, it would come
in some equivocal form—spite or pride or jealousy—sidling
up to her and leaving her nothing clear and direct that she could
do to fight it. This was the guide's last trip.

Jane studied the road ahead and saw the Loop coming. It
was the only hairpin turn on the highway, eight miles out of the
way to follow the course of the McDonald River and eight
miles back under Mount Cannon. "Pretty soon we'll be there,"
she said. "If you're not willing to do this, tell me now."

"I already told you," he said. "I want to live."

He drove the long curve, then climbed again, higher into the
mountains. When he pulled into the big parking lot at the
Logan Pass visitor center and stopped, Jane said, "Pull over by
the garbage Dumpsters and wait for me."

She opened the trunk and went through the suitcases one last time. She put Pete's pistol in his pack and the ammunition in hers to even the weight, then split his money between the two packs, closed them tight, and dropped the two suitcases into the Dumpster and covered them with garbage.

Jane used her Swiss Army knife to unscrew the Montana license plates and replace them with Colorado plates from a nearby car. She got into the car again and parked it as far from the road as possible, then handed Pete his pack, bedroll, and canteen. Finally she sprayed the inside of the car with the fire extinguisher and tossed it on the floor in the back seat, left the keys in the ignition, and walked away.

"What was that for?" asked Pete.

"The spray is just carbon dioxide. It'll be gone in a little while, but so will the fingerprints. If somebody traces the plates, they'll have a problem because the car's not registered in Colorado. It might buy us some time to make them trace it in other states."

"Why did you leave the keys?"

"Out of a million visitors, we can hope for one car thief. They must take vacations too." She handed him her canteen. "I'm entitled to one last phone call. Go fill these up with water from the tap over there while I make it."

She went to the telephone at the far end of the row, put in a quarter, dialed the private line on Carey's desk in his office, waited for the operator to tell her how many more she needed, and put those in too. Change made noise in pockets, and there would be no more collect calls for her. She couldn't be entirely sure that the shooters weren't using the telephone company's billing system to trace her.

"Hello."

"I love you," she said.

"What?"

She laughed. "I said, I love you. At least I hope it's you, or I just made a fool of myself for a perfect stranger."

"No," he said. "Not perfect. Do you have time to talk?"

She looked around to see if anyone was near. "Not much, but probably more than you do."

"Good for you," he said. "Having fun?"

"Not much," she began. Then she stopped herself. Could she tell him that a few hours ago she had watched a rifle bullet churn its way through a man's head because he looked like Pete Hatcher? Not if she wasn't also going to tell him it was over. "We're not out of the woods yet. Literally. I won't be able to call for a few days. We're traveling on foot, and there won't be any phones."

She could hear him breathing on the other end, then: "Why on foot?"

"It's safer. I'll tell you all about it in excruciating detail when I get home."

"That's what I was wondering," he said. "Can you tell me when you're coming home?"

"We've got to go about twenty miles, but that's measuring it straight. I figure two or three days to get up there, and then two weeks more to finish this for good. Then I'll be home."

"Why do you need two weeks?"

She sighed. "Because I never, ever want to do this again. If I do it right, it's over."

She waited a long time for his answer. Finally, he said, "I understand," as though he didn't. "Just promise me one thing."

"What's that?"

"Before you get on the plane, give me a call. I want to pick you up at the airport."

"I can probably find a phone before then."

"I know, but that's something else. Promise?"

"Sure," she said. She had spent her adult life inventing lies, and she could tell when somebody was hiding something. If Carey wanted to arrange a surprise for her, it was worth playing dumb to keep from ruining it. "I promise."

"Good. Do you need anything? Money or something?"

"No, thanks," she said. "I'd better get going. I love you."

"Me too."

"Bye."

They both hung up. As she walked away from the telephone, she fervently sent a wish across the mountains. Let the surprise be flowers and champagne. Don't surprise me by having the upstairs bathroom remodeled. Then she felt guilty and unworthy. The man she loved and wanted to spend her life with was planning a surprise. Whatever it was, she resolved to smile and throw her arms around his neck and kiss him as though all future happiness depended on it. She was not foolish enough to think that it didn't.

Jane walked out of the park building and found Pete Hatcher on the steps with their two full canteens. She cinched hers onto her pack and did the same for Hatcher.

"I thought you were supposed to wear them on your belt."

"Soldiers have to put up with two quarts of water whacking their butts, but I don't," she said. "Unlike them, we can stop and take off our packs when we want without getting shot."

"I hope," he said.

She walked across the lot and waited at the edge of the road. "Did you feel the change yet?"

"What change?"

"We just stepped across the Continental Divide. If you spill your canteen now, it goes into the Mississippi instead of the Pacific."

"I'll try to be careful to preserve the levees."

There was a break in the traffic and they hurried across the road. Pete stopped beside a wooden sign that had nothing on it but HIGHLINE TRAIL and an arrow pointing north. "Just how long is this trail?"

She began to walk on the soft, irregular ground, under hemlocks and cedars. It forced Pete to take the first step off the pavement, then hurry to catch up with her, and then they were walking along and the decision was over. "How long?"

"Long."

"What does 'long' mean to a woman like you in miles?"

"On the map it looks like twenty as the crow flies, and

maybe thirty if you take it in sections, point to point. The map isn't big enough to take into account all the meandering, which is what trails through wilderness do. And it's two-dimensional, so I can't tell just how hard the climbing will be. It could be fifty miles and seem like three times that."

"Do you mind if I keep asking questions?"

"Nobody can hear us, and the trail is shorter if you talk."

"What if they find the car?"

"Then they have to make a guess. If they think we changed cars, then they'll drive fast away from here to try to catch up and see the new one. If they think we abandoned it and walked off into the mountains, they have to guess which trail we took. If we went north toward Canada, there are a dozen branches ahead that come out pretty far from each other. But most likely they'll think we left the car so it would look as though we headed north for Canada, but turned south or east or west instead. Those trails all reach roads at some point."

"What if they don't fool themselves, know we headed for Canada, and pick the right trail?"

"Then they have other choices. They have to guess where we'll surface when we get to Canada, drive up there, and wait, or come up the trail after us."

"That's the one I don't like: some guy with a gun coming out here after us."

"Even if they do, they still have choices. We're carrying about what a cautious person would take on a day trip. A smart person would know there was the possibility of not making it back by dark and having to spend one night out there. Anybody who follows could choose to travel lighter than that for speed, or they could carry tents and heavy clothes and a week's food and water. If they travel lighter than we are, they could easily have to turn around and give up. If they load themselves down with lots of gear, they'll have a very hard time catching up with us."

"Especially with all those guns."

She laughed. "I wasn't going to mention those." She looked

at him for a moment as they walked along. He seemed calm. "But you're right. Good sniper rifles are heavy—ten to fifteen pounds with the scope. The ammo isn't light, and this guy isn't likely to scrimp on that. It's usually made for the military, so it's 7.62 millimeters wide and 50 millimeters long. He'll also carry a sidearm of some kind, and ammo for that. I'd say he'll be carrying an extra twenty pounds of metal that we're not."

"Maybe we'll wish we were."

"I doubt it, because if he's carrying the weight, he probably won't catch us. What you do when you're running is put lots and lots of forks in the road behind you. Each time the hunter comes to one, your chance of losing him is fifty percent. Next fork, fifty percent. We've put a lot of forks behind us already. If we stay ahead of him, then even making all the right choices won't help him."

She looked up at him as they walked. He was tall and strong, and he was in acceptable physical condition, because all the women who got off airplanes in Nevada would have found that attractive. "How do you feel?"

"Scared."

"Me too. Are you dizzy or light-headed, sick to your stomach?"

"No more than I have been for months. Why?"

"Then you don't have mountain sickness. I didn't think you would, after three months in Denver. Are your muscles warm and loose?"

"Don't tell me," he said.

"I'm sorry," said Jane. "But we've only got about two hours of light left. I'd really like to get the first of those forks in the trail behind us." She began with a slow trot, the pack shifting at each step and making clanking noises. Pete trotted along, making even more noise. When Jane felt the sweat beginning to come, she lengthened her steps a little, watching the trail for rocks and roots and trenches.

He said, "We sound like a pair of skeletons on a tin roof."

"The noise is good," she said.

"It is?"

"Bears don't like surprises."

26

As Carey made his evening hospital rounds, he kept thinking about Jane. Here it was late summer, but in the Rocky Mountains it must be getting cold already. She had sounded well and confident that she knew what she was doing, but he suspected that she would never have called if she had any doubt that she could convey that impression. She had been perfectly capable of lying to him about what she was doing for over a decade, and he had never suspected her. That was a train of thought he decided not to follow. She would get her client to wherever he was going, and she would come back to him. She would be very surprised at how welcome she was going to be.

He left the room of Mr. Cadwallader and walked down the hallway toward the nurses' station to make his notes. He was pleased. Cadwallader would be moving around nicely by noon tomorrow, and home by the next day. As he pulled Cadwallader's chart from the holder, Nancy Prelsky tapped him on the shoulder. "Telephone, Doctor."

"Huh?" He looked up. "Oh, thanks."

As he took the receiver, he assumed it would be Joy at his office. "Dr. McKinnon."

"Hello, Carey." The voice shocked him. How could Susan Haynes have known where to call him? Of course. The main switchboard had tracked him down and connected her. He hoped they had done it because it was a slow evening, and not because she had implied it was an emergency.

"Hello," said Carey. "Look, I don't want to be rude, but

didn't they tell you I'm on duty right now? And this phone is at a nurses' station on a floor with some very sick people."

"I apologize for calling you at work, but I'll make it brief. After last night's fiasco I'd like to start over again, and invite you and your wife to a dinner party with a few friends. There will be about twelve, and that takes a little advance notice."

He winced. He hated dinner parties, and he was appalled that this woman would call a surgeon in the middle of his rounds to arrange some social event. "I think that's the sort of problem we ought to talk about at another time. If you'll leave your number with my answering service, I'll try to call you tomorrow."

"Please. You have to give me a way to thank you, and this is the way it's done. Can you tell me when Jane will be home?"

"I'm afraid I don't know."

"You don't know? Why in the world not?"

"I just don't."

"I'm sorry to be pushy, but this kind of dinner party takes a certain amount of thought and arranging. Would you please call her and ask?"

He found himself looking around to see if Nancy was still within hearing range. He glanced at the call board and saw that there was a trouble light flashing on the board to signal that an IV had come loose in Room 469. "I can't call her. She'll call me when she can—probably in two or three days."

"Two or three days? Where is she—in jail?"

He tried to be patient, but he could feel the anger growing. "She's hiking in the mountains, and the place she's going is about twenty miles away, by air. Since she doesn't have wings, it'll take that long to get to a phone, and then she'll call. I'll try to remember to ask her then, and let you know. That's the best I can do."

"Fair enough," said Susan. "I'll let you go now. I'm sorry to be such a pain, but I want to make it up to you for last night, and I'm warning you I won't take no for an answer. Good-bye."

As soon as she heard a fresh dial tone, Linda quickly punched new numbers into the telephone. She had wanted to goad him into making just one telephone call to Jane, instead of always waiting for her to check in. If he had agreed to call Jane, she could be sure he would have done it from his home telephone: he was too self-important about his work to do it from the hospital. Then Linda could have tape-recorded the tones of the number he dialed, just as she had done in Hatcher's apartment in Denver. The tactic had not worked this time. Jane had not brought Hatcher to a long-term hiding place yet, so she hadn't given Carey a number he could call. But what Carey had given Linda was better. It was fresher, harder to get, and so it proved that she was better.

As she listened to the telephone ringing, she began to tease herself with thoughts about what she could say to make Earl feel the way she wanted him to. By the time the hotel operator answered, Linda was already beginning to feel choked with the emotions she had induced. When she gave the room number, her voice came out in a brave, sad little sigh.

Earl sat waiting in Lenny's hotel room in Kalispell. He lifted the new British Arctic Warfare sniper rifle out of its fitted transit case and began to break it down so he could clean and oil it. He lovingly ran his fingertips along the smooth nylon foregrip, then loosened the Allen screws. He took out the trigger assembly and adjusted the pull and travel once again.

He had fired from a crook in a tree on the hill at five hundred yards through a window and drilled that guy's temple. If he could have propped him up again and taken more shots, he could have grouped them within an inch of the first. He had supposed that watching her client's head suddenly spout blood across breakfast would be sufficient for Jane for the moment, so he had not searched for her in the crowd and tried to hold her in the crosshairs. He wanted something more complicated and meaningful to happen to her.

The rifle had a simple, unambiguous integrity. The rifle was perfect. Earl was not. He had let himself be seduced by the beauty of it, the smooth, skinlike touch of the nylon stock against his cheek, the dull gleam of the barrel and the clear, soundless image in the scope. He had found the car in the parking lot, he had seen a man with light wavy hair sit down in the window with a dark-haired woman, and he had reached out and harvested him.

Earl had not needed to force himself to wait to make the shot true, because the rifle was perfect. He could exert three pounds of pressure with his finger and the man would certainly be dead. It was only after he had felt the recoil against his shoulder and the scope had settled on the window again that he had perceived that something had gone wrong. He had expected that the restaurant would be abruptly churned into turmoil, with people standing to bump into each other and spilling things, because he had seen it happen before. Seeing the second dark-haired woman pass across the field of the scope had not convinced him. It was driving down from the mountain and seeing that the car he had followed from Salmon Prairie was already heading up the road.

He pushed the knurled lever on the left side of the receiver, slid the bolt out of the rifle, and set it down on the table beside the Allen screws. Every piece of the A.W. reminded him by its weighty, elegant, and indestructable steel, machined to an exacting tolerance, that he was not its equal. This time it had not been a cop stumbling blind into the middle of the hit. This time it had been Earl getting so confident of his invincibility with the new rifle, and so eager to exert it, that he had reacted like a kid, popping the cap because his overheated mind had assumed that any creature that came along a deer run had to be a deer. People were a sorry commodity compared to precision rifles.

When the telephone rang, he glanced at his watch and noted that it was four o'clock. That made it six in Buffalo. He respectfully set the rifle on the bed and picked up the telephone. "Yeah."

"Honey?" She had called him that maybe twice. Her voice was wet and gulpy as though she had been crying.

"Yeah," he said.

"They're hiking in the mountains. They're going twenty miles if it were a straight line, but it isn't, so it will take two or three days. During that time they won't be near a phone."

"Hold on," he said. He stared at the map on the table. He tore off a sheet of paper from the pad with the hotel's name on it, measured twenty miles on the scale, then ran it in a circle from Swan Lake. "It can't be twenty miles from where I last saw them. There's nothing they couldn't have driven to in about a half hour."

"Is there any place that would look safe to them? A private airfield or something?"

"Nothing I can see. Maybe Canada." He ran his finger along the road they had traveled: Missoula, Salmon Prairie, Swan Lake, always north. What if, instead of going left at Bigfork toward Kalispell, as he had, they had gone right? He took the sheet of paper with the twenty-mile mark and ran it slowly along the top of Montana at the Canadian Border. "Glacier," he said.

"What?"

"They could have turned up into Glacier National Park by now. There's only one big road through the middle of it, and it takes a loop up about halfway across that would put them about twenty miles from the border." He held the map close to his face. "Logan Pass." He pushed his thumbnail into the map and left a crescent-shaped mark so he could find it again.

"I should go," she said. Her voice was low and whispery and quiet, like a child's.

"You mean he's there now?"

"He just fell asleep."

"Good." It was as close as Earl could come to a friendly statement. His relief was for himself, because now he wouldn't have to spend the rest of the night thinking about Linda spread out on the bed with that faceless stranger going into her, over and over.

He heard Linda give a little sob, then sniff it back. She said, "He wore himself out . . . on me." The sob came out again.

Earl found himself standing, and the telephone crashed to

the floor, but he could still hear Linda's voice, crying quietly. Earl could feel surges of blood pounding behind his eyes.

"He's a doctor, Earl. He knows things about a woman's body—the nerves and things. He brings me up, all the way up so I can't control myself, and then keeps me there, won't let me stop."

Earl squeezed his eyes closed. He wanted her to shut up. "It's okay," he said. "It'll be over soon."

"Ten minutes ago I begged him—"

"Enough." Earl's voice was harsh and dry. He wanted to tell her to drive a tenpenny nail through the man's chest while he was sleeping, and then walk out. He wanted to, but he couldn't. Not yet. "Just do the best you can. The minute I've got them, I'll call you there." He found a pen on the nightstand with the little questionnaire about the maid service. "What's the number?"

She read it to him off the telephone dial. "But if you call me here, he'll get spooked. Leave a message on the machine at home or at the apartment I rented."

"Right," he said, but he wrote the number on the question-naire. "I'll call you." His writing was a scrawl, so even he could barely read it. He was in a horrible confusion of jealousy of this McKinnon that somehow merged into his rage at Pete Hatcher for putting him into this spot. He felt disgust at Linda for being a woman—a creature that had no other way of get-ting what she needed from a man, but who could do it when-ever she felt like it, because any man would accept the offer. He felt shame and humiliation because he had been able to invent no better way to find Pete Hatcher than to let his own woman turn herself out as a whore.

He thought back on the shot he had taken at Swan Lake and wanted to bite his finger off. She had already given away everything she had just to buy him that shot, and he had squan-dered it. Then he had the shadow pass across his vision that maybe Linda, deep down, wasn't as miserable about this as she had to make him think she was. He brushed all of these thoughts into the back of his mind. "You just think about what happens to him the minute I've got Hatcher. You'll get to do the cutting. Keep your mind on that."

"You can bet I will," said Linda. Her voice was hardening now into cold, clean anger, and that made Earl feel better. But then her voice changed again, and he could tell her mouth was away from the receiver. "In the bathroom," she called. Her voice was soft and thick. "All right." To Earl she whispered, "I've got to go," and hung up.

Earl placed the telephone receiver into its cradle and put the telephone back on the nightstand, then stepped to the door to the next room and looked at Lenny.

He was lying on the bed staring at the television. The two black dogs lifted their heads and looked at Earl, but Lenny kept his eyes on the screen, where one man was chasing another one along a catwalk in a dark factory.

"Load up the car," said Earl. "Keep the camping gear on top."

"We going someplace tonight?" He said it as though the idiocy of loading the car at night would be self-evident.

"Yeah, tonight. And get the dogs into their carriers. They're going too."

Linda pushed her chair away from the kitchen table and stood to hang up the wall telephone. She smiled to herself contentedly. Linda looked around at the bright, clean surfaces. She loved the careful, economical use of the space. The pots and pans were all heavy and old; only French gourmet companies still made them that way, and they charged hundreds of dollars for them.

She padded around the kitchen in her bare feet, collecting the ingredients and implements she would need for this recipe. As she bent down to pull a big pot out of the cupboard, she acknowledged that Jane's blue jeans felt a little tight in the thigh and the ass, but she wasn't sorry. When Carey got home from the late shift at the hospital, that wouldn't be something that he minded. Even men who thought that wearing tight clothes made you stupid would look hard at whatever you let them see.

She filled the pot with water and set it on one of the back burners to boil, then opened the door of the big old-fashioned pantry. There, hanging on a brass hook, was Jane's apron. She slipped the loop over her head and tied the strings behind her back in a bow. She looked down at the apron and smiled. It was dark blue with a red ribbon border and little blue cornflowers and yellow buttercups embroidered on it. It was almost too pretty to use.

She began to open the drawers under the counter, looking for ladles. In the second one she opened, she found an old boning knife that had been sharpened like a razor. She recognized instantly that this was the perfect tool. It was simple to hide and felt good in her hand, too secure to slip, too sharp to be brushed away. She set it sideways just inside the drawer, where she could find it quickly without cutting herself, and opened the next drawer. "Now," she whispered. "Where do I keep my ladles?"

An hour later Earl drove the car past the sign that said GOING-TO-THE-SUN ROAD OPEN MAY 15–SEPTEMBER 15. Jane was about a day too early. Earl was simply too much for her. He forced himself not to acknowledge the way he had come by the information, because that would make him think about what Linda was doing right now. Earl was the one who was too much for all of them. When you won the pot it didn't much matter who put what chips into it.

He could drive quickly now that it was dark, gliding into the turns and accelerating out of them to keep his traction. Lenny gripped the door handle but kept silent. Earl reached the Logan Pass visitor center, pulled into the parking lot, and studied the cars that had been left there overnight. When he didn't find the one he had followed in the morning, he drove past the building and found it parked at the edge of the woods not far from a garbage Dumpster. "That's it."

Lenny said, "We going to do something to the car?"

"Yeah. We're going to look at it."

He parked beside the car and looked inside. The keys were in the ignition. He opened the door, took out the keys, unlocked the trunk, and found it empty. He could see that they had cleaned the car out thoroughly. He said to Lenny, "Don't touch anything. Just let the dogs out, but keep them behind the car. They don't let dogs in the park."

Lenny let the two big black dogs out of their traveling cages. They panted and huffed for a few seconds, wagging their tails and trotting in circles. Earl opened the doors of the abandoned car. "Get in," he said. *"Einsteigen in."*

The dogs leapt through the doors, sniffing the car, the upholstery, the steering wheel. Earl turned to Lenny. "Give them a few minutes to get the scent." He took a flashlight from Lenny's car, walked to the Dumpster, and opened it. He found the two suitcases covered with garbage. They would be of no use.

Earl gingerly reached down, pushed the garbage aside with his light, and opened the first suitcase. Clothes . . . they had left clothes inside. His heart beat faster as he took out his pocket knife.

In a moment he was back at the car. He said quietly, *"Herauskommen."* The dogs jumped out of the car and waited for his command. He held the two shoes up so the dogs could take their time sniffing them. *"Fund!"* he said.

The two big black dogs circled the cars for a few seconds, looking puzzled. They sniffed the ground and came back, then turned their wide heads to stare in various directions. Lenny looked at Earl nervously, but Earl said, "Give them as long as it takes."

The dogs finally agreed that the visitor center building was the right direction. They trotted to the door and sniffed the steps and nosed the glass. Earl said, "They probably walked over there, but they didn't come back."

Earl picked up his backpack, then eased his arms into the straps and walked to the visitor center. *"Auf den fersen folgen."* The dogs fell into place at his side. He crossed the road with them and watched their faces. They seemed not to smell the scent, but maybe to dimly suspect it.

Lenny joined him beside the sign that said HIGHLINE TRAIL. He gazed at the dogs. "Doesn't look like they picked up anything here."

"No," said Earl. "The two of them bought new shoes. The first time they wore them was probably when they got out of the car and walked over here."

"Then why did you get them to sniff the car and the old shoes?" The man's head might as well be a helmet. His was a mind that never failed to disappoint.

"Because in a day or so, when we need help, the new shoes are going to smell exactly like the old ones."

Earl stood and stared into the darkness where the trail led off under the trees. His mind formed the words, "I'm coming. You'll wish you had put a gun in your mouth while you could." He wasn't sure precisely whom he was talking to. The distinction didn't mean enough for him to try to sort it out. He would have all of them in their turns and in the ways that they deserved.

It seemed to Calvin Seaver that he had called Earl and Linda a hundred times—first from Kennedy Airport, then from his stopover in Chicago, then Denver, and finally from Billings. He had never gotten anything but the answering machine, and he could hardly leave a message telling two killers that Pete Hatcher was in Salmon Prairie, Montana.

It was in the Billings airport that he saw the story on the television news, and he was glad that he had been cautious. There was film of a lot of people milling around outside a restaurant in Swan Lake, just a few miles up the road from Salmon Prairie. The newsman, who looked enough like the one Seaver usually watched in Las Vegas to be his brother, said a sniper had fired through the window and killed a man. What caught Seaver's attention had not been the body bag being wheeled out on a collapsible stretcher. It was the woman with long black hair who was being helped into a police car beside the ambulance.

He checked into a hotel in Billings and watched the report over and over on every local channel. For the first couple of hours he could feel that although his mind was still unsure, his body was already celebrating, pumping blood through the arteries in hard, dizzying surges, his breaths tasting sweet and full.

Seaver had been in the trouble business for over twenty years, and he had developed a clear idea of the odds. Swan Lake was a tiny town in the middle of the mountains. The population of the whole state was just a bit over eight hundred thousand. There probably hadn't been a shooting in Swan Lake since the Indian Wars. How could it not be Earl who had done it? How could that dark-haired woman not be *the* dark-haired woman? But Seaver needed to be positive. He sat on the edge of the hotel bed, the remote control in his hand, switching from channel to channel for three hours.

At ten o'clock, when the local news came on again, there was a photograph of the shooting victim. It was a portrait of a man wearing a suit and tie, his expression in a forced smile. It looked a little bit like Pete Hatcher, but it wasn't. The newswoman was telling Seaver that it was just some guy who had gotten himself shot—some unsuspecting dope who had been eating breakfast in front of the wrong window. Seaver couldn't believe it.

His mind shuffled quickly through the possibilities, looking for hope. The picture was a fraud. Earl had hit Hatcher, but Hatcher wasn't dead. The dark-haired woman had slipped the newsmen a fake picture to keep Earl from trying again while Hatcher was in the hospital. Or Earl had shot Hatcher, and Hatcher was dead. The picture was taken off some stolen ID the police had found in his wallet, and that was why it was a picture of somebody else. The more Seaver thought about it, the more he liked that theory. It made a lot of sense, especially if Hatcher had been shot in the head. Most people could barely look in the direction of a fatal head wound without fainting, and even if they did, there was so much blood on the face and so much distortion of the muscles—a slackening at first and then a tightening into a rictus—that any resemblance the corpse bore to a photograph of anything alive would have been accepted as a match.

Seaver clung to this theory for another half hour, waiting impatiently for the newswoman to come back from a commercial and announce that the initial identification had been wrong. His hope ended when the newswoman came back from a commercial with, instead, footage of the victim's parents leaving the coroner's office after identifying the body.

He wearily leafed through the pile of tourist magazines the hotel maids had left on the coffee table. They contained very little except ads for stores and restaurants in the area, but finally he found one with three pages of maps in it and spent a few minutes studying them.

Tomorrow morning, after he had caught up on his sleep, he would drive up to Kalispell. It looked like the only town up there that was big enough to hide a stranger comfortably. He would check into a hotel there and spend some time trying to pick up signs of Earl and Linda.

27

Jane led Pete along the trail in the waning light. She kept them at a double-time pace, along the long high cliff the map called the Garden Wall and on to Haystack Butte. When she judged that they had traveled two miles, she slowed to a walk. She waited for her wind to come back and then listened while Hatcher's deep, labored breathing slowly became quiet. She said, "How do you feel?"

"Lousy."

"Does your head ache?"

"Yes."

"Dizzy?"

"Yes."

"Green spots on your hands?"

"Yes."

"Liar."

"Yes." He walked along at her shoulder, taking deep breaths and blowing them out. She listened to them attentively without speaking. There were no whistles, no bubbly liquid sounds that would mean he was in trouble. There were people who simply could not tolerate high altitudes. Unless they were brought down, their lungs filled up with fluid until they drowned. Starting Pete off with a two-mile jog probably had not been the safest way to find out that he wasn't one of them, but she had needed to know before they had gone too far to turn back.

She had not lied to him about needing to use the last precious hour or two of light efficiently, to put distance between them and the road. It was already getting too dark to run. A twisted ankle would make the next thirty miles a nightmare.

As she walked, she subtly increased the pace again. She tried to keep her steps regular enough on the uneven, winding path to hold her speed. The end of the long summer had come, so the trail was as beaten down by other boots as it would ever be, and it had been laid out at about seven thousand feet, along the ridges just below the treeline, where soil was thin and poor and the constant winds stunted the fir trees.

After another mile they had passed Haystack Butte, and in the dusky light she saw the change she was looking for in the slopes to her left. There was a low, lush dark carpet of bushes and evergreens—lodgepole pine, spruce, fir—all young and thick. Among them loomed tall, ghostly gray trunks like the masts of sunken ships.

"Look at that," said Pete. "I wonder why it looks like that."

"A fire," said Jane. "In 1967 this patch burned."

He craned his neck to look at her with ironic amusement. "You from around here?"

She shook her head and smiled. "Of course not. I spent half the day in the car looking at maps. This is one of the places I picked out to get my bearings. If we get lost up here we're not going to enjoy the experience."

"What do we look for next?"

"After another mile or two, we should be able to look up on our right and see glaciers. First a little one. That's Gem Glacier. Then a really big one, called Grinnell Glacier. Then Swiftcurrent Glacier, all in a stretch of a couple of miles."

"And after that?"

"If we get that far before it's too dark to travel, I'll be very surprised."

He walked along for a time, then said, "I guess I should be delighted at the news that I don't have to keep trudging along all night. To tell you the truth, though, the farther we get from that guy with the rifle, the better I feel. And there's even something about it getting dark that's comforting. I've been having a prickly feeling in the back of my neck, like he's back there looking down the barrel at me."

Jane turned and looked up at him with an enigmatic smile. "He wouldn't be looking down the barrel. Nobody puts a round through somebody's temple from that far out without a scope."

"You're a very strange woman. You know that?"

"Of course I do." She smiled. "It's something I've cultivated over the years. But I'll bet you want to keep going even more than you did a minute ago, don't you?"

He seemed to be consulting an inner voice as he walked. "You're right. It worked. I feel bad enough to walk for hours."

"Bad isn't exactly the feeling I was looking for, but that's the price. As long as you never let your brain stop working, thinking about what's behind you, you'll be very hard to kill."

"So the prickly feeling in the back of the neck doesn't go away."

"That's right. I have it right now."

Pete half-turned his head to look as he walked. There was nothing behind them but the empty trail as far as the last bend. "You think they're back there?"

"If I did, I'd be running for my life," she said. "I think they're good. They'll find out the car was left in that lot in about three days, when it's towed out of the park. By then the only road here will be closed to visitors, the nearby car crossings into Canada will be closed too, and the long detours that go up there don't go to where we'll be. What I think they'll do next is give up."

The sky was darkening quickly now, and she saw the glow of his teeth that had to be a smile. "Really?"

"They've been following you for about a hundred days. They've committed two murders they won't get paid for. They've exhausted the computer searches, because from here on we aren't going to use credit cards or even names, if we can help it. That means the hunting is going to get much harder. Following you into a foreign country adds a level of extra risk. I think for a professional, the point of diminishing returns has come. They're in it for the money, and if this goes on much longer, the money's not good enough. They could have made more of it more easily doing bitter divorce cases and premature life-insurance payouts."

"Won't Pleasure, Inc., hire somebody else?"

"There are several possibilities. One is that these killers will tell Pleasure, Inc., where they lost you. Pleasure, Inc., will decide that if you're in Canada, then you're not planning on talking to American police. A second possibility is that the people who are after us now will keep Pleasure, Inc., on the hook—tell them to be patient, they're on your trail—but not waste any time actually hunting. Once a month they'll use the computer to see if your aliases turned up again."

"So I should feel good, right? I'm not being stupid."

"No. Because in a week or so they'll probably be off stalking somebody else, and if they're replaced, the new ones will be starting at zero. This morning you were talking about a different feeling you had—that you were glad to be alive. It's not gone, is it?"

"No."

"The quiver in the back of your neck doesn't go away, but the good feeling doesn't either. Now that you've had it, every day is going to feel as though you won it in a world championship."

He laughed. "It already does."

"You'll notice other things later."

"What things?"

"Good things. The kind of ambition that's stupid, the kind that makes you want a fancy car and a big house and flashy clothes, goes away."

"Why?"

"Because having them makes you feel as though people are looking at you, and that's uncomfortable. Being average, normal, makes you feel comfortable, and it isn't very different unless you read labels very closely. That was always true, of course, but now you'll be able to feel it, because you know that being a regular guy is a million miles from being dead."

The trail led them up between thickets of berry bushes, across meadows of wildflowers now dry and well past blooming. As the light died for the night, Jane could see the higher peaks on her right, but the blue-white glacial ice was lost in the black silhouettes of the mountains. They walked on, sticking to the center of the path in the dark. Jane took her flashlight out of her pack and let it play on the ground in front of her. Finally, as the trail led them up into a stand of stunted pine trees, she stopped, knelt on the ground, and studied the map.

"Are we lost yet?" asked Pete. She felt his shoulder beside hers as he knelt down to look at the little circle of light.

She put her finger on the map. "We're here." It was a spot where twisting dotted lines seemed to radiate in all directions, like the strands of an unraveling rope. "The trail on the left goes back to the road, then up Flattop Creek. The one on the right goes through Swiftcurrent Pass and connects with this whole network of trails up here. This one in the middle is the one we want." She aimed her flashlight up the path, and in the glow around it, Pete caught a glimpse of a wooden sign.

"So what's the problem?"

She frowned. "Never give up a chance to deceive. This chance is a beauty. I'm just trying to figure out how to use it."

He said, "Switch the sign?"

"They wouldn't be looking for one trail or another. They'd be looking for us, probably our footprints. We've already put about seven miles of them on the path, and if they were following, by now they wouldn't have much trouble recognizing them."

Pete sat and waited while Jane stared at the map, then stood up, opened his pack, and handed him his flashlight. "This is probably a waste of time," she said. "But if they do follow us, it isn't. You go down the left path as far as you can until it gets so narrow you can't step off it. A quarter mile would be great, but at least a couple of hundred yards. When you get to that point step off, and come back parallel with the trail, never stepping back onto it. Meet me here."

Jane walked down the trail to the right alone. She stopped

once to listen for Pete's footsteps, and when she heard them they sounded as though he was doing what she had asked. One of the qualities that made Pete Hatcher worth saving was that he never resisted. He wanted to live, so if she was willing to help him, he would do what she asked. Simple.

As she walked, she imagined herself taking Carey out of the world. Everything he said would be a question too, but the questions he asked would come from a more complicated intelligence, one that would be sifting and evaluating and testing alternative logical paths. The problem with classically intelligent people was that they seemed to be able to discern too many alternatives to pick any of them during the brief periods when what they did still mattered. She wondered what she had meant by that, and was back to the night ten months ago when Carey had asked her to marry him. She had said she would not marry him right then. She would tell him about her last trip—about who she really was—and then give him a year to think before he asked again.

He had not listened and then said instantly, "I don't care about any of this. Marry me now." He had listened judiciously and then let the waiting period begin. When he had thought about it for a month, instead of sticking to the terms and letting her spend the year cutting her ties, he had realized that he didn't want to wait—not shouldn't, but didn't want to. He had been unfair. He had focused his intellect on convincing her to marry him while she still had no business marrying anyone.

Her mind abruptly collided with something and jumped to another track. That story was fictitious. Jane Whitefield walked through the world with her eyes wide open. She could not pretend she had not known what might happen, or what she would do if it did. She had always felt contempt for women who accepted the theorem that if they were unhappy it could only be because their husbands had not made them happy. This must be how it started: constructing convoluted proofs that their mistakes were not actually their mistakes but their husbands' failure to prevent them or cure them. Not me, she thought. I did this, because I wanted his love more than I wanted to be careful. Now I'm going to get through it and go home to my husband, who is impatient because he adores me.

She watched the path narrowing, the rock slope on her right rising into a wall, and the little margin of weeds on her left thinning into a ledge that bordered a steep chasm. She put the flashlight into her back pocket, leaned both hands on the wall, placed her toes on the weeds, and began to sidestep back the way she had come. She had inched along for fifty feet before she was able to stand upright again. Then she carefully took a diagonal course down a gentler slope and headed for the crossroads.

When she approached the rocky knoll, she saw Pete Hatcher waiting patiently for her. She switched on her flashlight so he would see her coming and not be startled. "Been waiting long?"

"No," he said. "Just got here. I went as far as a streambed, where it started to get wet. I came back through the woods."

"Very good," she said. She sat beside him. "Now we change our socks." He watched her untying her boots for a second, then did as she said. When they had their boots on again, she said, "Now put the old socks on over your boots."

"It's a tight fit," he said as he tugged and stretched.

"It's okay," said Jane. "Now stuff some of these dry weeds under the soles of your boots, inside the sock, for padding. Don't use leaves, because they'll squish and get juicy. No pine needles, because they're slippery."

When they had finished, she led him off beside the center trail. They did not step onto the trail again for fifteen minutes, at the start of a stretch of bare rock that extended beyond the flashlight's beam. Pete stopped and shone his flashlight back the way they had come. "No trail at all," he said. "You're amazing."

"It cost us a half hour, but it always makes you feel better to do what you can. And if we are being followed, it will do more than make us feel better. You have to remember this isn't the F.B.I. that's after us. It's probably just some guy who discovered early on that it was easier to pull a trigger than learn algebra."

As Jane set off across the rocky plateau, she discovered that what she had told Pete was a lie. Stopping to disguise their trail had not made her feel safer. She tried to measure the prickly sensation in the back of her neck, and her body gave a convulsive shiver. She pivoted suddenly in her tracks and stared back into the forest. The sight gave her no comfort: the individual silhouettes of the trees had merged together into a shadowy mass of twisted limbs ready to assume any shape her imagination gave them.

"What's wrong?" said Pete.

"Nothing," she said. "Just checking to see if you were keeping up." She turned and began to walk quickly, and as she walked she searched for a way to exorcise her uneasiness.

She caught herself wishing she could have spotted the shooter on the mountainside this morning—if only a running human form, a solid shape in the windshield of a speeding car. As it was, the restaurant window had suddenly imploded in a shower of glass, and a bloody hole had appeared in a man's head. There was nothing mysterious about the way that had been accomplished, but to some part of her subconscious mind, knowing the mechanical workings of rifles and silencers was information too meager to lay to rest the sensations she had felt.

Since she had left home it had not felt to her as though professional killers had been logically tracing Pete Hatcher's movements. It felt as though they had given up physical form entirely, and rode the wind, waiting to materialize wherever it suited them.

Earl readjusted Lenny's load. When he cinched the straps to make everything secure, he nearly tugged Lenny off his feet. "Think you can keep your balance?"

Lenny slipped the tumpline over his forehead and took a few steps. "Sure," he said. "In the army we used to pack ninety pounds of gear and add the extra ammo on top of it. This can't be much worse."

Earl's jaw worked impatiently. Whenever Lenny was feeling resentful, he would just happen to mention that he had once been declared worthy to sign up to get his head shaved and hang around Fort Leonard Wood in case they needed extra cannon fodder. Earl was never quite sure whether Lenny was implying that cleaning latrines had made him Earl's moral superior, or excusing his inadequacy by saying that those wasted years had set him too far back to ever recover. It didn't much matter. Whatever they had done for him in the army, it hadn't given him big enough balls to challenge Earl directly, so Earl tolerated the talk.

He said, "Just use your map and compass, like they taught you, and don't lose your own ass out here." He turned to T-Bone and Rusty. *"Raus!"*

The two dogs galloped down the trail to the first bend, then waited and stared back at him. Earl adjusted his own pack as he set off. Lenny's military career had brought Earl one benefit, anyway. It had made him think of moving through these mountains the way armies did. He had loaded Lenny's strong back with all the camping gear and supplies, so Earl could carry little and forge ahead with the dogs. If he wanted anything Lenny was carrying, he could meet him on the main trail.

Earl walked along the path after T-Bone and Rusty for a few hundred yards to let his pupils open to the dark and his muscles get warm. Then he stopped and did a few stretching exercises against a tall cedar. When he was ready, he began to run.

As he ran, Earl considered his circumstances, and he found them to his liking. Jane Whitefield and Pete Hatcher had graciously gone to a great deal of exertion and inconvenience to put themselves into a place where he was strong and they were weak. Hatcher had been saved twice by the simple fact that it was hard to kill a man in a public place without committing suicide. Now it was only one day before the whole national park closed, and there would be no more tourists setting out into the high country to get in the way.

Earl moved through the woods with a hunter's practiced lope. He had always been a sportsman who loved to take the long, difficult shot, so he had spent many cold mornings running patiently through rough country, trailing wounded deer until they began to choke and cough too much blood to go on. Tonight he used his dogs to find his way and keep him on the path. He could hear the difference when their panting came from higher or lower, left or right, and the thuds of their big paws told him the nature of the surface they were running on. Turning on a flashlight in these woods would have given his presence away to anyone looking back from the ridges above, and the glare would have made his pupils contract, leaving him half-blind for several minutes.

Earl habitually held his head a little to the side as he ran, because the best night vision was at the edges of the eyes, and none of the wind from his running distorted the sounds. He knew his long legs carried him farther at each stride than his prey could step, and his stamina would keep him going longer than any man who had spent his days lounging around in Las Vegas.

He knew that the two of them must have started hiking at least four or five hours ago, but that did not bother him. They would walk for a few hours, until the moon was high and the wind up here started to howl, and then they would take their own exhaustion as an assurance that Earl would be too tired to follow. They would camp, make a shelter and a fire, and curl up. Maybe they would be cautious enough to tramp a distance off the main trail first, but they wouldn't risk going too far.

They didn't know what was after them. Earl could just discern the black barrel torsos of Rusty and T-Bone ahead of him in the dark—beasts with as much mass and muscle as small men, that could hear a twig the size of a toothpick snap under a boot, smell a fire in the woods for miles, and see with a predator's vision that didn't bother much with subtle gradations of tone and color but had evolved to pick out unerringly whatever was alive so they could sink their teeth into it.

As Earl ran, he could feel the strange, triangular field between him and Rusty and T-Bone, the dogs' attentiveness to his sound and scent holding them in position. They were as alert to any change in his will as to the sights and sounds ahead of them. The dogs were part of him now. He was a creature with three heads and sharp teeth and a rifle and a man's brain, galloping through the forest sniffing the wind for the smell of live meat.

Carey had finished his hospital rounds at seven, but he had found over the past ten days that each night he went home a little later. The old, comfortable house where he had grown up now seemed cavernous and empty because Jane wasn't there waiting for him. Tonight he had gone back to his office and spent two hours making notations in the files of his patients, signing forms and letters that Joy had typed and left on his desk, then looking over the latest pile of medical journals for articles that he needed to study. At nine he walked back to the hospital lot, climbed into the BMW, and remembered that he still had not stopped to fill up the tank. In the midst of that Susan Haynes business last night, he had forgotten, and then in the morning she had managed to delay him long enough so that he had not had time.

He turned the key carefully with dread in his heart and listened intently. The engine turned over, and the car violated Carey's sense of the laws of physics by starting, then taking him to the gas station without running dry.

As Carey drove up to the big old house in Amherst he was thinking about food. It was nearly ten o'clock, and he had not had dinner yet. Maybe he would just make himself a sandwich and go to bed. He saw that there were lights on in a couple of the downstairs windows. Susan Haynes had obviously forgotten to turn off any switches before she had locked the door this morning . . . if she had remembered to do that much. He pulled into the long driveway toward the garage. As he reached the place where the drive turned the corner of the house, his headlights lit up the bright-red tail reflectors of the car parked by the back door. It was the big black Mercedes that Susan Haynes had leased.

Carey stopped his car, pulled it forward around the big Mercedes to keep from blocking it in, and killed the engine. He glanced at his watch again. It was nine fifty-six. This woman was in his house at nine fifty-six waiting for him to come home. He closed his eyes and felt a constriction in the muscles of his throat.

His mind surveyed his mistakes leading backward in time like stepping stones. He should never have given her his key. He should never have invited an unattached woman to stay the night, never have given her a ride, never even have let on that her car had been towed to clear his parking space. He batted away the excuses that his mind automatically fabricated and spit out for him, like a machine that had short-circuited: no, he had not done it because she had really needed his help. He had done it because she was beautiful and he had not wanted to stop looking at her; because she was smart and distracting and he was tired of being alone. He had liked her. The nervously clinical words of an old study of physiological responses came back to him. Affection—even the most innocent kind—was found to prompt a "slight tumescence of the genitals." And that, in turn, would probably prompt a rationalization.

He knew that he could not start his engine again, back out of the driveway, and abandon his house until this woman got tired of waiting and went away. The only other option he had was to go inside and find out what she thought she was doing. It took him a moment to identify the source of his reluctance to face her. It was the instinctive alarm that made animals shy away from one of their kind that was behaving strangely. It had probably kept a lot of epidemics from spreading to healthy animals and wiping out entire species. This time the instinct was serving no purpose. Neuroses weren't contagious.

He walked around to the front door, found it unlocked, and stepped inside. The smell of food cooking overwhelmed him and reminded him how hungry he was. Susan had sneaked into his house and cooked something for him. He was relieved. It was unwelcome, but at least it was comprehensible, possibly even within the boundaries of normal behavior. He tried to analyze his lingering irritation at her. What had she actually done? He supposed that what had annoyed him most was that she had playfully set off a sexual longing that he was not entitled to feel. As soon as he had admitted it, he felt ridiculous for resenting her for it: blaming women for stimulating impure thoughts had gone out with witch trials. Or it should have.

He detected that he was also straining against some primitive territorial reaction she had triggered by coming into his lair without permission. The hostility was misplaced—just another legacy from earlier primates that had begun to get in the way. She wasn't trying to harm him. She was trying to be kind, after all. A lot of people believed that the rules should be abrogated for surprises. Carey was not one of those people, but he had to live in the world. "Hello?" he called. "Anybody here?"

When he heard no answer, he ventured into the living room. He moved into the dining room, and saw her. She was facing away from him, wearing a pair of jeans and a sweatshirt that he recognized as Jane's. If it had not been for the long, golden hair he might almost have convinced himself that she was Jane. She was pouring champagne into two glasses. The table was elaborately set with the best silver, and the candles were lit. She turned and held out a glass. "Hi," she said. The reserved, distant smile was on her lips. "Have you eaten dinner?"

"No," he admitted. "To what do I owe all this?" He realized that his jaw was tight, the muscles working. He smiled to cover the tension.

She shrugged, and he wished that it had not made him aware of the movement of her breasts under the fabric. "I'm showing you my gratitude. You've been very nice to me."

"I thought you had your heart set on a big dinner party." He looked around the corner toward the living room. "Should I expect the Rotherbergs and Bortonis to leap out from behind the curtains?"

She grinned and shook her head. "No, it's not a surprise

party. It's just a surprise." She sipped her champagne and looked into his eyes. "For you."

"Why?" He tried to seem casual. "I mean, I guess I should just say, 'Thanks.'" Unexpectedly, the rest of it came out. "But, to be honest with you, coming in and finding someone inside my house is not my favorite experience. I suppose that for a lot of people, it must be an accepted custom: it seems to turn up in television plots almost as often as the Evil Twin or the Long-Lost Father, and nobody else seems shocked. But I am. If I want somebody to come, I invite them."

The suddenness of her smile staggered him. It seemed to come from absolutely nowhere, and to be immune to anything he had said. She shrugged. "I gave you every opportunity, but you don't seem to let yourself think about anything personal until after work, and that would have been too late, wouldn't it? If I'd known it would bother you, I would have done it another way." She turned away and began fiddling with the objects on the table again.

He was positive that he was right, but he began to regret having said the words. When she spun around to face him, she seemed to have forgotten he had spoken at all: the smile seemed more radiant. "This doesn't get you out of my party, by the way. When your wife comes home, I'm still going to have a bunch of the local gentry over for dinner. That pays you back officially for helping me last night."

He waved his hand at the table. "Isn't this enough?"

She cocked her head at him. "This isn't the official thanks, which will be completely insincere and self-serving, and which Jane and I will like more than you do. This is something I thought of after I called you today. You're all alone and you don't know when your wife is coming back, and you sounded unhappy. Now is the time when a woman can offer something that will actually do you some good. So I decided to cook you a meal. Big deal."

She pointedly set her champagne glass beside the nearest plate and pulled out the chair at the head of the table. "I've done enough explaining and I'm hungry. So sit while I serve you."

Carey sat in the chair and she reached over his shoulder, then ceremoniously placed the linen napkin on his lap. "This is really something," he conceded. He turned his head as he said it, and found her still leaning over him, her face much closer than he had anticipated. He could smell the subtle scent of her hair, see the big liquid green eyes glinting in the candlelight.

"It's meant to be," she said. "No empty promises."

He was relieved when she brought out the big pot and began to serve the food. She had made bouillabaisse, and it had certainly not gotten worse during the hours after she had expected him to arrive. He tasted it.

"A small, neatly inscribed thank-you note would have been more than sufficient, but the food is wonderful," he said.

She tasted it too. "It turned out okay. I gave myself a tour of the house while you were out. When I got a good look at the kitchen, I figured I'd have to take this seriously if I was going to give you what you were used to."

"Well, thank you. You really know how to cook. You must like to."

She shook her head. "I hate it. I learned because men like to eat, and I like men."

He hurried to change the subject. "I just remembered that I saw your car in the driveway. Did everything go all right?"

She shrugged. "It was pretty much what you said in the morning. They were there all the time. The man I paid the ransom for my car said they don't always hear the phone ringing from outside."

"How much was it?"

"Three hundred. Isn't that outrageous? A hundred for towing the car down there, and two hundred for the fine. And they don't take credit cards."

Carey said, "I feel terrible. It was partly my fault. I'd like to pay for it." He had a strong impulse to make all accounts even, so the give-and-take would stop.

Her amused look returned. "That's very chivalrous. But it's

not the money, it's the effrontery." She seemed to realize something that hadn't occurred to her before. "And anyway, the whole point of the evening was to get out and meet people, and I guess it served its purpose. I met a lot of people, and made one friend."

He gave a noncommittal smile and a little nod. He tried to decide why the idea made him so uncomfortable. Maybe living in a small city all his life had made him conservative and timid about meeting new people, but he had known Susan Haynes little more than twenty-four hours. The word "friend" sounded premature, almost presumptuous.

There was also an element of danger in it that he did not find appealing. She was enormously attractive, and her conversation always had a sexual edge to it that seemed uncalculated but that his common sense told him could not be. It wasn't entirely clear whether she was overtly tempting him or treating him as though he were asexual. Maybe she was just behaving with a kind of adult openness that he had become entitled to as a married man, and he wasn't used to it yet. Maybe when you were happily married, women simply accepted you as safely ineligible for sexual relationships and became less guarded. But it was difficult to imagine a friendship with Susan Haynes extending into the future. Conversations would be full of tension and ambiguity. He suspected that Jane would take one look at her, listen to about three sentences, and announce that she hated her.

Carey realized that the silence had gone on for too long. "Did you make more progress in getting settled today, or just slave over a hot stove?"

"Not much progress. I spent most of the day thinking about you."

"Oh?" Trouble.

"Oh?" she mocked. "As if you weren't thinking about me."

He decided he had better not evade that one. "To be honest with you, over the years I've gotten to be pretty good at keeping my mind focused on my work during the day. I find I lose fewer patients that way."

"I'm sorry," she said. She shook her head and stared down at her lap. "I'm doing it again. It's like a reflex. I guess that's why I couldn't get you out of my mind—you're the witness to my gaffe. I made such a mess of things last night. It was completely unfair."

He noticed that Susan had stopped eating some time ago, and he had eaten as much as he wanted. "What was unfair?"

She smiled apologetically and shrugged, then looked at him from behind a strand of blond hair. "Sometimes when you meet somebody—even though you like them, or maybe because you like them—you start off wrong, and just keep going that way. You know it isn't the way you want to be with them, but somehow you can't figure out how to stop and start all over again. What I should have done last night was have a pleasant dinner with you, then call a cab and go home."

He silently agreed with her. He fervently wished he had made some excuse and called her a cab. "I really didn't mind giving you a ride," Carey lied. "None of this was any trouble at all."

"Of course you minded," said Susan. "I was being childish last night. Teasing you, instead of being honest and direct. So now I'm trying to start all over again."

"I don't even know what you mean," said Carey.

Her smile was beautiful, a little embarrassed. "Let's just say that I didn't really need your help undressing last night."

Carey felt his collar tighten as the blood rushed up to his head. He nodded. "I see." He had to find a way to end this. "Forget it," he said. "I admire your sensitivity very much. And I'm in awe of your honesty. Now we're more than even. And I really appreciate the wonderful dinner. I had almost forgotten how hungry I was until I was here. Thanks a lot."

Susan stood up and stepped toward the door of the dining room, carrying her glass. She stopped and looked back at him. "Is it time for a new start?"

"Absolutely," he answered. Anything to get past this. He picked up his glass and followed her into the living room.

She sat down on the couch by the fireplace. He hesitated,

then chose the easy chair on the opposite side, ten feet from her. He took a sip of his drink and glanced back at the dining room.

"Don't worry about the dishes," she said. She stood up and slipped the sweatshirt over her head and off. "I'll do them in the morning." She was wearing a black lace bra that made her white skin look somehow more bare than it should have.

He suddenly realized that he was gaping. He shook his head. "No," he said. "That isn't what I meant."

"We're being honest now, Carey," she said. "You wanted me last night. If you hadn't, then nothing I did would have made the slightest difference."

"I think you misunderstood," he said. "Or maybe I did."

She unbuttoned the jeans, slipped them down, and stepped out of them. More black lace, more smooth, milky skin. "I'm making up for teasing you last night. I'm not teasing now."

"Hold it," he said. "Could you please stop taking your clothes off for a minute and let me talk?" He took a deep breath. "I'm married."

"So am I." The full lips formed themselves into the reserved smile he had seen when he met her. "You're looking, though, aren't you?"

"It's hard not to."

She seemed to take this as permission to continue. She unhooked the black bra and slipped it off. Her breasts were round and full, whiter even than the rest of her, and the nipples were like rosebuds. She saw the alarm in his eyes and her voice went lower, almost a whisper. "It's okay. It's perfectly okay."

"No," said Carey. "It isn't okay." He resolutely kept his eyes on hers, but her eyes were teasing him now. "This isn't what I want. This could wreck my life."

She smirked, confidently aware that her nudity was power, and words were only a way of keeping him faced in her direction. "No, it couldn't. I'm married too, and that's what makes it perfect. You don't have to remember my birthday, and I don't have to entertain your poker buddies. My husband and your wife are thousands of miles away. Tonight, we can do any-thing, and it's free. There are no possible consequences."

"Your marriage may be ending, but mine's just beginning. I love my wife."

She smiled at him again. Her hands had moved to the waist-band of the panties, and as she spoke, her thumbs hooked over it and began to slide slowly along the inner side of the elastic, toward her hips. "Good for you," she said. "I'm sure she'll be panting for you when she's here—just as I am—but tonight she's not. So this doesn't take away anything of hers. This is just for fun. To be alone together in this house and not do it would be unnatural." Her smile disappeared. Her eyes low-ered, she bent toward him slightly to slip the panties down past her hips, then stepped out of them, naked.

Carey was gripped with self-loathing. He did not belong here, listening to this nonsense and watching this woman strip. He stood up abruptly, then moved to the couch. He saw her smile return and the lids of her eyes go down like the eyes of a purring cat. "You're one of the most beautiful women I've ever seen in my life," he said. "You're funny, clever, and very per-suasive. If I were ever going to cheat on my wife, this would have been the time." He snatched the pile of clothes off the cushion of the couch and tossed them to her. "Now get dressed and go home."

He walked to the dining room and began to carry dishes out to the kitchen and set them on the counter. On his third trip into the dining room, he heard some rustling sounds, then the front door closing. He closed his eyes, took five deep breaths, poured another glass of champagne, and drank it down. Then he went to the living room and looked: yes, she had left his key on the end table.

28

Jane found a shelf above the trail that was sheltered by big rocks on the north and west, where the cold mountain wind was coming from. "This is a good place," she said. "Does it look homey to you?"

Pete stopped and looked up at it doubtfully. "I could keep going for a while," he offered.

"We've come at least eight or nine miles in the dark," she said. "We might run out of steam in the middle of an ice field or on a mountaintop, and then be worth nothing by the time we find another safe spot. That's how you get hurt."

"Sold," he said. "Should I build a fire?"

"The rocks will protect us well enough from the wind." She reached into his pack and handed him his knife. "Go collect boughs from the fir trees down there. Not branches, just the soft parts near the tips. I'll get us unpacked."

Pete carefully made his way down onto the trail, then disappeared into the trees. In a moment she heard the whispery sound of pine boughs tossed onto a pile.

She had wanted Pete to be gone while she used her flashlight and a forked stick to search the cracks and crannies along the rock shelf. It was the sort of place where a rattlesnake would curl up to get out of the cold, then sun itself in the daytime. When she was satisfied that they would be alone, she searched the packs for the items they would need and laid them out.

Pete labored up the little path carrying a pile of boughs the size of a hay bale, dropped them on the rock, and saw her sitting cross-legged in front of a group of small packages. "What's that?"

"Canned beef, biscuits, dried fruit, and nuts," she said. "The bad news is that it's dinner. The good news is that if we eat it, we don't have to carry it."

"You should have been in marketing." He sat down across from her and imitated her as she opened cans with her Swiss Army knife. He took a bite of meat and a bite of biscuit. "It's kind of frightening. That stuff they've been saying about fresh air and exercise all these years could be true. This actually tastes good."

When they had finished, Jane stood up, sealed the empty cans and packages into a plastic bag, and put it in her knapsack. "More bad news: the garbage truck isn't due until a road is built—figure a thousand years or so. We have to pack the trash out with us." She looked at the pile of pine boughs. "Time to go to bed. Watch carefully."

She spread the boughs like a mat on the rocky shelf, then laid one of the waterproof ponchos on top of it and set the other one aside. "Unless it rains, most of the cold and damp comes from below."

Jane took off her jacket and boots and propped the boots under the rock shelf. "Your boots need to dry out while you sleep or you'll get blisters. You put them in a place where you can reach them and rain can't. You wear as little as possible while you're in your sleeping bag, and an insulated jacket makes a great pillow." She pulled her watch cap on. "This helps. You lose most of your heat through your head, so it'll keep you warm."

She fiddled with the zippers of the sleeping bags for a moment, then zipped the two bags together and slipped inside. "You sleep on that side, where you're farther out of the wind. Your blood is probably still thin from living in the desert."

Pete sat at the foot of the sleeping bags and looked up at her while he arranged his boots and jacket and put on his hat.

She could feel him staring at her in the darkness, trying to read her mind. She sighed, then said in the kindest voice she could summon, "No, I haven't."

"Haven't what?"

"Changed my mind about . . . anything. All I want is your body heat. This is the way to sleep if you want to be warm without a fire."

"Sure," he said. "I've heard that somewhere."

He carefully slipped in beside her, holding himself in a straight, rigid position so far from her that a cold breeze blew under the taut surface of the sleeping bag and chilled her toes. She laughed. "I'll tell you what. If this is too weird, we'll each go it on our own. I don't think we'll freeze tonight."

"No, no," he said. "It just takes a certain mental . . . what's the word? Insensitivity." He nodded sagely. "I can manage that."

"Good," she said. After a long silence she said, "But if I wake up with a hand on my ass, I'm going to pinch it. The one who says 'ouch' had better be me."

It worked. She heard him shifting on the bed of boughs and then felt the sleeping bag regain some of its slack and warm her back. She closed her eyes and listened to the wind blowing past above her head and the sounds of trees moving back and forth, whispering like the sea. In a moment she was asleep.

She was not cold anymore. She felt the hot, mild breeze where her skin was exposed to the air, then sank lazily beneath the surface. The warm water supported her, made her feel as though she were flying. She slowly, effortlessly glided above the bottom of the pool, the light resistance of the black water running along her body like a warm touch.

She looked up at the silvery underside of the surface, saw the bright moon wavering above it, and let herself rise up to meet it.

She came to the surface and took in the first dry, sweet breath, then let her muscles relax and floated. She was in suspension now, drifting passively, waiting. She reveled in the knowledge that he was sure to be here, and fretted, teasing herself with the lie that he would not.

She heard the water sloshing somewhere behind her head and looked up at the moon, her body going tense with anticipation and longing. When his big arm slipped around her waist, she let out a gasp that was certitude and joy and laughter at the same time. She let him pull her close. She could feel his chest against her back, his lips softly kissing the back of her neck. She leaned her head back on his shoulder. He was strong and gentle, and warmer than the water. She could feel his hands moving, never leaving her body, instead touching her lovingly everywhere from her scalp to the tips of her toes, the hands returning, lingering on each of the places she would never have let him touch.

He slowly turned her around and she looked into his eyes. There was no question in them, no uncertainty that would force her to speak. They did not have to talk, because they had been through this before, and he had somehow sensed this time that her answer had changed. She had just misspoken, forgotten on that other night that this was all right. The first kiss was slow, their lips drawn together and barely meeting at first, then staying together. She let it go on as long as she could bear it, feeling so safe, being cradled in his arms and cherished.

She slipped the straps of her bathing suit off her shoulders, then took his hand and made him peel it down and off. Pete's bathing suit came off too, or maybe it was already off. They embraced again in the warm, dark water, and this time it was so much better, with the water tickling the exposed skin to remind her it was bare. She felt so free that she was surprised at how constricted and uncomfortable she must have been before. She and Pete floated weightlessly, and something about the motion of the water seemed to make them drift together.

She let herself savor the moment, the world so dark and quiet around her, but her feelings so bright and hot and clear. She was so glad she had found out that this was allowed. But then she sensed that off in the dark beyond the pool, there was some kind of disturbance. Maybe someone was coming. "No, not yet," she pleaded. "Just a little longer." But Pete seemed to lose his solidity, to slip away from her. She reached for him.

Jane felt cold. Why had the water turned cold? She slowly rose toward consciousness to investigate her surroundings and opened her eyes to a terrible sense of loss. Then she was suddenly, abruptly, wide awake. She was shocked—frightened—not by the dream but by the realization that she was the dreamer. It was an enormous relief that it had not happened. She had not committed adultery, thrown her marriage away. She had not betrayed Carey. She had not done anything at all.

She sat up, as careful not to touch Pete as though he were a rattlesnake that had slithered in beside her for warmth, and extricated herself from the sleeping bag. She felt deeply depressed as she slipped her jacket on and walked across the cold stone shelf to retrieve her boots.

The Old People had studied dreams the way they studied every other event that passed before their eyes. When somebody awoke from a dream, he would immediately do his best to interpret it and fulfill whatever command it had brought him. Something was bothering the dreamer, something he had not given sufficient attention to while he was awake. Now that he was conscious again, he had to correct the oversight—overcome the inertia, the fear, or the inhibition that had prevented him from seeing clearly before. If Jane had lived in the Old Time, she would have been required to wake Pete up and demand that he act out the dream with her to set her mind at rest.

As she tied her boots, she looked over at Pete Hatcher. He was lying on his side facing her, his eyes closed and his jaw slack in sleep. He would be one of the seventeen men on the planet who looked good when he was asleep. She fought off the urge to resent him. None of this was his fault. She was just lonely for her husband, and she had been alone with Pete so much that her misguided subconscious mind had somehow drafted him to stand for Man. No, she thought. The dream had been too convincing and too specific for anything so abstract. Pete was an attractive guy who had the morals of a stallion and had made it disconcertingly clear that she was the one he wanted. Some part of her mind obviously had not taken her refusal as final but had been mulling the offer over.

She found her watch in her jacket pocket and consulted it as she strapped it to her wrist. It was only four o'clock, but she wasn't going to crawl back into that sleeping bag with him right now.

She heard the distant screeching of birds. She cocked her head to listen, but she could not identify their kind. She did sense that they weren't singing, they were frightened. Something must have come too close to their nesting place. She heard the wings of a flock of them passing overhead in the dark. It was too early for the birds she knew to fly.

"Pete!" she said. "Get up. It's time to move."

It was dark and still and cold, and as Jane and Pete rolled their sleeping bags and ponchos and put on their jackets, she could see thick clouds of steam puffing into the air from their nostrils.

Hatcher whispered, "Why are we in such a hurry?"

"Some birds woke me up," she whispered back. "I think something scared them."

As Jane gathered the pine boughs and carried them below the trail to hide them, she knew that she was not being foolish. This was unfamiliar country, but she had begun to get used to the sights and sounds, and the birds were behaving strangely. When she had removed every sign of the campsite, she used the last pine bough as a broom to sweep the rock shelf, then all of the footprints that led to it from the trail.

Jane set a brisk pace as they moved up the trail in the frigid predawn stillness. She led Pete northward, past thickets of berry bushes in alpine meadows, up rocky inclines that skirted the treeline. When the sky began to take on a blue-gray luminescence and she could see objects in depth, she began to hear other birds. She listened to them as she walked, trying to detect any sudden calls from behind that might be warnings. When the sun had turned the peaks to her left a dull orange, she said, "Are you up to a little run?"

Pete said, "Ready if you are."

They jogged until the sun was high, going single file on the narrow footpath. Jane listened harder for sounds that came from behind but heard nothing. When she saw a mountain that might be Iceberg Peak on her right, she stopped running and walked while she studied the map.

"Where are we?" asked Pete.

She pointed to the spot. "What we want to look for next are more glaciers: Ahern Glacier, Ipasha Glacier, and then Chaney Glacier, all middle-sized, close together on the right. Then we take a fork in the path. It looks like a good five miles from here."

"It's rough country," said Pete. "Are you planning to run all the way to Canada?"

"I wish we could," she said. "I'll probably feel better when we've passed that fork in the trail—one more chance to send a tracker in the wrong direction."

"Do you seriously think somebody could have followed us this far?"

"I honestly know some people could do it. I don't think it's likely that these people made all the right decisions and did it, but I've decided that it's stupid not to minimize the risks."

"How do we do that?"

"Move faster, stop less often, and keep traveling as long as the light lasts."

Pete walked along beside her, ducking now and then to shrug a branch past his shoulder. After a moment she realized he was trying to get a close look at her face, so she turned it to him. "Something wrong?"

"I was just having a fantasy."

"Pete . . ."

"It was about dancing. Honest."

"Pretty tame, for you. It must be the lack of oxygen up here."

His hands came up to gesture as he described it. "See, we're at this ballroom. It's got one of those old-fashioned spinning balls in the center made out of mirrors. The light is dim, except for that. I've got a tuxedo on. You're wearing—"

"A blue business suit."

"A black velvet dress: straps, just low enough to hint that the endowment is adequate."

" 'Endowment is adequate'?"

"Nice tits."

"Sorry I asked. Are we done yet?"

"No. I walk up to your table. You smile. You stand, you hold out your right hand—"

"And wave good-bye."

"No. I take your hand. The music begins." He hummed a waltz as he walked, his eyes closed. Jane waited, but he kept humming, the waltz going on and on.

She looked at his face. "Is that smile supposed to make me uncomfortable? Pete?"

"Sssh. Don't interrupt my fantasy. I finally got to lead."

She stared at him for a moment, then the laugh fought its way out and she slapped his arm. He opened his eyes and shrugged happily. "A guy can dream."

"I'm sorry," she said. "I apologize. I'll let you make the decision. Do you want to get to Canada quickly, or do you want to stroll along like this for a few hours, sleep on a frozen rock in a forty-knot wind, and maybe get killed?"

"Lead on," he said.

She pulled ahead of him again. For the rest of the morning she tried a new routine. When they were in thick cover among the evergreen trees she walked, striding along with a purposeful gait, trading the time lost for the chance to catch her breath. But when the trail led them up into grassy fields or onto bare, rocky ridges, she broke into a run, taking them across the open ground as quickly as she could. She never let herself forget the rifle.

Earl sat under the set of trail markers and rested while his dogs sorted out the conflicting sets of footprints. T-Bone raced off up the right-hand trail and Rusty took the left, sniffing the ground methodically. It was good to see that Jane had tried to throw him off like this. It had certainly taken her longer to do it than it would take him to find the right path. Almost as soon as he had formed the thought, he saw both dogs coming back, sniffing the grass beside the trail.

The dogs converged again beside the third path, the one that didn't have a sign anymore, and Earl stood up to watch the dogs work. They were staying beside the trail instead of on it, and in places Earl could look ahead of them and see spots where the weeds had been pushed aside by feet.

Earl found the first footprints a hundred yards farther on. The first ones were hard to see, so he wasn't positive yet, but his heart beat a little faster and he hurried on. He found the next set in a muddy depression, and they were much clearer. They had wrapped something around their boots to disguise the zigzag treads. He took in a breath that tasted thick with tantalizing possibilities. *"Auf den fersen folgen!"*

Rusty and T-Bone scrambled to his side, and he knelt by the prints while the dogs sniffed. He saw their eyes brighten, as though the smell were some kind of drug that actually conjured an image in their brains. They looked at Earl, ran ahead a few steps, then came back, panting and pleading with him. He was sure now. Hatcher and the woman had done the worst thing they could. Maybe it was a piece of a shirt, maybe even a sock. But it wasn't something they had picked up along the way. They had tied something around their boots that had touched their skin, something they had worn and sweated on. Now the dogs had their scent.

Earl adjusted the straps on his pack, tightened his belt, and said, *"Jagen!* Hunt!"

It took the dogs fifteen minutes to reach the place where the prey had spent the night. At first Earl was not sure, because there was no sign of charred wood or scorching, but the dogs showed him the pine boughs, and then he knew.

He headed down toward the trail, and the dogs hurried to beat him there. They galloped off along the trail, no longer set in motion by his command or the pleasure of running along a smooth dirt path in the woods with him. They had picked up the scent, verified it, and found it again. They were eager now, because at each leap they were closer, the scent was fresher.

Earl worked himself back up to a jog. He held his head up, staring into the middle distance and breathing deep, easy breaths. He gauged his speed to keep the dogs in sight and let them work without inhibition. He had no apprehension that they might forget their training. When it was time, they would let him come in and join them in the kill.

29

J ane kept Pete moving through the afternoon, running across the open spaces and walking quickly among the thickets and the stands of gnarled, stunted trees. In midafternoon the air turned cold. She found Chaney Glacier and then the fork in the path appeared as though in answer to a wish.

Jane stopped and turned to Pete. "This is the last place we can hope to fool them if they're on the right trail. Want to do a good job?"

"Of course," he said.

She sent him down the slope to uproot small bushes while she began to dig with her knife. She took the trail markers down the path that branched off to the right, then transplanted small shrubs in the middle of the trail that went north. She worked quickly, planting them in random patterns wherever the ground was bare, then spreading dead leaves and pine needles from the adjacent grove to cover the fresh dirt at their roots.

When Pete came back, trying to peer around the thick bushes in his arms to see where to place his feet, she sent him off again to gather rocks.

Jane stuck clumps of weeds into the ground in a second random pattern among the shrubs, then told Pete, "Don't just set the rocks into the mix. Bury some of them enough so they look like they've always been here."

When she was able to step back along the trail and look at the camouflaged spot without distinguishing it from the surrounding brush, she and Pete went back into the forest and collected more leaves and debris to spread among the bushes.

They stopped to look at their work. "I should take you home with me to landscape the yard," she said.

"If you get me through this I'll remodel your whole house."

"Let's go. Take the trail signs."

They set off below the trail into the undisturbed woods, then made a turn to angle back and rejoin the trail a few hundred yards farther north. They moved quickly now to make up for the time they had spent. Jane found a deer run along the trail a half mile on and stuck the trail markers into the ground there.

They moved on faster, and finally Pete said, "We seem to be going down."

"That's right," she answered. "This stretch goes almost due north for ten miles along the Waterton River."

He gave a tired snort. "Then it goes straight up, right?"

"Wrong. It flows into Waterton Lake. The lake is long, like the Finger Lakes in New York. Ready for even better news?"

"More than ready."

"It straddles the border. About two-thirds of it is in Canada."

"Let's do some more running."

They jogged along the trail, feeling the lower altitude and hearing it. Somewhere among the big cedars and hemlocks, a woodpecker rapped on bark. In places they had to slow their momentum to keep from losing their footing.

They reached the riverbank as the light was fading. "Are you hungry?" Jane asked.

"Starving."

"Don't you want to stop for dinner?"

"I want to do what you said this morning, before dawn. I want to use the light, wring every last bit of distance out of this day. Then I'll stop and eat a moose or something."

She grinned as she moved along the trail.

"What are you smiling at? Don't tell me it's your turn for a fantasy."

"Don't you wish. No, I was worried about you, but now I'm not. You're doing great."

"I told you a couple of days ago that I don't feel like giving up. I like living too much."

"That wasn't a couple of days ago. It was yesterday."

"See? I'm getting more out of time now. I feel as though I've lived a year since then."

Jane said nothing. Exercise was one of the therapies that doctors prescribed for depression, because it increased the flow of oxygen and released some chemical into the blood that fooled the brain into an unfounded sense of well-being. Whatever had happened to Pete Hatcher, she hoped it would last.

It was deep darkness when they reached a deserted campground. Jane pulled out her flashlight and played it around the big clearing until she found the sign.

Pete read it aloud. "Goat Haunt?"

"Beautiful, isn't it?" she said. "We made it. The tip of the lake should be right up there."

Pete waited, but she didn't move. "Are we going on, or are we going to sleep here?"

She looked around her with the flashlight. "There's a lot to be said for official campgrounds. The rangers generally put them in the best places they can find, so this is probably the most sheltered spot around here. It's a lot colder tonight than last night. There are hearths for fires, so if we build one, our ashes won't be a sign of anything to anybody once they're cool. People have built fires here all summer."

"You don't sound sure."

"I'm not."

"Why not?"

"I don't know," she admitted. "Maybe because I'm so exhausted from walking and running. Maybe because in order to get through that I had to get scared." She swept the area on all sides with her flashlight again. "I guess it's just nerves. I guess we're not going to accomplish much by tromping on in the dark. Let's eat and get some sleep and try to cross the border when we can see it."

This time Pete set off to find soft boughs without her saying anything, while she rummaged in the packs and unrolled the ponchos and sleeping bags. They ate the rest of their canned food with some powdered soup Jane heated over the small fire she had built.

They joined their sleeping bags and slipped into them after Jane had carefully cleaned the pot and put all of the cans into the plastic bag.

Jane lay on her back, closed her eyes, and felt the warm, living mass of Pete's body beside her, breathing deeply, then almost immediately falling asleep. In another few days she would be out of this life forever, lying safely every night beside Carey in the big bed with the maple tree outside the window.

The night breeze blew cold, and she could feel it caressing her face. She tugged the watch cap lower, pulled the sleeping bag to her chin, and let the wind soothe her to sleep. Tonight part of her was waiting for the dreams to come, but sleep was a jumble of images that never seemed to coalesce.

Sometime during the night the constant mountain wind disappeared and the air turned cold and still. It was three in the morning when Jane heard the howl.

She opened her eyes and lay still, then began to take inventory of her surroundings. The fire was out, and the dew had frozen on the ground. Her cheeks were tingling, so she rubbed them to get the circulation back. She decided it must have been a dream and rolled over, pushing her face deeper into the sleeping bag for warmth. Then she heard it again. It was a high, long yowl, and then it broke off into a series of yelps. She sat up quickly and listened.

There were supposed to be a couple of packs of wolves that had come back into the wild country above the border in the past few years, but the call hadn't sounded like a wolf, exactly. There was no shortage of coyotes anywhere in the country, but as soon as she had thought of them, she knew it was wrong. She heard another bark, but this one was closer, off to the left. It sounded like an answer to the first. She pounded Pete's shoulder, then kicked her way out of the sleeping bag. He sat up quickly and looked around.

Jane tossed his boots into his chest. "Dogs!" she said. "They've tracked us with dogs!"

She pulled on her boots, snatched up their packs, and used her flashlight to find the sign she had seen when they had reached the campground: "Boulder Pass Trail."

Pete had his boots on now, and he began to roll up the sleeping bags.

"Leave them," she said, and handed him his pack.

Jane began to run. She heard Pete fall into step behind her. When she had passed the sign and taken a few steps onto the forest trail she turned off the light and slipped it into her pack. She tried to wake herself and consider the implications as she ran.

All of her ruses and misleading trails had meant nothing. A man would have been fooled and walked on past the shrubs and plants and rocks she and Pete had carefully placed to cover the path. A dog would not even pause, just plunge on through them, following the scent. The spot had probably served the dogs as a beacon, because the sweat from the hard work must have been all over the rocks and shrubs they had moved. She had a sudden vision of herself moving trail signs along the way. All the effort and all the delay would have been worth it if only dogs could read.

"Couldn't it be somebody else?" The low, raspy whisper from behind reminded her that she had to keep him from being confused.

"No," she said. "Dogs aren't allowed in the park." She heard a bark and tried to gauge the distance. It sounded as though the dog was far behind them, but when she tried to decipher what that meant, she found that she couldn't. The dog had a deep-register voice, but that didn't mean it was loud; there was no way to know if the dog was even facing in their direction when he barked.

She ran harder, ducking and weaving to avoid low branches but making no attempt to keep her footprints off the trail. She searched her mind for strategies she could use to fool the hunter. The only one that offered any hope was to outrun him.

She and Pete had traveled half of one night and a full day, from before sunrise until late evening. They had wasted only enough time to try to disguise their trail and eat and pee. That thought made her feel worse. That was how dogs marked their territories. The occasional smell of human urine in the bushes along the trail had probably been overwhelming to a dog.

Running was the only answer. If she and Pete had traveled quickly for thirty-six hours, then this hunter and his dogs had traveled faster. In order to be anywhere near the campsite at Goat Haunt by now, they must have kept going through the cold and darkness for five or six hours while she and Pete had eaten and slept. The hunter must be an intimidating physical specimen, but she and Pete were warm and rested now, and ready to run. He would be worn out and hungry.

She ran on as quickly as she dared in the darkness. The trail wound upward through the trees against the path of a small creek she could hear to her left. Sometimes she could see a brief glimpse of moonlight on water.

She ran until the sun began to throw her shadow on the trail ahead of her, then she walked for a few minutes, listening to the harsh huffing sound of her breathing. Pete's breath was louder and deeper, and she could tell by his heavy footsteps that he was tired enough to stumble now and then. She pulled the pack off her back and onto her belly, found the map, and studied it.

"If we stay on Boulder Pass Trail, we'll reach a fork in the path, then go west to Kintla Lake or swing south to Bowman Lake."

Pete looked over her shoulder at the map. "They both look like a long way."

"Maybe twenty-five miles. Neither one leads to what I would call civilization, but I would be very glad to see a few park rangers with guns about now."

She studied the map more closely. There was a thin, jagged line like a crack in a teacup that crossed Boulder Pass Trail and zigzagged north to the border. "There is a closer way, if we wanted to take a big chance. See this line?"

"What is it? Another path?"

"No such luck. It's the border between Glacier County and Flathead County." Her finger followed it northward. "In Canada it separates the Kootenay District and the Lethbridge District."

"What are we looking at an imaginary line for?"

"Because it's not straight and regular and even. See the Canadian border? It's the forty-ninth parallel, because some politicians drew a neat line on a map in a comfortable building thousands of miles from here. But this line is all sawteeth and wiggles. That means it wasn't done that way. Surveyors actually went there. Somebody walked that line. Even if it was a hundred years ago, somebody was up there."

"Sure. It was probably one of those old-time mountain men that looked like Bigfoot and smelled the same, and his faithful Indian guide."

Jane shrugged. "They've got nothing on us."

"What do you mean?"

She answered the question she wanted to. "We've done pretty well so far. We just had food and a little sleep. The guy behind us didn't."

"How can you know that?"

"He was still up and chasing at three A.M. He was trying to make time and kill us in our sleep. If we want to outrun him, then the rougher the country, the better."

"I'm not so sure."

"Did you ever watch a dog climb a ladder?"

"I don't think so."

"They're lousy at it. If we have to do any heavy climbing, they'll hold him back, and maybe stop him."

"So this is where he's going to give up?"

"No," said Jane. "That's what I used to think. I don't believe that anymore."

30

Earl followed T-Bone and Rusty into the deserted campsite at Goat Haunt. The dogs streaked across the clearing and nosed the two sleeping bags that lay in a pile on the ground. Earl hurried to the stone hearth beside them and held his hand over it. He felt no warmth. He picked up a pine bough from the nest they had made and stirred the ashes. Sparks rose from glowing embers and ignited the pine sap on the bough. He set it in the hearth to burn and watched his dogs.

The scent was fresh, probably no more than an hour old, so the dogs were wide-eyed and impatient. He sat down to rest and gave them a chance to investigate all of the smells and sort out the trail. T-Bone kept dashing to the edge of the forest and stopping to look back. Rusty went back and forth across the campground methodically sniffing the ground, then trotted over to join his brother under the trail sign.

Earl read the trail marker and took out his map. They must have heard the baying of the dogs, got up, and run. The question was, Why had they chosen the Boulder Pass Trail? He traced the long, meandering line with his finger. There was a fork in the trail at Brown Pass. The south trail swung down along Bowman Lake, then Bowman Creek, to a patrol cabin and a road. The north fork went at least twenty-five miles, then to Kintla Lake, another patrol cabin, and a road.

They knew he was coming now, and they had chosen to try outrunning him. He sighed. It wasn't a bad strategy. He had been on the trail all night while they had been resting up. If they had not both been in reasonably good condition, they would not have gotten this far.

Lenny was a problem. By now he was hours behind, walking up the Highline Trail loaded like a pack animal. Earl considered resting the dogs and curling up on these sleeping bags while he waited for Lenny. But that way he would risk losing his two targets. He studied his map. Even if he waited for Lenny and set him on Boulder Pass Trail, Earl could be fairly sure that Lenny and his supplies would be of no use now that they were running.

Earl opened the two cans of dog food that he had left, dumped them out on two flat stones, and whistled. Rusty and T-Bone trotted over and ate. Earl found an old-fashioned pump and pumped some water into the trough underneath it for them. Then he filled his canteen, dropped in a water-purification tablet, and sat down to eat jerky and trail mix. Rusty and T-Bone licked the last of the meat from the stones, leaving wet swaths from their tongues, then walked over to lap water and lay down at Earl's feet.

"Decisions, decisions," he said to them. That was it. Jane was presenting him with choices. If she presented enough of them, one time he would make the wrong choice and go tromping off in the wrong direction. He was not going to do that. He hurried to the sleeping bags, gathered them up, walked with them into the bushes, and tossed them there to keep the sight of them from distracting Lenny. He covered them with the pine boughs.

Lenny would come up the Highline Trail, see no sign that anyone had been here, and keep going north beside Waterton Lake into Canada. When Earl wanted him, he would be able to find him at the Waterton Township campground.

Earl emptied his pack. He quickly assembled the A.W. rifle and attached the sling to it. He clicked one box-style ten-round magazine into it and put one more into the left side pocket of his jacket. He put the .45 pistol into the right pocket and slipped his knife into his belt at the small of his back. He put his map and compass into one breast pocket and then filled the remaining spaces with jerky and biscuits. He slung his canteen over his shoulder to counterbalance his rifle, then hid the pack with the sleeping bags.

Earl tested the weight of his load. He was twenty pounds lighter, with nothing rattling or slowing him down. It was a gamble to set off on another unfamiliar mountain trail with no more than this, but people always carried enough to get them there and back, so he didn't need to. After he had killed them, he and T-Bone and Rusty could have a feast on whatever was left in their packs.

He walked toward the trailhead, then called over his shoulder, "*Jagen!* Hunt!" The two big dogs bounded past him up the trail. Earl gave them a chance to get a good head start before he, too, began to run. After a time, he knew, the man and the woman would wear themselves out and see that all the running was doing them no good. Then they would go to ground and prepare to make a stand. He smiled. Nobody had ever ambushed a dog.

It was ten o'clock before Jane and Hatcher reached the fork in the path at Brown Pass. "This is it," said Jane.

Pete looked at the two paths leading west and northwest. "Which is it?"

"Neither." She pointed up to her right at the high rocky promontory above them. "That snow up there is on Chapman Peak. We climb from here. We'll have to go up about a thousand feet in a mile, moving almost in a straight line until we get to the lower edge of the glacier."

She watched his eyes move upward. Then he turned his head to take a longer look back up the trail. "After you," he said. It confirmed her suspicion. He was trying to keep his back between her and the bullet. She set off along the hard, rocky ground that began to rise in front of her immediately. Let him be noble. She would be quick.

They climbed through the zone of deciduous forest, up into the belt of pines and subalpine meadows, each of them stopping now and then to look out over the green treetops without appearing to be looking for anything specific.

By the time the sun was at its midpoint they stood at the foot of the glacier. Pete looked up at the field of ice above him as Jane studied the map. "You know what I'd like right now?"

"An ice-cream cone?"

"A big box of dynamite. I'd wait until this guy was standing right about here and roll an avalanche down on top of him."

Jane surveyed the bright, frozen expanse. "It's a dumb idea, but keep thinking. If he gets close, we'll have to do something." She folded the map. "We move west from here along the ridge."

"What sort of landmark are we looking for? I'd hate to miss it."

"We won't. It's called Hudson Glacier."

They moved rapidly along the jagged, rocky area below the crest of the mountain, their eyes down to watch where they planted their feet. It was another hour before Jane heard the bark of a dog, then a second dog answering. Pete turned to look behind them, but Jane grasped his arm and pulled him ahead.

"If you do see him, he'll already have seen you. The best hope is to keep moving." This time her voice was tense, tight in her throat. She had been wrong again. The way up the mountain had not been hard enough. There had been no stretch where a dog couldn't scamper up, so the man had not been held back at all.

She tried not to think about the man, but it was impossible to keep him out of her mind. He must have been up all night, and most of the day before. He didn't seem to need sleep, food, or shelter. He never gave up, he never guessed wrong. He killed anyone who might be Pete Hatcher, and anyone who might get in the way, and still kept coming.

A chill suddenly made the hairs on the back of her neck stand. She had never actually seen the dogs. She had heard howling in the forest as something followed their scent. The rangers didn't even allow anybody to bring dogs through the gate into the park. She shook her head to get rid of the feeling.

She knew she had climbed to about nine thousand feet now, and the air must be making her giddy. There were crazy, malevolent people, but their craziness didn't buy them the power to turn into dogs. They took shots at strangers with high-powered rifles. That was what she had to worry about, not old superstitions.

When they rounded the slope at the foot of Hudson Glacier she began to feel stronger. If she was maintaining their lead, then for a while the slope of the mountain would be between them and the rifle.

They turned northward, moving along the ridges, staying high, where there were plateaus with dead grass and stunted trees. The north wind picked up as the sun moved westward, blowing hard into their faces and making their progress slower.

At two o'clock, she heard the dogs again, and they seemed to be closer. She turned, but she could not see them. She said, "Ready to run again?"

As she ran into the wind, her steps were shorter, as though the air were catching her in midstride and pushing her back. She and Pete leaned into it, trying to stay low, but before long they were just scrambling over rocks and climbing up steep grades, buying each yard with too much of their strength.

At four fifteen, when Jane had Mount Custer on her left and Herbst Glacier on her right, she looked back and saw the man. He was little more than a small vertical line of darkness against the horizon. She could see two more spots of darkness ranging ahead of him, low to the ground. Jane took out her binoculars and found him.

She watched as he stopped, then sat on the ground with his knees bent, fiddling with something. At this distance she could not resolve any of the details of his face. Very deliberately he raised both arms in front of him at once. The gesture seemed oddly familiar. When his head cocked to his right, she shouted, "Get down!"

They both dropped to their bellies, then heard the whip-crack sound as the bullet broke the sound barrier above their heads. Jane counted seconds, listening for the report of the rifle, but it never came. He still had the silencer. She lifted her head a little and saw the man running.

"Let's go," she said, and pulled herself to her feet.

She and Pete ran together, side by side. She heard the whip-crack again, and this time she saw chips fly off a boulder ahead of her as the bullet ricocheted into the sky. There seemed to be no hope. Each time they ran, he would shoot. Each time they stopped to hide, he would run closer.

"We've got to get out of the open," she said.

"Agreed."

They ran to the west, moving diagonally down the slope of the mountain. As soon as they reached the first stand of scraggly pine trees, the shooting stopped. Twice Pete let his momentum build up, tripped, and rolled, then stood and ran again. They ran until the sun was beyond the western mountains and the dim afterlight threw no shadows. They stumbled into a long, narrow valley meadow with thickets of berry bushes as the light began to fail.

The bear was a hundred feet away, busily rooting on the ground, snuffling and grumbling to itself. Jane stopped. Her mind seemed to explode into fragments that scurried in several directions at once, looking for a way out. She knew immediately that the enormous tan animal was not a black bear. Its back had a big hump on it, and the profile of its face was flatter, with the snout turned slightly upward. Jane remembered the warnings on the little flyer she had picked up at the park entrance.

Grizzlies stayed in the high altitudes in the remotest areas of the park, and if any place was more remote than this little trough between two mountains, then it couldn't be reached by a human being. There wasn't even enough animal traffic to make a path in the weeds. She could see the thicket was full of berry bushes. The bear seemed to be finishing off a low branch, and now it raised a paw and swatted the next one to shake the berries loose. That reminded her of another problem. This was the time of year when they were voracious, trying desperately

to fatten themselves for the winter. Never hike at dusk. That
was the part that had been printed in bold letters.

In her peripheral vision she could see Pete slowly reaching
into his pack for the pistol. She touched him and shook her
head. Then they began to walk toward the far end of the narrow
valley. It seemed hopeless. A bear could outrun a man. This
bear was hungry. The gun Pete was still searching for would be
about as much protection as a fly swatter if a bear like this one
decided to come for them. Nobody even knew what made a
bear decide to amble away one time and attack another time,
but there were theories. Suddenly she remembered the rest
of the warning. This was the reason no dogs were allowed in
the park.

She whispered, "Keep going. Don't run, don't stop."

He looked alarmed. "What are—"

She pushed him forward, and he kept walking. She was
aware of each pace he took as he moved farther away from her.
Jane slowly turned her head to look back at the way she had
come, then across the field to the far end. She carefully chose
the spot where she would make her stand.

The bear stopped eating the berries, shook its wide, shaggy
body, and raised its head to stare directly into her eyes. She did
not know if she was held in the huge animal's gaze for a few
seconds or a minute. The bear's undistracted intensity brought
back to her phrases from stories her grandfather had told. Bears
could read minds. Probably in the Old Time, the listeners
would all have known what it was like to stumble on a bear
in the forest. They would have nodded their heads, maybe
chuckled nervously at the memory of this stare. It was said that
if he knew your real name, you couldn't escape him, and to her
it felt as though he were probing her mind for it now. The stories were proof that what was happening was unchanged since
the beginning of time. There was only one bear, and one small
woman walking through the wild country.

The bear sniffed the air and smelled her fear. It took one step
toward her, then another, tasting the breeze. She could see its
ears move back and its face elongate, and she knew what was

about to happen. There would be no chance to run, no way to fight. Her only chance was the one that had existed since the first Nundawaono woman and the first bear. Nothing had changed. Those who lived, lived by their wits.

Jane knelt in the grass, slipped off her pack, and watched the bear erupt into its charge. It surged forward with growing speed. As she fumbled in her pack, she watched the progress of his huge, powerful body across the field of dry grass, and said aloud, "Is it the truth, Nyakwai? Are the old stories true?" She whispered, "They had better be."

Her hands shook as she tore open the packets of honey and peanut butter, raisins and dried meat, then dropped them into the plastic bag with the garbage.

The bear was almost on her when she sprang to her feet. As Nyakwai always did in the stories, this one reared back on its hind legs. It seemed to Jane to be eight or nine feet tall as it towered over her, its thick, powerful forelegs opened wide to grasp her in its claws and hold her while it gnawed through her neck.

Jane flung the plastic bag of food and garbage hard at the bear's chest. As they always did, Nyakwai's lightning-quick animal reflexes clapped his big paws together and caught the bag between them, his long claws digging through it into the pungent mess it held.

Jane pivoted and sprinted for the far end of the field. She judged it was a hundred yards of open grass before the ground again rose into rocky outcroppings and sheltering trees. By the time she had finished making her estimate it was eighty. . . . Now it was sixty. She clenched her teeth and pumped her arms, making her toes dig in and tear at the ground with each stride. Forty. . . . Thirty. Just before the trees began, she glanced over her shoulder, then kept running.

In the stories, the trick was to get the bear to catch a small log, and then quickly swing a war club down on the top of its skull. But this bear was still in the spot where she had left it, peacefully rooting deep in the plastic sack, lapping out the fatty meat and peanut butter, the sweet, sticky honey and the crumbs of biscuits.

Jane took one last look at the bear. "Stay right where you are, Nyakwai," she whispered. "Something is coming— something evil."

Earl trotted down the steep hillside after the dogs. Everything seemed to come hard to him this trip, like the stiff north wind smacking into his face all afternoon. He had run until he had thought he would have to stop, and then he had at last spotted them on the bare ridge ahead. He had kept his head and run on, trying to gradually shorten the distance and buy himself the best shot. But he had seen the woman stop and turn around, so he had gone low and used the telescopic sight of the rifle to see what she was doing.

When he saw that she was holding a pair of binoculars, he'd had no choice. The range must have been a thousand yards. He had known that even though he was holding the best sniper rifle that money could buy, he was aiming it into the sunset at a receding target bobbing up and down over uneven ground with a forty-mile-an-hour wind blowing at him. He had tried to hold the man's back in the crosshairs long enough, but it was a ridiculous shot, and the round had gone high. When the gun had settled from the recoil and he had found them again in the scope, he discovered they had dropped to their bellies.

He had sprung to his feet and run toward them, using the time to shorten the distance and get into reasonable range. When they got up to run again, he had taken a second shot to make them go down again, but the tactic had not worked. Jane had obviously figured out that hiding while he moved closer could only end one way.

She had dodged to the left, moving across his field of vision to make his shot even harder, and then scrambled down here into the gulch. The sparse smattering of scraggly pines on the slope would not have provided cover from fifty yards, but from eight hundred, the tree trunks had multiplied in the scope's optics into an impenetrable wall.

Jane was a clever bitch. She had taken Hatcher from a mountaintop, where he'd stood out against the sky, down into a narrow mountain pass the sun had not reached for an hour and where enough soil had been deposited over the eons to let thick, leafy vegetation grow.

This was the moment he had known for days would come. Some runners would just keep running until they dropped, and then lie there to get their throats cut. But Hatcher had already shown that he wasn't one of those. Linda had taken a gun off him in Denver, and that meant he was the sort that would probably make some lame attempt at fighting. Jane was a pro, so it went without saying that when running got to be pointless, she would still not concede that she had used up her options.

Earl took long, leaping steps, almost flying a few feet and landing on both heels to stop himself, then taking a running start and doing it again. When he reached the bottom he moved out of the trees into a long, narrow meadow. The light was fading quickly, and the sky above him had already dimmed into that gray opaque surface that would turn deep later when the stars began to show.

A shiver of anticipation began in his spine and moved up to the back of his neck. He could feel that they were straight ahead, waiting for him. He cocked the slide on his pistol to chamber a round, then lifted the precious rifle across his chest like a skeet shooter and held it ready. Then he turned his face to the dogs.

"T-Bone," he whispered, and swept his hand to his right. "Rusty," he whispered, and swung his hand to the left. The two big black dogs began to advance through the meadow on either side of him. He could see they smelled something ahead in the meadow.

They stalked with their ears pricked forward, their necks extended, and their bodies held low to the ground. This was it, all right. He saw that there were bushes growing in big clumps, like haystacks here and there in the open field. Most likely the man and woman were crouched behind one of them, or even in the middle. Hatcher would be clutching the one little pistol he had bought that Linda hadn't gotten, probably sweating so much he could barely keep the grip in his hand.

Manhunting was all strategy, and Earl had them this time. If they stayed put, the dogs would sniff them out and Earl could lie prone out of pistol range and keep piercing the bushes until he had bagged them. If the dogs flushed them, they would have to run the whole length of this narrow valley to get out of the open. Earl could fix them one at a time in his flashlight beam and pop them at his leisure. It occurred to him that he didn't even have to do that. He could let the dogs run them down and tear them up first, then shoot them on the ground.

T-Bone and Rusty both stopped, stood stiff-legged, and began to growl. At first it was low, a sound like anger building. But then they began to move forward again, still low but faster now. He could see their muzzles contort to bare their long, glowing teeth—not just the biting fangs this time, but the big jagged grinders in the back for gnawing through bone.

Earl rasped, "*Abschuss!* Kill!" The word was more a cheer than a command, because they seemed already to be in motion when it began, streaking forward toward the big thicket ahead of him.

Earl chose a standing position so he could sidestep quickly to either side. He held the flashlight in his left hand under the foregrip of the rifle so that it would throw its beam wherever he aimed. He pushed off the safety and waited. The dogs tore into the thicket from both sides.

In the dim remnants of light from the sky he saw T-Bone take a hard run forward, his teeth bared to emit a sound that was half growl and half cry of joy. As T-Bone left the ground, Earl knew he was leaping for a throat. At almost the same time he saw Rusty dash in low from the other side of the thicket, and he knew they were attacking the way he had seen them go after the bloodhound—one for the throat and the other for the hamstrings. Earl danced to the right, trying to create a better angle in case the dogs had left one of the runners unoccupied.

Earl heard a sound that made him drop the flashlight in his haste to push the switch. The air seemed to turn thick with it, a noise that had a groan in it like the roar of an enraged man, but a noise that had fangs and hair, far too loud and deep to have come from a human throat.

Earl saw T-Bone fly through the air, spinning a little to land in the tall weeds. Then Earl saw the bear. It charged out of the thicket after Rusty, its maw wide open in a crocodile gape as it tried to corner the dog.

Earl found his flashlight and caught the bear in it. The head, a foot wide with a wrinkled snout and tiny black eyes, turned to him in a snarl. The flashlight seemed to have enraged the bear, but it had blinded Rusty. The bear's thick paw shot out, the black claws gleaming in the light like the teeth of a rake, and swatted Rusty's side. Then the bear, with astonishing speed, disappeared behind the thicket again.

Earl thought he saw the bushes move. He raised the rifle, fired, cycled the bolt, and fired again, but the bear had somehow gotten ahead of him in the dark. The bear found the dazed T-Bone and, in a second, reared up with his jaws clamped on T-Bone's throat, gave the dying body a neck-breaking shake, then dropped the carcass and headed back toward Rusty on four feet.

Rusty crouched, barking and snarling as the bear trotted toward him, then seemed to realize that he had finally met something he could not even injure, let alone kill. Rusty wheeled and began to run.

Earl turned on the flashlight again. In the rifle scope he could see the bright reflection in the dog's eyes. He could see its long tongue hanging out, and bright, honey-thick slaver dripping from it. Behind Rusty, the bear was methodically building speed, bounding along now, first both forefeet, then both hind feet, its close-set black pig-eyes gleaming. Rusty was running for his life now, to the only place where he would be safe. His idea of sanctuary was leading an eight-hundred-pound bear right back to Earl.

Earl steadied the rifle and held the running animal's head in the scope. He placed the crosshairs between the two rust-brown spots above the eyes and fired.

Rusty's forelegs crumpled and he collapsed, dead before his muzzle hit the ground. The bear stopped, gave a quick swat with his claws, and made sure the dog was dead.

Earl quickly switched off the flashlight and crouched, holding the scope on the big black shape. The wind was blowing from the bear's direction. Earl made no noise. As he watched the shape of the bear he tried to remember. He had fired once at Pete Hatcher, then once more. He had fired at the bushes twice: four. Then one for Rusty: five. But was he really sure he had started with ten rounds? Old hunting stories came back to him. People had shot grizzly bears ten or twelve times in places that were supposed to be fatal and they had not even slowed down. Earl kept his eye in the scope, slowly and quietly released the box magazine from the rifle, found the full magazine in his pocket, and clicked it in place.

He knew that if the bear charged, there was no way he could outrun it. He had to kill it before it reached him. He went to a prone position with his flashlight against the foregrip again, and waited.

As he waited, the third possibility, the one he had almost forgotten, occurred. The enormous dark shadow seemed to rise and grow as it lifted its snout from Rusty's carcass and turned its head toward Earl. It had finished feeding on the dog. It sniffed the air, turned, and slowly walked away.

31

Earl lay curled up on the top of the ridge, sheltered from the wind by a rock outcropping. It was cold enough to snow now, and he was almost sure the flakes would begin to fall before sunrise. A man could easily freeze to death up here with no sleeping bag, no tent, no tarp, no ... He decided not to make a list. All of the gear was on Lenny's back right now, somewhere behind him on the other trail. If the dogs had been alive, he could have lain between them and used their body heat.

The slaughter of his dogs was the very last offense that Earl was going to suffer. He knew who had done that. Jane had fed the bear something to keep it in Earl's path. She had known that the bear would kill the dogs and probably Earl too. Great upwellings of rage came out of his chest with each breath like convulsions, making his head pound with anger.

About now she would be certain Earl was either being eaten or clinging to a tree limb someplace down in that valley waiting for the bear to go away. A woman like her would be too smart to try to make her way north down there in the dark, through a forest that had never been cut. She would have to travel up here where the vegetation was almost nonexistent and she could take a step with some confidence about what was going to be under her foot when she put her weight on it. She would have felt the change in the wind and the drop in the temperature too, and she would want to be out of the mountains before the snow hit.

Earl lay still and kept his eyes focused on the long expanse of bare ridge ahead. When he heard the first sounds below the heights, he held his head up a few inches and listened, trying hard to pick out the noises he had sensed were different. Their footsteps were slow coming up, as though they were picking their way with difficulty. No, it was caution. Jane was that smart. She knew that if Earl was alive it was because he had backed away from the bear, staying downwind and heading for the heights, where there was nothing for bears to eat, so he wouldn't repeat the encounter.

She seemed to satisfy herself after a minute. He heard her footsteps begin to quicken, and then the bigger, heavier steps came faster too.

Earl took his hands out of his pockets, where he had been warming them, then slowly rolled onto his belly and pushed the A.W. against his shoulder. This was the sort of shot he had waited for. They would be moving away from him with their backs fully exposed.

He listened and strained his eyes to see, but he could not quite tell where they were. He picked up the flashlight and clamped it against the foregrip with his left hand, then turned it on.

For an instant he saw them: the man on the left, the woman on the right. But the flashlight had an unforeseen effect. The woman seemed to pitch forward onto her face, and the man crouched beside her and fired. Earl saw the first bright flashes as the man fired the pistol at his flashlight.

Earl ducked low and switched off his flashlight. He heard the ricochets as the next two bullets pounded off the rocks behind him. Then, after one more shot, there was silence.

Earl thought hard. Hatcher had fired. Jane had not. It had been a reasonable shot—certainly the best they could hope to get. Why had she held her fire? Earl crawled a few feet away to a new hiding place and peered over the rocks. He could see nothing.

He steadied himself, aimed the rifle, and switched on the light. Hatcher leapt up from his crouch and ran, but Jane stayed on the ground. Hatcher dashed to the left, back toward the woods. Earl followed him in the scope, but suddenly sensed something was wrong: Jane could have sent Hatcher off to draw Earl's attention while she rushed him in the dark. Earl held his fire and quickly swept the light toward the woman. She wasn't dashing toward Earl. She was still lying there. When the light hit her, she rolled to her side and screamed. "Pete! Don't leave me here!" There was no answer, and her voice came again, lower and with less hope. "Please!"

Earl swept the light along the slope of the mountain, but Pete Hatcher was gone. Then he turned the light back on the woman. She still didn't fire, and she still didn't get up. She began to drag her body along on the rocks, using her left leg and her hands to try to slither out of the beam that pinned her there. She couldn't be faking it. She knew as well as he did that if the bright white beam could reach her, the bullet could too.

Earl's heart beat faster. He knew exactly what had happened, because for two days he had been afraid it would happen to him. She had been startled when the light went on, turned her head to look at it, taken a blind step, and twisted her ankle in the rocks.

Hatcher had certainly emptied his pistol firing at the light. That could not be faked. When he had no bullets left and Jane was not about to do any running, there wasn't much he could do but take off and hope Earl took his time killing her. No, Hatcher probably didn't even have that much calculation in him. He had panicked, as they always did at the end. Now he would run until he was exhausted and lost before he remembered there was such a person as Jane.

Earl began to walk toward her. He could probably have bagged her from this distance, even in the dim light of the flashlight and with her lying down, but doing it that way made no sense. He had only ten rounds left, and after that the beautiful precision rifle would be seventeen pounds of useless metal. He began to relish the chance to look into her eyes before he killed her. He could afford to do that. Pete Hatcher was going nowhere. He would never have gotten this far without professional help, and now he was alone with an empty pistol in mountain wilderness with a snowstorm coming. There was a good chance he didn't even have the map and compass. Jane never would have let an amateur do the navigating. Earl would search her body and find out.

When Earl was fifty feet away from her, he turned on his flashlight again. Her eyes squinted against the glare and she struggled rise to her knees, but she didn't seem to be eager to put weight on the ankle. Earl moved closer.

"Don't bother to get up on my account, Jane," he said.

"How do you know my name?" She could not keep the fear and shock out of her voice. How could he possibly know her real name?

Earl kept walking. "I know everything about you. You've been mine for months. Since June, I think."

As he approached, he watched her. She fidgeted in the beam as though it were intense heat instead of ordinary light.

"What are you waiting for?" asked Jane.

"I was just trying to decide. One part of me says you ought to go just the way my dogs did—gutted and left to lie there for a while before you die."

He could see that Jane had to force her mouth into that unconvincing skeptical smile. "We're both professionals. You won, I lost. You can afford one bullet to the head and be on your way. Those are the stakes, not torture."

He set his rifle on the rocks, took his pistol out of his jacket pocket, and came closer. He was within fifteen feet of her now. "Is that so? What you've been putting me through—is that just business? You've been slowly sawing my balls off."

He began to pace on the rocks. The flashlight's beam whipped across her face, then bobbed up and down on her body.

She tried to make her voice sound calm, almost cheerful. "I'm sorry," she said. "It wasn't personal. I don't know you." She could see that his agitation was growing.

He stepped quickly toward her. "Well, you're going to, because I'm going to do just what he did to Linda."

She tried to decipher the words, but her mind stumbled, and gave her nothing but the terror. "Who? Who's Linda?" The grimace on his face and the abrupt, jerky movements of his body told her that whether Linda was a real person or "what he did to Linda" was just a slang way of saying something awful, what this man was planning was not a mere execution. She watched, mesmerized, as he bent his knees to set his lighted flashlight and pistol on the ground a few yards from her feet, where she could never hope to reach them.

As he stepped away from them toward her, his big silhouette caught in the dim aura of the flashlight, Jane brought Pete Hatcher's pistol around her body and fired it four times into his chest.

Earl's eyes squeezed tight with pain, then opened wide with knowledge. He knew why Hatcher had still been kneeling beside her in the dark after he had emptied the pistol, when he should have been running. It was to hand it to her, so she could reload it and lie there with her body hiding it.

He toppled forward across her legs.

The weight was smothering, confining. She used all her strength to lift his torso an inch and pull her legs out, then dropped him. It was not until she had stood up and taken a step backward that she was sure he was dead.

She took two deep breaths and heard Pete's running footsteps, coming along the ridge. He had completed his circle to come up behind the hunter, and now he was carrying the sniper rifle. He sidestepped around the body, keeping his eyes on it, horrified at the body and still frightened that the man might be alive.

She bent and picked up the hunter's flashlight and his pistol. She said, "I'm going to ask you two questions. No matter what the answers are, I'll show you how to get out of here and leave you safe. But I have to know."

He looked at her, uncomprehending. "Anything. Ask."

She knelt beside the body, clutched the belt and the shoulder and rolled him over, then shone the flashlight on the face. "Have you ever seen this man before?"

Pete Hatcher stepped close and stared down at the blood that had soaked the front of the shirt. "Uh," he grunted. Then he kept walking around to the man's feet to see the face right side up. "No," he said. "Never." He seemed to shiver once to get the sight out of his mind.

Jane moved the light to Pete Hatcher's face. "Do you know somebody named Linda?"

Pete's shoulders came up in a shrug and stayed there. He seemed to search the night sky for a moment. "A few. Linda Horn. I dated her in college. Linda Becker. She used to do my taxes, but she married a lawyer and they moved to New York. I don't know. . . . Give me a hint."

Jane didn't move the light. "We're miles from anywhere, where nobody can hear. Obviously I'm not going to tell anybody about any of this, ever. Is there a reason somebody named Linda might wish she'd never met you?"

She could see he was genuinely confused, searching his memory over and over without finding an answer. "No. I don't think so."

Jane switched off the flashlight. She looked up. The moon and stars had never come out, and the cold wind was pushing low, dark clouds in an endless stream across the sky. "You'd better go find a soft place and start digging a hole for him." She looked back down at the body and began searching the pockets.

"What are you looking for?"

"Hurry. Snow is coming."

Jane searched the man's pockets, pulled up his shirt and his pant legs to search for anything that might be strapped to his body, took off his jacket. She found a map like hers and a good compass, a magazine for the rifle with six rounds in it. There was a knife stuck in the belt at the small of his back. The coat was stuffed with jerky and crumbled biscuits. When she had taken them out, she felt a stiff spot in the lining, so she sliced it open with his knife and found a thick plastic packet full of money and identification cards.

Jane picked up her flashlight and searched the plateau carefully and methodically, beginning with the spot where she had first seen the man, then the hiding place where he had opened fire, then backtracking until she found the tracks where he had come up out of the valley, then simply walking back and forth to sweep the rocky, windblown expanse with her light.

When she returned, she found Pete waiting for her. They each took an ankle of the corpse and dragged it to the hillside. Pete had rolled some big stones aside and dug in the soft earth beneath them, filling his jacket with dirt, then dumping it out and filling it again. He had managed to dig about three feet down before he had hit bedrock. Jane helped Pete drag the body into the hole and push all of the dirt over it, then roll the big stones into place.

They walked back to the spot where they had left their packs, and Jane began to redistribute the gear. She put all of the money and most of the food in Pete's pack with his pistol and his ammunition. Then she handed him the dead man's map and compass. He said, "Why are you giving these to me?"

She turned on her flashlight and held it on the small pile of belongings the dead man had been carrying. "Besides the map and compass, he had identification, money, biscuits and jerky, bullets."

"So?"

"Think about what he didn't have. No tent, no bedroll, no pack, not even a change of socks. No car keys. There's somebody else, coming along the trail carrying the heavy stuff."

"Then let's get moving," he said. "If they're carrying all that stuff, it should be easy to keep ahead of them."

She handed him his pack. She pointed north along the ridge. "Go as straight as you can, to the north. In an hour, maybe three at the most, you'll be able to see a lake below you on the right. That's Cameron Lake. It's in Canada, and at the end of it is a big, modern road."

"But I can't leave you out here alone, waiting for some killer."

"You can't do anything else," she said. She put on her pack, stuck the killer's .45 pistol in her jacket pocket. "I don't work for you anymore. I quit. If you walk in that direction until dawn, you can be in Lethbridge by noon, and on a plane by dinner time. Head for Dallas. Rent a place like the one I told you about. If you use the papers in your pack, you'll be safe."

He held her shoulders. "Come with me," he pleaded. The next words came out as though he thought they would be a surprise. "I love you."

She bobbed up on her toes and kissed his cheek. "I love you, too. You're my brother." She slung the big sniper rifle over her shoulder, turned away, and began to walk.

Pete Hatcher stood and stared after her as long as he could, a tiny human form diminishing along the dark, rocky plateau. Twice he watched her drop onto a lower shelf where he could not see her, then reappear, climbing the next one. The third time, he did not see her again.

32

Lenny made his way along the trail with difficulty. It had been hard enough to walk ten miles a day carrying a hundred and fifty pounds of gear along a rough trail, but during the night a steady snow had begun to fall. The rocks and tree roots had acquired a thin glaze of ice and a covering of feathery snow that could turn an ordinary step into a broken leg. The path was getting harder to see, and in a few hours it would look just like the sparse pine forest around it. He stopped frequently to consult his compass and look for identifiable landmarks, but the snow whitened the air and hid the crests of the mountains like a fog. He was beginning to feel more and more uneasy.

At six in the morning he had calculated that if he kept to the trail, he would make it to the campsite at Goat Haunt by eight. Now it was after ten, and he was not sure he was even on the trail. The scraggly evergreen trees were beginning to look ghostly and unclear. A packing of white along one side of each trunk had made them begin to fade into the stillness of the landscape.

The fact that he had allowed himself to be put into this predicament was a source of amazement to him. He tried to follow the logic of events backward, but his mistake—his share in the blame for this disaster—could not be found in the recent past. It wasn't anything he had done. It had only been his vulnerability to people like Earl.

A month after he had gotten out of the army, he had begun his long search for something to do that didn't involve some guy who was no better than he was giving him orders. He had driven a cab for a while, but then a cop had pulled him over one night at the Burbank airport. The cop had said he didn't have the right kind of driver's license and then asked to see his cab permit, and then started writing tickets. There was the fine for the license, the fine for the business permit, and a ticket that said he couldn't even ask for permission to get into the cab business unless he spent twelve hundred bucks repairing the cab. Lenny had not argued with him, because he was afraid the cop would search the cab and find the gun. Driving a cab at night in a big city was dangerous, and he had already needed to flash the little SIG Sauer P 239 to save the cash box on two occasions, but the cop wouldn't have cared.

Lenny had used the cab to deliver pizzas for a while, until the expenses had outpaced the tips so dramatically that he'd had to sleep in it. Then he had traded the cab for an old pickup truck, a skimmer, and sixty feet of hose and become a pool man. That was how he had met Earl and Linda. At first Earl, at least, had seemed almost normal. When Lenny had come to clean and backwash the pool, Earl had generally been out working or training the dogs or something. But soon he had noticed that Linda never seemed to have anything at all to do. He would see her behind the curtains in her room, just standing there for twenty minutes, brushing her hair and watching him.

At first, the pool business had seemed to be right for Lenny. Just about every house in the San Fernando Valley had a pool behind it. If he could build up a list of forty clients, allot an hour a week for each one, and charge seventy bucks a month, he would clear twenty-eight hundred a month. With tips at Christmas and a markup on chemicals, he could stretch it to maybe thirty-five hundred. The best part was that it didn't take Lenny anything like an hour to clean a pool. It took twenty minutes, tops.

After a few months Lenny had become convinced that it was virtually impossible to work the pools; keep replacing customers who moved away, got pissed off, or never paid at all;

buy the chemicals; keep the books; and still live a decent life. If he drank too much one night, he couldn't call in sick. He still had to spend the next morning squinting against the glare of the sun that flashed off the shimmering surface of some swimming pool.

He was just at the point of admitting to himself that the business was not as practical as it had looked, when Earl had begun to toss him tidbits to keep him solvent. Earl did it with the same manner that he used when he tossed a chunk of meat to his dogs: "I got something for you, if you want it." At first it had just been watching the house and feeding the dogs while Earl and Linda were away.

For a long time he had not even known what business they were in. He could tell they made money at it, but sometimes it seemed to Lenny that everybody in the world was making money except him. It was like a joke that they had all heard and he hadn't. Linda had been the one to tell him they were detectives.

Earl had asked him to watch some guy's apartment. He had sat for three days listening to people on the radio bitching about the government, told Earl when the guy came home, and collected a thousand in cash. Another time, Earl had asked him to go pick up a package in Chicago. Lenny had received another thousand for taking a plane ride. The ease of it had suggested to him the plan of transforming himself from pool man to detective. The only way to get a license was to serve an apprenticeship consisting of two thousand hours of work for a detective agency, but he was, in a manner of speaking, already working for one.

It was only after Earl had agreed to put him on a time sheet but just pay him when he needed him that he began to see that the detective business was not what it seemed any more than the pool business was. He had logged barely a thousand hours on Earl's fabricated time sheets before the day came when he called Earl to say he had found a suspect, and then watched Earl walk to the window, poke a shotgun through the screen, and blow the guy's head off. That had been five years ago.

All of his history up to then—as soldier, businessman, entrepreneur—and all of the experiences he had endured since then that he didn't especially want to enumerate at the moment had led him to this. He was loaded up and slogging through snowy mountains like a damned Sherpa, and he was becoming more and more suspicious that he might be lost. The world around him seemed inconceivably enormous—much bigger than it seemed in the city—and yet he felt hemmed in by it, because moving across it was a matter of inches and heartbeats. Going in any direction in this snowstorm was like making a colossal bet. If he was wrong, there would be no recovery. But already, when he picked out his spot on the map, he could not be positive that he was pointing to where he was, or where he wished he were.

He devoted the next mile to hating Earl. It was Earl who had done this to him, left him here laboring through the snow, probably toward his death. Earl's method had not been much different from the alternation of fear and gratification that he used on his dogs. It was mortifying. For a second he hoped that Earl was lost somewhere out in the deepest wilderness, freezing to death.

Without warning, Lenny experienced a moment of clarity. That was what Lenny's personal story was about: Earl was going to get killed—maybe not on this job, but some time—and Lenny was going to inherit Linda. He would also take possession of all of Earl's stuff, as a matter of course. There was money, the house, the detective agency, and so on. None of that was important in itself. Its only purpose was to allow the man who had Linda to keep her comfortably.

As soon as he had discerned his destiny, Lenny began to feel better. He marched along with a dreamy certainty, thinking ahead in time rather than space. As long as he kept his face pointed toward the north, he would survive. He began to develop a notion. It was too new, too vague and unformed to call a plan. He would meet Earl somewhere on this trail. He would learn that Earl had caught up with the man and woman

he was chasing and bagged them. Earl would start off along the
trail toward home. Maybe Lenny would let him get five or
even ten miles before he pulled the P 239 out of his pocket and
fired it into the back of his head. Lenny would hurry back to
California and console Linda.

When he reached a hundred-yard straight stretch between
parallel rows of trees, he set off more quickly. He must have
been on the trail all along. With the unbroken snow ahead, the
path looked like a sidewalk. He had taken ten steps before the
woman separated herself from the trees. She stood absolutely
still and erect, and at first he wondered whether he had imagined her.

He kept walking, and he was sure. She was gazing at him,
but her eyes never moved. For a few seconds he squinted at
her, and his mind insistently offered him interpretations so
frightening that he forgot to stop walking. Maybe she was
dead, frozen to death leaning against a tree. Maybe Earl had
killed her, and this was her ghost, lingering on the spot. Maybe
she had always been something not quite human, and she had
lured Earl away from the trail to get lost and die and was
waiting to do the same to Lenny.

For the next few seconds he calmed himself. She was not a
spook. She was a woman. He could see the long black hair
streaming down from a navy watch cap, and there was a strap
across the front of her chest that had to be her pack. Spooks
didn't need to wear packs. She must have circled back and
come out on the trail behind Earl, and now Lenny had her.

She must have seen him by now, but still she didn't turn to
run. Maybe she didn't know Lenny had seen her. He had seen
rabbits behave the same way in the first snowfall of the year
when he was a kid in Michigan. They seemed to think the snow
had made them invisible, so you could walk right up and knock
them on the head. He kept his eyes fixed on her and kept
walking, narrowing the space between them.

At seventy yards, with less snow falling between them, he
could see her more clearly. She was definitely staring straight

into his eyes. Then he recognized the strap across her chest. The dark line above her shoulder that his eyes had interpreted as a branch of a tree was the barrel of Earl's new rifle.

Lenny shrugged off his heavy pack and heard it hit the ground. He pulled his pistol out of his jacket and charged her. He paid no attention to what was under his feet, just dashed toward her. He fired at her as he ran, a loud, echoing blast. He saw the snow kick up five feet from her. He fired again as she stepped to the side, and a small gash of white opened on the pine tree behind her. She stopped a pace away, beyond the snow-plastered trunk of a dead tree.

He saw her swing the rifle sling over her head and grasp the big sniper rifle in her left hand. He saw her put the fingers of her right hand between her teeth and pull the glove off to bare her trigger finger. She raised the rifle to her shoulder, brought up the bolt, slid it back, forward, down. He had to keep her pinned behind that tree, afraid to stick her head out.

Lenny fired twice more, quickly. He was so close now that he saw her push off the safety. He heard her yell, "Stop! I want to talk!" and then, "Stop or I'll shoot!" She was staring at him through the scope, but her small, female voice reminded him that he could do this. If he could make her flinch, duck for better cover—anything—he would be on her before she could recycle the bolt and take aim again.

Lenny raised his pistol again and tried to hold it on her as he ran. He fired again and again, his shots going wide, high, low, hitting bark and snow and rocks. She stood as still as the trees. He saw her finger start to tighten, and then he stopped seeing.

When Jane reached the trailhead at Logan Pass, it was night and the snow was a foot deep. The visitor center was dark, and the windows had been boarded over for the winter. She found the car that she and Pete Hatcher had left, and she could see that the keys were still in the ignition. She decided that it was best not to leave it here, where the search for lost campers it prompted might lead to shallow graves, so she drove to the next trail at Siyeh Bend, drove it into a snowbank, and walked back to Logan Pass.

She used the key she had taken off the body of the second man to open the rented four-wheel-drive Toyota and start the engine. She sat for a minute enjoying the sensation of being out of the cold wind, then drove out onto Going-to-the-Sun Road. At two in the morning, she reached the row of yellow steel stanchions set into the pavement to block the road for the winter. She had hoped the barrier would be fragile enough to crash through, but this one had been made with people like her in mind. She found her way out by backing up a quarter mile, driving through a small wooded grove and an open field, then coming out on the highway beyond the gate.

Jane drove ten miles from the park before she found a level, paved turnout on an exposed plateau, where the wind had swept away enough of the powdery snow to bare some of the blacktop. She stopped and left the motor running while she completed a cursory search of the vehicle. Under the seat was a key to a room at the Rocky Mountain Lodge in Kalispell, and in the glove compartment was a rental receipt for the Toyota.

She arrived in Kalispell before dawn, carried everything that had been left in the vehicle into the motel room, and began to study it. The men had left nothing in the room, but Jane had not expected them to. People in professions like theirs—or hers— didn't leave things where other people were likely to find them. She opened the two men's suitcases and sliced the linings enough so she could fit her hand inside to feel for hidden papers. She slashed the insoles of the shoes to see if they had been opened and glued back. She took apart their flashlights, the carrying case for the sniper rifle, then held up each piece of clothing and shone a flashlight through it to be sure nothing had been sewn into it.

When she had finished, she walked back out to the Toyota. She knew that there had to be a hiding place. After ten minutes of studying the engine compartment, removing door panels and carpets, taking out the spare tire and the gas-tank cover, she realized that she had looked at it and missed it. These killers wouldn't simply have hidden their secrets: they would have wanted them guarded.

Jane hurried inside and began to dismantle the dogs' travel cages. By the time she had pried out the false floor of the second one, she had confirmed her assumption that the licenses and credit cards the men had been carrying were counterfeit. The ones she found in the dogs' cages were older and bore scrapes and dull finishes from being carried in men's wallets.

She read the name on the cards in the first packet: Leonard Tilden. Leonard Tilden's California driver's license said he lived at an address in North Hollywood with an apartment number tacked onto it. He had only one credit card, and it carried the name of a bank that Jane recognized. The bank advertised credit cards for people with bad credit ratings who deposited enough to pay the limit. Tilden's picture on his license identified him as the man who had been following along behind to carry the gear. He wasn't a serious professional killer, he was a caddy. It was possible that she could use him to find out if the cards were real.

She stepped to the nightstand by the bed, picked up the telephone book, found the area code for the northern part of Los Angeles, and dialed Information.

A young man's voice came on. "What city, please?"

"North Hollywood."

"Go ahead."

"Do you have a number for Leonard Tilden, T-I-L-D-E-N?"

The young man was gone, and in his place was the familiar female voice of the information computer. "The . . . number . . . is—" Jane hung up.

The man she was interested in was the other one, the man who had carried the fancy sniper rifle. The little packet that contained his license, three gold credit cards, and one platinum card also contained fifty hundred-dollar bills. She dialed the Information operator again and asked for the number of Earl

Bliss in Northridge. The computer came on and said, "We're sorry. That number is unlisted."

She slipped the two men's identification cards into one pocket and the money into the other. Then she repacked the suitcases, making sure that everything the men had left here was inside. As she was about to go and load all of the luggage into their vehicle, she heard a sharp rapping on the door. She dropped quietly to the floor, held her breath, and listened.

Calvin Seaver waited on the doorstep and knocked again. He had stopped in Missoula to buy a down jacket, but his feet were wet and cold after the short walk from his room to Earl's. He listened at the door but heard nothing. He thought about the size and configuration of his own room, tried to imagine not hearing a knock on the door, and found that he couldn't. He rapped on the door a third time, harder, but he had already admitted to himself that his wait was not over yet. He had thought that maybe the new vehicle he had noticed in the parking lot had meant that Earl and Linda had returned, but apparently it hadn't. He stepped back along the snow-covered walk, placing his feet in his own footprints, opened the door of his room, and went inside.

He stepped to the corner of his room, where his suitcase sat on a folding stand, opened it, and took out his other pair of shoes and a dry pair of socks. He looked at them, then put them back. The snow had not gone away. He had heard that once it began to fall in the Rockies, it often never went away until spring. A dry pair of shoes wouldn't stay that way long enough to get him to his car. He was going to have to drive down the street to one of those upscale sporting goods stores and buy himself a pair of warm waterproof boots and some wool socks. If he got going right away, there would probably be some places open.

He sat at the desk and tried to anticipate the mistakes he might be making. After a moment of thought, he quickly wrote a note on a sheet of paper from the phone pad in front of him and looked at it. "Come see me in Room 3165." He fretted for a long time about the signature. He had been very careful so far. He had not left a message on Earl's answering machine or put anything in writing that could connect him to Earl if anything went wrong. He had paid the up-front money in cash that had come in across the tables in the casino. He had found Earl here without speaking to outsiders.

He had been able to do it because of a combination of luck and curiosity. When he had met with Earl and Linda in Los Angeles, they had made the deal in the car and had eaten lunch in a restaurant without saying anything that could be overheard. When the waitress had brought the check, Seaver had pulled out a credit card to pay it. But Earl had shaken his head and said gruffly, "I'd better pay that." Seaver had hesitated, but Earl's eyes had told him that he considered this a part of their business relationship, so he had put away his wallet. He had expected Earl to pay in cash so no record of the meeting would be created, but Earl had used a credit card, added a big tip, and signed with a flourish. It had caught Seaver's attention that the name he had signed seemed to be much longer than Earl Bliss. As Earl and Linda had stood up to leave, Seaver had surreptitiously opened the leather folder, glanced at the receipt, and seen that the name was Donald R. Brookings. As soon as Seaver had arrived in Kalispell he had called Pleasure, Inc., and asked that the credit department add to today's long list of names for credit checks the name Donald R. Brookings. When he called again, he learned that Donald R. Brookings had charged meals and rooms in Lake Havasu, Denver, and various places in Montana. The last ones were for this motel in Kalispell.

Now Seaver was in a delicate situation. If Earl Bliss got a note that was not signed, he might think just about anything. He might imagine it was a note from Hatcher and the dark-haired woman, inviting him to talk about a buyout of his contract. That could not be anything but an ambush. Earl would know that, and he would respond by arranging to have something ugly happen in this room suddenly and without warning.

And Earl had been in this business for a long time. There might be any number of loose ends and potential paybacks swimming around in that fevered brain of his that Seaver didn't know about. Earl might kill Seaver tonight in the dark just because he was about the size of one of Earl's loose ends. What was already happening was risky enough. Seaver was showing up and surprising Earl Bliss either just before or just after Earl had killed somebody.

Seaver tried to look at the issue of the signature from a positive point of view. Would leaving an unsigned note in the room down the walk protect Seaver from suspicion if the ones who found it were the police? No. It had his room number on it. He wrote "Seaver" clearly at the bottom of the page. Seaver looked at it for a moment, crumpled it up, and threw it into the wastebasket. What had he been thinking of? This was not the time to get impatient and do something foolish.

Seaver walked back past Earl's room and slogged off through the snow toward his car. When he got to it, he had to clean the snow off the windshield and the rear window with his bare hands. He started the engine and then sat in the car holding his cold fingers over the defroster for a minute or two until the numbness went away and he felt ready to drive. While he was at it, he would buy some gloves, too, and a hat.

Jane crouched behind the door and listened. When the knocking on the door had stopped, she had watched the man walk off and disappear into Room 3165. She had waited a few minutes, then returned to the work of packing up the men's belongings. She'd had a half-formed plan to take all of them out the back window of the room and bring the Toyota around the building and out of sight before she began loading.

But then she had been startled by the heavy crunching sound of footsteps outside the door. She crouched beside it and clutched the pistol she had taken off the second man. She stayed where she was, barely breathing, until she heard the footsteps again, this time getting fainter as the man moved off across the lot.

She recovered a little of her composure as she watched the man ineptly sweep the thick layer of new-fallen snow off his windshield and rear window onto his own feet, then drive off and have the pile of snow he had left on the roof slide down to cover his rear window again. The snow meant that the car had been here for hours, and the dress shoes and suit pants the man was wearing meant that he had probably come here from somewhere else and been caught unprepared by the early snowfall.

Jane's eyes rested on the elaborate carrying case for the fancy sniper rifle. She put on her gloves, knelt on the floor beside it, opened it, and began to take out the rifle parts that she had hidden in her pack and place them, one by one, in the precisely shaped indentations of the travel case. Magazine here, suppressor here, foregrip here, bolt here, buttstock here. There was a peculiar satisfaction to the task. It was like feeling the pieces of a puzzle slip perfectly into the spaces where they belonged.

When she had finished, she loaded all of the items she had found in the room into the Toyota. Then she carefully walked down the snowy pavement, stepping in the man's footprints to Room 3165. She used a credit card to open the door and looked around her: a single suitcase, a suit hanging in the closet. She searched the suitcase, but there was nothing in it but men's clothing with brand names that could be bought anywhere. She went to the closet and looked at the label sewn inside the coat of the suit: Callicott Haberdashery, Las Vegas. It could hardly be a coincidence that a man who bought his clothes in Las Vegas had knocked on the door of the two shooters she had met in the Montana mountains. He must be one of the team.

She went into the bathroom and looked at the items he had left on the counter: razor, toothpaste, comb, hairbrush, deodorant—just the usual stuff. She stepped back into the other room and noticed the wastebasket. She reached inside, unfolded the single piece of crumpled paper, and read it: "Come see me in Room 3165. Seaver."

She had heard that name. Seaver was one of the names that

Pete had mentioned when he was talking about the casino. Seaver was the one who had been told somebody was a problem just before Pete had read an obituary. But he hadn't been some hit man. He was the chief of security for the whole company.

Jane put the crumpled paper back into the wastebasket. Seaver was the customer, the one who had hired the killers. He was the one who had been sitting in Las Vegas all this time, comfortable and immune, while they had gone out to hunt Pete Hatcher for him. They had murdered a young policeman in Denver and some unsuspecting tourist in Swan Lake, but nothing they had done could ever reflect on Seaver. He had kept his distance until now. What was he doing up here? Was he checking up on his employees? No. What could he say that would have made them try harder, and what sanctions could he apply if they failed? Probably he had considered it safer to hand them their final payment as soon as they came out of the mountains so they wouldn't knock on his door in Las Vegas. It didn't matter. He was here.

Jane hurried out to the Toyota, took one piece of luggage out of the cargo bay, went back into Seaver's room, and knelt to slide it under the bed.

Jane drove to a supermarket in Whitefish, unloaded the rest of the men's belongings into the big Dumpster behind the building, then drove back to Kalispell. It was the middle of the night when she parked the Toyota outside the gate of the rental agency. She threw the key over the fence so it hit the door of the office and dropped to the top step, where they couldn't help finding it. Then she walked to the small airport at the edge of town and paid in hundred-dollar bills for a seat on the first flight to Los Angeles.

It was not until she was sure the weather had cleared enough and her flight was boarding that she went to a pay telephone and made her call to the police. She said quickly, "There's a man in Room 3165 at the Rocky Mountain Lodge. He told me last night he killed that guy over in Swan Lake." The woman on the other end was talking over her insistently, saying, "Your

33

Seaver was in a daze. None of this felt real to him. The cell was like something out of the movies: old, with things written on the walls that had come from a succession of madmen stretching back at least a generation, thoughts that no functioning brain could contain scrawled in letters like shrieks, with every fifth word misspelled, and anatomical pictures that made him queasy.

Seaver couldn't be here, not in his waking life. When the door had burst inward onto the floor he had been lying in bed, so maybe he had been asleep and what he saw now just proved that his subconscious was getting better at constructing nightmares. The guns had all been pointed at him as the intruders sidestepped to spread out around the bed. Some of the men had looked at him with cold contempt, but the faces of others were empty, just concentrating on lining up the sights with his chest, his head, his belly, waiting to fire.

He had known enough to lie motionless on his back, both arms stretched out from his sides as though he were being crucified. He had known that speaking was a bad strategy, not only because he might say something that would come back to haunt him but also because it was in his best interest to keep the ones with the empty faces calm. They would do the job they had been sent to do, and then they would realize they had the wrong man and leave.

Then one of them had dropped to his belly, slithered under the bed, and dragged out a long, narrow case, opened it, and nodded to the leader before he closed it. "He's got it," he said.

Rough hands had rolled Seaver onto his belly, applied the handcuffs, dragged him to a car, and driven him to the local police station.

While he had been fingerprinted and photographed and searched and pushed into the cell, he had been thinking frantically, trying to catch up with time. They had to be after Earl. Somehow Earl had done this to him—read the note, slipped the gun under the bed, and left. Then Linda had called the police on the way out of town. He wanted to shout, "But why?" loudly enough so they could hear it. Was it just because he had violated the unspoken terms of their agreement and come to Montana? Or could Earl have thought that Seaver had grown so impatient that he had come here to get his advance money back?

Seaver kept reminding himself that it didn't matter. He was in trouble, and he had to concentrate on what was going on now. The police had found his false driver's license and credit cards. They had performed a trace metal detection test on his hands by swabbing them with hydroxyquinoline and holding them under ultraviolet light. He was fairly sure he was in the clear on that one, because the glowing purplish specks that indicated steel and brass were small enough to be ambiguous.

But they had also done an atomic-absorption test on his clothes. That was bad. He knew they must have found antimony, barium, and lead. The only defense he could think of was that he had worn the same clothes for legal target practice at home in Las Vegas and not gotten them cleaned. He could hardly say he hadn't fired a gun in them. He had, but it had not been a rifle. It had been the pistol he had fired into the two men in New York City. The shorter barrel, close range, and downward angle probably accounted for why so much powder residue had stuck to his clothes.

Seaver might be able to account for most of the evidence in a trial if he got the right lawyer, but the rifle was like a mathematical problem that he couldn't figure out how to approach. When the ballistics tests were completed, he knew they would show a match between a test-fired bullet and the bullet that had killed the man in Swan Lake. Otherwise there would have been no reason for Earl to plant it in his room. As Seaver reflected on it, the whole issue of the rifle was perhaps his biggest problem. The lieutenant who had first interrogated him had mentioned, almost casually, that it had come with a silencer. If it had a factory-made suppressor on it, then it had to be a military or police-only model. The prosecutor would drag out Seaver's record and reduce his years of honorable service as a policeman into a set of connections that would make it possible for him to get his hands on a rifle like that—something not a lot of people could do.

He reviewed his own record from the point of view of a prosecutor. They could drag out his expert marksman ratings. Those would be far from enough to prove he could put a round through some guy's temple at five hundred yards, but there wouldn't be any other suspect around who could have done it on the best day of his life. The prosecutors would be sure to dig up his four shootings in the line of duty. The fact that four boards of inquiry had cleared him would mean nothing. Juries looked at internal investigations as what they were: routine, obligatory checks just to be sure there was nothing so obviously wrong with a shooting that the public was sure to recognize it instantly. The shootings would establish that Seaver had dropped the hammer on other men at least four times and not been turned into a shaking wreck by the experience.

The longer Seaver thought about his prospects, the worse they seemed. He had enlisted in the service, done fifteen years as a police officer, then eleven years in a responsible, respectable executive position in an American company with a recognized name. But to the twelve Fundamentalist farmers, old women in pearl necklaces, and fish-bait salesmen who would make up a jury around here, being vice president for security at a Las Vegas casino would sound like he was a gangster.

And what the hell was Seaver doing up here in the first place? The only thing strangers did up here was nothing—go on vacation. What was there to choose from? Hunting, fishing, skiing, horses. Could he salvage the whole rifle issue by saying he'd lied about it at first because he had planned to use an illegal weapon on a hunting trip? No. If rounds from the gun matched the bullet in a murdered man's head, it wouldn't matter why he said he had brought it. He had to stick to the story that the gun wasn't his. He had no fishing tackle or skis, no clothes he could wear to ride a horse even if he had known which end of one to climb onto. He had to say he had been here on business. But what sort of business didn't involve meeting with anyone?

He pondered what he knew about the way Pleasure, Inc., was run, but his mind kept getting mired in the depressing details of the one-of-a-kind project in upstate New York that had gotten him into this mess. Then it occurred to him that this wasn't such a bad project to think about. He could be here in Montana scouting for a place that Pleasure, Inc., could develop as a resort. Companies like Pleasure, Inc., really did keep that kind of scouting a secret. If word leaked out too early, the price of land would triple overnight, competitors would start nosing around, and the local lunatics who always turned up when any-body built anything would begin to organize. A scouting trip accounted for all of his aimless driving, and for his not being dressed or equipped to do any goofing off. A scouting trip would account for his using a false name: it kept competitors and speculators from suspecting anything.

Suddenly, the angle Seaver had been sifting for appeared to him. The sleazy reputation that clung to Las Vegas casinos could be used not to hang him but to make him a victim. It was not Seaver but unscrupulous competitors who had used the rifle to whack that guy in Swan Lake. They had done it so they could plant the rifle in Seaver's room and discredit Pleasure, Inc., seriously enough so the company could never build in Montana.

Seaver knew he would have to retrace all of his movements since he had arrived in Montana to find anything that supported his story and lose anything that didn't. He had arrived in Mon-tana when? Two days before they had arrested him. He had gone right to his hotel in Billings. Could he verify that? Yes. He had flown under a false name, but the police had found identification in the name he had used. If necessary, his lawyers could find somebody in the airline or even on the flight who remembered his face, so that proved it wasn't a lie. The hotel would have his check-in time. Then what had he done? He had gone to his room and watched the television . . . and seen the report of the killing! It was already on TV. The guy had gotten himself killed before Seaver got here! How could Seaver have forgotten the most basic step in proving a murder charge? He had an alibi!

Seaver was free. He was as good as out the door. He rehearsed his story again and again, adding tiny bits to it that he could be sure came from his memory and could be cross-checked by the police later. As he did, he discovered that the rifle had been magically transformed from a damning piece of evidence to a complete exoneration. If Seaver had not been here, he could not have fired the rifle. But the ballistics would show that somebody had fired it through that guy's head in Swan Lake. If the person who had fired it decided the best thing he could do with it was put it under Seaver's bed, then Seaver certainly was no friend of his. Presto! No murder charge, no conspiracy to commit murder, no accessory to murder, not even a felony charge for possessing a silencer.

It wasn't until many hours later, after Seaver had told the police the whole story and walked out of the police station, that his euphoria began to wane. He had only gotten himself out of one small scrape. He had been sent out by the three partners to handle a problem, and he had not handled it yet. He had gotten himself arrested instead. While he had been in jail, it was possible that things might even have gotten worse. There had been photographers on the jailhouse lawn, and men with video cameras that had the call letters of television stations on them.

If Earl Bliss had seen those reports, he would also see the reports that Seaver was free. He might decide that failing to frame Seaver meant he had to kill him. If Pete Hatcher was alive, even he could figure out that the reason Seaver was in Montana was to find him. It might be enough to drive him into the arms of the F.B.I. And if the Italians in New York had seen the reports, they might start asking questions too. He might have to think of a whole new story just for them. He was going to have to check with Foley, Buckley, and Salateri as soon as possible to find out where he stood.

As soon as he was out of Kalispell and down the road to Missoula, he checked into another hotel and walked down the street to a convenience store where there was a pay telephone. He called the private number of the partners' offices in the Pleasure Island casino, but nobody answered. He tried calling their houses but got nothing except the voices of servants who told him politely they were writing down his name. Then he tried the operator at the hotel.

"This is Calvin Seaver," he said. "I need to have you reach Mr. Foley, Mr. Salateri, or Mr. Buckley for me. Any one of them."

"I'm sorry, sir. The resort owners can only be reached through their assistants during normal business hours."

"I know better than that. They can be reached any time of any day of the year. If you don't know me, call up the emergency notification list. I'm at the top."

"Your name, sir?"

"I just told you. Calvin Seaver."

"I'm sorry, sir. I've been instructed to inform any callers that there is no Calvin Seaver connected with the hotel. All inquiries regarding a Calvin Seaver are to be immediately referred to Mr. Bennis in hotel security."

"So refer me. Get him on the line."

There was a silence, and Seaver could tell from the duration that the operator was talking to Bennis's office. No, damn it, that was Seaver's office. Bennis was a flunky, a man Seaver had picked out of the ranks because of his canine loyalty and his ability to keep his mouth shut.

"Bennis," said the voice.

"This is Seaver. I'm at a pay phone, so there's no tap at this end. You might want to check your bug detector."

"I already did," said Bennis. "It's clear."

"I'm in Missoula, Montana. The police got convinced they had the wrong man and let me out. I wanted the big guys to know. I'm coming home."

"Cal—" There was an unpleasant sound to Bennis's voice that Seaver had not noticed before, almost a whine.

"What?"

"You've been good to me, so I'm paying off the favor. Don't come here."

Seaver felt as though he'd had the wind knocked out of him. "What does that mean?"

"They hired some people."

"They were going to kill me in jail? Without even hearing what happened or giving me a chance to fix it?"

"Look, I don't know any more."

Seaver's field of vision had a red aura at the edges, and his heart beat so hard he could feel it. "They didn't hire them. They don't know who to hire, and they wouldn't let themselves get within a mile of anybody like that. You hired them. They called you into the office and told you I was a problem, a serious liability. Did you even tell them I wasn't? That I would never talk?"

Bennis's voice was calm. He sounded as though he were on the other side of a huge chasm, watching a disaster that had nothing to do with him. "You know them, Cal. They make a decision, and that's their decision. You don't talk them out of something like that."

"You're right," said Seaver. "I'm glad you told me. And you know what else? I'm glad you're the one they picked to replace me. You deserve it."

Seaver hung up and took two steps back toward his hotel. He was tired, and had to sleep. No, there was no way he could go back up there and sit around all night. He had told Bennis he was in Missoula. He had to get on a plane.

He looked at his watch. It was three in the morning. What was the date? September 16—no, 17. It was a date that he would always remember. As he walked toward the hotel, he shook his head, and was surprised that the violent movement traveled to his shoulders and spine. He probably looked like an old dog shaking water off his back.

Seaver gave a quiet snort of a laugh at the thought. That was about right. For eleven years, since the day he had gone to work for Pleasure, Inc., he had been moving a third of his salary into accounts in the Caribbean under the name Luther Olmstead. How could men as smart as Buckley, Salateri, and Foley not have guessed that? When they had met him, he had just finished fifteen years as a cop, where there had been no opportunity to put away a dime. Then he had landed a job that paid over two hundred thousand a year with virtually no expenses. The taxes alone would have been more than his old salary.

He would stop in Los Angeles just long enough to pick up traveling money and his passport. That was the main thing—getting out. After that, he would consider what else he wanted to do. The three big guys probably thought that, given his history, his impulse would be to call the police. They would be busy in a few hours getting rid of evidence. But his experience as a policeman had not given him an interest in calling the police. And that was not his only option. He might not know the names of the old men in New York that the three partners were afraid of, but he did know the names of some similar men in Los Angeles, and he just might decide to give them a call. They would appreciate the opportunity to give their friends in New York a timely warning. He had always heard that the Mafia worked on reciprocity and favors, and this was a time of his life when it would not hurt to have them think of him with gratitude.

34

Jane found Earl Bliss's address in the early afternoon. She drove past it slowly, looking for signs of danger, then continued up the road to study the next few houses. Out here on the northern rim of the San Fernando Valley, the stretches of pavement could hardly be called neighborhoods, because the houses were set at the ends of long winding gravel driveways on weedy parcels that seemed to her to be five acres or more. Some of the places consisted of old, rundown frame houses surrounded by the bodies of half-assembled cars, while others were like Earl Bliss's, little fenced-in compounds with sprawling suburban houses in the middle. Two miles down the road she turned around and came past the house in the opposite direction. The house remained as she had first seen it: no curtains had moved, no cars had suddenly appeared in the driveway.

She had no evidence of how many people had been engaged in the hunt for Pete Hatcher. Committing murder for money was not a business that lent itself to large teams. But she did know that at least one person was not accounted for: the one who had trapped Hatcher in Denver had been a woman.

Jane did not return until after midnight. She turned off the lights of her rented car, pulled far enough up the drive to keep a passing cop from getting curious, and walked toward the house. The chain-link fence was topped with barbed wire, but there were no insulators for electricity, so she pried off ten feet of it with the tire iron from her rented car, climbed it, and dropped to the lawn.

There was a kennel in the back yard with a pen and a long exercise run, but she knew that the dogs were far past barking, so she skirted close to it and studied the house. It was a five- or six-bedroom one-story ranch structure coated with white stucco. She walked around it, looking for motion sensors, automatic lights, indications of the sort of alarm system it had. There were no security company's signs anywhere on the property, no stickers on any of the windows. Most of the windows were dark, but she could see two with dim lights glowing behind them. She cautiously approached the first and peered inside. Through the curtain, she could just see a lamp on a desk. She moved to the other side of the window and looked at the place where the cord led to the electrical outlet. She could see the little plastic box and the circular dial. The light was on a timer.

She walked to the other lighted window and saw another lamp on a timer. She considered. The timers meant that nobody was home. There were no signs of an alarm system. It made sense that a professional killer would not want to have his house wired with devices whose sole purpose was to summon the police. And most of the time, the dogs would have warned him long before any intruder came close enough to enter the building where he slept.

She decided to take the chance. Earl and the second man were dead, but there was a strong likelihood that they had left some notes, some information about Pete Hatcher that could give a new set of killers a start. And there was still the woman who had trapped Pete in Denver. The woman might not be the sort who would come after Pete alone, but unless Jane found out who she was, there would be no way to predict anything about her.

Jane walked to the kitchen door, swung her tire iron to shatter the upper pane of glass, reached inside, unlocked the door, and entered. There was no noise, and there was no electrical contact in the frame that could have set off a silent alarm when the door opened.

She felt for the light switch and turned it on. The kitchen was modern and very expensive—a professional-size Wolf stove, Sub-Zero refrigerator, vast surfaces of green marble, the dull gleam of stainless steel—but when she looked in the drawers and cupboards there were few containers or implements to indicate that much cooking went on here.

She walked into the living room. There was electronic equipment, all small modular boxes piled up into towers and banks along one wall. Some of it she recognized—television monitors, VCRs, speakers, compact disc players, cable TV descrambler, tape recorders of various kinds—but among them were other boxes and monitors that seemed to belong to computers. To her it appeared that the man who lived here simply bought things. It occurred to her that each item in this house probably represented some person's life. People had been changed into leather couches and marble counters and electronic gadgets.

She moved up the hallway and found Earl's bedroom. Her nostrils picked up the faint scent she remembered smelling when his body had fallen on her, a mixture of sweat and gun oil and some kind of hair tonic. She waited for the wave of nausea it induced to pass, then began her search by the telephone, but she found no paper in the room for writing down numbers or messages.

She opened the sliding door beside her and found a custom-built closet with drawers and racks and hanging clothes. It was the hat rack that caught her eye first. There were a dozen baseball caps with the logos of teams and manufacturers of trucks and farm machinery, but others that said FBI, POLICE, or SWAT TEAM. In a bottom drawer she found two black ski masks with eye and mouth holes and a wide selection of gloves. He didn't wear those in southern California to keep warm.

She stepped to the rack of hanging clothes and confirmed the impression that had been building in her mind. There were clothes of all kinds—conservative suits and moth-eaten wool hunting shirts, a tuxedo beside an army field jacket that was in a plastic bag because it was covered with dirt. Earl had uniforms. There were the midnight-blue shirt and pants of the Los

Angeles Police Department beside the hot-weather version with short sleeves, a khaki Highway Patrol uniform, a blue windbreaker with the word POLICE in bold reflective letters like the ones plainclothes cops slipped on for raids. There were work clothes for the Department of Water and Power, Southern California Gas, Pacific Bell. Earl had been able to impersonate virtually anyone.

She left the bedroom and went up the hall to see what Earl had kept in the other rooms. She reached the door on the end, turned on the light, and drew in a breath.

It was a woman's bedroom. Earl had not lived in the house alone. It was inconceivable that a man like Earl would have one woman who lived in a house with his collection of police uniforms but asked no questions and a second who went out with him to kill people. This was almost certainly the woman who had ambushed Pete Hatcher in Denver. Jane opened the nearest closet. The clothes on the hangers were like everything else in the house: they bore very expensive labels without being especially appealing or tasteful choices, and all of them seemed too recent. There was such a profusion of new clothes that Jane wondered how anybody could spend so much time shopping. She tried to focus her mind on the immediate need to use her time efficiently. If the woman lived here, then there was a strong possibility that she could show up without warning. She had been in Denver, but Jane had seen no sign of a woman in Montana.

Jane spent ten minutes searching for framed photographs, albums, anything that might tell her what the woman looked like, but she found nothing. She looked more closely at the clothes in the hope that they would help her form an image of the woman's size and shape, but it was a pointless exercise. It seemed to Jane that every woman she had seen in California was a size eight, between five feet six and five feet eight.

She kept searching. The woman was vain and a bit self-indulgent. The room beside this one was a dressing room with a huge lighted mirror. The cosmetics, creams, perfumes, and oils in tiny jars and bottles were all brands so expensive that most women would not have recognized them.

She went into the bathroom connected with the bedroom and found it to be the same. There was a glass shower with marble walls that would have held five people and complicated fixtures for spraying water at different intensities and different angles. There was a sunken bathtub with Jacuzzi jets, a steam machine for facials, and here, too, the same profusion of unguents and lotions and oils, enough to last several lifetimes.

The door on the far side of the bathroom opened into the exercise room. There was a stationary bike, a treadmill, a Nautilus machine, weights, padded benches, step-stairs, pulley contraptions. The whole inner wall was one immense mirror with a ballet barre. Jane tried to understand this woman. The size of her clothes indicated that she took care of herself, but the equipment in this room was not of the quality or variety that most people put in their homes. It was all the industrial-grade gear that gyms bought. She lifted the bar of the exercise machine. If the setting was for the woman, then she was a specimen, Jane thought. Maybe Earl had used the equipment too. Through the French door on the outer wall, Jane could see a thin strip of moonlight on water—a pool, too, right at the woman's doorstep. But it wasn't the pretty kind, or the sort where people had fun swimming together. It was a single-lane lap pool. It reminded Jane of the dogs' exercise run by the kennel.

Jane moved back into the woman's bedroom. The whole house made her uncomfortable, vaguely afraid. She was fascinated and repelled by the mundane details, the fixtures of the man and woman's daily life here. She could not get herself to set aside the thought that each extravagance looked like a single spree, as though one day they must have come home from killing someone and used the money to buy a room full of exercise equipment. Another day they would come home and hire a contractor to remodel the woman's bedroom. She wondered if they thought about the people afterward: this room was cutting John Smith's throat, and this one was shooting Bob and Betty Johnson through their heads in their sleep.

She looked around her at the place where the woman slept. The woman dressed as other women did, and liked the amenities that other women liked, but there was too much of everything, and it all seemed a little bit off. It seemed to Jane that it was like the room of a man impersonating a woman: transvestites never seemed to wear an oversized sweatshirt and blue jeans. She remembered the weights in the exercise room: maybe she had stumbled on the truth. She took a pair of slacks out of the closet and measured the ratio of the hips to the waist. No, the clothes would not have fit on a body that had not been born female.

But everything in the house was wrong. The kitchen was not a place where anything was cooked. It was a hoard of appliances and glossy surfaces. The living room looked as though no one ever sat in it. The furniture was all too well matched to have been bought any way but at once, and it was spatially arranged to be neither attractive nor comfortable, just placed so that there would be room for a lot of it. She looked at the bed. It was king-sized, too big for one person, but she could not imagine the people who had lived here doing anything so human and comprehensible as sleeping on it together.

Jane opened the second closet and found the boxes of wigs. The woman had good ones, all genuine human hair. There were short ones, falls to take on and off, curly ones and straight ones. Jane took a quick inventory. The woman had light brown, dark brown, red, black, auburn, even gray. The only kind missing was blond.

Jane pushed aside some clothes and saw the door of a gun cabinet. It was built like a safe, with a five-digit combination lock. There was no hope of looking inside, but Jane decided that she had seen enough of Earl's arsenal already: what she wanted would be on paper. But the gun cabinet struck her as part of the impersonation. The room was so aggressively, insistently feminine, so exclusively the domain of a woman, that it was a perfect place for a cache of weapons.

She still had rooms to account for. She closed the closet and left the bedroom, then walked down the hall into an office. It had two desks, two telephones, two computers. There were no photographs here, either.

The filing cabinets were full of records of payments—some made by Earl Bliss, some made by Northridge Detectives—but no records of receipts, no notations relating to income, no lists of clients. Whatever useful information existed, it was probably in the computers. She searched the desk drawers. At first she found only office supplies, but the deep one on the right side of the second desk was full of electronic gear. There was a box of tiny short-range audio transmitters for hiding inside household objects, more powerful ones with prongs for plugging into wall sockets, even one that had been disguised as a night-light for a child's room. There were receivers and long-range microphones. She closed the drawer.

The place had once been a bedroom, so there was a closet here, too. She opened it, and the sight made her shiver. There was a handyman's pegboard. On it hung handcuffs like the police used, thumbcuffs with jagged inner edges that could do terrible damage if a prisoner struggled, a two-foot coil of piano wire with handles on both ends, a couple of long spikes like skewers. She lifted a small box from the shelf and took off the top. There were hypodermic needles and bottles. She read the labels and she could see they had been stolen from a hospital: anectine for stopping the heart, insulin for inducing shock, heroin for an overdose the L.A. coroner would find familiar and explicable. She put the box back and found the little press.

She looked at it without understanding until she opened the box beside it. Inside was a stack of blank gold plastic cards, all bearing the symbols of Visa and MasterCard. The machine was a die for pressing names and numbers into fake credit cards. Her breath caught in her throat. Maybe some of the blanks had the woman's picture on them. She shuffled through them eagerly, but found no picture. Her eyes passed across the little press. There was still type clamped in the die. She read it backward: Susan Preston Haynes. Of course it was a false name, or the woman wouldn't have needed to make the credit card at home. Knowing a false name was not going to get Jane any closer to the woman.

She looked around her at the room. The malevolence of the house was strongest here. The perverse eagerness to hurt, to render human beings into money made her sick. She glanced at the computers. Without codes and passwords, they were locked as tightly as the gun cabinet.

Jane sat at the nearest desk and tried to defeat the sick, nervous feeling in her stomach. Her mind had been calmly, logically working its way toward the conclusion that she had to wait as long as it took for this woman to come in the door, and then kill her. It was simple, practical, rational, and utterly wrong. She had just shot two men. But there was an immense difference between shooting back at a killer and crouching in this horrible place with the lights out, waiting for the door to open so she could bring a knife across a person's throat. She was not going to do it.

She looked around her, and her eyes rested on a small sheet of paper that said Federal Express. It was a receipt, the carbon copy of the mailing label on an overnight package. The date on it was two weeks ago. She picked it up and looked at it closely. The address box said, "Susan Haynes, Meadowgreen Suites, Orchard Park, New York 14127." Orchard Park was seven or eight miles from Buffalo, no more than fifteen from Amherst.

Jane found herself standing. She had to stop herself from dashing outside and running for the car. She looked around her at the walls that enclosed her. This house seemed as much of a threat as though it were alive. The computers were probably full of information about Hatcher and about Jane, but there were undoubtedly backup disks hidden somewhere else in the building. The building was full of hiding places, locks, and secrets that she could never hope to break. There were probably photographs of Hatcher, and maybe of her too. There might even be electronic equipment that was running right now, taking videotapes of Jane's visit.

She stepped to the kitchen, where she remembered seeing

books of matches with the names of restaurants on them. Then she went outside, sliced off five feet of the garden hose attached to the house, went into the garage and syphoned gasoline out of the tank of the Mercedes into a bucket.

Jane poured the gasoline liberally around the office and on the computers, in the two bedrooms, in the closets. She filled the bucket again, then poured gasoline along the inner walls of the living room, the exercise room, the bathrooms. She poured another bucketful along the baseboards and carpets at the outer walls of each room.

She dribbled a trail of gasoline down the hallway, across the living room rug, and through the kitchen to the back door. She poured gasoline on the kennel and along the walls of the garage. Finally, she poured a stream of gasoline from the kitchen steps to the garage, to the kennel.

Jane climbed back over the chain-link fence, lit a match, and tossed it on the back lawn. The vapor ignited with a *poof!* and a flash before the match could land, and bright yellow and blue flames raced in three directions. Jane hurried to her car. She saw the bright flare-up when the fire reached the kitchen floor, the flames licking up the kitchen walls.

As she started her car and backed out of the driveway, she saw the quick, purifying flames lighting up one window after another. When she reached the first turn in the road, she glanced in the rearview mirror and saw flames billowing out of the front windows, illuminating the clouds of black smoke that rose into the night sky.

35

Jane stepped into the airline terminal, stopped near the door, and scanned the monitors for the schedule of departures. There seemed to be no flight for hours that stopped in Buffalo, so she chose a nonstop flight to New York City that was leaving in ten minutes. She bought a ticket under the name Julie Sternheim and ran for the gate.

As soon as the plane was in the air and the seatbelt sign above her head went out, she used the Marie Spellagio credit card to activate the telephone built into the seat in front of her and dialed the number of the house in Amherst. She heard the phone ring ten times, and she let it ring five more before she gave up. She glanced at her watch. It was already four A.M. here, so it would be seven in Buffalo. By now, Carey had probably scrubbed and entered the operating room.

If the woman had been in Buffalo for two weeks, she must have gone there straight from Denver—been sent there from Denver. Earl Bliss had been the designated shooter, and he seemed to have had all the money, so probably he had been the one who made the decisions. He must have been smart enough to know that from the moment Pete Hatcher had seen the woman's face, she had become a liability. So he had sent her to western New York.

As Jane followed the path of logic, she felt her stomach tightening. The woman had not simply been excused from the hunt and sent home: she lived in Los Angeles. She had not been bundled off into hiding in a place that just happened to be near Jane's hometown. They had sent her something there by overnight mail. People in hiding didn't need anything urgently enough to require that it be sent in a way that left a record.

Jane tried to invent coincidences that would confute her logic. Had she given Pete any false identities that could have tied him to the western part of New York State? That was impossible. She never sent chasers across her own trail. Did Pete have any close friends or relatives there? When she had asked him about friends and relatives, there had been none east of Nebraska.

The address in Orchard Park might mean something. Orchard Park wasn't a big, bustling city where people came and went by the thousand without attracting attention. It was a suburb, a small upper-middle-class bedroom community. It wasn't a place to remain anonymous. It was a place to establish an identity.

This woman could not have been sent to spot Pete Hatcher. She was the only member of the team whose face he had seen. There was only one reason Jane knew of for this woman to be in western New York. That night on the mountaintop, when Earl had been deciding how to kill her, he had called her Jane. The woman must have known much more.

Jane began to sweat. The woman had been there for two weeks. She'd had enough time to find out—what? Where Jane lived, certainly. And that meant she knew who Jane was married to. Jane snatched up the telephone again and inserted her credit card. When she had punched in the area code, she stopped.

Every time Jane had taken Hatcher in a different direction, Earl had turned up with the rifle. Jane's throat was dry, and her head was throbbing. She had made some terrible mistakes. The woman had probably found her address in a day, and on the next day had broken into the house and bugged the telephones. Jane had obligingly called every few days, and that had somehow given her a location. Now this woman was waiting in Buffalo, probably watching Carey, and Jane could not even call to warn him, because the woman would be listening.

Jane forced herself to be calm and tried to think of another way. She could call Carey's office. No, that was foolish. If the woman had been listening for a call from Jane, she could not have assumed it would come to the house. The woman would also have tapped the lines in Carey's office.

Carey was at the hospital right now. There were hundreds of phone lines at the hospital. Tapping into all of them would be a job for a team of electrical engineers, not one person who knew how to plant a bug. Jane searched for a way to use the complexity of the place. Carey would be in surgery for the next couple of hours, where an outside telephone call could not reach him. After that, he would be all over the building, walking the halls to examine and discharge patients, read charts and scribble in files, look at X rays and test results. There was no way to predict precisely where he would be. If the operator didn't have a pretty clear fix on him, what would she do? She would page him.

Jane could not let that happen. The person this woman wanted to find was Jane. The woman could not assume that Jane would not show up in person instead of calling. The woman could monitor her telephone taps with a tape recorder, but she would have to watch Carey with her own eyes.

Suppose Jane didn't call Carey directly. She could call the nurses' station in the recovery room. Carey would certainly show up there immediately after surgery, and then again later to clear the patient to be transported to his own room upstairs. But what could Jane say to a nurse? She could hardly ask some stranger to tell Dr. McKinnon he might be in mortal danger because his wife hid fugitives.

For the moment, Carey was as safe as he could be. Nobody could get into an operating room. The big metal doors wouldn't open unless someone inside hit a switch on the wall. After that, he would be surrounded by people, going about his business as he had been doing for two weeks while this woman had been watching him.

The woman had not come to Buffalo to harm Carey McKinnon. There was no extra pay for that. She had come to watch him and use him to find out where Jane was. Carey was only valuable to this woman if he was alive and unsuspecting. He would be safe until . . . when? The moment when the woman saw Jane.

She sat strapped in her seat, rigid. Maybe she should not be going home. Maybe the best favor she could do for Carey McKinnon was to stay as far away from him as possible. If she stayed away for long enough, the woman would have to give up and go away. But then Jane realized that she was wrong. If this woman had been keeping Carey in sight for two weeks, then the woman could not be sure that Carey had never caught a glimpse of her, never seen her face. If the woman got tired of waiting, she would not just go away. Before she did, she would put a bullet in Carey's head.

Linda stared at the red zero on her answering machine. If Earl had done it and gotten back to civilization by now, he should have left a message for her. But maybe he had called home. There was no question that he would call as soon as he could reach a telephone. He would be thinking about what she might be doing to keep Carey McKinnon occupied, and he would want that to end as soon as possible.

She dialed the number of her house. The telephone rang once, twice, and then there was an unfamiliar high-pitched tone. A recorded voice that sounded like a middle-aged woman came on and stated authoritatively, "The number you have reached is not in service. If you think you have reached this number in error, please hang up and dial again." Linda took her advice.

After the third try, Linda began to feel panicky and worried. Was it possible that in all this traveling she had forgotten to pay a phone bill? Her mind searched for a way to reassure itself, but it came back with nothing. She weighed the danger of calling the long-distance operator in Los Angeles and explaining the problem. She could think of no reason not to, so she did. After a few seconds she was connected with the billing department. The woman on the other end consulted a computer and said, "You're right. I'm seeing it as out of service. It's not a billing problem. I've already checked your records, and you're up to date on your payments. But the phone is out of service."

"Doesn't whatever you're looking at say why?" asked Linda. "I'm expecting a very important call, and if they can't get through I'm going to be a very unhappy customer."

"I'm sorry," said the woman. "They don't tell us what the problem is. It could be a lot of things—a malfunction in the equipment in your home, for instance. Or with the line that goes to your house. If a tree on your property fell and pulled it down, I would have no way of knowing from here."

"Well, I certainly have no way of knowing from here, do I?" asked Linda.

"I understand that," said the woman.

"Can't you send somebody to check?"

"Is there anyone there now to let the repair technician onto the premises?" Linda could tell it was an official question, the sort that brought some rule into play.

"No."

"Then we wouldn't be able to send anyone, no."

Linda closed her eyes and let her voice carry some of the frustration and defeat that she was feeling. "If you were me, what would you do about this?"

Now that the woman had her victory, she issued a reprisal. "When you go out of town it's a good idea to leave a key with a friend or relative. You might call a neighbor and ask her to look across the street to see if there's anything obviously the matter."

The defeat was complete. "Yes, thanks," she said. "Maybe I'll try that. Good-bye." She hung up. Something was very wrong. She goaded her imagination to think of a way to find out what it was from the other end of the continent. She couldn't call the police and have them check the house, because what they might find would send her and Earl to jail. She and Earl had always been so careful to remain unapproachable and anonymous that she not only had no acquaintances among the people who lived nearby, but she could not now recall any of their names.

She used her laptop computer to call up the Los Angeles telephone directory Northwest section and scanned it. Finally she called the number of a florist a half mile from her house, ordered a dozen roses to be delivered to Linda Thompson from Earl Bliss, and charged it to the Northridge Detectives credit card number she retrieved from the memory of her computer. She made it sound like an afterthought when she asked to talk to the delivery driver. She heard the man turn his head away from the receiver and shout, "Enrique! Phone!"

She explained to Enrique, "These flowers are supposed to be a surprise, so it has to be done in a certain way. It's a house with a high gate. Drive up to the gate. Ring the bell. If anyone is home, give them the flowers. If nobody is home, there's a great big mailbox right by the gate. Put the flowers inside, so she finds them when she looks for her mail. Can you do that?"

"Sure," said Enrique. "Anything else?"

"Yes," said Linda. "When will you be back from your deliveries?"

"About an hour from now."

"Fine. I'll call you, because I need to know where you put the flowers. Okay?"

"Okay."

A little over an hour later, Linda called again and asked for Enrique. If a line was down, he could hardly have avoided noticing it. If—God forbid—there was a bigger problem, he would have seen something she could interpret. If the time for killing Pete Hatcher had run out and the one waiting in the house was Seaver, or if the house was under police surveillance, somebody would have appeared at the gate to talk to the delivery man. She waited for a minute and a half before Enrique picked up the phone and said, "I'm sorry, but I couldn't deliver the flowers. The boss says he'll cancel the order and credit your card for the money."

"What do you mean, you couldn't deliver them?"

"There's nothing there. The lady's house burned down. You want to find where she's living now, we'll be happy to deliver them there." He paused. "Lady?"

Linda stared at the wall of her apartment, but no words came to her, because her mind was moving too quickly. "No thanks," she said at last. "Just cancel the order."

She tested each of the possibilities. Had it been a simple accident—a short-circuit or something? But why would it happen now? The odds against that were astronomical, with nobody in the house to leave anything turned on. Maybe Earl had failed again, and decided it was time to burn the house with two bodies in it that matched his description and hers. No. That had not been a plan, it had just been talk. Earl never panicked. More likely, he should have done it but hadn't, and this was Seaver sending them a message.

What would Earl want her to do now? The answer came to her slowly, in simple, incontestable statements. Earl never gave up. If the house had simply burned by itself, she and Earl would need the money for killing Pete Hatcher more than ever. If Seaver had burned the house, then Earl would want to kill Pete Hatcher so he could add the cost of rebuilding to the fee and make Seaver pay for it. No matter what had happened in California, when Earl came for her, he would want to see some evidence that Linda had been doing what he had told her to do in New York.

She stood up and began to pack her belongings. When she had finished, she locked her suitcase in the trunk of her car and came back to put the items she would need into her purse. She walked to the door and looked back before she turned off the light. The only thing left in the room that she had brought with her was the telephone answering machine. With the house gone, it could be Earl's last way to reach her.

36

Jane was already standing when the hatch of the plane opened. She lockstepped up the aisle with the others, then broke free and hurried along the accordion tunnel and into Kennedy Airport. She rushed along the concourse, took the escalator two steps at a time, stepped to the ticket counter, and found that there was not a flight to Buffalo until 3:30. She bought the ticket, then walked to the bank of telephones along the opposite wall.

Jane called the toll-free reservation number of every airline that flew from Kennedy, then worked her way through the ones that left from La Guardia and Newark. Only two airlines had flights that were scheduled to take off earlier than hers, and both were already full. Jane was not surprised. Buffalo was not the sort of place people visited on impulse, so the flights tended to be booked in advance. She would have to wait three hours— no, only two hours, now.

She used the rest of her time to work the airport shops. She found some leather bomber jackets and selected one a size too big for her. It had big map pockets that started at the belly and ran up her ribs. The jacket would pass as cute if a woman wore it, but the look was decidedly male. The big shoulders and the roomy fit would disguise her shape; the thick, stiff leather would provide a distinct advantage against a knife. Anything metallic she put in the map pockets would serve as body armor. She found a smaller shop that sold monogrammed clothes, picked out a black wool baseball cap, and declined to have it monogrammed. She found a pair of soft black leather gloves. It was often a woman's hands that gave her away at a distance. She decided the blue jeans she was wearing were sufficiently nondescript, as were the boots she had worn in the mountains.

The flight to Buffalo took less than an hour, but to Jane it was endless. Carey was out of surgery now, and probably in his office down the street from the hospital. If she wanted to warn him, this was the time. She could avoid his telephones entirely, by calling Jake Reinert. There was absolutely no chance that the woman had tapped Jake's telephone. She could speak freely to Jake and ask him to go to Carey's office and tell him in person. The problem was that she still was not sure what to tell Carey to do.

The woman was a professional, so she would be watching for particular signs, and she would know what she would do if she saw them. What would she do if Carey received a visitor, then abruptly closed his office and left for the day? She would follow him. The answer always seemed to come out the same.

The plane began its descent just west of Rochester, and in ten minutes it was gliding up the runway at Buffalo International. Jane hurried past the car rental desks and went outside to flag a cab. The woman had been here for two weeks, and it was likely that she had rented a car at the airport. If she had, then she would have come out and seen the three or four fleets of nearly identical cars lined up behind the terminal. When she saw one of those four models in the right color, it was possible she would know the person in it had just come from the airport, and begin to wonder.

Jane had the taxi driver take her to an agency close to the center of the city, where she rented a Dodge minivan with tinted side and rear windows. If she was going to use it to watch for the woman, then she had to be able to look without having her head visible in the driver's seat.

Jane drove up the street toward Carey's office, her gloved hands clutching the wheel, the collar of her new jacket up, her hair tucked under her hat and a pair of sunglasses over her eyes. She circled the block, trying to take in all of the sights at once. There was nothing out of place. The cars behind the building belonged to Carey's receptionist and three nurses. As she came up the next street, she noticed that the lights were off in the examining rooms and in the little office where Carey talked to patients. He was gone.

Jane glanced at her watch. It was five forty-five, and Carey had undoubtedly gone back to the hospital. As she drove past the big white building she admitted to herself that it was getting dark. She would have to take off the sunglasses before she went inside. She had hoped not to need to go inside at all. She didn't know most of the people who worked in the hospital, so the woman would have a fair chance of picking Jane out of the crowd before Jane noticed her. The few people Jane did know were all old buddies of Carey's. If she walked in and one of them called, "Jane!" ugly things could start to happen.

Jane parked her van. She was on the same side of the street as the hospital's front entrance, so she wouldn't have to hustle Carey across the open, empty pavement, but the distance was greater than she would have liked. She glanced at her watch again and tried to steady her nerves. This was just like taking a runner out of the world. She had done this before. It should be easy. The doctors always went in and out of the rear entrance, where their reserved parking spaces were. If the woman was watching the car, she would be in the back. Jane would find Carey, push him into an elevator, and lead him to the front door. She would do it about ten minutes before he usually left, get him into the van, and whisk him off to a place where he would be safe.

Jane walked to the doors with a group who seemed to be relatives of someone who'd had a baby. There were a white-haired couple wearing the benevolent grandparent expression and a young dark-haired man who carried a bouquet of roses in a florist's vase so that water dripped on his coat. He seemed to be looking through objects rather than at them, while his mind made a rare visit to the realm of philosophy.

Jane judged that they would make a good camouflage. She opened the door for the parents before the man could transfer the roses to his other hand. He grinned apologetically and she grinned back at him in understanding. She said softly, "Are you a new daddy?" and he nodded proudly. "Congratulations," she said. She pushed the roses up. "Carry them this way, so the water doesn't leak out."

The little family group kept Jane surrounded all the way to the elevator, while Jane scanned the lobby for anyone who could possibly be the woman—blond hair, five foot six to five foot eight, size eight. But the lobby was only beginning to fill up with the early evening visitors now, and none of the women were the right age or size. She slipped away from the family and into the stairwell.

Jane hurried up the steps to the second floor, then the third. Carey's recovering patients were always on the third floor or the fourth. She stepped out of the stairwell and walked purposefully along the third-floor corridor. She turned the corner and stared down the next hallway at the nurses' station to be sure Carey wasn't there, reading charts or talking to someone. She went back the way she had come, then turned the other three corners, looking in each open door until she could see the nurses' station from the other side. She caught a glimpse of Nancy Prelsky hurrying across the hallway and into a patient's room. Jane waited a few seconds to be sure Nancy was occupied in there, then stepped across the hallway and into the other stairwell.

Jane repeated her tour on the fourth floor, but she saw no sign of Carey. There were three orderlies pushing head-high carts loaded with trays full of covered plates along the corridor, then stopping at each room to make a delivery. She looked at her watch: six twenty. Carey wouldn't come in to examine anybody during dinner.

She waited until the orderlies had moved around the corner to the rooms on the other side of the nurses' station, then stepped to a door. There was a chart with notes on it, and she recognized Carey's scrawl. She hesitated, then decided. If the person in here was eating dinner alone, then he wasn't too sick and he wasn't asleep. She knocked and heard a muffled response. She took off her hat and opened the door just enough to stick her head in.

The man was in his thirties, and his leg had a cast on it that went from a metal stirrup at the ankle nearly to his hip. He had a fork in his right hand and a television remote control in his left. When he looked down from the television at her, he seemed pleased.

"Excuse me," said Jane.

"Sure," he said.

"I'm just checking to see if Dr. McKinnon has been in to see you yet."

The man nodded and let his eyes be drawn back up toward the television screen above the bed. "Yeah. About . . . a half hour ago."

"Thanks," said Jane. But this time she did not smile. She was looking past the man on the bed. The windows on this side of the building looked out on the parking lot. Through his, she could see Carey's empty parking space. She closed the door, slipped into the stairwell, and began to run down the stairs.

At the bottom of the stairwell, she paused, put her cap on her head, then stepped out and stared at the floor as she hurried across the lobby and out the front door. She trotted to the van, climbed in, and started it. She spent five seconds checking the mirrors before she threw the van into gear and drove off.

It took twenty minutes to get to Amherst, and while she was driving the last glow of the sunset disappeared and late afternoon turned into evening. As she made the turn onto the street where she and Carey lived, she studied the parked cars, noted the houses that had lights on and the ones that didn't, searching for anything that seemed wrong or out of place.

Jane parked a few doors away from the house and moved to the back of the van to look at it. Carey's car was not visible in the driveway, and there were no lights turned on. Then she saw Carey's BMW make the turn at the corner and come along the street. She moved back from the tinted window and watched it glide past her.

Jane forced her attention away from him. Her eyes devoured

the sights of the neighborhood, scrutinizing them for the tiniest change. Had a shadow passed behind the set of blinds in the window across the street? Had a curtain moved? She pivoted to stare up the street, then down it to see if a new car had come around the corner after his. His arrival had not prompted any visible response.

The sky was black now—as dark as it would get tonight— and it was still early enough so that the normal activity in the neighborhood would keep her from standing out. It was time to move. She switched off the dome light in the van, slipped to the passenger side and out the door. She kept her body in the deep shadow of the van and studied the street again. When she was sure that there were no headlights approaching, she drifted quickly across the open pavement and up the driveway along the tall hedge that hid even her silhouette.

As she approached the rear corner of the house, she saw a square carpet of light suddenly splash onto the grass in the back yard. He had turned on the kitchen light. She would step in the back entrance, let him see her, but cover his mouth before he could say her name. She would tug him outside, out of the house before she spoke, in case that woman had planted a microphone like the ones she had found in the house in California.

Jane turned the corner of the house and looked at the big maple tree in the back yard. The glow of the red and yellow leaves above her made her stop and step back into the shadows along the house. She looked up. The light had come on in the bedroom.

Carey had come in the front door, walked through the living room, the dining room, and into the kitchen. He had not had time to climb the stairs and turn on the light in the bedroom. Jane quickly moved to the kitchen door, unlocked it, and stepped inside. The room was empty.

She hurried to the dining room, but he had already passed. She heard his footsteps above her on the upstairs landing. She ran across the living room to the stairway and climbed, taking the steps three at a time. As she reached the top, she saw him—

the long legs, the familiar shape of his back, the unruly light-brown hair that stood up from his head, glowing in the light from the bedroom doorway.

Jane quickly moved along the second-floor hall as he stepped into the room. She heard him say, "What's going on?" It was too late to prepare, too late to think. She slipped into the room and stepped in front of him.

The woman's pretty face contorted into a mask of fright as she snatched the bedsheet to cover herself. Her green eyes shot to Carey's. "Who is she?"

Jane's mind fought to sort out what she saw: blond hair, size eight, the right age. But this wasn't the way she had expected to find her—in bed, with her clothes in a pile on the chair. This had to be some kind of deception, and Jane sensed instinctively that she had to make the woman believe it was succeeding. Maybe she would not think she had to kill them if she thought they were fooled. Jane could only play the role that the woman had invented for her, and pretend to be the wronged wife. Jane said, "I'm just the woman who lives here—his wife." After a pause she added, "You seem to have us mixed up."

But Carey was gulping and staring, his face longer and emptier than she had ever seen it. "Jane. I just got here myself. I didn't—"

Jane kept her eyes on the woman, but she patted Carey's arm. "Stop," she said. "I know you didn't arrange this."

"I'm glad."

"You might come home late for dinner, but you wouldn't have been late for this." She struggled to figure out what was going on. The woman had been in here with the lights off until Carey had come in the house. The woman had come into the house to do something or other, and Carey had interrupted her.

Jane's heart beat faster. If the woman had been interrupted—surprised—then pretending she had come to seduce Carey would be a good tactic. All she had to do to be convincing was take off her clothes. But she had seen Jane now, and she wasn't doing anything. Jane stared at her. It was just possible that she wasn't armed, and that she was afraid Jane might be.

Maybe she just couldn't reach the gun. Jane kept her eyes on the woman and walked to the chair by the wall where the woman had left her clothes. There were suede leather pants, a silk blouse, underwear, a black leather purse. Jane reached down and tossed the clothes onto the bed where the woman could reach them. She squeezed the purse and tested its weight, then tossed it on the bed too. She felt her muscles go slack with relief. She had been right. The woman had not brought a gun. Jane could still get Carey out alive.

Jane took Carey's arm and began to lead him out of the room. "She's going to want to get dressed."

The woman's voice startled her. It was soft and low, teasing and seductive. "Aren't you going to say anything, Carey?"

Carey and Jane both stopped and turned as the woman swung her legs out of the bed. She stood up, casually naked. Jane felt shock, a flash of rage. Just what did this woman think she was doing? The woman seemed to read her mind. She shrugged. "He's not seeing anything he hasn't seen before." She reached into the pocket of the suede pants and held up a key. "I guess I won't be needing this anymore. Did you find the one I left the other night?"

"Yes," said Carey irritably. He walked toward her, but kept the bed between them and reached across it for the key. The woman's eyes were on Jane, and the big red lips began to turn up at the corners.

The sights in the room seemed to burn themselves into Jane's brain. The familiar shapes—the chair, the picture of Carey's parents on the bureau, Carey's golf bag full of gleaming silver clubs in the open closet beside her—all were distractions now. The key. What did the woman gain by the business with the key? Forget the key. Jane lifted her eyes toward the bed.

The woman was standing beside it now. She had pulled on the suede pants, and she was buttoning the white blouse. She stopped and tilted her head in a pantomime of false sympathy. "I know how this must make you feel. But it really wasn't anything serious. I just saw a chance to have some fun, so I thought I'd borrow him. We never thought that this could happen."

Jane stared at her, mystified. Why was she trying to make it look as though they'd already had an affair? What did it buy her? She should want to get out of here. Jane's heart beat faster. Something was wrong.

Carey moved to his dresser and opened the box on top where he kept small things he didn't want to think about—single cuff links, loose screws, keys that fit nothing. As he reached into his pocket to find the key, he said coldly, "Please don't imply that something went on between you and me. It's bad enough that you're here in the first place, but you're not going to—"

Jane raised her hand and shook her head. "Please. Stop." She tried to sound annoyed, but she was feeling a growing fear. "There's no point in discussing this. Let's leave this woman alone so she can get dressed and go."

The woman glared at her. "Not 'this woman,' " she said. "Susan Haynes."

Jane's body grew tense as she stared at the woman. She couldn't know that it was the name Jane had seen on the machine for making false credit cards. But she shouldn't be saying it. She should not want Jane to hear any name.

Jane saw the woman's hand slip under the bedsheet and grasp something hidden underneath, and she drew in a breath as she recognized the shape of it. As the hand began to come up off the bed, Jane was aware of Carey, still turned away to put the key in the small wooden box on his dresser.

Jane's right hand shot out beside her and plucked a golf club out of Carey's bag. The three-iron flew up inside her grasp until the handle reached her hand. She tightened her grip and swung it downward, hard.

Jane's eyes caught everything during the instant when the shining club swung down. She saw the woman's eyes read the trajectory, fix on Jane's eyes, and convey the terrible message: Not you . . . him! The gun had already begun its move to the left toward Carey, so Jane's swing sliced through empty air and onto the wooden footboard of the bed.

The club struck on the metal shaft, and the heavy head broke off, bounced once on the bed, and fell to the floor. Jane saw the woman's thick lips curl upward as the gun continued its rise toward the back of Carey's head.

Jane screamed, "No!" as she hurled herself toward the woman. She jabbed out at her with the only object she had. She felt the long, thin metal shaft stab into the woman's body below the rib cage. The woman shrieked and shrank backward, but the pistol swung around toward Jane's face.

Jane had committed herself. She could only push the shaft of the broken golf club harder, up under the rib cage and into the heart. The woman clawed at it, tried to push it out, then fell backward.

Jane watched Carey hurtle across the bed, kneel beside the fallen woman, touch her carotid artery, put his ear on her chest. He turned to stare at Jane, and his face was a mixture of horror and incomprehension.

"She's dead," he said. "I can't . . . Why would she—"

"She was staying near you because she thought I would call and tell you where I was," said Jane. She looked away so she did not have to see the expression of shocked understanding forming on Carey's face. As she surveyed the room, she tried to sound calm. "Since the easy way wasn't working, I'll bet she planted something in here . . ." Her voice sounded as though it belonged to someone she didn't know.

Carey stood up, his big hands held toward her, the fingers open in an unconscious gesture as though he wanted to stroke her and soothe away her hurt. "Oh, my God, Jane . . . I let her in. Days ago, before I knew—or thought I knew—that she was out of her mind." He seemed to have an afterthought, and it startled him. "I didn't sleep with her, I just didn't think—"

She came to him, put her arms around him, and rested her head on his shoulder. "I know," she whispered. "I got fooled, and you got fooled." It felt wonderful to be in his arms, familiar and new at the same time and, most of all, safe. She wanted to close her eyes and stay like this, but she could not. She released him and frowned thoughtfully at the dead woman on the floor as she walked around the bed.

Carey stood stiff and still, staring at the body. "This is what it is, isn't it? It's not just helping somebody run away." He paused. "That was what you were trying to tell me that night before you would marry me. That some day I might have to watch my wife stab somebody to death in our bedroom."

She stared at him, her face expressionless, waiting.

His eyes flicked away from her toward the body on the floor, and Jane could tell he was seeing its last moments again and that what he had seen was different from what she had seen. Jane had seen the cruel eyes narrowing, and quick hands in motion and then a gun muzzle that looked cavernous, and Carey had seen the beautiful, smooth, living white skin being pierced, running with fresh, bright blood, and then turned into this cold, waxy effigy of a woman.

Jane said, "Say what you're thinking. In a few minutes it will be too late."

Carey held up his hands, his eyes full of pain, but he was not able to find the words he wanted. He seemed to know he had to try. "I love you." So he had discovered it too, she thought. That was what you said when you couldn't say anything else. He tried again. "You're the best person I ever met . . . and this was the worst thing I've ever seen anyone do. And you did it for me, and that makes me feel awful, and grateful, and sick. And if we somehow get through this, I'll do everything I can to make sure you never do anything like it again. No more fugitives."

She turned her face for a second. Then she picked up the telephone, unscrewed the earpiece, removed a small electronic transmitter, set it on the floor, and stepped on it. "So much for that mystery. We'll probably be finding these for months." Then she sat on the edge of the bed and screwed the earpiece back on.

Carey came closer. "Maybe I should be the one to talk to them," he said. "I'm the one who knew her." He held his hand out for the telephone.

Jane set the receiver back on its cradle, then looked at Carey sadly. "I'm not calling the police."

"Why not? It was self-defense."

She took a deep breath and let it out. "This is a time when we don't have the right kinds of answers for the questions they would ask. This woman was a professional killer. If the gun has ever been registered, it wasn't to her. And if we get our names and pictures in the newspaper, there will be other people coming—ones who knew her, maybe others who have been looking for me."

"Then who are you calling?"

"Nobody." She watched his eyes. They looked as though they were gazing into the emptiness for the first time: there was nobody to call, no agency or institution that could do anything now but hurt them, no friend they could burden with this knowledge, because the risk it carried was too great. Jane said, "Here's what you do. Go right back to the hospital. Check on your patients again, haunt the nurses' stations, read charts, write notes. Act as though you had never left. Don't come back until after ten."

He shook his head in amazement. "You think I can leave you here alone?"

Jane stood and walked toward him. "Neither of us wanted this, but here we are. We're in trouble. I know the way out, and you don't." She pushed him toward the doorway, hard. "So go. We have to use every second."

He stopped, took a last look at her, then turned and walked down the hallway toward the stairs.

At ten thirty, Carey McKinnon unlocked his front door and stepped into his house. He called, "Jane?" but there was no answer. He discovered that he did not want to raise his voice and try again. It took an extreme act of will to ascend the stairs and enter the bedroom. For a moment it seemed as though he had lost his senses. There was no corpse, no blood. The bed had been made with crisp new sheets and blankets. The floor had been scrubbed. It was as though nothing had happened.

Gradually, he began to sense that he was not alone. He whirled and saw Jane standing in the doorway. She was wearing a blue dress with a flower print that he had always liked, but which she hardly ever wore. At her feet was a small leather overnight bag. She said, "Come on. We're not sleeping in that room tonight. You're going to take me to a hotel."

He waited. "That's all you're going to say about it?"

She shrugged, picked up the overnight bag, and handed it to him. "I'll just say it's the last thing you'll hear from me tonight that includes an order, or the word 'no.'" She turned and walked down the hallway of the old house toward the stairs.

"What about tomorrow?"

He could hear the smile returning to her voice as she said over her shoulder, "Ask me tomorrow."

The radiance of the sun just rising behind the horizon outside the east windows made entering the big conference room at dawn feel like walking into a dream. The light was beautiful, golden. In a few minutes it would shine through the broad, moist leaves of the jungle plants outside the glass with such intensity that the droplets left over from the three-thirty watering would evaporate in minutes. But the sky to the west was still that deep purple-blue of the desert night that made the colors of the Las Vegas lights glow brighter, like millions of flares burning at once.

Max Foley looked around the room and verified with mild satisfaction that he was the first to arrive. He supposed it wasn't surprising. The complexity of Buckley's mind seemed to Foley to have been built up like a muscle by a lifetime of worrying about eighty things at once. He had probably spent much of the night getting up over and over to see if any news had come in. Salateri had probably spent most of his night screaming into his telephone to find out why it hadn't. All three partners had been living in their suites upstairs for two months, and it was starting to feel like a siege.

Foley walked to the private bathroom at the far end of the room and knocked, then opened the door with his key. He glanced at the key, as he often did, before he put it back in his pocket. There were only three copies of that key. He had seen them listed once on the roster for the hotel complex: Universal Grand Masters. They were the keys to the kingdom. They would open any lock that any other key in the hotel would open, and a few more besides. "We three kings of Orient-Tar," as his kids used to say. That was—what? Two marriages back, before he had become rich enough to make giving away half his visible assets too steep a price for getting laid now and then. Foley stared in the mirror at his shave, combed his hair, and went back out into the conference room, then looked at his watch. It was after five o'clock, and he was getting impatient.

Foley walked to the end of the vast conference table and sat down in his chair. He glanced at the three identical piles of newspapers that had been left here for the partners and picked up the paper on the top of this morning's pile. It was the *Idaho Statesman*. He thumbed down the pile, reading the mastheads: *Salt Lake Tribune*, *Denver Post*, Spokane *Spokesman-Review*. It looked as though the staff had just bought every paper within a thousand miles of Kalispell. He returned to the top and spotted the words in the lead article that had been circled.

"Montana State Police confirmed that Calvin Seaver, the Nevada man held for questioning in the shooting, has been ruled out as a suspect and released."

The muscles in Foley's shoulders and elbows locked. He let the newspaper drop from his hands as he tried to reconcile what he had read with what he knew. Foley and his partners had sent Seaver out to find Hatcher and kill him. A man had been shot. Seaver had been caught a few miles away with the murder weapon in his motel room, powder residue on him, and false identity papers. Foley had always acknowledged that there was some remote possibility that Seaver might not be convicted of the murder—there could be warrant problems or something—but the notion that he would be released had never entered Foley's mind.

Foley's eyes fell on the pile of newspapers in front of Buckley's seat. He leaned forward and lowered his head to be certain. Yes, if he looked at it from the side, he could see an indentation in the shape of a circle. Buckley had set his coffee cup on the newspaper. Buckley had been here and gone.

Foley studied Salateri's pile of newspapers, but they seemed to be untouched. He swung his chair around, picked up the telephone, dialed Salateri's suite, and let the phone ring fifteen times.

He walked out of the room to the partners' private elevator and used his Universal Grand Master key to activate it, then rode it back up to the thirtieth floor. He rapped on Salateri's door, then kept knocking until his knuckles were sore and the knocks grew fainter. He took out his key and unlocked the door.

Foley pushed the door open, stepped into the big living room, and surveyed the rest of the suite through doors left ajar. Drawers had been yanked out of the built-in dressers to be dumped into suitcases, then thrown on the floor. Salateri had not even bothered to close the floor safe and push the antique Persian rug over it after it was empty.

Foley went out, locked the door, and walked along the hallway and up the fire stairs to Buckley's suite. He unlocked Buckley's door and took in a sharp breath. The place looked untouched. Maybe Buckley was asleep in one of the bedrooms. Foley stepped in, closed the door behind him, and took two steps toward the master bedroom before he noticed the painting over the sideboard. The Matisse on the wall had been replaced by a reproduction of a Watteau. Foley spun around to look at the lighted glass display case on the wall behind him. The spot that Buckley had designed as a shrine for his Fabergé egg was now occupied by a small black-and-orange urn that had curly-headed Greek wrestlers squaring off along the sides. To Foley it looked about as real as the ones in museums, but he knew better. It was a cheap fake, and Buckley was gone.

Foley stepped from room to room in the suite and savored Buckley's premeditation. He had left nothing here that was likely to be of value, but a casual observer would not have noticed that anything was gone. Buckley must have spent several nights packing up treasures, slipping them out of the hotel, and replacing them with junk. No, Foley decided. This was all too elaborate. Buckley had probably been preparing for something like this for years, the way people in flood zones kept a bag packed.

Foley closed this door behind him too and locked it, then walked down two flights to his own suite. As he packed his suitcases he tried to estimate the dimensions of his problem.

Seaver had been hired because he was a cold-blooded, competent watchdog. Now he was a watchdog with rabies. He was already locked inside the house with the family, and he was certain to be getting the urge to bite somebody. He must have used his cop experience and credentials and connections to cut himself a spectacular deal. But a spectacular deal was something like a short sentence, or even a reduced charge, not a free ticket on a murder. What did Seaver have to offer that the cops wanted more than they wanted the man who had shot some hapless schmuck through a restaurant window? There was only one possibility. He must have given them a sniff of the project in upstate New York.

Foley tested the opposite point of view. Suppose Seaver had not turned informant? If Seaver had an alibi, the cops would have had to let him go. God knew, if anybody could set up a solid alibi and go kill somebody, it was Seaver. But the thought only gave Foley a sick feeling. Hiring a couple of killers to go after a nice, gentle kid like Pete Hatcher was one thing. Sending a team of thugs to stab a man like Calvin Seaver in jail and having them arrive after he was loose was another. Seaver was an old pro, and the ones looking for him were a pick-up team of second-stringers hastily assembled and sent into the game without a plan. Even if he didn't know yet that his bosses had sent killers to silence him, by now he knew that they had cut him loose when he got arrested. He had been made into an enemy.

If Seaver now had an impulse to come here and get past the security to pay his respects to his bosses, it was hard to imagine a way to stop him. He had designed the whole system personally, supervised the installation of the hardware, hired the men and told them where to stand. Making Seaver into an enemy had been the wrong decision.

Foley stopped himself. He had to fight this new, neurotic tendency to construct ways to blame himself for everything.

This problem was not Foley's fault. It wasn't. He and Buckley and Salateri had been absolutely right to assume that Pete Hatcher was a threat. After waiting three months for the threat to be removed, they had been right to send Seaver out to handle it. That was his job, and they paid him more than enough to be entitled to assume he would do it. When Seaver bungled it and got arrested, they had been right in acting immediately to disassociate themselves from him and act to cut their losses. The only way Seaver could have gotten out of that mess was to talk.

Now Foley had to assume that Seaver was sitting in some secret, safe location—didn't they usually put people like him on some military base?—giving investigators from Washington everything. In a day or less, there would be the F.B.I., the Justice Department, and the police agencies of several states. They would make travel impossible and staying here unthinkable.

A couple of days after that, there would be raids at the offices of politicians in Albany, New York. A few powerful old men in New York City would start to notice that there were a lot more parked delivery vans, and city crews digging up the streets near their favorite haunts. Those old bastards wouldn't wait around for some grand jury to vote an indictment. They would do exactly as Foley would do in their position: act to cut their losses.

Foley packed very efficiently and methodically. He had never seen the attraction of sinking enormous amounts of money in paintings and bric-a-brac like Buckley, and he didn't have fifty pounds of gold jewelry hidden under a Persian rug like Salateri, so he didn't have to think very hard. He nearly filled his two suitcases with cash, threw on top an accordion envelope that contained a few passbooks for offshore banks, last month's stock and bond statements, and his passport. He slipped a few personal papers in with them, put on his favorite sport coat, stuck his prescription sunglasses into the pocket, and walked out the door.

As he stood in the private elevator and felt it descend thirty floors, he marveled at how simple and inevitable it suddenly had become to walk away from a two-billion-dollar company. There really was no decision to make. If Seaver had not talked, he would probably be on his way here to kill whoever was left. If he had talked, the police were on the way, and so were people a hell of a lot scarier than police. And if Seaver hadn't talked, and wasn't mad, then Pete Hatcher had probably heard of Seaver being caught running around the country with a gun, and that would convince Hatcher that *he* had to talk. And as of this morning, even if none of this happened, Foley would have the problem of explaining to the world the disappearance of his two partners. Foley's position had become untenable. This was like walking away from a burning building.

The elevator opened and he dragged his two suitcases out on the garage level. Then he thought about selecting the right car to take to the airport. His Saab was probably the best one for this, because it didn't look like something a man like Foley would drive.

He took the keys off the board and carried his suitcases over to the dark-green, stubby Saab. It was the name of the car that suggested his first destination. He would go to Sabi Sand Game Reserve in South Africa. He would stay at the Singita Lodge and begin making calls to find his next stop while he was there. For the moment he had a strong interest in places where he could see people coming from a long way off.

Foley opened the trunk. As he lifted the first suitcase in, he had a sudden, uncontrollable urge to look over his shoulder. It was like a chill at the back of his neck. He whirled quickly. There was nobody in the dark behind him, no visible shape at all on this level except his four other cars. But there could have been. It could have been the first F.B.I. agent, or Calvin Seaver waiting to get even, or some nightmare guy that the Mafia had sent to get rid of a bad memory. It could even be nothing more than a thief, somebody who knew that Foley had a lot of money. In a day or so, when the word got around that the three partners had bailed out, there would be a lot of people like that. He would have to watch for them, too.

It occurred to him that he was never going to be able to stop

SHE WILL HELP YOU DISAPPEAR,
IF IT HELPS YOU STAY ALIVE . . .

The Jane Whitefield Novels

by
Thomas Perry

Published by Ivy Books.
Available in bookstores everywhere.

Jane Whitefield is in the one-woman business of helping desperate people disappear. Thanks to her membership in the Wolf Clan of the Seneca tribe, she can fool any pursuer, cover any trail, and then provide her clients with new identities, complete with authentic paperwork.

VANISHING ACT

But when Jane opens a door out
of the world for an attractive fugitive
named John Felker, she walks into
a trap that will take all her heritage
and cunning to escape.

Jane Whitefield is the patron saint of the pursued, a Native American "guide" who specializes in making victims vanish. Calling on the ancient wisdom of the Seneca tribe and her own razor-sharp cunning, she conjures up new identities for people with nowhere left to run.

DANCE FOR THE DEAD

But when a calculating killer stalks an innocent eight-year-old boy, Jane faces dangerous obstacles that will put her powers—and her life—to a terrifying test.

The Jane Whitefield Novels

by

Thomas Perry

Published by Ivy Books.
Available in your local bookstore.

Dear Reader:

Backfire is the sixteenth FBI thriller—and believe me this one's going to knock your socks off. The action kicks off when Special Agent Dillon Savich receives a note at the Hoover Building that says only, "FOR WHAT YOU DID YOU DESERVE THIS." Is it a threat against him or against his wife, Special Agent Lacey Sherlock? Is it payback? For what, exactly?

Then Savich and Sherlock must race to San Francisco when their longtime friend, Judge Ramsey Hunt—aka Judge Dredd (from *The Target*)—lies near death after being shot in the back on the same day he postponed a high-profile murder trial because he suspected the federal prosecutor had been compromised. And now, that federal prosecutor is missing. What is going on here? And the big question: Why would anyone shoot the judge?

When Savich and Sherlock discover one answer, more questions arise until they must face the final shock.

Backfire is a doozy. Please let me know what you think. E-mail me at readmoi@gmail.com or visit me on Facebook.

Do enjoy this one,

BACKFIRE

"*Backfire* had me hooked right from the beginning. I could not put the book down, missed meals, stayed up too late. I loved it and did not want it to end."   —J. Mace

"The twists and turns in *Backfire* make it yet another true page-turner! Savich and Sherlock find themselves increasingly in danger, and the suspense makes the words fly by on the page. Once again, an excellent job keeping the readers on the edge. If I had three thumbs they'd all be up!"
                                              —T. Fontana

"*Backfire* was amazingly good! How can you not adore Sherlock and Savich, two of the best FBI characters in the genre? They are like family since I've been engrossed in their exploits from the very first book. Waiting to get [the next FBI thriller] is excruciating!"   —L. DiMezza

"Yet another page-turner from Catherine Coulter! *Backfire* is full of twists and turns that keep you guessing. It's just one of those books where you say 'one more chapter and I will put it down,' then hours later the book is finished and all you can think of is 'WOW, when does the next one come out?'"   —S. Wagner

"I just finished *Backfire*. I can't even begin to tell you how much I loved this one. I couldn't put it down. I was sneaking pages while I was working. I love every one of the FBI series books. How can you not love Savich and Sherlock?"
                                              —S. Munson

continued . . .

"I could not put *Backfire* down for long. I think it's your best yet. I recommend your books to everyone I know who loves to read. I really don't think I can come up with the words to say but, Catherine, you did it again. Thanks again for writing another wonderful, suspenseful FBI book."   —S.

"I LOVED *Backfire*! What a great book! It definitely kept me on the edge of my seat. I love that so many characters reappear in your books. Thank you so much for Savich and Sherlock. I am totally hooked and will be anxiously awaiting what comes next."   —K. Thompson

"I don't know how you continue to put out such riveting books, but please don't ever stop. I am addicted to Savich and Sherlock and all of their family and friends. Once I got hooked on your FBI series, there was no stopping. I recommend them to anyone who wants a fabulous read."   —J. Reichardt

"*Backfire* was phenomenal. It has the perfect mixture of suspense, humor, and romance to provide the sense of being with the characters, experiencing their fear, the thrill of the chase, and the ties of family, while always keeping the reader glued to the pages until the very end."   —N. Elkins

"*Backfire* fires you through a fast-paced plot with numerous twists and turns . . . Only Catherine Coulter can spin such a web and tie up the loose ends in an incredibly believable manner."   —*Fresh Fiction*

"An exciting suspense-laden whodunit . . . Fans will enjoy this twisting . . . fast-paced thriller."   —*Midwest Book Review*

"Series fans will applaud the strong female leads and the nifty teamwork of Savich and Sherlock."   —*Publishers Weekly*

TITLES BY CATHERINE COULTER

THE FBI THRILLERS

Bombshell (2013)

Backfire (2012)

Split Second (2011)

Twice Dead: Riptide and Hemlock Bay (2011)

Whiplash (2010)

KnockOut (2009)

TailSpin (2008)

Double Jeopardy: The Target and The Edge (2008)

Double Take (2007)

The Beginning: The Cove and The Maze (2005)

Point Blank (2005)

Blowout (2004)

Blindside (2003)

Eleventh Hour (2002)

Hemlock Bay (2001)

Riptide (2000)

The Edge (1999)

The Target (1998)

The Maze (1997)

The Cove (1996)

BACKFIRE

CATHERINE COULTER

J

Jove Books / New York

THE BERKLEY PUBLISHING GROUP
Published by the Penguin Group
Penguin Group (USA) Inc.
375 Hudson Street, New York, New York 10014, USA

USA | Canada | UK | Ireland | Australia | New Zealand | India | South Africa | China

Penguin Books Ltd., Registered Offices: 80 Strand, London WC2R 0RL, England
For more information about the Penguin Group, visit penguin.com.

BACKFIRE

A Jove Book / published by arrangement with the author

Jove Books are published by The Berkley Publishing Group.
JOVE® is a registered trademark of Penguin Group (USA) Inc.
The "J" design is a trademark of Penguin Group (USA) Inc.

For information, address: The Berkley Publishing Group,
a division of Penguin Group (USA) Inc.,
375 Hudson Street, New York, New York 10014.

ISBN: 978-0-515-15301-9

PUBLISHING HISTORY
G. P. Putnam's Sons hardcover edition / July 2012
Jove premium edition / July 2013

PRINTED IN THE UNITED STATES OF AMERICA

10 9 8 7 6 5 4 3 2 1

Cover design by Andrea Ho.

To my splendid other half, Anton,
with your sharp brain and, thankfully,
ultimate knowledge of all things medical

ACKNOWLEDGMENTS

I would like to thank the following consummate professionals for their infinite kindness and patience in making *Backfire* richer, and, super-important, accurate. Thank you all so very much for coming into my life. I worship at your feet.

Let me add that if there are any factual goofs in the book, it's my fault. I mean, I'd like to blame someone else, but alas, it's on my head.

Deputy U.S. Marshal Dave Key—your experiences and exploits are amazing. Perhaps even more amazing is that you're still alive and smiling and ready to take on more.

Marshal Donald O'Keefe, U.S. Department of Justice, U.S. Marshals Service, Northern District of California—El Jefe, your willingness to provide me with everything I needed is appreciated.

Chief Judge James Ware, U.S. District Court for the Northern District of California—you are thoughtful, eloquent, and you answered every one of my crazy questions, and even some I hadn't thought of.

Ms. Uyen Trinh, judicial assistant for Chief Judge James Ware—you are the great facilitator. I appreciate all your assistance and your wonderful enthusiasm for my books.

Lieutenant Donald Wick, Marin County Sheriff Department—I was told you were The Man, and I find I must agree. You added richness and verisimilitude to the Marin County scenes.

Ms. Angela Bell, FBI Office of Public Affairs, Hoover Building, Washington, D.C.—thank you for your plot-saving idea to get the letter into the lobby of the Hoover Building without breaking any rules, and for telling me the CAU moved to the third floor.

Mr. Alexander DeAngelis, director, China Office, National Science Foundation—I'm not just saying this because you're my brother-in-law. Your brain and succinct insights are a pleasure to behold. Thank you for providing me accuracy in all things Chinese.

1

Sea Cliff, San Francisco
Late Thursday night
One week before Thanksgiving

Judge Ramsey Hunt listened to the lapping water break against the rocks below, a sound that always brought him back into himself and centered him. He stood at this exact spot every night and listened to the waves, as unending and as infinite as he knew he wasn't. Only the sound of the waves, he thought. Otherwise, it was dead silent, not even a distant foghorn blast from the huge cargo ship that was nearing the Golden Gate through a veil of low-lying fog.

A light breeze ruffled the tree leaves and put a light chop on the ocean below. It was chilly tonight. He was glad Molly had tossed him his leather jacket on his way out. A week before Thanksgiving, he thought, a week before he would preside over the turkey carving and feel so blessed he'd want to sing, which, thankfully, he wouldn't.

Ramsey looked up at the low-hanging half-moon that seemed cold and alien tonight. His ever-curious son, Cal, had asked him if he could sink his fingers into the pitted surface. Would it be hard, like his wooden Ford truck, he wondered, or soft like ice cream?

At least his day had ended well. In the late afternoon, he'd met Molly and the twins at Davies Hall to hear Emma rehearse Gershwin's *Rhapsody in Blue* with the San Francisco Symphony, smiling and nodding as they listened. Ramsey had long thought of her as his own daughter, and here she was, a prodigy, of all things. He had to be careful or he'd burst with pride, Molly always said. Remarkably, Cal and Gage hadn't raised too much of a fuss at having to sit still during the rehearsal. Well, Cal did yell out once, "Emmy, I want you to play 'Twinkle Twinkle Little Star'!" which had brought warm laughter from the violin section.

They'd enjoyed enchiladas and tacos an hour later at La Barca, the family's favorite Mexican restaurant on Lombard, always an adventure when the three-year-old twins were anywhere near chips and guacamole.

Ramsey rested his elbows on the solid stone fence built when his boys had reached the age of exploration a year and a half ago. Better than nightmares about them tumbling off the sixty-foot cliff into the mess of rocks and water below.

He looked out across the entrance to the bay at the Marin Headlands, as stark and barren as the half-moon above them. Soon the winter rains would begin to green things up, as green as Ireland in some years, his second favorite place on earth after San Francisco. It was a blessing that this incredible stretch was all a national recreational area so he would never have to look at some guy sipping a nice fruity Chardonnay across from him on a condo balcony. He noticed a Zodiac sitting anchored below him, nearly as still as a small island in the ocean. There were no other boats around it that he could see. Who would be out so late, anchored in open water? He saw no one aboard, and for a moment, he felt alarmed. Had someone fallen overboard? No, whoever motored over in the Zodiac could easily have swum or waded to the narrow beach. But why? Not to get a suntan, that's for sure. He wondered if he should call 911 when he heard Molly open the family room door behind him. "Goodness, it's cold out here. I'm glad you're wearing your jacket. Is your favorite sea lion talking to you again?"

Ramsey smiled. Old Carl, that was the name he'd given this giant of a sea lion that liked to laze about in the water below. He hadn't seen Old Carl in several days now. He called back, "He's probably at Pier Thirty-nine, stretched out on the barges with his cousins. What's up?"

"Gage had a nightmare. Can you come and tell him the spinach monster isn't lurking in his closet? He doesn't believe me."

He turned to her, grinning. "Be right there—"

Molly heard a shot, cold and sharp as the moon, and saw her husband slammed violently forward by a bullet. Molly's scream pierced the night.

2

Denny Roper from Security came into Savich's office and handed him a plain white legal-sized envelope. Savich studied the big black block-printed handwriting: DILLON SAVICH, CRIMINAL APPREHENSION UNIT, THIRD FLOOR. That was it. No address.

Roper said, "A visitor told Briggs at security check-in in the lobby that he noticed this envelope propped against the outside door on the Pennsylvania Avenue entrance. Briggs wanted me to look at it before it came to you, just in case.

"We put it through the X-ray, checked it out for biologics. There's nothing gnarly like anthrax on the envelope or on that one piece of paper—but it's curious,

Savich. The person who sent it knows not only the name of your unit but your location—third floor."

Savich unfolded the single white sheet of paper. The same black block printing: FOR WHAT YOU DID YOU DESERVE THIS.

"I hope you've got some idea what that clown is talking about."

Savich said, "Not a clue. Tell me you have the visitor who handed over the envelope to Briggs."

"No, the guy walked away while Briggs was looking at the envelope. You know there are lots of tourists coming in this time of morning. Briggs called out, but the guy was gone, disappeared in the crowd. But we've got lots of good camera coverage of him, a close-up when he's speaking to Briggs. You think he was the one who wrote it?"

"Since it isn't possible to get into the lobby without a thorough security check, why not do it this way? Hey, I found this envelope, not a clue what it is or who left it."

Roper said, "Would you like to have a look-see at this surveillance video?"

Savich nodded.

"Since he spoke to Briggs, we also have his voice on tape, nice and clear. He looked and acted like an ordinary guy, according to Briggs, but I wanted some of you experts to double-check it for us." Roper paused, looked up at all the faces focused on him and Savich, not more than two feet outside of Savich's office. "It looks like your people are already interested. I'll get things set up in the conference room," and Roper walked out, waving the disk at the agents as he passed them.

Savich read the note again:

FOR WHAT YOU DID YOU DESERVE THIS

He sat back in his chair, closed his eyes, and thought: *What* had he done? Exactly *what* did he deserve? It was clearly a threat, but from whom? It had been only two weeks since they'd brought down Ted Bundy's mad daughter, Kirsten Bolger. There was her mother, her stepfather, and her aunt Sentra to think about. Anyone else? Well, there was the family of her lover and partner Bruce Comafield, but both families were solidly middle-class, with a great deal to lose. When he'd met with them after Comafield's death and Kirsten's capture, they'd been in a state of shock. Sometimes shocks like that upended a person's whole world, but no, those folks just didn't seem likely.

Who else? Behind his closed eyes, Savich saw a kaleidoscope of tumbled vivid memories of blood and death and brutal faces, too much and too many. *We're a failed species,* he thought, not for the first time. He opened his eyes to see his wife, Sherlock, standing in front of him, her eyes on the open sheet of paper.

Sherlock said, "Denny's got the DVD ready, said we might all want to see it. What's going on? What's in that letter?"

"It's a weird threat. What I don't like is that it was delivered personally. Come on, let's have a look at the guy who gave it to Briggs in the lobby."

He watched Sherlock shove a thick corking curl of hair behind her ear. He'd give it two seconds before another curl worked its way out of one of the clips and sprang forward. The clips never seemed to work very well. She said, "Everybody watched Denny come in and give you this envelope. Good thing you're involving all of us, or you'd be mobbed in here."

"That's what Roper seemed to think. It shouldn't take very long. We'll see if that brainpower can figure something out." She gave him a long assessing look, then turned and walked out of his office. He watched her walk in that no-nonsense stride, a traffic-stopper in those sexy black boots of hers. She was wearing her signature low-cut black pants and white blouse. He felt his heartbeat quicken. Could Sherlock be in danger because of something he'd done?

When Savich walked in with the envelope, Sherlock said, "Okay, Dillon, tell everyone what's in the letter before we watch the video."

Savich unfolded the single white sheet and said in an emotionless voice, "*For what you did you deserve this.* That's it, nothing else. Now, let's see what we've got, Denny."

There were nine agents, including Shirley, a gum-chewing grandmother and the unit secretary, with bright red hair this week, because, she'd said, she wanted everyone to confuse her with Sherlock, and one of the two unit clerks who would bet on anything with you and usually win. Denny Roper hit play and they all leaned forward to watch the sharp, high-res picture. Lots of tourists in the security line, all of them talking, dozens of conversations overlapping. The two security guards behind Plexiglas greeting and questioning everyone, handing out IDs, a smooth, practiced routine. Roper paused the DVD. "It's exactly nine-fifteen this morning. Here he comes."

A man—or a woman; it was hard to tell—came through the Pennsylvania Avenue entrance ahead of a dozen or so tourists. He stood in line, speaking to no one. When he reached the Plexiglas, he handed the envelope to Briggs. He was wearing loose jeans, an FBI hoodie pulled up over his head, and sunglasses, all of which would have had to come off if he went through security, which he'd had no intention of doing. He, or she?

Roper said, "I had them filter out everything but Briggs's voice and the man's. Listen again."

"What can I do for you, sir?"

"I found this envelope propped against the glass right outside. I brought it to you before it got trampled or tossed or whatever." A low voice, not particularly deep, but clear as a bell. A nice voice, really, calm, unhurried. And young.

Briggs accepted the envelope, studied it for a second, and the man blended into the group of tourists behind him. They saw him walk out the Pennsylvania Avenue exit and disappear. Roper said, "All slow and easy, not a care in the world. And that's it." Roper turned off the video.

Dane Carver said, "You've figured out his size?"

Roper said, "He's five-eight, weighs about one hundred thirty-five pounds. So what do you think?"

Ruth Warnecki Noble said, "I'd like to watch this a dozen more times, but first impression? He's slight for a guy, but I'd say he's male, twenty to twenty-five."

Dane said, "Or a pretty average female. But I agree, the walk makes you think man. But who knows? He never took off his hoodie and sunglasses."

Savich said, "We'll get the DVD to Operations Technology at Quantico. They'll enlarge, enhance, depixelate the face, do some reconstruction for us. The lab at Quantico can work on the audio recording."

There was a knock on the conference room door. It was an audio tech, Chuck Manson, who swore every single week he would have his name changed, but he never did. Savich suspected it was because he really enjoyed the attention. "Ninety-eight percent chance it's a man, and under thirty," Manson said, and disappeared.

"Okay, if Chuck says it's a guy, I'll take his word for it," Roper said. "I've asked for possible brands on the pants and hoodie, we'll see."

Lucy Carlyle said, "He has to look up when he speaks to Briggs, then his head goes down again. He knows he's on camera. It's a giveaway."

Savich's second-in-command, Ollie Hamish, said, "Denny, did you speak to the other security guard behind the Plexiglas? His name's Brady, right?"

Roper nodded. "Brady remembers the guy, what with the envelope delivery, but neither Brady nor Briggs can tell us much that's helpful."

"I'd like to speak to both Briggs and Brady myself later," Savich said as he stood.

Roper nodded. "I'll send both of them up."

Savich shook his head. "No, let me come down to the mezzanine to your turf."

Cooper McKnight sat forward. "Unless this guy's a loon, he's got to be from one of our cases. We could start with the most recent gnarly one—Bundy's daughter. Even though Comafield's close relatives seemed normal as apple pie, who knows? Maybe there's a nutso in there."

Roper looked at Savich. "I'll leave the video. Let me know when you want to speak to my people." He paused in the conference room doorway, a big man, built like a thick, knotted rope, Savich had always thought, and added, "I don't like this punk coming into our house like that. There are a lot of brains in this room, so take care of this for us."

Sherlock read the note again. "*For what you did you deserve this.* Something *you* did specifically, Dillon, so it's got to be a case you were personally involved with. There's Lissy Smiley, for example—that was up close and personal. But it could take weeks to make sure there's no one, absolutely no one, who would care enough about any of the dozens of perps we've brought down to do something this nuts."

Dane Carver said, "I wonder what the threat is, exactly? *For what you did you deserve this.* What is *this*? Is he targeting someone specific?"

All eyes turned to Sherlock.

Sherlock splayed her hands in front of her. "It doesn't have to be me. All right, all right, I'll be really careful.

We've got the guy on camera, we'll get a good facial reconstruction. It's our best lead."

Savich saw everyone was looking at him now. He tried to keep his face blank, but it was hard. He realized he was clutching his pen too tightly. It was Sherlock, he simply knew the threat was directed at Sherlock. Who else? He wanted to say something, but nothing came out. He couldn't stand himself. *Get it together.* He said, his voice sounding calm and in control, "If any of you come up with anything we haven't mentioned, let me know. I'm going down to the security section, speak to Briggs and Brady. Sherlock, you and Dane start work on possible names and cases."

On the elevator ride to the mezzanine, Savich remembered the shoot-out in Mr. Patil's Shop 'n Go in Georgetown. Was it only three weeks ago? The woman he'd had to shoot, her name was Elsa Heinz. Who else knew Savich had shot her? Everyone, of course. It was in the papers, his name included. Was someone who knew her out for revenge against him? A loved one for a loved one?

He put her out of his head. Threats were part of the job. Both he and Sherlock knew that. They and the CAU would deal with it.

3

Georgetown
Washington, D.C.
Friday morning
Five a.m.

Sean leapt impossibly high, caught the football from his mother, and took off toward the end of a park that was really a baseball field, with Savich on his heels. Savich couldn't catch him because Sean's legs were stilt-long, eating up huge swathes of ground, and he was rounding bases for some reason, clutching the football tight to his chest, heading for home, and John Lennon was suddenly singing into Savich's left ear in his flat whiny-smooth voice about imagining people getting along, like that would ever happen.

Savich reared up in bed and automatically looked at the clock. *Five a.m. Not good. No telephone call was ever good at five a.m.*

He picked up his cell. "Savich."

"Dillon, you've got to come, quickly, it's bad, it's really bad, I'm afraid—" Molly Hunt's voice, choking and thick with tears and fear. Dillon thought, *Not little Emma, who'd survived so much—*

"I'm putting you on speakerphone so Sherlock can hear you. Tell us what's happened, Molly."

Sherlock was leaning up beside him, her face pale in the predawn, her hair tangled wildly around her face.

"Someone shot Ramsey in the back. I don't know if he's going to make it; he's in surgery. Everyone's here, but I need you and Sherlock. You've got to come and find out who did this to him. Please, please, come quickly."

Ramsey shot? Savich couldn't get his brain around it. He hadn't seen Ramsey for six months, since he, Sherlock, and Sean last visited San Francisco. It had been more than five years, he realized now, since Ramsey had saved six-year-old Emma's life and hooked up with her mother, Molly.

Ramsey shot?

"Molly, take a deep breath. That's right. Now slow down and tell us exactly what happened." But he was thinking, *Why Ramsey? He's a federal judge, removed from that sort of violence—but a man who judged others was a man who gathered enemies.*

"He's in surgery," Molly said again. "The nurses say they don't know anything yet, but I know it can't be good. He was shot in the back—" she said, and broke off. He heard her breathing, harsh and fast, and then her voice, choked, frantic: "Please, Dillon, you and Sherlock, you've got to come."

Savich and Sherlock both asked questions and let her ramble, knowing she was trying to get it together. She told them Lieutenant Virginia Trolley was there with her, and they realized she was probably listening to their questions and Molly's answers. They'd met Virginia and her husband a couple of times when they'd visited San Francisco over the past five years.

"Molly, let me speak to Virginia." Virginia came on the line. "Dillon, the SFPD responded and arrived at Ramsey's house right after midnight. I arrived ten minutes later. Since it was dark, we didn't bother to look for footprints while I was there. No one wanted to mess up the crime scene bumbling around with flashlights."

"Have you spoken to Cheney?"

Virginia said, "Cheney arrived at Ramsey's house when I was leaving. He called me a couple minutes ago, told me he's assigned Special Agent Harry Christoff to lead the case, but he, Cheney, will be monitoring every detail. He wondered if shooting Ramsey was a revenge deal. It's too soon to know, but I'll tell you, it sure feels like it." Virginia's voice dropped lower. "Molly needs you guys. Can you come out here?"

"We'll be there as soon as we can."

When he punched off, he took Sherlock in his arms and held her close, stroking his hand up and down her back.

"He'll make it," Sherlock said against his neck. "Ramsey's got to make it. He's one of the good guys, Dillon. He will make it. How could this happen, and right on top of this threat to you?"

No, the threat's not aimed at me, it's aimed at you. Or Sean.

Cheney Stone called back as Savich was stepping out of the shower. He'd made it back to the hospital and learned that Ramsey had survived surgery and was in the surgical ICU. Molly, though, was a mess. "I asked the doc to give her Valium to calm her. You know what? He did. It seems to have helped her.

"Ah, here's Virginia. Let's go to speakerphone."

"Is Emma all right?" Savich asked.

Virginia said, "She was bordering on shock at first, with everything that was happening, but Emma's a tough little nut, she'll hold it together. When I was at the house I heard her tell her brother Cal she'd play him the theme from Harry Potter on the piano this morning—with variations—if he stopped shining a flashlight into Gage's eyes. Cal said he wanted to see if it would cause seizures." Virginia's voice hitched. "Where'd a three-year-old kid hear about lights and seizures?"

Savich said, "Don't ask. Our flight gets in this afternoon. You playing nice with Cheney? And Harry Christoff?"

"Oh, yeah, Cheney's a nice guy"—pause—"he'll throw us some crumbs, even though you FBI guys are going to have jurisdiction. All I hear about Christoff is that he came off an ugly divorce a year and a half ago, and he's been a nasty git ever since."

Savich heard Cheney say in the background, "Crumbs? You know what we know. Hey, and Harry's not a nasty git any longer, he's just nasty."

Virginia said, "And you, Mr. SAC? You're newly married. That means you're stupid happy all the time. Wait till you're married a few years, then I'll check back in with you. My guess is you'll still be stupid, but the happy part isn't a given."

Cheney said, "I'll be sure to pass that along to Julia."

Stupid happy? Savich liked the sound of that.

Savich said to Virginia, "Since you've known Ramsey for a long time, you know his habits, his friends. Cheney and Agent Christoff will see you as a valued resource."

Virginia gave a curiously charming snort. "Sure, like I'll expect to see that from any of his precious special agents." She sighed. "Every single cop in San Francisco wants to help get this crazy craphead, Dillon. You know Ramsey's a hero, even after five years, he's still Judge Dredd to all of us."

Savich remembered how Ramsey had been dubbed Judge Dredd by local and world media after he'd jumped down from the bench, black robes flying, and single-handedly took out the three gunmen who'd invaded his courtroom with guns and violence and death.

He said, "Keep repeating that to Cheney and Christoff."

"Just saying, Dillon. This is tough, really tough. It's personal, not only for me but for most of the force."

"We'll get the crazy craphead together, then, Virginia," Sherlock said. "See you later today."

Ramsey, Savich thought, *who did you push over the*

edge? And then he realized he and Sherlock would be three thousand miles away from the guy who'd written the letter to him. And they could take Sean with them, to stay at his grandparents'. That was a relief.

Cheney called again when they were on their way to Dulles. "Here's what I know so far. Ramsey postponed a hearing at a trial yesterday morning because he believed the federal prosecutor wasn't conducting the case properly, that he might have been threatened. He met with the federal marshal and the U.S. attorney, who are all in the same building with us, as you know.

"Now the prosecutor is a twelve-year veteran, Assistant U.S. Attorney Mickey O'Rourke. Ramsey had asked to speak to him in chambers, naturally, after he came to suspect Mickey might be purposefully jeopardizing the case. Mickey made an excuse. According to Olivia, Ramsey's secretary, Ramsey told O'Rourke he wanted him and his people at the meeting he was calling. Mickey didn't show, and none of his staff had any clue where he was. They hadn't seen him since Ramsey adjourned the hearing, and they were worried about him. His second chair said Mickey seemed off. But this? No one could believe it. In any case, we can't find O'Rourke. He's now officially missing. There's quite an uproar, as you can imagine."

"The name of the defendant?"

"There are two co-defendants, Clive and Cindy Cahill, up for the murder of a rich software geek here in

Silicon Valley. Either the Cahills have lots of money stashed offshore or they have some rich friends, because they have hired a first-rate counsel."

But once the prosecutor was suspected, Savich thought, what would it matter which judge presided anymore? And O'Rourke's disappearance would mean only a delay. None of it made sense yet to Savich.

He asked, "Why are the Cahills a federal case?"

Cheney said, "Because there's espionage involved, that's why. The murder victim, Mark Lindy, was working on a top secret project for the government, and was probably murdered because of it. That's why the FBI handled the case and not local law enforcement. We've got the Cahills pretty cold on the murder, but we could never find out the particulars of the project Lindy was into, because it involved national security. You know the CIA—they refused to tell us anything at all, even with CIA operations officers out here digging around.

"Even if a foreign government did set the Cahills on Mark Lindy, I don't know which one. I'll be speaking to O'Rourke's team again while you're in the air, see exactly what they have, if anything, that might help us find him."

"All right, Cheney, see you this afternoon," Savich said. He and his laptop MAX had a lot of reading to do about the Cahills on their way to California.

And flying with Sean was always a treat.

4

Before they left for the coast on the 8:19 a.m. United flight out of Dulles, Sherlock called her parents in San Francisco. "Lacey, you're flying into a real mess here," her father, Judge Corman Sherlock, said. "Ramsey's shooting is all over local TV, and everyone is out for blood. What with his martial arts heroics in his own courtroom five years ago, you'd think most of the media around here would imply he's unevolved and uncivilized. Go figure.

"There's lots of speculation, as you'd expect, but no one knows a thing yet, and the FBI hasn't said a word.

"The police commissioner's got a press conference scheduled at noon. We'll see if she's going to try to squeeze the SFPD into bed with the FBI. It would be a good career move.

"I saw Ramsey yesterday. He was on his way out to meet his family to go listen to Emma practice with the symphony at Davies Hall." He paused. "I told him I'd heard he'd postponed the murder trial, but he didn't tell me anything, only shook his head, said it was too sensitive and too soon to talk about.

"We're looking forward to seeing all of you. Your mother and I will get to take good care of Sean, of course, while the two of you are out finding the people responsible. I know you'll nail whoever did this."

From Dad's mouth to God's ears, Sherlock thought.

"This is an awful thing, Lacey, an awful thing. I'm wondering if it has anything to do with the trial he postponed. Do you think that's possible?"

By the end of the very long flight, Sherlock and Savich agreed they would rather eat week-old frozen artichoke dip than compete against Sean in another computer-based adventure of *Atoc the Incan Wizard,* a young Incan boy who used numbers, magic, and nerve to unravel the knottiest arithmetic problems and bring down an endless number of villains. Sherlock called Atoc the Harry Potter of Machu Picchu. During most of the flight, she played with Sean while Dillon read files on MAX and Skyped Cheney, working out what the Criminal Apprehension Unit could do. Cheney said, "It would help us for MAX to work on trying to locate any offshore stash the Cahills might have, and what talent they could have called in on short notice. We've had no luck as of yet."

"Eggs all in the Cahill basket, Cheney?"

"No, but it makes more sense than some sort of foreign government conspiracy to shoot Ramsey. I mean, if a foreign government was paying the Cahills for Mark

Lindy's top secret materials, and they threatened to talk if they weren't somehow found innocent, said government would more likely have them eliminated, not a federal judge or a federal prosecutor. There could be too much hell to pay for that."

Savich said, "The Cahills are the obvious suspects, but what would it gain them to kill Judge Hunt?"

"Maybe they were afraid O'Rourke had already told Ramsey too much," Cheney said. "But you're right. We're being thorough. We're looking at mail threats to Judge Hunt, letters and emails going back three years, and we've started a review of his cases going back even further. I'm making sure the SFPD is in the loop, passing along some assignments to them. We can use the manpower." He sighed, then added, "There are already endless complications, since Ramsey isn't an anonymous federal judge like most of his confederates. Nope, he's Judge Dredd, superhero. The mayor, the police commissioner, the major news outlets, even the conductor for the San Francisco Symphony have called me, wanting to know what progress we've made. The police commissioner is pushing for a task force, composed of the SFPD, the FBI, and the federal marshals, with the commissioner herself in charge. As if that's going to happen. I'm already getting an ulcer."

Savich asked, "Any progress on the missing federal prosecutor yet? Mickey O'Rourke?"

The answer was no.

When Savich ended the call, Sherlock said, "A federal prosecutor missing—it sounds like a spy novel. I'm very grateful my father wasn't the one judging the Cahill case."

"Mama, you weren't paying attention. I got you!"

Savich smiled, listening to Sherlock wail. "Oh, dear, Sean, how am I going to save myself this time? Atoc's shoved me in a pit of purple-headed Amazonian hippo snakes. Ah, here's what I'll do," and Sherlock walloped one of the writhing hippo snakes with a canoe paddle. Since she was the master Incan mathematician, Professor Pahuac, and rotten to the bone, she knew her end probably wouldn't be a good one.

5

San Francisco
Friday, early afternoon

Lieutenant Vincent Delion of the SFPD, and a longtime friend, met them at airport baggage claim. He told them he'd talked Cheney into letting him come get them. He told them the San Francisco Feds didn't know squat yet, and neither did the SFPD, and he told them about the task force Police Commissioner Montoya announced she'd like to form, just a couple of hours ago—with the FBI's assistance, of course. He tossed Savich a copy of the *Chronicle*. "Read this." Savich and Sherlock looked at the big block headline: JUDGE DREDD SHOT.

Delion soon pulled his Crown Vic into the heavy 101 traffic north to the city. "At least Ramsey is holding on. None of us wanted a murder case, particularly not his. I can't imagine what would happen to Emma, Molly, and the twins if he died." There was a punch of hard silence, then, "No, they won't lose him, they can't."

Delion shook his head, lightly stroked big fingers over his pride and joy. He smiled, remembering Sean Savich telling him in grave confidence at the baggage carousel, "I think your mustache is shinier than Hercule Poirot's."

Delion told Sean he was a fine judge of mustachios and that his was particularly shiny this morning in honor of meeting the bigwigs from Washington, D.C., their kiddo included.

Delion plowed his hand through his hair. "I'm hoping Ramsey will be ready to speak to us soon at the hospital."

Sherlock said, "How's Molly?"

"She's trying to show she's solid for the kids' sake." He paused for a moment, then added, "After what happened to Emma years ago, they all try to watch out for each other."

"Is Uncle Ramsey all right, Mama?"

They'd told Sean they were coming to San Francisco because Ramsey had been hurt, nothing more. "He will be all right, Sean. He's injured, but he's going to start getting better now." *Please, God, please, God.*

"Is Emma okay?"

"She's fine, Sean. She's watching Cal and Gage."

"No wonder," her five-year-old said. "Cal and Gage are babies. They need all the watching they can get. I'll help her."

Sherlock said to Delion, "When we flew out here for Memorial Day weekend six months ago, Sean spent three hours with Emma and the boys, and announced to us he was going to marry Emma and help her teach Cal and

Gage about life. I asked him about Marty Perry, his girlfriend next door, and the love of his life. I also asked him about Bowie Richards's daughter, Georgie, also the love of his life, up in Connecticut. Sean just smiled, didn't you, kiddo?"

Delion said to Sean, "I agree with you, Sean, Emma's a champ. As for Marty and Georgie, they sound pretty cool, too. Hey, kid, the older you get the more you look like your old man."

Sean considered that. "Mama says I'm more handsome than Papa, since I have her smile. She says that makes all the difference."

Delion laughed.

"Handsome is as handsome does," Savich said, and Sherlock saw Sean repeating his father's words to himself. She rolled her eyes. She leaned over and ruffled Sean's thick black hair.

Sean said, sounding a bit worried, "I hope Emma didn't forget she's engaged to me."

"Not a chance," Savich said. "Do you think your mama could have ever forgotten she was engaged to me?"

"Not a chance," Sean said.

When they passed by Candlestick Park, Sean said, "That's where Dwight Clark made *The Catch* way back in the old days, right, Papa?"

Savich grinned. "It sure is."

Sherlock said to Delion, "Can you believe he remembers that?"

Delion said, "Yeah, well, his hard drive works better because it isn't as full as ours."

All the adults realized any more discussion about Ramsey's shooting had to wait. Delion was talking about the upcoming 49ers-Seahawks game when Sean said, "Marty asked me when I was going to have a sister because she's going to have a new brother in March."

Now, that was a conversation starter.

6

San Francisco General Hospital
Surgical ICU
Friday afternoon

Savich didn't want to count all the lines that tethered Ramsey Hunt to life. There were IV lines in his neck, and an oxygen mask on his face. Savich recognized a kind of suction device connected to the end of the tube coming from Ramsey's chest, a Pleurovac, they called it. Ramsey lay on his back, still and pale, his immense life force badly faded. At least it wasn't extinguished. A light sheet was pulled to his chest, not quite covering his wide white surgical bandages. He was breathing lightly and steadily, a relief, but his eyelids looked bruised, perhaps from when he'd fallen. Savich hated it.

The SFPD guard outside the cubicle had given them the stink eye before Lieutenant Trolley introduced them to Officer Jay Mancusso of the SFPD. Since only two visitors could go into the small cubicle at a time, Savich went in first to stand beside Molly. She didn't look away from Ramsey, merely took Savich's hand in hers and squeezed hard. "Thank you for coming so quickly. The Valium Cheney suggested the doctor give me—it's magic stuff. It's helped unparalyze my brain. I'm sorry I lost it when I called you."

"Don't worry about it," Savich said. "Ramsey's breathing is solid and easy, Molly; that's a good sign."

Ramsey had told him once that Molly's hair was as vibrant a red as a sunset off the Cliffs of Moher in Ireland, and Ramsey was right. You'd think Ramsey was describing Sherlock's hair, but it wasn't the same color at all.

She turned into him, and he closed his arms around her. She felt fragile. It was odd, he thought, but Molly's hair didn't feel the same as Sherlock's hair, and didn't smell like her hair, either—it was jasmine he was smelling, jasmine mixed with lemon, not the faint rose scent of Sherlock's. "He'll make it, Molly," he said against her hair. "He'll make it. He's strong and determined, and he wants to stay here with us."

She pulled back in his arms and smiled up at him. "I think he will, too. But I'm so scared, Dillon. What if—"

"No what-ifs. Has he been awake at all?"

"In and out, mumbling words I can't understand for the most part, then saying Emma's name over and over. I think he's remembering back to the time he found her unconscious in the forest near his cabin."

"Has Cheney come in yet?"

"Yes, we spoke briefly. I told him what I could, which

wasn't much of anything at all, and he said he'd see me later today after Ramsey was awake and the doctors were satisfied he was going to be okay. I think he wanted to give me more time to consider who and why, but I can't think of a single person who would want to kill him. Cheney told me about the Cahills and how Ramsey had postponed the trial and how that federal prosecutor was missing. Ramsey hadn't said a word to me, but in all honesty, there wasn't time." She walked away from him, then turned, her hands fisted at her sides. "No, there was time, but damn him, he's always trying to protect me. He knew something hinky was going on, and he kept it to himself. I will have to seriously consider hurting him for that."

She picked up Ramsey's limp hand. "He's so strong," she said, more to herself than to him, "so tough, always a rock, you know?" A beautiful man, she'd always thought, with his dark hair and brilliant dark eyes, and his laugh, his seductive laugh. "Can you believe we've been married for five years? Goodness, Emma's eleven and the boys are three. The boys are scared, Dillon, they don't understand." Her voice hitched, then smoothed out again. "Emma's taking care of them. She's more their second mother than their older sister. The babysitter, Mrs. Hicks, is with them, too." She raised wet eyes to Savich's face. "They won't let the boys come see him, Dillon, and that only makes them more scared."

Ramsey moaned deep in his throat.

She leaned over him, lightly kissed his cheek. "Ramsey? You have a visitor. Come, wake up now."

His eyes opened slowly, blind and empty of knowledge, but they cleared slowly and focused. Savich leaned close. "I'd rather we were fishing in Lake Tahoe and I was catching that four-pound trout and you weren't."

An attempt at a smile, but he didn't quite make it. "I don't remember it like that."

"Okay, I'll give you the trout since you were the one who fried the sucker. It's nice to have you here with us, either way."

Ramsey whispered, "Molly?"

"I'm here," she said, squeezing his hand.

Ramsey looked back at Dillon, and now his voice was stronger, some of the familiar steel sounding through. "I remember now, someone shot me."

Molly said, "You were turning when I called out to you and someone shot you in the back."

"I went down like a rock, lights out," he said. He looked thoughtful. "I was shot once before in the leg—and, you know, wherever you're shot, it doesn't feel too good." He closed his eyes against a vicious lick of pain. "My chest feels like it's been flattened by an eighteen-wheeler."

Savich put the morphine plunger in his hand. "Squeeze this, it's your PLA, and it'll cut the pain."

Ramsey had never seen one before. He closed his eyes in gratitude and pressed the button. They both waited silently until he said, "That's better already. I can control this if I don't move too much."

Savich said, "I'm glad you turned when you did. Do you know what direction the shot came from?"

Ramsey looked blank. "The direction? I suppose it had to be from the ocean. Someone in a boat? It's hard to imagine someone firing at me from a boat, what with all the motion from the waves. That would take a professional, and still I can't imagine it'd be a sure thing."

Savich said, "Did you see a boat?"

Ramsey looked perfectly blank, not totally with them, and then pain hit him again, and he went stone silent.

Savich said, "You feel a little muddled, Ramsey, don't worry about it. The important thing is you're alive, and you're going to get better every day."

"The Cahills?"

"It's possible. We're checking."

"I don't know why, Savich. Do you?"

"We don't know yet, either."

"Have they found the prosecutor, Mickey O'Rourke?"

"Not yet."

Molly lightly shoved Savich away when Ramsey's eyes closed. She whispered next to his cheek, "I want you to think about healing yourself, Ramsey. Think about tossing me and Emma around on the mat—you need to get better to do that. And you need a shave."

He managed a rictus of a grin.

ICU nurse Janine Holder said from the doorway, "I like the dark whiskers. They make him look tough and dangerous. Dr. Kardak is here to see you, Judge Hunt."

Savich introduced himself, stepped back to let Dr. Kardak examine Ramsey. He was an older man, tall and thin as a whip handle, and he looked tired, like he'd gone ten rounds with death and just barely won.

When Dr. Kardak noticed Ramsey's eyes on him, he said, "Ah, Judge Hunt, you're awake and with us, excellent. My trauma team and I operated on you last night, and I've come to check how you're doing." Without waiting for an answer, he started to examine the IV lines and the fluid in contraptions Ramsey was tied to. All the while, he kept up a running monologue about what they had found at surgery, the broken ribs, the torn lung, the blood in the chest cavity, as if it were all business as usual and nothing to be worried about. When he at last listened to Ramsey's chest and examined his dressings, he said, "You sound good, Judge Hunt. I'm hopeful your lung will stay fully expanded and that we can pull out the chest tube this weekend. You need it for now, but I know it can hurt like the dickens."

When Dr. Kardak straightened, Savich asked him, "How close a thing was it, Doctor?"

Dr. Kardak said, "Tough to say, but he got to us—a level-one trauma center—in what we call the golden hour." He touched long, thin fingers to Ramsey's pulse. "Your major risk was blood loss, Judge Hunt, and that's behind you. You're going to live. That's not to say you're going to be happy for a while, but it beats the alternative."

"Amen," Ramsey said. "Thank you."

"Make full use of the morphine. We can give you something else if it doesn't hold you."

Ramsey pressed the button again. "Now that I know about this magic button, I'm thinking I'll empty it pretty fast."

Dr. Kardak said, "Not a problem. Three of us worked

on you in the OR, Judge Hunt. Dr. Janes kept reminding us you were Judge Dredd and we'd be tarred and feathered and ridden out of town if you went down on our watch." He gave Ramsey a fat smile, then turned to Molly and took her hands in his. "Your husband is strong and healthy, and, trust me, the team here is excellent. Try not to worry. Oh, yes, I forgot to tell you. I heard your daughter play Bach's *Italian Concerto* at the children's concert with the symphony two years ago. My wife still remembers how well she played it. In fact, I remember she wept when Emma played the second movement. I read she'll be playing Gershwin with the symphony in early December. Congratulations. She is incredible. Now, Agent Savich, Judge Hunt should rest."

Ramsey said, his voice low, a bit slurred, "Special Agent Dillon Savich is a longtime friend of ours. He knows all about gunshot wounds, and he's here to help."

"Is that so?" Dr. Kardak shook Savich's hand again, even though he'd already met him. He said, "I met your wife in the hall. Hard to believe two FBI agents married, as in to each other. How does that work?"

"I'm her boss. It's up to me to make it work."

"And how do you do that? Men everywhere would like to know."

"I tell her to suck it up when she disagrees with me."

This brought a laugh and a "Good luck with that" from Dr. Kardak. He said, "I'll be in the hospital all day if you have any questions or concerns."

Molly grabbed his sleeve. "Why is that? You said Ramsey would be all right."

7

San Francisco General Hospital
Friday afternoon

U.S. Federal Deputy Marshal Eve Barbieri leaned against the hallway wall, outside the SICU, her knee bent and her arms crossed over her chest, waiting for her turn to see Judge Hunt. His surgeon, Dr. Kardak, had told everyone Judge Hunt was doing fine, but she still wasn't over the soul-wrenching fear she'd felt when she'd been called at four a.m. to be told Judge Hunt had been shot. *Would he live?* Her boss, Carney Maynard, didn't know, but Hunt had survived surgery and he had a chance, he told her matter-of-factly, because Judge Hunt was made of pure titanium. *Thank all the powers that be, and thank Dr. Kardak's team.*

Maynard had told her the SFPD would be part of the protection detail along with the U.S. Marshals Service while Judge Hunt was in the hospital, but she was to stay close, as any questions about coverage or assignments would be directed to her. When Judge Hunt was discharged, she would be officially responsible for his and his family's protection. She looked through the windowed door of the SICU at Officer Jay Mancusso of the SFPD, seated by Judge Hunt's cubicle, and watched him study every face that came near. He looked angry, like most other cops she'd met since Judge Hunt had been shot. She wondered if every single law enforcement agency in the city would try to be involved in hunting down the man—or woman—who'd tried to kill him. Judge Hunt was a big deal, an American hero. She closed her eyes for a moment, thankful Ramsey would live and thankful for how well she had gotten to know him and his family over the years. When he was shot, she'd promised a real biggie if he would live—to be pleasant to her ex-mother-in-law if ever she saw her again, something she hoped would never happen. Eve and her ex-mother-in-law's son, Ryan, had been married for about half an hour before Eve booted him out. She could still hear the woman's outraged voice: *A good woman would forgive her husband his small transgressions.*

As she waited, she asked herself again for at least the twelfth time—had the Cahills hired the shooter? If so, it meant their defense attorney, Milo Siles, had to be in on it. How else could the Cahills have gotten hold of the talent and money so fast? She'd met the prosecutor, Mickey O'Rourke, several times, on the volleyball court. She remembered his laugh when his team had won—a really big laugh. He didn't laugh in the courtroom, though, he was all business, a veteran who wielded a bullwhip. He had a good conviction rate. But none of that mattered now. He was missing, simply gone, no word, no emails, no nothing. She sighed, wishing just this once she was FBI and had the assignment to lead this case.

She pushed off the wall and began to pace, aware that Mancusso was watching her through the window. She wanted to see Ramsey, see for herself he was breathing, that his excellent brain was working behind his smart dark eyes, but it was one cop after the other trooping in. Lieutenant Virginia Trolley, SFPD, was in and out because she was also a trusted family friend. Eve knew it made Molly feel better to have Virginia close, another trained body to protect Ramsey. And those two FBI agents from Washington had been in, Savich and Sherlock were their names, a husband and wife, and wasn't that a kick?

Eve looked up to see two men approaching—yeah, they were definitely Feds; you couldn't mistake their private club dress code—dark suits, white shirts, usually dark ties. They were striding toward her, self-assured and arrogant as toreadors entering the ring. She recognized both, of course; she'd been introduced to the new SAC, Cheney Stone, but not the other agent. She'd seen the other one driving out of the parking garage a couple of times, but that was it.

She moved to stand against the wall again, waiting, all indolent and loose-limbed. Let them come to her. She whistled between her teeth. She wondered who'd cornered the market on the federal wingtips.

She heard the agent walking beside Cheney Stone say, "That picture we found in the bushes, the newspaper clipping of Judge Dredd with an X through his face—it's like he's sticking it in our faces and laughing."

Hmmm, there was a clipping of Ramsey left at the crime scene? It was the first she'd heard of it. Not that she expected to know much about what the FBI had found, since she'd never even been inside the locked door on the thirteenth floor in the Federal Building. No, that space was inhabited only by the San Francisco FBI tribe. The U.S. Marshals Service occupied the twentieth floor, their digs only one floor above the senior federal judges' offices and courtrooms. She didn't care much for that FBI attitude, one of the reasons she hadn't considered signing on with them six years before. She'd heard too many stories about some of the special agents—and wasn't that a self-important title? For the most part, the FBI got results, but too often, it was their way or why don't you take a leap from the Golden Gate Bridge? Were they prepared to deal with her, or would they try to plant their big Fed feet on some part of her anatomy? She'd see. She'd go around them, or through them, if necessary.

Cheney Stone stopped. "And here's Deputy Marshal Eve Barbieri."

He remembered her name, and that was a surprise. Eve shook hands with Stone. "Congratulations on becoming special agent in charge, Agent Stone."

Cheney gave her a grin. "Thanks. It's already been two months and I'm still alive and breathing, for the most part. But my once predictable life now consists of herding pit bulls."

Eve could only agree, her opinion clear on her face even though she kept her mouth shut.

"Since we'll be working together on Judge Hunt's shooting, call me Cheney."

First name? Nice smile, white teeth, seeming sincerity, but with a new SAC, it was wise to be cautious. She nodded, too soon to offer up her own first name.

Cheney said, "Eve Barbieri, this is Agent Harry Christoff. Harry, this is Deputy Marshal Eve Barbieri. She's worked with Judge Hunt for three years and is a friend of the family."

8

Eve took a good look at Special Agent Harry Christoff. He was in his early thirties, tall and lean, with dark brown hair and bright green eyes. He kept himself in very fine shape indeed. Although he was dressed in the obligatory dark suit and white shirt, he wasn't wearing wingtips. Instead he wore black boots that looked as old as he did, but the ancient boots sported a high shine. As for his tie, it was bright yellow with black squiggles. A rebel? She didn't think such an animal existed in the Big Machine.

So the new SAC was trying to herd Christoff—good luck. She'd heard of him before, most had. He was known as a loose cannon, and that sparked her interest. He looked as mean as any of the other pit bulls, like he could kick the crap out of you while chowing a pepperoni pizza and washing it down with a Bud. But he had to have something going for him in the brain department, since SAC Cheney Stone had assigned him to this case.

"I know you by rep," Eve said. "They say you're a wild hair."

"Good to know," Harry said, and stuck out his hand. Eve shook his hand, strong, with tanned, long fingers.

Cheney continued to Eve, "You guys are fast. We've already started looking at those boxes of threatening letters to Judge Hunt you sent over."

She nodded, but she was still distracted studying Christoff, still evaluating—was he smart? Intuitive? Did this particular pit bull have any common sense? Did he have nerve?

She realized, of course, that Agent Harry Christoff was looking her over as well. "Ever have any problems before?" Christoff asked her.

Eve shook her head.

"Looks like the first time a problem cropped up, none of you were around."

Nice shot. She said on a yawn, "Guess I was out drinking grappa in North Beach, not camping out in Judge Hunt's backyard, stroking my Glock."

Not bad. Harry eyed her. She hadn't taken the bait, hadn't tried to belt him. He liked attitude, wanted to grin at her amused in-your-face, "you're not worth my time, Agent Moron" look. He'd seen Barbieri before and thought she was a real looker, but he'd never seen her up close. The close-up reality surprised him. With her long legs in black pants and her black boots that put her close to six feet tall, she nearly reached his eyebrows. They were really shiny black boots, too, maybe shinier than his. Nah, probably not. She wore a raw-looking red leather jacket over a black turtleneck, topping off the tough U.S. marshal look.

But her face spoiled the effect. Despite the outfit, she looked like she should be serving ice cream and cake to kids at a birthday party, smiling and tending them, her blond ponytail bouncing. She was real pretty and sweet-looking and—wholesome was the word, like some former Ohio State cheerleader, like the girl next door voted beauty queen at the state fair. Until you looked at her eyes, dark blue stormy eyes that weren't at all trusting, and the U.S. marshal showed through again. They were eyes that had seen a lot, though the good Lord knew she couldn't have seen more than he had in his eight years with the Bureau.

Harry stuck out his hand, wondering if she'd bite it, but she shook his hand, hers cool and dry, all business.

"Why are you grinning?"

"I was wondering if you would bite my hand."

She arched a dark blond eyebrow. "Only if you try to feed me."

Harry said, "So you think I'm a wild hair, do you? There's a story around about you, too, Barbieri. Something about a fugitive in a shopping mall in Omaha last year who tried to take a hostage in a Dillard's women's room? And you ended up sticking the woman's head in the john and not letting her up until she dropped her gun?" He grinned at the visual. "Talk about the pot and the kettle."

Cheney laughed, couldn't help it, watching the two of them. If they could manage to avoid bloodshed, they might work well together. Barbieri could stand up to anybody, and as for Harry, well, despite his reputation, he had gotten some remarkable results, and that's why Cheney wanted him on Judge Hunt's shooting.

Cheney said to Eve, "Your boss told me you'll be heading up Judge Hunt's protection team."

Eve nodded.

"Good. The media is gathered in the lobby. I don't doubt they'll try to sneak up."

"We've got that covered," Eve said. "Look at Mancusso's face—show him a lurking reporter and he'll stuff him into one of the laundry carts."

"We've also had Agent Dillon Savich, chief of the CAU back at the Hoover Building—that's the Criminal Apprehension Unit—and his wife, Agent Sherlock, fly out to help us with the case. You'll be working with them as well."

"Yes, I know," she said. "I saw you with them earlier." Eve had watched Cheney hug the woman with the rioting red hair and shake the big man's hand, all chatty and full of bonhomie, best buds.

Great, Harry thought, he'd be working with Savich and Sherlock from Disneyland East, too, as if there weren't already enough noses eager to poke under the tent.

Cheney said, "Harry, do you think you can manage to work with Barbieri? Work *with* her, not make her want to knock your teeth down your throat? Given it's Barbieri we're talking about here, she probably wouldn't hesitate."

"You're recommending caution around Suzie Cheerleader? Not a problem. She's only heading up the protection detail, so that's not a lot of work we'll need to do together."

Suzie Cheerleader? Eve gave him the fish eye. "I'll get

the job done, whether you work with me or not," and she shrugged as an eyebrow went up. "The question is, will you, Christoff?"

"In the FBI, we have cases, not jobs." He held up his hand and said to Cheney, "Like I said, there's no problem here. I can work with anybody, even cute little cheerleader types."

Cheney eyed them both, wondering if he was making a mistake. No, but he'd talk to Harry again privately, and ask Marshal Carney Maynard to make sure Eve Barbieri would work with Harry, not go haring off on her own. He had to admit there'd been a time or two when he'd wanted to rip Harry's face off himself. He said, "Deputy Barbieri, Harry will be point man on this. Your boss has asked that you assist him, as time allows. No hotdogging from either of you, especially you, Christoff, all right?"

Harry said, "Me, hotdog? Not a single lick of yellow mustard on me."

Eve took one last look at Harry, gave a little finger wave to Cheney, and turned away down the hall.

Cheney said, "I'm serious about this, Harry. Not only does she know Judge Hunt, she knows about most everything that goes on inside and outside the courtroom. You want to use her."

Harry nodded. "Sure, but bottom line, she's just the protection." He gave his boss a maniacal grin and strode off. "Hey, Barbieri, wait up! You and I got stuff to work out here."

9

San Francisco General Hospital
Friday afternoon

The first thing Eve heard when she slipped into Ramsey's cubicle was the sound of machines, some beeping, some humming. Then she saw all the lines running into and out of his body. She couldn't imagine trying to rest like that. She saw Molly standing over Ramsey, her head lowered, speaking to him quietly. She looked up when Eve came in.

"Eve, it's good to see you. Do come in. Ramsey, it's Eve."

Thank the good Lord he was awake. Eve nodded to Molly, leaned over Ramsey, and felt her throat clog. Not a single word could get through without risking tears. She stared down at him, taking everything in.

Ramsey saw her fear, and he wanted to reassure her, at least smile at her, but it was hard to make his mouth muscles work. He felt oddly detached from his own body.

He thought it was all the drugs that were making it hard to focus his mind on anything. But there was no pain, and that was a profound blessing, thanks to the magic morphine pump. He felt her clasp his hand and squeeze, felt her warm breath, like lemons, he thought, when she leaned close. "You're looking good, Ramsey. I gotta say I'm really happy about that."

For a moment, he couldn't find words. Where were the words? "So are you, Eve. Don't worry, I'm going to pull through, Molly told me so. And don't cry. I don't want to walk into the men's room and read 'Barbieri's a weeping wuss' scratched on the wall. What would that do to your reputation?"

She started to say she never cried, but that lie would perch right on the end of her nose. His voice was thin, insubstantial, and that scared the bejesus out of her. The last thing he needed was for her to fall apart. "We got a regular hoedown outside, FBI everywhere. They're all huddled together, so I slipped in to see you."

"I'm glad you did."

"I can't imagine why anyone would want to shoot you, of all people."

Ramsey frowned. Eve squeezed his hand again. "I know, why shoot the judge?"

"Can you tell me what happened, Ramsey?"

Surely he could try to do that again for Eve before his lights went out. "It was late, nearly midnight. I was out back, staring up at the stars and over at the Marin Headlands, and I was remembering Cal asking if he could sink his fingers into those pits on the surface of the moon."

Was it her imagination or did he sound stronger? Pits in the moon? This hard-as-nails federal judge was wondering about the pits on the moon?

"I didn't hear a thing out of the ordinary, nor did I see anything or anyone. One shot and I was down and out." He paused, and the pain suddenly surfaced. He jerked, gritted his teeth, but it didn't lessen, it was pulling him down. He pressed the morphine button.

Molly said, "If I hadn't called out to him, Eve, he wouldn't have turned and moved, and the bullet would have hit him in his chest." Saying the words broke the dam. Molly burst into tears.

Ramsey said, "No, sweetheart, I'll be okay. No need to cry." He hated to see her cry, but there was nothing he could do, only lie there helpless, wanting to howl. "Eve—I remember now. There was a boat. A Zodiac, pulled up near the beach. I saw it."

Eve's heart speeded up. A Zodiac—now they had a place to start. She saw his eyes were squeezed tightly shut, his mouth in a thin seam. "Just a moment," he said, and she watched him press the button again. But she couldn't stand it. She went to get the nurse, but when she came back he was out again.

Molly was huddled over him, her shoulders shaking. It nearly broke Eve's heart.

10

Emma Hunt pushed back her piano bench and rose. She couldn't concentrate on Gershwin's *Rhapsody in Blue*, though she loved the sheer romantic exuberance of it, how the music built and built until its grandeur, its firecracker opulence, made her fingers tingle and her heart beat faster. But not today. Emma sighed. Ever since her dad was shot the night before, she'd felt deadening fear. She heard Cal and Gage squabbling in the next room, speaking their twin talk, taking pleasure in knowing their mother had no clue what they were saying. Neither did she, but the two of them understood each other perfectly. Did they realize no one else could understand them? Oh, yes, she'd bet a week's allowance on it.

"Emma?"

She turned to see her mother standing in the

doorway, holding Cal and Gage's hands. Both of them looked grubby from playing underneath the big oak tree outside the music room door. Her mother looked frazzled, but she was trying to pretend she was fine.

Emma smiled, though it wasn't easy. Her brothers didn't need to see that she was afraid—no, not just afraid, she was terrified—their father would die. "Mama, do you need me to do something with the boys?"

"No, sweetie, I'm going to clean them up myself. I wanted to tell you the Gershwin sounded wonderful. Do you know I listened to Gershwin himself playing *Rhapsody in Blue* on iTunes and sometimes you sound just like him? Maybe better."

Emma rolled her eyes. "You're my mother. Of course you'd say that. You know I'm not as good as Gershwin. Mrs. Mayhew says he was brilliant."

Molly said, "Ellie will be here soon to watch the boys so you and I can go back to the hospital." She glanced at her watch. Emma knew her mother hadn't wanted to leave her dad at all, that she'd rather have stayed beside his bed, holding his hand, telling him he would be all right. But it was better for the twins that she came home to see them. The hospital staff always patted Emma's head, her shoulder, telling her every other minute that her father would recover. She was grateful everyone cared so much. She closed her eyes for a moment. Her father's stillness scared her the most. He was never still, always in motion, laughing or using his hands when he talked. She always clutched her mother's hand when they were with him.

Cal and Gage pulled away from their mother and ran

to the corner of the music room, where they had stacked piano music into two equal piles, one for each of them. What on earth did they plan to do with those piles? They knew better than to tear the pages; she'd yelled at them too much about that over the past year. The boys were arguing now, and about what? Emma said, "I wonder when they'll start speaking English to each other?"

Molly smiled. "They already say your name and *Mama* and *Papa* to each other."

"And ice cream."

That got a small smile. "And ice cream. Don't worry about the Gershwin, you're ready to play for the audience and the orchestra. You know they love listening to you. The concertmaster, Mr. Williams, told me you were a miracle. Naturally, I agreed."

"That's because Mr. Williams doesn't have perfect pitch and he wishes he had mine," Emma said matter-of-factly. "I sure hope Giovanni will like my *Rhapsody in Blue*."

"Of course he will. Emma, I really don't think you should be calling the conductor of the San Francisco Symphony Orchestra by his first name. Maybe best to call him Mr. Rossini. You're eleven. You want to show him respect."

Emma was silent for a moment, a frown between her eyebrows, identical to her mother's. "I know I'm only a kid, but he asked me to call him Giovanni. He said he'd like me to go to Milan to study with Pietro Bianci." She said the name slowly, careful to get the pronunciation right.

Molly went on alert. "When did this happen?"

"Yesterday at Davies Hall, while you and Dad were trying to get Cal and Gage to behave—before Dad—" Emma swallowed. "He doesn't think Mrs. Mayhew is the right teacher for me anymore."

Molly, momentarily distracted, said, "Not only does Mrs. Mayhew know every single serious piece of music for the piano in the universe, she's played most of them, including Gershwin, both in Paris and London."

"Mrs. Mayhew is very old, Mama; that's what Giovanni—Mr. Rossini—said. He told me her teaching isn't what it used to be."

Emma's eighty-two-year-old piano teacher had elegance, style, and immense talent and goodwill. She had *known* George Gershwin. Who cared if she didn't play as well as she did fifty years ago? As for Emma going to Italy to study at her age? Not a chance. She wanted to tell Emma she wasn't about to let her out of her sight until she was twenty-one, maybe even thirty-five, not after what had happened five years ago, but the words fell out of her head. She swallowed. She would have a talk with Mr. Rossini, but even that didn't seem important now. Ramsey was fastened to more high-tech machines than she'd ever seen in one place. He could still die. Tears gushed up into her throat, and she had to swallow to keep them down.

But Emma knew, of course. She rushed to Molly, squeezed herself against her. "Dad will be all right, Mama." She pulled away a bit. "I had a dream about him on Wednesday night, the night before—it was Thanksgiving, and we were all sitting around the table and he was carving a turkey about as big as our backyard, and he was singing 'Roll out the Barrel.' He looked really good, Mama. He looked happy."

Molly drew in a deep breath. Thanksgiving was six days away. She was not going to lose it again in front of her child. "I've never heard your father sing that song."

"Neither have I, but he sang it in a big deep booming voice. It was sort of catchy."

"I wonder how much that turkey weighed," Molly said. "Do you think Safeway will have one that big?"

Emma smiled. "Not a chance. That turkey must have weighed one hundred pounds. I think we'd eat leftovers for a year. I hear Mrs. Hicks."

Molly called out, "Cal, Gage, would the two of you stop trying to break each other's heads? Are you ready to go, Em?"

But Emma wasn't looking at her mother, she was staring out the window.

11

Harry smoothly turned his beloved dark blue Shelby Mustang onto Geary Street.

"Why don't you tell me about the old newspaper photo of Judge Dredd with an X through his face you found at the scene?" Eve said.

He whipped around and looked at her. "How'd you know—well, yeah, I'm surprised that bit got out. Yeah, that's what we found. Sitting under the big hydrangea bush in the backyard."

Eve wasn't about to tell him she knew because she'd overheard him and Cheney talking about it. "The shooter rubbing our noses in it?"

"That's what I think." He gave her another surprised look.

Eve said, "So we're going to meet the two FBI hot-shots at Ramsey's house in Sea Cliff, check out how the photo got in the hydrangea? Check out the beach for signs of the Zodiac?"

"The forensic team couldn't find anything on the

beach, so no need to traipse down there," Harry said. "You ever hear of Savich and Sherlock before?"

"Who hasn't? Only two weeks ago they were front and center on the Kirsten Bolger case, and can you believe it, Bolger grew up right here in San Francisco?" She'd savored the colorful reporting, even felt a good dollop of envy, although she'd never admit it, at least to an FBI agent, particularly this FBI agent.

Harry said, "At least the local coverage has finally run out of juice on Kirsten Bolger's family. They'll be taking a rest until the trial begins next year, when they'll light up their torches again."

Eve marveled at the two agents—married. What could two people in such stress-filled, dangerous jobs possibly have to say to each other after, say, a violent shoot-out, like the one with Bolger in a North Carolina tobacco field? *Hey, sweetie, you want to go get a beer to celebrate we're still alive?* She wondered if Sherlock painted her toenails, and imagined a nice French. And Savich was big, tough, hard as nails, good-looking. "Is Savich as fast as he looks?"

Harry nodded as he braked for a red light. "He is. He's a fourth-degree black belt. Sherlock is a first-degree, a *shodan*—"

"Yeah, yeah, I also know when you're a sixth *dan,* you wear a red-and-white belt. I mean, come on, why care so much about the color of your freaking belt? One big show, a business, that's all it is. The bottom line in the real world is to beat the crap out of your opponent, however you can."

"How do you know about a sixth *dan*?"

"From a book I saw at my boss's house."

"At Maynard's?"

"Yep. He hosts these big barbecues, feeds all hundred of the deputy marshals regularly."

"That's a lot of spareribs." Harry shot a look at her. "Cheney is new at his job, but I wouldn't mind if he picked up on the barbecue ribs idea from Maynard. So that's what marshals do? What about fighting?"

She gave him a fast smile, gone in the next instant. "We've got martial arts experts of our own, with all sorts of belts and colors. Lots of our deputy marshals are scrappers who like to show off their ripped-up knuckles and bruised kidneys."

"And you're not into martial arts?"

"Don't know about that. I fight dirty, real dirty. Like I said, you want to put your opponent on the ground, his knees around his neck, as fast as possible." She started to ask him if he'd like to visit her in the marshals' gym, wear a couple of his prized belts, then remembered her boss telling her, *Play nice, Barbieri, play nice.* She cleared her throat. "So Savich is a computer expert, right?"

She fought dirty? He thought of her toilet adventure in the Dillard's women's room in Omaha and smiled. "Give Savich a motherboard and he can make bread with it in no time at all."

"Hey, that was sort of sweet."

"Sweet? Hey, I tell you what. Let's mix it up one of these days, Barbieri. I'll get you feeling a little respect for the discipline. Because you're so cute with that blond cheerleader ponytail swinging around, I'll go easy on you."

She batted her eyelashes at him, very effective, since she was so damned pretty. "Your best shot is I'll be dazzled by your multicolored karate belt. Turn right here, we're nearly there."

When Harry pulled his Shelby into the Hunt driveway a few minutes later, he couldn't help it, he gawked. "Some digs."

"It's got about the best views in Sea Cliff—the ocean, Marin Headlands, and the Golden Gate Bridge. Looks like all the news people have left. So has the SFPD. I don't like this; someone should be here." She pulled out her cell, punched in Carney Maynard's number, and then she dropped her cell and pointed. "Hey, that's Emma—she screamed!"

Eve was out of the car before Harry could turn off the motor, her Glock 22 in her hand, her long strides eating up ground.

12

Molly jerked open the front door, saw them, and thought she'd collapse in relief. Molly said, "He was staring in the window at us! He ran over toward Mr. Sproole's backyard!"

Eve said, "It'll be okay. I'll take care of it. Get back inside, Molly!"

Eve saw a man running, a blur of black. And he was carrying something black—a gun? He jumped the fence into the neighbor's backyard. Harry started to yell for her to wait up, but he didn't waste his breath. He watched her leap the stone fence smooth and high, like a hurdler. He ran after them.

"Federal agents! Stop!" Eve shouted.

But the man didn't stop. He ran straight for the fence at the back of the neighbor's yard, vaulted over it, and disappeared.

Eve didn't hesitate. She jumped that fence, too, right after him.

A scratchy old voice yelled from the yard, "Be careful or you're dead!" He turned to see Harry running toward the fence after them. "Hey, fellow, there's a snaking little trail down to the water, but it isn't safe. Who's the guy she's chasing? You're all federal agents? Is that the guy who shot Judge Hunt?"

Harry waved off the old man and jumped the fence, stumbled on some loose rocks beyond it, and nearly fell on his face. He windmilled his arms, and managed to gain purchase. He looked down—at least sixty feet to the beach—not a beach, only a thin strip of dirty sand covered with a mess of black rocks and huge boulders.

Below him, Eve was tacking back and forth down the side of the cliff, shortcutting the windy little path. She stumbled once, and Harry's heart seized. She caught herself, but she had to drop her Glock to do it and stopped to pick it up before she started down again. Harry saw the man had reached the beach and looked up to see Eve coming toward him. He scooped up a rock to hurl at her, thought better of it, and ran. Eve yelled back at Harry, "Call it in! I'm going to get him!"

She would catch him, Harry didn't have a single doubt, even though she was a good twenty yards behind him. Harry dialed 911. The SFPD would get here faster than the FBI.

He watched Eve jump onto the strip of dirty sand and rocks and sprint after the man. Was that a gun in his hand? Then why hadn't he shot her instead of picking up a rock? Surely the guy could tell, even from this distance, that she was moving way faster, gaining on him quickly. The putz looked like he was going to drop, he was breathing so hard. In that moment, Harry felt kind of sorry for the guy. He had no clue what was in store for him in about twenty seconds.

Eve felt the wind sharp and cold off the water, and was happy to see the guy in front of her was flagging big-time. She shouted, "Stop it right now, or I'll shoot you in the leg. Do you hear me?"

The guy looked back at her, faltered, slowed, and finally stopped. He bent over, trying to catch his breath.

"Well, now, isn't this easier?"

"I didn't do anything!" he managed to say between breaths.

Eve jogged up to him, her Glock pointed at his chest, and threw him to the ground. She went down on her haunches beside him and ripped a camera from his hand. "That was for making me chase you, you brainless moron. Do you realize it looked like you had a gun? And, oh, my, would you look at this—it's a really expensive camera you're carrying."

Harry was grinning when he climbed back over the fence and saw the old man again, a golfer's cap on his head, a newspaper spread open on his lap, stretched out on a red-and-green striped chaise longue.

Harry said, "She's trying to prove she's tougher than I am."

"I gotta say she proved it, since you're not screaming she's dead. That fence is there to keep idiots from flying off the edge, but that first idiot headed to it like a homing pigeon. Didn't even see me, he was moving so fast. You said you're federal agents?"

Harry pulled out his creds, introduced himself.

The old man said, "FBI Special Agent Harry Christoff. I think I've seen that girl before. Who is she, another FBI agent?"

"She's a U.S. marshal, and a friend of the Hunt family."

"Yeah, I've seen her over at the Hunts' house. I'm Decker Sproole. You people are here because of Judge Hunt, aren't you? Was that guy the one who shot him? Why would he come back? I haven't ever understood that old saw about a criminal returning to the scene of the crime."

Harry said, "I don't know who he is yet. We've got to wait until she brings him up." They heard voices from over the fence, and watched Barbieri heft a young man over it, his hands cuffed behind him. He was skinny as a flagpole, a baseball cap pulled low over his forehead, his black clothes bagging off him.

Harry eyed the guy. He didn't look much like a professional killer. He said to Eve, "Glad you didn't break your neck."

"No thanks to this pathetic bozo," she said, and smacked his shoulder.

Mr. Sproole said, "Is he the man who shot Judge Hunt?"

"I didn't shoot anybody! She knows it!"

"Yeah, I guess I do. After all my running around, it looks like I didn't haul in our perp. What I landed was a would-be paparazzo. Imagine this fine upstanding young man wanted to take pictures of the grieving family."

"I'm not young, I'm older than you are! I'm a professional photographer."

"Yeah, and a trespasser who resisted arrest." She pulled the camera from his hand again. "After I remove the memory card and press delete a few times, you'll be all set to go sneak around someplace else and cause aggravation."

Harry said, "What's your name?"

"Robert Bacon. Like I said, I'm a professional, a freelance photographer. These photographs might be worth something, though there aren't that many since Emma Hunt saw me and yelled her head off."

"Well, Robert Bacon, did you know there are laws against doing that on private property?"

Bacon stood tall and proud. "I'm a professional. Have you ever heard of freedom of the press?"

Eve smacked him again on the shoulder. "Quiet, Bobby." She quirked an eyebrow at Harry. "Bobby Bacon? We got us the real live Bobby Bacon, the photojournalist."

"I go by Robert. Hey, if you give me back my memory card and take off these cuffs, I'll shoot a couple photos of you, you know, doing your job," and he looked at Eve hopefully.

"Thanks, Bobby," Eve said, "but I don't think I'd take such a good photo right now, since I'm all sweaty and windblown because of you," and she slapped him on the back of the head with her open palm.

He staggered, then straightened. "Listen, a photo of

Emma Hunt playing the piano, I coulda paid my rent for two months, what with her history."

Eve put her hand on Bobby's shoulder. "Bobby, you don't want to mess with Emma or her family. Don't you know who her grandfather is?"

Bobby Bacon looked blank, then pointed to Mr. Sproole. "This old guy?"

"Nope. Her grandfather is Mason Lord. Look him up. If you got a photo of Emma published he didn't like, he'd carve out your pea brain and make you eat it."

Bobby swallowed. "But I didn't think—"

"Well, now you know. If you've got a brain, you'll stay away from Emma."

Harry introduced Eve to Mr. Sproole, who eyed Bobby Bacon. "If I had my daddy's Remington, I woulda blasted you between the eyes, shooting Ramsey in the back like that."

"You crazy old duffer, you know I didn't shoot anybody. I'm a professional photographer."

"Yeah, well, I would have shot you on spec. Maybe you carry that camera around as camouflage. Maybe you got a gun hid in your shorts."

"I didn't wear shorts today. I'm commando."

Mr. Sproole said, "I got a feeling I don't wanna know what that means. You trespassed on my private property, too, and for calling me crazy, I'm going to press charges myself, put your skinny butt in the slammer."

"I was only trying to make a living. I'm sorry I called you crazy. She's the one who's crazy. I mean, who would come rocketing down that path like that over some photographs? I practiced climbing that trail twice in case I had to use it."

"And where did you think you were going to go from there, Bobby? Swim to Marin?" Eve said.

"You're a wuss, Bobby," Mr. Sproole said. "This little cutie brought you back, all trussed up." He eyed Eve. "And look at you, Deputy Barbieri. I've got to say, you're prettier than any of my four granddaughters ever were."

Harry wrote down Mr. Sproole's number and address, gave him a salute. They walked through the garden gate and back to the sidewalk with Bobby Bacon, his wrists now uncuffed, clutching his camera, minus the memory card, walking between them.

Harry said, "Prettier than any of his four grand-daughters? He must like cheerleader types."

"Shut up," Eve said.

"All of them?" and Harry laughed.

"Hey, he's right," Bobby said. "You are pretty. Your hair is a nice natural blond. So how come you're such a bitch?"

"That's Deputy Marshal Bitch to you, Bobby."

They kept him on the sidewalk until three squad cars, sirens blasting, rolled into the driveway. Six cops jumped out, guns drawn.

"That was fast," Harry said, his creds raised high over his head.

Eve said, "It's because everyone knows it's Ramsey's address."

There was pandemonium before everything got sorted out. They watched two officers drag Bobby Bacon to a squad car, Bobby yelling about police brutality and freedom of the press. He was still yelling as one of the officers shoved his head down to get him into the backseat. "I want my memory card back."

Eve grinned, tossed it to one of the officers.

When Eve and Harry walked to the Hunt home, Molly was standing in the doorway. Behind her stood Mrs. Hicks, the babysitter. She looked ready to kiss them. They heard Gage and Cal talking up a storm, and Emma's voice over theirs, telling them to be quiet, but they didn't.

Eve took Molly's arms in her hands, steadied her.

"He's a paparazzo. He didn't get any photos. The cops have taken Mr. Bacon downtown, where he'll be booked for trespassing and trying to escape a federal marshal."

Gage shouted, "Was that bad Bacon man here to shoot us?"

Eve went down on her knees in front of Cal and Gage, gathered them to her. "Listen up. That guy was a rude photographer, nothing more. The policemen hauled him off to jail. He wasn't here to hurt anyone."

Cal said, "But why'd he want to take our picture, Aunt Eve? Daddy's not here, he's in the hospital."

For the almighty buck. "You and Cal are so cute, I'll bet he was going to hawk them in Union Square. I bet he could get a buck each for them, at least. Hey, I'm glad you're speaking English today."

They gave her an identical look. Gage said, "We're not stupid, we have to if we're talking to you. I think he wanted to see Mama cry, didn't he, Aunt Eve? He wanted to take a picture of her crying." Cal shook her sleeve.

"Maybe, but we don't have to worry about him anymore. Now, this man is Special Agent Harry Christoff. He's FBI, and he's going to help me find out who hurt your dad."

"But he's a stranger, he could be another Bacon—"

Emma rolled her eyes. "You guys want some ice cream?"

Once Emma herded the twins out of the room, Mrs. Hicks, looking stalwart, following after them, Molly said, "They were terrified the man was here to shoot them."

"So were we," Harry said.

Molly blew out a breath. "The jerk. What will happen to him?"

"Probably not much," Harry said. "A bail hearing. Maybe a plea bargain."

Eve said, "Now that the excitement's over, Harry and I can start taking a look around outside. Agents Savich and Sherlock will be here anytime now. If you want to go back to the hospital, Molly, go right ahead."

Harry said, "I think it'd be a good idea for you guys to have some protection right now, not wait until Judge Hunt is home from the hospital. They can keep the Bobby Bacons of the world out of here."

"The media, too," Eve said. She'd assumed there'd already be coverage here. She'd been wrong. She pulled out her cell phone.

13

It was late afternoon and chilly, with only a few wispy tails of fog coming through the Golden Gate when Savich and Sherlock joined Eve and Harry in the Hunts' backyard. Sharp gusts of wind blew off the water. It was too cold to think much about the incredible view.

Savich said to Harry, "The SFPD out front aren't fooling around. They stopped us and looked us over pretty closely since they didn't know who we were."

Harry said, "There was a paparazzo here who caused a commotion only a half-hour ago. The police are here to keep everyone else off the property. Deputy Marshal Barbieri here—Eve—will be heading up security."

Savich said, "Good to know. I can see from that police tape and the height of the stone wall pretty much where Ramsey had to be standing when he was shot. He said he saw a Zodiac anchored off his little slice of beach. He didn't mention hearing anything, which means the shooter had to have motored in before Ramsey came out, and waited. Ramsey is about my height, and he was shot from the rear under his right shoulder blade, with the exit wound higher." He looked over the wall and studied the terrain below. "Maybe sixty to seventy feet up from the rocks, with a steep angle down."

"Have you heard about the rock with a newspaper photo of Judge Hunt tied to it, his face marked through with an X?" Harry said, and pointed.

"We've heard," Savich said, looking over at the bush.

"The conundrum is, do we have two people, the shooter from the beach and someone else who dropped the rock up here? Seems like an awfully risky thing to do just to leave a message. There's an active neighborhood watch, according to Mrs. Hunt, that she herself helped start five years ago. Even though it was near midnight, there's a chance one of the neighbors would have seen a second perp."

Eve said, "You can bet someone in a neighborhood like this one would have gone on alert if they saw a stranger near Ramsey's property. I'd wager my Sunday hat if the shooter dropped the message, he came up the trail from the beach on Mr. Sproole's property next door and over his fence into that backyard, since that's the only trail for a good distance. And if he risked Mr. Sproole seeing him, then why would he bother to shoot him from down below in the first place? Why not right here, then drop the rock and head back down to that Zodiac? It's a conundrum, like Harry said."

Sherlock said, "Show me where they found that rock."

Eve touched the leaves about halfway down the huge hydrangea and pushed them aside. "I wasn't here, but that flag marks the spot, there."

Sherlock turned to Harry. "You were here when the rock was found. Tell me how the rock was set under the hydrangea. Did it look carefully placed, or like it was simply tossed there, like an afterthought?"

Harry said, "The note attached to the rock was actually upside down and set partially into that soft soil. It looked freshly placed, not covered by any dirt or leaves. The forensic team didn't find it until it was full daylight, because the rock was under the hydrangea."

Sherlock stuck her hand in among the leaves, felt around with her fingers. Then she went down on her haunches and continued to carefully poke around inside the hydrangea.

She looked up and cocked her head to one side, something Savich had seen her do many times, a sure sign she was picturing what had happened. "How did the shooter know Ramsey would be outside, by himself, late Thursday night? Surely he didn't simply hang around to see if his target happened to come outside? So did Ramsey have a habit of coming out here at night by himself? To look at the Marin Headlands, the Golden Gate?"

Eve pulled her cell out of her pocket and dialed. "Molly? Did Ramsey have a habit of spending a few minutes outside every night, before bed?"

She listened. "Thank you. That helps. I'll tell you later, I promise. We're still out here at the house trying to make sense of how this all happened. I'll see you soon."

She punched off, slipped the phone back in her red jacket pocket. "Yes, every night. Molly said it was a ritual, that Ramsey came out sometimes even in the rain. She said it made him feel blessed to be able to look out from his own Wuthering Heights, like it was the center of the world."

Harry said, "That means the shooter, or the people who hired him, knew that. They had to know his family well, or they had to be watching his house long enough to be sure he would be there. Are the Cahills even a possibility? Could they have found out a detail like that about Ramsey's habits from jail?"

Eve said, "You're right. How many people could have known about Ramsey's habits at night, in his own back-yard? And Ramsey was shot within twenty-four hours of his closing down the trial. That's a small window of opportunity for the Cahills."

"So what is it you've been thinking about down there, Sherlock?" Savich asked.

She pulled her arm out of the hydrangea bush. "I've been thinking about why the picture, why the message. Someone seeing it sitting handily under the bush, not twenty feet from where Ramsey fell, might conclude we've got two people involved, as Harry said. But if the second man's job was to plant the picture for the police to find, to make some sort of statement, why on the ground under the bush? And what message were they sending?"

"The first impression it leaves," Eve said, "is that Ramsey was shot because of what he'd done as a judge, because of his reputation and what it means to people. The crossed-out picture is a sort of in-your-face sneer; that's what Harry thought."

"I suppose," Harry said, "that it could be some kind of misdirection, to point us away from the trial or from some personal motive."

Sherlock nodded. "Here's the deal. I agree the Xerox itself could be misdirection, but what about where it was found? It makes it seem like there were two people involved, but the fact is there was only the shooter, and he was on the beach."

Harry said, "Then how'd the rock get here? Did the guy climb up the cliff to drop it under the bush, then scramble back down to the beach and climb back aboard his Zodiac before the cops got here?"

Sherlock smiled. "There's a freshly broken branch inside that bush, and I doubt it was one of our forensic team who broke it. Something heavy broke it from behind, from the rear, and it's maybe two feet directly up from where the flag on the ground marks where they found the rock. That means the rock wasn't just laid on the ground under the bush, it hit the bush hard."

Savich said, "So it came from a distance." He looked down over the wall again. "It's too far down to throw it up and hit the bush with much force. But a small rock could easily be shot up here with a slingshot, say. One of those leather Trumark models they use to hunt jackrabbits and such. It would reach up here easily, aimed at the hydrangea, a nice big target. Good going, Sherlock."

Eve stared at her. "How'd you think to even look for that?"

Sherlock said matter-of-factly, "There had to be a solution to Harry's conundrum, and this was the only one I could think of. The shooter was careful, he studied Ramsey and picked his spot carefully, so it didn't make sense he'd give up that advantage by climbing up the trail to drop a message."

"Amazing," Eve said. "So much for our second perp." But Harry wasn't convinced.

Sherlock said, "Answer me this, Agent Christoff. If there was a second man, why didn't he come out from his hidey-hole to make sure Ramsey was dead? No, what the shooter wanted was to kill Ramsey, and didn't care too much if he missed with that rock. In the grand scheme of things, that attempt to sneer at us, to misdirect us, or whatever, wouldn't have worked if we didn't find the rock. So what?"

Everyone chewed on that. Harry said, "Okay, one shooter, then. I can't get over the timing—Ramsey postponed the trial and he gets shot. It's got to be the Cahills behind this, or someone they're involved with. The timing makes it too coincidental, and I, for one, don't believe in coincidences."

"I don't, either," Savich said. "But as Sherlock pointed out, a stranger couldn't predict Ramsey would be standing out here exactly when he needed him to, and so someone's been studying him for at least a week, I'd say."

Eve rubbed her hands over her arms. "Someone who followed him around for a week? That's hard to take in."

Harry said, "Okay, say it isn't the Cahills. But the timing is still what it is—even if it was planned for some time, someone may be cashing in on a wonderful opportunity, since the Cahills are hanging over the crime scene like a black cloud."

"Judge Hunt closing down the trial was mentioned on the local news at noon yesterday," Eve said. "If someone had already planned to kill him, they moved very fast."

"There's another big question with the Cahills," Savich said. "The way it looks now, there'll be a mistrial because the federal prosecutor may have been compromised, and now he's missing. Ramsey's being shot doesn't change that. It will all begin again for them, with a different set of players."

Eve said, "Molly said that was one of the first things out of Ramsey's mouth when he woke up. Why shoot him? A judge's job is to be impartial, unlike the prosecutor who'd spent months preparing for the trial. What difference did it make to the Cahills who was sitting up there in the black robe?"

Eve looked over at the crime scene tape that marked where Ramsey had fallen. "Whoever it was made one big fat mistake."

Everyone looked at her.

"The shooter didn't manage to kill Ramsey. He failed.

Now what's he going to do? Try again? If it was the Cahills who targeted Ramsey, for whatever reason, they've already won, because he's out of the picture for the near future. What if it was someone else?"

"That's why we've got to protect him, Eve," Harry said.

"No one will hurt Judge Ramsey Hunt on my watch," Eve said. "No one."

Sherlock said, "I'll be checking on the Zodiac, and Cheney has feelers out for any word about a shooter for hire."

"We need to talk to the Cahills," Eve said. "Regardless, they're certainly people of interest. It's a place to start."

14

Sherlock's eyes were closed as she listened to Emma play George Gershwin's *Rhapsody in Blue* on her parents' magnificent Bösendorfer grand piano, which had been purchased for Sherlock when she was about Emma's age. When Emma hit the final notes, there was a long moment of silence, then applause, Sherlock's parents the loudest.

"It's been too long since I've listened to you play," Judge Corman Sherlock said. "Thank you, Emma."

Harry couldn't believe what he had just heard. An eleven-year-old kid, her thick dark brown hair veiling her face, had knocked his socks off. How could those small hands play with such passion and purity, even reach all those racing chords, those endless runs and trills?

Evelyn Sherlock was still smiling. "That was grand,

Emma. Thank you for the preview. We'll be there to hear you at the symphony, of course."

Emma gave them a small smile, but it soon fell away. "I don't know how well I'll play with Daddy in the hospital." She looked down at her clasped hands. "He smiled at me this afternoon, but it was so hard for him, and I knew it hurt him."

Eve said, "Say your dad can't be with you at Davies Hall. We'll fix it so he can be listening to you on a live feed."

"But what if something happens? What if he's still in the hospital? How could I play then?"

Eve said, "If he isn't home—and believe me, that's unlikely, since your daddy's such a tough dude—we'll take the live feed to the hospital and hook it up there. Can't you see all the nurses and doctors, all the other patients cramming into his room to see you play? Believe me on this. Wherever your daddy happens to be in a week and a half, you know he'll be right onstage with you."

What a perfect thing to say, Savich thought. Eve didn't even hint that Ramsey could possibly be well enough to actually attend her performance, and that was smart. He squeezed Sherlock's hand.

Emma tried to smile at Eve. "That means I can't make a single mistake."

"You never do," Eve said.

Sherlock said, "Do you like the Bösendorfer, Emma? My parents got it for me a very long time ago."

"It's too bad you aren't here very often to play it," Emma said. "Mrs. Mayhew—she's my teacher—she says a piano has to be played or it goes stale."

"Do you think the Gershwin sounded stale?"

Emma shook her head. "No, it sounded perfect. I'm used to my Steinway, but I like this piano, too. I wish Mama were here."

Eve said, "Look at the big picture, Emma. Your daddy needs her attention right now more than we do."

Emma thought about that and nodded. She touched middle C. "The action's perfect."

Evelyn Sherlock said, "Emma, would you like to have Lacey play for you?"

Emma's eyes shone. "Oh, yes. Do you know Bach's *Italian Concerto*?"

Sherlock rolled her eyes. "I haven't played that killer in a long time. I can feel my fingers yelling at me not to try it."

Harry said, "Tell your fingers to man up. I'd sure like to hear you play, Sherlock."

Sherlock took Emma's place at the black piano bench. She played some scales, ran some chords, and realized the feel of the keys on this magnificent instrument was a deeply embedded memory that came back quickly. Still, she wasn't about to try the first movement, far too wild and hairy without practice. She played the second movement, slow, evocative, and sorrowful. As she played, she felt the power of the music burrow into her. When she finished, Sherlock slowly lifted her hands from the keyboard, letting herself settle for a moment, another embedded memory she would thankfully never lose.

Emma jumped to her feet. "Oh, goodness, that was beautiful. I can play that movement, but not like that, not like it makes everyone want to cry."

"The last time you played that second movement for me, I cried," Eve said.

"You're easy, Aunt Eve," Emma said, and gave her a fat kid grin.

"Yeah, your music is my downfall."

Sherlock hugged her. "You're eleven years old, Emma. You'll make everyone weep when you have more life under your belt."

Molly arrived at nine o'clock to take the children home. Savich brought down Cal and Gage, both deeply asleep, one draped over each shoulder. He saw Molly speaking quietly to Sherlock. Molly even managed a smile. *Excellent.* Then it was his turn.

An SFPD black-and-white was parked across the street to follow Molly home.

Sherlock asked, "What were you talking to Molly about, Dillon?"

"Ramsey was more lucid this evening. He described the Zodiac to Molly again." He cupped his wife's face in his big hands. "Cheney will find it. Now, I don't think I woke Sean up when I fetched Cal and Gage, but he's got ears like a bat; we should check on him again."

15

Russian Hill
Friday night

It had been a lovely evening, Eve thought, as she unlocked the front door of her condo on Russian Hill, only a ten-minute drive this time of night from the Sherlock home on Mulberry in Pacific Heights. She couldn't get over Agent Sherlock playing the piano like that. She pictured Agent Savich—no, Dillon, he'd told her—his eyes never leaving his wife's face. He said that after you shared a dinner of barbecued pork spareribs and finger licking, only first names sounded right. "But you're a vegetarian," she'd said to him. "You didn't eat any of those delicious ribs."

He said, "Licking your fingers is the operative image here."

Eve wondered what Harry had thought of the odd evening—an FBI agent playing Bach, and no talk of who had tried to kill Ramsey. When she'd mentioned that to

Dillon, he'd said only, "Don't you think your brain does better when it gets to stir a different kind of stew for a bit?"

Good people, she thought, full of life, so much of it. Some people seemed to have more of life in them than others, and that included Sean, brought downstairs after dinner, beaming at all of them in his Transformers pajamas.

She saw Harry in her mind's eye, frankly astonished when Emma had played Gershwin's *Rhapsody in Blue.* Then he'd closed his eyes and leaned his head back on the chair cushion as he listened to Sherlock play that incredibly sad second movement.

She heard a noise, something close, something dangerous—she jerked around, her hand going to the Glock at her waist. Harry said, raising his arms, palms toward her, "Don't shoot me. It's only ten o'clock. I thought we should talk. Sorry to alarm you, I thought you saw me following you here."

Her heart was pounding. She couldn't make him out clearly, but she recognized his voice. "I can't believe I didn't hear you sooner. I can hear ants nesting. I never noticed you behind me, and here you were driving that hot Shelby."

"How can you protect Judge Hunt if you don't pay more attention to who's on your tail?"

He got her, curse him. "Yeah, you're right, but that'll be the last time. Talk would be good. Come on in. I'll put on some coffee. So it's only ten o'clock? What does that have to do with my shooting you?"

"No shooting until after midnight, that's the rule."

"Haven't heard that one. I think it's smart to talk about the case."

"So what do ants sound like when they're nesting?"

She grinned at him over her shoulder as she unlocked the door to a small lobby with a black-and-white tiled floor, black mailboxes set against a stark white wall, and a half-dozen palm trees in green and blue pots stationed in the corners. She waved him in. "The elevator's a 1920s job that creaks and groans all the way up. Scares most people, but I love it. Still, I prefer to walk up. Keeps yummy things like spareribs from making a home on my thighs." They walked steep, wide stairs to the third and top floor.

"I'm on the end." The corridor was wide, covered in a red carpet splashed with cabbage roses that should have made Harry bilious. Instead he found it curiously charming. She stopped in front of a blue door, unlocked it, and stepped in. She flipped on the light, waved him in.

Eve's living room wasn't what Harry was expecting, although he wasn't quite sure what that would be, since he'd only met her earlier in the day. Maybe a black leather sofa and chairs and lots of gym mats on the floor? No, the living room was light, airy, filled with color. There was a view of the city through the big windows and a sliver of a view of the bay. He followed her to the kitchen, streamlined but softened with fresh flowers in a vase on the two-seater kitchen table, herbs in small pots lining the windowsill over the sink. It was painted a soft yellow.

"Nice apartment."

"It's mine now, bought it when the building went condo five years ago. It's the right size for me."

Eve smacked the heel of her hand to her head. "I'm an idiot." After she turned on the coffeemaker, Eve pulled out her cell, and typed on the small Google screen.

"Well, okay, that's only because you aren't FBI. What are you doing?"

She stared at him.

"What? Oh, I'm picturing you lying flat on your back, out like a light, me standing over you rubbing my bruised knuckles."

"That's a pretty solid fantasy scenario. What are you doing really?"

She punched in numbers she'd looked up on her cell. "Calling the Port Authority to see if there were any cargo ships coming through the Golden Gate about midnight last night."

He hadn't thought of that. He guessed he was an idiot, too.

"Here we go." She dialed, got a message, punched off her cell. "It's late, no one there. I'll call in the morning."

She laid her cell phone on the counter. "Where do you live, Harry?"

"Over in Laurel Heights."

She knew it was a lovely area near the Presidio, with streets named after trees. "You have a house?"

He nodded. "After my wife left—" He cut off like a spigot run dry, nodded at the coffeepot.

As Eve filled two large mugs, a hank of her blond hair fell along the side of her face. He watched her tuck it behind her ear. "This is decaf, so we'll both have a shot at some sleep tonight. What do you take in your coffee?"

"Black is good."

When they were seated across from each other at the kitchen table, Harry waved his hand toward the window. "What have you got planted in that first pot?"

"Thyme."

"Yeah? You put that in birthday cakes?" Again, he saw her in a pretty swingy summer dress, long legs in open-toed sandals, serving cake up to a noisy herd of kids at a party.

"Not unless my specialty was pasta primavera cake."

He laughed. "I called the hospital on the way over. Judge Hunt is sleeping. No setbacks so far. I hope he makes it out of the hospital in time to see Emma play at Davies Hall."

"If he can make it without causing a stir and disturbing the audience, he'll be there," Eve said. "With the paramedics, if he needs them."

"He's a local hero. The paramedics would be thrilled. Emma blew my mind tonight."

"I guess I've heard her play so many times I'm used to it. It was Sherlock who blew me away. Made me feel inferior. Judge Sherlock told me she chose being an agent over trying to make it as a concert pianist. When I asked him why, he only smiled and shook his head. I wonder what happened."

"Who knows? Maybe in the pursuit of her blood?"

Eve said, "It's hard to imagine Savich and Sherlock are actually married."

"Cheney told me he's heard stories about Sherlock going toe-to-toe with Savich when she disagrees with him, that she can be as stubborn as he imagined his mother-in-law would be if he had one. But despite that, he says what impresses him the most about Sherlock is her loyalty." He studied his coffee, swirled it in his cup. "Imagine that, loyalty in a woman."

Whoa. Best move right along.

"Tomorrow's Saturday," Eve said. "Virginia Trolley has asked to be part of our protection team. She'll have officers stick close to Ramsey's house, keep people from sneaking in when no one's home. Did you know Virginia Trolley is a longtime friend of Ramsey's? She's a good cop, too."

Harry said, "I met Lieutenant Trolley. She acted suspicious, didn't much like me."

"What did you do?"

"Nothing at all. I was my charming self."

"Yeah, I can only imagine."

"She's like you, wears a uniform."

"What does that mean?"

"Look at you, all in black with that kick-butt red leather jacket. I'll bet your socks and your underwear are black, too."

He'd nailed that one.

"You didn't tell me what you did to make Virginia dislike you."

"Strange, really. I only happened to mention that the San Francisco cops are really good at writing parking tickets."

Eve rolled her eyes, then grinned. "Yeah, no secret there. Got to raise money to support the city budget."

"Good coffee, even though it's decaf. Cheney told me he put Burt Seng with Sherlock on finding that Zodiac. Fact is, Burt could find a contact lens in a swimming pool. He'll be updating us at the meeting tomorrow."

"I hadn't heard about a meeting. Do you think I can be in on that? When? Tomorrow morning?"

He couldn't help himself. "That'd be okay, if you don't forget your place."

She leaped for the bait, coffee sputtered out. She wiped a napkin over her mouth and gave him a look to fry his liver.

He quickly raised his hand, smiling. "You gotta learn control, Barbieri. You can't lose it every time someone makes an innocent comment that rubs you the wrong way."

The jerk, but he'd done it on purpose, and she'd been ready to go for his throat. She dredged up a smile and a sneer. "And when do you interview the Cahills? Can I go with you for that?"

"Savich and I planned to do that in the morning. That actually is why I followed you home tonight, so I could ask you about the trial. I'd wanted to be there from the beginning, since it was my case, but something else came up. Since Judge Hunt isn't in any shape to tell me about it himself yet, could you tell me exactly what was happening to make him so suspicious about Mickey O'Rourke?"

Eve said, "Ramsey never talked to me about it directly—of course he wouldn't—but I can tell you what I saw.

"The trial was still in the final pretrial motion stage. They hadn't impaneled a jury yet. Milo Siles, the Cahills' defense attorney, had been making all sorts of motions for discovery. He'd demanded proof of everything the government accessed from the murder victim's computer, especially anything that was considered top secret. He kept going on about the *Brady* rules giving the defense the right to any documents it needs to defend their clients, even in the case of espionage. It was pretty obvious, really, Siles was trying to force the government to disclose exactly what Mark Lindy—the murder victim—did for them."

"Yeah, I know all about Mark Lindy, since it was my case, like I told you. So it sounds like Siles was trying to get the government to drop the case rather than have what Mark Lindy was working on compromised? That sounds nuts."

"Just you wait. There was a lot of talk then about the Classified Information Procedures Act that provides protection for the government and for defendants in these kinds of cases. There were a bunch of conferences, some of them in camera—that means in Ramsey's chambers—and after that, Ramsey started getting more and more hard-nosed with O'Rourke. You see, Ramsey had ruled some of that information admissible, but O'Rourke had repeatedly failed to provide it to the court. At first his excuses seemed reasonable, but then he had no more excuses, even bad ones.

"I'll tell you, it was quite a sight seeing Ramsey lambaste a federal prosecutor like that. He said the court would have to impose sanctions, possibly dismiss the federal indictment, and you could tell that really burned Ramsey, and that's when he suspended the trial, the same day he was shot."

Harry nodded. "Since Judge Hunt's known O'Rourke pretty well after working with him for years, he realized he wouldn't behave like that—ignoring the judge's directives time after time—if something weren't seriously wrong. No way would a federal prosecutor want a case dismissed, except if there was bad stuff going on, and he was directly involved. Yes, that fits nicely.

"Thanks, Eve. I've got a better handle on it now. About the Cahills: Savich wants to meet with them as soon as possible, before they have a chance to talk all this through with their lawyer. We're going to offer them a chance to spend some time together if they're willing to talk to us immediately, without waiting for Siles. They're going to want to see each other real bad, one reason is so they can both be sure they can still trust each other. A lot has happened in two days. Who knows what they know? What they've heard? What they're thinking? Maybe they're ready to deal."

"Maybe," Eve said.

Harry rose. "Gotta go. Thanks for the coffee."

She followed him to the front door. "Do you think I could go interview the Cahills with you?"

"That'll be up to Savich."

Eve didn't think her chances were that good. Besides,

there was so much to do, best not to overload anywhere. She dropped it. "Hey, what tree are you heading for?"

An eyebrow went up, and then he grinned. "Yeah, yeah, my street name. I live on Maple—my house is in the center of the block. I'm really close to pizza and Szechuan, and the dry cleaner's. All the comforts, lots of people driving around, parking to shop or eat. The cops love to ticket in that neighborhood."

"Imagine Virginia not liking you when, I'm sure, you happened to mention that to her."

She heard him whistling as he walked away down the corridor. She was in bed ten minutes later.

So his wife had left him the house on Maple and he'd stayed there.

16

Two guards walked Cindy Cahill over from county jail number two to the interview room on the sixth floor, where the men were housed in the Hall of Justice. She shuffled into the room ahead of the guards, wearing her prisoner's three-piece suit—cuffs, belly chain, and leg irons. She looked up and saw her husband, Clive, dressed as she was, sitting in one of the uncomfortable chairs.

"Clive," she said, and tried to move toward him, but the guards stopped her. Clive rose slowly, smiling at her. "Hi, gorgeous. I liked you in the blue suit Milo brought you to wear in court last week, but hey, orange looks great on you, too. You okay?"

"I'm okay, but I wish I knew what's—" Cindy shot a look at Savich and shut up.

Savich rose slowly as the guards seated Cindy beside her husband, then left the small room with Savich's nod.

Savich introduced himself and Eve to the Cahills. He said, "Before we begin, I'd like you to confirm you've both agreed not to have your attorney, Mr. Siles, present. Is that correct?"

"Sure," Clive said. "Like I already said before my sweet wife arrived, we don't need Milo for this. We didn't do anything wrong, and we have nothing to hide. And how could I pass up the chance to spend some time with Cindy? Even talking to you clowns is better than being bored."

He sat back in the uncomfortable chair, like a seasoned lounge lizard.

Savich asked, "Mrs. Cahill?"

"Okay with me," Cindy said. "So call me Cindy. I heard the guards talking about you, Agent Savich; said you were from Washington, and you were real important."

Clive said, "Hey, where's Special Agent Christoff? That boy needs manners, you know? He's a hard man, that one, not much fun at all."

Savich watched them look at each other for a moment—affectionately? Wondering if the other would spill the beans? He didn't know, but allowing them to be together in the same room without their lawyer present was a good start. With everything that had happened— suspension of the trial, the federal prosecutor O'Rourke gone missing, and Ramsey shot—Savich knew both of the Cahills would want to find out as much as they could about what the Feds knew. He doubted they'd fold their tents and want to deal given what had happened, but maybe they'd let drop something—anything—to give him some leverage, particularly with Milo Siles, since even on a good day the chances of getting the truth out of a defense lawyer were harder than getting a bipartisan bill out of Congress.

Savich said as he sat down, "You needn't worry. Agent Christoff won't be joining us. There will be only myself and Marshal Barbieri."

As Savich spoke, Cindy didn't look away from his face. She rested her cheek on her long white fingers, her fingernails not so lovely now. Those dark eyes of hers saw deep into a man's soul, no, not his soul, Savich thought, she made a direct connection to his sex, and the pull of her was powerful. He recognized he was new prey to her, and so Savich clicked away, knew she recognized that he'd turned her off, and hoped she would work really hard to snare him. He wanted to observe her methods.

When Cindy turned her eyes to Eve, with her fresh, very pretty face and blond ponytail, she didn't look happy, and he was pleased. What came out of her mouth pleased him even more. "Well, now, aren't you the cutest little thing? All blond and blue-eyed, like a little princess, and yet here you are, a big U.S. marshal all dressed up in red and black, like a hard-ass. I thought all you marshals did was chase bad guys who escaped from the real cops. Like Tommy Lee Jones."

"My hero," Eve said. She was pleased Savich had decided to bring her even though Harry had been

major-league ripped until Savich had calmly said it was
obvious Cindy would have the advantage with two male
interviewers, plus she would be instantly wary of anything that came out of Harry's mouth, since he'd led the
case against them and interviewed her at least a dozen
times. Savich wanted to shuffle the deck, pull out a joker,
and present Cindy with another woman. Hopefully
Cindy hadn't noticed her in the courtroom. Unspoken to
Harry was the message that since Eve Barbieri was a
looker, why not try to rattle Cindy Cahill, who firmly
believed she was God's gift to all men? Harry hadn't said
another word. On their way to the interview room, Savich had said only to Eve, "Rattle her."

"And would you look, you've got a little holster where
you carry your gun. Isn't that delicious? I always liked
macho girls. I mean, men can be so difficult, don't you
think? Tell me, Eve, what do you do with a difficult
man?" And Cindy Cahill slanted Savich a sloe-eyed look.

Eve smiled at Cindy, recognizing pure sex on the hoof
when she saw it. She was sure men vibrated to full alert
when Cindy waltzed into their vicinity. She was also
beautiful, despite so many months spent in jail. Her dark
eyes were exotic, slightly slanted, full of sparkle and high-
voltage tease. She looked at you with incredible focus,
and that focus was now turned on Eve. Eve sensed a formidable intelligence behind those hot, dark eyes—and
something else when Cindy looked at her—calculation,
and hatred. *Hatred?* Was Savich right? Was this incredible woman jealous of *her?* She said nothing.

Savich smiled. "Maybe what we should be talking about, Cindy, is how you thought you could get away with threatening a federal prosecutor."

Direct attack, Eve thought, and took due note.

Cindy Cahill answered Savich, her voice dripping Southern Savannah honey, "Threaten the federal prosecutor? You mean Mr. O'Rourke? I'm sure I have no idea what you're talking about, Agent Savich. Do you, Clive?"

Clive said through a yawn, "Not a clue."

"What you both must have figured out by now," Savich continued smoothly, "is that your whole plan to get the murder charges dismissed has blown up in your face. Judge Hunt saw through it, and now there will be a mistrial. You will be tried again, with even greater security, and you'll be convicted. If you had anything to do with Judge Hunt's shooting or with O'Rourke's disappearance, we'll find that out, too. I would think two people facing the death penalty might be asking about a deal right about now."

Clive and Cindy exchanged glances. Clive said, "We already told you we had nothing to do with any of that. Mr. Siles has already told us to sit back and wait awhile, see what happens now. Right, darling?"

Cindy said, "Right. We wouldn't want to disappoint Mr. Siles."

Savich said, "You've got to know your lawyer doesn't want to end up in prison with you, if he was involved. If you could help us find Mr. O'Rourke, or to find Judge Hunt's shooter before he can do any more harm, I'm sure the U.S. attorney would be very interested in possibly removing the death penalty from the table, maybe even reducing your sentences. And I'm sure the government would very much like to know who you sold that information to from Mark Lindy's computer."

Clive said, "We don't know what happened to Mr. O'Rourke. I'll tell you, though, I think maybe he went off somewhere and had a heart attack. He was real intense, always impatient, always demanding. I saw him start shaking once in the courtroom, looked to me like the poor boy was about to fall apart. Do you know he threatened me? I laughed at him, because what could he do? I was already in jail."

Cindy said, "O'Rourke's a schmuck, no sense of humor. Clive's right, he's probably dead in a ditch somewhere of a heart attack. If he is, I sure won't miss him."

Eve said, "I guess you don't know Mickey O'Rourke's a great volleyball player with a serve like a bowling ball, and he can spike the ball down your tonsils. His wife tells him he's a killer, then she punches him, and he laughs. He's a nice guy, loves his daughters. Did you know he has two daughters, teenagers?"

Clive shrugged and began whistling.

Cindy continued to study Savich, but Eve knew she was well aware of her. She'd come out swinging at her, Eve thought, something she had to admire. *Well, then, time to go for it.*

Eve said, "I've wondered exactly what you did, Cindy. I mean, you had sex with Mark Lindy—it's your tried-and-true method, isn't it? And then Mark did most anything you wanted because he was so pleased with himself that this beautiful woman was sleeping with him, telling him he was a stud. Did he let you look over his shoulder while he worked on a classified government project, never suspecting you were writing all his user IDs and pass-words on your sleeve while you were cooing in his ear?

"And then you put him to sleep with a nice cocktail you made with your own little hands, a bit of Rohypnol with a knockout drug, didn't you? Poor Mark, he didn't have a clue that his sex goddess was knocking him out so she could get to his key fob to tunnel into his computer, and access all his data. I'll bet you called in Clive to help you with that part, didn't you? This is all really Clive's deal, isn't it, Cindy? He's the brain in your duo, right? He does the planning, makes the decisions, deals with the buyers, handles all the money, doles out spending money to you, his sex kitten?

"Do you even know who the buyers are?"

Cindy rose straight up, slammed her fist on the table, rattling her chains. "You bitch! I do the planning, I do everything, do you hear me?" Clive grabbed her hand. She shut up, even managed a twisted smile at Eve.

Nice start, Savich thought. Cindy Cahill looked like she very much wanted to kill Eve. The investigative train-ing the marshals were given at the marshals' academy at Glenco looked to be good; either that or Eve had learned a few things growing up with a marshal as a father. Prob-ably both.

Eve said, "Was it Clive who targeted Mark Lindy for you? Or did some foreign agent set you up with Lindy?

Did you know, Cindy, that those top secret materials were headed for a foreign government?"

Cindy Cahill didn't leap to the bait this time, but she couldn't keep the rage from her eyes. She tried on a sneer for size, but she couldn't mask the mad. "You're making up a story. The same story that ridiculous CIA operations officer told, too. Do all of you read off the same script?

"Listen up, little girl. What I mean is that Clive is my husband, my partner." She gave Clive Cahill an adoring look and patted his hand, making the chains rattle again. "He's my sweetie pie, not my boss, never my boss."

Eve arched an eyebrow, gave her a *yeah, right* look. "Your sweetie pie didn't mind you sleeping with Mark Lindy so long as there was a big payoff? Sorry, Cindy, but come on, now—that was your only role, wasn't it? That is, until something went wrong. What happened? Did Mark Lindy realize what you were doing and threaten to call the police? And so you gave him the last cocktail of his life?"

Cindy gave Eve a girl-to-girl smile. "In my experience, guys usually prefer beer."

Eve sat back in her chair. "That wasn't a bad comeback, Cindy, but maybe Clive could give you a cooler line, since he's smarter. *Hmm,* I wonder what your folks would think about how you've grown up, what you've finally done."

17

Cindy Cahill never looked away from Eve's face. "Since dear old Dad started coming to my bedroom when I was eleven years old, I don't think he'd care one way or the other."

Interesting, Savich thought. Did the shrinks know she'd been abused? He started to rein it back, since he didn't want the Cahills to demand their lawyer, but he wanted to see what Eve would say next. He gave her a small nod.

Eve said, "Clive, if it wasn't you running the show, what were you doing, anyway? Did Cindy have you fetch her coffee, slide her slippers on her dainty feet, make up her schedule of seduction for her?"

Clive was shaking his head, looking from his wife to Savich, then finally back at Eve.

Eve continued. "Then what is she doing with you, Clive? You're nearly old enough to be her father, aren't you, nearly as old as her father who abused her? Tell me the truth, now, Clive, I know it must be tucked in the back of your brain. You're afraid of her, aren't you? Afraid she'll tire of you, afraid she'll start seeing a guy who's younger than you? Afraid she'll take her chances and talk to us, leave you here by yourself on death row?"

Clive's pale face turned red. He yelled, heaving, he was so mad, "I am not afraid of her! She's my wife. She'd never do anything to hurt me! I'm the one who found her, who taught her everything—"

"Did you teach her how to kill? Probably not, since the scene at that murder was a mess, not well done of you at all. Poison doesn't always make a person just fall over and die. No, Mark Lindy fought when he realized what you'd done to him. He tried to take you down, but the poison got to him first, and it wasn't at all pretty, was it, Cindy? And that, Clive, led the police to both of you."

Cindy Cahill squeezed Clive's hand hard. "Don't you get all bent out of shape about anything, Clive. She's only trying to play you." She shook her head at them. "Aren't you two the cool team? How long have you worked this routine together? Have you ever had any luck with it?"

Eve sat forward now, clasped her hands in front of her. "Do you know, Cindy, one thing I'd never do is kill someone by poison. It's so—mean-spirited, cowardly, really, you know what I mean? And it's so tacky. So low-class. Give me a knife any day and let me face down the person I'm going to kill."

"I am not tacky!"

"No? Then what do you call using your body whenever Clive wants you to? Without the money, without the trappings, who would think you're worth any more than a fast in and out with a streetwalker against a wall in an alley?"

"You bitch! I'm not a whore. Sue thinks I'm perfect!"

Sue? Who is Sue? What is this?

Savich broke in, hard and fast. "And Sue is walking around outside in the sunshine while you two are on the road to a lethal injection. Was it Sue who tried to kill Judge Hunt?"

Cindy and Clive Cahill looked at each other again and pulled it together. Cindy studied her fingernails and sounded bored. "There is no Sue, it's a name I made up. As for Judge Hunt getting shot, I don't know any more than anyone else who saw the news on TV. I have no idea who shot him."

Eve said, "Come on, game's up, Cindy. Did Sue shoot Judge Hunt?"

"I'll tell you again—there is no Sue," Cindy said. "There wasn't even a reason for us to shoot the judge, was there?"

Savich said, "Are you so unimportant, Cindy, that Sue didn't even tell you why she wanted Judge Hunt dead?"

"There is no Sue," Cindy said yet again, calm as a stone now. "Like I already told you morons, why would we want the frigging judge dead? There's no payoff for us, you said so yourself. Me, I was sort of sorry to hear it. Judge Hunt was hot, the way he looked at me—" Her husband didn't say a word, only stared at the wall behind Savich's head. "I bet he doesn't look so hot now, does he?"

Eve wanted to leap over the table and punch her out. She forced herself to draw a deep breath instead.

Savich said, "Did Sue kill the prosecutor like you did Mark Lindy?"

Clive shrugged. "We don't know anything about the judge, and we don't know anything about the prosecutor. How could we? We're in jail, Agent Savich, not out drinking beer and dancing at clubs." He sat back in his chair and smirked. "That prosecutor, what a schmuck. O'Rourke would never have proven a case against us."

But Cindy was still enraged. "All the accusations—it's entrapment, nothing more. We didn't kill anyone—if that ridiculous judge hadn't stopped the trial, we would have been acquitted! Somebody else shot him—probably someone he put away." She turned to Clive. "You know what, darling? This has been fun, but we got to put an end to it. Agent Savich, we want our lawyer."

Eve wanted to kick herself. She'd been the one to screw it up, to push it too far.

Savich said as he rose, "I was hoping you two were behind the attempt on Judge Hunt's life, that you'd hired an assassin to kill him, with the help of your lawyer paying him from some offshore account we haven't found yet. Now I see that's impossible." He flattened his palms on the scarred table. "After spending some time with the two of you, the fact is I don't think either of you has the brains to pull it off by yourselves."

"We could do anything we wanted to," Clive shouted. "And what we want now is our lawyer!"

Eve rose and stared down at him, then at Cindy.

"Why don't you tell us about Sue? You really don't have to take the fall for her, not if she approached you, not if she's the go-between to sell the material you stole off Mark Lindy's computer."

Neither of them said a word.

Savich said, "Do you know Mark Lindy always liked to say he wasn't a wackadoodle, like Sheldon on *The Big Bang Theory*. He was more like Leonard, funny and kind?"

They looked at Savich blankly.

Savich shrugged. "Mark's sister Elaine said he readily admitted he was a nerd, and he'd laugh, say he loved Spock as much as the next nerd, but she said Mark knew he saw people more clearly, interacted with them more easily, than most nerds did. But he didn't see you clearly, did he, Cindy? And it cost him his life."

Still no word from either of them.

How had Savich known that? From the murder file, of course. Eve said, "Did this Sue tell you to poison him, Cindy? Clive? Did she watch you do it?"

Cindy said, her voice vicious, "There is no Sue, you little dyke."

Eve smiled at Cindy, turned to the door, and said over her shoulder, "You could be a model, Cindy, but not for much longer. Not if you stay in here."

"I wouldn't want to be a model. What idiot would want to live on yogurt and look like a refugee camp survivor?"

18

Savich and Eve walked into the FBI conference room on the thirteenth floor of the Federal Building a half-hour later, straight-up noon. Half a dozen FBI agents were seated around the long conference table along with Lieutenant Virginia Trolley and Lieutenant Delion of the SFPD, and the U.S. Marshal Carney Maynard. Savich gave a little finger wave to Sherlock and Harry, who were eating pizza out of the same box. Pepperoni, Savich knew; it was Sherlock's favorite.

There were stacked pizza boxes, a ton of paper napkins, and cans of soda scattered across the table. SAC Cheney Stone swallowed the last of his Hawaiian pineapple pizza slice and waved to them. "Come on in. Help yourselves, lots of pizza left, and probably still warm.

Savich, there's a couple of slices of veggie pizza for you if this crew hasn't scarfed them all down. Tell us how you made out with the Cahills."

Savich looked over at Marshal Maynard as he sat down. "Deputy Barbieri did an excellent job, sir, rattled them good. She got Cindy Cahill so angry she spit out a name—Sue. We're thinking she might be the operative who was the Cahills' handler."

"Sue?" Maynard said. "Sue is a foreign operative?"

Savich nodded at Eve as he picked up one of the three slices of Veggie Heaven pizza.

Eve said, "Well, Cindy implied she had a close— maybe an intimate—relationship with her, before she tried to deny that Sue exists."

Savich said, "Harry, you've been looking for their contact for months, haven't you?"

Harry said, "We thought there had to be someone working closely with them. Their backgrounds didn't fit high-level espionage. They've been talented grifters, that's all, who've been busy rolling drunks and using Cindy's charms to cheat some lonely men out of their money. This was way out of their league."

Savich nodded. "So now this Sue is our best bet for the one who made contact with the Cahills, maybe recruited them."

Cheney asked, "So this woman might be the shooter? You think the CIA knows about this and they didn't bother to tell us?"

"We can ask the CIA if they have a file on her," Harry said. "But so far the CIA hasn't even told us what it was the Cahills managed to steal. Only that it was in the area of cyber-security, quote/unquote. Maybe now we have something to trade them."

There were smiles around the table.

Eve said, "We might have gotten more out of them, but their survival instinct kicked in and they backpedaled like crazy and hollered for their lawyer." She sighed. "It was my fault, I handled it wrong, pushed them too hard."

Savich said, "You did good, Eve, lots better than Harry would have done. He'd have scared the crap out of them. This is good pizza, guys."

Sherlock, a slice of pepperoni pizza halfway to her mouth, said, "No last name? Only Sue, and Cindy Cahill just spit it out?"

Eve nodded.

Harry turned to Eve, his eyes narrowed. "What did you do? Swing your blond ponytail in Cindy's direction and watch her explode?"

"Close," Savich said.

Harry said, "Maybe she was making up the name Sue, playing you."

Eve could see he wasn't happy about having this sprung on him. He'd worked this case for more than a year, and he'd never gotten a name out of them.

Deal with it, Harry.

Eve took a big bite of her pizza slice. "Tell you what, Harry, you can listen to our recording of the interview, make up your own mind. Sorry there's no video showing my ponytail."

Cheney asked, "Harry, your team never came across this name Sue in your investigation?"

"No, and believe me, our agents"—he nodded to several agents across from him—"we checked through their known associates for months, in and out of jail. Clive Cahill isn't stupid. He's always used prepaid cell phones we can't trace to him, for example. If he was making contact with some foreign corporation or government or intelligence service, whatever, we have no record of it."

Ten-year veteran Agent Burt Seng said, "The whole operation was skillfully done until the Cahills screwed up and ended up with a dead body on their hands, and got caught. To get any of the confidential information off Mark Lindy's encrypted computer, somebody in the operation had to know a good deal about the information security system Lindy used to access the project he was working on. Not only his user IDs and passcodes, but enough about the access algorithms and the project itself to know what was valuable and how to get to it without alerting the security oversight team."

Savich said, "It means this Sue was super-careful. She had to pay the Cahills some upfront money, but you haven't been able to find any stashed funds, right?"

"Not a dime," Burt Seng said. "This 'Sue' name, though"—he turned to Agent Griffin Hammersmith—"you ever hear of a foreign spy with the name Sue?"

Griffin shook his head. "I'm thinking it's got to be a code name. Maybe it isn't even a woman, who knows?"

Eve said, "Cindy didn't shout it out like it was a code

name. It sounded like she knew this Sue person, and well."

Cheney was tapping his pen on the tabletop. "Savich, you agree with Barbieri?"

Savich said, "Yes."

Cheney said, "I'll call the CIA operations officers who worked on the Cahills' case, see if they recognize it."

Savich said, "I'm thinking I might throw out Sue's name to Siles, see his reaction, see if he recognizes the name. I told the guard not to let either Clive or Cindy Cahill have any phone calls until after we visit Siles today."

Cheney said, "Okay, let's shift gears for the moment." He turned to Agent Seng. "Burt has been waiting to give us follow-up on what he and Sherlock found out about that Zodiac Judge Hunt saw."

Burt Seng wiped his hands on a napkin, then clicked on the overhead to show a Google map of Sea Cliff. He pointed. "Judge Hunt's house is there on the point of land. You can see there are big boulders scattered all over the beach. Since Judge Hunt told us about the Zodiac, we can forget about whether the shooter drove down Sea Cliff Avenue, parked his car or motorcycle near China Beach Park, and made his way down to the beach." Burt grinned. "Man or woman, this Sue came in by water.

"If you've ever been on an inflatable with an outboard motor, you know it's capable of speed. He could have motored the Zodiac right up to the beach. He didn't care if Judge Hunt saw the Zodiac, since he planned to kill him. He walked around the ocean side of the bluff and positioned himself in the mess of thick rocks that stud the beach." He nodded to Sherlock as he put the photo of the Zodiac on the overhead.

"Now, a female Sue adds a new wrinkle to this," Sherlock said, "since Mrs. Moe, the owner of Bay Outings in Sausalito, says she rented a Zodiac to a man at two o'clock on Thursday afternoon under the name Bently Ames."

Burt said, "Mrs. Moe never questioned it was a man. She described him well. Here's our sketch." He projected the drawing on the overhead and passed around a sketch of a man described as five-foot-nine or -ten, on the slender side, wearing loose jeans, sneakers, an oversized blue Windbreaker, dark opaque sunglasses, and a Giants baseball cap.

"Bently Ames never took off the sunglasses or the cap. He had a flat voice, Mrs. Moe said, no particular regional accent she could identify. He was polite, paid with an AmEx. He needed the Zodiac only one day, wanted to do an evening run on the bay with his girlfriend, who'd grown up on Zodiacs in Hawaii, he told her. She remembered he was wearing a big honker diamond ring on his pinkie finger, could have been fake, she didn't know, but why would a man wear a fake diamond? Again, Mrs. Moe didn't question this was a man. She thought he was middle-aged, maybe even older.

"Now, Bently Ames returned the Zodiac Friday morning right on time. Mrs. Moe said they didn't even have to wash it down, it was so squeaky clean."

Sherlock picked it up. "We had our forensic team scour the Zodiac for any sort of evidence anyway, but like Burt said, Bently Ames was thorough in his cleaning, so we don't have anything."

Burt said, "We'll show this photo of the Zodiac he or she rented to Judge Hunt, see if he can positively identify it. That's unlikely, though, since Zodiacs look similar, for the most part."

Sherlock said, "We found the real Bently Ames in his Tiburon real estate office. He said his wallet wasn't missing. We asked him to check. Turns out his wallet was in his pocket, but his AmEx was gone. He said he'd had dinner with his sister at Guymas, a Tiburon restaurant on the water, on Wednesday evening. Then he remembered that after he paid the bill, he'd stopped in the men's room. He said there were maybe four guys in there using the facilities but for the life of him he couldn't remember anything unusual. Then he stopped cold, said a guy bumped into him in the small hallway outside the restroom."

"Bingo," Virginia Trolley said. "Was he wearing sunglasses and a ball cap?"

Burt nodded. "Yep, a Giants baseball cap. Again, Mr. Ames described him as a man.

"Since Sue had to park someplace, we checked the parking lot closest to Guymas first," Sherlock said. "No luck. We didn't think he'd use the parking lot next to the Tiburon Theater and take a chance of being seen, but we checked anyway."

Sherlock said, "The parking lot attendant in the big lot sits in a booth and takes the money." She gave a big grin. "Guess what?"

"He did park there," Harry said. "And the parking attendant noticed a license plate? Please? Please?"

"Nope, but this little freckle-faced kid struts out of the booth in his loose low-rider jeans and tells us sure, he remembered the dude, remembered the sunglasses and the baseball cap. Then Freckle-face told us he knew for sure it wasn't a rental, since it was a butt-ugly old Dodge Charger, with red paint chipping off. Unfortunately, no license plate, but Freckle-face did say it was a California license."

Cheney turned to Agent Griffin Hammersmith. "Griffin has been coordinating with the highway patrol and the local police departments to try to locate that vehicle. He's also got more news for us."

Sherlock thought Griffin Hammersmith was saved from being too pretty by his nose. It was off-kilter, probably broken when he was a kid. As for his eyes, they were bluer than hers. She wondered if he was used to women trying to chase him down. He said in his slow, melodic voice, "I tried to put myself in the shooter's shoes. If I came to San Francisco to murder a federal judge, I'd want to draw as little attention to myself as possible. I'd probably want to stay outside the city, unless I had to be there. And I wouldn't stay anywhere near where I was going to snatch a credit card, like from Bently Ames in Tiburon. So, south of the city, probably near a major highway. A nice enough place but not big or fancy.

"So that's where we focused. And after a couple of hours of phone calls, we found a small boutique inn off Highway 280 near Atherton, called Pelican Eave. The manager remembered the man, and the car. Yep, the same car the parking attendant described to us. 'Overdue to be traded in,' she said. She said he introduced himself as James Connor and he always wore his sunglasses and ball cap—though she remembered it as an Oakland A's cap—even when he drank tea by himself in the front parlor. Since he paid in cash upfront, for two weeks, she never asked to see any identification. A pity.

"We have agents out there surveilling the inn. She hasn't seen him since Thursday, the day of the shooting.

"We've got an APB out for the car as we speak, and his drawing and description at the local airports and all the cop shops in the Bay Area. I don't think we'll find him anywhere close to Atherton."

Sherlock looked at Agent Griffin Hammersmith. "Why?"

"It's my opinion he's not about to take the risk of going back to the Pelican Eave." Griffin cleared his throat. "Well, I'll bet this guy is alarmed. I mean, he knows now Judge Hunt is alive, and if he wants to try again he has to stay in the area. He also knows it's riskier for him now, and I think he might dump the old Charger and stay closer this time, more in the center of things, where he can blend in with the tourists. If I were this guy or this gal, I might change how I look and stay at one of the dozens of small hotels and motels on Lombard Street or at Fisherman's Wharf." Griffin splayed his hands. "This is all a guess, guys, so—"

Harry laughed. "And your point would be, Griffin? Your so-called guesses are almost always right."

Griffin said, "The thing is, though, our guy—or this Sue—has been in and out of San Francisco for at least a week, maybe longer. That's long enough to learn how to keep out of sight.

"We've got agents canvassing the hotels starting on Lombard and at Fisherman's Wharf, with his drawing. Thanks to Lieutenant Trolley, we've got us a half-dozen SFPD to help." He nodded to her, and Virginia said, "Our pleasure."

Harry sighed. "I'm wondering why don't you just tell us which hotel Sue's staying at, Griff, so we wouldn't have to waste all this time?"

This time everyone laughed.

Now that he'd seen Griffin Hammersmith in action, Savich was wondering if he could get him to relocate to Washington. He bit into the last slice of Veggie Heaven, now cold, and said, "Honestly, I don't think putting that drawing through the facial recognition program will get us anything, what with the ball cap and sunglasses."

Cheney said, "Maybe we'll get lucky and Sue will drop the ball cap; then we could try the FRP. One last note: We still don't have anything about our missing prosecutor, Mickey O'Rourke. We've talked to his prosecution team, his co-workers, his family, his friends. We have him on camera leaving the Federal Building by himself late Thursday morning, though he never told anyone in his office he was going out. We're examining his phone records, his credit card bills, but as of yet we don't have anything very helpful. His wife, as you can imagine, is a mess.

"Her name's Melissa. She told us Mickey had seemed distracted the last week or so, but he wouldn't tell her what was wrong. She did remember he kept asking his two daughters where they were going and when they'd be home every time they stepped out of the door, which makes it sound like O'Rourke was frightened. Because of the Cahills or this Sue? We don't know if he skipped or if he was taken by someone, but the longer he's gone, the worse it looks."

19

Agent Dane Carver studied the young man sitting opposite him and Agent Ruth Warnecki Noble in one of the small interview rooms on the third floor of the Hoover Building. Ted Moody was bouncing his leg up and down, and kept his eyes on his bouncing leg, as if afraid if he looked them in the eyes they'd shoot him.

Dane sat with his arms crossed over his chest, his expression hard. "You don't look like a street punk, Mr. Moody, but I've been wrong before. How long have you been doing crap like this?"

The young guy flinched, raised his head, his eyes blinking furiously. "I didn't do anything wrong, not really. I mean, I don't know why those agents came and forced me to come with them. I have to get to work or Mr. Garber will fire me."

Ruth said, "I spoke to Mr. Garber, told him you were assisting us, so your job is safe. But you did do something you shouldn't have done."

Dane said, "It's called a felony, and you're a criminal, Mr. Moody."

"No, I'm not, sir, Agent, I'm not a criminal. Maybe you think—no, I—nothing I did was wrong."

Ruth leaned over the table, put her hand over his and smoothed it out. He had long, slender fingers and fairly clean fingernails today, but his hand was moist with sweat, he was so afraid, mostly of Dane, who looked perfectly ready to shove his tonsils into his sneakers. *Good.* "Ted—may I call you Ted?"

He whispered, "My mama calls me Teddy even though I'm grown up and even have my own apartment now, since last April, over on Washburn Street. It's not much, but I pay the rent on it all by myself, and I've got a bed and a couch and a TV."

"Teddy, then," Ruth said in the same gentle voice she used with her eldest stepson when he lost a ball game. "We really need your help. We need to know who hired you to deliver that envelope into the Hoover Building and recite that story to the security guards."

"But I don't know, I mean—is it national security?"

Dane opened his mouth to blast him again, but Ruth gave him a look she made sure Teddy saw, and Dane made do with a silent message to Teddy: *Fear me.*

Ruth kept touching Teddy's hands, kept her voice gentle. "Teddy, was it a man or a woman who gave you the envelope?"

Teddy shot a look at Dane, grabbed Ruth's hand like a lifeline. "All right, ma'am, I'll tell you. It was a man. Look, I really needed money because I lost most of my pay in a poker game and I didn't want to have to ask my mom to help me with the rent. He offered me two crisp one-hundred-dollar bills, and all I had to do was deliver that envelope here. I didn't have to run over anybody or break any laws, nothing like that, which I wouldn't do anyway."

Ruth beamed at him, patted his hand. "Tell us about this man. What did he look like? Was he young, old?"

Teddy leaned really close to Ruth. "I never saw him, I swear."

Bummer. Both Dane and Ruth knew he was telling the truth, so there was no reason for Dane to pound the table and yell at him.

"Then how do you know it was a man, moron?" Dane asked him, sitting forward.

"He sounded like a man on the phone. I mean, why would a woman do something like that? Really, he sounded like a man—honest."

Dane said, "All right, then tell us how you happened to connect with him."

Teddy said, "You know I work at the Union Seventy-six gas station over on Bowner Avenue. Mr. Garber hired me because I'm real good at figuring out what's wrong with a car, so anyway, this guy called me on my cell phone—said he'd seen me work, said he'd heard people say they could count on me, that I was reliable." Teddy Moody tried not to puff up, but he did. "Really, ma'am,

Agent ma'am, I don't know anything about him, but he said he knew I was good to the bone, and he surely admired responsible young people like me, that's what he told me, exactly. My mama's always telling me I was good, but you can't always believe your mama."

And that made all the difference, Dane thought. It was strange logic, but he understood it. A nerdy twenty-year-old kid with one shining skill and the guy had the brain to praise him, drew him right in. That was clever.

"So then he told me what he wanted me to do, and I didn't see anything wrong with it, I swear I didn't."

Ruth said, "He called you only once?"

Teddy nodded.

"Did he tell you his name?"

"I asked him who he was, and he laughed. He said people used to call him the Hammer, but his name didn't matter. He told me he would mail me an envelope inside another envelope, and in the second envelope there'd be two one-hundred-dollar bills and a script—that's what he called it, 'my script'—and all I had to do was tell the security guards in the lobby exactly what he'd written on the script."

"And that was, exactly?"

Teddy closed his eyes and repeated word for word the conversation Ruth and Dane had heard on the security tape.

"That's very impressive, Teddy," Ruth told him.

"The Hammer told me to practice the script in front of the mirror until I had it memorized and it sounded all natural, and so I did. That was all, Agent ma'am, I swear." Teddy's eyes shimmered with tears. "He promised I couldn't get into trouble. He said it was only a joke on this Agent Dillon Savich. He said no one would ever even find out who I was. How could they? I'm a law-abiding person, and I could just walk out. I believed him. I was in this knot of tourists and everything happened like he said it would. I simply slipped back into the crowd when the guards were talking about the envelope." He dropped his head again, studied his hands. "I wanted to believe him, you know? I mean, I really did walk out and nobody said a word to me. And there were the two brand-new hundred-dollar bills—I really needed that money. What was in that envelope? Was it bad?"

Ruth said, "Yes, very bad. The Hammer wasn't trying to help you out, Teddy, and deep down, you knew that, didn't you?"

Teddy swallowed. He looked scared and miserable. "Yeah, I worried about it, Agent ma'am, but it was two hundred bucks and I didn't think it could be that bad. I mean, it was only a dippy white envelope, nothing lumpy in it, like a bomb or anything. I'm sorry, I really am." He looked from one to the other. "Am I in real bad trouble?"

The kid looked so scared Dane hoped he wouldn't pee his pants. He said, "Let's see if you can redeem yourself. Agent Warnecki asked you if the guy sounded young, older, or really old. Tell us what you can and we'll see."

Teddy's head snapped up, hope beaming out of his eyes. "He sounded—well, I never knew my pa or my grandpa, never had either one of those, though I guess everyone has to, even if they've never met them, right?"

Ruth smiled. "So he sounded what, forty? Sixty? Eighty?"

"In the middle, I guess."

"Did he have an accent?"

Teddy shook his head. "No, he didn't sound like anything I recognized, and his voice was kind of raspy, you know, like a longtime smoker's voice, not very deep, but scratchy, like I said."

"Do you have the script the Hammer sent you?"

Teddy shook his head. "I'm sorry. He told me as soon as I memorized it I had to burn it, and so I did. It sounded kind of neat, you know? Kind of like I was a spy or something, and so I borrowed Mr. Garber's Redskins lighter and burned it out in back of the station."

Dane pushed over a sheet of blank paper. "Was the script written in pencil or pen, or on a computer?"

"He handwrote it—a pen. It was black ink."

Dane pulled out his pen and handed it to Teddy. "I want you to copy his handwriting the best you can. Write the script down as close to the way it looked. Take your time, Teddy. This is very important."

Dane's unspoken message this time was *Do it well and I might let you live.* After five minutes Dane and Ruth studied the script. The lettering was cramped and slanted really far to the right, like the Hammer had fisted the pen and written nearly upside down. A left-hander? Or someone who was trying to deceive?

Dane said, "Not bad," and Teddy looked suddenly like he might survive.

Ruth said, "Now, Teddy, I want you to write down everything the Hammer said to you when he called you on your cell, from beginning to end. I know it's been a couple of days. Do the best you can."

Teddy scrunched up his face and labored. After another five minutes he had written phrases, some single words, and some complete sentences, enough for them to see exactly how he drew the kid in.

Ruth said, "Think a moment, Teddy. What was your impression of the Hammer? What I mean by that is what did you think while you spoke to him? Did he frighten you? Did he make you laugh? Was he sincere? Did you believe him?"

Teddy fiddled with Dane's pen as he thought about this. Finally, he said, "He sounded like I always thought my daddy would sound if I'd ever known him."

Good enough, Ruth thought. Confident, probably some hardnose expecting obedience, and he'd gotten it from Teddy Moody.

Teddy said, "I didn't think you'd ever find me. I mean, I know there are cameras everywhere, but I've never even been arrested for anything, and why would anyone in the lobby know me? The Hammer told me you'd never find me, since I was just another tourist. See? I wrote that down, right there." And he pointed. "How did you find me?"

Dane said, "An agent who watched the security video saw something black under a couple of your fingernails.

Once we enlarged your hands, we saw it was something thick and oily. We had photos of you. All we did was show them around some of the gas stations and body shops in the area. There aren't that many. We found you on the third try."

Teddy Moody blinked. He looked from Ruth to Dane and back again. "That is so cool," he said simply. "I'd sure like to do stuff like that."

Ruth smiled at him as she patted his shoulder. "You're still too young, Teddy, but maybe in ten years or so, if you don't take any more money from strangers, you could try out."

Dane leaned over the table close to his ear. "You better keep your poker game stake at fifty bucks, Teddy, no higher. You don't want any more Hammers searching you out. If something had gone wrong, believe me, he would have slit your throat and walked away, whistling."

Teddy looked like he was going to faint. "But you're not going to arrest me or anything, are you, Agent sir?"

"Not this time," Dane said.

Teddy gave both Dane and Ruth a blazing smile. "I got rent money and I won't have to go to jail, either. What a great day."

Ruth and Dane's eyes met when the elevator doors closed on Teddy Moody and the security guard who was escorting him from the Hoover Building. They both smiled.

"That's one lucky kid," Dane said. "And so are we. I have an idea where to look for this guy."

20

Harry carefully steered his Shelby into a parking space in the California Street garage of the Mason Building, which housed Milo Siles's law firm. He looked over at Eve. "Savich told me he hates driving that rental car, says it hurts his soul."

Eve laughed, flipped her hand one way, then the other. "Well, red Porsche, uck-tan rental—tough choice."

Harry cut the engine, fiddled with his keys. "Congratulations, by the way, on what happened with Cindy and Clive. You did good."

"It was Dillon who told me to rattle her. I'll tell you, though, when she spit out Sue I nearly fainted."

Harry fiddled some more with his keys. "I guess I never made her mad enough. Yeah, I scared her, but she never stopped trying to play me, and all the while Clive sat back and grinned like a fathead, and watched her work me over. What she did to the other agents who interviewed her was just as sad." He hit his fist hard against the steering wheel, then looked closely to see if he'd done any damage. Luckily, he hadn't. What, Eve wondered, would he do if he'd wounded his baby?

He looked out the window, watched Savich pull the uck-tan Taurus into a parking slot. "I'd like to have been there when she lost it."

Eve grinned. "She claimed right away she'd made it up, then she tried to provoke me back. She's really pretty good at it. What I liked best was when she asked me what I'd do with a difficult man, like Savich. He'd turned her off, you see, and she saw he wasn't interested, and couldn't stand it."

"You can tell me later how you answered that," Harry said, getting out of the Shelby. He said to her over the roof of the car, "But none of that means you need to be along on this interview."

She tilted her head, swinging her ponytail, and one of her eyebrows went straight up. "What? You don't want my incredible brain at work on Milo Siles? Hey, he might spit out Sue's name, too. How can you afford to miss out on that chance?"

Harry was being a dog in the manger. He knew it and wanted to punch himself out. He sighed and stepped away to join Savich.

Savich said, "I like the Shelby, Harry, it oozes style. How do you like driving a stick in San Francisco?"

"Newbies around here tend to pray hard when they have to stop on a steep incline, but not us old-timers. All we old-timers ever worry about is how often we have to buy new tires."

Eve poked him in the ribs. "You're telling me you never pray when you're stopped dead on one of those Pacific Heights inclines?"

He shook his head and gave a tug on her ponytail. "I guess you drive a wuss automatic."

"And I'm proud of it."

"Siles's law firm has the entire eighteenth floor," Savich said. "There are a total of ten equity partners, a gazillion assistants, lawyers, and secretaries on salary. I verified Siles is in, but I didn't make an appointment; better to catch him by surprise. It seems a lot of folk work on Saturdays, including Silas's secretary. Harry, this guy knows you very well. Eve, how about you?"

"The Cahills' trial is the first time I saw him in federal court. I doubt he'll recognize me. I always sat in the back of the courtroom."

"Harry, any advice?"

"He's fast on his feet, and trying to pin him is like nailing Jell-O to a tree."

Savich grinned. "We're here to try anyway. Harry, Cheney says you do contempt and scorn really well. Feel free. A little fear couldn't hurt, either. Eve, go with your gut, depending on how he reacts to you."

"And what will you do, Dillon?" Eve asked, as she swung her black bag over her shoulder.

He thought about that for a moment. "If you guys leave any blanks, I'll try to fill them in."

They were greeted on the eighteenth floor by a stylish

young woman with dark hair, the only receptionist manning the large, curving mahogany counter on this fine Saturday.

Savich looked at her name badge, smiled, and showed her his creds. "Alicia, we'd like to see Mr. Siles."

Alicia drew back, alarmed. "Do you have an appointment, Agent? Ah, Special Agent?"

Savich said, his smile warm, "We don't need one. Isn't that handy?"

She looked at Harry, then at Eve. "Who are you?"

Eve and Harry showed her their creds.

"But—"

"Point us to his office, Alicia."

They followed her along a wide hallway with polished wooden floors to the end office, both Savich and Harry admiring her red power suit, her stiletto heels, and her walk. Eve poked Harry in the ribs.

Before Alicia could precede them into Siles's office, Savich gently pushed her to the side and opened the door himself. "Thank you, Alicia. Please hold his calls and any clients that show up."

Milo Siles shot to his feet when the three of them walked into his bragging-rights corner office with its magnificent San Francisco Bay view. The fog had burned off earlier, and it was a postcard day, warm by San Francisco late-fall standards, in the upper sixties.

Milo liked hypermodern, Harry saw, like his own ex-wife. Show Nessa any piece of furniture that combined glass and chrome in a weird shape, and she'd embrace it, while Harry hunched over with a belly cramp.

Savich introduced the three of them to Siles.

Siles said, "I recognize Deputy Barbieri. She sat at the back of the courtroom during our very short trial. I didn't know you were a marshal. I pegged you as a TV reporter.

"Of course I also know Special Agent Christoff. I believe I've seen him perhaps too many times." He looked hard at Savich. "You, however, I've never seen before. You're not with the local FBI, are you?"

Savich shook his head. "I'm from Washington."

"What may I do for the three of you?"

Somehow, Eve thought, Savich knew it should be she who answered, and he gave her a small nod. She said, smiling at Siles, who, even in his lifts, was a good three inches shorter than she was, "Cindy told us about Sue, but she forgot to give us a last name. Could you please provide that, sir?"

Savich wouldn't have seen the flash of horrified recognition in Siles's eyes if he hadn't been watching him closely.

Gotcha.

Siles paled a bit, too, if Savich wasn't mistaken, but for only an instant. Then Siles turned his back on them, got himself together, and said over his shoulder, "Would any of you like a glass of water?"

They all declined.

Milo Siles drank, or pretended to, then sat behind his impressive glass desk framed with a beautiful dark wood that looked like it should be on the endangered list. Black paraphernalia was set precisely on the top of the desk—a computer, a phone, a fancy black desk set that looked like an expensive Christmas present from someone who didn't know what else to buy for him but didn't want to cheap out.

Siles waved them to chairs. There were only two. Without hesitation, Eve fetched another chair. She noticed that all the chairs were lower than Siles's, so he could, quite literally, look down on them. She remembered clearly her father telling her once, "You don't have to hunt for red buttons to push with short guys. And short guys wearing lifts are the easiest of all."

Eve glanced at Siles and saw from his look that he seemed to have downgraded her to gofer, a pretty girl with no particular importance, even though she was a deputy marshal. And so she said to him, her voice deferential, "I have to tell you, sir, I admired watching you sparring with the prosecutor. O'Rourke didn't have a chance against you even though he's probably a good eight inches taller than you and doesn't have to sit on a stack of books."

Bravo, Savich thought.

Whatever Siles would have said stuck in his throat. He turned red, then yelled, "I do not sit on a pile of books!"

Harry said, his voice lazy, "Come on, now, Deputy Barbieri, no reason to insult him. I'll bet his dad was short, so what could he expect? It's not very nice to rub his nose in it. Look at his office. He's a very successful man. He could probably convince the devil to buy charcoal for a barbecue."

Siles tented his fingers, regarded each of them in

silence, smoothing himself out. "You're all quite good. But these insults, they're rather immature, don't you think? I'm a busy man. What can I do for you?"

"Tell us about Sue," Savich said.

"I heard about your interview with my clients without my being present," Siles said. "I don't care that they told you it was all right, because it's not. If that happens again, I'll take it up with the court."

Savich said, "It seems to me a big part of the court is missing, and another part has been shot. So I'll repeat what Deputy Barbieri asked you for, a last name. We know Sue is very likely an agent of a foreign government. Attorney-client privilege won't protect you for long from Homeland Security and the CIA if you're abetting espionage against the United States."

Siles said easily, "Isn't there an old song about Sue? I wonder why Cindy mentioned a girl named Sue?" And he laughed.

Savich said, "Because Sue is involved, a go-between. The Cahills' handler. She probably hired the Cahills to help her get the classified documents from Mark Lindy's computer, or maybe the Cahills looked her up when they realized what they had. I'm sure you can tell us how this all worked. You don't want to be tried for treason, Mr. Siles."

Milo Siles sat forward, clasped his hands atop the huge black desk pad. "I have never heard either of the Cahills mention a woman named Sue. I don't know personally who this Sue might be, well, unless she was referring to my wife. There is no question of treason or of selling any of Mark Lindy's computer data to anyone. The Cahills were being tried for murder, not treason." He sat back, grinned at them. "My wife, by the way, is a bitch, and I'm taking steps to see she won't be my wife for much longer. Trust me, I'd hardly be involved in some conspiracy with her."

His desk phone rang, and Siles picked it up, listened, and said, "I'll be there in a few minutes." He set the phone gently back into the receiver. "Poor Alicia. I'm a busy man, even on Saturday. She was afraid to put through the call. Are we done here?"

"And here I thought we've only just started," Eve said.

Milo Siles looked amused. He studied Eve Barbieri's very pretty face, her blond hair whipped back into a ponytail, showing off her well-shaped ears that sported small gold studs. Her red leather jacket was open, show-ing her black turtleneck. "When I first noticed you in the courtroom, Deputy, I thought you were real cute, all bouncy and clean like some of the female TV anchors, all tits and no brains, a girl next door every guy dreams about marrying. But let me be honest here. You're not in Cindy Cahill's league. She makes men forget their names from twenty feet away. She'd have no reason to be dis-turbed by your looks, such as they are. And you're what, five, six years older than she is?"

She's got him taking shots at her, Harry thought. *Good work.*

Eve smiled at him. "I guess that'd place me closer to Clive's age, like I could hook up with him and it wouldn't look quite so obscene. Is that what you were thinking, sir?"

She watched him quickly rethink his approach. She saw when he'd decided how to deal with her, all in about two seconds. Siles had defended some of the smarmiest, most dangerous people on the planet, drug dealers, extortionists, and murderers. Few people could shake him.

Savich could, maybe, but she? To him she was nothing more than a fly buzzing around him.

Siles said, "Who cares about ages, Deputy? They're a loving couple. Wouldn't you say you're being rather sexist?"

Eve shook her head. "Not me. You want to know what I think? I think Cindy drives the bus and Clive has been expendable for a while now. I looked at him and wondered how long it would take before she dumps him. Not that she'll get the chance now. I mean, she's never getting out of prison unless she talks to us, right?"

"I have a client waiting outside—" He looked down at his Piaget watch. "Do either of you gentlemen have anything to say, because I'm finished talking with Ms. Ponytail here—Deputy Marshal, ah, what did you say your name was?"

Savich said smoothly, "Mr. Siles, why don't you tell us what you think about Federal Prosecutor Mickey O'Rourke's disappearance."

"I don't know anything about it, Agent Savich. How could I? Mickey has never shared his emotional sensitivities with me. I did hear through the grapevine that he was having an affair with a law clerk last year, though I don't know if that has anything to do with this. Look. I know people are starting to get alarmed, since Mickey hasn't showed up anywhere. I'm as concerned as anyone else." He paused for a minute. "We all noticed he was behaving pretty strangely in the pretrial hearings, like ignoring Judge Hunt's direct orders to hand over needful documents so I could give my clients the best defense. I chalked all his balking up to the intense cutthroat competition in the federal prosecutor's office finally getting to him. They have about a hundred federal prosecutors, and they're always jockeying for position. Did you know the prosecutors themselves keep actual records of their wins, who gets the toughest prison sentences in the least amount of time for the least cost? This is a death penalty case, and Mickey was going to have to convince a jury without using any of that classified information, information I'll bet he couldn't even access himself, information he either couldn't or wouldn't turn over to me. Can you imagine the stress?

"I think when Judge Hunt finally called him on the carpet, O'Rourke panicked. Once he failed to show up in chambers without a good reason, his career was over. I wouldn't be surprised if Mickey took off, and kept going."

Siles smiled and sat back in his chair, his fingers laced over his Italian vest, obviously pleased with himself.

Eve said, "You said your wife's name was Sue. It isn't, sir. It's Marjorie. Her middle name isn't Sue, either, it's Ann. And she's divorcing you, sir, not the other way around. I understand finances are the big bone of contention between you. Seems you have reasons to feel stressed yourself."

Siles looked momentarily poleaxed, then wiped the look off his face. "Didn't think you'd know that," he said slowly.

"Yes, sir, I do. Why did you make that up?"

"A joke, Deputy, only a small joke." Siles looked at his Piaget again, and rose.

Savich said, "It's not a joke that Mrs. Siles's divorce attorney plans to strip you down to your boxers. With those very embarrassing photos they say they have, I'm wagering you know you're going to need a lot of money soon."

Harry picked it up. "And what better way to get it than to join in a little conspiracy and earn a couple of million getting the Cahills off?"

"I'd like all of you to leave now," Siles said.

Savich paused in the doorway. "I'm sure if we find your offshore accounts, Marjorie will be very interested. She'll probably help us any way she can when we tell her you're colluding in selling information to a foreign government."

Before he closed the door, Eve said over her shoulder, "So many bad things can happen in federal prisons, Mr. Siles, you know that. And a lawyer who defends traitors, who's maybe a traitor himself? Can you begin to imagine what would happen to you? I can't see you defending yourself that well in prison." She paused, turned back to him, and gave him her card. "Think about it. Call me."

Siles found himself taking her card. He said nothing, watched her blond ponytail swing as she walked out his office door in those kick-ass boots. He walked to his desk and picked up his phone to dial his divorce lawyer. He'd have had his bigmouthed wife, Marjorie, killed months ago, easy enough back then, before the spotlight. It was only his two sons, both of them now taller than he was, who had kept her alive. He'd waited too long for that now.

21

Morphine-induced euphoria was a fine thing indeed, but Ramsey didn't want to cruise around in oblivion anymore. It left his brain fuzzed and stupid, not at all what he wanted now that Molly and Emma were coming to see him. Without drugs he was better able to cast about his brain to figure out who had shot him. Had someone picked out a judge with a certain reputation, or was it something about him, specifically?

And then there was the other big question: What had happened to Mickey O'Rourke?

Ramsey felt an ache building behind his left eye, and he gritted his teeth against the pain. He looked up to see Emma and Molly standing at the entrance to his cubicle. He felt a leap of pleasure and set himself to forget about his chest and his headache.

He called to them, "No need to tiptoe, I'm not

zombied out on drugs. In fact, I'm doing so well the SICU nurses and doctors don't want me around any longer. They need my bed for someone who really needs to be here, not a slacker like me. They're going to move me very soon now to the biggest private room in the hospital. They call it the Taj—can you imagine? They're gathering the troops right now." He didn't mention the long conference at his bedside that morning with Dr. Kardak and Marshal Maynard, debating the pros and cons of moving him. There was too much traffic through the ICU to suit the security team, and too many interruptions by law enforcement to suit the nurses and the medical staff. They had compromised by agreeing he would leave the ICU a bit early, for a secure room on one of the inpatient floors, with an extra staff nurse assigned to him.

He said, "Come here, Emma, and give me a big hug."

She ran to him, drew up short. Was she afraid to touch him? Probably so. She studied his face as she reached out her hand and lightly laid her fingertips on his forearm. When she realized his eyes were clear and focused on her, she seemed to accept that he wasn't lying to her because she was a kid. "If they're going to move you away from all these machines, it for sure means you're getting better." She moved her fingers to hover over his whiskered cheek.

"I don't want to hurt you, Daddy."

He grinned up at her. "Nah, no chance of that. Do you remember a long time ago when I told you I was tough and you could always count on me? Forever?"

She swallowed, nodded.

"Nothing's changed, Emma. I'm still the same. There's nothing here your old man can't handle."

He knew even a small movement might hurl him into a well of pain, but he raised his hand to gently stroke her face. Slowly, Emma leaned down and hugged him. "Doesn't it hurt to lie on your back?"

"Not much. They wrapped me up like a mummy. Don't be afraid, Emma. Everything is all right now."

But how could everything be all right? Emma wondered. Whoever had shot her father was still out there, and he might try again. Would there be guards around him forever?

Emma said, "Officer Hughes told us he heard you laugh this morning. He said it was a good sign."

He'd laughed? He couldn't remember. Ramsey had probably been riding the morphine express to LaLa Land and heard a nurse say something funny, or not funny at all, it wouldn't matter.

"There you go," he said, looking over at Molly, who cocked her head toward Emma and nodded. She was pleased he was finally getting some alone time with his daughter. Emma's fingers stroked his face, as light as butterfly wings.

He said, "Your mom told me you're keeping a close eye on Cal and Gage in case she gets so worried about me she forgets to feed them. I tried to think what Gage would do if food didn't magically appear whenever he wanted some. It wasn't a pretty picture."

Emma laughed. "They'd both go next door to Mr.

Sproole's house and out-cute each other so he'd clean out his refrigerator for them."

Ramsey laughed along with her and managed to hug her again, though the pain in the back of his chest spiked. Pain tasted foul, he thought, not for the first time, and how odd was it that you could actually taste pain? It wasn't coppery, like blood. Maybe like rotted asparagus? He said, "I know Mr. Sproole is an ice-cream junkie; he's always got some in his freezer. Do you think he'd break out his chocolate-chip cookie dough ice cream for Gage and Cal?"

"No, that's his favorite. He'd give them an old carton of vanilla. They'd be happy enough with that." She settled herself on the bed beside him, still clutching his hand like a lifeline. "Sean was over at our house this morning, playing with Gage and Cal while I was practicing. When I finished a piece he tapped me on the shoulder. He was real serious and polite, Dad. He said he still wanted to marry me, and even though he would have three wives he could promise me that I'd be his number one wife, since I was older than his other two. He said if I agreed, I couldn't date any other boys until he grew up and came to fetch me." Emma giggled.

A laugh spurted out of Ramsey's mouth. He couldn't help it, though it made him groan. He breathed slowly in and out, and when the pain settled into a steady throb again, he asked, "So what did you say about being Sean's number one wife?"

"Sean wasn't done. He asked me if I wanted a big wedding. When I told him I probably would, he said he was going to have to get three jobs, since both Marty and Georgie wanted big weddings, too."

Emma looked thoughtful. "Maybe two other wives would be good, since they could keep Sean company while I was practicing, or away playing somewhere."

His practical girl. And that twinkle in her eyes. It wouldn't have occurred to her to dismiss a five-year-old boy and make him feel small. Lucky Sean. Ramsey said, "I wouldn't be surprised if Sean grew up to be as cool as his daddy."

"And his mama."

"And his mama. Trouble is, your Aunt Sherlock told me she doesn't want her son to go to jail. Three wives could push him right into the slammer."

Again, Emma looked thoughtful. "That wouldn't be good. Sean couldn't work three jobs to support his wives if he went to jail."

A nurse appeared in the doorway beside Molly. "Judge Hunt, are you ready for your trip to your very own private corner room? It's the same room the president would be given if something happened to him in San Francisco. It even has Monet reproductions on one of the walls. There'll be room for half a dozen guards to buzz around you." She frowned at him, seeing that he was in pain and guessing he hadn't used the morphine pump recently. Then she sighed. She understood why. She smiled at Emma. "Your daddy's so buff and strong he'll be better in no time, so don't you worry."

"My dad's real tough, and he's going to have my back all my life; he told me so."

ICU nurse Janine Holder hadn't cried in the hospital for a long time because it never helped, but she felt tears come to her eyes. This beautiful young girl was hovering protectively over her father, and what he'd said to her, so simple, so heartfelt—Janine swallowed and smiled. "If you're ready, Judge Hunt, I'll call everyone in and get it done. Mrs. Hunt, you and Emma need to come with me."

Two days was long enough in the surgical ICU, Ramsey thought. Too much beeping and clanging and buzzing all day and night. At least he hadn't heard any flatline whines, hadn't heard anyone dying. He'd have some peace and quiet now, even if there would be half a dozen guards. If he wasn't yet ready to be released into the wild, at least he would have a more comfortable cage.

Ramsey heard Molly say outside his cubicle, "Emma, we'll go get some sandwiches in the cafeteria, then go to your daddy's new room and wait for him there. Did you know Uncle Dillon and Aunt Sherlock are outside? We can say hello."

Ramsey wasn't stupid—he pumped in some morphine for the move. No matter how careful everyone was, he imagined there would be jostling, and it wouldn't be fun.

Officer Mancusso came to stand in the doorway. "You're not to worry, Judge Hunt. Hughes and I will be accompanying you. Nothing will happen to you, sir."

Ramsey could only marvel at the odd mix of pride and promise in the young officer's voice. He realized he didn't know his first name, and asked him.

"It's Jay, Judge Hunt," Mancusso said.

It looked like an honor guard, Sherlock thought, when they finally got the bed wheeling down the hall toward the east elevators. Officer Eddie Hughes was on one side of the bed and Officer Jay Mancusso on the other side. Eve and fifteen-year-veteran Deputy Marshal Allen Milton walked at the head of the bed, and a muscular orderly with a big Fu Manchu mustache steered and kept an eye on the IVs dangling from the headboard and the chest tube pinned to the sheets. Ramsey had tried to smile at them as they wheeled him by.

Sherlock saw Ramsey's face was white with pain. At least Molly and Emma weren't here to see him. But Ramsey would live, and they would catch his shooter. She wondered how she'd be holding up if Dillon had been the one shot and nearly killed. She gave him a fast kiss.

Savich, Sherlock, and Harry got in the back of the line behind Ramsey's bed. Eve stood beside him, her hand resting lightly on his arm. She leaned over for a moment to say something to him and her ponytail swung down to lie against her face. Sherlock smiled. After the interview with Milo Siles, Dillon had told her, "I learn something new every single day. Do you know there appears to be power in the ponytail?" And he'd grinned like a bandit.

When they reached the elevator, they looked up and down the now-empty hospital corridor. They watched the doors open, and five people squeezed into the elevator around the bed. The doors closed behind them.

An SFPD officer waited with them for the other

elevator, which seemed to be tied up on the seventh floor, while yet another deputy marshal used the stairs. They stood quietly, watching the arrow of Ramsey's elevator leave the fourth floor and hover at the fifth floor.

They heard a loud clanging noise and the sound of muffled gunfire.

Savich ran to the stairs door, yelling over his shoulder, "Sherlock, Harry! Find out where the shooter got access to the elevator! Get him!"

When he burst out of the stairwell door onto the fifth floor, he was greeted with the yells of hospital staff and the screams and shouts of patients standing at the doors of their rooms, staring at smoke seeping out between the closed elevator doors. Half a dozen hospital personnel were trying to pull the elevator doors open, but no luck. Savich ran to the fire extinguisher case and pulled out the ax. He shouldered through and slipped the edge between the doors and pulled down across the safety beam. The doors sprang open.

Thick black smoke billowed out. When it was cleared enough to see inside, Savich saw blood spattered everywhere.

22

A shout came out of the chaos. "The shooter's on the roof of the elevator! Officers down!" Officer Eddie Hughes stumbled out, panting and coughing, holding his bloody arm and trying to keep Deputy Marshal Allen Milton upright, blinded by the blood streaming down his face. Both men still had their guns in their hands.

SFPD officer Jay Mancusso staggered out, his Glock at his side, his eyes tearing from the smoke, coughing. He wheezed out, "He threw a smoke bomb down through the top of the elevator and opened fire. Barbieri, she's with Judge Hunt. I don't know—" And he bent over in a fit of coughing. At least he hadn't been shot that Savich could see.

The orderly was trying to pull himself up, blood soaking his white pants.

All of it had happened in seconds.

Savich was coughing, fighting to see through the gray haze of smoke still clouding the elevator. A frantic voice came through the chaos, "Judge Hunt! How is Judge Hunt?"

Savich managed to push his way in, and his heart stopped. Eve was lying stretched out on top of Ramsey, and she wasn't moving. He was afraid to touch her. "Eve? Answer me!"

Slowly, Eve raised herself off of Ramsey. She was in pain, obvious to Savich, but he didn't see any blood. She turned to look at the myriad faces staring down at her, then settled again on Savich's face. He helped her slide off the bed. She stumbled, and he helped her right herself. "Sorry, the bullets knocked me silly. I'm okay." She pulled away from him and looked down at Ramsey's white face. "Ramsey—talk to me."

He opened his eyes. "Hi, Eve."

"Are you all right?"

A doctor and a nurse squeezed into the elevator beside them and eased them aside to tend to Ramsey. "Yes, I'll live." He coughed and moaned. "All the smoke and gunfire. How is everyone else? How are you, Eve?"

"I'll live, too. He shot me three times in my back, missed my head, thank goodness, or I'd be a goner. The impact knocked the breath out of me, that's all." She gave a wild grin, even though she felt like she'd been whacked by a two-by-four too many times. "Thank the good Lord for Kevlar."

A doctor tapped Eve on the shoulder. Ramsey gave her hand a squeeze, and reluctantly, Eve released his.

They wheeled him out of the elevator. He said to all of them, "I'll be all right, don't worry about me." Three doctors, including Dr. Kardak, panting from running from surgery to get here, hovered over him as they wheeled his bed down the hall, two SFPD officers and one deputy marshal flanking them.

They heard Ramsey say, "You'd be wheeling me down to the morgue in the basement if not for Eve. I'm going to kick her butt for taking such a chance."

Eve waved into the elevator car. "It looks like a war zone in here." She pointed up, nearly groaning at the pain in her back. "Would you look at the ceiling? Our guys shot the crap out of it. They fired nonstop, but I don't know if we hit him."

She closed her eyes. It had looked like the end, but no one was dead. She sent a prayer of thanks upward. "Please tell me you got this idiot."

Savich said, "Sherlock and Harry are on it; they'll be here soon."

Harry Christoff gently picked up an elderly man by his elbows and set him aside. He shoved two police officers out of his way and stood in front of Eve, panting from running down three flights of stairs. He took in her tearing eyes, her blond straggling ponytail, her smoke-blackened face. "Good grief, woman, look at you. You're all right, aren't you?" He saw that she was hunched over and touched her arm.

Eve smiled at him. "I'm okay, thanks to the miracle of Kevlar. We all survived."

Sherlock burst out of the stairwell, panting.

Savich said immediately, "Ramsey's okay. Everyone's alive. Is he still inside the building?"

She started toward Eve, but Eve said quickly, "I'm in one piece. Did you get the guy?"

Sherlock ignored the god-awful mayhem in front of her and forced herself to calm. "He made it out of the elevator shaft. We started a search, but we can't lock down the whole hospital. He's probably out on the street by now."

"How could he have pulled this off?" Eve asked.

Sherlock said, "Okay, he had to case out the elevators and hang out close enough to the ICU to find out when Ramsey was going to be moved. It looks like the shooter called both of the east elevators to the roof. There's an access hatch up there for servicing. He immobilized one of them and settled himself on top of the working elevator when it was called down. He loosened the ceiling hatch and waited. We don't know how long he was up there, but he must have cut this pretty close, otherwise someone would have called for service on the immobilized elevator, and he didn't want that."

"But how did he know?" Eve smacked the side of her head. "Am I an idiot or what? I'll bet even the dishwashers in the cafeteria kitchen knew when Ramsey was being moved."

Sherlock said, "It's even better than that. He didn't even have to look in. The shaft acoustics are incredible, so he could hear Ramsey being pushed into the car, got himself set. The moment the car started up, he shoved the hatch aside, dropped the smoke canister in, and started firing. He couldn't see any better than you guys could through all the smoke, but he must have seen where Ramsey's bed was, focused his fire there. Eve, what happened inside?"

Eve tried to straighten, but a jab of pain punched her ribs. She felt Harry's hand tighten on her arm. She said, "I didn't think; I threw myself on top of Ramsey, and right away three shots hit me in the back—in the blessed Kevlar. He kept firing, but our guys were firing back, so his shots were pretty wild. Whatever he hit was random after that. I'll tell you my heart nearly stopped while I was lying there, thinking of how helpless Ramsey was." She paused for a moment. "You know, I'm betting the shooter thinks he killed Ramsey."

Sherlock stared at the blood splattered on the elevator walls, stared at Eve and at Harry standing behind her. She knew that three close-range shots in the back, even through Kevlar, would make you feel like you'd been beaten with a baseball bat. "If you hadn't been wearing the vests, he'd have killed all of you." She felt such rage she was shaking with it.

Sherlock asked Officer Mancusso, "What about Hughes and Milton? How badly are they hit?"

Officer Jay Mancusso said, "Deputy Milton's head wound looked bad, but they always do. I heard one of the doctors say it was only a scalp wound, though. Eddie Hughes—he got it in the arm, through and through. The orderly who got shot in the leg went right off to the ER."

A nurse, still looking on, called out, "Doug was

pressing on his leg wound himself. You'd better believe he was hollering for the trauma team. He'll be all right."

Jay said, "Both Eddie and I got two shots in the Kevlar, but we're okay. We didn't get hammered like Deputy Barbieri."

Savich said, "Eve, tell us what else you remember."

"Jumping on Ramsey, covering him as best I could, screaming at the orderly to take cover. There was so much gunfire after a second or two, most of it from our guys, shooting wildly upward through the thick smoke, and then there wasn't any more return fire. The shooter was gone."

Sherlock patted her arm. "Yeah, he got out, but guess what? I've got some good news I haven't told you—one of you wounded him. I saw some blood drops on the top of the elevator car, bloody handprints on the shaft ladder, and a couple of drops on the roof and in the stairway. Then he must have managed to get himself bandaged enough so he didn't spill anymore. That means we can spot him on the security cameras, see how badly he's hurt, but best of all, we'll have his DNA." She cocked her head to one side. "Or Sue's DNA."

"Excellent," Savich said. "At last we've got a break."

Harry cupped his elbow around Eve's arm and said without looking at her, "You think you got any broken ribs?"

"They feel like they're in splinters. Don't worry, I'll get it checked out." She knew she wouldn't be up for smelling the roses for the next couple of days. Bruises would cover her back. She prayed no ribs were cracked.

She wondered who'd managed to nail the shooter. DNA. Dillon was right, at last they'd caught a break.

The last people Eve wanted to see here came running up in the next moment. She walked toward them, away from the elevator, and said quickly, "Emma, Molly, Ramsey's all right. The doctors took him back to his new room. He wasn't hurt, I swear. He's okay."

Emma clung to her mother and swallowed, but she couldn't stop shaking. Neither could Molly. Emma stared at Eve and the drifting dirty smoke, and then she looked toward the elevator. "How can everything be okay, Aunt Eve? I can see the blood."

"I'm not lying to you, Emma."

Emma still stared into the bloody elevator.

One very old man called out from a doorway, "Is Judge Dredd dead?"

Emma turned on him. "Don't you say such a thing! My daddy's fine."

Eve said, "Some people were hurt, Emma, but not your dad. I promise."

They looked up to see Dr. Kardak walking toward them. He said, more to Emma and Molly than to them, "Judge Hunt is well. We're all a little shaken, but we've checked him out thoroughly, and he wasn't injured. We're settling him in his new room." He gestured toward Molly. "I suggest, Mrs. Hunt, that you and Emma stay here awhile longer before you come back.

"As for you, Deputy Barbieri, I understand you were injured. You need to come with me."

Once they stood in an empty hospital room,

Dr. Kardak said to Eve, "Take off the vest, Deputy Barbieri. Let's see the damage."

When Eve and Dr. Kardak came out a few minutes later, three pairs of eyes fastened on them. The doctor said, "She won't be having much fun for a couple of days; there's going to be a lot of bruising from the impacts. I didn't feel any cracked ribs, and that's good. We're going to get an X-ray to be sure." He pulled a pad out of his coat pocket and wrote a pain prescription for her. A nurse trotted over and handed her a pill. "Take this, it'll help." She closed her hand over Eve's wrist. "Thank you for saving Judge Hunt."

23

Hospital security chief Ron Martinez walked into the small security office off the hospital lobby, where Savich, Sherlock, Harry, and Eve sat in folding chairs waiting for him. He loaded a disk into the office computer and almost immediately paused it and pointed. "We think this is our guy. He walks straight to the two elevators on the right, no hesitation, like he knows exactly where he's going. Less attention from anyone at the reception desk that way."

Martinez reversed the disk and paused it where the camera got a close-up.

They stared at a man of indeterminate age wearing loose pants, sneakers, a loose navy Windbreaker, dark sunglasses, and a Giants ball cap.

"Bingo," Harry said. "He fits the description of the guy we've been looking for."

"He's well disguised," Eve said. "He knows you're

getting him on film. He's not even trying to avoid the cameras, and I'll bet he knows where every one of them is. He looks middle-aged to me. What do you think?"

"Maybe older," Harry said. "Thin, maybe about five-foot-nine. I can't see his face or his hair with the sunglasses and the pulled-down cap, but we get a glimpse there of part of his neck—does his neck look saggy to anyone?"

"An elderly assassin?" Martinez's eyebrow shot up.

Savich said quietly, "Listen, it might even be a woman."

Martinez's other thick black eyebrow shot up. "A woman? In a shoot-out like that?"

Savich said, "Since we've got DNA, we'll soon know everything about him or her, including the time of birth. That is, if he's in the system."

"Or about Sue," Eve said.

Chief Martinez pressed the play button again. "Sorry, guys, but we don't have cameras on the roof of the hospital where he accessed the elevators." He fast-forwarded. "The next time we have him on camera, he's exiting the west stairwell into the lobby and waltzing out of the hospital. This is within a couple of minutes of the shooting." A new camera angle showed the shooter walking quickly out of one of the hospital entrances on the west side.

"But look at this. He's holding his arm. That's got to be where they hit him."

Sherlock said, "Yes, and the Windbreaker covers any blood."

Chief Martinez told them the security people, SFPD officers, and deputy marshals were showing hard copies of the photos of the shooter to everyone who might have seen him, questioning the garage attendants, even people on the street. It was plain to see no one held out much hope of that happening, but on the other hand, it was worth a try.

They left Martinez singing a happier tune about what the DNA might show, and all returned to Ramsey's room. They passed a deputy marshal and an SFPD officer sitting on each side of the door, talking about Deputy Marshal Allen Milton's head wound. "The bullet slicked along the side of his head. Allen's blaming his head, said if it wasn't so big he could have tucked it inside his vest where it belonged."

The big corner room—the Taj—looked north toward the city. It was blessedly quiet now, with only six people and Ramsey. Molly and Emma were standing on either side of Ramsey's bed, not speaking, merely holding his hands, staring down at him. Two deputy marshals had positions by the windows, and Dr. Kardak and a nurse were speaking in low voices, reviewing Ramsey's chart.

Ramsey's eyes were closed. He knew his wife and his daughter were standing next to him, felt the warmth of their hands, but his brain seemed to be operating on a twenty-watt. He decided that was okay for the moment, a fair trade-off for the pain in his chest being magically gone, thanks to a shot of morphine. He opened his eyes as they approached and said in a slurred voice, "Eve?"

Eve, still hurting despite the pain pill, made herself walk upright and not hobble to his bed. He looked shell-shocked, she thought, as if the wild shoot-out in the elevator couldn't really have happened. She understood completely. When Emma and Molly stepped back, Eve placed her fingers on his forearm and smiled down at him. "I'm here, Ramsey. No need to worry about me. I might look on the scruffy side, but all my working parts are operating fine. Looks like you're okay, too.

"We have some news for you, if you haven't already heard. We shot him, Ramsey, and we found his blood in the elevator shaft, and that means we'll have his DNA. There's a really good chance we'll identify him." Eve looked over at Dr. Kardak, and raised a questioning eyebrow. The doctor nodded his consent for her to keep talking to Ramsey.

"Was it this Sue person?"

"We don't know yet, but it's possible. On the security video, he looks like maybe an older guy, but that could have been a disguise. I'm glad we were all so lucky."

Molly touched Eve's arm. "I will owe you forever."

"Me too, Aunt Eve," Emma said, swallowing down tears.

Marshal Carney Maynard came running through the door, Virginia Trolley on his heels. Maynard studied Ramsey, then, satisfied, said, "There's a media frenzy downstairs. My guys and hospital security have cordoned off the elevators, and we're putting security stations around the floor. We'll hope it works to keep them out. And I called Cheney Stone. He'll be here any minute. Maybe we can talk him into making a statement."

Better him than me, Savich thought.

Virginia Trolley said, shaking her head, "Our police

commissioner will probably beat him to it. She's always eager to be the face of law enforcement in the city."

Savich said, "Ramsey."

When Ramsey focused on Savich's face, Savich continued, "I know you're close to floating up on the ceiling, but you're the one who had the unusual visual perspective, looking up. Can you tell us what you saw?"

Ramsey wondered for a moment—had someone said something to him? He looked at all of them, then focused again on Savich. Yes, Savich had asked him to speak. He had to think about that. He willed away some of the mental confusion, and everything became clear, too clear, really. "Eve had her hand on my arm, Eddie was talking about the Forty-niners, and then I saw the roof hatch lift and I caught a glimpse of a face staring down at me, but only for a split second, right before all the smoke and gunfire—" He lost himself in the words, but that was all right, because in the next second the rest of him was lost as well.

Marshal Maynard said, "Your forensic team has five slugs from the Kevlar vests, all of them from a Kel Tec PF-9, chambered for the nine-millimeter Luger cartridge. As you know, it's the lightest and flattest nine-millimeter ever made and has a single stack holding seven rounds. That means he had three or four magazines with him and he was fast changing them out."

Eve looked at her boss. "If you hadn't insisted on Kevlar vests for everyone—" She stopped, which was okay, because everyone in the room knew what she meant.

24

Five-foot-nothing veteran forensic blood expert Mimi Cutler rushed into the room, her wrinkled lab coat flapping, her short spiked dark hair sticking up at odd angles where she'd run her fingers through it countless times throughout more hours than she wanted to count. But she was smiling, and that made Sherlock's heart leap. She looked ready to make everyone's day.

Cutler caught her breath, smoothed her hair, straightened her coat, and beamed at the people in the office. She waved a sheaf of photos in her hand. "After a wild and hairy all-nighter, here you go, hot off the press." She fanned herself. "Okay, let me back up. The very first thing we did when we arrived at the scene yesterday was collect all the samples of the shooter's blood. We processed some of the blood, then ran the DNA through the CODIS and bang!—look at this photo, it just came through my email." She beamed as she handed each of them a copy. "Here's our shooter."

All of them stared at an eight-by-ten colored police booking photograph of a young bruiser who looked like he'd lost a fight—his face was a mass of blotchy purple-and-green bruises, his split swollen lips dark red with dried blood. His head was shaved bald and sat on a neck that looked wider than Sherlock's waist. The height chart behind him showed he was six foot four inches, and he looked like he had to weigh two hundred and sixty pounds. "His name is Paul, aka Boozer, Gordon. He's an amateur boxer, has anger management issues. It looks like he lost a fight the night he was booked, doesn't it? He's been arrested and jailed for assault three times to date. He lives here in the city, on Clayton." She beamed at them.

There was dead silence in Cheney's office.

"What? We've identified your guy! What's wrong?"

Harry said, "Sorry, Mimi, but we don't think this is our shooter. Our shooter is lots older, lots shorter, weighs maybe half what this guy weighs, and his neck is about as thick of one of this guy's wrists."

"But this is an exact match; the probabilities are off the wall. You've got to be wrong."

"I guess it's time to back up again, Mimi," Sherlock said. "I don't suppose there's a chance of a lab error, or a mix-up with the samples?" She added with a smile, "Maybe more than one person's blood?"

"Naturally not," Mimi said, not appeased by the smile. "I collected the blood myself, and we ran samples from three different sites. All the samples matched."

Savich said, "Let's find this guy. Cheney, can you get some people working on his last known address? And Sherlock, get on the phone to the hospital, find out if Paul Boozer Gordon was there this week, maybe as some kind of patient?"

Mimi grabbed her hair and tugged on it. "A patient? How would a patient's blood get in the elevator shaft?"

There was only one possibility, Savich thought, far-fetched, but still. He said slowly, "Mimi, did you happen to test the blood samples for traces of heparin?"

"Heparin? No, why?"

Savich said, "There's lots of blood in a hospital—in the blood bank, in the laboratories, at nursing stations waiting to be picked up. And that includes heparinized blood that wouldn't clot right away. You wouldn't be able to tell as easily if the blood was older, that it was planted there, would you?"

"Are you telling me the shooter brought the blood *with* him into the elevator shaft? Someone else's blood, to plant on the scene? That he added heparin to the blood to fool me? Do you realize that would mean this frigging shooter would understand *blood analysis*? You're saying he purposefully set out to mislead us? To mislead *me*?" She paused for a moment, her rocket brain filling in the possibilities. "Goodness, even if he actually managed to get hold of someone else's blood, think of how careful he had to be to leave blood splattered at the scene in a way that wouldn't be spotted by the forensic team as looking wrong. All that work, all that study and practice—for what? Nothing, really."

Savich said, "Unless this Boozer Gordon was shot in the elevator shaft, how else does this make sense?"

Harry said, "If that's true, Savich, the shooter had to know we'd see through the deception sooner rather than later. He couldn't have hoped to frame someone else for the shooting that way. It reminds me of that newspaper picture of Judge Dredd we found in his backyard. Another way to give us the finger again, not give *you* the finger, Mimi, but us. He wanted to show us how smart he is, and what tail-chasing loser dogs we are in comparison. Another thing, apparently the shooter wasn't wounded after all." Harry cursed under his breath.

Cheney was off his cell first. "DMV still has Boozer Gordon's address on Clayton Street. Now, you're saying our shooter somehow got some of Boozer's blood, enough of it to create believable blood splatter?"

Savich nodded. "Only explanation I can think of."

Sherlock closed her cell. "Medical records has Boozer Gordon discharged from the hospital late Friday morning, the day before Ramsey was attacked in the elevator. He came in through the ER, apparently looking beat up as badly as in that mug shot. I spoke to an ER nurse. She was not very happy with my question. She said no one had ever walked in and stolen blood from them, for heaven's sake, that it simply couldn't happen. Then Miss Manners got huffier, told me it was ridiculous to think someone could simply waltz in there or into a patient's room and draw his blood. Couldn't happen, never in this lifetime. But I agree with Dillon. I think that's exactly what happened, I'd bet my hair rollers on it."

"No," Savich said, "not the hair rollers."

Harry said, "So our guy put on a white coat, walked in, and drew Mr. Gordon's blood?"

Sherlock thought for a moment. "However he got it was an elaborate pretense, especially with the huge risk he took in that elevator shaft. I'm thinking that even if he'd planned Ramsey's murder for a long time, there was very little planning in that attack on the elevator, since of course he couldn't know he needed to play it."

Harry said, "Would a professional take on an armed guard like that? We're working on the assumption that Sue is a professional, but, you know, this really feels like it's personal."

"Personal, or maybe desperate," Savich said. "An act of rage, or delusion."

Harry nodded. "And he didn't leave that blood behind on the fly, since he added heparin to make us think it was fresh. It's like some kind of crazy what-if scenario that he'd played through in his mind, maybe even read about and practiced. That would have taken time, and that could be the key here, he had to have time on his hands. Sherlock's right, why would Sue the master spy go to all this trouble?"

Sherlock's eyes locked with Savich's.

He said matter-of-factly, "You mean the shooter was in prison."

Harry said, "Until recently, I suspect. If Sue the spy has nothing to do with this, then we may be talking about a guy who came out of prison knowing exactly what he wanted to do, everything all laid out."

Cheney said, "And, bottom line, what he wants to do is to kill Judge Hunt."

"A guy," Harry said. "I'd just gotten my brain wrapped around this Sue. Doesn't matter, if he was in jail, we can find him."

Mimi Cutler, who'd been standing by the door, began pulling on her hair again. "Do you guys know I had to *cancel* a date last night—my first date in four and a half months—and the guy is *hot*. I didn't tell him what I do for a living, since he'd probably freak. He's a stockbroker and only sees blood if he nicks himself shaving. I gave him a lame excuse about a sick mother, and would you look at this—it turns out I couldn't even find my mom."

She shook Boozer Gordon's photo and ripped it in two.

Sherlock said, "Mimi, tell your guy you do blood analysis for DNA, that you were working on the Judge Hunt incident at the hospital yesterday—it's all over the news. He'll be so impressed and excited to know someone in the thick of things, he'll be camping out on your front porch. Trust me on this."

Mimi stopped pulling on her spikes of hair. "You think?"

At Sherlock's solemn nod, Mimi smoothed down her

hair. "You don't mind if I tell him about Judge Hunt? Give him the gory details?"

"Like I said," Sherlock added, "it's all over the news, so why not cash in?"

Mimi left, fluffing her hair and humming "Girls Just Wanna Have Fun."

Harry stared after Mimi, shaking his head, marveling at how you could be in the pits one second and laughing out loud the next.

25

He was glad for the drizzling rain, cold and wet on his neck. It made shoveling dirt over Mickey O'Rourke nice and easy. Finally he stepped back, studied the mound he'd made. Not good, too high, too easy to find. He began pounding the back of the shovel on the wet dirt, flattening it down, scraping some of it away. Once he had the dirt as flat as he wanted it, he dragged branches over to cover it.

"RIP, Mickey," he said, as he kicked a chunk of sod under a branch.

He stood for a moment, marveling at the near-perfect silence, the only sound the rustle of leaves and the rain dripping off his arm and striking a rock beside his booted foot. He could hear himself breathe. The air was heavy with wet and green, not even a whiff of an exhaust fume. And here he was, only eleven miles from the interstate and its endless stream of cars. Not a bad place to be dead, he thought, like in a faraway forest.

He would miss this place, home for nearly a year and a half now, especially his small apartment in San Rafael, just a block from the Mission San Rafael Arcángel. He'd visited the old church quite often, not to pray but to focus his mind. It was as quiet as a tomb in the dark of night, cool and peaceful, as if the spirits settled there knew their own worth, and kept order.

He considered what to do with the shovel. Not leave it in the trunk of his Jeep; that wouldn't be smart. He would dump the shovel, but not around these grassy hills, and not in these woods. They were too close to Mickey in his tatty shroud. No, he'd dump it in some thick trees on his way back to San Rafael. Maybe a hiker would find the shovel and think it was good fortune.

He turned his face to the sky, felt the cool drizzle seam down his cheeks. Then he shook himself like a mongrel and trotted the quarter-mile back to his Jeep.

26

Boozer Gordon didn't look so hot. The tiny black stitches on his chin running up his cheek to his ear looked like one-sided beard bristle. The bruises covering his face were now a faded purple, and both his eyes were still black. He was wearing an ancient green fleece bathrobe, and his big feet were in thick black socks. Boozer was very big. Savich had to look up at him.

"Yeah, what do you clowns want? It's Sunday; you're supposed to be in church or at least getting out the chips and salsa for the football games."

Sherlock gave Boozer her patented sunny smile. Savich thought, *We'll see if your smile is as powerful as the blond ponytail.*

"We're not just any clowns," Sherlock said, "we're FBI clowns, and we labor every day to bring criminals to justice—what you see is your taxpayer dollars at work. We have some questions for you about a shooting that happened yesterday." And she flipped out her creds. After a thorough study, Boozer looked at Savich. "You her bodyguard?"

"That's right," Savich said, and handed over his own creds.

"Just what I needed," Boozer said, and sighed. "Federal cops on a Sunday, doesn't that make my day. It will only get suckier if the Forty-niners lose.

"Listen, you're wasting your time. I'm innocent of anything that's happened in the past two days—look at me, I've been in the hospital. I got the crap beat out of me, not in the ring, but in a stupid bar. Four morons whaled on me. Don't get me wrong, I coulda taken them if I didn't have beer leaking out my ears."

"Six sheets to the wind?"

"Yeah." He smiled down at Sherlock. "Only lucky thing is I never get hangovers."

Savich thought, *You're only twenty-three. You just wait.*

Boozer stepped back and let Savich and Sherlock walk into a small hallway with a living room off to the right, a long, narrow room that, surprisingly, had a big window that gave a sliver of view of the Golden Gate Bridge.

The room, even more surprisingly, was neat, down to the Sunday *Chronicle* stacked beside a big black La-Z-Boy with a beautifully crocheted dark blue afghan hanging over the arm.

Boozer waved them to a pale green sofa with three

colorful throw pillows set just so along the back cushions.

"Nice pillows," Sherlock said.

"My mom," Boozer said. "She comes by when I'm not here to water my plants, and she does stuff, like brings pillows and changes the sheets and dries out the towels."

"The ivy looks good, too," Savich said. "Sit down, Mr. Gordon. We need your help."

Boozer's look was disbelieving. "My help? I told you, I've been out of commission for the past two days. I've never shot anybody—well, I couldn't have even tried if this happened in the past two days." He eased himself down in his big chair and pushed up the footrest. He gently unfolded the afghan and pulled it over his legs and leaned his head back against the headrest.

Sherlock and Savich sat on the sofa, careful not to disturb the artful placement of the throw pillows.

Sherlock said, "You were in San Francisco General Hospital until noon Friday, isn't that right, Mr. Gordon?"

His head came up and his eyes popped open. "Listen, I didn't hurt anybody at the hospital, I was too out of it even to get pissed off at anyone, and, well, everybody was nice to me."

Sherlock said, "That's good to know. I'm nice, too. Now, Mr. Gordon, we need you to think back. You're lying in your room on Friday, you're by yourself. You've got some nice pain meds working, and you're feeling pretty good, right?"

"Yes, but it didn't last all that long, maybe four hours; then I hurt again."

Savich said, "This is very important, Mr. Gordon. While you were lying in your hospital bed did any hospital technicians come in to draw your blood?"

That roused Boozer. "Oh, man, did that torturer accuse me of having bad blood? Did the hospital send you over because I've got that avian virus?"

"No, your blood is splendid," Sherlock said. "No viruses. We need you to tell us about the torturer."

Boozer looked from one to the other. "Why should I? You're cops, like those other yahoos who hauled my butt to lockup for no good reason. My manager had to bail me out, and he was yelling at me, too, and there I was, hurting since I was the one that got knocked crazy, not those four other bozos who ganged up on me. At least the cops sent me to the hospital. Why should I tell you anything?"

Savich said, "We think the person who drew your blood has tried to murder Judge Dredd twice."

Boozer blinked raccoon eyes at them. "Judge Dredd? You're kidding me, right? I mean, they used to have a poster of Judge Dredd at the martial arts school since he used to work out there. You're telling me the dude who took my blood is the one who tried to shoot him in the elevator yesterday?"

"Yes," Sherlock said. "Judge Dredd is okay, for the moment, but we want to find the shooter before he tries again. You called the man who drew your blood a torturer. Tell us about it."

The front door opened, and a very beautiful woman strolled in. She was wearing a black pantsuit and low-heeled shoes, and she was as blond, porcelain-skinned, and fine-boned as a storybook princess. She was carrying a bag of groceries under her left arm with what looked like a pair of folded boxers sticking out of the huge tote in her right hand.

"What is going on here, Paul? Who are these people? You're not one of those missionary groups, are you? If you are, you're out of luck. Paul's a devout Catholic."

"Oh, hi, Mom. These here guys aren't Christians, they're FBI agents, and they need my help to find the guy who's trying to kill Judge Dredd."

Now it was her turn to stare. "Goodness me," she said finally, and accepted their hands to shake and their introductions and creds.

Boozer said, "Oh, yeah, this is my Mom, Cynthia Howell. She doesn't have my name because she divorced my pa for being a mean drunk and married Daniel, my stepdad. He gave me that black Ford One-fifty last Christmas. You saw it in the driveway, didn't you?"

Savich said, "A fine machine."

"Well, that about sums it up," Mrs. Howell said. "My Paul can help you? Really?"

"Mom, it turns out I saw the guy who shot Judge Dredd in the hospital. He drew my blood."

"I see. Paul, you tell these agents everything you know about this man while I get you another pain pill. Oh, I brought over two homemade pizzas, with lots of pepperoni, the way you like it. I know you're hungry, but let me warm them in the oven for about ten minutes." And she walked out of the living room and into the kitchen.

His mother made him pizza? Pepperoni? Sherlock felt her mouth water.

Mrs. Howell came right back with a glass of water with three ice cubes and a slice of lemon wedged on the side of the glass. Boozer took the pill, drank the water, and gave his mother a sweet smile. She gently cupped his face. "It doesn't look as bad this morning. I'll get your pizza in the oven now, sweetie. Don't wait for me. You can tell me everything later."

Sherlock said, "The tech who came to draw your blood?"

Boozer leaned his head back and looked at the ceiling. "He was a little guy."

Savich said, "Being as how you're on the tall side, what do you mean, exactly, by little?"

"I don't know, shorter than you, lots less than six feet. Kind of scrawny, not all that much to him, you know what I mean?"

You're a behemoth. Even Dillon looks scrawny compared to you. Sherlock said, "Tell us about his face. What did he look like?"

"I can't tell you much about his face because he was wearing one of those surgical masks, you know, like he needed protection from me, like I was contagious or something. That's why I thought when you showed up the hospital had found something was bad."

Savich said, "No, Mr. Gordon, there's nothing wrong with your blood. How about his hair? What color?"

"He had a green scrub hat on his head."

"Could you see his hair at all?"

"I remember thinking the cap was too big for him. It covered his whole head, came down over his ears. If he didn't have that big needle in his hand, I would have said something, like why didn't the hospital give him caps that fit him, but I kept quiet."

Sherlock said, "How tall is your mom, Boozer?"

They heard a lovely voice call from the kitchen, "I'm five-foot-nine, Agent Sherlock. Paul is tall, too; he takes after me."

Sherlock smiled at Boozer. "Picture the guy in your mind, he's standing by your bed. Is he taller than your mom?"

Boozer thought about this. "Nah, he's about the same as my mom, maybe a little bit shorter."

"Is there anything you can tell us about him that stood out when you met him? You called him a torturer. So he wasn't very good?"

"That's for sure. He would have really hurt me if I hadn't been a little looped from all the drugs. He had a real hard time getting the needle in a vein, had to go to my other arm. I don't know how many times he stuck me. I was wishing I could knock his block off, even with the drugs."

"But he finally got the needle in a vein," Savich said. "Do you remember how many blood vials he filled?"

Boozer shuddered, scrunched up his face like a kid. "I didn't want to look, but after a while I did. Three of those vacuum vials with the purple stoppers. I asked him what all that blood was for, and he said something like,

'I guess they want to make sure your insides didn't get as wrecked as your face.'

"I remember that because I thought it sounded kind of nasty what he said; then he left, didn't say anything else to me. I guess he was the only one at the hospital who wasn't nice to me."

Savich studied Boozer's face for a moment. He could see the pain meds were starting to work. Boozer was sitting more easily in the big chair, his muscles loose, his hands smoothing out the afghan. He said, "Go ahead and close your eyes, Mr. Gordon. Relax. Imagine you're watching him draw your blood. Is there anything unusual about him?"

"I heard him cursing under his breath when he couldn't find a vein."

"Anything else?"

"Well, he stopped in the door when he was leaving and turned around."

"Look at him, Boozer. Was he old?"

"Hard to say, over fifty, I'd say, somewhere in there."

Sherlock wanted him to compare his age to his mother's, but she wasn't stupid. She looked up to see Mrs. Howell coming into the living room carrying a huge tray with a pepperoni pizza so hot you could feel the cheese dripping off your chin.

"I have another pizza in the oven, so there's plenty for all of us. Agents?"

Boozer had his slice of pizza in his hand when he said, "I remember now, the guy was wearing this butt-ugly

ring on his finger, and another ring with a big diamond
on his pinkie finger. I saw them when he pulled out those
surgical gloves to put on his hands."

*The same diamond pinkie ring Mrs. Moe described the
man wearing when he rented the Zodiac in Sausalito.*

Sherlock chewed a bite, then asked him, "How big
was the butt-ugly ring?"

Boozer studied her face for a moment. "You have a
piece of cheese on your chin, Agent Sherlock."

She laughed, swiped her napkin over her face. "Thank
you. The pizza is delicious, Mrs. Howell. Now, the ring,
Mr. Gordon?"

"It looked like a religious ring, you know. It looked
real old and solid, with some dull jewels sticking up in
the middle."

"Why do you say religious?"

Boozer shrugged. "I don't know, just a feeling, I
guess, when I saw it. I was flying sort of high and it
popped out of my mouth—'You an ex-priest?' He asked
me why I thought that, and I pointed to his ring.

"He said, 'Nah, it's just a ring I won off this old guy
in a poker game.' Nothing more, that was it. I didn't
really care because I was worried about that needle in his
hand and I wanted it over with."

Twenty minutes later, the pizza settling happily in
their stomachs, Mrs. Howell showed them to the door.
Sherlock simply couldn't help asking her, "May I ask you
how old you are? You look like Boozer's sister instead of
his mother."

Mrs. Howell laughed. "If I told you it might get back

to my husband. It's the strangest thing, but it embarrasses him that I look so much younger than he does. The joys of cosmetic surgery, but don't tell Daniel. He thinks I'm perfect, and I don't want him to think otherwise. Isn't my Paul an amazing young man?"

As they walked away from Boozer's apartment, Savich stopped by their rental car, pulled Sherlock against him, and kissed her. "Yep, pepperoni."

"I got to eat all yours, too. Poor Mrs. Howell, she was mortified that she hadn't brought a vegetarian pizza, just in case. Do you think our shooter really won that butt-ugly religious ring in a poker game?"

27

After four long knocks, Eve opened her door to Harry Christoff.

"I had this feeling it was you, but I was sort of hoping I was wrong."

"Why? You wanted maybe the postman? It's Sunday, no delivery on Sunday."

A laugh spurted out of her. "No, I'm not really up to acting all social and civilized. I'm sorry I missed the meeting this morning; you'll tell me everything?"

"I will, but you have to invite me in first. I figured you'd be in pretty bad shape, so I came bearing gifts." He held out a bakery bag and a covered go-cup that sent the aroma of dark roast coffee wafting to her nose.

Eve took the bag first, looked upward, and said "Thank you," then, "You're amazing, Harry, and you even brought coffee. No, you're more than amazing, you're a prince, Agent Christoff. Are there any glazed?"

He looked down at her scrubbed face, her hair hanging loose around her shoulders over a faded red robe, her bare feet. "You look like the homecoming queen on a reality show. I'm glad you slept in this morning. How's your back?"

She forced herself to stand up straight. "I'll be good to go after three donuts and this wonderful coffee. Come in, let's go to the kitchen. Are there maybe more than one glazed?"

"There are three, but I was hoping for one myself," he said, as he followed her into her kitchen. He still couldn't get over how streamlined and cool it looked, with pale green granite counters shot with black, and hanging copper pots over a small center island. He said, "My kitchen's right out of the forties."

"As long as everything's clean and works, who cares what decade it comes from? It's all about the food and the person making it, right? You want milk in your coffee? You don't want a glazed donut, do you? You somehow knew it was my favorite?"

"Nah, give me a chocolate with sprinkles. I'm a real man."

"How many donuts?"

"Six."

She set everything out on the small kitchen table, and they started in on the donuts and coffee, neither saying much of anything until only one donut, not glazed, was left on the paper plate between them. Eve wiped the sticky glaze off her mouth and her fingers, laughed, and leaned forward to flick a red sprinkle off his chin. She sat back and sighed, contented. "Thank you. Before you came, I'd just gotten out of the shower and wondered what I was going to make for breakfast. Nothing appealed, then you showed up."

She toasted him with her coffee cup.

He asked, "How'd you sleep last night?"

"In the arms of the angels, with the help of two aspirin and a sleeping-pill chaser. I'm trying to stay away from the codeine." She stretched, froze, then began, very slowly, to stretch again.

Harry stood up. "Let me see how bad the bruising is today."

She stared up at him. "You mean you want me to drop my bathrobe?"

"Well, yeah, but don't feel like you have to put on a show for me, even though I did let you eat all three of the glazed donuts. No, just show me your back. You know, if you can't think of me as your doctor, you can pretend you're an artist's model draped with a towel. Come on, Barbieri, I'm not going to jump you. You're safe. I'm not desperate enough, and, fact is, you're too pathetic-looking right now."

She stood up, turned her back to him, and let her robe drop to her waist. Harry pushed her hair out of the way, even though he didn't need to, and studied the shades of her green, black, and yellow back. "You got a modern art painter living with you?"

She tried to look back over her shoulder. "That bad?"

He lightly touched his fingertips to one bruise. She didn't flinch. "Do you have some muscle cream?"

She pulled her robe back up. "Yeah, I do, for all the good it did me. I can't reach the bad areas."

"Get it. I'll do it for you."

She gave him a look, then left him in the kitchen to finish his coffee and stare out at her small back garden with its six-foot stone walls and single cypress tree. Everything looked dormant now, but he imagined there'd be lots of color in the summer.

He ate the last donut since it was chocolate.

She came back into the kitchen in a minute, handed him a white tube. It was brand-new.

"It's supposed to be good stuff, not only for muscle soreness but for bruising as well. I bought it yesterday before I realized I couldn't reach anything."

She again dropped the robe to her waist. She grinned over her shoulder. "Am I really that pitiful?"

"Not quite; you combed your hair."

"Well, I looked in the mirror and nearly fainted. I had to do something."

Harry covered his fingers with the cream, stared at her long stretch of back, closed his eyes for a moment to get a grip on himself, and touched his fingers to her skin. *I'm a solid, consummate professional, doing my job.* He wished she did look pathetic, but the fact was, she didn't, not at all. He reminded himself he was looking at a deputy marshal's back splotched blue and green, but, unfortunately, that didn't help.

"Am I rubbing too hard?"

She said over her shoulder, "No, it feels grand."

"Would you like to lie on your stomach? Speaking as one solid professional to another?"

She laughed, then groaned. "Not a good idea, even speaking as a professional. You've got really good hands, Harry."

Really good *professional* hands. He started whistling as he continued rubbing the cream on her back in steady smooth strokes, deepening when he realized he wasn't hurting her, and if his hands went a bit lower than the bruises, surely there were sore muscles at her waist, and the massage couldn't but help.

"You can't see the bruises now," he said. "You're all white since I've used half the tube on you."

"Feels like it, nice and hot."

He didn't want to stop, but he did. He stepped back. Slowly, she shrugged back into her robe. She turned. "Thank you. Look at me, I think I can straighten without groaning."

He went to the sink to wash his hands. He could feel the heat deep and knew it must feel good on her back.

"Tell me more about your meeting this morning with Cheney, Savich, and Sherlock."

So he told her, answering her questions until she had no more. His cell phone chimed.

"Yeah?"

"Cheney here, Harry. They found Mickey O'Rourke. Two kids in Nicasio saw a man bury him. Thank God they had the sense to keep quiet so he never saw them.

The Marin County sheriff, Bud Hibbert, had a photo of Mickey on his desk, recognized him, and called me. I called Savich and Sherlock. They've finished interviewing Boozer Gordon. I don't want to call Barbieri; she's probably still flat on her stomach, high on codeine."

"Actually," Harry said, "I'm with her now, and she's doing okay. She's got to get dressed, but we'll be there as soon as we can."

"Good. Ask Eve to requisition a Chevy Suburban out of the marshals' pool, that way the five of us can ride up together."

Harry punched off his cell. He looked up to see Eve standing in the doorway to the kitchen, unmoving, her face set.

"You heard what Cheney said?"

She nodded. "I didn't want to believe Mickey could be dead, it hurt too much, so I tried not to think about it." She swallowed. "But I knew he had to be. Harry, he's dead, just—dead. That monster murdered him."

Harry said, "Yes, the monster murdered him. But we've got two kids who saw him. We've got witnesses, Eve. Cheney wants us to go up there. We'll catch him; you know we will."

She turned to go into her bedroom, saying over her shoulder, "I can't stand this, Harry, just can't stand it."

Harry thought of Mrs. O'Rourke, thought of Mickey O'Rourke's teenage daughters, thought of the uncertainty they'd been living with for the past four days, the soul-eating fear, and now they had to face the death of a husband, a father.

When Eve came out, she was dressed in her black and red, her hair in a ponytail, no makeup on her face. Her eyes were puffy from crying.

He walked to her and lightly rubbed his fingertip over her cheeks. "I'm sorry, Eve. Believe me, I know how you feel."

28

Harry turned the U.S. Marshals' Chevy Suburban west off Highway 101 on Lucas Valley Road, drove about ten miles, then turned right on Nicasio.

Sherlock looked out over the rolling hills of cattle and horse country. "The hills are still all gold and brown, even with the rain."

Cheney said, "The rain was a little late this year. By March, the hills will be as green as Ireland." He saw Harry turn the windshield wipers on intermittent, and said, "I hope we stay with this light mist. A full-on downpour would really make things difficult." He waved a hand as Harry curved left. "There's Nicasio, one square block, really. Its claim to fame is the 1871 red school-house. It's a historical landmark."

Harry said, "The Nicasio Reservoir is up ahead. You'll

see this area is a real mix, with a few exclusive, expensive homes sitting next to farm country and to old hippie hangouts."

Eve said, "Hard to believe we're so close to the gazillion people living in San Francisco."

They were all thinking, *We're talking about the ridiculous weather and the scenery because Mickey O'Rourke is dead.*

Harry pulled in to what looked like a makeshift parking lot, climbed out of the Chevy, and opened a gate. "Here it is. Ranch Road." And he got back into the SUV and drove through the gate. He followed the narrow, dirty road through trees and fancy horse pastures and hills dotted with cows. They came across a white Crown Vic with a green sheriff's ID on the side, parked at the edge of the road.

Bud Hibbert, the Marin County sheriff, was tall and runner-lean, with a full head of iron-gray hair that glistened with a light film of rain. He had a craggy, weathered face that announced he sat squarely in his fifties, and dark, smart eyes that looked like they'd seen about everything.

"How'd the FBI get hold of a U.S. Marshals' SUV?" he asked, nodding toward the big black Suburban.

"I'm Deputy Marshal Eve Barbieri," Eve said, and shook his hand. "I'm their procurer." She introduced everyone, and Sheriff Hibbert introduced his three deputies, all from Civic Center Main Station.

Hibbert said to Cheney, "I got the particulars you sent out on Federal Prosecutor Mickey O'Rourke Friday afternoon. When we realized the body was O'Rourke, I pulled our guys back immediately to preserve the crime scene for you. You've got a forensic team coming?"

Cheney nodded.

Sheriff Hibbert said, "The two kids who saw the killer—we knew they weren't blowing smoke because Rufino Ramirez's dad is a deputy sheriff in our Point Reyes Substation.

"We haven't seen this kind of thing around here, Agents, since the trailside murders. It's already all over town."

Hibbert raised his face. "It's been raining on and off all morning. I'm afraid I can feel more coming. No choice, let's do this," and he turned toward his cruiser. He said over his shoulder, "Deputy Sheriff Ramirez took his boy, Rufino, and his friend, Eleanor, back to his house; then he called the other parents over, so they're all together, waiting for you. How far behind is your forensic team?"

Cheney said, "They're only a few minutes out. I called Joe Elder, the forensic team leader, told him you'd have a deputy waiting here for them at the same place where you met us."

Sheriff Hibbert nodded, climbed into his Crown Vic, and led them slowly past a few more dirt tracks before turning left at the fourth, which threw them into a mess of thick oak and bay trees. Soon they saw half a dozen more cars pulled onto the grass along the dirt tracks, their passenger sides pressed up against the trees. The tracks narrowed to a dirt path.

The sheriff pulled over, got out of his Crown Vic, and waved them forward. He said, "We figure the killer parked some twenty feet down this trail; that's where we found tire tracks, nice and clear before the rain picked up. Our guys are taking the tire casts now. He carried O'Rourke's body about a hundred feet farther into the woods. This is private land, but you can't see the house from here."

They followed him along a narrow trail, the trees so thick overhead it looked like twilight in the woods. There was no wind to speak of, but the air was pregnant with rain, and a light drizzle continued to fall. When they reached a small clearing, Sherlock looked up, hoping to see a bit of sun, but she knew that wasn't going to happen. She hoped heavy rain would hold off for a while longer to give the forensic team time enough to set up some cover.

Marin County officers circled Mickey O'Rourke's grave, talking, drinking coffee. Savich saw the hole was maybe three feet deep, deep enough to keep Mickey O'Rourke hidden in this desolate spot for decades, if it hadn't been for those two kids. He wanted to meet them. He nodded to the deputy, then leaned down and pulled back a white tarp. They stared down into Mickey O'Rourke's bone-white face and the obscene red slash across his neck. The deputies around the grave looked on with them.

Eve couldn't bear it. She swallowed, turned away. She said, "Ramsey is going to hate this. Why did he have to die?"

There was no answer to that.

They all turned around at the sound of footsteps coming up the trail.

"That'll be our forensic team," Cheney said, and waved when he saw Joe Elder.

"What are you standing in our way for!" Joe yelled, still from a distance. "Move your carcasses, let us through."

Joe was nearing retirement now. He was impatient with fools, impatient with everyone, as a matter of fact, and would generally snort at anyone in his vicinity.

They listened to him bark out orders to his team of two men and two women, snarl at the deputies who happened to get into his space, and shout for some coffee for him and his people.

There was silence when they at last lifted Mickey O'Rourke out of his grave. Eve crossed herself, a habit ingrained from her childhood, and said a prayer. She looked over at Harry. His face seemed to be carved from stone. His hands, though, were clenched at his sides.

Since there wasn't anything more for them to do, Sheriff Hibbert led them to the Ramirez house. It was a mile away off another dirt road, a small clapboard house set pressed against a knot of bay trees.

They heard the two kids' high, excited voices before they got through the front door. After introductions and their assurances no one would browbeat the kids, Julio Ramirez led them in from the kitchen.

They were eleven years old. Emma's age, Sherlock thought, and skinny as skateboards. They looked both scared and excited, like their parents. Eleanor looked a great deal like her mother, small and fine-boned, quite unlike her father, lucky for her.

Rufino was a good-looking kid, the image of his deputy father. A future heartbreaker, Eve thought.

It took about ten minutes before Deputy Ramirez convinced the other parents to adjourn back to the kitchen and wait. Finally they got the kids settled at the ancient mahogany dining room table, each with a soft drink and within easy reach of a plate of chocolate-chip cookies provided by Eleanor's mother.

In another few minutes, they gently got Eleanor and Rufino to the point in their story where their explorations took them near the clearing.

Keep it light, Sherlock thought. "You two were smart not to call out to him."

Rufino said, "We almost did, then Ellie grabbed my arm and pointed. We both saw the shovel and the big mound of earth. Ellie nearly peed her pants, she was so scared."

Ellie punched him in the arm. "Yeah? Well you did, too, Ruf."

Sherlock grinned at both of them. "I can sure understand that. Can you tell us what the man was wearing?"

Eleanor said, "A raincoat, it was brown, and he was wearing a Giants ball cap. It was drizzling."

Rufino said, "We were trying to find a double rainbow, but we didn't. We never saw his face because he had his back to us. He was pounding down a big pile of earth, then he pulled branches over the—"

"The grave," Eleanor said, and squeezed Rufino's fingers. "It was really gross."

Rufino said, "And we knew right away it was a grave and we knew this man wasn't good, so we were real quiet."

Eve thought, *You're both alive because he never realized you were there.* There was no doubt in Eve's mind the man would have killed both children and buried them with Mickey O'Rourke. Her ponytail swung forward as she leaned toward the kids. "Did you see any part of his face? Like his profile?"

"No," Rufino said. "We were always behind him. His boots were real dirty. His feet were small, like my dad's."

Harry asked, "Was your impression that he was tall? Short? Fat?"

"He was kinda tall," Ellie said without hesitation, "and he wasn't fat, but not as skinny as Ruf's dad."

"Was he about your dad's height, Rufino?" Eve asked.

Rufino wasn't sure; the guy was pretty far away. He knew the deputy marshal was disappointed, but he didn't want to make anything up, and she smiled at him when she realized it. He smiled back. Yes, indeed, a girl slayer, Eve thought again.

She said, "Did he seem old to you? Young?"

"Old," both kids said at once.

"Older than your parents?"

Neither child was sure about that. To these kids anyone over twenty was old.

Cheney said, "Then what happened?"

Rufino drank the last of his soda and wiped his hand across his mouth. "After he put some branches over the grave, he leaned down and picked up the shovel."

Ellie said, "He said something, then he walked away."

Harry felt his heart pick up. "Did you hear what he said?"

Ellie said, "Yes, sir, but it didn't make any sense to Ruf or me. It was something like RIP and then a name—Mickey I think. We were afraid to move, so we sat there for another five minutes."

Rufino said, "We heard a car motor start, it was a long ways away, but we heard it. We figured he was leaving so it was okay to move."

Ellie said, her small voice trembling, "It was horrible. We sat there and stared at those branches and all that black earth and knew there was a dead body under the ground."

Rufino leaned over and patted her back. "It's okay, Ellie, it's okay."

Cheney said, "Let me tell you, kids, you're both heroes. Without you, the man you saw buried would probably never be found. And you've really helped us."

Rufino patted Ellie's back again. "Since you're a girl hero I guess it's okay for you to be scared." The little girl stopped shaking.

Another chocolate-chip cookie each, and everyone at the table knew the kids were tapped out. They were still excited but wrung out. They all went out into the kitchen to thank the parents and tell them how incredible and smart their kids were. Sherlock studied Rufino's dad—maybe five feet ten inches, give or take, one hundred fifty pounds, give or take. Was Sue the taller of the two?

When they returned to the grave site with Sheriff Hibbert, they stared down into the empty hole. The rain had picked up, and the dirt was fast becoming mud and sliding into the hole. "*RIP, Mickey,* that's what he said over Mickey's grave." The sheriff looked at each of them. "I really want you to nail this bastard."

There was a moment of silence. Sherlock said, "The killer matches the general description of Ramsey's shooter. More or less."

Harry said, "If it is the same guy it's got to tie in to the Cahills. But it could be a woman, this Sue, I suppose." He pushed one of his fists into his palm.

Savich nodded. "Okay, we don't know exactly when O'Rourke died yet, but my guess from seeing the body is he was murdered fairly recently. Did the killer head back from the hospital after his attempt to kill Ramsey on the elevator to where he'd stashed Mickey O'Rourke in order to kill him?"

Yes, he had, Harry thought, and nodded.

Eve turned to Sheriff Hibbert. "So he might have stashed Mickey O'Rourke somewhere near here. You have any ideas about that, Sheriff?"

Sheriff Hibbert nodded. "Deputy Ramirez told me there's an old farm shack in the woods near here, on property that belongs to a new house a developer built some six years ago. As for the shack, it's been deserted for years. Let's go see."

They fell in behind the sheriff's car and soon turned

off another dirt road onto a rutted path. They slowly made their way about fifty feet until they couldn't go any farther.

Sheriff Hibbert leaned out the window. "We can't see the new house from here because the dirt road—Mason's Cross—is set at a ninety-degree angle in the middle of a bunch of oak and bay trees. We've got to walk the rest of the way to the shack."

They climbed out of the Suburban into the drizzling cold rain and mud and trudged after the sheriff for about twenty yards.

Hibbert stopped. "There it is."

They stared at a dilapidated wooden shack, probably older than Sheriff Hibbert's parents.

29

Sheriff Hibbert motioned them back. He opened the creaking wooden door, his gun drawn. They heard him suck in his breath.

He stepped back, his face set and pale as death in the dim light. "You're not going to like this."

The shack was a single room, maybe twelve by twelve, the floorboards rotted through. Part of the roof had caved in, probably years before, and rain flooded in. A single metal cot was shoved against the back wall, beneath some remaining roof. There was a dirty blanket hanging off the bed, nothing else.

The blanket and the mattress were soaked with blood, dried black. There was blood splattered on the wooden floor planks, even on the walls.

Cheney pulled out his cell phone. "Joe? We found the kill site. I need you to bring a couple of your people over to us." He handed Sheriff Hibbert his cell.

"Ask Deputy Millis to show you the way. The shack is off Mason's Cross Road. You'll have to walk a ways." He handed the cell phone back to Cheney.

None of them said any more. They all knew Mickey O'Rourke had spent the last three days of his life tied down to that cot, alone, knowing in his gut he was going to die. And he had. He may have wanted to die at the end. By the look of the shack and the spattered bloodstains, he'd been beaten. For information?

It was difficult to step back, cut off the rage and sadness, to force their minds to focus on what was in front of them. Sherlock said, "There's a chance he left fingerprints."

Eve said, "He hasn't missed a single trick so far, but he never expected anyone to find this shack. So maybe you're right."

Harry asked Sheriff Hibbert, "Do you have any idea how long this shack has stood vacant?"

"At least twenty years, maybe longer. I haven't heard of anybody staying out here since I've been sheriff. We get some homeless people squatting in our abandoned buildings now and then, but not here, it's too remote." He looked up at the boards sunk in on the crumbling ceiling. "It'd be safer to camp under a tree." He looked toward the bed. "How I hate this smell, the smell of death."

Cheney took one last look around the room, and said, more to himself than to the rest of them, "It's up to me to tell Mrs. O'Rourke her husband's dead. I'll take a chaplain with me." He sighed. "As if that will help." He looked up. "This guy doesn't deserve to walk the earth." He paused for a moment. "I know a woman didn't do this. If this was Sue, then Sue is a man."

It **was odd**, Eve thought, looking out the Suburban window as Harry drove them back to the city, how the ride home always felt quicker.

She listened to the windshield wipers clapping steady as a metronome, the rain, now that they weren't getting soaked standing in it, oddly soothing, somehow comforting.

She saw Cheney's eyes were on his hands, clasped in his lap. He had to be thinking about Mrs. O'Rourke and the girls and what he would say to them—it couldn't be the truth, at least not all of it.

Harry looked stiff, mechanical, as if he was afraid to express anything for fear he'd yell with it. Savich and Sherlock, too, were without expression, but Dillon was pressing his wife's open palm against his thigh. She wondered how much horror they'd seen. Too much, she thought. What were they thinking?

Eve felt a wave of despair, not only because of the bloodbath they'd found in the shack but because it was the naked proof that some people were simply evil, some people were simply missing all compassion or any human feelings at all. How else could this monster have killed Mickey so brutally?

RIP Mickey. She wanted to kill him herself.

She met Sherlock's eyes. Sherlock said, "How's your back, Eve?"

She snapped back from the edge. "Thanks to Harry the Hands, I'm feeling fine." She added, "Harry was at my condo this morning, and let me tell you he's got the greatest hands. I think he even got a moan out of me, it felt so good."

No one said a word.

Where had that come from?

Eve cleared her throat. "What I meant to say was that he massaged my back with muscle cream and—"

"Let it go, Eve," Harry said. "No one thinks there were any prurient thoughts in your head or mine. Your back is purple and green, and you were hobbling around like a crippled old deputy marshal retired lady."

Insanely, Eve wanted to laugh.

When they arrived at the Federal Building, Cheney said, "I'm going to pick up the chaplain in my own car and drive over to see Mrs. O'Rourke. As for the rest of you, it's Sunday. Take some time off, try to let go of all this. We need all your brains ready tomorrow morning. We can bank on hearing from forensics and the medical examiner first thing." He paused for a moment. "Wish me luck."

They did, all of them grateful they weren't walking in his shoes today.

Eve said her good-byes and went walking in the rain. She realized her mistake a couple blocks later when every step made her back hurt. She saw a taxi, and, miracle of miracles, it stopped for her. She directed the Ukrainian driver to Saint Francis Church on Larkin, a fixture in her Russian Hill neighborhood for nearly a hundred years. The rain was coming down heavier when she opened the side door and slipped inside. It was warm and dim and ancient. She breathed in the soft air scented with incense. She always felt safe here. She sat awhile, absorbing the quiet and gazing at the many symbols of hope that surrounded her, hope she knew was embedded in the very walls. She eased forward on the pew and sent a prayer of gratitude that Eleanor and Rufino were alive. She prayed to find this man who'd wantonly killed Mickey O'Rourke, who'd tried to kill Ramsey. She didn't pray that she would kill him; she didn't think she should push God on things like that. And she prayed for Mickey O'Rourke's soul.

When she walked back to the vestibule, she saw Father Gautier standing by the big closed double doors, arms crossed over his chest, an umbrella open at his feet to dry. He was St. Francis's longtime pastor, always softspoken and patient. Father Gautier gave her a long look. "I hope you found what you needed, Eve. I noticed you weren't in church today. Is something troubling you?"

She told him that Mickey O'Rourke, whom Father Gautier had known as his parishioner far longer than she had, was dead, a violent death. She gave him no details.

He took her hand as he closed his eyes a moment. He whispered, "I am so very sorry, for his family, for all of us. *Requiem in pace.*"

They stood quietly for a moment, then Father Gautier said, "You're wet," and his voice held a touch of humor, bless him.

Eve said, "Not so much now. It's so very warm inside. I think I'd like to stay that way."

When Father Gautier left her, she pulled out her cell.

30

Sean was lying boneless against Savich's shoulder, Savich stroking his back. He'd fallen asleep between his grandparents in front of the TV watching Sunday Night Football.

He took Sean to the second guest room next to his and Sherlock's bedroom, gently eased him down on his back on the twin bed, the crib long stored away in the basement. He pulled the dinosaur sheet and two blankets over him, since Sean liked to be warm when he slept. He kissed him, breathed in his kid smell, and straightened. He felt the light touch of Sherlock's hand on his arm.

"He's so beautiful, so perfect, and we made him," she whispered. "Isn't that amazing?"

Savich turned and hugged her. He said against her ear, "I was thinking that right now it'd be good to be as innocent as Sean." He closed his eyes and pressed his face against her hair. "I can't get Mickey O'Rourke's face out of my mind, or that farm shack where he was beaten and murdered." He hugged her more tightly. "Life is so fragile. You're here, then you're not, and it's final, no going back, no changing anything at all."

She held him, stroking her hands up and down his back and said against his cheek, "Dillon, I've been thinking about what Cheney said—that a woman wouldn't have killed Mickey O'Rourke like that. I don't see it, either. Not only was the killing savage, she would have had to carry O'Rourke back to the car, a good distance from the shack, and then she would have had to carry him an even longer distance to bury him. Remember, Ellie and Rufino said after he left O'Rourke's grave, they heard the car start up from a good ways away? Even with superior upper-body strength, I don't see how she could have managed. O'Rourke was a big guy—taller than you. What does it mean?

Savich said, "It means our Sue isn't a woman."

31

Eve's back hurt so badly when they arrived at her condo she didn't think she could walk a step until Harry's hand cupped her elbow. "Harry's hands are here to minister to you so you have a chance at some sleep tonight. First, though, you need a long, hot shower. I don't want you getting sick."

"I can make you some coffee."

"I'll make it while you shower. After you're dry and warmed up, I'll see to your back. I'll call Feng Nian Palace and get us some Chinese delivered. We can stretch out in front of the TV, watch what's left of the football game, and munch on egg rolls."

After her shower, Eve walked into the living room to see the Patriots' QB Tom Brady complete a pass to Wes Welker and gave a small cheer. "I think Wes Welker would make a great marshal," she said. "He's strong and fast, and you can tell that brain of his is high-voltage." She grinned down at Harry as she tossed him the tube of muscle cream. She carefully sat beside him on the sofa, eased her robe off her shoulders, and leaned forward. Her hair was loose down her back. He looked at her hair for a moment, then shoved it over her shoulder and began smoothing the cream over her back. He stroked her until the final whistle blew. She really didn't want him to stop, but finally she said, "Your hands will cramp up. I'm fine now, thank you. I can't believe how stiff I was. Goodness, it's almost nine o'clock. Are you hungry yet?"

"Dinner should be here any minute. You feel okay?"

"Better," she said, "much better." She realized her robe was still down. She quickly shrugged it back up, closed it, and tied the belt. She turned to face him, lightly laid her hand on his arm. "You're very kind, Harry, thank you."

Harry was silent for only a moment, then said, "Sherlock told me about Mrs. Howell's homemade pizza for her son, Boozer, how delicious it was at eleven o'clock this morning. I was thinking we eat too much pizza—so we're having Szechuan. That okay with you?"

"It's great. Do you know I can't imagine an amateur trying to find a vein in my arm and poking that needle in a dozen times? It's too bad the guy had his face and head covered up."

Harry said, "Yeah, but we were real lucky today—if

those kids hadn't seen him, we'd still be looking for Mickey O'Rourke."

"Yes, forever. Hey, what do you want with your fried rice? A beer?"

Harry asked for water. He watched her walk to her kitchen. She looked looser, walked more easily. He said, "I called Cheney while you were in the shower. He said Mrs. O'Rourke was brave, that was the word he used. I guess he was expecting her to fall apart, but she didn't. She told him she wanted to be the one to tell her daughters. The chaplain stayed, but Cheney's home now."

"I hope I don't ever have to tell someone their husband or wife is dead. By violence."

"Agreed. I called Officer Mancusso and asked him to unplug the TV and call if Ramsey happens to find out something. He said he'd alert the nursing staff to keep quiet as well."

"That's good, Harry. I'll tell you, Molly looked so beaten down, so afraid for Ramsey today, that she shouldn't have to handle any more tonight."

"We should be okay until morning now," Harry said.

Eve handed him his water. "I'm thinking our killer has been making a few mistakes. Like the kids seeing him today. You know he never wanted Mickey O'Rourke to be found. And he failed to kill Ramsey twice."

Harry took a drink from the Pellegrino bottle. "I can't help but think he's not altogether sane." He stopped, shook his head. "Shoot me. I don't know what to think anymore, but I do know this has got to be a huge hit for him. Any time now he's going to listen to the news and hear about Mickey O'Rourke being dug up. So what does he do now?"

Eve said, "Good question. He isn't going to give up, that's all I'm sure of. If Savich is right, he's in the spy business. I don't imagine you can survive very long doing that unless you're real careful. But he hasn't been careful, has he, at least with his two attempts on Ramsey's life?"

Harry said, "He tried to be with burying Mickey O'Rourke; bad luck for him there."

"We'll find out from forensics tomorrow if he left any prints in that shack. And if Sherlock is right that he's spent time in prison, we'll have him."

Eve took a pull of her beer. "Why did you and your wife divorce?"

The doorbell rang. The food.

She said, "Give him a big tip, Harry, I'm really hungry."

They were eating hot-and-sour soup when Eve said, "I'm sorry I asked you about your wife. I didn't mean to. It popped out."

"My ex-wife," Harry said mildly, and finished off the bottle of Pellegrino.

"Nevertheless, it's none of my business. I've only known you for a matter of days. Isn't that amazing? So much has happened, it seems much longer."

He said nothing, but she was right, it felt very odd.

Eve sat back against the sofa and immediately sat forward again at the stab of pain in her back. "I hate not having control. My dad's the same way. I'll tell you,

Mom had to belt him lots over the years when he tried to be her camp commandant. I'll bet they've both lost count.

"My four brothers are all grown up, and they laugh at him now when he tries to throw his weight around." She drank the last of her beer. "My dad's amazing. He reminds people of Tommy Lee Jones, though the two marshal movies came out before he started his service there."

"Service where?"

"In Chicago. Didn't you know? My dad's the U.S. marshal in Chicago? He's served as marshal there through two presidents."

"I thought the marshal changed out with every new administration."

"Once in a great while, an appointed marshal is so well regarded he's left in place. My dad says he's trained the toughest hard-asses in the United States Marshal Service right there in Chicago. He says they take no grief, since they have a responsibility to Tommy." She paused for a moment. "He's very good, my dad."

"How does your dad treat you?"

Eve gave him a big smile. "You heard Dillon talk about the power of the ponytail? Works on my dad every time."

32

Ramsey blamed himself. Eve saw it clearly on his freshly shaved face, just as she'd known he would.

"It's obvious to me that by suspending the trial, I alerted the Cahills or whoever is working with them that I suspected something going on with Mickey's prosecution. If only I'd held off that day, let the pretrial motions continue until I could talk to him privately, he might still be alive."

Eve said, "It isn't like you to sit back and watch a train wreck, is it, Ramsey? You did what was appropriate, what your experience and your training told you to do. Who could have known what would happen?"

Ramsey plowed right over her, shaking his head back and forth. "No, no, I should have thought it through better. I should have realized that with the death penalty on the table, whoever was controlling Mickey wouldn't draw the line at anything. It's my fault they killed him, no one else's."

Eve said patiently, "Ramsey, say Mickey had succeeded in manipulating you, and you had ruled to dismiss the federal case against the Cahills. Do you think they would have let Mickey live? I think you know as well as I do after what happened that Mickey was dead the minute they threatened his family. If he'd come to you, maybe it would have turned out differently, but he didn't."

Slowly, he shook his head. She hated it. He looked defeated. "I should have approached him differently, gotten him to confide in me—if he'd told me, I could have made sure he'd be safe. And his family."

She lightly tapped her fist against his arm. "Stop this, Ramsey, you're pissing me off. A monster hiding in a human skin did this. No more blaming yourself or I'll have to punish you for it when you're well again."

He didn't smile. "I've been thinking about why they shot me, of course. I'm a judge, and if a judge is doing his job, he's providing an even playing field to give the jury the best chance of arriving at the truth, not to influence the jury in any one direction.

"So why me? Most of my pretrial rulings had been in the Cahills' favor, in fact. And the bigger question—why did they try to kill me after the trial was dead in the water, at least in my court? We were done with each other, so why?"

He looked at each of them. "The only answer I've come up with is that they think Mickey may have talked to me before they could grab him, told me something dangerous for them, either about the case itself or implicating whoever had threatened him. That would also explain why they tried to shoot me again on Saturday, while they could hope I was still too ill and drugged to have spoken to anyone."

"That's a reasonable scenario, Judge Hunt," Harry said. "We're certain someone was working with the Cahills, probably a professional. And the man—we're calling him Sue for the moment—might have a great deal to lose if he's exposed. As a matter of fact, Sue did try to find out if Mr. O'Rourke told you anything before he kidnapped him, but O'Rourke didn't have any information to give him, and so he ended O'Rourke's life."

Ramsey said, "So whoever this Sue is, you can be sure the Cahills are up to their earlobes in this with him; there's simply no other explanation." He paused for a moment, his eyes narrowing. "Molly already knew Mickey was dead last night, didn't she? She knew, and she kept quiet about it."

Eve said, "No, I didn't tell Molly."

"The TV didn't work, either. I wondered why not. What'd you do, Agent, unplug it?"

"I asked one of your guards to unplug the TV, Judge Hunt," Harry said.

"I hate lying here feeling helpless, everyone guarding me, shielding me. I'm pretty sick of it." He smacked his fist on the bed and swallowed.

Eve waited a moment until he had himself together

again, then looked him straight in the face. "I had nothing to do with it. It was all Harry's idea."

What moxie. Harry had to work hard to keep the laugh in. She was a piece of work, fast on her feet. He couldn't help but admire that. She'd succeeded in distracting Judge Hunt. Harry saw incredulity, disbelief, and then humor in his eyes.

Harry said, "Yes, sir, it's true. I ordered Deputy Barbieri to keep her mouth shut, and I told everyone here in the hospital to keep this from you or I'd have them all fired."

"But still—" Ramsey said, but Eve overrode him. "You want guilt? Give me a big share, okay? I allowed you to very nearly get killed in the elevator only two days ago."

Ramsey frowned at her. "Get real, Eve."

"I will if you will. Listen, we all do our feeble best, and sometimes things simply don't go the way we planned or we prefer. Did your recovery take a hit from that fiasco Saturday?"

"No, the elevator business didn't faze me, Eve. Dr. Kardak even told me I was such a superb physical specimen he felt comfortable taking out the chest tube this morning. They took away my morphine pump, too. I'm on oral pain medication now, and I'm thinking a lot more clearly." He looked from Eve to Harry. "You two are quite a team, aren't you?"

"We're not a team," Harry said. "That's a vicious rumor."

"That's right," Eve said. "If we were a team, Harry would be saluting me by now."

"In your dreams," Harry said.

Ramsey didn't laugh. He knew how bad it would make him hurt. He said, "So you think Sue is a code name for a man? That simplifies things, doesn't it?"

"It's a start," Harry said. "All we can do is keep digging."

"If we were a team, Ramsey," Eve said, "you could count on me telling the boy here where to dig."

A laugh came out this time. Ramsey closed his eyes and took some light shallow breaths against the stabbing pain in his chest where the tube was removed. Slowly, too slowly, he eased. He said, "Emma's performance is in a week and a half. I keep telling my body to get over it and stop whining at me. I really don't want to miss it." He managed a smile. "Do you know what a pain it is to have to lie here and let people come in and out and torture you? Amazing that the hospital makes you pay them for it." He realized he had come full circle. "Sorry for the complaints. I'm a loser. Just belt me."

"Nah," Eve said, "not until you have a prayer of belting me back." He was exhausted, Eve saw it, knew Harry saw it, too. Not only exhausted, he seemed flattened emotionally, like Molly. She knew he'd think about Mickey O'Rourke's murder and blame himself for a very long time.

She watched Ramsey close his eyes. He said, barely above a whisper, "You've got to find the worthless son of a bitch who did this."

She took his hand, squeezed it. "We will, Ramsey, I swear we will."

There were two marshals and two SFPD officers nearby, two outside and two inside the room. Of course they'd been listening. She knew they'd all discuss the O'Rourke murder with Ramsey after she and Harry left. Perhaps they'd come up with something. She knew the deputy marshal who was stationed outside Ramsey's room was smart and committed to keeping Ramsey safe. Not a single sign of trouble, he'd said when they'd arrived to see Ramsey. She hoped it stayed that way.

She said to the guards standing by the window, "Hey, has Judge Hunt talked you into playing poker with him yet?"

Ramsey groaned.

"What, you haven't stripped them of their paychecks, Ramsey?"

"No, not our paychecks," Officer Mancusso said. "We told him he'd have to fix parking tickets for our wives."

Ramsey said, "I tried to tell them I couldn't fix a thing since I'm a federal judge, not a state judge."

Mancusso winked at her. "We don't believe him. We figure a federal judge has got friends everywhere."

"If you win, Ramsey, what will you get from them?"

Ramsey didn't open his eyes. "I'm thinking maybe they can get one of their buddies in Contra Costa County to ticket my chief judge's boat in Discovery Bay. He's having way too much fun on *Cyrano*—his big bad cabin cruiser—and drives way too fast. Scares the crap out of the fish. He deserves a couple of tickets, and he needs to spend more time in here commiserating with me."

Mancusso said, "I heard the chief judge has friends everywhere, too, sir."

33

Federal Building
Thirteenth floor
San Francisco
Monday morning

After the forensic team leader Joe Elder and the M.E. Dr. Martin McClure had left the conference room, one back to his beloved lab, the other to his sanitized and very quiet morgue, Cheney summed it up. "So all we have from Joe is a smudged partial palm print that may be identifiable and we know isn't O'Rourke's." Cheney clicked off his second finger. "The M.E. confirms Mickey was tied down and beaten during the two days before he died early Sunday morning. The killer sliced Mickey's throat with a sharp knife at least six inches long, not serrated, right to left, suggesting he's left-handed. And last, Sheriff Hibbert let us know the tire tracks were made by a worn Goodyear All Weather, a popular replacement tire for a whole lot of SUVs. So we haven't got a lot."

Savich said, "Nothing from Hammersmith about the Dodge Charger he's been looking for?"

"He's had no luck with that," Cheney said. "And no useful leads yet from any of the hotels in the city on the man—or woman—who was driving it."

Savich said, "After what the killer did to Mickey O'Rourke, we should stop talking about a woman. We all think you're right, Cheney. It's a man who killed Mickey O'Rourke."

Burt Seng said, "Still, guys, it could have been a very strong woman. Hey, Eve here could carry lots of dead weight."

"Not that much," Eve said. "And not that far."

Savich said, "Mickey O'Rourke weighed two hundred and ten pounds, and everyone has described the perp as slender, not real big, so it's got to be a man, a very fit man."

Harry said, "I agree; even the ponytail couldn't have managed it."

Eve said, "Yup, it's a man. For sure. Now, I don't think Cindy was putting us on, either, about the name Sue—it was too raw, too fast. I don't know who this Sue is, but I agree, she can't be O'Rourke's murderer. Maybe an accomplice, but not the killer."

Sherlock said, "Boozer Gordon described a man, too, not a woman; there was no question in his mind. So, yeah, good-bye, Sue."

"Without those kids," Harry said, "not only wouldn't we ever have found Mickey O'Rourke, but, bigger yet, we still would have been trying to fit our killer into a female body."

Cheney said, "I say we buy those kids tickets to a Forty-niners game."

Savich repeated slowly, "If Sue is an accomplice, was she with the killer when he beat Mickey? Did she question him? Did she tell him to slice Mickey's throat? If so, then why wouldn't she go with him to bury him? As his lookout, his helper, whatever? But she didn't." Savich stopped cold. He looked very thoughtful, then, without another word, he started quickly typing on MAX's keyboard.

Sherlock cocked her head at him, since she knew that *Eureka!* look well. He'd thought of something, something big. She said, "We've been working on a bit of information Boozer Gordon gave us. When the man was putting on plastic gloves to draw Boozer's blood, Boozer noticed two rings on his fingers. The diamond pinkie ring sounds like the one Mrs. Moe described the shooter wearing when he rented the Zodiac. As for the other one, Boozer said it looked sort of 'religious' and actually asked the man if he was a priest. The man said no, he'd won it in a poker game. But still it could be an easy lie. Since it was an odd sort of ring to wear, it could have significance, it could be important."

Eve said, "Priests don't wear rings, not in the Catholic Church, though bishops do."

Sherlock nodded at her. "We sent a police artist to meet with Boozer and get a sketch of the ring. Here it is, to the best of Boozer's memory."

While everyone looked at the drawing, Sherlock said, "Even though it's pretty rough, we sent the sketch back to the Hoover Building. Given all the ecclesiastical rings I looked at on the Internet, Boozer's description of the ring isn't far off. We should know soon if our people can find anything." But Sherlock didn't look hopeful.

Harry pointed to the sketch. "The ring does look faintly religious. I hope you're right and it's important to this guy, for whatever reason."

"Well, well, would you look at this," Savich said. He looked down at MAX again for a moment, then smiled at everyone. "In all the talking we've done about Sue, we've assumed Sue is an American woman because it's an American name, short for Susan. But it occurred to me to ask if there are names in other languages that sound like Sue, since this case revolves around espionage. I ran it as a search through MAX, and it turns out there are names in Chinese that are pronounced *Sue*, or close to it. The closest one is a family name, written in English as *X-u* or *S-u*. Either way, since it's a surname it can be a man or woman's name, but no matter, I'd say Xu is a man and very probably Chinese."

Cheney rose straight up, slammed his fist to the table. "That's got to be right! It fits too well not to be. It all makes sense now. The Cahills had a Chinese handler named Xu who probably recruited them to get access to Mark Lindy's classified information. Question is, why is Xu still in the country? Why is he still around more than eight months after the Cahills were arrested?"

Eve said, "To stay here over eight months, he'd have to be an American citizen, whether he's working for the Chinese or not, or have excellent fake papers."

Harry said, "The reason he's still here is because the Cahills know exactly who he is, and they could announce his identity to the world at any moment they liked. I think he's trying to clean things up before he checks out."

Savich said, "Say Xu is an agent for the Chinese. They can't be happy with him that the simple retrieval of information of Mark Lindy's data—meant to be done with stealth and alert no one it was even taken—turned instead into the very messy murder of a U.S. citizen, one working for the federal government. Imagine if it got out that Chinese intelligence was responsible, and the press got ahold of it—heads would roll. This Xu's continued usefulness to his employer, maybe even his life, might depend on the Cahills keeping their secrets. He had no choice but to stay here."

Cheney said, "So Xu had to try to get the Cahills off, or make them think he would, to prevent them from giving him up."

Cheney said, "I wonder if the CIA already suspects Chinese involvement? If so, they probably beat us to this Xu name days ago."

Savich said, "I'll speak to Billy Hammond at the CIA again, give him a heads-up. They're much better placed to follow this up quickly, if they haven't already."

"Will he tell you the truth?" Eve asked him.

"I suppose it's a vague possibility. On the other hand, Hammond was a stone wall when I asked him what kind of intelligence the Cahills were after on Lindy's computer."

"It's possible they don't know," Eve said. "I mean, who knew the Forty-niners would be having a winning season?"

They were interrupted by a knock on the door.

"Come," Cheney called.

The door opened to Agent Andre Devereau. Behind Andre stood Molly Hunt.

"She needs to see you, Cheney, so I brought her back." Cheney nodded, and Agent Devereau closed the door behind Molly.

Eve was on her feet. "Molly? What's happened? Are you all right?"

Molly was wearing jeans and a sweatshirt, sneakers on her feet. Her vivid red hair was wild around her head, no makeup on her face. She looked like a freaked-out teenager.

She said to Eve, "A phone call came in a half-hour ago. You told me never to pick up, and to record every call, and I did. I didn't want to stay there and wait, so I came right over. Eve, call my home number. The voice mail access code is one-five-five-nine."

Eve picked up the landline and punched the speaker-phone. She dialed Molly's number, and they all heard it ring, heard her punch in the code. There was the date and time, then a muffled gravelly voice.

"Mrs. Hunt, the mole on the back of your left thigh is very sexy. I'm thinking you and I will get together after your murderer husband is underground. It will be you and me and Emma. She can teach me to play the piano, and I can teach her—other things. The murdering bastard won't be with us much longer, Molly—may I call you Molly? I'll come for you, I promise."

Eve pressed the stop button.

Molly stood as pale as the morning fog snaking over the bay behind her, her hands clenched at her sides. But when she spoke, her voice was calm. "I can't figure out why he called Ramsey a murderer."

"He said it twice," Sherlock said. "Does he believe Ramsey is a murderer because he was presiding over a death penalty trial—namely, the Cahills'?"

Eve walked to Molly, placed her hands on her shoulders. She looked her right in the eye. "Molly, how could this guy have seen you naked?"

Molly ran her tongue along her bottom lip. "The bathroom has a large window looking out at the ocean, right beside the Jacuzzi. Ramsey and I like to—" She broke off, swallowed. "There are blinds, but we never use them. There are no neighbors to look in, after all, and it's a direct view to the ocean and the headlands beyond."

Harry said, "Too far from the water to see a mole, even with binoculars. So he may have managed to sneak up to the back of the house and look in on you without your seeing him. It could have been any time, even before he shot Ramsey. Think, Molly. Do you remember anything—maybe a shadow you couldn't identify, a flash of movement out of the corner of your eye?"

Molly shook her head. "It was raining last night while I was bathing. When I looked at the window, I only saw the raindrops streaming down the glass, nothing else, I'm sure."

"He could have managed to get to the window unseen by the deputies guarding the house," Eve said. "It's a big property, with lots of ways in, if one climbs the cliff or sneaks through Mr. Sproole's yard. It's a huge risk to take, though. It's more likely he saw you a week or more ago. When he was planning to shoot Ramsey."

Sherlock said, "Molly, did you tell the marshals?"

Molly nodded. "They weren't happy. They checked around the house right away, but they didn't find anything. You know the rain was heavy."

Molly stared at each of them in turn. "He's going to kill Ramsey unless you find him. How many more times can he fail? He was promising me, you heard the certainty in his voice. He's going to kill Ramsey."

Savich hated the despair in her voice, and he snapped her back. "Molly, have you taken a bath every night since last Thursday night when Ramsey was shot?"

She started. "Well, no. I've been so exhausted, I've hopped in and out of the shower, but last night—" She gave a hoarse laugh. "Last night I needed to calm myself down, get it together for the children. I soaked for a good thirty minutes. And maybe he was outside, watching me, and I didn't know it—I was lying there, my eyes closed, and I was so thankful Ramsey had survived the elevator attack—" She looked at them blindly. "I know he was there watching me, all the time, *he was watching me.*"

And in everyone's mind—*Could he have gotten to her last night, broken into the house without alerting the marshals outside?*

Sherlock said with infinite calm, "He's not going to try to take you. His whole purpose is to terrify you, to scatter your focus, and our focus. The best thing for your peace of mind, and for ours, would be to take you and the kids to a safe house for the duration."

Cheney nodded. "I'll arrange it."

Molly said, "That's like in the movies. I can't believe any of this, it's all so surreal, and Ramsey—" She broke off, pulled herself together, cleared her throat. "All right. Good. I'll try to make the boys think it's a mini-vacation, maybe down by the zoo? We'll need to transport Emma's piano, since she plays at Davies Hall in a week and a half."

Harry said, "It'd be less risky to rent one, bring it to the safe house."

"No, that wouldn't work. Emma's piano—it's been her lifeline since Ramsey was shot."

Cheney said, "Don't worry, we'll figure it out."

"Thank you. I'll head home, then, and get everything ready. But what if he's watching the house? What if he sees us leave? And follows us? He'll know you're taking us away; he'll know it."

Savich said, "No, Molly, he won't know where you're going. Listen to me, this guy isn't some kind of superman who knows all, sees all. He's only one man, and we've done this before. Trust me, this is going to throw him off his game."

But not for very long, Eve thought. They had no idea whether his game included continuing trying to kill Ramsey, or even what his game was. Not that she would say that to Molly. He knew they would all hear his phone call to Molly. If he thought about the consequences at all, which, of course, he had, she knew they were going to have to be very careful while moving her.

Molly slowly nodded. "I don't want to tell Ramsey about this. There's nothing he can do. I can't stand worrying him more when he's helpless. It would destroy him to know he can't protect us. All right, I'll get Emma out of school now."

34

*Damn her eyes, I'm one of the most famous defense lawyers
on the West Coast. How can she do this to me?*

Milo Siles mashed the elevator button once more,
then another couple of times for good measure. The elevator doors opened, and he stepped in. Eight other people surrounded him, most taller than he, and he felt the
familiar punch of claustrophobia. He closed his eyes and
thought about the .38 he'd left in his glove compartment. He'd managed to wheedle a permit for it, not an
easy task in San Francisco. It was a good thing he'd left
it there or he might have shot the selfish cow and her
greedy moron of a lawyer. How demeaning it was to be
forced by a lamebrained judge to meet with a lamebrained mediator on the twelfth floor of the Crandall

Building, in *her* lawyer's conference room, to listen to *her* lawyer demand half a million dollars from him every single year for the rest of her selfish self-centered life, plus the house in Claremont, plus the shares in the vineyard in Sonoma, plus support for their two boys until they were eighteen.

Half a million dollars. A year.

Milo was so angry at his soon-to-be ex-wife's outrageous demand, he'd nearly outshouted his own divorce lawyer. And that officious cow of a mediator had counseled that they all take a deep breath and sit back and close their eyes for a moment. And then what? Sing "Kumbaya"? He wouldn't be surprised, not in San Francisco.

He'd taken that deep breath and closed his eyes anyway, and that did help him relax, because what he saw was a huge number of zeroes flashing in front of his eyes—the ten million dollars or so he had stashed in his holding company in the Grand Cayman Islands. No way Marjorie or her lawyer would find out about that. He'd been very careful through the years that it couldn't be traced to him, not by anyone.

He grinned to himself. You never knew when you went the extra mile to make some real money in this business if you might have to make a quick exit. This trial with the Cahills was a disaster, but at least it had pushed his nest egg up to that nice round number, more like the nest omelet he'd always wanted. He should never have taken the risk of defending the Cahills' worthless butts after they screwed up and got themselves indicted for murder. The case was hopeless from the start. He should have known that for all that money there would be risks far beyond keeping the Cahills quiet and cooperative, making his motions, and sitting back to wait. Well, he'd done everything as agreed, and he deserved that money. It was Marjorie's overspending that had pushed him into it, wasn't it?

He pictured his wife staring at him across the table, her eyes narrowed beneath her dark brows, which always needed plucking. It made bile rise in his throat. He'd supported her lazy butt for seventeen years, and what had she done to earn it? Be a housewife? As in be the loving wife who tended the house, took care of the children, maybe cooked the occasional dinner? That was a joke. Marjorie had a maid, a cook, and a gardener—and a nanny when the boys were younger. She did nothing at all useful, spent her hours on herself and on her idea of playing, whatever that happened to be. She'd probably had a half-dozen lovers, all of them buff and twenty years younger than she was, he knew it to his gut, and it was *he* who had paid for them. When he'd stormed out of that ridiculous mediation session with her lawyer, the lead-faced dyke who didn't make any bones about hating him, Marjorie had come up behind him and whispered in his ear—easy for her to do, since she was two inches taller than he, the cow—"I know more than you think, Milo, about this Cahill trial, about how you've cheated your firm. Think about it, dear. Five hundred thousand dollars a year is a lot better than sharing a cell with Clive."

He'd turned on her, his mouth working with no

coherent words at first. "I let you do what you want, what's in this for you?"

She laughed. "Let me paraphrase Nicole Kidman when they asked her how she felt about splitting up with Tom Cruise—I don't have to wear flats any longer."

He'd nearly decked her.

Tom Cruise wasn't that short, and neither was he.

Milo would have smashed his fists against the elevator doors, but he couldn't lose it since there were too many people looming over him in the elevator. Marjorie was divorcing him because he wasn't tall enough for her?

He had to get hold of himself. She'd overheard a conversation with Clive? He couldn't remember any such conversation, but obviously he hadn't been careful enough. Well, she'd keep her mouth shut. If she spilled to the cops, then the Feds would seize all his assets under the RICO Act and she wouldn't see a bloody dime. Maybe sharing a cell with Clive would be worth it, knowing she'd have to get a job, maybe selling bagels in one of those outdoor kiosks at her favorite mall.

Milo walked a block over to the Mason Building, which housed his law firm, and directly into the underground garage to his new Beamer parked next to the express elevator. He admired its sleek lines for a second, still got a kick out of how the door opened for him with his key fob still in his pocket. As he squeezed in, he saw Marjorie's smiling face again, her smile so big she showed the gold tooth in the back of her mouth she'd never bothered to change out. He smacked his fist on the dashboard. This wasn't his fault; none of this was his fault.

He was a good provider. And he would still send his boys to Princeton, his alma mater.

He buckled his seat belt and settled smoothly onto the sinful dark gray leather seat and pressed the magic button—that's what his youngest son called the ignition. No, he wouldn't worry about his sons. They'd get over this. They were old enough to understand. He would make them understand.

His baby roared to life. *Calm down, calm down. So what if you give the witch half a million dollars a year? You can afford it.* But it was his hard-earned money, and she would spend it on those vacations she was always taking by herself, with the boys, with her frigging friends. Never with him after the first five years. All right, so he was usually busy; he had to support his family, didn't he? He had no interest in being one of those idiot tourists who walked around with a guidebook in their hands, always pulling out their cell phones to take stupid pictures no one cared about.

He backed out of the garage and eased into traffic. He crossed the Golden Gate twelve minutes later, and headed north toward Bel Marin Keys, to the beautiful little clapboard house he owned, with its own private boat dock and its one inhabitant, Pixie. She would make him feel better. She listened to him, really listened, and she knew he was suffering today. She cared about his feelings and what his wife was doing to him.

It wasn't raining, but it was cold and overcast, and promised rain. He was glad he'd gotten the coupe and not the convertible now that it was getting toward winter. This was San Francisco, after all.

35

If Bill Hammond at the CIA was to be believed, the CIA hadn't made the connection that Sue could be a Chinese name spelled Xu, hadn't even known for sure that a foreign government was behind the attempted theft of Mark Lindy's materials. He assured Savich the CIA would of course follow up on that possibility, search out every Chinese national with diplomatic cover whose name sounded anything like Xu.

Savich doubted the two CIA operations officers who'd come to San Francisco some eight months before to conduct an extensive investigation had left not even knowing a foreign government was involved, let alone which one. It really didn't matter now, Savich thought, since the game had changed. Now that they had a name, the CIA would be back in the investigation, trying to crash the party and take the cake. Savich figured he had one last shot at the Cahills before CIA operations officers arrived. They were the only ones who knew Xu, the only ones other than Xu who knew what had happened to those files off Lindy's computer.

He sat with Eve again at the same scarred table in the interview room. "I'm glad you're still wearing a ponytail," he said to her as the guards brought Cindy and Clive Cahill in.

The first thing out of Clive's mouth when he saw them was, "The guard said you wanted to see us again, Agent Savich. You wouldn't believe—or maybe you would believe—what kind of language Milo Siles used when he found out we'd talked to you without him on Friday. He tried to make us promise we'd never do that again. But Cindy and I—we're beginning to wonder a bit about Mr. Siles, and that's why we agreed to see you without him."

It's about time you're finally realizing Mr. Siles isn't in your corner. Savich said, "Tell you what, Clive, after we talk, you and Cindy can consult with Mr. Siles if you feel the need, how's that?"

Clive and Cindy shared a look, and Clive slowly nodded. "No harm in listening, at least until you bore us." He looked at Eve. "You're quite the little hero, aren't you, doll? It's all over the news how you saved Judge Hunt's life, threw yourself on top of him in that elevator and took three bullets in the back. How good are the Kevlars nowadays? You sore?"

Eve smiled at him. "You bet."

Cindy said, "A pity the guy wasn't a better shot and splashed your brains all over the judge."

Eve turned her smile to Cindy. "My brains are relieved that didn't happen. It's true, I'm still a bit sore, but you, on the other hand, are still wearing chains and brushing your teeth with your fingers."

"Nah," Clive said. "This is a class joint. We even got toothbrushes, but you have a point, they're not electric."

Eve said nothing more. She didn't want to tangle with either of them, at least not yet.

Cindy noticed Savich was looking at her and leaned slightly toward him. "Isn't that sweet, Clive? Little Miss Sunshine with her bouncy ponytail doing her good deeds. She saves a life, then visits us poor put-upon prisoners again with her sidekick, Mr. Tough Guy."

Savich said, "Actually, we wanted to thank you in person for blurting out the name Xu. So how does he spell that? *X-u*? Or *S-u*? *S-o-o*, maybe? At any rate, he's Chinese, and he's your handler. We know he's fluent in English and no one has yet pegged him as Asian, so he's either very good at disguises or he's an American. Is he American?"

Cindy and Clive didn't say anything.

Savich continued. "It's only a matter of time before we find him. If we do that without your help, you won't have anything left to trade."

"I don't remember any Xu," Cindy said. "Xu—who is that, Clive, do you have any idea?"

"Not a one, sweetie. You look beautiful today. I've missed you." He started to lean over to kiss her, but there was a firm fist smack against the glass window in the door and he pulled back. What would the guards do, Eve wondered? Come in and physically distance him from her so he couldn't reach her? Probably. The guards couldn't know when violence would erupt, and wouldn't take that chance.

Savich said, "You know we found Mickey O'Rourke, your federal prosecutor, dead yesterday."

"We heard about that," Cindy said. "Gossip moves at the speed of light in prison, makes my old neighborhood look like slo-mo. Imagine O'Rourke getting himself killed. I didn't find out too many details, because the cops on TV are keeping a lid on it. Only that he met with *foul play.* I've always thought that phrase sounds wussy, don't you, Agent Savich?" She said it again: "Foul play—like they're going to hand out some kind of football penalty.

"Clive, did you hear about poor Mr. O'Rourke getting whacked? That idiot man who preened and strutted around in court and only finally managed to get himself in big trouble with the judge?"

Clive nodded, his lips seamed. "How did he die?"

Eve said, "Xu cut his throat."

Clive's hand went unconsciously to his neck; his fingers lightly rubbed against his skin. "That wasn't very nice."

"No, it wasn't." Savich sat back and regarded the two of them. "You can't think this is part of some master plan to get you out anymore. It seems to me Xu is snipping off loose ends, killing anyone who might know who he is.

Do you want to know who the big whopper loose ends left are?" He suddenly sat forward, pointed at one, then at the other. "You and Cindy."

The Cahills' eyes met briefly, then Cindy laughed. "That's a stretch, isn't it, Agent Savich? Unbelievable, that's what it is. We've been in this lovely facility now for eight months, fourteen days—"

"Thirteen days," Clive said.

Cindy shook her head. "You know I believe thirteen is unlucky, Clive. Nope, this is the fourteenth day. Being here means we're safer than you two are driving on Highway 101 at rush hour. Do you know, if I were this mythical Xu you talk about, I wouldn't be too worried about your catching me, any more than you could catch a box of smoke."

"Smoke—did Xu describe himself that way to you?" Savich said.

Cindy smiled broadly. "Oh, I don't know any Xu. That's only what I say—I mean, he is leading all of you around by your noses, isn't he?"

Eve said, "Xu has managed to get away so far. But smoke? When we take him down we'll ask him how he wants to style himself then."

Clive said, "Yep, the guy sure made you look like incompetent morons. Oops, I guess I shouldn't say that, should I? You might order up the waterboarding."

Eve leaned forward. "You might as well know we wounded him"—*Well, not quite, but close enough*—"we have his DNA, and when we match it we'll know exactly who Xu is. You know the CIA will have his prints, even if Xu is a brand-new alias for him. As Agent Savich said, it's only a matter of time." And Eve sat back, crossed her arms over her chest, and continued, "The CIA is coming back soon to talk to you again." She gave an elaborate shrug. "Waterboarding? I hear they don't use that anymore, old hat now. The CIA has much better methods.

"You know they've got a lot of motivation to find out everything you know, since Mark Lindy's project was highly classified. They won't even tell us about it. Believe me, everybody wants to catch this guy before he leaves the country. So Agent Savich and I have been talking with the U.S. attorney, and he's willing to make you an offer if you tell us what you know."

The Cahills were silent again, but there was something in the air between them. Fear? Of Xu getting to them?

Savich picked it up. "Suppose for a moment you get out by some quirk, even on bail. Xu would have every reason to kill you."

Eve shrugged. "Of course, if you wait until the CIA gets here, they could bollix everything up. Or Xu could be captured or killed. Either way, we wouldn't have anything to offer you then."

Cindy Cahill yawned. Her wrist chains rattled as she raised her hand to pat her mouth. She froze. Too bad the rattling chains always ruined a good performance.

Cindy said, "Agent Savich, we don't have any idea what you're both talking about. We're United States citizens, and we haven't been convicted of anything. You can't think we believe the CIA is going to haul us off to Guantánamo Bay?"

"And we didn't steal anything," Clive said, his voice parroting Cindy's tone, as convincing as his lawyer's. "Cindy and I have maintained our innocence throughout this debacle. We know nothing of this Xu or O'Rourke's murder or the two attempts on Judge Hunt's life. We don't know anything at all. We're in jail. Get over it."

"I'm getting bored, Clive, honey," Cindy said.

"Me, too, sweetie," Clive said, "but, hey, at least we get to see each other."

Eve knew they weren't getting anywhere fast. It was time to get down and dirty. She said, "Surely you two are smart enough to realize you could be convicted on half the evidence the prosecutors have. You are both going down, and that means all the way down to a lethal injection."

Clive smiled at her. "I thought you said the CIA was going to haul us away, never to be seen again?"

Eve turned to Cindy. "Tell me, Cindy, do you have any idea what you're going to look like in five years? Ten years? In fifteen years, right before you get the needle in your arm?

"Let me tell you what I've seen. You'll probably exercise for another year to keep your body in shape, but you'll be fighting a losing battle. They feed you lots of carbs and fat, and you'll gain weight because there's not much else to do in prison but eat. After a while, you'll stop exercising, I mean, why keep it up? Who is there to admire you? A bunch of women who could view you as too pretty and hate your guts and hurt you?

"Your skin turns pasty in jail because there isn't much sun available to you, and no good beauty creams. In five years, you'll be a fat slob and anyone you know now who sees you will hardly recognize you. Clive will, and because he might still care about you, in theory, he'll try not to gag.

"When they finally put that needle in your arm, you'll be a ruin, and they'll be putting you out of your misery. You'll end up only a name and a carcass to be disposed of."

Eve kept quiet and waited. They were crude threats, but they were all she had left. She listened to Cindy Cahill's pumped-up breathing, watched the appalling comprehension in her eyes before she managed to smooth it away. But Cindy couldn't veil the rage that followed. It beamed out of her eyes like a flashing beacon. She said, "I hope Xu cuts your face up before he kills you, bitch."

"That's not going to happen, so listen up. Tell us about Xu and what he has, and you won't have to worry about him, or about dying in here."

There was a heavy lump of silence, while the two of them looked at each other. Clive gave Cindy a small shake of his head.

Eve felt Dillon's hand pat her knee. He said, "You know what I admire about you, Clive? You're a real gamer. You know how to spot the perfect mark; you know how to manipulate your mark into doing exactly what you want. You picked out Cindy, didn't you, because you knew you could mold her to be exactly what you needed?"

Clive said, "Then I'm smart enough to know when I'm being gamed, right, Agent?"

"Sure you are. There'll be lots of games in prison, Clive, but you won't win many of them; you won't even get to play because you'll be the game. The inmates will recognize you fast enough as a *GQ* sort of guy who's used to the good life and sees them as a bunch of low-life yahoos. Believe me, they'll detest you on sight. They'll make you very sorry you look good, Clive.

"The chances are they'll make you their bonus buddy, at least for a while, as long as you're looking good. After that, it depends on how bored and sadistic they are."

Eve heard the tension in Clive's voice. "Come on, that sort of thing doesn't happen anymore. I've been here eight months. No problems like that. Sure, there are disagreements among the inmates, but nothing violent, nothing sexual."

Savich shook his head at Clive. "This is local lockup, Clive, not a big bad federal prison where you're headed. Did Milo Siles try to convince you that if you're found guilty, you'd be headed to one of the federal country clubs for B felons? If he did, he lied.

"No, you're going to a place designed for people like you—violent felons and cold-blooded murderers, there to mark time on death row.

"You're a thinking man, Clive, I told you I admire that. But you're not a tough guy. You won't be able to protect yourself. And you won't have any money to buy yourself out of bad situations.

"Actually, I doubt you'll even last to the end of all your appeals unless they put you in solitary. At least you wouldn't get a hunk of soap pushed down your throat in solitary. On the other hand, who wants to spend the rest of his life in a concrete box by himself?"

The only sound in the small room was the hitch in Clive's breath.

Clive cleared his throat. "What sort of deal are you offering?"

Cindy hissed at him, but Clive didn't look at her.

Savich said, "The death penalty's off the table. You'll get twenty-five years, but it will be in a kind of prison you can look forward to walking out of instead of being carried out in a green body bag."

Clive looked at Cindy, but her eyes remained on Savich's face. "This is bull, Clive. Don't listen to them, they're playing us." She said to Eve now, venom pulsing in her voice, "When I get out, I'm going to kill you if it's the last thing I do."

Eve's eyebrow shot up. "What did I do to you? I've told you the truth, nothing more, nothing less." Eve sat back, touched her fingers to her ponytail. "Do you hate me because I look healthy and clean, and my breath is fresh and I can drink Starbucks coffee every morning if I want to?

"Get off your high horse, Cindy, I'm not the one here who murdered Mark Lindy. Tell us the truth, and you might survive to see the light of day outside of a prison."

Savich watched Clive lean again toward his wife, but at the bang on the door window, he pulled back. He licked his lips. They were dry and peeling. *Not that handsome now, are you, Clive?*

Cindy Cahill rose to her feet, her chains rattling. "I know twenty-five years is way too long. You bring the prison time down with the possibility of parole and we'll think about it. Clive, keep your mouth shut."

He nodded at his wife, but Eve saw him swallow convulsively. *Good.* He was scared, as well he should be.

So was Cindy; she was simply a better actress. Eve wondered if Dillon could get the federal prosecutor down even more. She was of two minds on what should happen to these two violent, greedy people, but protecting Ramsey trumped everything else.

Savich watched the guards walk them out. He doubted either of them would be speaking to Milo Siles about the offer.

36

Saint Francis Wood
San Francisco
Monday afternoon

Emma hovered around the three big men as they tenderly eased her prized ebony Steinway out of the moving van, positioned it onto the big roller board they used for pianos, and carefully pushed it from the driveway onto the side flagstone walkway.

The drizzling rain had stopped for a while, which was a relief, since Molly knew Emma would have tried to plaster herself on top of the waterproof tarp over her piano to make sure it stayed dry.

As for Molly, she was relieved to see the pinched look gone from Emma's face. When Emma had come into the principal's office at her school on Lake Street, her face had been frozen with fear until she'd seen Molly standing there, smiling. Still, Molly had said immediately, "Your dad's okay, Emma." She'd pulled her shaking daughter against her and said again, "He's fine, I promise you. Now, I've decided it's best for us to leave our home for a little while. We're going to stay in a lovely house in Saint Francis Wood. Remember, we've driven through the neighborhood and admired all the older houses, and the big yards, just like ours?"

Emma raised her face. "They're afraid the man is going to try to kill us, aren't they?"

So much for sugarcoating the truth. "Everyone wants to make sure we'll be safe. That's all there is to it."

Emma said with great patience, "Mom, I'm nearly twelve. Tell me what's happened."

Molly nearly lost it then, but she wasn't about to tell her daughter about the message the man had left on the machine. "Nothing happened. I only want all of us to be safe."

"You trust me to take good care of the boys, but you won't tell me the truth? So I'll know what's going on? So if something happens I won't be surprised?"

Good point. "It's possible a man came onto our property last night. Everyone wants us out of there until they catch the man."

"The marshals didn't see him?"

"You know how many ways there are to sneak close to our house. He may have climbed up the cliff, and there'd be no one to see him unless he went around to the front of the house. It will be much easier for everyone in the house we're moving to."

Emma squeezed her mother tightly to her. "It's all

right, Mom. We'll get through. The boys will think it's a cool game. I'll help."

Molly had hugged this precious human being tightly in return, whispered against her hair, "We're bringing your piano."

Those few words had earned her a quick smile from her daughter.

Molly watched the men maneuver Emma's piano to the base of the three front steps of the large Mediterranean house.

Savich looked at Harry, and they tried to join them in carrying the piano up the steps, but the foreman held them back. "Thanks, gentlemen, but we can't have you hurting yourselves. We've got this."

One of his young assistants, who had a tall red Mohawk, said between grunts, "It's the insurance he's worried about. You're right, though, this freakin' sucker's heavy."

Emma hung back, ever watchful. Molly was standing inside the doorway, one eye on the twins, who were examining every inch of the living room, and the other on Emma. The Steinway had never been moved an inch since it was reverently placed in their home in Sea Cliff five years before. This was a huge deal for Emma, and on top of everything else. How could Emma function? How would she react? Could she still see herself playing in front of a huge audience at Davies Hall in nine days? Molly saw her smile at Red Mohawk, who was grunting big-time, just for her, and hoped.

Once they carried the piano into the entrance hall, Red Mohawk grinned down at Emma. "Your mama said you're a big deal, that you're so good you even play with the San Francisco Symphony. That true?"

Emma never knew what to say to this sort of question. She was aware her mother was watching her, ready to speak for her, but she knew she was old enough to answer for herself. "I'm not playing with the orchestra this time. I'm playing by myself—George Gershwin's *Rhapsody in Blue,* a week from Wednesday. I don't know if there are still tickets left, but you could ask. What's your name?"

The young man laughed and touched his bush of hair. "You can call me Mohawk. Let me see the size of your hands." Emma held up her hands. The young guy studied them, placed them palm to palm. "Unbelievable," he said.

The foreman said, "Do you know what my name is? I'm Sam Davis, but there's no relation."

Emma stared at him. She didn't have a clue what he was talking about.

"Sammy Davis Jr.; he was one of the Rat Pack," he said, but Emma was still in the dark.

He grinned at her. "Ask your dad or maybe your granddad; one of them will know."

Once they lifted the piano back onto the roller board, Emma trailed behind them as they steered the Steinway through the doorway into the long living room.

"Here," she said, "in this corner, wide part of the case out."

When the piano was placed exactly, Red Mohawk

brought in her piano bench and set it just so in front of the keyboard.

Emma looked at each man in turn. "Thank you for taking such good care of my piano."

Red Mohawk said, "Play us something if you really want to thank us."

Gage, whose hand was now being firmly held by his mother, shouted, "Emmie, play them the theme from *Star Wars*."

Cal shouted louder, "No, the theme from *Jaws*!"

Emma grinned at her little brothers, sat down, and played "Nobody Does It Better." There were whistles and applause, and a couple of boos from Cal and Gage.

When the movers left, Emma took Gage and Cal upstairs to show them their new bedroom, the twins chattering away in the twin talk they spoke when they didn't want anyone to know what they were saying.

Molly waved her hand around the living room. "This is very nice. However did you manage to get us this beautiful house on such short notice?"

Savich said, "The house is for sale. When the owner found out Judge Dredd needed it as a safe house for his family, he offered it to us immediately."

"It has some of the feel of our home," Molly said. "Built a long time ago and beautifully remodeled." Her voice hitched, and she added quickly, "Come along, I'll make us all coffee. Tea, Dillon?" She motioned away Sherlock. "No, let me do this. At least I still have control over making coffee."

When they were all seated around the authentic-looking

fake Chippendale dining room table, Molly said, "The red-and-cream walls blend so well with this rich furniture. It makes this room oddly peaceful. Thank you all so much for coming here with us. It makes this all less difficult."

Sherlock said, "The backyard is fenced in, so the boys will be fine. The owner is sending over a jungle gym for Cal and Gage, said his granddaughter's outgrown it."

Savich's cell phone rang, and he left the room to answer it.

Sherlock said, "We're hoping for a phone call from Clive Cahill, telling us he's ready to deal. It's been nearly an hour since Dillon and Eve talked to them."

"Not Cindy?" Molly asked.

Sherlock shook her head. "Dillon thinks Clive's the weak link in this chain, or maybe he's the more realistic."

Harry nodded. "Eve said her money's on him as well. I know she has all her digits crossed. She wanted to be here, but she's meeting Marshal Maynard, going over plans for Judge Hunt's protection. Last time I saw she had her cell phone attached to her ear."

Molly asked, "Do you think the Cahills will talk?"

Sherlock said, "We'll know soon. We tried to reach Milo Siles, their lawyer, but his secretary told us Milo was in a divorce mediation session with his wife and her lawyer this morning and hasn't returned to the office yet. She let drop he was probably in a rage and she'd bet he'd turned off his cell until he calmed down. Still, Dillon tried to call him, but it went right to voice mail."

Molly said, "What do you think is going on?"

Sherlock said, "Since Siles was angry, it could be as simple as his sitting in some bar somewhere sulking."

When Savich walked back to the dining room it was to tell them it was Cheney, who'd gotten a call from his buddy, Marin County Sheriff Bud Hibbert.

It wasn't good.

37

A chill, thick mist cloaked the golden Marin hills in gray. They hit heavy rush-hour traffic on the approach to the Golden Gate Bridge. Harry passed Cheney the emergency light bar, and Cheney stuck his arm out of the window and plopped its magnetic base on the roof. Traffic, thankfully, made way for them as best it could. Harry always got a kick out of using a magic blinking light bar, made him feel like Moses parting the Red Sea.

Cheney said, "Let me give you some background on Pixie McCray, some of which I learned from Milo Siles's secretary. Pixie was divorced, no kids, and she was a legal secretary for Mifflin, LaRochette, and Kent, a firm Milo has litigated against many times over the years. That's how they met. We don't yet know how long they've been together, but I found out Milo bought Pixie's house about four and a half years ago. He bought a Sea Ray

Sundancer to go with it, a fast luxury yacht that even has a swimming platform. It's parked right on his own private dock on the lagoon."

"Pixie—a charming name," Sherlock said. "And now she's dead, along with Milo Siles, just because he was visiting her."

Savich said, "I wonder if Milo's wife knew about Pixie."

Cheney said, "Even though his wife was using photos to get more leverage in the divorce settlement, according to Siles's lawyer, my guess is neither of them cared much about what the other was doing for the past five years or so. That's from Siles's divorce lawyer. He said Milo left really mad about his wife's demands at the mediation session, and that's the last anyone saw him."

Sherlock asked, "How did Xu find out about Pixie McCray?"

Cheney cut his eyes to her. "Funny thing is, it wasn't a big buried secret. The house in Bel Marin Keys is in Milo's name, and so is the Sea Ray Sundancer, both easy to find out."

Sherlock said, "I gather this house and boat weren't part of her demands?"

Harry said matter-of-factly, "Milo Siles's wife is obviously having an affair, too, maybe even a long-term affair, like her husband, so they seemed to treat it as no harm, no foul."

Sherlock closed her eyes for a moment. How could anyone live like that? Were Milo Siles and his mistress, Pixie McCray, dead because the Cahills had told him too much about Xu? Had Milo tried to blackmail Xu? Or was it simply because he'd known who Xu was and what he'd done that had signed his death warrant?

She said, "We need to keep checking on whether Siles had any hidden accounts, see if he got himself killed because Xu paid him to keep his mouth shut."

Savich nodded. "If Milo hid any money in his own name, he was pretty sophisticated about it. It could take some time, but MAX will find it eventually."

Sherlock said, "I'm hoping we don't find any accounts. That would mean Milo wasn't so stupid as to imagine he'd come out of this whole-hide if he was dealing with Xu."

And Pixie McCray, who probably hadn't known anything, hadn't done anything to anyone at all, was dead, too.

Cheney kept the lights flashing until they turned east off 101 on the Bel Marin Keys exit. They drove through an industrial area, then wetlands, and finally past some palm trees lining the road on both sides. The closer they moved toward San Pablo Bay and its myriad waterways, the heavier the fog became. The roadways crisscrossed around the lagoons, the fog blending with the water like a surrealist painting. The rain picked up and the gloom deepened. It was nearly dark now.

Cheney said, "On a sunny day, this is a beautiful area, fairly affluent, with hundreds of homes sitting either on a lagoon or on Novato Creek. All the lagoons have access to San Pablo and San Francisco bays, as you can see from all the boats. I have a friend who lives not far from Pixie's house, on her same street. I wonder if he knew Pixie McCray. Maybe he's even seen Milo Siles at her house."

Cheney turned left off Bel Marin Keys Boulevard onto Calypso Shores. The houses were set close together, the landscaping mature and well maintained, a great place for both families with kids and retirees. Cheney pulled Eve's Suburban up to the curb about a half-block from Pixie's house, the closest available spot. The houses blocked the view of the lagoons and the boat docks, but they could see the water at the end of the street, and the lock where boats came through. They huddled under umbrellas and walked quickly to the house. There were half a dozen Crown Vics, a couple of them haphazardly parked in the driveway, others against the curb, one up on the lawn. The county coroner's van and the county's Crime Analysis Unit van were parked in the middle of the street, blocking traffic.

Neighbors were standing around, staring and talking, looking generally horrified, huddled beneath umbrellas and awnings as the rain beat down.

The white wooden house was a single story with a big solar panel on the roof, built some thirty years ago. It still managed to look stylish, its three palm trees in the front yard adding a bit of tropical charm.

Sheriff Bud Hibbert met them at the front door. "I'd just as soon not have seen you guys until the Christmas party. What this guy did, how fast he moved—it's frightening. They're in the bedroom."

They left their umbrellas on the front porch and

walked around two forensic techs and a sheriff's deputy through the country feminine living room and a small country kitchen with a connected eating area, and down the carpeted hall to the end of the corridor.

Sheriff Hibbert asked for the photographer to stand back for a moment and motioned them around the big king-size bed. It was a god-awful scene, Sherlock thought, so much blood. There was always so much blood. She sometimes wondered how a human body could hold that much blood.

The sheriff said, "I haven't let them touch the bodies. The crime scene's just as it was when a deputy arrived after we got a call from a neighbor who heard Pixie's dog carrying on and came to see what was happening."

None of them really wanted to, but they looked closely at what had once been two living, breathing people until Xu had slit their throats.

The sheriff said, "All their clothes are in place, so no sexual activity had begun even though they were lying on the bed. Look at the blood splatter, the way their bodies ended up when they died. Siles's head has nearly fallen off the near side of the bed, and she's fallen nearly off the other side of the bed. I've been trying to figure out exactly what happened."

Savich pointed at Sherlock. She was standing quietly at the foot of the bed, and he knew she was putting it all together in her mind, using her special gift to picture what few people could see at a crime scene.

"Sherlock?"

She said, "He came in quietly, saw them. He was fast,

silent, and smart—even managed to lock Pixie's terrier outside without alerting them. Milo was first. He grabbed him by his hair, jerked his head back, sliced his throat—again, right to left. Not even a second, that's all the time it took. He let Milo fall, reached over him, grabbed Pixie by her hair, jerked her head toward him, then back so violently it snapped her neck. When he sliced her throat he must have been staring down at her, watching her eyes as she realized she was dying. The coroner might be able to determine which of those things killed her, not that it makes any difference.

"You can see the dried tears on Milo's cheeks. He was crying, his head probably against Pixie's shoulder. She was—comforting him."

Sheriff Hibbert stared at Sherlock for a moment. He said slowly, "Yes, I can see that now. Thank you."

Cheney said, "Milo came to her for comfort. And he got her killed."

Sheriff Hibbert said, "Let's back out now, let the coroner and the CAU people do their jobs."

Sherlock paused. "The CAU?"

"Yeah, the Crime Analysis Unit; that's what we call our forensic section."

Sherlock said, "Of course. We're from the CAU in Washington, the Criminal Apprehension Unit."

Sheriff Hibbert said as he walked them to the back of the house that gave onto the waterway and the boat dock, "The neighbor—Mrs. Dee Kotter—saw Pixie's terrier, Bob. He was locked out of the house, and that surprised her, since it was raining. She knocked on the door, found it wasn't locked, and found them. She told us Milo was a twice-a-week fixture at Pixie's house, her longtime boyfriend. He was always polite, spoke to the neighbors who spoke to him, and made Pixie happy. She said it was sort of a joke with Pixie, always saying why marry a man and put up with the toilet lid being up all the time? Better to have him visit, orderly and planned, and that was the way she liked it. The neighbor didn't know Milo was married.

"Mrs. Kotter took Bob. Last time I saw her, she was petting him, kissing him over and over, and crying.

"It's nearly dark, so canvassing the neighborhood is tough. And the damned rain doesn't help. We don't believe it was raining when the killer got here, so hopefully someone saw a stranger, a car, something.

"We also have men over on Caribe Isle—that's the spit of land across the water—interviewing everyone along the street. There's a small park at the end of the spit, and a narrow beach with a nice view of the back of all the houses along this street, including Pixie's house.

"Even though there was a break in the rain, I don't know if anyone was in the park or on that skinny beach. So far, we don't have anything."

Savich cursed. Sherlock was so surprised she nearly tripped over a Christmas cactus on the wide back porch.

Savich said, "I just realized, Xu's got two major loose ends left—the Cahills. You know he's going after the Cahills. Ramsey, at least, is safe from him for the moment."

He got Eve on the first ring.

"Barbieri."

"He's going after the Cahills next. I know in my gut he's got a pipeline into the jail. Xu has to know they're going to flip on him now he's killed Siles. Eve, get over to the jail, get them to safety."

When Savich punched off, he said, "She's going to bring the Cahills to the twentieth floor, put them in one of the pre-court holding cells."

They stood under the wide porch and looked out over the water to Caribe Isle, listened to the waves bumping against the dock. It was dark and miserable, the rain coming down in torrents. A deputy sheriff strode through the rain from the neighbor's yard, a black umbrella over his head.

He shouted, "Sheriff, we got a winner!"

They'd found an old gentleman on Caribe Isle who'd been walking on the narrow beach beyond the small park. He had a straight view to the back of Pixie McCray's house and her dock. He was chewing on his pipe since he didn't smoke anymore, he told the deputy, hurrying because he knew the rain was going to start up again, and that wasn't good because Purlie, his bulldog, hated to do her business in the rain. He said it was nearly four o'clock when he saw a small outboard motorboat come through the lock, turn left, and motor to Pixie's dock. He saw a man climb onto the dock and go into the house.

Did he see the man leave?

Nope. Purlie was through doing her business, and it started drizzling again, so he took her home.

Xu had come by boat, just as he'd done the night he'd motored the Zodiac to Sea Cliff and shot Ramsey.

They went to speak to Mrs. Dee Kotter, Pixie's neighbor, but she was in shock, numb. She was crying again, holding Bob close, both of them shivering in disbelief and horror at what had happened, here, in Bel Marin Keys, and nothing ever happened here.

38

San Francisco
Monday night

Xu stood beneath the striped awning of Morrie's Deli on Seventh Street, looking through the rain at the Hall of Justice across the street, and waited. It really didn't make any difference that he was there because there wasn't anything more he could do. But even if he couldn't control what would happen, he wanted to be close.

He hated feeling impotent. He'd had no choice but to put his trust in people he hardly knew to carry out his plans, too often a recipe for disaster. His Chinese trainers had dinned into his head over the years never to give anyone else a task that was critical to a mission. And nothing could be more critical to him than Cindy and Clive Cahill dying tonight.

It was at moments like this that he wondered what his life would be like if he had stayed Joe Keats, the name he'd picked for himself when he was eighteen and tired of having Xian Xu mangled and then mocked as a girl's name by the uneducated idiots in Lampo, Indiana. No one ever mispronounced Joe Keats. Except for some of the braying asses he'd trained with in Beijing, who thought it shameful that he, with a Chinese father, had taken on an American name.

He drew a calming breath. He had done what he could, and if his plans went south, he was ready to run, from the FBI, even from Chinese intelligence, if he had to. He would survive.

Joyce Yang, the girl who'd turned him to the dark side, she'd say and laugh her husky laugh that made him mad with lust, and why not, he'd been only twenty years old. He'd loved her with everything in him, at least in those long-ago days before she'd betrayed him with a mid-rung operative, Li Han, in Chinese intelligence, and Xu had cut her throat and buried her deep near her precious hometown of Beijing, where he knew the choking sand from the Gobi Desert would score her grave until her bones were uncovered in the years to come, a fitting place for her, he'd thought at the time. As for Li Han, a man who looked like he was supposed to—Chinese through and through—Xu had left him with a slit throat in an alley in one of the many nasty parts of Beijing where murder was as common as girls selling themselves for a bowl of rice. Would their kids have looked Caucasian like him or like their mother, a full-blooded Chinese?

He looked at his watch. Nine-twenty on this dark rainy night in San Francisco. Soon he'd be drinking scotch at the Fairmont Hotel, watching the football wrap-up of the Monday-night game on the big flat-screen TV in the sports bar.

He whistled, realized he didn't have enough spit in his mouth. For twelve years he'd survived—indeed, he'd thrived—working undercover in the American section of Chinese intelligence. They had taken to calling him *mingzing*—the star—because of what he'd accomplished for them. He'd learned to be ruthless in the way they respected, and yet he was charming enough to talk people out of their paychecks. Maybe his black hair was a bit too glossy and coarse, but no one would question that he looked entirely American, just like his mother, Ann Xu, who'd been an American history teacher at Lampo High School. The principal, fat Mr. Buck, hadn't made fun of him like his peers had, since Xu was the school system's expert in cyber-security. Buck even managed to get him a computer science scholarship to Berkeley. Xu wondered sometimes what Mr. Buck was doing these days. He smiled now. No way Mr. Buck, the bulwark of American conceit and smugness, could know his prized student had killed three students on his watch. Even then, Xu had been good at making people simply disappear.

Joyce poked into his memory again, those beautiful almond eyes of hers, whispering her flawless English in his ear how it would astound her trainers that he could so easily pass for a Caucasian. Like him, she'd been born in the U.S., not twenty miles from Berkeley. Ah, those days at Berkeley, hoisting up the Chinese flag, screaming with other protesters about the brilliance and honor of the Chinese people and the profligacy and corruption of Americans. He'd learned over the years, though, that it was the Chinese who had the market cornered in corruption. He wasn't like the Chinese, he wasn't corrupt, he carried his assignments out promptly and professionally—but now he was watching in disbelief as his life spiraled into the crapper in the span of five short days.

He'd failed in his mission—his *anli*—his superiors had told him, because he'd chosen defective tools, yet they'd happily approved Xu's plans when he'd assured them Cindy Cahill could focus her attention on Mark Lindy and he'd be stuttering to do whatever she wished. And he'd been right, Lindy couldn't resist her, just as his handlers couldn't resist trying to get their hands on the latest generation of the Stuxnet worm Lindy was working on. Even the original Israeli worm had infected sixty percent of Iranian computers and slowed down their production of nuclear fuel for years. Having the access codes to Lindy's work was as important to their industrial security as having the hydrogen bomb.

But his superiors had ended up being right about those two losers, Cindy and Clive Cahill. To cover themselves, they said they'd known Lindy would be too smart and too cagey to fall for a Mata Hari, that he'd be as careful with his passwords as the devil with a bowl of ice cubes.

Xu remembered as clearly as if it had happened today when he'd gotten a call from Cindy more than eight months ago, hysterical, screaming—Lindy was dead, that it wasn't her fault he'd been called in by some sort of incident response team and they'd questioned him about accessing private networks that Lindy knew he hadn't accessed, and he'd accused her of calling up the Stuxnet program on his computer. She'd called in Clive, and he'd held Lindy down while Cindy had poured the poison down his throat. Idiots, both of them, asking to be caught, and they had, of course.

All his superiors in Beijing had wanted was to have him steal the information and leave the country, with no one the wiser, if possible. They blamed him that a high-ranking American cyber-intelligence officer had died. They made it clear they wanted no more killings, and so he'd made a deal with the Cahills, hired Milo to keep them quiet, gotten O'Rourke in line, and waited.

Until everything went to hell. O'Rourke had pan-icked, ready to spill his guts to that damned judge when he'd suspended the trial. He'd fixed that problem, but he still couldn't be sure how much Judge Hunt knew, or suspected.

From the moment he'd slit O'Rourke's throat, he'd been on his own. From that point on, the Chinese would be more likely to have him killed to prevent his arrest than to help him. Perhaps if he succeeded tonight, the Chinese would see he'd acted in their best interest as well as his own.

It will be all right, Xu, you'll see, it doesn't matter that those silly kids are making fun of you, my darling, that just makes them stupid. And his mother had rocked him when he was small, and he'd believed her, but he'd started to feel a simmering rage, a rage that seemed to encase him like a tunnel, and he knew he wanted to kill them all for mocking him. When Xu was fourteen, one of the bullies with a brand-new driver's license had died in an auto accident, or so it was ruled. He remembered his mother had looked at him as if she knew what he'd done, but she'd said nothing. But he remembered now, she was watchful, always watchful after that. He'd been more careful with the other two bullies.

Xu shook his head, wondering why he'd think of his mother now, wondering, too, if she would rock him now, tell him he was smart, that he'd figure his way through this fiasco, and everything would be all right. Had she known then he would kill again? And again?

As for his father, he was grateful to the loser for two things—he'd forced him to learn Mandarin and had sent him to Beijing to visit his grandfather before the old man dropped over dead during Xu's last visit when he was seventeen.

He looked down at his watch again, saw a streak of blood on his left wrist. How could he have missed it? He scrubbed his skin until the dried blood flaked off. Was it Milo's blood, or the woman's? What was her name? Pixie, that was it, like some lame rip-off of Tinker Bell.

No matter. Soon Billy Cochran would be dispatching Clive Cahill to hell. He knew Cochran as an angry man who'd killed before, a three-time felon set to transfer out to San Quentin in the morning. Cochran had very little to lose, and was enough of a veteran inmate to know how to kill Clive without being caught. Cochran had been eager enough to accept the offer Xu had made when he'd visited him—he was leaving an aging grand-mother who needed money badly. Cochran was vicious enough and would feel no remorse, but there was always the question of whether he could pull it off. He'd been caught three times, after all. Xu wished he could do it himself, but it wasn't possible.

Nine-twenty-nine—one minute until Cochran killed Clive. Xu himself had set the time. That was when the TVs were turned off and the prisoners were herded to the showers before they returned to their cells for the night.

Nine-thirty exactly. Cochran should be smoothly slip-ping his shiv into Clive's back to penetrate his heart, and he'd fall dead without a sound, leaving trails of his blood to mix with the water going down the shower drain. Cochran would be gone in the morning, and there was no missing that fool. Xu looked through the big window into Morrie's Deli and thought about a corned beef on rye. He realized he hadn't eaten all day, but not yet, not just yet.

Cindy's death might be more problematic, and a pity, really. He thought of the last time he'd had sex with Cindy, what a delight she was as she slid her fingers beneath her thong and shimmied it down her legs. Yes, a pity. Once, a long time ago, he'd thought they might work together again.

The best he could find was a scared little Asian woman, maybe five feet tall, and one hundred pounds. She'd spoken to Cindy to gain her trust; he'd made sure of that. He'd found Lin Mei himself, out on bail, and he'd found she had a little boy. She didn't have Cindy's physical strength, and that might be a problem if Cindy spotted the blade at the last second. Still, he had more faith in Lin Mei than in Cochran. She was an immigrant, and he'd been right to think she'd believe him absolutely when he looked her directly in the eyes and told her in fluent Mandarin her son would die if she failed in her task.

It was nine-thirty-five now, and it was over, one way or the other. He looked into the rain-soaked night and imagined fireworks, bursting balls of sparkling red shooting out of the top of the Hall of Justice.

He prayed the whole nightmare was over.

He pulled his collar up on his Burberry rain jacket and walked down Seventh Street toward the Bayshore Freeway, where his Audi was parked in a safe underground garage.

As he cranked the engine he realized he'd forgotten the corned beef on rye. It was a cop deli, too, probably delicious.

39

Harry pulled his Shelby into the driveway, cut the engine, and turned to face Eve. She had asked him about every detail of the crime scene in Bel Marin Keys. They had fallen back on talking about the brutal murders as dispassionately and professionally as they could, but it was difficult.

Eve said, "At least Savich should have a real shot with the Cahills tomorrow morning. We've got them isolated in the marshal holding cells, out of contact. They shouldn't find out about Milo's murder until Savich springs it on them. There's a good chance one of them will talk, since Xu killed their lawyer this time, their only contact with Xu and the person they've been pinning their hopes on to get them out. What's left for them to try?"

Eve opened both her car door and her umbrella, and ducked under it. She stepped onto the driveway and took her first good look at Harry's house. Even in the dark with the rain pouring down, she could see enough to be surprised at how big it was, probably worth a bundle even in this depressed market. She liked the shake roof and the big windows that gave it a colonial sort of feel even without the columns. She ran through the rain from Harry's Shelby to the front door. A bright porch light was a welcoming beacon. There were even ferns hanging from under the porch ceiling, still looking perky, though it was nearly Thanksgiving. She imagined the tree-filled yard would be spectacular in the spring and summer.

"I like your house; it's the showcase of the neighborhood, isn't it? You'll have to tell me how you snagged it."

He gave her only a curt nod. It was odd, Eve thought, but Harry had seemed a bit unwilling to bring her here, but, as she reminded him, he'd been to her condo, and now it was time for her to see his digs.

His wife's digs, he'd said, not looking at her.

Since she'd left the Suburban at the marshals' pool at the Federal Building, he'd offered to take her home. She knew he hadn't realized he would be making a stop first.

"Everything is beautiful. You have a gardener, don't you?"

He nodded. "His name is Mr. Sanchez. He's been with me six years, comes once a week. His son helps him now." He paused for a moment as he stuck his key in the front door, looked over his shoulder at her. "I just realized I don't know his first name. He's always been Mr. Sanchez to me. His son goes by Junior Sanchez." He smiled. "Not Sanchez Junior."

He pushed open the door, turned off the alarm, and stepped back for her. "Come on in."

Eve shook out her umbrella and slipped it inside a copper umbrella pot. She stood in a small square entryway with a mirror on the wall above a curvy modern table for mail and flowers, but the beautiful Italian cachepot was empty. The gardeners didn't work inside. He pointed her to the living room, where a big easy chair, an ottoman, and a big-screen TV were displayed front and center, and a pile of newspapers had been tossed in a haphazard stack on the floor beside the chair. Sure, there was a sofa, chairs, and a coffee table, all with an Italian country flavor, but it was obvious he never sat there. Other than the pile of newspapers, nothing else was out of place. No beer cans, no running shoes. Two *Sports Illustrated* magazines sat on the coffee table. She gave him points when she saw that neither one was the swimsuit issue.

Still, everything was so "guy," she had to smile. She looked at the walls, saw they were covered with framed travel posters—of Lake Como, the Alps, Parliament on the Thames—all in full color, inviting you to step right in. She waved toward the posters. "Do you like to travel, Harry?"

"Yes."

She turned to him. "Only a simple yes? No explanation, like whether you've been to all these places and which one is your very favorite in the whole world?"

"That would be Lake Como, I guess. The hiking is great around there. I like Inverness for hiking, too."

She said, "I've never been to Inverness."

"It's stark, usually cloudy, often raining, and almost, well, painfully real. Would you like some coffee?"

She checked her watch. "I'd be a moron to drink coffee this late. You have nonfat milk? Splenda?"

He had both.

Eve watched him grind coffee beans, then measure the ground coffee into the filter and dump water in from the sink tap.

Harry said, "Funny what Savich said about Billy Hammond, his friend at the CIA in Langley. He wouldn't verify anything at all about the information Xu obtained or was after, even though he's known Savich for a hundred years, give or take. That kind of secrecy, it's enough to make you gag in your soup."

"At least he apologized," Eve said. "It must be incredibly sensitive stuff if they're putting tape over his mouth. I'll bet they already know exactly what was accessed, since it would be recorded on their servers. They just don't want anyone else to know, though, even us."

"According to Savich," Harry said, "they weren't much interested in interviewing the Cahills. They probably know the Cahills didn't know about the information Xu accessed, or how valuable it is. But maybe they know enough to help us find Xu."

"That's all we want from them, really," Eve said.

Suddenly he was staring at her as they stood in his kitchen, listening to the coffee perk, shaking his head.

"What? Do I have rain still dripping off my nose?"

He said, "The first time I saw you I thought you looked like a homecoming queen from somewhere in the Midwest, someone who should be frosting cupcakes for her kid's birthday party. I wondered, how can she possibly be a deputy U.S. marshal?" He shook his head again. "You're so damned pretty." Then he waved his hands, as if he were trying to wave away his words.

Since it was obvious to her that Harry wished he'd kept his mouth shut, Eve waved her own hands at his kitchen cabinets. "You said you liked my kitchen. I had it remodeled last year, you know. I found a really good contractor who came in on budget and on time. You want her name?"

"Nah, everything works fine. Once in a while the sink clogs, but that's no big deal."

She grinned. "You're right. Nothing wrong with cooking in the 1940s. Now that I think about it, if you wait another couple of years, all your kitchen appliances will be back in style as retro, except maybe for those green-tinted cabinets."

He handed her a mug of coffee, gave her nonfat milk from the refrigerator, and dug out a couple of packets of Splenda from his stuff drawer. As she stirred her coffee, she said, "What you said, Harry—do you know my brothers are always saying the same thing? They still call me Miss Suzie-Q.

"When I told my dad I wanted to be a U.S. marshal like he is, though, he looked at me up and down and said, 'That would make me very proud, Eve. It's a great career choice for you. You'll be one of the best.'" She paused for a moment, looked down into her coffee mug. "Yes, that's exactly what he said, straight up. I've never forgotten." She cleared her throat and drank some coffee. "This is very good, Harry. Do you cook?"

"When the need arises. What did your mom say?"

Eve took another sip of her coffee, enjoyed the zing of caffeine, though she knew she'd be cursing herself at two a.m. "When my dad told her what I wanted to do, she laughed. And laughed. She was happy. I saw her kiss my dad and shake her head and say something about the apple not falling far from the tree.

"I look just like my mom, you know. It's funny what you said, Harry, because my mom was a college cheerleader. And I can still see her cutting our birthday cakes at our big kid parties, hear her singing at the top of her lungs, leading all the kids in a sing-along. I might add that everyone adored her. She was so beautiful, so bouncy and fun. She still is."

Harry said, "So you fell pretty close to both trees. And your dad's the U.S. marshal in Chicago?"

"Yep. Like I told you, he's an anomaly. He's served under two different presidents now, unlike most of the ninety-four marshals countrywide. Tell me about your folks, Harry."

He shrugged. "They live in London—well, they do for most of the year. They love to travel, always have, and they took me with them. I guess they gave me the travel bug."

She could only gape at him. Parents lived in Harrisburg, Pennsylvania, for heaven's sake, or Minneola, Florida, not London, England. "Why do they live in London?"

He looked like he wanted to tell her to leave it alone, but he said finally, "My dad's a financier. It sounds old-fashioned, I know, but that's what he says he is."

"What does he finance?"

"Well, he runs Willet, Haversham, and Bayle."

She let out a whistle. "They're so big even I've heard of them. They're worldwide. And they survived the bankers' rape of the world with fairly clean hands, from all I've read. Your dad's CEO?"

"Well, not really. He's the chairman of the board. Actually, he pretty much is Willet, Haversham, and Bayle."

"But your name's Christoff."

"Willet and Haversham are his first and middle names, the middle name from his own father, and Bayle is his best friend. They picked the name because Dad liked the sound of it, all snooty and English, like one of their ancient law firms."

"So your dad is Willet Haversham Christoff? And what's your full name?"

"I'll tell you on my deathbed."

"That bad? Does your name sound like an English duke? All right, I'll wait. Do you have any brothers or sisters?"

"I'm an only child."

"All right, I'll keep pulling hen's teeth. Your mom?"

"Sylvia is my mom. She's a fashion consultant."

She stared at him. "You're kidding."

He shrugged. "She'd take one look at you and want to haul you off to be photographed for *Vogue*. And she'd be right. The camera would love you, she'd say. You've got great bones."

"How would you know that?"

"She took me with her on photo shoots, showed me all the subtle clues in a person's face, actually. I've found it all very useful to a cop."

"With that background, why'd you want to be a cop?"

Harry said, without hesitation, "My uncle Roy, my mom's brother, is FBI. When I was six years old he told me I had the heart of a cop. He was right."

Harry's cell rang. "Yeah?"

His face remained impassive, but his eyes hardened. "We'll be there in twelve minutes."

"What?"

"You put the Cahills in a holding cell in the Federal Building, right? Someone evidently cleared the Cahills to go back to the San Francisco jail. Cheney called, found out they were transferred at eight-forty-five tonight."

"No, that's not possible. I mean—what happened?"

40

Hall of Justice
Women's jail
Monday night

Cindy Cahill shook her hands to regain some circulation as plump mean-as-a-snake Annette in her too-tight uniform trousers unlocked her wrist chains. "Welcome home," Annette said. "Hey, you weren't over in the Federal Building for very long. What was that all about?"

Cindy shook her head. "No one said a word, dragged me and Clive over there, then brought us back."

"Your hubby okay?"

"Clive would be thriving if it was World War Three." She and Clive had been taken to the holding cells on the twentieth floor because Savich had wanted to scare them, and not about the CIA, either, but about Xu, as if he'd have a chance of getting into the jail and killing them. Of course, no one had said that, but she'd known it to her toes. Why hadn't that bitch marshal Barbieri told her what this was all about? Because Barbieri was only a drone, and drones kept their mouths shut, if they even knew the answers.

As she knelt down to unfasten the ankle chains, Annette said, "Maybe this moving you around has to do with your lawyer being murdered up in Bel Marin Keys this afternoon. Both him and his girlfriend."

Cindy's heart stopped, her breath caught in her throat. She put her hand out to the wall so she wouldn't fall over. Milo was dead? Murdered? Of course Xu had killed him, she knew it, and that meant he was cleaning house: O'Rourke, Judge Hunt, Milo—she and Clive were the last ones left. Well, Judge Hunt was alive, but why Xu gave a crap about the judge was a huge question in her mind, since he had nothing to do with anything. Had Milo tried to blackmail Xu into giving him more money? Could he have been that stupid? Or was Xu ready to leave the country? He didn't want to take the chance of anyone finding out his name or anything about him?

And now she and Clive were the only ones left who could tie him to anything at all. It was bad enough Xu had murdered O'Rourke, but she'd believed he'd had to, since O'Rourke had screwed everything up and alerted the judge. It even made sense to her. Both she and Clive had believed Xu would find some other way to get them out. But to murder Milo? Even though in the last couple of days both she and Clive had begun to have doubts about Milo, he'd always calmed her, always made her feel like she was in charge. And he always reminded her that Xu was backing them, the man who had all the money and would spend as much as it took. Xu wasn't bad in the sack, either.

Now he'd murdered Milo.

"Hey, you hadn't heard? That's amazing. The lieutenant burps and everyone in this place knows a meatball sub was delivered before he's finished it off."

"No, I hadn't heard," Cindy said, and she thought, *Screw the twenty-five years.* She suddenly didn't care how old she'd be when she got out of prison. At least she'd have a chance of getting out. Were she and Clive really safe here? If Xu really wanted them dead, could he somehow make it happen? She felt fear so corrosive it was like her stomach was turning in on itself.

"I need to use the phone. I need to call Agent Savich at the FBI."

Annette gave Cindy her patented "I can do whatever I want with you since I'm the boss" look and shook her head. "Nope, sweetheart, you can make your call to Agent Savich during business hours tomorrow. This isn't a hotel. Come on, time for you to shower and get your butt to bed."

"But it's urgent; it's a matter of life and death—"

Annette simply sneered at her. "Like I said, Cindy, this isn't a hotel. Let's go."

Cindy knew Annette wouldn't budge, and so she bowed her head and followed her to the showers. She'd call Savich first thing in the morning.

She didn't pay attention any longer to the guards seeing her naked; it hardly even registered. There were several other women in the showers before lights-out, some of them sullen and quiet, others usually loud and foul-mouthed. She'd learned to avoid the two or three bullies, to stick with those who stayed quiet and left her alone.

How could she get Savich to agree to fifteen years now he knew she was terrified of Xu?

She managed a bit of lather out of the crappy soap bar as she considered what she'd say to Savich. Better to leave Clive out of it, let him deal on his own. She'd known yesterday Clive wanted to tell Savich and Barbieri everything he knew, down to Xu's sock size. And she'd stopped him. Had that been a mistake? No, no, tomorrow morning it would be fine. She knew Savich would interview Clive separately soon enough after her to make sure she'd told him the truth.

She'd still try to bargain for fifteen years. No more, fifteen years. It wasn't a lifetime of years. She could get through it, she *would* get through it. If only Mark Lindy hadn't found out what was happening and freaked out—

Cindy put the bar of soap back on the shelf and turned to see a tiny Asian woman she'd noticed hovering in the background since yesterday, always deferential and polite to her, trying to get Cindy into a conversation. What was her name? She couldn't remember. The woman was standing naked in front of her, something in her hand. In a blur Cindy saw it was a blade. She jumped back, but she wasn't fast enough. The blade sank into her chest even as she slipped and fell on her back onto the wet tiles. She stared at the woman, whispered, "Why did you do that?"

The woman said, "For my son. I'm sorry."

Xu, she thought. Xu had done this. Her last thought was of Clive. Was he dying, too?

41

San Francisco General Hospital
Monday night

Clive Cahill was dead, and Cindy Cahill was fighting for her life in surgery because of a stupid mistake, and it was all her fault, no one else's.

Eve sat in the waiting room with Harry, playing the "if only" game—if only she'd stayed longer with the Cahills at the holding cells on the twentieth floor of the Federal Building, if only she'd thought to read the Cahills' transfer papers from San Francisco jail carefully enough, Xu would never have found them.

No, Miss Brilliance had looked with only one eye and half a brain at the transfer papers, never seen the error that had to be there that returned the Cahills to the San Francisco jail instead of leaving them right here. She had only glanced at the paperwork, really, then trotted out with Harry, excited to think she'd finally see his house. She hadn't even thought to double-check; no, she'd happily hopped into Harry's Shelby and gone with him without another thought about the Cahills' safety. *Her fault*. She'd fire herself if she were her own boss.

Cheney walked into the surgical waiting room with Sherlock and Savich behind him. Before Eve or Harry could open their mouths, Cheney said, "We don't know yet who got to Clive. It was clean and fast, and before anyone knew anything, the guard heard a yell and there was Clive lying dead on the shower floor, a shiv lying beside him in bloody water.

"They found an Asian woman by the name of Lin Mei standing over Cindy, crying, still holding a bloody home-made blade. Lucky for Cindy she stuck her in the chest only once with it, then jerked the blade right out."

Eve said, "Did she say why she did it?"

Savich said, "Lieutenant Clark in the San Francisco Sheriff's Custody Division spoke to her while the EMTs were transporting Cindy Cahill to the hospital. He said her voice sounded like she was drugged or in shock, that she couldn't seem to speak above a whisper. She told Clark a man who looked American told her in fluent Mandarin in the calmest voice she'd ever heard that he would slit her son's throat if she didn't stab Cindy Cahill to death. He handed her a photo of her son shooting bas-kets in a friend's driveway. He even told her where she would find a blade to stab her with tonight—in a drain next to the women's shower. She said she didn't have a doubt he'd do exactly what he said if she didn't kill Cindy."

Sherlock said, "It seems so unlikely, but we know now

that Xu looks American. No one who's seen him thought he looked Asian, but he was always wearing glasses before. So it means he's Chinese American, with Causasian features."

Eve said, "So Xu visited this woman in prison?"

Savich shook his head. "Clark told me that Lin Mei had been out on bail until yesterday. Then she showed up after missing her court date, on purpose, it looks like, told by her court-appointed lawyer, who told her she'd see a judge in the next couple of days and be rebonded. Xu approached her while she was working at her job at the bakery at Whole Foods. He waited patiently until she was on break and stepped in front of her."

Savich shook his head. "Do you know she was arrested for kiting a check for her brother to get him out of trouble with a Chinese gang because she didn't have any money? Now she'll be up for murder."

Eve said, "Hopefully attempted murder with mitigating circumstances. Didn't she think about what would happen to her and her son if she got caught?"

Cheney said, "Caught? She never tried to hide that she'd stabbed Cindy. She was paralyzed by what she'd done, that she'd tried to kill another human being. Lieutenant Clark said after she described what she'd done and why, her eyes rolled back in her head and she fainted. When she woke up she didn't say another word. He said he asked her over and over why she hadn't come and spoken to one of the guards, but she only looked at him with great sadness. He had her brought here to the emergency room."

Eve looked up to see her boss, Marshal Carney Maynard, standing in the doorway. He looked tired, she thought, and unhappy, and she couldn't blame him at all. Maynard said, "There aren't any nurses around who know anything about Cindy Cahill. Is she still alive?"

"She's still in surgery and hanging in," Eve said. "That was all the OR nurse could tell us. She said when the surgery's done, the surgeon will come out and speak to us. It's nearly one a.m., sir, you didn't have to come." *Of course he had to come, you idiot. He's here because of you.*

Maynard said, "I did have to come, Eve. Cindy Cahill is here because my people screwed up."

Nice way of putting it. "No, sir, your people didn't screw up. I screwed up, and I'm singular," Eve said, and looked him straight in the eye. "Let's do this in front of everyone, I deserve it."

Marshal Carney Maynard eyed her back and frowned. "How do you figure you suddenly rule the world, Deputy Barbieri?"

"Sir, the truth is I only glanced at the transfer papers. I should have studied them as carefully as I would if they had been papers bringing Qaddafi's body to the U.S., but I didn't."

Maynard waved a hand to cut her off. He was more frazzled than tired, and here was Barbieri desperately trying to shoulder all the blame. It'd be easier if he could heap it all on her head, but he couldn't. He said, "Since the proverbial buck stops with me, Deputy Barbieri, I'm the one responsible. I knew the importance of this transfer, but I was watching the Monday-night football game.

This was the classic definition of a snafu. I'd hoped never to have one with such disastrous results under my watch, but it's happened, and now we all have to deal with it.

"So dial it down, Eve." He laughed. "We've given our FBI contingent a fine show. Here's what happened. Turns out we had a new deputy driving the prisoner van. His partner didn't look closely at the paperwork, and so they did the run they normally do. They drove Clive and Cindy Cahill straight back from one of our holding cells to the San Francisco jail. That simple. No, Deputy. You did your job. I didn't do mine."

Sherlock said, "No one wins in a blame game, Marshal Maynard. Not even the FBI contingent."

Nurse Camp looked in from the doorway. "Dr. Elba is tied up and asked me to speak to you. Cindy Cahill is out of surgery. Dr. Elba thinks she has an even chance, though she's still oozing blood because of a clotting problem she's developed from all the bleeding. We moved her to recovery. You won't be able to speak to her until morning, all right?"

Harry asked, "Could you please find out about a new patient for us, a Mrs. Lin Mei, probably having a psychiatric evaluation?"

Nurse Camp said, "Not in my bailiwick, Agent. The people at the reception desk can help you find her."

Eve thanked her and watched Savich dial Bill Hammond at the CIA. They could hear a man's voice loud and clear: "Are you nuts, Savich? It's four in the damned morning!"

Harry and Eve looked at each other, knew they didn't

42

Judge Corman Sherlock said to his son-in-law the next morning across the breakfast table, "You're frustrated, Dillon, and no wonder, after last night. How about I give you my membership card for the Pacific Heights Club over on Union Street and you get a good workout? I can call Mr. Eddie, he's usually there, and he's been looking forward to mixing it up with you. He outweighs you by a good twenty pounds, all of it muscle. Even though he's older than you, he's one tough bald bugger."

Savich hated to say no; he couldn't think of anything he needed more than a sweaty hard workout. He shook his head. "I've got to take a rain check with Mr. Eddie. Lacey and I have to get over to the hospital as soon as we can. Cindy Cahill's awake, more or less, and this is our first chance to talk to her."

Five minutes later, after Sean had demolished a bowl of Cheerios and started to rag on his grandmother about the visit to the zoo she'd promised him, even though the zoo wasn't open yet, Sherlock started up their rental car for the ride across town to San Francisco General Hospital.

Savich booted up MAX as they drove toward Market Street. "Cheney is already working on getting a sketch of Xu from Lin Mei. He said he'd have it out to Hammersmith about now, but it doesn't look like he's posted it yet. I wonder how Cindy will react to it."

"I only hope she'll be able to talk to us," Sherlock said. "Cheney said she wasn't doing well."

"If she can, I know in my gut that now she'll tell us everything she knows about Xu, since he tried to have her killed."

He sat back for a moment, closed his eyes. "Until Xu murdered Milo Siles, and his game plan became clear, it was a nightmare trying to predict him. Sometimes he was controlled and logical, sometimes not. What he pulled off last night was an act of desperation, beyond his control. He was lucky it worked out as well as it did."

Sherlock turned onto 101 South. "Ripping up an elevator ceiling, throwing down a smoke bomb, and firing down on a bunch of marshals and Ramsey sure wasn't a logical, controlled act. I still can't figure that one out."

"I can't, either. It's so over-the-top and out of character for him. Why was he so desperate to kill Ramsey in such a crazy way? Bottom line, he's a spy, probably has been for quite a while, and a spy's first watchword, it would seem to me, is discretion. He buried Mickey O'Rourke in a spot no one would ever find. Bad luck for him those kids were there.

"But then he murdered Milo Siles and Pixie McCray in broad daylight when he could easily have been spotted. He's all over the place."

Sherlock said, "I think with Milo it boiled down to eliminating anyone who could hurt him as fast as possible so he can get out of Dodge. It was desperation, like you said. I think if he'd thought he had a choice, he'd have waited until he could get Milo alone, bury him deep, like he did Mickey O'Rourke. I'll tell you, Dillon, it gives me a headache."

Savich grinned at her. "I'm hoping Xu is deluded enough or desperate enough to make a try to kill Cindy in the ICU. I doubled her guard. She's as well covered as Ramsey. If Xu shows up, we'll get him, no doubt in my mind."

"You know he's got to try. The last thing he wants is for her to talk to us, and he's got to know she would talk, since he tried to have her killed."

"Ah, here comes the sketch."

Sherlock looked over at MAX's screen at the man's face. "Not very distinctive, is he? Not a single Asian facial characteristic except maybe for the thick black hair. Green eyes, and a thin, longish face. What age would you say, about thirty-five?"

Savich said, "Yeah, that's about right." He stared at the man and found himself wondering how Xu had hooked up with the Chinese government, and why he'd become a traitor to his country of birth. *Does he feel more Chinese than American? Or is it all about money?* Savich knew neither was the whole of it. Fact was, though, Xu was a psychopath who happened to be half Chinese and had found a perfect fit getting paid to do what he took pleasure in.

43

They found Cindy Cahill in the surgical ICU only one cubicle away from where Ramsey had fought for his life, shot by the same man who'd ordered Cindy killed. Officer Colley looked them over from beside Cindy's cubicle and smiled at them. He'd also done a guard shift when Ramsey had been here.

"Good to see you, Agent Savich, Agent Sherlock. Agent Christoff and Deputy Barbieri have been waiting inside for you for a couple of minutes. There've been lots of doctors and nurses in and out. I think she's in trouble." He held up his cell phone to show them the sketch of Xu. "Just got it." He nodded to Sherlock. "No sign of him. You can bet they'll strip-search any guy who looks like him before he leaves the lobby, ball cap or not."

Cindy looked white as death, her eyes closed, her eyelids bruised, her hair matted down. There was a plastic oxygen mask over her mouth, and when she breathed, it was with effort, as if it was hard work for her. The single sheet pulled over her was stained pink where it touched her chest, and looked to be draped over a maze of gurgling tubes, packings, and pressure dressings, some of them stained pink as well. One of her IVs held a bag of blood that was slowly dripping into her arm. Without makeup, without a show of her usual attitude and the force of her personality, she looked young and vulnerable, and gravely ill.

Savich nodded to Eve and Harry. "Has she been asleep since you got here?"

Eve shook her head. "She's awake, but she hurts and she's dopey from all the drugs they're pumping into her. The doctor told me he didn't know whether she'd make any sense or not."

Sherlock said, "All we can do is try."

"Ah, there's an eye opening." Eve leaned over her. "Good morning, Cindy. You want to blink at me so I know you're there?"

Cindy Cahill blinked. "I'm here," she whispered.

"Are you in pain?" Savich asked.

Incredibly, she smiled. "It doesn't feel like I'm swimming in Bali with the sun beating down on me, if that's what you mean. I've always wanted to go to Bali, but I don't know if I'm going to make it there now. Do you know she apologized to me after she stuck that knife in my chest?"

Everyone felt a pang of pity until Cindy whispered, a heap of venom in her voice, "I even went out of my way to talk to that skinny little bitch. I mean, I didn't have anything better to do, so why not? And all she did was yak, yak about her son, as if I cared." The real Cindy, attitude and all, had snapped back into focus, as ill as she was.

Harry grinned. "Sounds like you're getting back to normal, Cindy," he said, and kept his fingers crossed she'd stay with it.

"I won't be back to normal ever. Look at me. At least the bitch didn't kill me."

"Her name's Lin Mei," Sherlock said.

"Who are you?"

"I'm an FBI agent."

Cindy said, "I like your hair. I once had red hair, well, more auburn, really, but I didn't curl it like you do yours." She cut her eyes to Eve. "What I hate is blond ponytails. I mean, it's so dated, like a woman trying to regain her girlhood. It's pathetic."

Eve said, "The reason Lin Mei tried to kill you is because Xu threatened to murder her little boy if she didn't."

They all saw how quickly Cindy computed this, even as sick and drugged as she was. "Poor kid's dead now. I mean, since I'm alive, it means Mom failed, and Xu will find that out fast enough."

"Her boy is being protected," Sherlock said. "He'll be fine."

Eve continued, "Do you know Lin Mei's in shock and here in the psychiatric unit?"

"She's probably faking it. I hope she goes down hard

for this." They saw a hand clench. "I actually pretended to *listen* to her! I actually paid her some attention, and this is how she repays me."

Savich said, "I'm sure you agree she was smart to pay more attention to Xu. She didn't think the police could protect her son from him."

"All right, so she was smart to believe him. I mean, he shot Judge Hunt, murdered Mickey O'Rourke and poor Milo, the greedy idiot. Wait—" Sudden panic bloomed in Cindy's eyes. "Clive. Where's Clive?"

Savich hadn't wanted to go there, not yet, but Cindy's face was flushed, her eyes focused on him. He didn't have a choice now. He said, "Xu hired a prisoner to stab him in the shower, as he had Lin Mei stab you. Clive didn't make it. I'm sorry, Cindy."

Cindy's face went perfectly blank. She tried to shake her head at them but couldn't seem to make her head move. She closed her eyes and didn't make a sound, except for her labored breathing. Tears seeped from beneath her eyelids and streamed down her white cheeks.

Eve thought, *So Cindy hadn't been simply using Clive after all.*

Savich said, "You can't help Clive now, but you can help yourself. I've got that offer from the U.S. attorney for you, Cindy. Are you ready to tell us what you know about Xu?"

Cindy whispered, her eyes still closed, "Is it fifteen years, like I wanted?"

"Yes, since Xu's now a serial killer, fifteen years is on the table if what you tell us helps us find him."

"You got that in writing?"

"There hasn't been time, Cindy, and we don't have much of it now. He could be leaving the country as we speak."

"Can I trust you, Agent Savich?"

Savich leaned down close to her face. "You can trust me."

Cindy opened her eyes and studied his face. She whispered, "Xu's first name is Xian, *X-i-a-n*, but he'd always been called Xu, said it was easier than Xian. He's a lot younger than Clive, but he didn't tell me his age. I teased him enough for him to tell me he was from Indiana, got out of there when he was eighteen. He said he changed his name to Joe Keats, but when he was working, he was Xu. I don't know if he's using Joe Keats now, since I never saw his passport. I think he's got lots of aliases."

"Does this look like him, Cindy?" Savich showed her the sketch of Xu on the cell phone.

"That's not too bad. He's handsomer, though, really pretty green eyes. He did tell me he got his eyelashes from his mom, Ann."

"Do you know where he's staying?"

"No, he never told us that. He showed up when he wanted to. I think he moved around."

"What was Xu after from Mark Lindy's computer?"

"He never told us that, either. He said the less we knew about it, the better for everyone. Lindy did tell me he was an expert on computer worms and viruses, stuff like that. He bragged to me once when he was lying on top of me after sex that he was one of the major designers of the worm that shut down Iran's nuclear bomb plans."

An alarm went off on one of the electronic monitors Cindy was connected to, and a nurse and resident rushed into the cubicle. "Please leave now," the doctor said. "She needs some help."

The four of them were hurried out of Cindy Cahill's cubicle. They stood motionless outside the cubicle. "Is she going to die?"

No one had an answer for that.

Savich punched the elevator button. They said nothing more, waited until they were inside. Savich said, "Since there's nothing we can do about Cindy, I need to sit down somewhere, run the information she gave us on Xu through MAX."

As they walked to the cafeteria, Eve said, "I want her to make it, I really do. I'll admit I was surprised she was so upset about Clive. I always thought she was using him, like he was some sort of father figure to her. It's all so—useless."

Savich shook his head. "I'd say they had a mutual dependence, strange as it was."

Eve nodded. "I also think she had a bit of contempt for him, since she knew very well Clive was weaker than she was—but yeah, she depended on him, he was always there for her. I wonder what will happen to her now."

44

San Francisco General Hospital Cafeteria

Sherlock set down her coffee cup as she looked over Dillon's shoulder. Xu had been born and raised in Lampo, Indiana. He was the son of a Caucasian mother, Ann Xu, a history teacher at Lampo High School, and a Chinese father who had first immigrated to the Gulf-side town of Paxico, Florida, before moving to Indiana and buying a gas station.

At eighteen, Xu and his parents had left Lampo for a long summer vacation at Bronson Lake, fifty miles from Lampo, Mrs. Xu had told neighbors.

The family had simply never returned. The gas station Mr. Xu had owned remained vacant; the history position at Lampo High School had been filled when Ann Xu hadn't returned for the fall term. No one ever heard from the son. Cursory inquiries were made, but there was simply no sign of the Xu family after they'd gone on vacation. They were eventually forgotten, since no one knew of any family on either the mother or father's side to contact.

Sherlock said, "Do you think Xu killed his parents?"

"Oh, yes," Savich said. "There's no trace of Xu after that. If he changed his name legally to Joe Keats, we'll find him."

The critical thing was that they had Xu's first Indiana driver's license, with a photo taken of him when he was sixteen. Dillon had already sent the photo to the image-processing lab at the Hoover Building to have it updated to show how he would look now, nearly twenty years later. They were waiting for the aged picture now, ready to compare it to the sketch Lin Mei had given the police sketch artist, and then would forward it to Hammer-smith and his team as soon as it arrived.

"His features really are Caucasian," Sherlock said, looking at the driver's license. "Look at those green eyes. There doesn't seem to be any resemblance at all to his Chinese father, except they are both on the slight side. He's a good-looking kid, isn't he?"

"Look closely," Savich said. "He's already got an arrogant tilt to his head, and there's a dead-on look in his eyes, staring you right in the face, like he doesn't care what you think or about much of anything."

A message notification popped up, and they were soon looking at the same face, though more filled out, lines about his mouth and eyes, yet his eyes were more intense, and still had the same dead-on look, easily recognizable.

Savich forwarded it to Hammersmith, waited a few seconds, and called him on speakerphone.

Savich said, "Griffin, did you get that picture of Xu I sent you?"

"It's going out over the network now. I was wrong about Xu moving from the Atherton B-and-B to a middle-of-the-road motel on Lombard or down by the wharf or any of the motels in the Tenderloin. We've checked; he ain't there.

"I'm still convinced, though, he's got to be close by. I don't think he knows we've identified him yet. It could be he's staying at one of the most exclusive hotels, like the Stanford or the Fairmont or the Mandarin, figuring we wouldn't expect that. I'm thinking the Fairmont."

"Why the Fairmont in particular?" Sherlock asked.

A pause, then Griffin said, "A feeling, just a feeling. No guarantees."

None needed, Savich thought.

"Also, from what we know about him and his contacts, he's not short on money, so why not be comfortable?"

"Then why did he stay at that bed-and-breakfast in Atherton when he first arrived to kill Judge Hunt?"

"I don't know. I've realized he's not so easy to figure out." Griffin sighed. "Until he killed Mickey O'Rourke, I had him pegged differently. We'll canvass all the hotels we can, this time with Xu's photo in hand. We'll have them put up his photo behind the registration desks. He might still be wearing that ball cap and sunglasses—well, there's nothing we can do about that except give them a heads-up."

"Griffin, do me a favor."

"Sure, Sherlock, whatever you need."

"Be careful, Griffin. He's a very dangerous man. Please don't forget that."

"I will. Listen, I could be all wrong about the Fairmont."

"They tell me that doesn't happen often," Savich said. "Call when you get something."

When Eve and Harry got off the elevator on the fourth floor, Eve looked up the hallway at an SFPD officer and a deputy marshal, on their feet when they spotted them.

Once inside Ramsey's room, Deputy Marshal Haloran said quickly, "What's going on?"

Eve said, "I really made a mess of it, Joe."

Harry squeezed her arm. "She means Cindy Cahill is pretty bad off. But she may have finally given us something useful. We'll know soon."

To Eve's surprise, Ramsey was reading a spy novel, and wasn't that perfect? She wondered what Savich would find out about Xu, the spy and cold-blooded murderer who wanted Ramsey dead.

She leaned over and kissed his cheek. "You look really hot, you know that?"

He also looked tired. But he was back, all hard, dark edges, and the killer smile, Judge Dredd in the flesh. "I look hot? That makes you as much of a liar as my wife.

Happy to see you, though, liar or not." He paused. "Eve, I can tell by looking at you that something's happened. What?"

Eve said, "Cindy Cahill told us the man who's been trying to kill you is called Xian Xu. He's Chinese American, born in Indiana, and looks as WASP as you do. Dillon and Sherlock are trying to track him down. I don't suppose the name means anything to you?"

"Not any more than the name Xu by itself," Ramsey said. "If they can find him, maybe I can start making some plans to get out of here and back to work."

"We should get him now, Judge Hunt," Harry said. "He won't come after you again." Ramsey stared from Harry to Eve, considering that, and Eve said, "Hey, do you think you'll be going home in time for Thanksgiving?"

Ramsey became aware that the pain meds were tugging on his brain, and evidently his hearing as well, because he thought in that moment that Eve had a beautiful speaking voice. He forgot about Thanksgiving, forgot everything but her voice. He stared up at Eve. "You ever have voice lessons?"

"Me? Goodness, talk about playing a rusty saw. That's what my vocal cords feel like. Ramsey, have you had your pain meds recently?"

"Well, yes, a couple of minutes ago. You're lucky I'm still awake."

She took his hand, squeezed it. "Hey, Haloran. If you want to play more poker with Judge Hunt, now's the time."

Sherlock and Savich were seated in the security office off the lobby, Griffin on the phone. He sounded so hyper she hoped he wasn't driving.

"We've got him! Amazing what a difference that picture made."

Sherlock said, "Let me put my cell on speaker, Griffin. Okay, make our day."

"Xu's here at the Fairmont Hotel. The registration clerk on duty recognized him after studying the photo. She was used to seeing him in sunglasses and his ball cap, but this morning, he came trooping out of the restaurant after he'd had breakfast and asked the concierge a question. She said good morning to him. He said good morning back to her and smiled. She added he had a very nice smile. So it appears our Mr. Xu either forgot his sunglasses or he didn't care this morning about hiding his face from prying eyes. Maybe he doesn't intend to stay much longer."

They cheered loud enough for Griffin to grin. The guard at the hospital video console turned toward them and toasted them with his coffee, since they looked ready to high-five the world.

Sherlock said, "Griffin, you're a genius. I worship at your feet. Tell us everything."

"He's not at the hotel now. The registration clerk told us the last time she saw him, he was headed toward the hotel front doors."

Savich asked, "Griffin, did the registration clerk say he was carrying anything, like luggage?"

"I didn't ask her. Hold on." Two minutes later, Griffin came back on line. "She doesn't remember seeing him carrying anything."

Savich said, "If he believes Cindy is dead, he may think his job here is done. He could have put his luggage in his car before he went in to breakfast. Griffin, speak to the concierge. Find out what question Xu asked."

Griffin was back on the line in a minute. "The concierge who spoke to Xu is off-duty. I'll try his cell to see if he remembers what Xu wanted. I'll get back to you."

Savich said, "Griffin, stay around the lobby. If Xu comes back, call us, but don't try to apprehend him, okay? How many agents are with you?"

"There are two of us."

"Make sure you all look like happy tourists. Cheney or I will call you."

When he punched off his cell, Savich said, "I'm thinking keep it simple. We wait for him in his room, that way there's no chance of any bystanders getting hurt."

Sherlock cocked her head at Dillon. "Do you think he's leaving for good?"

"I don't know. He's careful and he's smart. He didn't check out when he left the Fairmont this morning, but if he's got luggage with him in the car, he may not go back."

"I would bet he knows Cindy is alive by now, and of course Ramsey is, too. Do you think he's giving up on it all, running?"

"Nothing he does would surprise me. There are only three places we know he might go—back to the Fairmont, one of the airports, or here, the hospital."

"He's got to know we're ready for him here, Dillon, and that Ramsey and Cindy Cahill are well protected," Sherlock said.

"So was Ramsey in the elevator. Call Eve, have her alert the deputies with Ramsey. Something big is going to happen today. We just don't know where."

They were walking toward the parking lot when Savich got a call from the ICU.

Cindy Cahill had gone into convulsions. She hadn't made it. She was dead.

45

San Francisco General Hospital

Xu walked at a brisk pace through the San Francisco General Hospital campus to Potrero Avenue. He turned right and walked to Twenty-second Street, where he'd parked his Audi on a quiet residential side street.

The San Francisco air was fresh and chill, clouds scuttling across a gray sky. Finally he could take a second to look at them and breathe a sigh of relief. He grinned. He'd taken a huge risk coming to the hospital, and now that Cindy had had the grace to die, he hadn't had to take the even greater risk of trying to kill her himself.

That little scrap of a woman, Lin Mei, had ended up a murderer after all.

He'd worried at it like a dog's bone. Cindy would have had every reason to talk to the FBI now, and if she had told them what she knew, they would eventually have found the Xian Xu who became Joe Keats. The National Security Agency would have no record of a Joe Keats or of his connection to Chinese intelligence, but he could never have been Joe Keats again. He would have become an international fugitive wanted for murder, dependent on the Chinese for his very life, if they chose to let him keep it.

Had Cindy managed to speak to the FBI agents he'd seen leaving the ICU before she died? He couldn't be sure, but it was unlikely. She'd had major surgery; she'd had a tube down her throat until this morning. If she'd been conscious at all, it wasn't for long. He'd heard the frenetic beeping from the monitors, watched the staff rush to her cubicle. They'd been in there a long time. When they'd come out, he knew she was dead by the expressions on their faces.

Cindy had gone to meet her maker, whoever that was, and she'd taken his secrets with her. He thought about her death, wondered if she'd even known she was dying or if she'd been too drugged out to even recognize what was happening to her. To his surprise, Xu saw his mother's face, saw her heaving for breath as he'd stood there, a bloody knife in his hand, watching her in the kitchen of their small vacation house, grabbing her throat because she couldn't breathe as she sank to her knees on the floor.

He walked faster. His mother's death was long ago, long over and done. He'd been trained to block out memories that were of no use to him, to focus on what was important, and immediate, not wallow in the past, reliving moments he couldn't change. His immediate task was to get back to his superior in Beijing, Colonel

Ng, a tough-as-nails little man with a gold tooth in the front of his mouth. He would have to rehearse carefully, convince Ng that there were no more witnesses to hurt them, that Ng's cyber-intelligence unit could not be tied to anything that had happened. Xu had, after all, brought them a great prize, the latest American Stuxnet research, or a good part of it. Who could fault him if he'd had to dirty his hands, so long as they were all safe? In the end they would do as they wished, of course, but he hoped they would find him too useful to waste.

After eight long months, things had finally turned around for him, and he no longer needed to stay. After he picked up his luggage at the Fairmont, he and his Audi would make the six-hour trek to LAX. No way was he going near SFO airport. He momentarily pictured himself waving good-bye from thirty-three thousand feet on his way to Honolulu to the idiot FBI agents still looking for him.

Xu was whistling when he reached his Audi ten minutes later. He fobbed open the door and slid in. He paused for a moment, staring out the windshield. The sun had peeked out from behind the clouds, full and hot. He loved this beautiful city, with its swirling pristine fog that rolled in through the Golden Gate and left again. No one should live in Beijing with the lung-rotting pollution and its sandstorms blowing in from the Gobi Desert that turned the sky brown, choking its people even through the masks they wore. Crowds of people, endless millions of them scrabbling to survive in a city where buildings seemed to go up every second, so poorly constructed they began to fall apart around you the next day—that is, if some unscrupulous local officials didn't evict you first.

As he drove north toward the city, he thought back to his college days at Berkeley, where he'd protested with all the vigor and ignorance of youth against the cause du jour, usually a variation of the theme of America as a decadent wasteland. He smiled now at how he'd lapped it up, with Joyce's help, both of them ardent young Communists. Except Joyce had been more, so much more. He hadn't realized until he'd lived in Beijing that the Chinese government at all levels could give the bozos here in America lessons in corruption. His idealism had died there, drowned in all the bureaucratic inanities and the fraud that permeated everything. He'd watched groups protest, watched them shout their pitiful truths, watched them get the Chinese government's boot on their necks. How could you continue to believe in a society in which you couldn't even trust the food you ate, or the air you breathed? The only people you could trust in China were your own family, and he had no family left.

During his year-and-a-half stay in the area, Xu had come to hope he could live here, though it would surprise his masters that he would leave behind the splendid apartment they'd given him near the Forbidden City. Perhaps in a year or two, when all of this was behind him, he could think about working for himself. He had a reputation in some important circles. He would see.

He honked at a driver who cut in front of him as he turned onto California Street. He knew the locals thought the traffic here was insane, and he snorted a laugh. Even L.A. couldn't compete with Beijing, the traffic-snarl capital of the world, with its endless streams of bicycles weaving in and out of traffic on the overcrowded roads. Once he'd even seen a skinny little kid pedaling away on top of a thick stone wall.

He looked at the people walking on the sidewalks, most of them with phones attached to their ears, most of them busy with the little problems in their little lives. They had no idea what was going on in the world around them.

It was time to go back to Beijing and make his case. He hadn't contacted them since he'd taken O'Rourke, and now he decided he'd wait. Best to do it in person.

Xu felt a taste of fear in his mouth. It was viscous, foul, like the pumping blood from Mickey's throat spraying the walls of that miserable little shack.

He started whistling again. He'd be in and out of the Fairmont in ten minutes, no longer, and on his way to LaLa Land.

46

**Fairmont Hotel
California Street**

Xu left his Audi with the valet. He'd be back in ten minutes, he told her, pressing a ten-dollar bill into her hand. Pretty girl. He walked through the elegant hotel lobby, with its yellow granite columns, scattered huge palm trees, and sculpted seating arrangements spread throughout, and arrived at the elevators. He punched the button for the sixth and top floor. There were two couples in the car with him who obviously knew one another, the men carrying shopping bags, the women flushed and happy and chattering about lunch.

Both couples got off at the fifth floor. He wondered if they had views as incredible as his. He'd miss seeing the Golden Gate in the distance, and the downtown beneath him to the east, a tight knot of multifaceted buildings shining with reflected light in the bright afternoon sun.

He got off the elevator and walked down the

beautifully carpeted hallway to his suite at the end of the wide corridor. He didn't see a soul except a maid standing beside her cart in front of the door across from his suite. He didn't recognize her, and he always made a point of knowing who was around him when he was in an unfamiliar place, staff included.

She looked up at him, smiled and nodded, then said, "Is there anything you need, sir?"

He shook his head and thanked her. He watched her sort through a stack of towels. There was something about her he couldn't quite pinpoint that was a bit—off. Was she new? Was it simply because she was working a different shift? Or had he simply not seen her before? He smiled back at her. "You having a good day?" he asked.

"Oh, yes, it's splendid today, after the rain," she said, and turned her back to him to open the room across the hall.

Something was definitely off, but what was it? They couldn't have found him, simply couldn't have. But he hadn't stayed alive for the past twelve years by taking chances. He carefully eased a small canister out of his jacket pocket, slipped his finger through the ring and pressed it against his thigh. When he slid his key card down the slot, the green light flashed and the door opened, quiet and smooth, as it always did. He let the door open a crack.

He stepped into the very modern living room of his suite, with its view of the city spreading out before him.

A man's voice yelled, "FBI! Hands in the air! Now!"

"Don't shoot me!" he yelled. He flung his hands into

the air, and let the safety ring remain on his finger as the canister crashed to the floor. There was a deafening blast, and thick smoke billowed like a black curtain in front of him. A sheet of flames burst out hot and high, and Xu was down, rolling. He'd closed his eyes as he'd hurled the canister and turned his head away, but he still saw lights, felt his eardrums throb from the deafening noise.

He heard shouts, heard bullets flying around him through the flames and smoke. He knew they couldn't see him any more than he could see them, even less if they were still blinded by the light with their ears ringing. But they'd know if they didn't do something fast they'd burn to death. He felt a bullet sting his arm, ignored the shot of pain, crawled to the front door, and rolled out into the hall. His last view of his suite was through a wall of flames, the FBI agents yelling to one another from the other side.

He jumped to his feet to face the maid, who was raising her SIG. "Freeze!"

A shout and three more bullets came through the smoke, striking the wall behind her close to her head, and she flinched. He kicked the SIG out of her hand, backhanded her face, knocking her to the floor, and took off down the nearest stairs. His left arm hurt like the devil, but he took two, three steps at a time, hoping he wouldn't go flying on his face. With his useless arm, he'd break his neck if he did. He forced himself to slow and straighten his clothes before he reached the lobby, and took a second to regain his breath. He saw blood had soaked through his jacket sleeve. It was a dark material, thankfully, it wouldn't be all that apparent at a glance, but it hurt, really hurt. He knew he should be applying pressure, but there wasn't time.

He forced himself to walk, not run, across the lobby and toward one of the smaller front doors. The fire alarm went off, the people in the lobby started looking around uncertainly, wondering what to do while the staff took their places to usher them to the doors. Very soon there would be pandemonium, he would see to that, enough craziness that even the FBI agents would be too busy trying to save their own butts and protect all the innocent bystanders to care about catching him. He heard a shout from behind him over the alarm bells. "It's Xu! Stop, FBI!"

He kept walking as he reached into his pocket and pushed a preset number on his cell phone. There was a loud explosion, and soon there were screams and the sounds of people running—the chaos was beginning, and the FBI agents waiting for him in the hotel lobby would be drowned in the stampede.

He held his arm as he walked quickly to the valet station. He saw his car, but the girl wasn't there, no one was, none of the bellmen, none of the valets. He saw her then, but she was dashing back into the lobby, yelling something to the doorman. Where were the keys to his Audi? He didn't see them, and he couldn't wait. He had to get out and grab a taxi, and where was a taxi stand?

He didn't register the dark van parked across the

street until the van door slid open and a redheaded woman jumped out. He saw a gun pressed against her side. Another fricking FBI agent, he thought, and she was running right at him.

Xu took off, weaving through the growing crowd of panicked people clogging the sidewalk. He heard sirens in the distance. How had the FBI found him? How? *Cindy,* he thought, she'd been able to talk.

He could hear her, knew she was gaining on him. She was a woman, and if she made the mistake of getting too close, he could kill her in an instant. He could nearly smell her now. He heard angry, panicked voices as she shoved people out of her way.

Sherlock heard an explosion. Her heart stopped as she looked up to the top floor and saw a window flying outward, sending shattered glass raining down, smoke and flames gushing out after it.

It was Xu's room. What had he done? Eve, Harry, and Griffin Hammersmith had been in that room waiting for Xu, and Agent Willa Gaines outside in the hallway, dressed as a maid. Were they still there?

Sherlock couldn't believe it was Xu she saw coming out through the luggage door of the hotel. She saw people running out of the hotel behind him, heard yells, felt the rising panic.

She jerked open the van door and jumped down. Two agents monitoring the hotel exits shouted after her, but she paid no attention. She ran full speed after Xu. He was fast, but there were so many people around, all of them excited and looking up, wondering what had happened.

He disappeared for a moment. She stepped around a couple of tourists, saw a blood trail on the sidewalk. Good, he was hurt. Who else was hurt? *Stop it. Focus.* Sherlock saw him again, holding his arm as he ran. She took a flying leap past two civilians who stood in the middle of the sidewalk gaping up at the flames and landed on his back, her arms around his neck. The force drove him to his knees. He was larger than she was, and stronger, even wounded, but she was well trained, her adrenaline level off the charts. She had to flatten him, get his face against the sidewalk.

She struck her fist as hard as she could against his wounded arm, and he howled. He fell to his belly, yelling in fury and pain, cursing, trying to flip her off him. With his good arm, he tried to grab her to pull her beneath him, but she didn't let that happen.

People were standing around them now, looking to see what was happening, but not understanding. "Keep back!" she yelled. "FBI! This man set the bomb in the hotel!"

Sherlock raised her SIG, shoved it against the back of his head. Xu froze. Sherlock leaned down beside his ear. "Give me an excuse, Xu, come on, twitch or move your finger, anything. Let me blow your brains out."

"How did you know?"

"We're FBI. You're not." She leaned back and clipped a handcuff around his right wrist. "And it turns out you're not as good as you thought you were. You have

47

Something was wrong. Savich double-parked the Taurus and ran toward the FBI van across from the Fairmont, where he knew Sherlock and two other agents were positioned. He heard the explosion, saw the glass bursting outward from the sixth floor, followed by gushing smoke and flames.

And then he saw Sherlock through the throng of panicked people, barreling through the crowds, shoving people aside. She was after Xu, and Sherlock was catching him. Savich watched her leap forward and tackle him. They disappeared from sight.

He shoved people out of his way, yelling Sherlock's name. Then he saw her astride Xu's back, cuffing him. Suddenly there was a loud cracking sound from somewhere behind him, a rifle shot, he registered it in an instant, and he saw her head bloom red. His heart froze in his chest. Xu threw her off and scrambled to his feet, one handcuff dangling off his right wrist, and disappeared into the crowd.

Savich couldn't believe what he'd seen, simply couldn't

accept it. He had to get to her, had to see her smile at him and tell him it had all been a dream, nothing more. Above the mayhem he heard a ferocious growling sound he realized was coming from his own throat. He saw frightened faces staring at him, but he ignored them. People dove out of his way. His vision narrowed to an arrow of misting red, like blood—no, not blood. He'd get to her, he'd find it was all a mistake, that what he'd seen was a lie his own brain had spun together, nothing more than that. When he burst out of the last scattering knot of people, he saw three teenage boys huddled over Sherlock, protecting her from the stampede.

He grabbed one of the boys' arms, pulled him back. "I'm FBI. Keep the people away—you, call nine-one-one."

Savich stared down at all the blood streaming down her face, matting her hair to her head. She was lying on her side, utterly still, and he was afraid in the deepest part of him that she was dead. He couldn't breathe, couldn't think. He was afraid to touch her, afraid that when he pressed his fingers against her throat there would be no pulse, there would be nothing, and it would mean she was gone. His fingers hovered, then finally touched the pulse point in her neck, pressed in. He felt her pulse. Yes, she was alive. He ripped a sleeve off his white shirt and pressed down on the blood streaming from her head. His hands were steady and strong, but his brain was a wasteland of chaos. But she was alive. Nothing else mattered.

One of the boys asked, his voice shaking with a mixture of fear and excitement, "Is she dead?"

Savich barely registered the question. It was outside of him, not important, only she was important. He could see he was pressing on a deep gouge the bullet had made along the side of her head. But how deep? There was so much blood with a head wound, too much. He pressed down harder on the wound and put the fingers of his other hand against her bloody neck to find her pulse, to reassure himself again it was there. He touched her vivid hair curling over his hands, wet with blood.

He said, more to himself than to anyone else, "She's alive." Saying the words helped to make them real.

One of the boys said, "The nine-one-one operator said everyone in the city is rushing to the Fairmont."

"Billy, what are you doing? What is going on here?"

"Mom, we're okay. We're helping the FBI. One of the agents got shot."

Savich blocked out the parents' voices, leaned close to Sherlock's bloody face. "It's okay, sweetheart, you're going to be fine. You've been shot—well, let me say it's more than a graze, but still, the bullet didn't hit your brain." He pressed his cheek against her bloody hair, and thanked God the shooter's aim wasn't true. He wondered for only an instant who the shooter was.

"Savich! Where's Sherlock?"

It was Eve. Billy's parents pulled him and the other two boys out of the way. Eve fell to her knees beside her.

Savich raised his face, now nearly as bloody as his

wife's. "I saw the explosion blow out that window in Xu's suite. Are you all right?"

Eve waved that away. "Your face—"

"It's Sherlock's blood," he said.

Eve said, "Is—is she okay?"

He made himself nod. "The bullet didn't kill her. She's alive, but she's out—" There weren't any more words. He pressed his shirtsleeve hard against the wound, his eyes not leaving her face.

He didn't care about Xu, didn't care if the Fairmont burned to the ground, only about Sherlock. *No, get yourself together, Sherlock's alive. You have to take charge, there's no one else.* She'd captured Xu and then someone else had shot her. Who? It didn't make sense; Xu was alone, always alone. Wasn't he?

He looked over at the three boys, Billy's parents standing protectively behind them, and Savich registered that Billy was as redheaded as Sherlock, tall, gangly, and skinny as a plank. He nodded at them, and manufactured a calm, steady voice. He said to Eve, "These boys protected Sherlock from the crowd. Get their names." He managed a smile at Billy's mom.

"Ma'am, your son is a hero, all three of them are heroes. Thanks, all of you."

He looked back down at Sherlock. "Eve, where's Harry?"

"He went after Xu."

No more words; he never looked away from Sherlock's face until Eve touched his arm. "The EMTs are here, Dillon. Let them take care of her."

48

EMT Nathan Everett lightly touched Savich's shoulder. "You all right, sir? Yes, okay, I see now it's her blood. You need to let us take care of her now."

Savich raised his face to a man he'd never seen before in his life. "She's going to be all right."

"Yes, sir, yes, she will," Nathan said, and turned to direct two other EMTs to bring a gurney.

Eve pulled Savich to his feet. He watched them lift Sherlock onto the gurney. She looked nearly lifeless. No, she would live, she had to. "I got the boys' names and addresses."

Savich forced himself to focus on Eve's face. "Are you okay, Eve? And Harry and Griffin?"

"Yes, we were just rattled."

"Have Harry and Griffin gone after Xu?" He looked at her face, really registered it for the first time. "You look like you've been in a war."

She nodded. "All three of us do. The fire and smoke was from an incendiary device, but we made it through.

Xu even had a bomb rigged in the room. Luckily, we'd gotten out before he blew it."

The crowd melted away from Sherlock's gurney as they rolled her to the ambulance. Savich walked quickly after her. He said over his shoulder, "Who shot her? It sure wasn't Xu, since I saw her cuffing him. So who was it?"

"We'll find him," Eve called after him, as he climbed into the ambulance with Sherlock and they shut the door.

It was slow going getting through the snarled traffic, the gawkers milling around, but finally the ambulance pulled onto Market Street on the way to San Francisco General.

Savich held her hand between his, never looking away from her face.

"I know it's a lot of blood, sir," Nathan said, "but head wounds are nasty like that."

"Yes, I know," Savich said. "I've seen them before."

He watched the EMT check her pupils again and look at her head wound. He prepped her arm and slid a needle into a vein at her elbow. "My name is Nathan. The bleeding from her scalp has stopped. She needs this IV in case we have to give her medication. She's getting saline now, nothing more."

Savich nodded. "My name's Savich. Give me an alcohol pad and I'll wipe the blood away."

Nathan Everett wanted to say *No, you shouldn't touch her,* but he saw the big man with only one shirtsleeve, his black leather jacket on the floor beside him, was desperately trying to keep control. "Sure, here you go. But stay away from the wound; we don't want it to start bleeding again."

He watched Savich lift up her hair and wash it with sterile dressings Nathan had soaked in saline from a plastic bottle. He was gentle, his touch light. After a half-dozen dressings, he'd only gotten some of the blood cleaned from her hair.

Nathan handed him another dressing. "You need to wash your face as well, sir."

Savich did as he said. *So much blood,* he thought, as he wiped his face.

Thank goodness, Nathan thought; the wound wasn't as bad as he'd feared. It was a deep gouge along the side of her head. But was her skull fractured? Her brain injured? Was she still bleeding inside her skull from a lacerated artery? Nathan didn't know, but he did know the bullet had passed only a few millimeters away from exploding her head open. Nathan swallowed. The important thing now was that she wake up soon. The sooner she woke up, the better the chance she was still the person she was. He said aloud what he was hoping for. "It isn't fatal, but she needs to wake up. Are you an FBI agent?"

"Yes, I'm Agent Savich, Dillon Savich."

"You work with her? Is she an agent, too?"

"Yes, she's an agent. I live with her as well. She's my wife."

Nathan nearly fell over backward when he said that.

"You're kidding."

Savich only shook his head. He listened to the ambulance siren blare loud and insistent as traffic pulled over in front of them. Odd, but he hadn't heard the sirens before now. He wiped a streak of blood off her face. She was pale, nearly as white as Sean's two percent milk. It looked obscene. It nearly broke him.

Her eyes opened. She looked dazed, like a prizefighter who'd gone too many rounds.

Savich leaned in close, his hand squeezing hers. "Sherlock?"

She blinked, licked her lips. "Why are you up there, Dillon? Or why am I down here? What happened?"

"You don't remember? It doesn't matter. You were shot, but you'll be fine."

She looked confused, as if she hadn't understood what he'd said. "Dillon, my head really hurts."

"I know, but we're nearly to the hospital now. You had a small accident—nothing, really—only a small hit."

"A small hit?"

Nathan said, "That's right. Try to stay awake. That's right, can you focus on my face?"

"Her name's Sherlock."

"Sherlock, what color are my eyes?"

She didn't say anything, simply closed her eyes again.

Nathan saw Savich's face go blank and said quickly, "She woke up, she was herself, and that's an excellent sign. Six more minutes and we'll be there. She's not going to die, Agent Savich."

For the first time, Savich looked and actually registered the face of the man beside Sherlock. He was in his early forties, on the heavy side, with pockmarked skin, deep brown eyes, and a reassuring smile, but most important, as he'd spoken, Savich hadn't seen any lurking doubt in his eyes.

Nathan cleared his throat. "Who shot her?"

"I don't know," Savich said. "I don't know much of anything except there was a bomb in the Fairmont and she caught the man who blew it up and someone else shot her."

Nathan said, "Was the man a terrorist?"

A terrorist? "No," Savich said. "He's a very careful, very well-prepared man who deserves to be in shackles." He added, never looking away from Sherlock's face, "I hope no one died in that hotel."

Sherlock jerked, took a hitching breath.

Savich felt her hand tighten briefly around his fingers before she let go again. He clasped her hand tighter, and his own breath hitched. He was terrified.

He felt Nathan's hand on his shoulder. "I do, too, Agent. We're here, sir."

49

Fifteen minutes later, half a dozen FBI agents rushed into the emergency room, thankfully not at all crowded, Cheney at their head. Savich was standing by the registration desk, speaking quietly to a nurse.

Cheney forced the words out: "Eve said it's a head wound. How is she?"

Savich looked at Harry, Eve, and Griffin, with four other agents whose names he didn't know crowding in behind them, some of their faces and clothes blackened with soot. One of them had blood smeared on his shirt. His or someone he'd pulled out of the hotel?

Virginia Trolley and Vincent Delion came running in behind them.

Savich said, "She's awake. I'm not with her because they're doing a neurological exam and the doctor said there wasn't room and since I couldn't add anything useful, I needed to be out here." He nodded to the nurse. "Nurse Blankenship is going back and forth, telling me exactly what they're doing and why."

"How bad is it?" Virginia Trolley came up to put her hand on his shoulder.

Savich said, "The bullet gouged a trench along the left side of her head, above her left ear." He touched his fingers to his own head to show them. "If it had been a couple of millimeters to the right, she'd be dead." Savich felt his throat close. He swallowed. He stood as stiff as a fence post, trying to get himself together. "She was a little groggy when I left her, but she seemed okay. They were shaving off a square of her hair so they could put stitches in." Odd, but saying those words nearly broke him. He said nothing more. He knew he needed to stop to keep control.

Nurse Blankenship looked from Savich to the group, and said to all of them, "As I told Agent Savich, the fact that they're ready to stitch her scalp so soon is great news. They're not taking her to CT right away, and that means they're not worried about a skull fracture and her neurological exam must be normal, or nearly so."

"Is there something wrong with her exam?" Savich asked.

Nurse Blankenship hastened to say, "No, sorry—I only meant she's had a concussion, that's all. I tell you what, I'll go back in and check on them again, so you'll know what to expect, okay?"

She smiled at them all, walked quickly down the hall into Sherlock's cubicle, and returned in under a minute.

"They said she'd be going for a CT scan in a few minutes, just to be sure. The doctors say the odds are good the scan will be normal and that she'll be staying for only a day or two, that she'll make a complete recovery with only a small scar for a souvenir.

"Now, if all of you would repeat to Agent Savich that his wife should be up within the week, I would appreciate it." She patted Savich's arm and excused herself.

There was a collective sigh of relief. Harry studied Savich's face, saw he'd finally accepted Sherlock wasn't going to die. Savich turned toward them, focused again. "What information do you have? Do you know who shot her? Do you know what happened to Xu?"

Harry said, "A couple of Virginia's officers who were positioned two blocks up on California ran into a young guy waving his fists and yelling after a white Infiniti that was fishtailing down the street. Xu had jerked open the guy's car door, clouted him in the head, and shoved him into the road. We've got an APB out on the car and the license plate number.

"Xu is hurt. One of us"—Harry nodded toward Eve and Griffin—"shot him in the suite from behind a wall of flames. Agent Gaines, our maid in the hallway, said Xu was shot in the upper arm and bleeding pretty heavily when he took off down the stairs. He broke her nose but didn't kill her. When she got herself together, she came in to help us get out, a good thing, since Xu had left a bomb to detonate when he got clear. Griffin's singed a bit around the edges; we all are, inside and out, coughing a bit, but nothing worse.

"We followed Xu's blood trail down the stairs to the lobby, and we were in the stairwell when he detonated the bomb. There was pandemonium in the lobby, but we didn't stop to help, we ran directly outside to find Xu. You were already there, leaning over Sherlock." Harry looked at the others. "That's all we know."

Agent Kain, who'd been one of the agents manning the van with Sherlock, said, "Sherlock spotted Xu. She didn't say a word, jumped out of the van and took off. We ran after her fast, but there were people clogging the road and the sidewalk. Then that window blew out on the top floor, and people were screaming and trying to escape the flying shards of glass. When we got to you, Savich, you were with her along with those three teenage boys."

A second agent said, "She had him flattened on his belly with one of the cuffs already snapped on when we heard that single shot. It sounded like a rifle, which meant it could have been fired from anywhere behind us. We'll have a trajectory as soon as they get forensics out there."

Savich said, "But who? Xu didn't know we'd be there at the Fairmont waiting for him. How could he have arranged for someone with a rifle to be covering his back?"

Cheney said, "I don't know, Savich, but how likely is it that a brand-new player suddenly shows up when Sherlock has Xu down and nearly restrained and then, for whatever reason, shoots her?"

Savich slammed his fist down on the counter. "She

had him, it should be over, but now he's in the wind again. And it must be that Xu isn't flying solo."

"The Chinese?" Eve asked.

"It's possible," Savich said, "but I don't see the Chinese doing this. In their position, I would have shot Xu, if anyone, not Sherlock."

Virginia Trolley said in a voice that could cool boiling water, "We've got half the force out near the Fairmont. Someone must have seen him, seen something. Keep the faith, Dillon."

Cheney said, "It's a mess at the Fairmont, the streets blocked with fire trucks and police cars. We moved your Taurus, Savich, not to worry. So far, Sherlock's the only one they seem to have ambulanced out. There were only cuts and bruises, from what I could see."

"The media were already there when we left," Eve said. "It's national by now, since it's the Fairmont Hotel in San Francisco. They've got everything going for them with this story—a bomber they're calling a terrorist and an FBI agent shot in the head."

Cheney's cell rang. He glanced down and frowned. "It's KTCU." Savich watched him think for a minute, then answer. He turned away from them as he said, "Agent Stone."

Almost immediately, Cheney said, "Yes, yes, but I'm not there. What do you know for a fact, so I'll know if I can add anything?"

Smart, Savich thought, *pulling information from the media for a change.*

Cheney punched off his cell, rejoined the group.

"That was the anchor of the six-o'clock news. He told me only a corner suite on the sixth floor of the Fairmont was badly damaged. Naturally, he had no idea it was Xu's suite. I didn't tell him I already knew from my own people it was completely gutted, a lot of smoke and water damage on that whole floor, but he did tell me the fire's out.

"The anchor wanted to know if a terrorist was holed up in the Fairmont and if he managed to shoot the FBI agent in the street. He wondered if the FBI had bombed the suite to get the terrorist to come out."

Cheney grinned at them. "Where do they get this stuff? Like the FBI carries grenades around with them in their holsters. I told him I was only now finding out anything, and to give me an hour."

Eve asked, "What will you do when he calls back?"

"I'm going to give him our photograph of Xu to put on TV. Given the bomb was at the Fairmont, you can bet everyone will be watching the news to find out what happened, which means everyone will know what Xu looks like by tonight. If the media wants any more than that, I'll tell them to talk to the police commissioner."

"Many thanks," Virginia said.

Cheney said, "Now, tell me about the bombs, Harry. Was the first one a hand grenade?"

Eve wondered how the devil Harry would know, when Cheney added, "Harry was in Special Forces before he joined the Bureau."

Harry said, "It wasn't a conventional grenade or some of us would be dead, Xu included. There was no shrapnel, too much boom, and too much blinding light. It was a flash-bang. We used those suckers a few times in Afghanistan, when the situation called for something debilitating but not fatal, like cleaning out an enemy nest.

"Flash-bangs are powerful, they're effective, and they're pretty small. I'll bet Xu carried one around in his pocket, in case he ever found himself in trouble.

"I'm thinking he must have suspected something wasn't right when he got to his room at the Fairmont; maybe our agent in the hall spooked him. Anyway, he must have had the canister in his hand when he opened the door to the suite. He threw it at us, and there was a deafening noise and a blinding light. I knew what it was, but that didn't stop my ears from buzzing or help me see any quicker, and, of course, it hurt.

"There was instant fire everywhere, walls of it, and that was Xu's doing, too. Flash-bangs make a great incendiary device if you wrap them in an accelerant, like Sterno in a Ziploc bag, and duct-tape the bag to the canister. It would make the canister that much bigger, but not too big to carry in a jacket pocket. The Sterno ignites and gets blasted in all directions. It's a potent weapon.

"Since Xu knew what was coming, he had a second to turn away, prepare himself. We didn't, but we did manage to fire through the flames even though we couldn't see anything. Luckily, one of us hit him."

Nurse Blankenship returned and nodded to Savich. "Agent Savich, your wife will be going to CT now, before she's admitted to her room. You can go with her. She'll be out in a second."

"There she is," Eve said.

Sherlock was lying on a gurney, a white sheet pulled up to her neck, what looked to be rolls of cotton bandage wrapped around her head. There were streaks of blood at its edge, probably from her hair. She looked pale. "Give us a moment," Savich said to the orderly and nurse.

He slipped her hand out from under the sheet and squeezed it. "Sweetheart, are you awake?"

She whispered, "Yes. I was only resting my eyes." She looked around at everyone. "All of you guys are here? Hey, is this some kind of party? Is it my birthday?"

Savich knew she was trying to make a joke but was too woozy to pull if off. He said, "Yes, it's a party, and you're the guest of honor. After you get this dinky head scan to make sure your brains are in good working order, we're going to cut you a slice of your birthday cake."

Her eyes dropped to half-mast, her voice faded, but Savich, who knew her as well as he knew himself, heard the whisper of humor when she said, "I sure hope it's carrot cake."

"Yes," Eve said, "with butter-pecan ice cream."

Savich leaned close. "After the scan, the doctors want you to camp out here for a couple of days. Is that okay with you?"

She closed her eyes, and her voice was starting to fade out. "I don't think I want to stay here, Dillon. The light's too bright and I don't know anybody and my head hurts. Well, maybe I'll stay if you stay with me and bring me birthday cake." She attempted a grin. "I'll share it with you."

Savich smiled. "You know what? I'm going to see if you can't camp out with Ramsey. Would you like that?"

"I like Ramsey," Sherlock whispered. Her words sounded like they were floating up from the bottom of a well.

Harry said, "Sherlock, do you remember chasing Xu down? Tackling him?"

"Yes, of course I remember Xu. I got him on his stomach, and he was bleeding all over the place and I was cuffing him and then—" She frowned. "I saw a really bright light, it was beautiful, and then, all of a sudden, I was here getting stitched up and waiting for my birthday cake. Do you really think they'll let me camp out in Ramsey's room? I've never heard of anything like that before."

"I'll see if you can sit with him by the campfire."

"Please tell me Xu didn't get away. Please."

Eve said, "He did, but not for long. Now neither will the man who shot you."

Sherlock couldn't say anything because it was suddenly all too much. She closed her eyes again and breathed deeply. The orderly said, "We need to get her to CT now, Agent Savich. You'll have to clear it with admissions if you'd like her to stay in the Taj with Judge Dredd. You really know him?"

There was a bit of laughter, which felt very good to everyone. Cheney said, "I think it's a great idea, her rooming with Judge Hunt. Dr. Kardak might go for it, if only to keep even more law enforcement officers out of the hospital. There's already a battalion of marshals and

SFPD officers hovering on that floor. We can fit her in without adding a single man, and still be sure she's safe."

Eve said, "Ramsey can get her into their poker games. Does she play?"

Savich smiled at Eve. "She's a killer at Texas Hold 'em."

Cheney said, "Okay, listen up, everyone. There's no way Xu gets away from us. We'll have his picture all over the news in an hour. He's wounded, and he needs medical care. He's in a stolen white Infiniti with an APB out on him. All he's got with him is what he was carrying in his pockets. A passport, if he's lucky. But he's not going anywhere until he gets his wounded arm taken care of. That's got to be where we focus."

But it wasn't Xu who had shot Sherlock, Savich thought.

50

San Francisco General Hospital
Tuesday evening

Sherlock's head thrummed to a steady beat. If she tried to move her head, it felt like electric jolts were frying her brains. The stitches felt like they were pulling her scalp too tight. On the other hand, she was alive, and breathing trumped everything.

Savich had kept her parents away with the promise she'd be home tomorrow. Really it was Sean who'd kept them away. Her parents had looked at him and known to keep still, and put on a good show. Savich told her he'd lied clean, telling Sean his mother was staying with Molly and Emma because they were scared. Sean had listened thoughtfully to this smoothly delivered lie, Savich told her, and said, "But Papa, I want to protect Emma. Can't I go over and stay with them, too? We can have cocoa and I can show Emma *Flying Monks,* my new computer game."

Sherlock's mother said, "But Sean, you promised to go with me to the movies tonight to see *Rory and the Last Duck,* don't you remember?"

Torn between impressing Emma with his computer game and the movie, Sean was seriously conflicted until his grandfather said, "Your grandmother promised to buy me kettle corn, Sean; that's my favorite. Yours, too, right?" and so Sean's conflict melted away. He did think to ask, "Papa, are you coming with us?"

No, Savich told him, he was going to help his mother make Emma and Molly and the twins feel all secure, but not to worry, he'd be back to tuck Sean in. Since Sean was five years old, matters of life and death and hospital stays with a huge white bandage around a parent's head weren't about to be a part of his reality. When they'd wheeled Sherlock into the room, Molly had been there with Ramsey. She was horrified at what had happened, and question after question came pouring out until she saw Sherlock had gone quietly to sleep, providential, since the last thing she needed was Molly hovering over her.

When Sherlock woke up, the nurse gave her two Tylenol, a net, the nurse told her, to keep her safe, the only pain meds she would be getting for now. Hence the dull roar in her brain when her dinner was delivered thirty minutes later.

A fillet of sole sat in the center of a hospital plate, with half a lemon on the side, and vegetables. Who wanted vegetables when you felt down and out? When you could have been dead, your head shot off? No, you wanted ice cream, and a birthday cake, not runny chocolate pudding. She said to Ramsey, who sat in his bed eight feet from hers, "How are you surviving on the hospital food?"

He smiled, having seen the limp fish on her tray. "Since I'm Judge Dredd, one of the nurses asks me every day what I would like for dinner. The chef either makes it himself or picks it up on his way in to the hospital."

"That's not fair. Nobody asked me what I wanted to eat. What did you get for dinner?" Despite the hot wire slicing through her head, she leaned up. "I see now, it's a big steak, medium. And a baked potato. This isn't fair, it's not right. Can I have a bite?"

Ramsey looked at the steak left on his plate, looked over at her, and said, "Nah, I'm far more in need of red meat than you are, Sherlock. I've got to build up my strength. Getting shot in the chest trumps a little head wound any day. Eat your fish and leave the real patients to chow down the meat and potatoes."

Deputy Morales said from the window, a hamburger halfway to his mouth, "We were nice as could be to the nurse, but she kissed us off, said we had a per diem, and we should order in what we wanted for ourselves."

Savich appeared in the doorway, carrying two big pizza boxes. "Ramsey told me you'd try to steal his dinner, so here you go, sweetheart, enough for you and your guards and maybe one slice for Ramsey, if he's still hungry." He studied her face. She was still pale, but she was sitting up, with the bandage wrapped around her hair, looking faintly ridiculous. Today he liked ridiculous; it was a great look.

Soon there were four guards standing around the two patients, all chowing down on pizza, including Savich's vegetarian pie. Savich stood at the foot of the bed knowing he should eat, but his thoughts of what had happened wouldn't let go of his brain. He couldn't imagine eating, and so he stood there, watching her, listening to their chatter and laughter fill the room. Everyone was distracted, and that was a good thing.

The pizza tasted wonderful and settled nicely in Sherlock's stomach, despite her headache. She saw Dillon wasn't eating, and she wanted to tell him she was all right. He leaned down to kiss her, and she saw the fear lurking behind his smile as he said, "I'll be back after I've tucked Sean in for the night."

She took his hand. "Will you bring my birthday cake?"

"So you remember that, do you?"

She smiled at him. "Don't forget the butter-pecan ice cream."

There was a knock on the door. A young cop none of them had ever seen said, "Agent Savich? I'm Officer Holt. I found a folded piece of paper on the sidewalk where Agent Sherlock was shot. I took it immediately to Lieutenant Trolley. After she read it and dusted for prints, she told me to bring it to you right away." He handed Savich the paper. "You can see it has your name printed on it, nothing more. No one has any idea who left it."

Officer Holt looked over at Sherlock. "Hello, Agent Sherlock. I'm glad you're okay." He looked then at Ramsey and swallowed. "Sir, all of us are glad you're going to be all right," and he swallowed again.

Without thought, Sherlock turned her head to see how Ramsey was reacting to this show of adoration, and froze at the jolt of pain in her head. She managed to smile at him when Ramsey thanked Officer Holt for his concern, but her focus was on Savich as he unfolded the piece of paper.

"What's in the note, Dillon?"

He looked up, his brow furrowed. "Remember last Thursday, that note delivered to me at the Hoover Building?"

Sherlock said, "*For what you did you deserve this.* What about it?"

He handed her the note.

51

It was quiet, the light dim in the hospital room. Sherlock and Ramsey lay quietly, waiting for the sleeping pills the nurse had just given them to pull them into sleep. The guards by the windows were reading by shrouded reading lights. Savich hadn't returned yet from tucking Sean in. They'd brought in a cot for Savich.

Sherlock said, "Ramsey, I was going to wait until Dillon got back, but I don't think we should put it off. We need to talk about this other person in the mix, this man who shot me—he was already here in San Francisco, waiting, I suppose until he had the setting he wanted. Shooting me—it was revenge, Ramsey. It's got to be revenge. Against Dillon."

No sleeping pill could compete with what she said. Ramsey's brain snapped to full alert. "I gathered you thought that, from that bizarre note, but I don't understand. You don't think the man who shot you has any connection to Xu, that they don't have anything to do with each other?"

"It's possible, I suppose, but I don't think so.

Everything Xu has done is business to him, a matter of survival, but for the man who sent Dillon that note, it's personal; something in the past is driving him. *For what you did you deserve this.* How do you like that for over-the-top drama? He wants to terrorize us; he's taking pleasure in it."

Ramsey turned toward her, immediately regretted it, and held himself very still. He hated the sharp pain, but he hated more having to lie like a slug, helpless and impotent. And he hated having to be shaved and bathed each morning because he wasn't strong enough yet to take his own shower. He reminded himself both he and Sherlock were lucky to be alive. He said, "So shooting you was revenge against Savich. But why here, why now? And why you, rather than Savich himself?"

"Well, there's more to it than that, Ramsey." She looked up to see Dillon slip into the room through the partially open door, saw the guards move quickly, then throttle back.

Savich nodded to the guards, said quietly, "This was his second note, Ramsey, that's what Sherlock was going to tell you. What did you call it, Sherlock? His second notice of doom? He sent me one before he shot you."

Ramsey tried to take it in. He said slowly, "You're saying I was this madman's first victim? You're saying he shot both Sherlock and me to gain revenge against you?"

Savich nodded. "The first note was delivered to me last Thursday at the Hoover Building. That night, Ramsey, at midnight, you were shot. We didn't connect the note to you until tonight, when he proudly sent us the second identical note after shooting Sherlock.

"We couldn't ever be sure of a motive for Xu to try to kill you in the first place. All of us wondered why shoot the judge? But his connecting your shooting to the Cahill trial, making it seem the Cahills were responsible, I'd say it was fortuitous for him. Shooting you succeeded in getting Sherlock and me to fly out to San Francisco, and that wasn't fortuitous, it was planned. He's been watching us ever since."

Ramsey said, "But if the man was in Washington delivering the note to you, he'd have had to move fast to get to San Francisco and set everything up to shoot me from the beach below my house the same night. There wasn't enough time."

Sherlock said, "He wasn't in Washington. He paid a young auto mechanic to deliver the note to the Hoover Building on Thursday. We found the guy and brought him in, but we couldn't track down the man who'd paid him."

Savich said, "In fact, we know he was here in San Francisco, studying you and staying at a B-and-B in Atherton for about a week, enough time to do the reconnaissance he needed of your habits, your home, for planning the Zodiac rental, all of it. What's terrifying is that he would have succeeded if Molly hadn't called out to you at the last moment."

Ramsey said, "So my being shot the same day I shut down the Cahill trial, the same day Mickey O'Rourke disappeared, it was all a coincidence?"

Savich said, "Yes, and one he took advantage of. The shooter was following your trial closely enough to decide that Thursday night was the perfect time to shoot you to throw us off making the connection to the note for a while. He couldn't have scripted it better."

"Like Dillon said, he'd already been here a week before any of that. And he had to have been to Washington before he came here, checking out the neighborhood around the Hoover Building, learning enough about Teddy Moody to pick him out as his mark."

Ramsey said, "Why didn't he leave a note with me, so you'd know this was his revenge, like he did with you?"

Sherlock said, "I imagine he was getting a real kick out of the confusion he'd created since we immediately connected your shooting to the Cahills. I guess when he shot me, he was ready to take the credit."

Ramsey said, "And that leaves us the big question. Why me? We've been friends for a long time, Savich, but there are other people closer to you. That must mean the shooter has a connection to both of us." After a moment, Ramsey said, "This is the same man who tried to kill me again in the elevator on Saturday, the same man we believed was Xu."

Sherlock said, "And that was an act of someone who's driven or unbalanced enough to take such a risk. Very unlike Xu." She closed her eyes for a moment, not in pain but in thought, though sleep was pulling on her. She became aware of Dillon stroking her forearm, his touch light and comforting. She continued. "It all makes sense now. Xu was very hard to predict, even to understand.

How could we profile a man, reconcile everything he had done, when he was two very separate men whose motives couldn't be further apart?"

Ramsey said, "Then that telephone message to Molly, that wasn't Xu, either."

Savich said, "No. The phone call was meant to terrorize, like the notes."

"It was a spur-of-the-moment dig at me, and my family?" Ramsey said.

Savich nodded. "That, yes, and more than a little unhinged, like that photo he left of you as Judge Dredd X-ed through under the hydrangea, and the blood he left in the elevator shaft. The man makes plans, but he's not rational. He's deranged."

Sherlock said, "The thing is, Ramsey, he took lots of time to plan this all out, to learn all about you. Lots of time—and that's the key. We think he was in prison, where he'd have nothing but time to spend in the library. He told the young man who delivered the first note to Dillon to call him the Hammer. That's a prison moniker."

Ramsey said, "Do you think it's someone I put away?"

There was silence in the hospital room, the two guards at the window listening intently.

Savich said, "Maybe, but it's got to be as much about me because he picked me to send the note to, and he shot my wife. I don't know why he went for you first, Ramsey. Forgive me, but if I'm to be blamed I would have thought he'd have gone for Sherlock first, but he didn't. It was you."

Sherlock said, "There's got to be a good reason he went for you first, Ramsey. We have to figure out what it is."

Ramsey said, "It means he's carrying a load of rage at me, maybe more than he has against you, Savich. It could be over something he thinks we did to him together."

Sherlock only nodded. Her head felt like a weight was pressing her down. "Yes, but what?"

Savich said, "We'll have to find out, but not tonight. You both look ready to fold your tents. Get some sleep."

Savich leaned down and kissed Sherlock's mouth. "Sleep well, sweetheart. We'll get this all figured out in the morning. Ramsey, don't snore so loud you wake her. I'll be back in a moment," and Savich followed Deputy Babcock and Deputy Cluney out of the room. Deputy Babcock said, "This is hairier than my mother-in-law's legs. Two killers, not just this Xu character. Have you told Marshal Maynard?"

"Cheney will."

"Barbieri called a few minutes ago, said they'd found the Infiniti on one of the winding streets above Sausalito. Sounds like he was on his way to find a doctor to take care of his arm. I hope Xu hasn't invaded someone's home. I can't imagine a doctor would have a fully equipped office in his own home, but I guess he'd have enough stuff to help him with an arm wound. I sure hope he hasn't killed anyone."

Savich said, "I hope Xu won't think it's prudent."

"We'll find out soon enough, either way," Babcock said.

Savich said, "Xu's got to be somewhat panicked. No,

don't listen to me, I'm too tired to think straight. He's survived this long by staying cool and always using his brain. Everyone is focused on small medical offices and walk-in clinics, especially those with a Chinese clientele. He probably knows some doctors who cater to people at the Chinese consulate, take care of their families. I wonder if we can find out who those doctors are."

"Probably already done," Babcock said. "I wonder how he expects to get out of here?"

Officer Cluney said, "I would drive out of California, maybe to Utah or Nevada, stay away from the airports for a while."

Savich said, "You're probably right, if he's well enough to drive that far. Now that his cover is gone and we know he didn't shoot either Ramsey or Sherlock, it's the second shooter we have to guard against."

Cluney said, "If they don't know each other, how lucky is that for Xu?"

Babcock said, "I'll bet Xu's putting him in high on his nighttime prayer list. Agent Savich, you can relax. With four of us around the clock, how could this second guy possibly believe he could get to either Sherlock or Judge Hunt in here?"

"How? Remember the elevator?" Savich snapped his fingers. "He came this close to killing Judge Hunt. Don't forget, this guy prefers the elaborate over the simple and straightforward. The more convoluted and intricate he can make his plans, the bigger the rush he gets."

Babcock said, "But he's failed twice. Doesn't he realize that we all know now he's the danger and not Xu?"

Savich said, "But the only reason we do know is because he led us right to it, by shooting Sherlock with Xu in sight, and by leaving that note. Now he wants us to know."

Babcock said, "I don't understand why he doesn't simply wait. Say a month, even another year. If it's revenge we're talking here, what's the rush?"

Savich said, "That note was a challenge, and he'll see himself as a failure if he doesn't get it done before we get him. It's payback for him, and it will be fast, whatever he does."

"It won't matter," Babcock said. "Everyone guarding Judge Hunt and Agent Sherlock knows exactly what we're dealing with now. He won't get near either of them."

But when Savich drew the single blanket over himself on the cot, he wasn't so sure. He wasn't about to let Sherlock out of his sight.

If they were right and the man had been in prison, what was he in for? Murder? Who was his payback for? A son, a friend, a brother, maybe a mother? He and MAX would find out.

52

San Francisco General Hospital
Wednesday morning

Sherlock touched strands of dried bloody hair at the edge of the white bandage wrapped around her head that made her look like she'd walked out of a war zone. She wanted to do something about that before Dillon returned. She said to the nurse, "When can I get this white towel off my head? When can I wash my hair?"

"Actually, you look sort of cute with the white towel," Nurse Washington said, patting her hand. "Once Dr. Kardak examines you, we'll get your hair washed and change out the dressing for an adhesive strip that will cover your sutures. So how are you feeling, Agent Sherlock? Any headaches, dizziness, nausea? Were you able to sleep?"

Sherlock said, "The headache's better this morning; it comes and goes. I felt a little dizzy when I first stood up. That's about it."

"Have you felt disoriented at all? Any mental side trips? Ah, here's Dr. Kardak, to look at both you and Judge Hunt."

Dr. Kardak said good morning to her and to Ramsey, then took her chart from Nurse Washington and hummed in approval as he read it. He looked up at her. "I heard Nurse Washington ask if you had any disorientation, any mental side trips? An interesting way of putting it, yet perfectly clear."

"Harry Potter World might be fun, but no, I haven't been taking any trips in my head. My orientation's fine."

Dr. Kardak nodded, pulled the curtain around them for privacy, and leaned down to plant his stethoscope on her chest. "You've had a mild traumatic brain injury," he said. "You can expect the symptoms you're having—what we call the post-concussion syndrome—to last a week or so, maybe longer. Now, I'm going to need your patience because we're going to repeat the neurologic exam you had yesterday and ask you a few questions to test your memory, okay?"

"As long as we don't forget to wash my hair," Sherlock said.

When Dr. Kardak finished, he straightened, studied her face silently for a moment. "Your balance, your strength, your reflexes, your memory, everything looks good. I have to say, Agent, you're the luckiest patient I've treated in some time. Your scan from yesterday looks normal, except for your scalp injury. To be shot in the head and sustain no structural brain injury or bleeding, no cracked skull, no visible swelling, is amazing. I would think, though, that most people who've had your experience might consider a career change."

Sherlock said, "I realize I was incredibly lucky and I am immensely grateful for that. To be honest here, what happened at the Fairmont, well, I guess you could say it came out of the blue, so there was no way to do my job and avoid it." She grinned up at him. "It could have happened to anyone."

He said, "In that case, Agent Sherlock, I hope your luck continues for your next three lifetimes. As for your husband, I must tell you the man's a wreck, but, naturally, he believes he has to appear calm and in control around you. My prescription is for both of you to take a break and hug each other really tight, all right?"

Sherlock nodded and felt a stab of guilt. With so much flying around them, they couldn't take a break, but she surely could hug him. She said, "Yes, I can do that."

"I want you to rest this morning, and by that I mean no chatting up Judge Dredd here. If you're not sleeping, you're to lie here nice and calm and quiet. I'll leave the curtain between the two of you so you're not tempted to talk shop. With a bullet wound such as you've had, I like to repeat the CT scan to make sure there's no delayed swelling or bleeding. I doubt there will be. If everything looks good I want you to continue resting this afternoon, let your brain and body settle and heal. Depending on how you feel, we can talk this afternoon about whether we'll have the pleasure of your company through Thanksgiving, Agent Sherlock. How does it sound if we plan to release you Friday morning?"

"No can do, Dr. Kardak. I've got a five-year-old son who doesn't need to see his mother lying in a hospital bed. I'd like to leave this afternoon."

He studied her face for a moment. "Five years old, you say? What's his name?"

"Sean. He's the image of his papa. He plans to marry three different girls. He's also planning on working three jobs so they'll all be happy."

Dr. Kardak chuckled. "Sean sounds like my kid Peter, all mouth and laughter and boundless energy. There aren't any girls yet on Peter's somewhat limited horizon." He looked toward the curtain, called out, "Judge Hunt, how long have you two known each other?"

"More than five years," Ramsey said from behind the curtain. "When I first met Sherlock, she was three months pregnant, throwing up whenever anyone in her hearing said the word *pregnant*."

"Oh, goodness, I'd forgotten," Sherlock said. "I remember belting Dillon a couple of times when he let the word slip out."

Dr. Kardak pursed his lips. "I'm going to mention that to one of my shrink friends." He rolled his eyes. "He's a practicing Freudian therapist. I shudder to think what he'll have to say." He studied Sherlock for a moment longer. "Very well, if nothing unexpected shows up, you may go home, but you're to rest, let everyone wait on you. You are not to bake even the sweet-potato casserole, you understand me?"

Sherlock nodded. "I won't even make my sausage stuffing. Promise."

"You may, however, eat as much as you want." He pulled the curtain open and nodded toward Ramsey. "As for Judge Dredd here, he gets to enjoy our hospitality for a while longer. I understand there's to be a Thanksgiving feast here in the room tomorrow. The floor staff can't talk about much else. The chef told my assistant he was even preparing a surprise for your dinner. I'm thinking I might drop by, see if there are any leftovers. Maybe watch one of the football games."

When he left ten minutes later, Sherlock heard Dillon speaking to Dr. Kardak outside in the hall. When Dillon came into the room, he was smiling and carrying two cups of coffee. Sherlock held her arms out to him.

53

San Francisco General Hospital
Wednesday morning

Molly sat beside her sleeping husband, her hand resting lightly on his forearm. He looked thin, she thought, even with all the extra meals the nurses brought in for him. He wasn't eating enough, despite their efforts. It was the pain and dependence and niggling fear, she imagined, fear for her, and for Emma, and for the boys.

Molly laid her cheek against his shoulder and wondered for the dozenth time who the man was who had shot him. Who hated him, and Dillon, so much?

At least Sherlock was going home after her brain scan. Molly looked at the big hand of the clock on the wall. Sherlock would be back soon. Deputy Marshal Ray Rozan was with her, her Kevlar vest, Sherlock called him. As for Savich, he hadn't budged an inch from her side until the phone call. The call was short. When he'd punched off his cell, he'd looked at his wife and she'd told him with no hesitation, "Go. I'll be fine with Deputy Rozan." That was it. Molly knew the call had to be urgent to make him leave Sherlock. She admired Sherlock's restraint. She hadn't asked him what had happened, and he hadn't said a thing.

Molly thought Sherlock looked perfectly fine to go home when they'd helped her into a wheelchair for her CT scan. Having all the matted blood washed out of her hair and the clunky bandage replaced with a strip of plastic tape had made a huge difference.

Molly looked toward Officer Lamar Marks standing beside the window, staring down into the parking lot. Was he thinking about Thanksgiving tomorrow? She knew he wasn't on duty tomorrow, since he had three kids and a truckload of relatives coming to his house. Another SFPD officer had volunteered. He'd eat very well for it, she thought, smiling.

But maybe Officer Marks was thinking about the same thing Molly was: *There were two separate killers.* It was difficult to accept that that could be possible, yet everyone had always wondered, *Why would Xu shoot Ramsey?*

"Molly?"

She looked up to see Dillon standing in the doorway.

"Sherlock's still getting her tests?"

She replied in a whisper, "She should be back soon, Dillon; that's what the nurse told me. Ramsey's sleeping, which is excellent. What happened? Who called you?"

He smiled at her shotgun questions, motioned for her

to join him at the door. "A Chinese physician was found murdered early this morning in his office in Sausalito. There was ample evidence Xu had been there yesterday. We understand the doctor closed his office that afternoon, sent everyone home. Xu was probably there already, demanding treatment. Given all the blood in the examining room, Xu was in bad shape." He paused for a moment. "Dr. Mulan Chu was a primary-care doctor that Xu knew somehow. Perhaps he'd treated Xu before. It's a pity Xu got to the doctor before he got the warning we were sending out."

Molly said, "Why would Xu murder the doctor who'd saved his life, a doctor he knew?"

"We're thinking Chu found out what Xu had done at the Fairmont. Virginia said there'd been a call from his number to the police department asking to speak to someone about the Fairmont fire, but the caller hung up. We're thinking Xu overheard Dr. Chu dialing the cops, and that's why he killed him."

Ramsey said from behind them, "Do you think Xu is out of control, Savich?"

Savich and Molly walked back to Ramsey's bedside. Savich said, "No, I don't. I think he did what he believed he had to do to save himself. I think all Xu wants is to get out of Dodge, and he's doing whatever he has to do to accomplish that. He's not insane or going on some sort of mad killing spree. Not that it matters to Dr. Chu or his family."

Savich looked over at Officer Lamar Marks, who looked like he'd been punched in the face. Savich knew exactly how he felt, since he'd felt the same way when Delion had first told him. Officer Marks said, "Xu better hope all he needs is this one doctor visit."

True enough, Savich thought.

Officer Marks said, "He could still end up in an emergency room somewhere."

Ramsey said, "Lamar's right. If he's that bad off, then he'll need more medical attention."

Molly said, "Even if he can weather through it, Xu could still be stuck in bed for another week, Dillon." She brightened. "Maybe he could die."

"He's certainly lost enough blood. Dr. Chu couldn't have transfused him in his office."

Officer Marks said, "No one saw him at the doctor's office? No other staff, patients, passersby?"

"We have nothing so far. We do know Xu went to Dr. Chu's clinic within an hour of his getting shot. The M.E. estimated Dr. Chu was dead within a couple of hours after that."

"I wonder where Xu is holed up now?" Officer Marks said.

Savich heard some voices in the corridor behind him and quickly turned. He expected Sherlock, but it was a couple of orderlies. Where was Sherlock?

Savich bolted from the room and ran to the nurses' station.

54

Sherlock was tapping her fingers. Why in heaven did everything take so long in a hospital? Well, okay, so she'd been sitting here in the patient waiting area only about ten minutes, but still. Where was a nurse, or the tech to wheel her in and get this business over and done?

She didn't even need another brain scan. She sincerely hoped it wouldn't include an injection. Her head was aching again, a slow series of dull thuds. She wanted to get out of here; she wanted to be able to kiss Dillon silly and hug Sean to her, have him pat her shoulder and ask her to play a computer game with him that it would be her responsibility to lose with dignity and guile.

Deputy Ray Rozan stood near the radiology waiting room door, his eyes always on the move, studying anyone for the slightest interest in coming within six feet of her. He was on edge, all the guards were, what with two maniacs out there. But it wasn't Xu, it was the other unknown man that scared him. They had only a sketch and a description of him: slender build, an American, maybe older, but no one was really sure. Whatever his age, he'd been capable of that mad spree in the elevator on Saturday.

Ray looked over at Sherlock, knew she wanted nothing more than to go home. He watched her pull her cell phone out of the pocket of a dark blue bathrobe with lots of dog hair on it that Savich had brought in for her along with her cell. He'd heard Savich had returned the previous night to sleep on a cot not two feet from her hospital bed. Rozan wondered if he'd told her why he'd been called away. He probably hadn't, since she didn't look upset, only a bit anxious. And hurting a little, too, from the fixed expression in her eyes. Her hair looked better without the blood—a soft riot of curls now, so thick it nearly covered the small bandage over the head wound. It was hard to imagine the person in that bathrobe tackling Xu and bringing him down.

"You want me to go see what's holding up these yahoos, Sherlock?"

She glanced down at her watch. "We can give them another couple of minutes. We'll make it fifteen minutes, tops. I think I'll call Dillon, see what's happened."

Rozan said it aloud: "Xu killed a physician, the one who treated him."

She nodded. "Yes, I was told." She closed her eyes against the stark knowledge of it. She'd been so close, she thought. She'd had Xu flat on his face against the sidewalk. If only she'd had time to get the other cuff on him. If only.

"We're ready for your test now, Agent Sherlock." Sherlock looked up to see a tall, lanky tech standing beside Deputy Rozan, wearing scrubs, a mask over his nose, green booties on his feet. He had a sheaf of papers in his gloved hand.

Deputy Rozan said, "I need to see your ID."

The man turned, clearly startled. "Are you her husband, sir?"

"No, I'm Deputy Rozan. She's in my care. Show me your ID, please."

"Well, you can see my name tag, and here are the orders for Agent Sherlock's CT scan, signed by Dr. Kardak."

"Why don't you have a hospital ID?"

"It's in my locker. I usually wear it, but no one ever asks for it."

"Then show me your driver's license."

Savich burst into the waiting room, saw the tech, masked, standing too close to Rozan, and raised his SIG. "Get back and drop to your knees!"

The man dropped Sherlock's chart and fell to his knees on the floor. Savich, panting hard from running, stood over him.

The man looked up at him, obviously terrified. "Who are you? What did I do?"

Rozan said, "He didn't have his hospital ID, and I'd just asked him for his driver's license when you, ah, came in, Agent Savich."

"Lose the mask," Savich said.

The man pulled the ties loose. The mask fell off his face. "My name's Terry Lempert; see, my name's on my name tag. Why are you pointing that gun at me?"

Savich put his SIG back in his waist holster.

A nurse came to the door. "What's going on here? Goodness, Terry, what did you do now?"

Sherlock said calmly, "Officer Rozan is my guard, and this is my husband. I guess you'd say he's part of the guard detail for me. He thought this man was a threat to me. Do you know him? Can you verify he's supposed to be here? To take me in for a CT scan?"

The nurse looked toward Rozan.

"Yes," Rozan said. "Can you identify this man for us?"

She said, "I've known him for nearly ten years. It's Terry Lempert. He's been known to flirt with pretty patients, though, and I thought he'd gone over the top this time." She watched the husband pull Terry to his feet.

"Very funny, Kaitlyn," Terry said, dusting off his knees. "I wasn't doing anything, really."

Savich said, "Sorry, Mr. Lempert. You really should consider wearing your ID, given all that's happened here the past week."

Lempert said, "Yeah, oh, yes, right. You nearly made me mess myself."

"He didn't shoot you," Officer Rozan said, and smiled, shook Lempert's hand. "You'll be fine. You did good."

Savich walked to where Sherlock sat smiling, of all things, in her wheelchair. She laid her hand on his arm. "My hero."

"Terry, go get your ID. Then you can take over Jonah's case in room three. Jonah can deal with Agent

Sherlock. Next time, don't wear a mask when you fetch a patient. I've told you it freaks them out." She shot a look at Savich. "And their husbands."

Savich rested one hand lightly on Sherlock's shoulder. "Sorry, Terry," he said. "But if anything happened to Sherlock, I'd lose my job."

Terry was very pleased to take over Jonah's case, even if it was a ninety-year-old curmudgeon from Fresno who did nothing but cuss at him.

55

Xu was trying to sleep, but it was hard, since he felt like crap. After leaving Dr. Chu's clinic yesterday afternoon, he'd barely made it across the Richmond Bridge and was glad to find this hole-in-the-wall motel near the highway. He wished he'd made it farther, but it was impossible, not until he was stronger. He had not taken enough oxycodone to kill his pain entirely because he couldn't allow himself to get completely helpless. It was what a stupid man would do, and he hadn't survived by being stupid. He would make peace with the grinding pain.

Xu knew what this pain would be like, since he'd been shot once before. One of his trainers in the army compound outside Beijing had accidentally shot him in the leg, the blind moron. He remembered his trainer Mr. Yeung had actually cried over him, which was the only reason Xu hadn't tried to kick his stomach through his backbone.

His arm would heal, Dr. Chu had assured him several times, and he'd be well enough to fly anywhere in three or four days. Xu knew from his other gunshot wound that he wouldn't have full use of his arm for several months. At least the bullet hadn't shattered any bones on its way out of his arm.

Dr. Chu had known not to ask what had happened when Xu showed him his wound and his gun. He'd calmly sent his office staff home before he ushered Xu into one of the clinic exam rooms, helped him out of his blood-soaked jacket and his shirt, and settled him on the examining table. He'd asked absolutely nothing while he'd worked on him, but Dr. Chu had known. The doctor had given him intravenous morphine and Versed. Xu had watched him as he began silently cleaning out and suturing his wound. Xu had floated away, only vaguely aware of what Dr. Chu was doing. He remembered lying stretched out on Dr. Chu's examining table until he thought he could drive safely. He'd asked to take a Windbreaker with him he'd seen on a hanger in a hallway, and Dr. Chu had helped him put it on. It was large enough to fit over his arm without too much pain and zip over the bandage, since his shirt wasn't salvageable. Dr. Chu had told him to wait while he brought him antibiotics and pain meds from his office. He hadn't realized Xu had followed him down the hallway and could hear him speaking.

He heard Dr. Chu say, "I need to speak to the police

about the fire at the Fairmont today. I know what happened."

Xu had no time for thought. He'd stepped into the small office, aimed his Beretta at Dr. Chu, who heard him and looked up and threw the phone at him as Xu pulled the trigger. Xu watched him slide down behind his desk. He heard a voice on the phone saying, "Sir, who is this? What do you want again? You said you knew about the Fairmont fire?"

Xu hung up the phone, took some antibiotics and oxycodone, and walked out of the clinic.

It was too bad about Dr. Chu. Xu appreciated what the doctor had done for him. The doctor was collateral damage, and he'd still be alive if he'd had better judgment.

The FBI knew who he was and knew what he looked like; they had to, since they'd found him, probably through Cindy. He'd been too late after all. His passport and his visa were useless to him, but he knew where he could get others. At least they didn't have a clue where he was now or where he was going to be soon enough. It was then he realized, paralyzed for a moment, that neither did he. He'd dumped the white Infiniti on one of Sausalito's curving streets and hot-wired a dark blue Honda parked nearby. He should have gone farther away to find a car, but he'd simply been too weak.

Xu pulled the cheap motel blanket up to his neck, settled his wounded arm on one of the skinny pillows. First he had to heal. He could hardly fly to Beijing into the arms of the Chinese, not now, even if a false passport got him through customs. The Chinese would sever all connections with him now and deny he ever existed, no matter how valuable the information he'd gotten them from Lindy's computer. They might even kill him if they could.

Xu forced himself to lie perfectly still on the rock-hard mattress, yet the pain in his arm continued to drum a steady tattoo. He wanted nothing more than to go to sleep, but the instant he closed his eyes, he was back at the Fairmont, watching each and every scene play through slowly. So be it. He examined each decision he'd made, an exercise his trainers had taught him early on. He thought of the flash-bang he'd long carried with him. He'd never really believed he'd need it, but his training had always pushed precaution, and that piece of insurance had paid off in spades. It had been a while since he'd used one, but he hadn't forgotten. That and the bomb he'd set up in his room had saved his life.

Should he have gone out the hotel through the back service entrance? No, there would have been FBI agents out there waiting for him, away from the crowds. He'd done the right thing there, too, getting whole-hide out of the lobby by mixing with the tourists who were running around like berserkers after he blew up his little surprise.

He let himself relive the awful pain he'd felt crashing down to the sidewalk when the FBI agent had tackled him and smashed her fist against his wounded arm. He felt again the humiliation and panic when she'd snapped the cuff on his right wrist and began reciting his rights to him, close to his ear, the bitch.

Even after all his training, perhaps because of it, there'd been no way he could have foreseen that agent chasing him down. It wasn't just any damned FBI agent, no, it was a woman, and it shouldn't have happened, wouldn't have happened if he'd been whole. He should have turned to face her, used his training to snap her skinny neck or his Beretta to shoot her dead, before she'd gotten him down.

A woman bested me. He looked down at the handcuff that still circled his right wrist. How to get the damned thing off? It would have to wait. He'd figure something out, he always did.

And someone had shot the bitch. It had looked to Xu like she was dead, a shot through the head, but of course he hadn't checked, just shoved her off him and run.

Who was he? Was it the same idiot who had shot Judge Hunt at the wrong moment and blown the Cahills' trial apart? Had he shot the agent purposefully to save Xu? Why?

Who was he?

When the knock came on the door of his motel room, Xu grabbed his gun, gasped at the rip of pain through his arm, and shouted, "Go away!"

Another knock.

Xu raised his Beretta, aimed it at the motel door. "Who is it?"

A hard rasping smoker's voice called out, "I'm the one who saved your bacon."

56

Xu stared at the man standing in front of him, his back to the motel door. He was wearing a Giants baseball cap, sunglasses, a loose blue Windbreaker, jeans, sneakers, and gloves. He smiled at Xu, not moving since Xu's Beretta was steady on his chest.

"Who are you?"

"I already told you, I'm the one who saved your bacon. Good thing I followed you here from that doctor's office in Sausalito, since it looks like you're going to need some more saving."

"How did you find me?"

"Well, now, I've got to admit I had a bit of luck there. My car was near that white Infiniti you stole—nice job, incidentally, yanking that guy right out, no muss, no fuss, and you were out of there. I lost you for a while because of all that snarled traffic you caused at the Fairmont, but then I thought about it and decided you'd probably headed to the Golden Gate, so I did, too. And there you were ahead of me, going through the tollbooth. I followed you off at Spencer Avenue, watched you leave the Infiniti and steal the blue Honda. Then I sat back and waited for you just down the block from that doctor's office.

"Yeah, I heard the gunshot. You killed the guy. Why? He saved your bacon, too."

Xu's arm hurt from holding the Beretta steady, but it didn't matter. The Beretta didn't move. "I overheard the moron calling the cops. I had no choice."

"Good to know you don't just go around shooting folk for no reason."

"No," Xu said, "there's always a reason. Then you followed me here?"

"Sure, not a problem. I was surprised you made it so far the way you were driving. Gotta say, you sure don't look so hot. You've still got some blood on your face from when that agent planted you on the sidewalk."

There was blood on his face? What did this guy want? Xu said slowly, "But that was yesterday afternoon. Why did you wait until today to knock on my door?"

The man said matter-of-factly, "The Feds might have been following you or you might have had some other help coming. I had to wait, seeing as how I'm not too fond of the cops myself. You know, there's a chance the clerk in the dinky motel office might have seen the blood on your face, and if he did, he must have wondered. Surely he wondered. If he sees your photo on TV, he'll know."

"Nah, the kid doesn't know anything; he was too busy playing video games when I checked in. I don't even remember a TV."

"Like I said, you don't look too hot. Do you want another pain med? Once we get you feeling better, we can decide where to go. Look, if I'd wanted you dead, I wouldn't have shot that agent off your back. I'm not here to hurt you. You're already in bad shape. I'm here to help you. Stop pointing that ridiculous gun at me."

Xu ground out the words "Why would you care?"

"I'm thinking we're a lot alike."

"That's crazy."

"Nah, I kill because I want to, and you kill because you have to. See? Not so different."

Xu stared at the guy for a long time, and nodded. "The pills are on the night table."

The guy shook two pills out onto his gloved palm, handed them to Xu, waited until he swallowed them, and gave him a glass of water.

Xu still didn't pull down the Beretta. He motioned the guy to step back, then held himself still and waited for relief.

"I see from the number of pills still in the bottle you've been going light on the pain meds. Not a bad idea, given who could come through that door."

"Take another step back. I don't want you so close to me."

Xu watched him take two steps back.

"Why did you kill that FBI agent who was on my back?"

"Well, you see, when she knocked you down, she was out there in the open. I had a nice clear shot, and I took it."

"You're saying it wasn't about me? You wanted to kill her?"

"Oh, yeah, I wanted her dead, but I figured what I was seeing was pretty interesting, so why not see where it led me? Hey, kill one bird and save the other."

He opened his mouth, but the man raised a gloved hand. "No reason for you to ask me any more right now. Maybe if we become BFFs, I'll tell you everything."

The medication was numbing the pain in his arm but blurring his brain as well. Xu said, "Were you the one who tried to kill Judge Hunt?"

The guy nodded. "I thought I nailed the bastard, but he turned at that last second. Can you believe the rotten luck? But still, it was a good shot, he should have died."

"But he didn't. Did you try to take him out again in the hospital?"

Xu would swear the guy puffed up with pride.

"I gave that plan a lot of thought, even got me some blood from a patient in the hospital to smear on the walls of the elevator shaft to drive the Feds nuts, but—"

Xu interrupted, "It was a ridiculous plan." He stopped talking at a fierce jab of pain, held himself perfectly still, waiting for the meds to kick in and kill the pain once and for all. This idiot who'd shot through an elevator hatch wanted to help him?

Xu said, "I want to see you. Take off those sunglasses and that ball cap now or I'll drill you between the eyes."

"Okey-dokey, fair enough, but ready yourself. You're in for a big whopper surprise."

The ball cap and the sunglasses came off. Xu stared,

so stunned that for a moment he didn't feel the pain in his arm.

"Got you, didn't I?"

Xu could only nod.

"Fact is, I mean, who can you trust in this sad world?"

"You," he said. "Maybe I can trust you. You're as bad as I am."

"No, you're wrong about that. I'm worse."

57

Sean was teaching Cal and Gage how to play *Flying Monks,* the latest computer game his grandmother had presented to him when they'd first arrived. It was always a treat for Sherlock to watch her five-year-old teaching younger children, and three-year-old Cal and Gage looked utterly absorbed, nodding and all serious about the rules Sean was laying on them. *Flying Monks—* another new game Sherlock would have to master.

She caught herself thinking that kids were so different now, an observation probably made by every single generation in man's long timeline. She smiled to herself. Time always passed, and everything always changed. No kid today could imagine the world without a small device called a cell phone that would soon do everything but make them Kool-Aid. And now you could ask your phone a question and it would answer. But people, she thought, people themselves never changed.

Cal shouted, "I got you, Gage. I've moved up two ranks. I'm flying! I'm a Major Monk now."

Sherlock felt bone tired, and was trying not to show it, but she didn't mind, because she'd succeeded in fooling Sean. She'd hidden her bandage well enough—thank God for all her curly hair—and he'd accepted her being gone Tuesday night, inquiring only if Emma had wondered why he hadn't come to see her. Sherlock had lied to him cleanly. "Of course Emma wanted to know where you were, Sean. I told her you'd promised yourself to your grandparents and you'd never break a promise."

"You didn't tell her I went to see *Rory and the Last Duck,* did you, Mama?"

"Nope."

"She doesn't know Grandpa and I ate two buckets of kettle corn, does she? I don't want her to think I'm a pig."

"Nope."

Sean looked thoughtful, an identical expression to his father's. "There's so much to do, Mama. Sometimes I just don't know."

His grandmother had walked in then with a freshly baked plate of chocolate-chip cookies, and Sherlock forgot to ask him what he just didn't know.

She sensed Dillon behind her and heard his deep voice. "Here, sweetheart." He leaned down, kissed her mouth, and handed her a cup of hot tea. "Drink it down.

Then I'm thinking it's time for you to hang it up for the night."

"But—"

"Dr. Kardak said you'd give me grief and I was going to have to be the enforcer. You've done well, stayed nice and quiet all afternoon and evening. Now it's time to let your brain and your body knit themselves back together while you have pleasant dreams." He paused for a moment. "I'm thinking I have some good ideas on how to help you make that happen."

She took a sip of tea, looked up at him. "You're going to read me a bedtime story?"

"I could, but I hadn't planned to."

"I wonder what you could possibly have in mind?"

He smiled at her. "You finish your tea and we'll see. Molly called, said Ramsey misses you since you were a civilizing influence on all those males around him. She'll be here with Emma soon to pick up Gage and Cal. Ah, if you like, I can remove Sean before Emma comes in."

"I'll watch Cal and Gage," Evelyn Sherlock said. "I've got the power as long as I've got these chocolate-chip cookies."

Sherlock said, "Maybe it'd be good to take Sean upstairs, otherwise he'll be so excited about seeing Emma it'll be difficult to get him to bed."

Half an hour later, Sherlock was lying in bed, the pill Dillon fed her quashing the remnants of pain in her head.

Now, what else did her husband have in mind, as if she

couldn't guess? She heard him singing a country-western tune in the bathroom, a song James Quinlan, a fellow agent and musician, had written about a man who loved wild broncos, wilder women, and black gold. When he came into the bedroom a few minutes later, he was wearing only pajama bottoms, slung low on his hips.

Sherlock thought she'd swallow her tongue. "Don't move, please."

He obligingly stood still, arms at his sides, backlit in the bathroom doorway, smiling at her. "I missed you scrubbing me down."

"Me, too." It was true. As a shower mate, Dillon was a keeper.

"How's your head?"

"What head?"

He was grinning when he came to stand over her. "Life's been a tangle, hasn't it? I say we take a small break from the madness. What do you think?"

It was amazing how good she felt in that moment. This was probably the best idea she'd heard in a very long time.

58

"You've got a burn just there." Harry lightly touched his fingertip to a red spot on Eve's neck.

She never looked away from him. "I could put some more burn cream on it, or maybe you could kiss it and make it well."

"Not a good idea," he said, and took a step back from her.

Harry, Eve, and Griffin had been treated by the EMTs at the Fairmont, had been pronounced good to go, had been debriefed at the Federal Building, and had showered and cleaned up at Harry's house before he'd brought her back to her condo.

Eve felt punch-drunk, both hyped and exhausted. The weird thing was, this potent mix had her seeing Special Agent Harry Christoff with new eyes. The new eyes really liked what they saw.

Harry knuckled his own eyes. "I keep seeing Xu coming into the suite, and then I hear Griffin yell for him to get his hands in the air. Then everything happens so fast, all at the same time—the explosion of bright light and that god-awful noise, and fire everywhere.

"I still can't believe Xu was carrying a flash-bang. And he knew exactly what to do with it."

Eve said, "I want to learn how to use one. Talk about effective; my ears didn't stop ringing for an hour. It was as if that light slapped right into my brain and I was as good as blind for five minutes."

Harry said, "Xu certainly came prepared, you have to give him that."

Eve said, "I don't have to give him a damned thing. However, I wouldn't mind shooting him in both knees. I guess you'd have to be in the military to learn how to use a flash-bang."

Harry said, "No Flash-bang Escape Weekends for civilians?"

"Not that I've heard of. You want a beer?"

He shook his head.

Eve waved him into her living room, eased herself down onto the sofa.

Harry sat in the chair opposite her and gave her a brooding look over his steepled fingers. "I'm wondering if the State Department can get the Chinese government to tell us anything about Xu now that he's blowing up hotel suites and killing people."

"I doubt they'd even own up to knowing who Xu is. If we pursued it, accused Xu of being a Chinese spy, they'd claim he was probably an innocent bystander the FBI was trying to nail as a scapegoat. I'll bet the State Department will back off, without more proof, and even then—"

Harry tapped his fingertips together. "I keep asking myself—is there anything we could have done to stop him?"

"If we hadn't been blinded and mule-kicked, we could have put a dozen bullets in his chest. That would have ended things nicely. At least one of us got him in the arm. I wonder which of us it was. I don't suppose the medical examiner will want to examine our weapons?"

"If it got out that the M.E. was going to check our SIGs, there'd be a pool started up to see which of us had popped Xu."

She got up, went into the kitchen. She called out, "You want some Fritos and queso dip?"

Harry laughed. "Sure, why not? I can't remember the last time we ate."

Eve brought in a tray with a huge bag of Fritos and a bowl with the queso dip, steaming from the microwave, and set the tray on the coffee table. "Well, come on over and sit next to me unless you want to drag that chair over."

Harry dragged over the chair opposite the coffee table.

Eve gave him a long look. "I usually like it when a guy is scared of me, but you? You won't sit next to me on the sofa, you won't even give me a mother's kiss on my neck to make my owie better again."

"Mama didn't raise me to be stupid."

She scooped up dip onto a big Frito. "Do you know I overheard Cheney saying you weren't a nasty git any longer, only nasty."

"When did you hear that?"

"At the hospital last Friday morning. I was standing in the corridor outside the ICU when you and Cheney came waltzing in."

"What I really am is a mild-mannered agent, only no one will believe me. Okay, maybe it's true I haven't been too much fun for the past year and a half."

"Amazing, we only met last Friday."

"We've seen each other on the elevators, in the Federal Building garage."

"Yeah, well, you pretended you were this tough guy who shaved himself with a hunting knife. Hard to reconcile that image with what all of us deputy marshals know to our guts, namely, that FBI agents are all wimpy clones made in the FBI factory."

"Oh, yeah?"

"It's common knowledge."

"You want to know what FBI agents think about the fricking Marshal Service?"

She grinned at him. "Nope."

When he opened his mouth, she raised her hand. "You asked and I answered, so keep quiet."

He said, "The few times I've seen you, I always thought you were too pretty to be a marshal, since nearly all of them are ex-military buzz-cut hardnoses. And look at you—you wear that black-and-red getup with your butt-kicker boots so you can be one of the boys. Have you found they take you more seriously?"

He was spot-on about that, she thought.

"It's the boots that win the day," she said. "No one messes with the boots."

"The fact is, though," he continued after eating a Frito, "the unmarried FBI agents keep trying to figure out how to get your attention. Word is, you never give any of us the time of day."

"Nope, you're all pantywaists. Who wants to hang around a pantywaist with wingtips on his big feet?"

"Yeah, yeah, blah, blah. You know what it is about you—it's that blond ponytail and those big blue eyes, makes all the guys want to take you home to Mama."

"The blond ponytail wouldn't have anything to do with it. Nope, Mama would admire my black boots."

He laughed. "Maybe."

She studied his face a moment and liked what she saw—the hard planes, the sharp cheekbones, and his eyes, green-as-the-Irish-hills eyes. There was an inbred toughness in him. She said, "You know, the past five days have made me understand a little why there were so many wartime marriages. Men and women thrown together in extraordinary circumstances—I guess to survive they needed to reaffirm they were alive by making connections, by making another human being matter to them so they were able to ignore death, if only for a little while."

Harry said, "Nah, it doesn't work like that."

"What? Hey, that was all sorts of philosophical and

you say 'nah'? Haven't you heard of the bazillion war-time marriages?"

"I think regardless of how people meet, they're either meant to be together or they're not." He ate his Frito, then quickly dipped another into the dip. "I'm starving and I hadn't even realized it." He toasted her with it. "Thanks for the best Frito I've had in a week."

"Nothing beats a Frito. So you weren't such a nasty git before your divorce a year and a half ago? It was the breakup that made you into one?"

"I've always been nasty. The git thing, that's all Cheney."

"That's why your wife left you?"

He paused with a Frito an inch from his mouth. "No."

She cocked her head at him, said slowly, "No, that isn't what happened, is it?"

"Why do you think that isn't what happened?"

She said, "I've known you only a short time and one thing I see very clearly is that you're not nasty. You're an honest man, Harry. You say you'll do something and you do it. You don't make excuses when things don't go right, and you don't expect to hear any. That's clear-headed, and it's tough, but it's not nasty.

"Well, maybe when I first met you I wanted to punch your lights out because you were posturing like a rooster. I think you enjoyed getting my reaction, you liked rubbing my nose in it, liked reminding me I was *only* the protection detail, not a member of the investigation team." She ate another chip, never looking away from his face. "Not that I really mind posturing for the fun of it, mind you. You know one of the things I like best about you? You're funny, you make me laugh. You have a good outlook, Harry."

"I was shot three years ago in an aborted bank robbery."

"Where?"

"At the Bank of America on Chestnut."

She threw a Frito at him. "No, idiot, on your body. Where were you shot?"

He gave her a faint smile, stood up, and pulled out his shirt. She looked at a four-inch scar on his left side over his lower ribs. It had to really hurt, she thought. She'd never been shot, only punched a couple of times. She kept looking at him, couldn't seem to drag her eyes away from that hard disciplined body.

He said as he quickly tucked his shirt back in and sat back down, "She freaked, and couldn't get past it no matter what I said. Our three-year marriage went downhill fast when I refused to resign from the Bureau. Bottom line, it was her ultimatum."

He picked the Frito she'd thrown at him off his sleeve. Then he looked at it in his hand and carefully laid it down on the tray. "I'd always heard it's nearly impossible for cops to stay married—but I'd never thought about it, since my parents have been married forever. I mean, we were both good people, weren't we? I was in love, and so was she. Before I asked her to marry me we talked about the high divorce rate among cops. I gave her all the stats, quoted a couple of articles. She scoffed at the idea that she—who had just passed the bar—could possibly be swayed by any of that. I told her my hours could be crazy and she said her hours wouldn't always be her own, either, but she was nothing if not levelheaded, she'd have no problem dealing with the chance of violence bumping into our lives.

"To be honest, the entire time we dated, it was more or less nine-to-five for me. I went out of town only a couple of times to do some undercover, but it didn't impinge much on our time together. But the threat, the reality of violence, it was always there, always lurking, and I knew it. I simply ignored it.

"I'll tell you, Eve, it sucks to be a cliché."

She wouldn't want to be a cliché, either. He was right, what had happened to them was all too common, and maybe why she hadn't ever set herself up in the marriage market again. "You want a beer now?"

"Sure." He got up with her to go to the kitchen. "Sorry to unload my sorry history on you. I didn't mean to. Actually, I have no idea why it popped out."

"Thank you for telling me."

"How old are you?"

"I'll turn twenty-nine on the twenty-sixth of January."

"You ever get close to getting married?"

"Yeah, I was married, right out of college. It wasn't long before I realized I wasn't going to be the last notch on the moron's belt. Truth is, after the moron, I don't think any guy could make it past my dad and my brothers. They'd make hash of him." She rolled her eyes. "They told me after my little misadventure—that's what my brothers called my brief marriage—if any guy did me wrong again they'd bury him deep, never to be found."

She got a couple of beers out of the refrigerator, handed him one. They clicked bottles and drank.

Eve said, "You ready to kiss my owie now and make it well?"

"Yes," he said, putting his beer on the counter, "I think I am."

59

Judge Sherlock's home
Pacific Heights
Early Thursday morning
Thanksgiving Day

Sherlock opened her eyes to see Dillon standing over her.

A big smile bloomed because, quite simply, how could it not? Sherlock yawned and stretched. "What time is it?"

"A bit after six a.m. How are you feeling?"

Sherlock queried her head. The wound itself throbbed a bit, but there weren't any voices inside her head screaming punk rock, and that was good.

"Like a million bucks. You tell a great bedtime story, Dillon. Every bone in my body is humming 'Ring My Bell.' What in heaven's name are you doing up? Helping my parents with the turkey?"

"No, Molly is keeping the turkey to herself. Your mom's in the kitchen, though, making sausage stuffing for you carnivores and a nice cornbread stuffing for me.

I woke up a couple of hours ago, realized we'd all over-looked something, and went to work on MAX."

She studied his face. "You know who he is? The man who shot me yesterday? The man who tried to kill Ramsey twice?"

He climbed into bed beside her, pulled her against him, and kissed her hair. "It's all pretty straightforward once you look at it the right way."

He was big and warm, his heartbeat steady against her chest. "What do you mean, 'the right way'?"

"Remember, it was you, Sherlock, who suggested a long prison stay fit the bill, someone who'd had time on his hands to plan the bizarre attacks on Ramsey. And we knew the person who had that note delivered to me at the Hoover Building had joked to Ted Moody about calling him the Hammer—prison slang."

She nodded.

"And Dane and Ruth have been checking inmates released since the first of this year, looking to find a father or a brother, someone with a relationship to one of our cases who was out now, who could be looking for revenge."

Sherlock said, "Ruth told me she and Dane were going nuts, that they couldn't find a prisoner who fit the profile."

Savich said, "There's a very good reason for that. I realized the one case that remotely connected Ramsey to me was more than five years ago, though I wasn't all that involved. Remember Father Sonny Dickerson, the pedo-phile who kidnapped Emma?"

Sherlock clearly remembered the obsessed ex-priest who'd sexually abused Emma until she'd escaped and Ramsey had found her and hooked up with Molly to save her. So much violence, so much deception, and it had all ended in Dickerson's murder in the hospital. And now Dillon knew. Sherlock snuggled closer, waiting. She enjoyed a good punch line as much as he did.

"I did a search on all of Father Sonny's relatives. His father's dead, his only other sibling, a brother, is dead. There was only one relative left who wasn't dead, and that's Sonny's mother, in jail for killing her husband. She's the Hammer."

That was a kicker. "You're kidding me—Sonny Dickerson's mom shot me in the head?"

"Yes. We all believed it was a man, of course, since everyone who saw her—from Ted Moody, who brought us that note in the Hoover Building, to the lady who rented her the Zodiac—described a man. We even heard what we all thought was a man's voice on that telephone message to Molly, never doubted it was Xu.

"She's got a gravelly voice she's learned to control, and she knows how to disguise herself as a man. She let us believe all the attempts on Ramsey's life were Xu until Tuesday, when she shot you with Xu on the ground under you." Sherlock came up on her elbow. "I can't get over it—Father Sonny Dickerson's mother. But, Dillon, why didn't her name pop right out when Ruth and Dane did their search, no matter if she's female?"

"Because her name is Charlene Cartwright. Like I said, she was in jail for ten years for the murder of her husband, evidently a miserable human being who not only abused Sonny and his now-deceased brother but also his wife, Charlene. She snapped and shot a dozen bullets in his face with his own gun.

"From the court transcript I read of her trial in Baton Rouge, I think her shooting him was justified. I don't know why her lawyer didn't plead self-defense, but he didn't. He went for the SODDI defense—Some Other Dude Did It—but the jury didn't buy it, and no wonder, since there was so much evidence against her. They wanted her to serve hard time, and so she did. She was given fifteen years, paroled after ten.

"Father Sonny was murdered when she'd been in prison for about five years, so she had ample time to figure out who to blame and how to carry out her revenge."

Sherlock said, "Why did she target you? Of course I remember most everything about the case, but you were hardly involved."

"That's why I didn't make the connection sooner. When I found her, I realized that she saw me as making it all possible because of the facial-recognition program I modified from my friend at Scotland Yard. Remember we didn't believe the sketch we inputted into the program would pay off? But it did, the program spit Father Sonny out right away."

Sherlock said, "So Charlene read about the facial-recognition program, saw your name and your connection to Ramsey, and decided you were the one who fingered her son, that without you, he wouldn't have been caught, which is totally wrong. Father Sonny tried to take Emma again in Monterey. In the end, that's what brought him down."

"Yeah, but we're talking a very angry woman here."

"Angry but irrational," Sherlock said. "She used you as her focus, the hub of the wheel. She was going to punish you by killing those who mattered to you, as you had hurt her by supposedly killing her son."

"Looks like. I guess there was no way she could know Father Sonny kidnapped the wrong little girl when he took Emma since he was ordered killed by Emma's grandfather for it. She must have believed Ramsey killed him, that I and everyone else protected him, covered it up, and that's why he was number one on her hit list."

Sherlock recited, "*For what you did you deserve this.* I wonder how many lines she played around with before she came upon this one. It sounds highfalutin, doesn't it? Like God is going to smite you and you deserve it. Why isn't her name Dickerson?"

"It was a common-law marriage, and she kept her maiden name—Cartwright. She served her ten years in Louisiana Correctional Institute for Women in Saint Gabriel, outside of Baton Rouge, until four months ago when she was paroled, completely rehabilitated, and, citing her exemplary behavior, willing to do whatever was asked of her, according to the warden himself. She was, naturally, a clerk in the prison library, spent many hours in there 'studying,' according to the parole board records."

Sherlock said, "And I was second on her list after Ramsey? To hurt you?"

Savich nodded. "She must have decided to put Ramsey on hold, since she realized there was no way she could get to him again in the hospital, not after the elevator debacle."

He shook his head. "I can't get over her preparation for that attempt. She even took Boozer's blood, remember, because she wanted us to think she was wounded, and that she was a man. She wanted to play with us."

"And Boozer described a man as well."

"Well, we thought Xu was a woman for a very long time, what with that Sue name mix-up. Turns out we were wrong on both counts."

Sherlock said, "That stunt in the elevator. Amazing, what she did."

"She failed, thanks to Eve and Kevlar."

Sherlock said, "Dillon, how do you know it was Charlene, though? I mean, for sure?"

"There were samples of her handwriting in the trial record. They matched the notes she sent us. And she's wanted in Louisiana again, for cutting out on her parole officer two months ago."

Sherlock said, "She must have been following the FBI van, no other explanation for why she was there and ready to shoot just when I was out and visible at the Fairmont."

"She would have had no idea you'd jump out of the van and go after Xu. That part of it was lucky for her."

"Lucky for both of them," Sherlock said. "And isn't that a happy thought?" *If her aim had been a hair better, I'd be dead*. Sherlock's hand was a fist on his chest. He felt her fingers tangle in his chest hair. He pressed lightly, flattening her palm.

Savich said, "I've got her photo. It will make a huge difference knowing who we're looking for. You know, Charlene doesn't look like a killer, not really. I saw two photos, one before her trial and one taken two years ago. She didn't look beaten down anymore, like a battered wife. She looked fierce, the set of her head and shoulders was proud, like she was on a mission for justice, like some old Joan of Arc."

Sherlock pushed off the covers. "Let me see."

"No, you stay put. I'll bring MAX in here to show you." He felt her hand moving over his chest. He leaned down, kissed her.

"No, don't bring in MAX yet," she said against his jaw. She kissed his throat. "Not yet."

60

San Francisco General Hospital
Judge Hunt's room
Thanksgiving

Nurse Natalie Chase was divorced. Even though her ex was a real loser, she'd loved his name, and since she didn't have any kids by him, she'd kept it. Thank heaven his gene pool wouldn't continue through her. She had no close family, only a couple of cousins who lived in Boston, so she always volunteered for holiday shifts. She liked holidays; there was usually something special going on, and she didn't have to be alone. This year she'd been invited to a Thanksgiving feast like no other she'd seen in a patient's room, with Judge Hunt and his crew. They were breaking more visiting rules than she cared to think about, but nobody was worried about it, not since it was Judge Dredd and it was Thanksgiving.

Sure, she had to keep an eye on all her other patients, but most of them were with family, chowing down on turkey and dressing if they could. Even her elderly patient with Alzheimer's was with his daughter, who was snacking on turkey and stuffing while she kept vigil. No one was alone today.

It baffled and angered Natalie that someone would want to kill Judge Ramsey Hunt. He was genuinely nice, a treat to the eyes, and, like everyone else taking care of him, she was thankful today of all days that Judge Dredd was doing so well. Another three or four days, she thought, and he should be well enough to go home. Home, maybe, but not back to his normal life. Not while there was a killer who might try for him again. She couldn't imagine living with that, couldn't imagine what his family was going through, knowing that a madman was still out there, waiting for another chance.

At first the TV news had showed a picture of a man, Joe Keats, who'd escaped from the Fairmont a couple of days ago, as the man who'd shot Judge Hunt. And today they were showing the picture of a woman instead, who was supposed to be the shooter. She looked, Natalie thought, a bit like her own mother.

Would there be another picture tomorrow? The news didn't seem to have any idea why she tried to murder Judge Hunt and the FBI agent, but she knew that by the end of the day there would be talking heads arguing over every detail on TV and plastering the Internet with so many opinions even the mullahs in Iran would see them. She could already recite the words: "Anyone with any information about the whereabouts of either of these people—"

SFPD Officer Gavin Hendricks waved his hand in front of her face. "You look a million miles away. Another slice of turkey?"

She shook her head at him, smiling. He'd been guarding Judge Hunt for the past three days. He was a tall black man with a pitiful excuse for a goatee, she'd told him, and he'd laughed and said it was his father's fault. She said, "If I eat any more I might pop a button, and that wouldn't be cool at all. What if an emergency turns up? What if a patient sees me with my pants button popped open? It wouldn't inspire much confidence."

"You're sure, Natalie?" Molly Hunt called out. "We've got lots."

"Thank you, Molly, but if I ate another bite, I'd have to find a bench to sit on because my butt would be too big for a chair."

Gavin laughed. Natalie saw Molly turn to her husband and touch his arm and then his cheek. She did that every few minutes. A lioness always watching.

The room should have been pandemonium with all the visitors—four guards, Judge Hunt's family, three kids, and a slew of FBI agents. They'd wheeled out the second bed and taken advantage of the largest patient room in the hospital to set up several folding tables provided by the cafeteria, spread a tablecloth over them, and crammed in a dozen chairs. It was a wonder to see in a hospital room, Natalie thought. The table looked like a family dinner, with everyone in fine spirits, except that many of them were wearing guns and darting their eyes to the door if anyone approached.

Agent Sherlock, the FBI agent who'd been her patient yesterday, was forking down some of the incredible sausage stuffing, laughing at something her husband said to her. *Lucky, lucky woman,* Natalie thought. Did she realize how near she'd come to death?

Not the time for grim thoughts, Natalie told herself. She looked back over at Officer Hendricks. He was coming her way, two slices of pumpkin pie on small Thanksgiving paper plates, with whipped cream on top. "I've decided both of us will trust our buttons not to pop," he said, and held a slice of pie out to her.

She considered turning it down, but naturally, she didn't. "Thank you, Officer Hendricks."

"Make that Gavin, ma'am."

"And you can call me Natalie."

He sat down beside her, and they ate pumpkin pie and chatted about nothing in particular until the football game came on. Gavin forked down another bite of pie, closed his eyes, and hummed. "Oh, man, that is fine. I hear Emma Hunt made the pie. Emma's a whiz on the piano and a good cook. I'd say the kid's got it made."

They looked over to where Emma sat beside her father, her small white hand on his forearm.

Her two little brothers, Cal and Gage, seriously cute identical twins, sat at the large table, currently hemmed in by three large adults and another little boy, Sean Savich. He would grow up to be as handsome as his dad, Natalie thought, looking from him to his father, Agent Dillon Savich.

"Emma Hunt's playing with the San Francisco

Symphony next Wednesday," Gavin continued, took another big bite of his pumpkin pie, and shook his head. "Hard to believe. Look at those small hands. What is she, eleven, twelve?"

"She's eleven, Judge Hunt told me. He's so proud of her he would pop his own buttons if the hospital gown had any. All he can talk about is being well enough to go to see her perform next Wednesday."

"He'll make it," Hendricks said. "The man's strong, he's got an iron will. I've gotten to know him. You know, I keep seeing him jumping down from the judge's bench in his black robes, flattening those yahoos who invaded his courtroom."

"I remember that. Goodness, everybody does. It was an incredible thing he did," Natalie said. Her wrist pager beeped. She smiled at Officer Hendricks—Gavin—rose, and thanked the cooks for feeding her an extraordinary dinner.

Natalie paused in the doorway for a moment, and looked back. She marveled at the bonhomie and good-will they were all managing, even with that woman lurking in everyone's mind, out there making more plans for murder. Even if the goodwill was paper-thin, it was valuable. She gave a last smile to Gavin.

Natalie took care of the emergency—Mr. Pitt in room 306B was hyperventilating at the news his grandson had happily delivered about his marrying a Las Vegas dancer—and walked back to the nursing desk. She studied the photo they had of Charlene Cartwright again. Soon this woman's face would be more familiar to people than the governor's. The woman had once been pretty, Natalie thought, but now she was beyond that, an odd thing to think, but it was true. She touched her fingertip to the smoker's lines fanning out from her eyes, the deep scored lines about her mouth. There was a message in the woman's eyes, wide pale green eyes, flat as a stagnant pond. Those eyes scared Natalie to her toes. The message was, quite simply, both the promise of death of anyone she wanted gone and the acceptance of her own death, should it be demanded of her.

She realized she'd seen eyes like Charlene Cartwright's once before during a six-month stint in a psych ward. She hadn't wanted to think about what was going on behind those eyes.

Ramsey was asleep, finally, an exhausted sleep that worried Nurse Natalie Chase a bit, but then she managed a reassuring smile at all his family hovering around his bed. "Don't worry. His vital signs are fine. His football team lost, that's what flattened him."

They all smiled and eased.

When Dr. Kardak came in a moment later to have the small slice of pumpkin pie he'd been promised, he looked down at the sleeping Ramsey. "I'd say he had too much fun." He looked over at Sherlock, lifted her hair off the butterfly strips she'd pressed over the sutures, and, thankfully, left them alone. "Still feeling well, I take it, Agent Sherlock?"

"Fit as a fiddle," she said, then, "I always wondered

why a fiddle was fit? I mean, what does health have to do with a musical instrument?" and Dr. Kardak, forking down a bite of pumpkin pie, swallowed and smiled. "Not a clue." He looked one last time at the sleeping Ramsey, nodded to the rest of them, and left.

Sherlock was tired. She wished she could curl up next to Ramsey and take a nice long winter snooze, but she knew it wasn't to be.

Savich said, "You look burned out, sweetheart. You ready to go home to bed?"

"Are you offering another bedtime story, Dillon?"

He lightly touched his fingers to her cheek, studied her exhausted face. "I think it's got to be sleep without dessert for you tonight." He turned to Eve and Harry, who were studying Charlene's photo.

Eve said, "A woman, all the time it was a blasted woman. I mean, it was okay for Xu to be Sue for a while, but Charlene Cartwright is giving our sex a bad name. And look at us, Sherlock, you've got an aching head, and I'm still nursing the bruises she shot into my Kevlar in the elevator. Do you think she's nuts?"

Savich slowly nodded. "She is now. Before she married her husband? If I had to venture a guess, I'd say no.

"You're right to be worried about Charlene. Xu has no more reason to be here that I can see, unless he's too weak to drive. Either way, he'll be out of the picture for a while unless we're lucky enough to find him.

"Charlene's a different matter. We are her purpose, her focus. She needs this fight or she might as well float off the planet, that or kill herself. But you know, I really don't think she'll give it up until we bury her." He pulled Sherlock close, closed his eyes for a moment.

He said, "All of us know that informants solve most of our cases. Since her photos are everywhere, we've got to hope she stays close."

61

Skyline Motel
El Cerrito, California
Nine o'clock Thursday night

Charlene looked through the glass into the small motel reception office. Her luck was holding. Only one skinny guy was inside, and from the description Joe had given her, it was the same guy who'd been deep in a computer game when Joe had checked in. He said he remembered the kid's name because it was so weird. Okay, she'd told him, but Jerol wasn't as weird as Xu, and she was going to call him Joe. He'd smiled up at her. And she'd started singing Johnny Cash's "A Boy Named Sue."

She didn't know where she was taking Joe yet, but it was too dangerous staying this close to the city any longer, now that his photo was plastered all over the TV. She figured he needed another couple of days before he'd be good for much, not that she needed him to help her, but he was smart, had lots of experience. If he could learn to trust her, maybe they could stay together for some time, like she'd planned to stay with Sonny. She'd be with Sonny now if not for that little kid, Emma. What a snooty name that was. Wasn't she to blame, too, for Sonny's being dead? It wasn't Sonny's fault he had this problem. The kid shouldn't have run away from him, selfish little cow, when she knew—Charlene shook her head to get her brain back on track. She was losing herself more often now in her thoughts. She'd think something, and then the thought seemed to grow and change, to branch out in all directions, like a spin-off of a TV show.

She focused on Joe, and her brain seemed to flip a switch. He really knew these FBI agents, he told her, knew how they thought, knew what they'd do in any given situation. He'd stayed one step ahead of them, no problem, just as she had. *But you didn't know about that little redheaded agent who slammed you down on your face, did you? Without me, the train would have left the station—you'd be on it dressed in shackles and handcuffs.*

He knew that as well as she did, so she didn't say it out loud. He'd thanked her twice already, and it came easily to him. She found him charming. She'd known Joe for such a short time, and she already liked him a lot better than she'd ever liked her miserable husband, bad memory that he was. Joe said he liked the big diamond on her pinkie finger, and she'd laughed, told him it wasn't real, told him it was as fake as her vicious long-dead husband who'd given it to her and that's why she wore it, to remind her of that wonderful day she'd shot his face off.

And he'd asked her about the other ring she wore that looked like it belonged to a religious order. She'd fallen silent, fingering the ring, then said, "It belonged to my son, before Ramsey Hunt murdered him." And that's when he'd asked her to tell him the whole story.

When he'd finally fallen into a restless sleep last night, she stretched out on the bed beside him and listened to him breathe. She realized she hadn't slept beside a man in a very long time. It felt strange to hear another's breathing so close beside her. He woke her up once when he started talking in his sleep. And now she knew something about who and what this man was—not only a killer, as she was, but mixed up with the Chinese—a spy, maybe? And he was piss-in-the-pants afraid of them. *I end up with the weirdest people,* Charlene thought. Her son was kind of weird, of course, but he wasn't stupid, he was—off. He hadn't deserved to die, hadn't deserved to be murdered by that miserable judge.

Her familiar rage kicked in, made her mind hiss and crackle. It wasn't right what happened to Sonny. What had happened to him was the real crime. Imagine a federal judge murdering a man in his hospital bed? And every one of those crooked cops had covered for him, nothing but sympathy for him because of pathetic little Emma. Emma—Charlene hated that name now. She figured the kid and her mom had moved to a safe house after she'd left that phone message for little Molly, since when she'd last driven by, the house was empty. She'd find them, follow the kid from school, maybe.

Emma, Emma, Emma, the name drummed louder

and louder in Charlene's brain. *Get it back, get it back, focus, focus.*

She blinked, again focused on Joe. He'd been thrashing around, a fever, and she'd fetched him three aspirin and some water, and cupped his head. He never opened his eyes, but she already knew his eyes showed a life ancient with violence, far more than she could imagine. As she'd looked down at him in the dim motel room light she realized he might have made a fine son. There was something about Joe Keats, whose real name was Xu—maybe his will to survive, she wasn't sure—but he impressed her. Regardless of what he was or what he'd done, he was a man who didn't whine or complain or strike out. Well, she'd see about striking out.

He healed amazingly fast, she'd thought, when she'd tended his wound earlier. The flesh around the wound was pink, and healthy-looking. She hadn't seen any blood crusted around the stitches. And now Joe was sleeping. He'd sworn to her he could drive. She'd told him he should get rid of that blue Honda he'd lifted in Sausalito. As soon as they were away, he'd told her—best not to leave it at the motel. Well, if he got himself killed because of that stupid car, it was his business. She was driving her own car, bought and paid for in Stockton from a little old man going into a nursing home.

The bell tinkled when Charlene pushed open the door and strolled into the motel office, cash in her hand. Jerol was sitting behind a counter loaded down with piles of brochures for local sights. Joe was spot-on about him—Jerol was playing a computer game, all his attention on some military figures fighting on the screen, its gunshots, loud bangs, and booms punctuated by his grunts and cheers.

Joe's Beretta was snug against her side, just in case, since you never knew when some snake might up and try to bite you.

She spotted an ancient TV propped up on a portable serving table. It was tuned to a local news channel. The weather report was segueing into the news. The spit dried in her mouth. Her photo appeared on-screen followed by Joe's. The volume was turned low, but she could hear the newsman talking about Joe. *Hurry, get checked out or the moron might look up, see the photos, and call the cops.* She moved to stand squarely between the kid and the TV.

"Hey, I was looking at that bad guy on TV."

Well, that settles that, she thought, feeling the Beretta warm against her palm. *No choice now.*

She smiled and said, her voice loud to drown out the TV, "Hey, do you have any brochures on Six Flags Discovery Kingdom up in Vallejo? That's the new name of the place, right? I'm thinking my friend and I would like to check it out tomorrow."

"Who's your friend?" Jerol Idling said, his voice impatient. He'd been close to scoring another hundred points and needed only one more good kill, but he'd happened to look up at the TV when she came in and there was a photo of some guy and they were blaring how dangerous he was, how he'd set off the Fairmont fire and murdered some people, and the weird thing was, the man looked familiar. Jerol knew he'd seen him, but where?

Charlene studied his face as she said, "My friend's name is Joe—" She stalled. What had Joe called himself when he'd checked into this place? Cribbs, that was it. "I'm with Joe Cribbs. He's in two-seventeen."

Jerol wanted to see the man's photo again on the TV, but this woman was standing right in front of him. "Mr. Cribbs didn't say anything about a *friend* coming." His mom hated guests coming in unannounced ever since six college students had snuck into one room to spend the weekend. He'd been only seventeen at the time, but he still remembered the mess they'd made. Not that this old lady was likely to make a mess, not like those beer-guzzling yahoos, but still. "When did you show up?"

Rude little bugger, Charlene thought, leaned toward the kid, showing him a cleavage she'd learned to make by pushing in her elbows and leaning over. She could push them nearly to her tonsils, and there weren't that many wrinkles. The two truckers in Bakersfield she'd tried it out on were distracted quickly enough. "Last night. So you got any brochures?"

"Yeah, we even got brochures for mud baths in Calistoga if you want. Is Mr. Cribbs feeling better? He looked pretty bad when he checked in yesterday. I mean, he was all hunched over, and I knew he didn't feel good. Do you know, he looks kind of like—"

Charlene said quickly, "He's fine, only a flu of some sort."

"Hey, aren't you a little old for Mr. Cribbs? I mean, like his mother?"

Well, now, that's quite enough out of you. Charlene raised her hand and shot him in the face with Xu's Beretta. As she fired, she jumped back. She didn't want his blood to splatter on her clothes.

62

Savich punched off his cell. He watched Sean happily playing an NFL video game with his grandmother, who knew squat about football, and he was winning. He wondered if Sean was smart enough to be on the 49ers' side in the game and not the Redskins'. He leaned down and said quietly to Sherlock, "Cheney said they're getting about fifty calls an hour on the hotline with sightings of Xu and/or Charlene. The SFPD has provided some manpower to sift through the calls, since the field office hasn't the staff to do it."

"At least we can discount the calls that have Xu walking around, since he isn't," Sherlock said. She rubbed her hands over her arms.

"Cold?"

"No, I guess someone walked over my grave. I

wonder where that saying comes from. It's pretty gruesome."

"But descriptive. What did you feel?"

"I'm worried that something bad's going to happen, Dillon. Soon."

He didn't say anything. He pulled her to her feet, then sat down and brought her down on his lap and held her. He knew she was right, something bad had to happen, with two armed and desperate people out there, their pictures all over TV.

After they got Sean bathed and buttoned into his Spider-Man pajamas, they got him down but, unfortunately, not out. He couldn't stop talking. He was too excited about how he'd stomped his grandmother at NFL football. He had, to Savich's surprise, gone for the Patriots. Savich finally sang him his favorite song of all time, guaranteed to put him out by the end of the first verse—"You've Got a Friend in Me" from *Toy Story*.

Sherlock was grinning when Sean's eyes closed. "Every time," she whispered.

They were getting ready for bed when Savich's cell rang.

"Savich here."

He was quiet, listening, his expression unchanging, but Sherlock saw his eyes darken. The bad something had happened.

She looked down at her watch. It was an hour and a half short of midnight on Thanksgiving night.

63

Eve looked at the cluster of cop cars surrounding the motel office, parked at all angles throughout the lot. The few motel guests were grouped together, talking, probably trying to figure out what had happened. They knew enough, Eve thought, looking at the M.E.'s white van. They just didn't know who had shot Jerol.

After they'd spoken to Mrs. Idling, Eve and Harry had come outside, primarily to get out of the way of the El Cerrito forensic team and the M.E. She said to Harry, "I hate this. That young man is dead because he must have recognized Xu on TV. But what I don't understand is why Xu came back to the office and shot him. Why not simply leave? Why even come to the office in the first place?"

Harry said, "Maybe Xu couldn't be sure about him,

didn't want to chance him making a phone call. The kid was another loose end." He watched them wheel young Jerol Idling out, already zipped into a green body bag. Savich and Sherlock and Cheney followed. They were speaking to the El Cerrito police chief, Glenis Sayers.

Eve said to Harry, "When Chief Sayers's detectives arrived at the scene, they found the name Joe Cribbs with the license plate number that Jerol had written down for him next to it. When they matched it to the blue Honda that was stolen in Sausalito on Tuesday, they called her. Bless her, she called Cheney right away, so it's thanks to her we're in the mix at all."

They watched El Cerrito police officers crowding around the chief, one of them with his arm around Mrs. Idling's shoulders. She was plastered against him. They could hear her sobs from where they stood. Life can be snuffed out from one moment to the next, Eve thought. It was horrible and scary, and true for each and every human being on this earth.

Harry nodded. "There isn't any doubt it was Xu. Everything fits. Mrs. Idling never saw him, but she knew a guy had paid cash to check into room two-seventeen on Tuesday. Jerol told her the guy seemed sick, favoring his arm when he checked in, said the guy seemed really out of it. The Joe Cribbs signature in the ledger is pretty illegible, as if written with the wrong hand. Remember Xu is left-handed, and he was shot in that arm. I'll bet ballistics matches the bullet to the gun that killed Dr. Chu."

Eve said, "But that doesn't help us tonight. Maybe Xu

doesn't know we've got him made, doesn't know we're looking for that blue Honda he's driving. I wish Mrs. Idling hadn't dismissed the shot she heard as a backfire for those precious minutes before she came over to investigate."

Harry said, "The corker is she saw two cars skidding out of the parking lot, with the door to Mr. Cribbs's room standing wide open."

Eve said, "It means he was too sick to ditch the Honda, but he wasn't too sick to call someone to the motel to help him. He's been here a day and a half. He could have called the Chinese for help. You think that second car was driven by a Chinese connection?"

Harry shook his head. "That doesn't sit right with me, doesn't feel right. But you know, if not the Chinese, then who? And was that other person the one who shot Jerol?" He thought about that, but no answer stepped up. He said, "That second car, Mrs. Idling is sure it's an older Corolla. Since there was no license plate matching it in the register, it wasn't anyone who was staying here, legally, at the motel. If they're smart, they'll leave the Honda somewhere and we'll have no way to trace them."

Eve said on a sigh, "Whoever it is, it's a game changer. With help, Xu can go anywhere he wants now."

Cheney called out, "Harry, we need you over here."

64

Eve kicked back, put her booted feet on the ottoman. She was wearing the same clothes she'd worn yesterday, and she felt grungy. She leaned her head back against the sofa back and said, "My head hurts."

Harry stood over her, a cup of coffee in his hand. "You ate breakfast an hour ago so it's okay to drink another cup of this fine brew. Then we'll talk."

Talk? That opened her eyes. *What did he mean, talk?* Eve didn't want to talk—a *guy* talk about two adults enjoying sex and no commitment? No, that wasn't Harry. Harry was honorable to his feet. Like big statue-of-David feet. No, Harry felt guilty because he'd made love to her and now it was morning and somewhere along the line he'd realized she expected more from him, and so he regretted ever pulling down her blue bikini panties. How was he ever going to explain that to her so she didn't shoot him?

She stared at him, unblinking. He hadn't said a word while he'd chowed down on his cereal, one of those health-food brands she'd never heard of, while she'd slathered strawberry jam on her toast. Not a single word about how incredible she was and it was the best night of his life, and how about now let's get naked right here, on the table? Would she climb up on the table? Yes, she would.

She continued to stare at him. To her eye, Harry radiated guilt.

Eve drank a bit of coffee and watched Harry walk to the chair opposite and sit down. He looked indolent and loose, his legs stretched out, crossed at the ankles, and he steepled his fingertips together. *Tap, tap, tap.*

Maybe she was wrong, maybe he didn't feel guilt about having sex with her, wanting now to shoulder the blame, to claim all the fault. Maybe she was wrong. Instead, maybe he was feeling cocky he'd scored with her. Was that better than his feeling guilty about seducing her? *Seducing* her? What had happened between them—what was it last night, three times? Talk about a busy two-way street.

Harry said in a brooding voice, "You're so pretty, it drives me nuts."

Pretty? He was beginning his guilt speech by telling her she was *pretty* and it drove him nuts? No, what she was was a mess. She needed a shower, she needed a couple of multivitamins, she needed to have Harry tell her it wasn't just because she was *pretty* that he was attracted to her; what she wanted him to say was something very different, like it was her insides that turned him on, and he didn't for a single instant feel guilty about making love with her, and he wanted more, he wanted—Eve pulled out her cell. "I want to speak to my dad."

"Why now?" His left eyebrow shot up. He still looked, she thought, loose and relaxed, indolent as a lizard, and she wanted to smack him.

She managed a credible sneer. "What do you care? Oh, I see, if Daddy asks me where I am, I'll have to confess to him I'm currently only twenty feet from a guy's bedroom, wherein lies a rumpled bed, and the guy's name is Harry Christoff, and sorry, Dad, he's not in the U.S. Marshals Service, he's a dippy FBI agent."

Harry grinned at her. "I love to listen to you spit out a hundred words without taking a breath. Actually I'd like to speak to your dad. Don't you think it's about time? He really doesn't like FBI agents?"

About time? To apologize to him for seducing his daughter, but, hey, it happened, so let's move on? She studied his face, took another slug of her coffee, and carefully set the cup down on a magazine to spare the shiny wood surface. He wasn't smiling. In fact, he was holding himself very quiet, his eyes focused on her face. No way was she going to let him speak to her dad. She said between seamed lips, "I was thinking you don't really like women except to sleep with them to add another notch to your belt. But that's not it—you feel guilty, right? You're sorry you seduced a colleague. Were you thinking about apologizing to my dad? And then you'd like me to just go away so you can forget it ever happened."

Harry couldn't help himself. He smiled at her. What was her idiot talk about his not liking women? About his feeling guilty he'd slept with her? He felt calm and steady, better than he'd felt in so long he couldn't even remember when or why. *Well, Eve, the truth is making love to you made me remember that life is really a very fine thing indeed. You think I feel guilty because I made love with a colleague? Don't you realize you're my entire bloody army of salvation? Bring on your daddy.* He said, "I'm now a reformed git. Here's to the power of the ponytail." He picked up his coffee cup, said slowly, feeling his way, "You think I took advantage of you?"

She thought about that for a moment. She had to be honest here. "Maybe not every time."

Harry wasn't about to dwell on each glorious time; he'd shake himself out of his chair and that wouldn't put the focus where it belonged. "That ponytail of yours—it's a big draw, Barbieri. I look into those big blue eyes of yours, listen to you smart-mouth me, and I find myself thinking I'd like to see that ponytail at the breakfast table for, say, the next fifty years, or so. Yeah, at least fifty years. I come from healthy stock, and so do you." There, he'd spit it right out, and waited.

Oh, no, no, that wasn't a guy's guilty speech or a cocky speech. What this was was way too fast, way too much, even with his light hand and that intent look in his eyes. Beautiful eyes, he had. No, wait, stop it.

What was he saying? Eve couldn't get her brain around it. He wanted to see her ponytail for fifty years? Across the breakfast table? As in marriage? Eve jumped out of the chair, grabbed her jacket, and was at the front door in under thirty seconds.

He called after her, "What about calling your dad?"

"He doesn't need to know yet what kind of deep trouble I'm in."

"Can you tell me about this deep trouble? Maybe it concerns me?"

She shook her head and was gone. Harry didn't go after her. He listened to her engine rev, heard her back too fast out of the driveway, and hoped she didn't knock over the azalea pot he hadn't brought in yet for the winter.

Harry sat back in his chair and smiled. Sitting across the breakfast table from Eve for fifty years. It sounded fine to him, more than fine, it sounded like he'd wake up smiling a whole bunch of mornings. He loved her brain, her smart mouth, her courage, and, well, her gorgeous athletic body as well, and her gorgeous athletic body's enthusiastic reaction with him was something to make a guy grin like a fool for a millennium.

He sat back and closed his eyes, wondering how long it would take her to come to grips with what they could be together, given a healthy chance. She'd thought he was going to give her the guy talk about not wanting it to be more than sex? How could she ever think that? *Well, there's your history, stupid.*

He drank the rest of his coffee, set the cup on his

knee. He closed his eyes and leaned his head back. He caught himself when Xu's face intruded clearly in his mind's eye. He was not that far away, and who was with him? The El Cerrito police had found the Honda downtown, but no trace of Xu or his companion.

There had been hundreds of calls yesterday, but nothing helpful in finding Charlene Cartwright, either. It was a manhunt now, pure and simple. Until the end played out, Judge Hunt, Savich, and everyone in their path was in danger. He had to get showered and shaved, get himself to the hospital.

As he lathered his face, he wondered what he could do that would really count. Other than chase Barbieri down and kiss her stupid and convince her it wasn't only sex for him.

He thought he'd ask Savich to write a country-and-western song about a girl with a swinging blond ponytail and shit-kicker black boots.

Time to get yourself together, Barbieri.

65

Dr. Kardak straightened over Ramsey and nodded, looking, truth be told, very pleased with himself. "You're healing very nicely, Judge. Your tube tract is closed and your lung sounds good, barely a crackle or two left. You're very lucky that bullet didn't wreck your lung, or worse. I see you've cut back on your pain meds, and you're smiling. I couldn't ask for more. Our chef said you were eating more of his wonderful meals.

"All in all, you keep improving like this, and you're going to have a front-row seat at Emma's performance next Wednesday." Maybe not front and center, Dr. Kardak thought, though he didn't say it aloud. With any luck at all, Ramsey should be able to sit upright for an hour or so.

Ramsey heard a cheer from the guards at the window as Dr. Kardak left. He grinned over at them. Both of them spent Thanksgiving here; in fact, they had both been with him for more than a week now, and he'd been cogent for at least four of those days. He knew just about everything important about all the people who were taking care of him and was wondering how he could pay them back. SFPD Officer Gavin Hendricks and Nurse Natalie were really hitting it off, and maybe he'd played some part in that. They made a nice couple.

He felt clearheaded again, he felt in control. He was able to think in a straight line without having to deal with pain trying to jerk him off the path. And his thoughts led him right to Father Sonny Dickerson's mom. Her name was Charlene Cartwright, and she had to be in her sixties. What kind of a person that age could hatch a plot like this and execute it? He tried to imagine her motoring a Zodiac to his beach, being a good enough shot with a sniper rifle to have killed him dead if he hadn't turned, and then using that slingshot with that absurd photo of Judge Dredd attached to it. Harder still to imagine her climbing down on the roof of the elevator, pulling up the ceiling hatch and firing down at him and escaping—she must have kept herself in very good shape in prison. Her audacity amazed him, even as a mother avenging her son. Father Sonny was a son who didn't deserve even a passing thought, much less a full-blown vendetta. Didn't she know full well that he'd been an obsessive insane pedophile? The fruit must not have fallen far from the tree, he thought. Charlene had to be as crazy as her son in her own way. He opened his laptop and began researching Charlene Cartwright's criminal record. He wanted to know everything about her, her murdered husband, and her children.

She'd planned and plotted for five years. Amazing. Thank the good Lord she'd failed. At least until now.

66

San Francisco General Hospital
Saturday morning

Sherlock sat in Dr. Kardak's small office on the fifth floor, waiting for him to come back from morning rounds and give her a final check. Thankfully, she didn't have to worry about having the stitches snipped out of her head, since he'd told her they would resorb by themselves. She'd sent Dillon on to see Ramsey, saying, "I'll be fine. There's no reason for us to sit here and twiddle our thumbs together. You've got a lot on your plate—go deal with it. Send up a guard if someone's bored; otherwise, I'll come to Ramsey's room when I'm done."

Savich had gently lifted her hair and lightly touched his fingertip to the small bandage. "I'll send a guard. You will not go anyplace without someone covering you like a blanket." He'd stared at her for a moment, kissed her hard, and left.

Sherlock knew he was still reliving those moments

when he'd thought she was dead, but what could she say? She refused to think what she'd feel and do if Dillon had been the one shot. She pulled out her cell and called Ruth, who was in Maestro, Virginia, with her husband, Dix, and her two stepsons on this fine Saturday morning.

Ruth said, "You guys have sure got yourselves in the middle of a big curdling mess out there. You swear to me you're all right, Sherlock?"

"Yes, don't worry, it was only a little tap on the head. Talk to me, Ruth, about Charlene Cartwright. What do you know?"

"Dane flew to Baton Rouge last night, then drove to the Louisiana Correctional Institute for Women in Saint Gabriel this morning. He said the warden was goggle-eyed to hear what sweet, good-natured Charlene had done. He had to admit that yes, it was true, Charlene had worked out in the gym like a trouper for the past five years or so, and was in excellent shape for any age, really, and remarkable for someone ready for Medicare. Dane didn't tell the warden she'd styled herself the Hammer. He should be about through with his interview with an inmate who was supposedly Charlene's best bud, so you should call him in a couple of minutes. You swear you're okay?"

After reassuring Ruth about herself and Judge Hunt and how he and his family were holding up, Sherlock dialed Dane, who answered on the third ring. "Hi, Sherlock. I just finished up a very informative interview with Charlene's confidant, Maria Conchas, so your timing is perfect. Let me search out a private place." He came back on a couple minutes later. "I'm in a supervisor's office. Maria's a piece of work, in prison now for eight years for shooting her neighbor for looking in at her sleeping through her bedroom window, or so she claimed. 'And I was naked, the nasty peeper!' Quote/unquote. Maria put the guy in a wheelchair for life with a bullet in his spine. Her punishment is another two years, after which she can waltz out of here on two strong legs.

"Moving right along. Maria and Charlene spent long hours discussing life and men and how the Big Bad brought you down until you took charge and decided to do something about it. Maria said Charlene wasn't shy at all, in fact, enjoyed talking about what she was going to do to FBI Agent Dillon Savich when she got out. She called him 'hateful bastard,' the one who was responsible for her boy's death, namely, Sonny Dickerson. Do you know she made Maria call her the Hammer? Said Charlene could turn so mean it scared her to death, but never in front of the guards.

"Now, I wondered why Maria was so eager to tell me everything about Charlene's plans, since she had been, supposedly, her best friend. Maria told me she looked up Father Sonny Dickerson in their newspaper files and found out what he'd done five years ago before he'd died, well, before he'd been murdered. *Good riddance,* she'd thought. She couldn't believe Charlene wanted revenge for that 'crazy pervert,' as Maria called him, even if Charlene was his mother. She told me she knew to her gut after reading about Sonny and what he'd done that

Charlene had to be mad as a hatter to want to avenge him. Charlene said this to Maria, and I wrote this down, 'I'm going to get it done. I blew off that vicious jerk's head who made my son the way he was, didn't I?' She was talking about her husband. Maria said she believed her and we should, too.

"I asked her if she knew about the note Charlene sent to Savich. She laughed, said Charlene worked on different-ent wordings for three months before she was happy. Maria recited the note in a dramatic voice, *For what you did you deserve this*. Maria said she even tried her hand at some variations, but Charlene didn't like anything she came up with. Maria shook her head and said to me, 'I mean, who would take that idiot threat seriously? Talk about sappy.'"

Sherlock said, "So she said Ramsey's name?"

"Yes, Maria said Charlene told her about some 'nasty bugger' judge she was going to kill, too."

"Was there anyone else on her hit list after she killed Ramsey? Had to be someone close. I mean, to make Dillon pay a stiff price, this person had to be close, right?"

"I'd say so," Dane said, "since it was you, Sherlock. I know we were all hoping it was random, that any FBI agent would have filled the bill—but it wasn't random, and I doubt you really thought that for a minute, not really.

"Charlene wanted you dead because you're Savich's wife, the most important person in his world, just as Sonny was to Charlene.

"Yes, I know it doesn't make much sense, since Savich

was three thousand miles away when Father Sonny was killed, but Charlene didn't care. If not for Savich and his fancy technology, her precious boy would never have been caught. She thought Sonny would still be flying high and free, and she would be there with him, together again."

Sherlock said, "Dane, even if there hadn't been a match in the facial-recognition program, Father Sonny wouldn't have cut his losses, disappeared, and flown free. He'd have done just what he did do—gone after Emma again, and that's why he was caught. Identifying him through the sketch was only a shortcut, and not a very important one."

"Didn't matter. Maria said when she pointed out to Charlene that Sonny had to get caught sooner or later, Charlene threw a ten-pound free weight at her. Maria gave me a manic grin, said she'd never argued with Charlene again after that. I wanted to ask her why she hadn't figured out sooner that Charlene was off her rocker, but I didn't, since Maria's train isn't exactly running on the tracks, either."

Sherlock said, "But that whole deal at the Fairmont; how could she possibly have found out I'd be there?" She paused, added, "I just gave myself a head slap. She was following me, of course."

"Yep, probably for a couple of days, waiting for her chance. She must have thought God was in her corner when you leaped out of that FBI van and took off after Xu. I'll bet she was already in position and she took her shot."

"I never saw her, Dane, never noticed. How good an agent does that make me?"

"Have you forgotten that no one even considered there was another shooter besides Xu out there, and certainly not an older woman? You know Charlene was very careful. She knew you were in the surveillance van, knew something was going down at the Fairmont."

"How long was she out of prison before she shot Ramsey, Dane?"

"Nearly six months. Maria told me Charlene planned to rob a couple of stores to get herself a big enough stake, then she was going to take shooting lessons. This probably all went down close to Saint Gabriel, but far enough away not to connect her. When she was ready, she skipped out on parole. I'd have to say she got good at the firing range, but not good enough to kill you."

"With me, that's true, but with Ramsey—she wouldn't have failed with Ramsey if he hadn't been just plain lucky.

"Is there someone else on her make-Dillon-pay list?"

She realized Dane didn't want to say the name aloud, she could hear it in the pulse of silence. She felt her heart speed up because she knew, of course she knew. She waited. Finally Dane said, "After you, Maria said Charlene was going to kill Sean. 'An eye for an eye,' she told Maria. She wanted Savich to suffer as much as she'd suffered. A son for a son. And that's why I was going to call you right away if you hadn't called me first."

Dr. Kardak walked in, smiled and apologized for making her wait, but Sherlock was already on her feet, halfway out the door. "I'm sorry, but I can't stay. Later, Doctor." And she ran out of his office.

She heard him call after her, "I guess if you can sprint like that I shouldn't be too concerned about you."

Two hours later, Corman and Evelyn Sherlock and grandson Sean were in the Sherlocks' SUV, headed for a visit to Yosemite National Park.

67

San Francisco General Hospital
Saturday morning

Harry wasn't at all surprised to see Eve sitting next to Ramsey's bed when he arrived at the hospital. He hadn't had a chance to speak to her since she'd taken off like a launched rocket out his front door that morning. His first thought was that she looked gorgeous wearing her signature red and black, her U.S. Deputy Marshal badge sparkling on her jacket whenever she moved, her blond ponytail swinging. Harry couldn't seem to remember the last time he'd felt, well, this light, like gravity wasn't quite pulling him down to the ground. Despite all the scary violence going down around them, despite Eve's wariness of him and of them that morning, Harry realized he was grinning like a loon at the two guards who'd seconds before looked ready to tear out his throat before they'd realized who he was.

He looked at Molly and Emma sitting on the other

side of Judge Hunt's bed, all their focus on husband and father. The two guards, at ease now, moved again to stand in front of the big window.

Eve, who'd been speaking to Judge Hunt, looked over at Harry, saw him smiling at her, and froze like a deer in the headlights. She rose, her black boots bringing her nearly to his eye level to make herself more of a force, Harry thought, and she snarled at him, "A little late, aren't you, Agent?" She got a surprised look from Emma.

Harry, all bonhomie, said, "I finally came to see if Judge Hunt is ready to bribe me to take him home."

"I'll get my wallet," Ramsey said, pretending to reach for it. He caught a brief punch of pain in his chest and laid his head back against the pillow again. "Maybe tomorrow morning would be good. I'll have to make sure Molly doesn't steal my money, though."

"I have your wallet along with your vast fortune of about sixty bucks," Molly said. "You can forget any bribes, no one'd take that pitiful amount of money, not when they'd have to face Eve. And me."

"Maybe I can pay in favors," Ramsey said.

"Yeah, yeah," Eve said, "like anyone in this room is going to end up being tried in front of a federal judge."

He laughed, regretted it immediately, and felt Emma grasp his hand.

Emma said to Harry over her shoulder, "Dad says he's going to be at my performance next Wednesday even if they have to helicopter him in."

"If need be, I'll fly the helicopter," Harry said, patted Emma's shoulder, nodded to Molly, and walked past Eve over to the guards. SFPD Officer Gavin Hendricks and U.S. Deputy Marshal Jimmy Purcell looked alert and serious as a gun barrel staring you in the face. You couldn't ask for more than that. "Everything quiet?"

"Yeah," Jimmy said. "Believe me, anything on two legs gets past the two guys outside, we'll throw them to the floor, strip-search them, male, female, you name the species, we'll strip it."

"And search it," Gavin added.

Harry answered their questions about what was new, what was happening and what wasn't, took a call from Savich and said to everyone in the room, "I'm doing guard duty for Sherlock while Savich spends some time with you, Ramsey. Then he's scheduled to call Disneyland East and update Director Mueller."

Harry was whistling as he left Judge Hunt's hospital room, but he couldn't stop himself from looking back. He met Eve's eyes, smiled at her, and would swear she was looking back at him like he was a big New York steak, and she was starving. That look, he thought, was surely an excellent sign. He spoke to the guards sitting outside the room, and walked toward the stairwell. As he took the stairs two at a time toward Dr. Kardak's fifth-floor office, he decided the time he was assigned to be with Sherlock was his best shot at being there if something happened, since Sherlock was right at the eye of Charlene's storm. There was no way she could get to Ramsey, and Sean was safe, on his way to Yosemite. Despite himself, he really wanted a chance at Charlene, then he wanted to haul Eve to Carmel for long walks on the beach, longer nights, and no sleep. Then maybe she'd agree to think about spending lots more time with him, maybe she'd even come around to giving a nod to a future. Why was she wary of him? Because she didn't see him as a good risk? He would convince her he was. He was reliable, he kept his promises, he wasn't a pig, and he even knew how to cook. Yes, his work could be dangerous, but Eve understood that, and he would have to worry about her as much as she'd worry about him, since she also carried a gun.

Yeah, he might get an ulcer worrying, but she might get one, too. Only fair. They'd share that worry, like Savich and Sherlock already did right now. Sherlock and Savich were solid, and Eve and Harry could be, too. They even had a little boy, Sean. A kid? Now, that was something to think about.

He raised his hand to knock on the door when Sherlock opened it. "Hi, Harry, I heard you coming. You walk heavy, so I knew it wasn't Charlene with an ax in her hands. You didn't see Dillon? No matter. So Dillon volunteered you to stick close." She shook her head. "Thing is, Dillon's very protective, but I really don't think—"

Harry looked at her beautiful serious face and its halo of rioting red hair and raised his finger to touch her mouth. "Stop. I'm here. Think of me as your overcoat. Is Sean safe?"

"Yes. He was so excited about his surprise trip to Yosemite, he was whooping and hollering around the house. Bless my parents. Dad simply called the chief judge and postponed his upcoming drug trial for a couple of days. Sean's safe."

Sherlock studied his face. "I apologize for trying to brush you off. Let's chalk it up to an idiot moment. I'm very glad you're here. And now that I look at you, Harry, I'd swear you look like you're about to burst. What's happened?"

He was that transparent? He shook his head. What was happening between him and Eve was nobody's business. It was private business, his business, and when he decided the time was right, he would make it Eve's business too. He said, "Eve is running scared."

"Not for Ramsey, I hope. He's better guarded than the president."

"No, she's scared about us. Maybe she thinks I'm a sucky risk."

Sherlock marveled. No matter how grim a situation, people still found each other. It was, she thought, one of the very fine things about being alive. She patted his arm. "Nah, you're not a sucky risk. Your first wife didn't have the guts to deal with your job, so you cut her loose. That was the right thing to do. It's time now you let yourself move on, Harry.

"If anything, Eve's probably scared her dad and her brothers will freak that she's allowing a pantywaist FBI special agent to spend quality time with her, as opposed to one of their own—a mighty macho U.S. Marshals Service deputy."

Harry blinked at her. "You think?"

Sherlock nodded solemnly. "I'd say from the way she's been looking at you lately, you don't need to worry."

And Harry realized his private business was now lying on the floor in front of Sherlock. Why had those words, his own business, popped out of his mouth? Was Sherlock right? He remembered Eve's snarl in Judge Hunt's room.

Sherlock lightly touched his arm. "Nice jacket," she said. "Harry, stop worrying, it'll work out okay. I've seen that look before. All of us pantywaist FBI agents will write you references for her family if you need them. Eve's something else, isn't she? She really impressed Dillon in those two Cahill interviews."

He didn't want to say anything more, he'd said too much already. His lips were now zipped. He said, "Savich was right, she's sharp, she's intuitive. I love her cheerleading ponytail, Sherlock, and her big heart. She's got a huge heart. Do you know, after my divorce I swore off women for as long as I drew breath, and would you look at what happened? I'm thinking about long walks on the beach a week after first seeing her. Is that insane or what?"

Sherlock wanted to laugh, she really did, but she saw he wasn't joking. She said calmly, "All I know is both you and Eve are smart and honorable, and that your heart's as big as hers. You've got a lot going for you. She wants you, Harry, and one reason is because you're sexy. And look at that Shelby you drive, that car's nearly as sexy as you are. Seriously, Eve will be fine. She just needs some time. Like you said, it's only been a week. Her family will be ecstatic once they meet you. You know that as well as I do."

He wasn't going to say another word, never again was he going to spurt all his thoughts out like a shaken soda bottle. "When I left Judge Hunt's room, it's true, she looked at me like I was a steak."

Sherlock laughed. "Talk about a positive sign. Harry, come sit by me and let me tell you what I've found out about Charlene."

Dr. Kardak came in ten minutes later to hear Sherlock say, "You wouldn't believe Sean, Harry. He made his grandparents both promise to let him use their cell phone cameras so he could take lots of photos of El Capitan in Yosemite to show his three girlfriends. Hello, Dr. Kardak. Sorry for the delay."

"I'd like to meet this pistol," Dr. Kardak said waving away her apology. "I hope there aren't any more emergencies, Agent Sherlock, and you won't be haring out of here again."

Harry rose to excuse himself, but Sherlock smiled up at him. "Nah, Dr. Kardak won't make me take off my clothes to see a head wound. Harry, please supervise, make sure he does things right."

And so Harry watched Dr. Kardak push back Sherlock's hair, remove the small bandage with a light hand, and probe around the stitches.

He did a quick neurologic exam, asked her a few questions, and pronounced her free of him. He looked down at his watch. "That took all of five minutes, and no emergencies to interrupt either of us. Call me if you have any concerns, Agent Sherlock, and do let me meet that son of yours sometime."

Sherlock was glad to be done with it all as they walked to the elevators. Done with the medical part, that is. Harry watched everyone, checking out any man or woman who even looked in her direction. They were far from done with the rest of it.

Sherlock said, "The hotline is getting reports of Charlene sightings from Fresno up to Redding and reports of Xu from as far away as Montana. They're following up on as many leads as they can.

"One thing worries me, though, worries me a lot. We still don't know who was driving that second car that screeched out of the Skyline Motel Thursday night."

Harry had fretted over this loose thread as much as Sherlock had. Everyone he knew was thinking about it. "No. We don't have a clue."

"According to Maria Conchas, Charlene is a guided missile. My gut says she won't stop until she's shot down. Probably she couldn't call a halt even if she wanted to. She's got herself hardwired."

Harry said, "Charlene Cartwright's crazy. Xu isn't. I don't know who's more dangerous."

"I guess I'm more afraid of crazy, since Charlene's the one who shot me and Ramsey."

Sherlock saw the same tech who'd had the misfortune to come into the CT waiting room on Wednesday walking toward them, whistling. He saw her, saw Harry, who was staring at him as if he was measuring him for a hole in the ground, and stopped in his tracks.

What was his name? She finally remembered. "Mr. Lempert, it's okay. This is Agent Christoff. Harry, this is Mr. Lempert. The thing is, Harry, last Wednesday Dillon was a little hard on Terry." The use of his first name brought him back, and he even managed a tentative smile. He came one step closer to her, shot a glance at Harry, and cleared his throat. "You're looking good today, Agent Sherlock. You must have come from Dr. Kardak's office."

He darted a look at Harry. "I'm not a killer—well, unless I feel threatened, that is." He cleared his throat when Harry didn't change expressions. "That was a joke, Agent. Really."

"And a good one, Terry," Sherlock said, and patted his arm. "I've got to tell you, I sure hope I don't have to see you again for a while—professionally, that is."

She spotted a women's room near the elevator and excused herself. "Harry, maybe you want to message Deputy Marshal Barbieri? See if everything's okay on the steak front?"

He grinned. "I'll message Eve after I see you're safe upstairs." He stuck his head in the door, didn't see anyone. He walked in, looking beneath each of the three stalls. He saw two feet in sandals with bright red toenails, young feet. He watched one of the feet tap to the sound of music he couldn't hear. Okay, then. When he came out he said, "I'll be right here if you need anything."

As Sherlock stood at the counter washing her hands, a woman came in. Sherlock automatically went on alert until she got a look at her. She was older, quite heavy, a scrub nurse in a loose green top and pants, down to the green booties covering her shoes. A surgical mask hung by its ties around her neck. She wore a name tag. Harry wouldn't have let her in otherwise, Sherlock thought. A green scrub hat was perched on her thick black hair. She wore black-framed glasses.

"Hey," the nurse said, looked around, then walked toward a stall.

The nurse was suddenly behind her. Sherlock felt a gun pressing into the back of her neck. A deep voice hissed hot rage in her ear, "How did you find me, bitch?"

This wasn't Charlene Cartwright; she knew her photo as well as she knew her own. She willed her fear and her pounding heart to the back of the bus. "Xu, I can't believe you came here. Why? Are you trying to get your manhood back?" She felt her breath clog in her throat. Was this the way to play him? What would he do?

She heard a sneering laugh. "I wondered if I'd ever get the chance to be alone with you, with that big guy outside following you around. But you had to visit the bathroom, didn't you? The only reason you got me on the ground was because I was hit real bad."

Good, he was talking to her, trying to justify how she had gotten him down. She sneered back. "Yeah, an arm wound's all you had, nothing to write home about. And you're still whining? I thought above all, Xu, that you were a professional, that you were doing only what you had to do to clean up the mess you'd made. But look at you, here, trying to show me up."

His left hand moved up to grab her throat. He

whispered next to her ear, "You and your people destroyed my life by finding me when it shouldn't have been possible. You're going to be my prize at the end of this wretched assignment. Tell me now. How did you find me so fast?"

She held his hot eyes. "Turns out you're not so special, Xu. Our profiler guessed you liked to treat yourself well and thought the Fairmont would be right up your alley. Before she died, Cindy told us about Lampo, Indiana. We found you within two hours of accessing your old Indiana driver's license."

His hand was shaking.

Pedal back. "Would you look at you now, Xu, no one would guess who you are. And you've succeeded in getting me alone. Who made you the ugliest nurse in the universe?"

Sherlock hadn't realized her voice had risen. He moved the gun fast, shoved it against her ear. He hissed, "Keep it down. If that bodyguard of yours comes in here, I'll blow his head off. You want him to die with you?"

She shook her head, whispered, "No, I don't want him to die. I don't want to die, either."

He laughed.

68

"You want to know who helped me?"

She nodded at the fat bedraggled scrub nurse with coarse black hair and puffed out cheeks and smeared dark mascara looking back at her. He met her eyes in the mirror, used his nose to push aside her hair, and whispered against her ear and the Beretta's gun barrel, "No one looks at ugly people. That's what she told me."

"Who?"

"Crazy Charlene. She told me this getup was my best chance of killing you."

Charlene? For a moment, Sherlock couldn't get her brain around it. "Charlene was driving the second car out of the motel parking lot?"

He grinned at her, worked the gun barrel a bit deeper into her ear. "She found me, took care of me. She's crazy as a loon, but the weird thing is, I like her. She's committed. She's got exactly two minutes to get to the roof. Then we can get this done."

The gun in her ear hurt, but it was the fear roiling in

her belly that was threatening to bleed panic into her brain. *No, you can't let fear kill you. Time, you need time.*

She whispered, "Charlene is here? Did she kill Jerol Idling at the Skyline Motel?"

"Yep. That gunshot brought down the house, and so we had to move out fast. I thought my arm was going to fall off running to the car. That's when I first thought of killing you, of watching the light go out behind your eyes. I gritted my teeth and knew before I left I'd come for you." He shoved the Beretta in hard. She couldn't help it; she made a small yipping sound of pain.

She didn't look away from his face next to hers in the mirror. He was standing so close she felt his hot breath on her cheek, saw his flat, dark eyes, eyes that had watched dispassionately as he'd killed. She knew she'd see death in them if she looked closely, knew she'd see her own death. She thought of Dillon, of Sean, of a stranger walking through the bathroom door and Xu calmly shooting her. She said, "Why isn't Charlene here wanting to kill me?"

"Charlene's got other plans. I promised her I'd provide a nice big distraction soon so we can both take care of business."

"Charlene won't get near Judge Hunt."

"Goes to show what a tiny little imagination you Feds have." His voice lowered. "You don't have much time, so I might let you in on it. You won the first round, I'll admit it, but the game goes to me."

"Why would Charlene follow you? Take care of you?"

He kept his voice low, whispered, "Charlene apologized to me for not killing you, but I didn't mind. It meant I'd get to kill you myself. All the others, they were just business, but not you. You're my bonus."

Ramsey's safe; no way can Charlene get to him. "What's your distraction?"

"A nice big boom, like at the Fairmont, but you won't hear it, you'll be dead. You think Charlene's going for that judge? Even though her brain visits Disneyland a lot of the time, Charlene realizes Judge Hunt is a no-go for now. She's willing to let the judge lie in bed, suffer for his sins. She's going to kill another man she blames for her son's death, and that's Agent Savich, your husband. Talk about hate, Charlene lives for it. I don't think she can live without it. She seriously wants him dead."

Sherlock's vision blurred, and her heart stuttered. She felt Xu's hand touch her hair. "A pity this pretty hair will be covered with your blood and your brains soon. Say good-bye to your hubby, if you want. You think Charlene's telling him right now to say good-bye to you?"

69

Savich was leaning against the corridor wall, a couple dozen feet from the guards outside Ramsey's room, speaking on his cell to Jimmy Maitland at the Hoover Building. Maitland put him on hold to connect him to the director, who wanted a status report directly from Savich. *Great,* Savich thought, *and what am I going to say? All I can tell you, sir, is that everyone you're worried about is still alive and at large, but there are lots of dead people, too, one of them a doctor who never hurt anyone in his life, and one a young kid who loved video games and worked with his mom in a motel.*

As he waited, Savich decided that as soon as he finished his attempt at raising Director Mueller's spirits he would put an extra guard on Emma. They had kept Sean safe from Charlene, and he would make sure she couldn't turn her attention to Emma. At least right now, she was safe in her father's hospital room.

He'd just finished giving Director Mueller a rundown when a skinny tech came slouching toward him in a long white coat and high-top sneakers. He had thick blond hair on the long side, and a stethoscope around his neck. Savich registered in that second that something wasn't right. Despite all that blond hair, the guy was older than he'd originally thought, lots older. The man looked at his watch, and Savich saw his wrist. It wasn't a man's wrist.

He wasn't fast enough. The man already had his gun jammed into Savich's side.

He leaned close. "No, Agent Savich, I don't think you want to do much more than breathe and accept that your trip through life is coming to a dramatic end. Long overdue, I'd say."

Savich didn't move. He said, "Hello, Charlene. Pretty good disguise, except that all that hair doesn't match how old you are. Why didn't you wear a white wig?"

The gun shoved hard into his side. "Smart mouth on you, but you're right, I could have done better than this wig, but I didn't have much time. Turns out it didn't make a lick of difference, now, did it? I might be older than you, baby boy, but I've got lots of experience handling punks like you."

"No," Savich said, "I don't think you do."

She gave a low laugh as she jerked his SIG out of his belt clip and slipped it into her coat pocket. "Now, don't you move or you're dead where you stand." She leaned closer. "I can tell you want to have a go at me. I read all about your martial arts demos and how everyone oohs and aahs over you, but you move a muscle and I'll shoot you, and then I'll kill those guards in front of Judge Hunt's room, then all the nurses down at the nurses' station. If one of the guards shoots me, who cares? I don't."

The gun jammed hard again against his kidney. Savich didn't make a sound, even though the shot of pain nearly sent him to his knees.

"Now, you and I are going to take a little walk to the stairs at the end of the corridor. We're going to walk up those stairs to the roof. I've given this a lot of thought, and I decided I'd like to see you do a lovely swan dive from seven floors up."

She moved behind him, kept the gun pressed into the small of his back. "Don't forget, I can pull this trigger faster than you can do any of your fancy kicks. You're real quiet, aren't you? You're thinking about going for it? Be my guest. At the very least you'd be strapped in a wheelchair for the rest of your days. That'd be okay, but I'd rather see you lying splattered on the ground seven floors down. You wanna know something really ironic?"

"Yes."

"Your little wife is enjoying herself with Joe Keats— you call him Xu, I think. Only he doesn't look like Xu right now. No, he's a butt-ugly scrub nurse with lots of black hair and glasses. I even put some lipstick on Joe, stuffed his cheeks to fatten them up, strapped a pillow around his middle, smeared on some eye shadow. Think it'll fool your little wife?"

Savich lost the spit in his mouth. *No, Harry will take care of Sherlock. No one's going to get past Harry, but Harry isn't expecting Xu. No, let it go, focus. You've got to get out of this alive before you can get to Sherlock. Pay attention.*

"Yep, Joe called me a few minutes ago. He should

have her away from her guard by now, and in a couple of minutes we're going to hear a big honker boom—this floor's going to turn to dust and ashes. That will roust and rumble all your buddies, make them think Judge Hunt's under attack. Joe's good with bombs. Then Joe and I are going to walk away.

"Hey, I wonder if she's bitten the big one yet? He was stone-cold pissed that she brought him down since she's half his size, not to mention she's a woman. She humiliated him. Joe told me a professional has to take pride in his work or he isn't worth spit. She stomped on his pride. A man like Joe shouldn't have to suffer humiliation like that unless he's as mean as a snake like that vicious bastard of a husband I had to shoot in the face—" She paused, shook her head. *Stop it, shut your mouth. He doesn't need to know all this, STOP IT.*

She snapped back and focused. "*For what you did you deserve this.* I'd say that sounds real good, don't you? Has a real ring to it. Killing you is going to beat shooting that judge who murdered my boy, because you're the one who made it happen. Keep walking. Up the stairs, boy. Move out."

A nurse called out, "Agent Savich, wait a moment. Judge Hunt asked to speak to you."

Savich saw the gun jerk in Charlene's hand and wondered if he or the nurse would be dead before he could answer her.

70

A toilet flushed. Both Xu and Sherlock froze. The stall door opened, and a hugely pregnant woman squeezed out the stall door. She was pulling out earbuds blasting the end of Barenaked Ladies. "Twins," she said. "Isn't that—"

She saw Sherlock, saw the gun, saw the ugly guy who was dressed like a woman and a nurse, and she opened her mouth and screamed as loud as she could, and didn't stop. Xu's gun jerked toward the woman. Sherlock pivoted, brought up her knee hard in his crotch, and slammed her fisted hands down on his wounded arm as the bathroom door burst open and Harry came flying through.

The woman didn't stop screaming, she kept it up, a lovely ear-splitting blast, but those screams were lovelier than the "Hallelujah Chorus" to Sherlock. Xu was trying to raise his arm from the floor to shoot Sherlock or the pregnant woman or Harry, she didn't know which. She kicked him in the head and stomped her boot heel down on his hand, heard the bones crack. The Beretta clattered across the linoleum. Xu was cursing her, an odd mixture of Mandarin and English, and she kicked him in the ribs.

Harry fell to his knees beside Xu, turned him on his stomach, and grabbed his hair, only to have it come off in his hand. Xu's hand came out of his pocket fast, a knife clutched in his fingers. He slashed out at Harry once and again, trying to break free. Harry wanted to kill him, wanted it very much, but instead he jumped back and raised his SIG. "Xu, if you don't throw that knife away and put your hands on your head I will shoot you in one second."

Xu froze. He didn't release the knife.

"You die holding a knife, that's rich." Harry brought his SIG down against Xu's face. "Hey, you got another flash bang with you?" Harry smiled. "Three, two—"

Xu let the knife fall. Harry kicked it against the counter. Harry was cuffing Xu as Sherlock grabbed her cell and punched in speed-dial. Dillon's cell rang once, twice, and kept ringing four times until it went to voice mail. Charlene had him, otherwise he would have answered. She had to get to him, but the pregnant woman was choking, gasping for air, she was so scared looking down at the man lying handcuffed on the floor moaning and cursing. She grabbed Sherlock, hugged her as hard as she could, and began, of all things, to pat Sherlock's back. She cleared her throat. "You're the greatest kicker."

Harry yelled, "Look what I found, a damned detonator." Harry disarmed it. "So much for this part of your plan, Xu."

She'd forgotten the bomb. Sherlock pulled away from the woman. "Thank you. Sorry, I've got to go."

But the woman grabbed her again and kept squeezing. "I'm sorry you can't get closer, but it's twins. I have to wear mules, since I can't even see my feet."

"I know." Sherlock knew the woman was going into shock, and so she said gently, "It's all right now, I promise." Then Sherlock simply lifted her away. In the next second, she pushed out the bathroom door. She shoved her way through the growing crowd of people and yelled, "Get security, fast!"

71

Savich called out to the nurse still walking toward them, "It's okay. Tell Judge Hunt I'll be in to see him in a few minutes. Thank you."

"Smart move," Charlene said out of the side of her mouth, watching the nurse give Savich a smile and a finger wave and turn back to the nurses' station.

"Cute little gal. From the look she gave you, I think she'd like to fool around with you. You faithful to your wife?"

Savich saw the nurse turn once more and look from him to Charlene, puzzled. *Keep going, everything's okay. Keep all your mad attention on me, Charlene.*

"Not going to say anything, huh? You're probably not faithful, no guy is, including that dog of a husband I had, and do you want to know what—" She stopped again in mid-sentence. *Shut up, shut up, Charlene.*

Savich opened the stair door and started climbing. What she was saying, it was bizarre, but it was more than that. It was as if her brain suddenly went skydiving, and she was barely able to bring herself back to focus. Could he use that?

They reached the fifth floor, two more floors to go. Thank God no one opened the doors. He wondered how much longer that luck would hold, kept glancing toward her, looking for his chance. His cell rang, and he felt her jump. He listened to it go to voice mail, then silent.

"Keep those legs moving, Savich. I heard your cell ringing; leave it alone. Two more flights, then we'll get ourselves a nice suntan. It's actually sunny today, and would you believe it this time of year in San Francisco?"

"Yes, it's remarkably pleasant." Savich could hear her breathing. She couldn't be as fast as he was any longer, no matter how trained up she was. *Only one more floor.* Should he try for her on the stairs?

He took another quick look back. She was walking three steps below him, her gun steady on his back. "What you looking at, Savich? Are you wondering about your little sweetie? I'd have to say there isn't much hope for her, Joe—Xu—is a remarkable man. Can you believe that, a real live spy for the Chinese right here in San Francisco, California? He never told me what he took, only that he'd had some problems. Everyone has problems, I told him, and I took care of him. I like him, he's a gentleman and he said thank you to me for it. So live and let live, I say." She paused, panting a bit, then, "It's sad, though, even though we're supposed to hook up after the bomb goes off, I don't know. I just don't know."

Did she realize she probably wouldn't get out of the hospital alive? She sounded philosophical about it. Let her talk, Savich thought, talking would take more breath and a bit of her attention. He said, "You don't think you'll see him again?"

She surprised him. "Joe asked me to come to Beijing with him, but I can't imagine such a thing anyway. I mean, all those people who don't look like me or talk like me and would probably hate me on sight, you know?"

"Yeah, I know. The thing is, Charlene, I think Joe is in trouble with those people. He's not going to China, no matter what he told you."

"You think he's lying to me? Well, he did say then that he was probably through doing what the Chinese told him to do, so maybe we'll go to Tuscany—that's a real pretty place in Italy where he told me he wants to buy a villa, become a local eccentric, he said, because he has lots of money saved."

"You're slowing down, Agent. Yeah, I can see you're thinking about jumping me. If you try it, I promise I'll shoot you in midair. You got that? I'd rather follow the plan I had with Joe. I mean, we're nearly to the roof, how about it?"

Less than one flight left. They heard a door open down a floor, heard fast footsteps going down.

"Lucky day for that bozo," Charlene said. She glanced down at her watch again, breathing heavily.

"Here at last. Now we exit. The roof stairs are to the left, down the hall. Shove open the door and don't move."

Savich did as she said.

She was right behind him. He felt the gun pressed against his spine. They walked only six feet to another, more discreet door that led to the hospital roof.

They heard a man's voice.

"Hey, what are you doing here? What's going on?"

72

A young man wearing a nice blue suit came striding toward them, waving his hands. "You're not supposed to be up here. Who are you?"

Savich knew Charlene wouldn't hesitate to shoot him. He said quickly, "I'm Agent Dillon Savich, FBI. We need to check out the roof. We'll be okay by ourselves." *Please believe me and turn around. Go back to your office.*

The man seemed to think about asking to see his ID, but then he shook his head at himself, said, "Hurry it up. No one's supposed to be up here. Security should have told us. Everyone's on edge, I guess. Sorry, do what you've got to do." He flapped his hand at them and walked away.

Charlene said, "Good dresser, but he's got a whine in his voice. I wonder if he's married. Bet he is and his wife can't stand him, probably wants to walk out the door and take some loser lover—" She looked blankly at him for a moment. "Now move it. That's right, you open the roof door."

Another disconnect, Savich thought, but it hadn't lasted long enough for him to make a move. He had to be ready when she did it next. She said, "Another dozen steps to the roof, then there's a door latched on this side.

"I know what you're thinking, but don't do it, not unless you want to live five minutes less. And you really want to live, don't you? Even if your little FBI wife isn't breathing anymore, you still want those five extra minutes for yourself."

He felt the gun shoved hard against his back.

He unlatched the roof door, thought about jumping out and diving out of her sight, but Charlene grabbed his jacket, stayed close to him.

They stepped out onto the graveled roof together and looked out at the sprawl of San Francisco. The wind was sharp, a chill in the air, but the sun was bright overhead.

"Let's walk over to the edge. See, they've got the thigh-high railing. I wonder what good they think that'll do? I mean, if you want to end it all, you just gotta step right over and then you're flying. Or in your case, you're going to get a little encouragement."

She poked the gun hard in his back. "Walk."

He walked. Savich knew he had to do something or he would shortly be dead. That couldn't happen. He had to get to Sherlock. She was alive, she'd managed to beat Xu, or Harry had, Savich knew it to his gut. He felt her, strong and whole. He saw Sean, so tickled he was going to Yosemite, his arms around his neck, giving him a big

73

Sherlock threw open the hallway door on the seventh floor.

"Hey, who are you? You've got a gun!"

"FBI! It's all right," she called to the young man who, after seeing her SIG, stood stock-still. "Did anyone go up to the roof?"

"Yes, another FBI guy and some sort of tech. The roof door's right there."

She ran to the door and pulled it open. Sherlock took the stairs two at a time, unlatched the roof door, and forced herself to lift it slowly. She saw Charlene, wearing a blond wig and dressed like a tech standing not a foot from Dillon, her gun aimed at his chest. He was too close to the edge.

He's alive; thank you, God.

Sherlock climbed out onto the roof, trying not to make any noise. She quietly eased the roof door back down, keeping low. The wind was strong up here, but she could hear Charlene saying, "I can put a bullet in your face and push you over if you'd prefer. Which way do you want it, Agent Savich?"

Dillon said, "Would you like me to tell you who murdered your son, Charlene?"

"Whether it was you or it was Judge Hunt, it doesn't matter. You're both murderers, and you should both be dead, and you will be—" She shook her head, and in that moment, Savich saw Sherlock, fell and rolled as Sherlock yelled, "Charlene!"

Charlene whirled around and fired, but Sherlock had already dropped to the graveled roof behind a ventilation shaft. Sherlock fired three fast shots, and one struck Charlene in her side. She yelled and leapt back.

Savich was on her. He kicked her in the stomach, sending her wheeling backward, but she didn't let go of her gun. She was wheezing and couldn't catch her breath, but somehow she managed to raise her gun and twist around to fire again at Sherlock.

Sherlock fired. She didn't miss.

Charlene Cartwright fell onto her back, breath huffing out of her mouth, blood splattering from her chest, spewing out around her.

Savich came down on his knees over her. "Judge Hunt didn't kill Sonny. Neither did I."

Charlene stared up at him. "Is Joe dead?"

Sherlock said, "No, he's not, but I imagine he'll end up on death row where he belongs. He's not the man you think he is, Charlene."

"He should have been my son," Charlene said, and she stopped breathing.

Savich said slowly, "When they do the autopsy, I'm thinking they'll find a brain tumor. She wasn't right, Sherlock." He rose, gave her a hand, and pulled her up hard against him. "I knew you were okay, I knew I would have known it if you weren't. Harry's all right?"

"Yes." She began feeling his chest, his arms, dropped to her knees and felt his legs, saying, "I had to get to you. The nurse on Ramsey's floor said you and another guy had gone into the stairwell. I came up as fast as I could."

"I'm all right. Thank you for coming in time." He pulled her to her feet.

Sherlock lightly laid her palm against his cheek and looked at his beloved face. "You would have saved yourself."

Would he? He didn't know. Savich held her for a very long time until the cold wind chilled them.

EPILOGUE

Molly looked out over the packed hall of beautifully dressed people, the orchestra in their formal black and white, and the conductor, the tall and aristocratic Giovanni Rossini, a charming rooster tail of silver hair rising straight up off his head, lustrous as a new coin under the glittering lights. She watched him raise his baton and listened to the opening chords of Tchaikovsky's Symphony No. 4 fill the vast hall. She couldn't take her eyes off the shining nine-foot ebony Steinway on stage, waiting there for Emma.

She had wanted to be backstage with her daughter, but Emma had clasped her hands between hers and said, "You know it makes me nervous when you're here, Mama. I know you don't understand that, but it's true. Please, you need to be with Dad tonight. He's really tense, and I know his chest hurts. It's the Christmas season, Mama, Dad is here, and everything is wonderful." And Emma had hugged her tight and smiled up at her.

My incredible daughter, Molly thought. She knew at that moment she needn't be worried for Emma. Her piano teacher, Mrs. Mayhew, would be there in any case to keep her calm and grounded. She kissed her daughter, held her small face a moment between her palms, kissed her again and made her way back up to the box to the right of the stage with its perfect view. She knew she had to suffer through a Dvořák and a Mahler before Emma played, and dug her fingernails into her palm. At least she didn't have to worry about the twins, who were at the Sherlocks' house, stuffing themselves with kettle corn and hot chocolate. As for Ramsey, he looked stoic, but she knew his stomach was roiling with nerves, and she could see the low hum of pain he still felt on his face. He looked thin, she thought, but still a sex god, she'd told him when she'd stood back and looked at him in his formal tux. Both Savich and Harry had helped him dress, a slow, laborious process, with Molly standing in the corner of the bedroom watching, trying not to show how terrified it made her that he was still hurting.

She squeezed his hand. He grinned at her, whispered, "Emma will be superb, you know it." Molly knew he was saying that as much for himself as for her. She forced out a smile and for a moment leaned her face against his shoulder.

The orchestra finished the Tchaikovsky, and Rossini

turned to bow and accept applause. Molly turned to smile at Dillon, who had Sean on his lap, and Sherlock and Eve and Harry sitting next to him, and they nodded back at her. She whispered to Ramsey, "We've never had such perfect seats in the hall. It was nice of the Vincents to lend us their box so all six of us could sit together."

Ramsey nodded, knowing the Vincents were in Paris, where they would most like to be, despite the cold December nights. He remembered squeezing into Notre Dame with them one Christmas Eve years ago along with thousands of other people, and then walking along the Seine to the Pont Neuf, where they'd stopped to buy a bag of chestnuts roasting on an open grill. Perhaps his family could do that together next year.

Rossini's baton came down, and Constantine's beautiful Christmas music filled the hall. Ramsey settled himself in to listen. He would have a next year now, to go to Paris if he wished. He was so grateful to be alive, here in Davies Hall ready to hear Emma play, that he wanted to shout with it.

Molly was fidgeting. Ramsey whispered, "Stop worrying. Emma's a pro, she'll be great."

Molly drew in a deep breath. "You're here, that's all that's really important to Emma, and to me."

Molly didn't know there were so many Christmas carols in the world, from England to Mexico, and the Arctic was probably next. Then it was over, finally. When the applause died down, Rossini turned his charismatic smile on the audience. He said in his charming Italian accent, "We are proud to present Miss Emma Hunt. She will play George Gershwin's *Rhapsody in Blue.* We are also proud and very pleased to see her father, Judge Ramsey Hunt, with us tonight. I was told he said he'd be helicoptered in if need be." Rossini bowed toward their box bringing every eye in the audience to them.

"Miss Emma Hunt." Giovanni Rossini held his hand out to welcome Emma as she walked toward him in her Christmas-red velvet dress, her beautiful glossy dark hair held back by two gold clips, like shiny silk beneath the lights. She wore black ballet flats on her small feet. Her only jewelry was the locket Ramsey had given her for her last birthday, a photo of her and her mother on one side, Ramsey and the twins on the other.

Molly could never adequately describe her feelings when her daughter walked onto a stage. Usually it was a strange mixture of so much pride she could burst with it, and such throat-clogging terror she thought her face would turn blue. And such elation, she thought, that she knew she could leap off the box railing and fly, and finally, utter blank-brained amazement that she'd given birth to this incredible being. She watched Emma take Rossini's hand and smile up at him, then turn to walk to the Steinway grand piano, shoulders straight, lightly running her fingers over its glossy black finish. She sat down in front of the keyboard, moved the bench an inch to the left. Before Emma lowered her hands to the piano, she looked directly at their box and smiled.

She began to play *Rhapsody in Blue,* Gershwin's magical, exuberant, full-bodied, passionate masterpiece. No one who heard it would think an eleven-year-old girl was playing. Slowly, drawn inexorably into the music, Molly began to breathe again and she wondered if maybe she couldn't fly after all. She knew every chord and every run by heart, she'd heard Emma play it so many times. When Emma struck the final chord, she sat quietly for a moment, something Mrs. Mayhew had taught her to bring her back and calm her racing heart, before she eased off the piano bench and turned to face the audience. She bowed.

Molly leapt to her feet, clapping madly, hearing the audience's huge applause as they rose in a standing ovation. If Ramsey had been able to, he would have jumped to his feet along with his beaming wife, and Savich, with a wildly clapping Sean in his arms, Sherlock, and Harry and Eve, but he knew he'd probably tip right out of the box and make a mess of it on the people below.

Emma bowed again as the applause continued, with shouts of "Encore!" She seated herself again at the Steinway. She played variations on a medley of Christmas carols she herself had written, from "Oh, Come All Ye Faithful" to "Silver Bells," which lifted every spirit in the house, and Molly decided she loved Christmas music after all. When she stood to bow again, the audience rose once more to applaud. Rossini presented her with a deep bow and red roses. Emma looked directly at her father, held out the roses to him, and gave him a bow.

As if choreographed, everyone in the audience turned to look up at his box. The applause, if possible, grew even louder.

When, at last, the audience settled into their seats,

P.S.

Within an hour of the end of the concert, photos and videos, with sound, appeared on YouTube showing Judge Ramsey Hunt's box in Davies Hall in San Francisco, Sean in his father's arms, nearly falling over the railing in his excitement, yelling to Emma. Within hours it went viral.

To escape the media, Savich and Sherlock took Sean to Disney World in Orlando. Unfortunately, a little girl recognized Sean, jumped up and down, and screamed, "Marry me, Sean!" and it started all over again.

Keep reading for an excerpt from

BOMBSHELL

The newest FBI thriller from Catherine Coulter
Available July 9, 2013 from G. P. Putnam's Sons

Maestro, Virginia
Very late Friday night

She'd drunk way too much. She was an idiot. Why had she, Delsey Freestone, a reasonably intelligent twenty-five-year-old supposed adult, swan dived into those last two margaritas? *Because the big cheese director of Stanislaus was treating you like his favorite student, making you his special margarita recipe, that's why, and you were afraid to turn him down. To be honest, you were flattered, too. And what was in those margaritas that tasted so good?*

She was very sure at that moment that she didn't want to know.

She didn't understand why Dr. Elliott Hayman, the new director of Stanislaus School of Music—*Call me Elliott, my dear*—had appeared to want to cut her out of the graduate student female herd at the party and bestow his margaritas and attention on her. Not only was Dr. Hayman in charge of the prestigious music school, he was also an internationally celebrated concert pianist, with a libido, she'd read in a critic's review, to rival his glissandos. When it came to renown, he was in a different universe than hers. She and Anna Castle, a violinist from Louisiana and her best friend in Maestro, had decided Dr. Hayman enjoyed the role of director because it appealed to his vanity, but they also both acknowledged it was only the older graduate students, like herself, who believed that he was, at the core, faintly contemptuous of the students. On the other hand, he was a sharp dresser, dropping in conversations that he shopped twice a year in Milan for his suits, always fashioned for him by Bruno Giraldi himself. Whoever Bruno was, Anna observed, Dr. Hayman certainly dressed to impress.

So why had Dr. Hayman dogged her all evening, giving her entirely too much attention until she was certain every student within hearing distance now hated her guts? Thank you, Dr. Hayman—Elliott—that was just what she needed. And what would Anna say about him when she told her about his behavior tonight? She'd laugh and say something like, "Smile, Dels, and suck it up," stretching it out in her lazy Louisiana drawl until Delsey would want to yank the words right out of her mouth. She'd wished all evening that Anna had come, but no, Delsey had had to fly solo.

Delsey supposed the sudden waves of gut-wrenching nausea combined with her flatlining brain had been heaven-sent, since it had gotten her out the door of Professor Rafael Salazar's sprawling ranch-style home on Golden Meadow Terrace in under a minute, with no one the wiser, only one arm in her coat when she'd quietly closed the back door behind her. She'd sucked in the cold winter air, grateful to be out of Professor Salazar's whooping and hollering party, away from both him and his twin brother, Dr. Hayman, and wasn't that a hoot? Twins! Separated as boys and ending up with different last names. The only thing they had in common, as far as she could see, was their incredible talent.

She drove very carefully until her head was pounding so hard and she was feeling so woozy she was swerving like a drunk, which, she supposed, she was. *No cops, please, too much humiliation.* She eased her ancient Spyder to the curb of Tinsel Tree Lane and shifted into neutral. She pressed her forehead against the steering wheel, willing the world to stitch itself back together for her, swearing to any power listening she'd go back to her one-drink limit. She'd made that promise when she was only sixteen after sharing a bottle of hooch with her boyfriend Davie Forman, and wanted to die, not have sex with him in his daddy's Mustang. Tonight was the first time in nine years that she'd broken that promise. *What an idiot you are. You deserve freezing your butt off and having your head explode, and the misery of hugging the toilet in the morning.*

She finally cracked an eye open to see the half-moon crystal clear overhead. It looked as cold and hard as the solid mountains of snow that blanketed everything around her—trees, street signs, cars, mailboxes. Big snow, the locals called it; unusual, the locals also said. Yet here it was, a big honking snowstorm. At least it had stopped pelting down for a while, but they said it would begin again hard come dawn. She'd come to realize after the first heavy snow in December that if she hit a snowdrift, she and her Spyder wouldn't be found until spring.

Looking at the unrelenting white made her miss the warm salty air of Santa Monica, scented with the night jasmine trellised on the stone fence surrounding her former apartment building. To top it off, her car heater was struggling to stay alive, her Spyder no more used to this circuit-freezing weather than she was. She sure wasn't helping any, staying out all hours of this frigid night—it couldn't be more than ten degrees, and counting down. *Houston, we have a problem.* She squeezed her eyes shut; what should she do?

She became aware of how very quiet it was, not a single owl hooting in the snow-drenched trees, not a single car or truck engine tunneling through the snow on the interstate only a quarter mile away. No wonder; it was nearly one o'clock Saturday morning. Only people she didn't want to know about were up this time of night. She looked around and sent a silent prayer of thanks upward that there weren't any cops, either. She knew she wasn't up for convincing anyone she wasn't drunk. She'd probably shatter the Breathalyzer.

She raised her head after a few minutes, held perfectly still for a moment, noticed she didn't feel as dizzy, and blessed be, her headache was throttling down. She shifted the Spyder into gear and drove slowly in a perfectly straight line, as only those who are impaired and know it do. After another six blocks, she turned off onto

Hitchfield Avenue and then onto Lonely Bear Court. She saw her building up ahead on the right, a duplex with her one-bedroom unit on bottom and Henry Stoltzen's on top. Built as a solid redbrick back in the twenties, the heirs to the old lady who'd lived there all her life had split it up in the late nineties.

She looked up to see Henry's light on. Henry and his prized six-inch goatee had helped her move in the day she'd arrived in Maestro, fed her hot dogs and beer, and quickly become a good friend. He liked the popular songs she wrote and sang even though he sat solidly in the classical corner, a gifted cellist who adored playing Jean-Baptiste Sèbastian Brèval's Sonata in C Major.

He seemed oblivious of most other people around him, only his music and his iPod tethering him to planet Earth. She turned into her parking spot next to Henry's, drew a deep breath, thanked the Almighty she was still alive and not in jail. She promised good works she told herself she wouldn't forget by morning, and slogged through the snow to her front door. She was shaking with cold when she finally fit her old-fashioned key into the lock and the door opened. She stepped into a blissful seventy degrees.

She locked the front door behind her, slipped on the two chains, and shoved the dead bolt home. She flipped on the light inside the door in the small foyer. *Home and warm. No more margaritas, no more one A.M. parties. I'm now a sensible woman, resolute and determined, and the director of Stanislaus can go compliment someone in the reed section.* She saw Eileen Simons of clarinet fame in her mind's eye, and knew she was interested in Dr. Hayman—*Elliott,* that is. Why hadn't Director Hayman loaded Eileen up with booze this evening and stayed away from Delsey? Eileen had been at the hoedown, as drunk as everyone else, and giving her the die-bitch eye all evening.

Now I'm safe.

Where had that left-field thought come from? Well, from being out alone and drunk in the boondocks of Virginia in the middle of the night, that's where. Delsey bypassed the living room and went straight to the kitchen, swallowed three extra-strong aspirin and drank two full glasses of water. The tap water tasted nastier than usual, but she drank it anyway. She wiped the back of her hand across her mouth and walked through the hallway to the bathroom, turning on lights as she went. When she flipped on the bathroom light she saw the colorful South Seas shower curtain was pulled closed around the bathtub.

She never left the shower curtain closed because it made the bathroom look too small—well, unless she hadn't cleaned the bathtub. Had she? Her brain was still fogged-in and she couldn't remember.

A hot shower, that was all she could think about. Jets of hot water pounding her face, clearing out her head, making her want to live again. She stripped off her clothes, paused on the clip on her bra when she heard something, movement, something. Maybe a sharp breath? She didn't move, listened hard. No, there wasn't anything. Her brain was still squirrelly with tequila. She got her bra off, left her clothes in a pile on the bathroom floor, pulled back the shower curtain, and froze.

She'd never believed she was a screamer, but a scream ripped right out of her mouth, and then another, her brain screaming in tandem, *Not possible, not possible.* Her breath caught when she heard the sound again and whirled around, but she didn't have time to be afraid before something hard as a brick smashed her on her head, and she didn't scream anymore.

From #1 *New York Times* Bestselling Author

CATHERINE COULTER

SPLIT SECOND

AN FBI THRILLER

A serial killer is on the loose, and it's up to FBI agents
Dillon Savich and Lacey Sherlock to bring him down. They
soon discover the killer has blood ties to an infamous and
now long-dead monster. And when Savich and Sherlock
are joined by agents Lucy Carlyle and Cooper McKnight,
the chase is on . . .

"Intricate plot twists pepper this spine tingler from one
of the masters of the genre." —*The Newark Star-Ledger*

"Realistic and . . . riveting." —*Booklist*

"The story line is fast-paced . . . and never slows down."
—*Midwest Book Review*

catherinecoulter.com
facebook.com/catherinecoulterbooks
penguin.com

M1115T0512